THE OXFORD LIBRARY OF
SHORT NOVELS

THE
OXFORD LIBRARY OF
Short Novels

Chosen and Introduced by
JOHN WAIN

Volume I
Goethe to Stevenson

GUILD PUBLISHING

LONDON · NEW YORK · SYDNEY · TORONTO

This edition published 1990 by
Guild Publishing
by arrangement with Oxford University Press

Introduction and selection © John Wain 1990

CN 2127

Printed in England by
Clays Ltd, St Ives plc

*These volumes are based on an idea from
Stan Remington, a man who loves books, and
who during a lifetime in publishing has
worked long and successfully to
awaken that love in others.*

Contents

INTRODUCTION

ALL these tales were written within the two centuries or so that witnessed the meridian of prose fiction in Western literature, the epoch when it was virtually unrivalled as a source of recreation and entertainment and at the same time an acknowledged force in promoting both self-knowledge and awareness of the needs of society. During those years, technology—such as it then was—worked in favour of the written story by providing it with rapid printing, easy multiplication of copies, speed of transport and distribution, rather than, as now, overwhelming it with a multiplicity of competition. During at least the first century of our chosen period, the novel grew like a joyously undisciplined tropical forest, unregulated, pushing higher and higher by its own hungry vitality. Compared with the steady flow of theory and critical analysis that had accompanied poetry and drama for thousands of years, since the very inception of our literary tradition, the novel grew from strength to strength on impulse and public appetite with no guidance, and equally no hindrance, from the critics. Nobody defined its aims for it or held up formal targets and norms. During its formative years it drew much of its strength from English writers and yet the most important English critics—Johnson, Coleridge, Hazlitt, Lamb, De Quincey, right through to Matthew Arnold in the middle of the nineteenth century—do not take it as matter for discussion. We can fairly say that as far as England is concerned, the novel had to wait for Henry James's subtle and penetrating essays of the 1870s and 1880s before it received the kind of criticism that seriously went into questions of form as well as of content and social tendency; and James came to the task from an apprenticeship in France, where a new and more conscious breed of fiction-writers, from Stendhal through Flaubert to the Goncourts, were approaching their work more rigorously than was common in England. Here, novelists tended to be regarded as a body of professionals like journalists or historians, with their own imperatives, pursuing their avocation slightly to one side of the concerns of the 'man of letters'. Not until Oxford University awarded a Doctorate of Letters to Ivan Turgenev in 1879 was there a public act which conveyed the recognition of the novelist's art by anything describable as an English Establishment. Turgenev was indeed the ideal choice, not only a cosmopolite but a supreme artist, a craftsman to set beside Flaubert, a writer's writer, a novelist for the connoisseur, who never puts a foot wrong or uses a word too many. Is it fanciful, I wonder, to see in Oxford's recognition of Turgenev some tangible fruit of Henry James's campaign to have the novel considered as an entirely mature literary art?

At all events, after James, serious criticism of the novel, serious weighing of its formal possibilities and attempts to discriminate between one strategy and another, become less unusual, and the late nineteenth and early twentieth centuries saw a good deal of consciousness of technique and approach. During the working life—roughly—of Stevenson, James, Conrad, Bennett, and later of Firbank, Norman Douglas, and on to the Bloomsbury writers, novelists paid attention to formal questions and pondered the aesthetics of their art, not as a refined game but in the search for precision of effect, economy, and energy of impact. This was the period when 'literary' fiction pulled sharply away from the mass market, when the stratification into highbrow, lowbrow, and middlebrow, always implicit in the economic and social structure of society but not necessarily fitting snugly over it, became most directly influential on writers and publishers. Since 1945, these classifications have tended to be blurred out of existence by the levelling power of television and the application of mass marketing techniques to literature as automatically as to pet food or deodorants.

For these reasons we begin this selection in the mid-eighteenth century and end as the echoes of World War II die away. (Our last story in fact contains mention of the closing battles of that war.) And this was the period that saw the haunting presence of an outline that never quite achieved actuality, a form that never became truly distinct. The long, capacious novel was a natural growth. The short, tightly organized novel, already finely achieved in Jane Austen, and going on to encompass such masterpieces as *Madame Bovary* and *A Passage To India*, was its natural corollary. But behind that, the collective literary mind was haunted by a shorter form still, one to which the name *nouvelle* or *novella* was sometimes given. This form was always seen as pitched consciously between the short story (which does have a definite nature, lives according to its own laws of being, and is as different from the novel as a drawing is from a painting) and even the shortest form of the novel proper. One's impression is that this form, lacking a tangible presence, lacking a local habitation and a name, nevertheless existed as—an idea? Not quite; a flavour, an aspiration, an emanation. It is more a matter of intention than anything else. Some of the tales here are quite simply short and economical novels; others are short stories which have grown until they have lost the immediacy of impact, the unity of impression, that make up the strength of that form, and gained in compensation some of the generosity, even prodigality, of the novel. But here and there—in *Heart of Darkness*, I believe, or in *Death in Venice*, or in a superbly crafted narrative like *The Member of the Wedding*, one senses the achieved or almost achieved presence of that shadowy form, the *nouvelle*, conceived and written as an entity on its own, product of a self-conscious and refining epoch, probably extinct in our unceremonious days. In our time it sometimes happens that a novelist writes a very short novel, or a short story writer writes a very long short story, but that's what they are and that's what they remain. In the heyday of the connoisseurship of prose fiction, there was briefly a separate, deliberately conceived form, and here and there in these three volumes I believe we can meet it.

But, as Yeats rightly says, 'names are nothing':

> But names are nothing. What matter who it be,
> So that his elements have grown so fine
> The fume of muscatel
> Can give his sharpened palate ecstasy
> No living man can drink from the whole wine.

Names, or at any rate sub-categories, are nothing. Essences, realities, are another matter. Whatever else they are, all the offerings in these three volumes are fiction, prose fiction, and what is it to be that? It is an important human activity: but what activity? The nearest I would venture to a definition of prose fiction as it has flourished in Western Europe and America since the 1720s would be: a long and detailed account of events that did not actually take place, performed by people who did not actually exist. But if these events and people never had concrete existence, if accounts of them are not 'true', why should we pay any attention to them? That question has proved a fruitful theme of discussion among critics and philosophers for centuries: long before the novel took recognizable form it was discussed in terms of poetry, the drama, and fine fabling generally. C. S. Lewis speaks somewhere of 'The long process whereby Europe became aware of fiction as an activity different from history on the one hand, and lying on the other.' This awareness has, in some quarters, always been fragile. The events and characters in an invented story may put you in mind, and may be intended to put you in mind, of specific events and real persons, and some readers enjoy fiction better as the element of invention is brought down and the element of factual correspondence is raised, till the novel becomes a crypto-document or is marketed by publishers interested in a quick turnover by the barbarous label 'faction'. In such books the façade of being a novel is retained, one suspects, largely as a cover for sloppy research ('That's not how it happened.'—'So what? I was inventing') or, even more simply, as a possible defence against the law of libel.

The people who write and market books of this quasi-documentary kind don't do so because they simply fail to see that an invented story can be 'true' in the sense of conveying the writer's vision of the truth about life and the world. They realize, presumably, though their own path lies elsewhere, that a writer may find in an invented story the freedom he or she needs to express a perception of the truth, to say to the reader, 'life is like this', and to say it with more conviction because the writer's art, unlike the historian's, is free to escape from the domain of the purely random and meaningless, the events that happen not because people are what they are or the world is what it is, but through one-in-a-million chances and coincidences. So Aristotle, at the very beginning of our literary tradition, remarked that fiction is more philosophical than truth. But this awareness, as I say, is not universal, even among those who read books, and among the general populace it has never taken root at all. It is quite clear, for instance, that many people believe, in a misty but altogether unshakeable way, that the action of their favourite TV soap opera is really going on somewhere, and that for thirty minutes a day they are somehow enabled to draw aside a magic curtain and look in on it. They take the characters they see there as actual people like themselves, sending them medicine if they fall ill and offering good advice through the post. And if they do this more rarely with novels than with television serials, then that is only because they read novels much more rarely. I had a proof of this very recently. Some months ago I published a novel, related in the first person, in which the narrator is shown as having been born and bred in Oxford and his parents as the keepers of a small pub. A woman who lives in the same village as I do knocked on my door the other evening and said she had come to talk about my book. I asked her to sit down. 'You were born in Oxford, I know,' she said. 'What pub was it your Mum and Dad kept?' Feeling that I must make a despairing effort to wrench apart the writer from the written, I told her I was not born and bred in an Oxford public house, that in fact I was a native of Staffordshire and that my father was a dentist. She looked at me for what felt like a full minute and then said, 'Well, *you're* a bloody liar.'

Quaint? Certainly—and yet we must all, if we are honest, admit to having felt now and then the tug at our elbow of that same impulse, the impulse to believe that an account of anything, to be true, must come from someone who has 'been there'. We feel it, for instance, in the (can we deny it?) slight surprise we feel when, after reading Stephen Crane's utterly graphic, utterly vivid and convincing, account of what it was like to take part in a Civil War battle in *The Red Badge Of Courage*, we learn from the nearest reference book that Crane not only had no experience of that war either as combatant or onlooker, but was not even born until some years after it was over. We shouldn't be surprised, but we are. The truthfulness of a literary account of something does indeed depend on the author's having been there—but to 'be there' is an affair of the imagination and of the understanding. This is underlined by the fact that the masterpieces of imaginative fiction, though indeed they deal in made-up stories, often contain very little in the way of invention. To recount the story of many a famous novel is a matter of uttering two or three sentences, not in themselves of any interest. The interest is put there by the author's profound understanding of them. Thus neither of the two great Russians we have represented here is working to invent anything, to 'tell a story'. This is not to say that their work is artless. Even in a tale with the simplest outline, the disposition of material, the constant problem of what information to feed into the reader's mind at what point, is always a subtle art. But the pattern they work to is the opposite of the thriller-writer's 'plot', which always involves a puzzle, or the unceasing obligatory pyrotechnics of the writer who woos us to abandon our hold on everyday reality and escape into the marvellous, whether by way of interplanetary travel or by hob-nobbing with Orcs. In Tolstoy and Chekhov it is life, ordinary observable life, that flows across the page as naturally and irresistibly as a river: except that 'ordinary' life turns out, under their compassionate and perceiving eye, to have nothing ordinary about it. Of the two, *My Life* has the broader canvas; it is the character study of an individual, but also the portrait, deftly and economically conveyed, of an historical situation. Behind the pathetic, comic, vulnerable lives of the cluster of characters in the foreground, we are made to feel the presence of Russia herself, so terrifyingly huge, unwieldy, unchangeable, unresponsive to individual human effort. The questions, 'Can Russia ever become civilized? Will life here ever become humane and orderly, even to the extent to which the flawed societies of Western Europe are humane and orderly?' recur again and again in one form or another, till in the end, as is usual with Chekhov, it becomes virually impossible to say what the 'subject' of the story is. The subject is life, humanity, the world; particularly Russian life, Russian humanity, the Russian world, but behind them always the inescapable generalization, the watching figure of Everyman.

Tolstoy's Ivan Ilych knows that, being Everyman, he will die. But like Everyman he lives from day to day by ignoring that knowledge, carrying it around him like an unopened parcel. It was left to Tolstoy, the greatest of all the writers represented here, to take Everyman up to the moment of actually opening that parcel and knowing what it contains. *The Death of Ivan Ilych* is one of the greatest works of fiction, perhaps *the* greatest, ever penned. But in what sense is it 'fiction'? Because Tolstoy has 'made up a story'? Rather, what he has done is to look with a courageous, perceiving, compassionate eye on the stories that people are continually unfolding around him simply by getting on with their lives.

Fiction as a gateway to truth: the made-up story as a deeper and stronger perception of actuality than a mere chronicling of the random drizzle of events: that is what Sir Philip Sidney meant when he said 'the truest poetry is the most feigning'. What the works gathered in these three volumes offer, then, is not only entertainment and enchantment—they are certainly here—but a view of truth in many of its forms: truth general and truth local; truth universal and truth particular: truths that hold good of human life in all epochs and under all systems, to the tracing of certain strands particularly important in the last two centuries. As examples we might take two, the strand of Symbolism and the strand of Science.

Symbolism does not have to be spread over a story, either by the writer or by the interpreter; it inheres there. Language is such a universal sign-system that it is hardly possible to make a statement, and virtually not possible at all to construct a story, without making a symbolic statement. To recount an incident is to recount, in diagram, the entire class of incidents to which it belongs; to explore the reactions of one human mind is to explore the reactions of all. The stories which were told to European children for centuries—Jack the Giant-killer, Snow White and the Seven Dwarfs, and the like—were never mere stories, if there was ever such a thing as a 'mere' story. They presented archetypes and patterns of behaviour; they were explanations of life which helped the developing mind to deal with the influx of experience.

In that sense, all writing is autobiographical. It describes what has happened to the author, and to the reader, and to everyone who walks the earth. It is true that at certain periods literature has shown a preoccupation with the morbid, the clinical, the monstrously exceptional, the kind of interest that Mario Praz documented in his pioneering *The Romantic Agony*. But very few of those works have become accepted into the canon of masterpieces. 'Nothing can please many, and please long,' said Johnson, 'but just representations of general nature.' And if we strip that judgement of its eighteenth-century full-bottomed wig and and transpose it into another idiom, however widely different, it remains a truth. The statement that holds good in the greatest number of instances will interest the greatest number of people. The individual can stand as the symbol of the species. The particular *is* the universal.

On Sigmund Freud's seventieth birthday someone made a speech in his honour hailing him, among other things, as the discoverer of the unconscious. In his reply Freud gently disclaimed the title. It belonged, he said, to the world's imaginative writers, who had explored the terrain of the unconscious and identified its features long before they were given clinical names. During the movement in thought and art which we have agreed to call 'Romanticism', this terrain was explored with a special energy. This was the generation who, in the words of Erasmus Darwin in 1791, sought to 'enlist Imagination under the banner of Science'. The words occur in the foreword to Darwin's poem *The Botanic Garden*, in which the poet, grandfather of the theorist of evolution, sought to pour the relatively new wine of Linnean botanical research into the old bottles of neo-classic verse. (The poem is not a success in this primary aim; there is a coupling, but no new synthesis.)

As the eighteenth-century Picturesque movement merged with the broader vision of Romanticism, the greatest cultural change in modern times—the turning from outer to inner landscape—was accomplished almost incidentally. The first thirty years of the Romantic movement were rich in writers who inhabited as a matter of right the country of the subconscious, the world of dream and symbol and life-enhancing fantasy. In doing so they not only pioneered the exploration of material which in the following century was to be the subject-matter of a new science, Psychology, but showed an unhesitating friendliness to scientific enquiry of all kinds. Only during the long reaches of the nineteenth century did the idea grow up that art and science were somehow mutually hostile and mutually exclusive. The opening of that century, and the closing years of the eighteenth, are rich in minds which found in the new material revealed by science a source of imaginative enrichment and liberation. The impact of microscopy alone provided miracles enough for a lifetime of wonderment.

Because the Romantic generations were interested both in new knowledge and immemorial dream and vision, the two can coexist in their work. It would have been pleasant, had the relentless struggle for space permitted, to reprint here Adelbert von Chamisso's *The Strange History of Peter Schlemihl* (1814), a curious and once celebrated mixture of folk-tale and scientific romance. The fable reaches a turning-point when Peter, the guileless hero-victim, has just become aware of supernatural power; he buys a pair of boots at a country stall, choosing old ones rather than new because he is short of money; once he has them on, he finds that landscape and vegetation around him change at bewildering speed, for the young man who keeps the stall has, in true *Märchen* style, sold him the fabulous Seven League boots, widespread fantasy of a world where travel was slow and difficult: those boots which, by transporting the wearer more than twenty miles at each step, would give the determinedly stepping walker a speed comparable with that of an aircraft. Up to this point we are in the Europe of legends, as firmly anchored in traditional belief as in the tale of the fatal bargain with the devil, with its roots in the Middle Ages, which Chamisso uses as the mainstay of his story. But at one seven-league stride we are in the equally magic world of scientific enquiry. Since he will not accede to the devil's demand for his soul, Peter must remain till his death an oddity and an outcast, unable to take root in any human society; his refuge is in the pursuit of knowledge, exploiting his marvellous rapidity of motion to survey the world of plants, minerals, and animals, and store up his observations for the benefit of mankind. Chamisso, who spent his own later life in such studies, brought his hero to this more tranquil end, the saint of this new religion, avoiding the desperate denouement of Mary Shelley's *Frankenstein* (1818), whose scientist hero dies in following the creature of his own making through the wastes of the Arctic, intent only on killing the monster and obliterating his own fatal act in synthesizing life.

Coming forward in time we find the same preoccupation with the workings of the mind in Stevenson's classic novel of split personality; while a more complex relationship of Art and Science, with the third element of puzzle-interest thrown in, is contained in the figure of Sherlock Holmes. Holmes's methods are drawn from those of Victorian science, but his motives from the Aesthetic Movement: he solves problems of crime and guilt not to confer benefit on society, but to enjoy the intellectual stimulus of pure reasoning, which affords him the same pleasure as his Stradivarius or, perhaps, more darkly, as his addiction to cocaine. He is an interesting hybrid, by Darwin and Huxley out of Poe and Baudelaire. Goethe, who in later life considered his own treatise on the nature of light, *Farbehnleher*, to be his greatest work, stood at the same junction of Science and Art.

But if these have been centuries of science, they have equally been centuries of political and social change on a scale, and at a pace, unprecedented in world history. Inescapable generalizations about politics, society, and history are forced on us when we consider the difference between the small German state we glimpse as the background of *Werther*, and the post-Bismarckian Germany which fought the two World Wars; or the Algeria we sense behind the philosophical radicalism of Camus and the Algeria of today. Literature *is* political, because life is political. Present-day readers of *Castle Rackrent* may feel that the essential cause of the sorrows of Ireland—the fact that so many of the decisions that really affect the lives of her people are made elsewhere and then inflicted on them—has not changed since 1800. To read this bundle of tales from end to end with an eye to the political and social lessons that can be learned from them would not be incorrect, since in the criticism of any art there are no 'correct' or 'incorrect' procedures, merely some that are more illuminating than others.

The Death of Ivan Ilych is, as it has to be, a critique of society as well as a piercing of emotional veils. Over much of its length, the story could just as well be entitled *The Life of Ivan Ilych*: naturally, for his death is what it is because his life is what it is. Tolstoy, like Chekhov, perceives the immovability of Russian (perhaps of any) society. Misail in *My Life* is angrily assailed by his father, by his neighbours, even by some of his workmates, because he steps out of his place in the social framework, takes to manual work which seems to him more useful and fulfilling than a meaningless desk job in the bureaucracy; but society exacts a price, because its signposting has been ignored. Ivan Ilych, for his part, congratulates himself, during all but the last days of his smug meaningless existence, on the tact and skill with which he has followed the signs.

A man would come, for instance, wanting some information. Ivan Ilych, as one in whose sphere the matter did not lie, would have nothing to do with him: but if the man had some business with him in his official capacity, something that could be expressed on officially stamped paper, he would do everything, positively everything he could within the limits of such relations, and in doing so would maintain the semblance of friendly human relations, that is, would observe the courtesies of life. As soon as the official relations ended, so did everything else. Ivan Ilych possessed this capacity to separate his real life from the official side of affairs and not mix the two, in the highest degree, and by long practice and natural aptitude had brought it to such a pitch that sometimes, in the manner of a virtuoso, he would even allow himself to let the human and official relations mingle. He let himself do this just because he felt that he could at any time he chose resume the strictly official attitude again and drop the human relation. And he did it all easily, pleasantly, correctly, and even artistically. In the intervals between the sessions he smoked, drank tea, chatted a little about politics, a little about general topics, a little about cards, but most of all about official appointments.

It would be easy enough to quarry from Tolstoy's story, or from Chekhov's, a root and branch dismissal of Tsarist Russian society. Certainly it was easy for the Soviet literary establishment, when after the Bolshevik take-over Russian literature had to be put through the meat-grinder of Marxist criticism, to demonstrate that all nineteenth-century writers had been saying in chorus, 'This is a society that needs to be changed.' But of course all societies need to be changed: they are imperfect human institutions, riddled with faults, anomalies, and injustices. Is there an important writer in French or English literature (to go no further) whose work conveys that the society it depicts need *not* be changed?

Even a story like *Vathek,* which would seem to be pure escapism innocent of any serious purpose, can yield a message about political and economic preoccupations; the appearance of tales about the Near East, in the late eighteenth and early nineteenth centuries, is a reflection of the fact that an expanding Europe was thrusting into conflict with a declining Ottoman Empire; only thirty-eight years after the publication of Beckford's romance, Byron was to meet his death preparing for combat against Turkish forces, and the legend of the English *milord*, product of an unjust system who gave his life fighting for justice, was to weave its way into the crazy patchwork of Anglo-Continental relations.

Moving forward into the twentieth century one finds the preoccupations of the eighteenth and nineteenth—nationalism, social justice, the search for personal happiness outside a formal religious framework—still demonstrably present, though often perceived in a different way, like the same objects grouped on a new stage under different lighting. The strands of Science and Symbolism are as firmly evident as before, with the interesting new development that a work like Tolkien's *Lord of the Rings* is eagerly devoured by many whose reading is otherwise mainly confined to 'science fiction'. Tolkien's reverie, welling up from a lifetime of rapt contemplation of Northern myth and legend, of Christian Anglo-Saxon poetry and Norse Edda and Saga, is instantly acceptable to a sci-fi public because, as a variant of 'enlisting Imagination under the banner of Science', science fiction has in fact revived the fainting *genre* of Romance, offering the reader an escape from the dailiness of life into a gleaming empyrean of fable. It has enlisted Science under the banner of Romance, and in the world thus created a Hobbit or an Orc is as natural as a Martian. With this kind of perspectival twist does the twentieth century carry on the themes of the preceding two centuries, and it has been a grief to me that some of the writers who bring out this continuity most strongly—Franz Kafka, for instance—wrote nothing of suitable length for our gallery.

One preoccupation that could be seen as an example of a novelty in twentieth-century literature, reflecting a new element in the culture, is the much stronger concern with sexuality. All literature has of course always given a central place to sex, to gender, to the general issue of the pairing of man and woman, but what the literature of our own century reveals is a more exploratory attitude, an interest in different sexual viewpoints (including among others the homosexual), an unwillingness to be bound by traditional views of the contrasting nature of male and female. That these traditions descended in slightly different forms in different areas of Europe—to say nothing of the East or even of Islam—is well brought out if we consider the case of Colette and the impossibility of finding anything corresponding to her work in the English novel of the time.

Colette has always been very popular in England, almost as much so as in France, and the reason must be that the English are accustomed to going to France for things they find difficult to obtain at home. One notices at once that Colette is not handicapped by the Anglo-Saxon tradition that sexual desire, in the physical sense, is an attribute of the male only. Already, in the first quarter of our century, she was producing novels which calmly postulated that women had sexual desires and had to make room for their fulfilment among their other fulfilments. If one looks for any such recognition in English writing, it is either not there or there only fleetingly and in texts that are difficult to interpret. The heroine of Cleland's *Memoirs of a Woman of Pleasure* is certainly described as receiving as much pleasure from her sexual activities as she bestows, and her psychology seems convincing—to a male reader; but then the book was written for a largely male readership (probably) and by a man (certainly).

Colette's deep understanding of her characters—combined with her skill in narration, description, every technical device of the writer—leave one completely convinced. She also has the advantage of being what the English call 'unshockable'. In *Chéri*, the *donnée* of the story (a spoilt youth has been given by his mother into the care of a fading *grande horizontale* who will supervise his journey across the perilous straits between boyhood and manhood) could certainly not be described as edifying. Both partners enter into the relationship for reasons of self-gratification; both are monstrous egotists and it never occurs to them to be anything else. When Léa is facing the loss of Chéri that she has always known was inevitable, she sees her relationship with him in terms of a strategic mistake. For a woman approaching fifty to have an affair lasting for six years is like going out to the colonies with one's husband; when she comes back, her friends have forgotten her and her clothes are out of fashion. So she reflects. But when the moment of relinquishment finally comes, and the pain bites deeply, there is a dimension of tragedy and even of nobility in her response to the situation.

Because *Chéri* is the most famous of Colette's works outside France, the English-speaking reader naturally thinks of Léa as being offered by the author as a standard-bearer of feminine sexuality. In fact, she is hardly a typical member of the female sex, if only because her life is spent in an atmosphere of over-sated consumerism that most women do not have the time and money, or perhaps the inclination, to inhabit. Perhaps it is the sheer vitality of the portraiture that makes her come across as a female figure as universal as Molly Bloom. In any case, the slight atmosphere of depravity which hangs about the tale serves to highlight an Anglo-French difference. English fiction has, as a matter of historical fact, been powered very often by moral fervour, by an urgent concern with questions of how to live and what to do. The French novel traditionally has less of this urgency. What it has instead is a penetrating curiosity about life. That Chéri and Léa are as nearly as possible worthless as moral and social types does not make them any the less fit subjects for the novelist. The fact that such people unquestionably do exist, and have the psychology and the emotions that they do have, are facts like any other, and deserve analysis.

For a complement to Colette on this side of the Channel, one's eye naturally falls on D. H. Lawrence, a writer who also put the relation of man and woman at the centre of his work, declared indeed that it was his main theme. Actually the subject of sexuality, fundamental as it is, stands in Lawrence as the surrogate or iceberg-tip of an even more fundamental concern, his sense of the pre-human and non-human sources of power in the universe, those forces which belong to (since we must use the word, loosened as it has been by the too various demands made on it) 'nature'. To Lawrence, human life became a succession of trivialities, a mere matter of going through the motions, unless it was plugged in somehow or other to these unknowable, undiscussable but palpably real and present sources of strength and instinctual knowledge. If one makes a list of the things Lawrence disliked in people, and constantly preached against (often to the detriment of his novels as novels) it reads at first like a string of random dissimilarities: will-power, intellectualism, idealism, frivolity, and the kind of wit that naturally accompanies frivolity. But one soon sees the common element that unites them. They are all attributes that go against, or are unresponsive to, the vibrations that come from the primeval realities, the 'dark gods'. That is why, though his work seemed so obviously to flout the respectability involved with church-going and religious belief, he could say with perfect sincerity, 'One has to be so terribly religious, to be an artist.'

At all events, Lawrence managed to overthrow with a single assault the convention that there is and ought to be no such thing as equally shared sexual fulfilment, even though he occasionally veers close to the traditional view of womanly submissiveness in those passages where he insists that the male driving force has 'authority' to which it is the woman's rôle reverently, even religiously, to submit. As against this, his work does at least abound in female characters who are alive to, or are in the process of being made alive to, their sexual nature and acknowledge it as essential to their completeness. People who have grasped this, and have disposed their lives so as to bring it about, win Lawrence's approval. They have ceased to be 'nerve-worn with consciousness'; they have instinctual wisdom. He speaks of them in the same tone as a nineteenth-century evangelical preacher from his own background might have spoken of those who were 'washed in the blood of the Lamb'. We are a long way from Colette, as far as Nottingham is from Saint-Sauveur-en-Puisaye.

Let me end with the ritual defensive gestures. Nobody will totally approve of this selection. The field of literature is so vast and full of surprises, and individual readers' tastes are so varied, that nobody is ever completely satisfied with any selection. Why this? Why not that? Surely you've forgotten the other? Yes, yes, of course. Many fine things have been left out. The only realistic hope is that nothing has got in that *isn't* a fine thing, and that the collection as a whole gathers a rewarding variety of fine things of different weights and colours and textures.

Quality has been the only criterion. The only non-literary factors that have led to exclusions have been considerations of length and date. Some of the greatest writers of the chosen period are missing because they did not attempt anything of a suitable length: likewise, the decision to halt in the mid-1940s has excluded some fine work by (for instance) Günter Grass, Marguerite Yourcenar, Gabriel García Márquez. Apart from that, quality has been my only thought. In particular I have been oblivious of the claims of fairness, making no attempt to balance the various linguistic and cultural groupings within the Western tradition; there is nothing here translated from Italian, or the languages of the Iberian peninsula, or Scandinavia. I regret these omissions. I regret every decision that has resulted in leaving out something good. I hope the works I have missed will be published elsewhere, and speedily, and frequently, for of first-rate imaginative work the world can never have too much.

The finished product is my responsibility, and its faults and inadequacies are on my head. Stan Remington had the initial idea for the collection and made many useful suggestions. I have also acted on suggestions from Frances Whistler of Oxford University Press, Roger Green, Christopher Gray, and William Wain, the last of whom gave me his help in every stage of the work. To all of them, my grateful thanks.

Oxford, 1989   JOHN WAIN

Johann Wolfgang von Goethe
THE SORROWS OF
YOUNG WERTHER
1774

ALTHOUGH this collection is in no sense a work of literary history, and, as we noted in the Introduction, makes no attempt to match up with any fairness the contributions of individual nations, it is, none the less, fitting that we begin with a famous story by a German genius: probably the greatest genius ever to arise among them, Johann Wolfgang von Goethe (1749–1832). In youth rebellious, impulsive, his untamed art the power centre of the short-lived *Sturm und Drang* movement, in later life Goethe filled out to a broad, inclusive, tolerant wisdom that shone upon the world of his time like the beams of the sun. To get a sense of his work one has to see it against a background of the Germany of the late eighteenth and early nineteenth centuries, not yet unified and welded into a formidable military and economic power, rather a cluster of diminutive states, only Prussia among them having much in the way of military power; a culture characterized by poets, philosophers, great musicians, and minor monarchs, the country admired by Coleridge and De Quincey. As late as the 1840s Queen Victoria, on her first visit to her consort's native Coburg, could speak of 'our dear little Germany'. But there was nothing small-scale about German energy or the German creative genius. In the new European mind that formed itself after the French Revolution, German energy, German philosophical, historical, and literary ideas were to the fore.

Goethe in his youth was in close contact with the torrentially enthusiastic critic and theorist J. G. Herder, who set a high value on folk poetry and believed that the soul of the nation spoke through its artists known and unknown—an idea familiar enough since his day, but largely because he and his generation made it so. The eighteenth century, when it considered the matter at all, seemed to believe that men of genius arose one after another by a kind of divine accident, with no need of any roots in the national temperament or the spirit of the age. Herder, who believed that the German-ness of all things German was their great strength and their great contribution, edited a volume of essays in 1773, under the title *Von deutscher Art und Kunst,* to which Goethe contributed an ecstatic essay on Gothic architecture, which he took (mistakenly, as it happens) to be an essential expression of the German spirit. The spread of German influence throughout Europe was strongly aided by the formidable Swiss critic and theorist of literature Madame de Staël, whom we shall meet again in the head-note to Benjamin Constant and whose amorous adventures also included one with Chamisso. Madame de Staël greatly admired the energy and originality of German Romantic writers and expressed this admiration in her book *De L'Allemagne* (1810), which was confiscated by order of Napoleon, but published in England in 1813 and translated into German in 1814.

The Sorrows of Young Werther is a product of Goethe's youth and his participation in the great wave of energy that swept across Europe in the first years of the Romantic movement. It was written in three months in the spring of 1774, and one might almost be able to tell from its intense, passionate, hurrying quality that it was written by a young man and in the spring. From the first onset of lyric joy at the verdant beauty of the rural scene, quickly followed by an overflowing of love towards a girl who typifies its loveliness and innocence but is promised to another, through to the final act of high heroic self-destruction, the story's energy never flags. The book became a wildfire vogue throughout all Europe; everywhere, young men adapted their appearance to what they hoped was resemblance to Werther, as a generation later they were to do with Byron.

Goethe lived for eighty-one years; it hardly concerns us to trace the details of his long and resplendent career after writing *Werther*, beyond noting that in 1775 the Duke of Weimar invited him to his court, and Goethe accepted and thenceforth spent most of his time there, engaged in a wide range of literary, theatrical, and scientific work.

[The text is prefaced by this note, ostensibly from the Editor.]

I have carefully collected and here present to you whatever facts I have been able to discover concerning the history of poor Werther, knowing that you will be grateful to me for doing so. You cannot withhold your admiration and love for his character, any more than your tears for his fate.

And you, noble soul who feels the same longing that he felt, take comfort from his suffering, and let this book be your friend, when, because of destiny or some fault of your own, you cannot find a nearer and dearer one.

BOOK ONE

HOW happy I am to have come away! Dearest friend, how strange is the human heart! To leave you, one so dearly loved, from whom I was inseparable, and yet to be glad! I know you will forgive me. Were not all my other personal relationships definitely chosen by fate to torment a heart like mine? Poor Leonora! And yet I was blameless. Was it my fault that, while the capricious charms of her sister provided me with a pleasant entertainment, her poor heart built up a passion for me? Still—am I altogether blameless? Did I not encourage her emotions? Did I not relish her perfectly genuine and naïve expressions which so often made us laugh, although they were anything but amusing? Did I not—but oh, what is man that he dares so to complain of himself! Dear friend, I promise you I will improve. I will no longer ruminate, as I always used to do, on the petty troubles which Fate puts in my way. I will enjoy the present and let bygones be bygones. You are certainly right, best of friends, that there would be far less suffering in the world if human beings—God knows why they are made like that—did not use their imaginations so busily in recalling the memories of past misfortunes, instead of trying to bear an indifferent present.

Be so kind to tell my mother that I shall attend to her business as well as I can, and that I will give her news about it soon. I have seen my aunt, and found that she is far from being the disagreeable person my family makes her out to be. She is a lively, impetuous woman, but very warm-hearted. I explained to her my mother's complaint concerning that part of the legacy which had been withheld from her. She told me the reasons and motives of her own conduct, and also the terms on which she would be willing to hand over everything, and even more than we asked. In short, I do not like to write more about it just now; tell my mother that all will be well. And again I have found, handling this trifling piece of business, that misunderstandings and neglect create more confusion in this world than trickery and malice. At any rate, the last two are certainly much less frequent.

Otherwise, I am very happy here. The solitude in this heavenly place is sweet balm to my soul, and the youthful time of year warms with its abundance my often shuddering heart. Every tree, every hedge is a nosegay of blossoms; and one would wish to be turned into a cockchafer, to float about in that sea of fragrance and find in it all the nourishment one needs.

The town itself is not pleasant, but all around it Nature expands an inexpressible beauty. This moved the late Count M. to lay out a garden on one of the hills which, intersecting one another in the loveliest natural diversity, form the most charming valleys. The garden is simple, and as soon as one enters, one feels that it was planned not by a scientific gardener but by a sensitive heart wishing to commune with itself alone. I have already shed many a tear to the memory of its former owner, in the crumbling summerhouse which was once his favorite retreat, and now is mine. Soon I shall be the master of the garden; the gardener has taken to me after only a few days, and he will not fare badly.

10 May

A wonderful serenity fills my whole being, like these lovely mornings which I enjoy with all my heart. I am quite alone, and pleased with life in this countryside, which seems to have been created for souls like mine. I am so happy, dear friend, so completely sunk in the sensation of sheer being, that my art suffers. I could not draw anything just now, not a line, and yet I have never been a greater painter than at the present moment. When the mist rises around me from the lovely valley, and the sun at high noon rests on the roof of my impenetrably dark forest, and only single shafts of sunlight steal into the inner sanctuary, and I am lying in the tall grass by the falling brook, discovering the variety of thousands of different grasses closer to the ground; when I feel nearer to my heart the teeming little world among the grass blades, the innumerable, inscrutable shapes of all the tiny worms and insects, and feel the presence of the Almighty who created us in his image, the breath of the All-Loving who sustains us, floating in eternal bliss—my friend, when everything grows dim then before my eyes, and sky and earth rest in my soul like the image of a beloved being—I am often overcome by longing and by the thought: could you only breathe upon paper all that lives so full and warm within you, so that it might become the mirror of your soul, as your soul is the mirror of the infinite God!—My friend—but it is more than I can bear; I succumb to the power and the glory of these visions.

12 May

I do not know if mocking spirits haunt this place, or whether it is the warm heavenly fantasy in my own heart which transforms everything around me into a paradise. Near the entrance to the town is a fountain, a fountain which holds me spellbound like Melusine with her sisters.—Going down a small hill, you find yourself in front of a vault to which some twenty steps lead down, where the clearest water gushes forth from the marble rocks. The enclosing little wall above, the tall trees which give shade all about, the coolness—all this makes the place so attractive and thrilling. Hardly a day passes without my sitting there for an hour. Then the girls will come from the town and fetch water, the most innocent task and the most necessary, in ancient times performed even by the daughters of kings. As I sit there, the patriarchal idea comes to life again for me: I see them, our forefathers, meet at the fountain and do their wooing, and feel how benevolent spirits hover around wells and springs. Anyone who has refreshed himself at a cool fountain after a long walk in summer will understand my feelings.

13 May

You ask me if you should send me my books?—My dear fellow, I implore you, for God's sake, do not bother me with them. No longer do I wish to be guided, excited, stimulated; my own heart storms enough in itself. What I need are cradlesongs, and I have found plenty of these in my Homer. How often do I lull my rebellious blood to rest, for you cannot imagine anything so erratic, so restless as my heart. My friend, need I tell you all this, you, whom I have so often burdened with the sight of my transitions from grief to excessive joy, from sweet melancholy to fatal passion. I treat my poor heart, moreover, as though it were a sick child, and satisfy all its desires. Do not tell this to anyone; there are those who would strongly disapprove.

15 May

The simple folk here already know me and have taken to me, especially the children. When I first joined them, and asked them in a friendly way about this or that, some thought that I wanted to scoff at them, and they sometimes even curtly rebuked me. I did not resent this; I merely felt most vividly what I had observed frequently before: people of a certain rank will always keep a cool distance from common people, as if they were afraid to lose their dignity by too much familiarity. On the other hand, there are superficial fellows and malicious jokers who seem to be condescending and only hurt the feelings of the poor folk all the more by their insolence. I know quite well that we are not and cannot ever be equal; but I am convinced that anyone who thinks it necessary to keep his distance from the so-called mob in order to gain its respect is as much to blame as the coward who hides from his enemy because he fears to be defeated.

A little while ago I came to the fountain and saw a young servant girl who had set her pitcher on the lowest step while she looked about for one of her companions to help her lift it to her head. I went down and looked at her. 'Do you want me to help you?' I asked. She blushed all over. 'Oh, no, sir!' she said.—'Why not?'—She adjusted the pad on her head, and I helped her. She thanked me and went up the steps.

17 May

I have made all sorts of acquaintances but have not yet found any congenial company. I do not know what there is about me that attracts people; so many like me and become attached to me, and then I am always sorry that we can travel only a short way together. When you ask me what the people here are like, I must answer: Like people everywhere! There is a certain monotony about mankind. Most people toil during the greater part of their lives in order to live, and the slender span of free time that remains worries them so much that they try by every means to get rid of it. O Destiny of Man!

They are a very good sort of people, however. Whenever I forget myself and enjoy in their company the pleasures still granted to human beings, can exchange friendly jokes in all frankness and candour around a well-set table, arrange a drive in a carriage or a ball at the proper time—all this sort of thing has quite a good effect on me; I must only avoid remembering that there are still many other forces dormant in me, all unused and rotting, which I must carefully hide. Ah! it contracts my heart, and yet—it is the fate of a man like myself to be misunderstood.

Alas, that the friend of my youth is gone! Alas, that I ever knew her! I should say to myself: You are a fool to search for something that cannot be found on this earth. But she was mine, I felt her heart, her great soul, in whose presence I seemed to be more than I really was because I was all that I could be. Good God, was there a single force in my soul then unused? Could I not unfold in her presence all the wonderful emotions with which my heart embraces Nature? Was not our relationship a perpetual interweaving of the most subtle feeling with the keenest wit, whose modifications, however extravagant, all bore the mark of genius? And now—Alas, the years she had lived in advance of my own brought her to the grave before me. I shall never forget her—neither her unwavering mind nor her divine fortitude.

A few days ago I met a young man by the name of V., an open-hearted youth with pleasant features. He has just left the university and does not consider himself a sage but thinks, nevertheless, that he knows more than other people. He has studied hard, as I can tell from many indications; in short, he has a pretty store of knowledge. As he had heard that I sketch a good deal and know Greek (two unusual phenomena in these parts), he came to see me and displayed all sorts of learning, from Batteux to Wood, from De Piles to Winckelmann, assuring me that he had read the whole first part of Sulzer's 'Theory,' and that he possessed a manuscript of Heyne's on the study of antiquity. I let that pass.

I have made the acquaintance of another good man, the Prince's bailiff, an honest, candid character. They say it warms the heart to see him among his children, of whom he has nine.

There is much talk about his oldest daughter in particular. He invited me to his house, and I am going to pay him a visit soon. He lives an hour and a half from here in one of the Prince's hunting lodges which he was permitted to occupy after the death of his wife, as he found life here in town, and in his bailiff's quarters, too painful.

I have also come across a couple of odd people whom I consider thoroughly repulsive, and quite intolerable in their demonstrations of friendship.

Farewell! You will approve of this letter, which is entirely historical.

22 May

That this life is but a dream is a thought which has occurred to many people, and I myself am constantly haunted by it. When I see the limitations which imprison the active and speculative faculties of man; when I see how all human activity is directed toward procuring satisfaction for needs that have no other purpose than prolonging our miserable existence; when I see, moreover, how any comfort we may derive from certain points of inquiry is merely a dreamlike kind of resignation, in which we paint our prison walls with gaily coloured figures and luminous prospects—all this, Wilhelm, leaves me speechless. I withdraw into my inner self and there discover a world—a world, it is true, rather of vague perceptions and dim desires than of creative power and vital force. And then everything swims before my senses, and I go on smiling at the outer world like someone in a dream.

That children do not know the reason of their desires, all the learned teachers and instructors agree. But that grown-ups too stumble like children on this earth, not knowing whence they come or whither they go, acting as little according to true purposes, being ruled like them by cakes and birch rods, no one likes to believe; yet to me it seems quite obvious.

I know your reply to this statement, and I willingly admit that those are the happiest people who, like children, live for the day only, drag around their dolls, putting their clothes on or off, tiptoe around the cupboard where Mummy keeps the sweets locked up, and, after having finally snatched the desired bit, stand with full cheeks and shout: 'More!'—These are indeed happy creatures. Nor are those people unhappy who, giving pompous names to their shabby occupations or even to their passions, pretend that these are gigantic achievements for the happiness and welfare of mankind. Happy the man who can be like this! But whoever realizes in all humility what all this amounts to, who observes with what pleasure every prosperous citizen trims his little garden into a paradise, how patiently even the unfortunate man struggles along his road under the weight of his burden, and how all are eager to see the light of the sun a little longer—well, such a man remains calm and shapes his own world out of himself; and he, too, is happy because he is a human being. And then, however confined he may be, he still holds forever in his heart the sweet feeling of freedom, and knows that he can leave this prison whenever he likes.

26 May

You know of old my habit of settling down in some pleasant region and living there in a modest way. Here, too, I have discovered again a place which has attracted me.

About an hour from the town is a village called Wahlheim. Its location against a hill is very interesting, and when you leave it by the upper footpath, you can suddenly overlook the whole valley. The good landlady of the inn, pleasant and brisk for her age, provides beer, wine and coffee; and the best feature of all is two linden trees, shading with their spreading branches the little square in front of the church, which is framed on all sides by peasants' cottages, barns and farmyards. I have seldom found a place so intimate and charming, and often have my little table and a chair brought out from the inn, and there drink my coffee and read my Homer. When I came for the first time, quite by accident, on a fine afternoon, under these linden trees, I found the little square deserted. Everyone was out in the fields. Only one little boy, about four years of age, was sitting on the ground, holding another child of about six months, who sat between his feet close against his breast, so that his arms formed a kind of chair for the little one; and the older boy sat perfectly still in spite of the sprightly way in which he glanced around with his dark eyes. I was amused by

the sight and, sitting down on a plough opposite the two, made
a drawing of the brotherly pose with great delight. I included
the nearest fence, a barn door, and a few broken cartwheels,
just as they came into view, and realized, after an hour, that
I had made a well-composed and very interesting sketch,
without having added the slightest invention of my own. This
confirmed me in my resolution to keep close to Nature in
the future. Nature alone is illimitably rich, and Nature alone
forms the great artist. It is possible to say a good deal in favour
of rules, about as much as can be said in praise of bourgeois
society. The person who takes his direction from rules alone
will never produce anything in bad taste, in the same way as
the person who allows himself to be shaped by rules of social
convention can never become an intolerable neighbour or a
conspicuous villain; on the other hand, any rule is likely to
destroy both the true feeling of Nature and its true expression,
whatever people may say to the contrary. You will object that
this statement is too severe, and that rules only restrain and
prune the overluxuriant vine, etc. My dear friend! Shall I
give you an analogy? It is the same with love. A young man's
heart is entirely attached to a girl; he spends every hour of
the day with her, wastes all his strength, all his fortune, in
order to prove to her at every moment that he is wholly
devoted to her. Should a philistine then enter the picture,
a man of some responsible position, and say to him: 'My
dear young man, it is natural to love, but you must love only
in a sensible way. Organize your day; some hours for work
and some—the hours of relaxation—for your sweet heart.
Calculate your means; and it is perfectly permissible to use
whatever is left over and beyond your personal needs to buy
her a present of some sort, only not too frequently—perhaps
for her birthday or a similar occasion.'—Should the young
man follow this advice, he will certainly turn into a useful
member of society, and I should advise any prince to take him
into his Cabinet; but his love is done with, and, if he is an artist,
his art as well. O my friends! Why does the stream of genius
so seldom break out as a torrent, with roaring high waves, and
shake your awed soul?—Dear friends, because there are cool
and composed gentlemen living on both banks, whose garden
houses, tulip beds and cabbage fields would be devastated if

they had not in good time known how to meet the threatening danger by building dams and ditches.

I am indulging, I see, in rapture, analogies and rhetoric, and I have forgotten to tell you the end of my story about the children. I had been sitting on my plough for almost two hours, completely absorbed in a painter's kind of perception which I described to you very fragmentarily in my letter of yesterday, when, toward evening, a young woman came up to the children, who had sat motionless the whole time. She carried a little basket on her arm and called from a distance: 'Philip, you are a very good boy.' She greeted me; I thanked her and, getting up, asked her if she was the children's mother. She said, yes, she was; and, handing a piece of bread to the older boy, she lifted the younger child on her arm and kissed it with motherly affection. 'I asked Philip to take care of the little one,' she said, 'as I had to go to town with my oldest son to buy white bread, sugar, and an earthen pot.' I noticed all these articles in her basket as the lid had fallen open. 'I wanted to make some soup for Hans (that was the name of the youngest child), but this oldest brother, the rascal, had broken the old pot yesterday while he was quarrelling with Philip for the scrapings.' I asked about the oldest boy, and she had hardly mentioned the fact that he was chasing the geese in the meadow when he came running up with a hazel switch for his younger brother. I continued my talk with the woman and learned that she was the schoolmaster's daughter, and that her husband had gone to Switzerland to collect his inheritance from a cousin. 'They meant to cheat him out of it,' she said, 'and did not answer his letters. That is why he went there himself. If only nothing has happened to him; I have not heard anything from him since he left.' I was quite sorry to have to leave the woman, but I gave a penny to each boy, and another to the mother to buy a roll for the younger one whenever she went to town; and in this way we parted.

I tell you, my dearest friend, when I am completely beside myself, the tumult of my emotions is soothed by the sight of such a woman, who is rounding the narrow circle of her existence with serene cheerfulness, managing to make both ends meet from one day to the next, seeing the leaves fall without any thought save that winter is near.

Since then, I have often gone back there. The children are quite accustomed to me; they get sugar when I drink my coffee, and share my bread and butter and my curdled milk in the evening. On Sundays they never lack their penny, and, should I not be there after church, I have asked the landlady to give it to them.

They are quite familiar with me and tell me all sorts of things. I am particularly delighted to watch their show of temper and their naïve outbursts of greed whenever other children from the village are with them.

I took great pains to convince their mother not to worry that they might 'bother the gentleman.'

30 May

What I wrote you the other day about painting is certainly also true of poetry; one has only to recognize what is excellent and then have the courage to express it, which is, of course, easier said than done. Today I have come upon a little drama which, if truthfully written down, would make the loveliest idyll in the world; but why talk of poetry, drama, and idyll? Do we always have to dabble in literature when we are allowed to witness some natural happening?

If you should expect something noble and distinguished after this preamble, you will again be greatly disappointed. It was only a country lad who strongly attracted my sympathy. As usual, I shall be a bad narrator, and as usual, you will think my story is exaggerated. It is again Wahlheim and always Wahlheim that offers these exceptional characters and incidents.

I had been invited to drink coffee under the linden trees. As the people were not quite to my liking, I had found some pretext for not joining the party.

A young peasant came out of a nearby house and was soon busy mending the plough which I had sketched some days before. As I liked his manner, I spoke to him about his circumstances; we were soon acquainted and, as usually happens to me with such people, were soon quite familiar. He told me that he was in the service of a widow who treated him very well. He told me so much about her and praised her in such a way that I could soon guess that he was heart and soul devoted to her. She was no longer young, he said; her first husband had treated her badly, and she did not want to marry again. It became more than evident from his words how beautiful and how charming she was in his eyes, and how much he wished that she would choose him as a husband so that he might efface the memory of her first husband's faults. I should have to repeat every word of his story in order to give you a true picture of the pure affection, love, and devotion of this man. Yes, I should have to possess the gift of the greatest of poets in order to depict to you convincingly the expressiveness of his gestures, the harmony of his voice, the hidden fire of his eyes. No, words fail to convey the tenderness of his whole being; everything I could attempt to say about this would only be clumsy. I was particularly moved by his anxiety that I might receive a wrong impression about his relationship to her or doubt her respectability. The delightful way in which he spoke of her figure, her physical charm, that irresistibly attracted and captivated him in spite of her lack of real youth, I can only repeat to myself in my inmost soul. Never in my life have I seen an urgent and passionate desire combined with such purity of heart; yes, I may well say, never had I myself imagined or dreamed of such purity. Do not scold me if I confess that the memory of this innocence and candour fills my soul with delight, that the picture of this devotion and tenderness follows me everywhere, and that I thirst and languish as if kindled by that flame.

I shall try to see her as soon as possible, or rather, after giving it a second thought, I shall avoid her. It is better that I see her through the eyes of her lover; she might not appear to my own eyes, in reality, as I now see her; and why should I destroy the lovely image I already possess?

16 June

Why do I not write to you? And you, a learned man, ask me this? You should be clever enough to guess that I am in a happy mood because—in a word—I have made an acquaintance who moves my heart in a strange way. I have—I do not know.

It is not easy for me to tell you, in chronological order, just how it happened, how I met such a lovely being. I am contented and happy, and therefore not a good historian.

An angel!—Nonsense! Everyone calls his loved one thus, does he not? And yet I cannot describe to you how perfect she is, or why she is so perfect; enough to say that she has captured me completely.

So much innocence combined with so much intelligence; such kindness with such firmness; such inner serenity in such an active life.

But all this is foolish talk—pure abstract words which fail to describe one single feature of her real person. Another time—no, not another time, right at this moment I will tell you everything. If I don't do it now, it will never be done. Because—between you and me—since I began this letter I have been three times on the point of laying down my pen, having my horse saddled and riding out to her. Although I swore to myself this morning not to do it, I am going every other moment to the window to see how high the sun has climbed.

I could not bear it any longer; I had to see her. Here I am back, Wilhelm; I will now eat my supper and then go on writing to you. What a delight it was to see her among the dear lively children, her eight brothers and sisters!

But if I go on in this way you will know as little at the end as at the beginning. Listen, then, while I force myself to go into details.

The other day I wrote you that I had met the bailiff S., and that he had asked me to visit him in his hermitage, or rather, his little Kingdom. I neglected to do so, and probably never would have gone there if I had not by chance discovered the treasure hidden in that quiet part of the district.

The young people here had arranged a ball in the country, and I gladly agreed to go. I asked a good, pretty, but otherwise uninteresting girl to be my partner, and proposed to hire a coach to drive out to the appointed place with her cousin and herself, picking up Charlotte S. on our way. 'You will meet a beautiful girl,' my partner said while we were driving through a broad clearing of the forest toward the hunting lodge. 'Be careful that you do not fall in love with her!' her cousin added.—'What do you mean?' I said.—'She is already engaged,' was her answer, 'and to a very worthy man who is not here at present. He left to attend to his affairs after the death of his father, and is also about to apply for an important position.' This information did not particularly impress me.

The sun was still a quarter of an hour from the top of the mountains when we drove up at the lodge gate. The air was very close, and the ladies expressed their concern about a thunderstorm which was evidently gathering around the horizon in small compact whitish-grey clouds. I dispelled their fear by pretending to be a weather expert, although I myself began to feel apprehensive about an interruption of our amusement.

I climbed out of the coach, and the maid who came to the gate asked us to wait a moment—Mamsell Lottchen would soon be down. I crossed the courtyard toward the well-built lodge. When I had gone up the outer staircase and entered the house, I saw the most charming scene I had ever in my life beheld. In the entrance hall six children, between the ages of eleven and two, were swarming around a handsome young girl of medium height, who wore a simple white dress with pink bows on her arms and breast. She was holding a loaf of dark bread and cutting one slice apiece for each of the children around her, in proportion to age and appetite, dealing it out so kindly, and each child cried out 'Thank you!' so artlessly, after having stretched out two tiny hands as high as possible before the slice was cut; after which they all cheerfully jumped away with their supper, or, if of a quieter nature, walked sedately towards the gate to have a look at the strangers and at the coach in which their Lotte would soon drive away.—'Please, forgive me,' she said, 'that I gave you the trouble to come for me, and that I keep the ladies waiting. While I was dressing and making all sorts of arrangements for the household during my absence, I forgot to give the children their supper, and they won't have their bread sliced by anyone but me.' I paid her an insignificant compliment while my soul was taking in her whole appearance, her voice, the grace of her bearing; and I had just enough time to recover from my surprise when she ran to her room to fetch her gloves and fan. The children meanwhile kept at some distance, casting sidelong glances at me, and I went up to the youngest, an extremely pretty little boy. He drew back just as Lotte returned from her room, saying: 'Louis, shake hands with your uncle.' The boy obeyed her most trustingly, and I could not refrain from kissing him with affection, in spite of his runny little nose. 'Uncle?' I asked, taking her hand. 'Do you consider me worthy of being related to you?'—'Oh,' she said with a merry smile, 'our circle of relatives is very wide, and I should be sorry if you were to be the worst among them.'—On leaving, she told Sophy, the next oldest to herself, a girl of about eleven, to take good care of the younger children, and to give her love to their father when he returned from his ride. She told the children to obey Sophy as they would herself, and some of them promised to do so; but a pert little blonde of some six years said: 'But she is not you, dear Lotte. We love you much more.'—The two older boys had climbed up behind the coach and, on my pleading for them, were allowed to accompany us to the edge of the wood if they promised not to fight with each other and to hold on fast.

Hardly had we taken our seats and the ladies exchanged their welcomes and their remarks on one another's dresses and particularly on one another's hats, and had gossiped a good deal about the people they expected to meet, when Lotte asked the coachman to stop and order her brothers to climb down. They insisted on kissing her hand once more, and the older one did so with all the tenderness which can be characteristic of a boy of fifteen, the younger one in a rough and boisterous way. Once more she sent her love to the younger children, and then we continued our drive.

The cousin asked if Lotte had finished the book she had recently sent her. 'No, I have not,' Lotte said; 'I do not like it; you may have it back. And the one before it was not any better.' I was amazed when, on my asking her what books she meant, she gave me the titles. I was struck by the show of character in everything she said; every word revealed fresh attractions, and her flashes of intelligence showed in her face, which seemed gradually to light up with pleasure when she felt that I understood her.

'When I was younger,' she continued, 'I liked nothing so much as novels. God knows how happy I was if I could sit in a corner on Sundays and share with heart and soul the fortunes and misfortunes of some Miss Jenny. And I won't deny that this sort of book still has some attraction for me; but, as I have so little time now for reading, whatever I read has to be to my taste. And the author whom I like most of all is the once who takes me into my own world, where everything happens as it does around me, and whose story, nevertheless, becomes to me as interesting and as touching as my life at home, which is certainly not a paradise but is, on the whole, a source of inexpressible happiness to me.'

I tried to hide my emotions at these words. I did not, it is true, succeed very well; for when I heard her speak casually, but with much truth, about *The Vicar of Wakefield* and about——, I lost all my reserve and told her everything I wished to tell, and only noticed, after some time, when Lotte directed the conversation to the other two, that they had been sitting all the while with wide-open eyes, as if they were not there at all. Now and then the cousin puckered up her little nose mockingly, to which, however, I paid no attention.

The conversation turned to the pleasures of dancing. 'If this passion should be a weakness,' Lotte said, 'I readily confess that I don't know anything to surpass dancing. And whenever I have something on my mind, I start strumming some *contredanse* on my clavichord (which is always out of tune), and then all is well.'

How delighted I was to look into her dark eyes while she spoke. How my whole soul was fascinated by her warm lips and her glowing cheeks! I was so deeply lost in the excellence of her conversation that I often did not catch the very words by which she expressed her meaning!—All this you can imagine, as you know me well.

I climbed out of the coach as if in a dream when we stopped in front of the house where the ball would take place, and was so lost in my dreams, with the twilit world all about me, that I hardly noticed the music which rang out to us from the illuminated ballroom above.

Two gentlemen, Herr Audran and another whose name escapes me—who can remember all those names!—who were the partners of Lotte and her cousin, welcomed us at the coach door and took charge of their ladies, and I escorted my partner upstairs.

We went through the steps of a few minuets; I asked one
lady after another for a dance, but it seemed that only the
most disagreeable ones could not decide to end the dance with
a clasp of the hand. Lotte and her partner started an *anglaise,*
and you can imagine how delighted I was when she was in the
same line with us from the beginning of the first figure. You
should see her dance! She concentrates so completely—heart
and soul—on the dance itself; her whole body is in harmony,
as carefree and as ingenuous as if nothing else mattered, as if
she had no other thoughts or feelings; and I am certain that
at those moments everything else vanishes from her sight.

I asked her for the second *contredanse;* she promised me
the third and assured me with the most charming frankness
that she was very fond of dancing in the German way. 'It
is a custom here,' she continued, 'that any couple belonging
together remain together for the German dance; but my
partner is awkward at waltzing and will be grateful if I spare
him the effort. Your lady cannot waltz either and does not like
to; but I noticed during the *anglaise* that you waltz well; if you,
therefore, want to be my partner in the German dance, do go
and ask my partner for the favour, and I shall do the same with
your lady.' I accepted the promise by taking her hand, and we
agreed that her partner should meanwhile entertain mine.

Now the dance began, and we enjoyed ourselves for some
time, interlacing our arms in various ways. With what nimble
grace she moved! And when at last we changed to waltzing,
and all the couples revolved around one another like celestial
bodies, there was at first, owing to the inefficiency of most
of the dancers, a kind of mix-up. We were wise, and let the
others have their fling, but as soon as the clumsiest had left the
floor, we stepped out and held the ground firmly with another
couple, Audran and his partner. Never have I danced so well!
I was no longer a mortal being. To hold that loveliest creature
in my arms and to whirl with her like the wind so that the
surroundings disappeared—truly, Wilhelm, I swore to myself
that a girl whom I loved, on whom I might have claims, should
never be allowed to waltz with another man save myself, even
if it would spell ruin for me. You will understand!

We took a few turns around the ballroom between dances,
to recover our breath. Then she sat down, and the oranges I

had secured for her, now the only ones left, had a good effect, except that whenever she shared a little slice in a dutiful way with a greedy lady sitting next to her, I was cut to the heart.

We were the second couple in the third *anglaise*. As we crossed and recrossed the lines of dancers and while I, God knows with what delight, clung to her arm and held her glance, which was reflecting the frankest and purest happiness, we met a lady who had caught my attention before, because of the amiable expression of a face not exactly young. She looked at Lotte with a smile, lifted a warning finger, and, whirling past, pronounced the name *Albert* twice with much emphasis.

'Who is Albert?' I asked Lotte, 'if I am not too bold to ask.' She was about to answer when we were forced to separate, so as to participate in the Great Figure Eight. I seemed to notice a thoughtful shadow on her brow as we kept passing each other. 'Why should I keep it a secret from you?' she said, offering me her hand for the promenade. 'Albert is a fine man to whom I am as good as engaged.' This was, of course, no news to me (the ladies having spoken to me of the matter in the coach), and yet it was now in some way new to me, as I had never actually thought of it in relation to her, who had become so dear to me in so short a time. At any rate I entangled myself in the dance, became absent-minded and stumbled in between the wrong couple, so that everything was at sixes and sevens, and Lotte's presence of mind as well as much pushing and pulling were necessary quickly to restore order.

The dance was not yet finished when the lightning, for some time seen in flashes on the horizon and which I had always explained away as mere summer lightning, became more powerful, and the thunder drowned out the music. Three ladies ran out of the ranks of dancers, and their partners followed suit. Confusion became general and the music stopped. It is natural, when an accident or something terrifying surprises us in the midst of our pleasures, for us to be more impressed than usual, partly because of the so vividly felt contrast, and partly, even more, because our senses are then susceptible and therefore react much more strongly. To these causes I must attribute the strange grimaces that I noticed on the faces of several ladies. The wisest one sat down in a corner, with her back turned to the window, and covered her ears with her hands. A second one knelt in front of her, hiding her head in the lap of the other. A third pushed herself in between and, bathed in tears, hugged her sisters. Some wanted to drive home; others, even more at a loss, did not have enough presence of mind to check the advances of some *gourmets* who were busy capturing from the lips of the pretty ladies in distress their anxious prayers destined for Heaven. Some of the gentlemen had gone downstairs to smoke a quiet pipe; and the rest of the company did not refuse when the hostess had the sensible idea of showing them into a room protected by shutters and curtains. Hardly had they got there when Lotte began to arrange the chairs in a circle, inviting everyone to sit down and join in a parlour game.

I saw more than one fellow purse his lips and stretch himself in expectation of a delicious forfeit. 'We are going to play "Counting",' Lotte said. 'Attention now! I'll go round the circle from right to left, and you all must count in that way round and round, each of you the number that falls to him; but its must go like wildfire, and the person who hesitates or makes a mistake gets his (or her) ears boxed, and so on to a thousand.' Well, it was great fun to watch her. She went around the circle with her arm outstretched. 'One' counted the first; his neighbour 'two'; 'three' the next, and so on. Then Lotte began to go faster, faster, and faster, until someone made a mistake—bang! a slap on his ear, and while the others laughed the next also—bang! and faster and faster! I myself received two slaps and, greatly pleased, thought that they were harder than those she gave to others. General confusion and outbursts of !aughter brought the game to an end before the 'thousand' had been counted. Groups of friends disappeared into the background; the thunderstorm was over, and I followed Lotte into the ballroom. On the way there she said: 'They forgot the thunderstorm and everything else while they played the game.' I did not know what to say. 'I was one of the most frightened,' Lotte continued, 'but by playing the brave one, in order to cheer up the others, I became courageous myself.'

We stepped to the window. The thunder could still be heard in the distance, and the blessed rain fell gently on the ground, from which the most refreshing fragrance rose to us on the fullness of the warm air. She stood leaning on her elbow, her eyes searching the landscape; she looked up at the sky and then at me. I saw her eyes fill with tears; she laid her hand on mine and said: 'Klopstock!' I remembered immediately the magnificent ode which she had in mind, and was overcome by the flood of emotions which she evoked in me with this name. It was more than I could bear. I bowed over her hand and kissed it, moved to the happiest tears. And I again looked into her eyes—noble poet! if you had seen the deep reverence in her eyes! May I never hear again from other lips your so often profaned name!

19 June

I have forgotten where I stopped in my story the other day. I only know that it was two o'clock in the morning when I went to bed, and that if I could have chatted with you instead of writing to you, I should probably have kept you awake until daybreak.

I have not yet told you what happened when we drove home from the ball, and I have not the time to tell you today.

It was a magnificent sunrise. The dripping forest and the refreshed fields lay all about us! Our companions were dozing. Lotte asked me if I would not like to do the same; I should not take any notice of her. 'So long as I see these eyes open,' I said, looking into hers intensely, 'there is no danger of my falling asleep.' And we both kept awake until we arrived at her gate, which was noiselessly opened by the maid, who assured Lotte that her father and the children were well and still asleep. Then I left her, after asking the favour of seeing her again that same day. She granted my request and I went. Since then, sun, moon, and stars may continue on their course; for me there is neither day nor night, and the entire universe about me has ceased to exist.

21 June

My days are as blissful as those which God reserves for his saints; and, whatever may happen to me, I shall never be able to say that I have not experienced the purest joys of life.—You know my Wahlheim. I am now completely settled here. It is only half an hour to Lotte's home, where I feel like myself and find all the happiness granted to man.

Had I known, in choosing Wahlheim as the goal of my walks, that it lies so near to Heaven! How often, in my wanderings near and far, have I seen the hunting lodge which now encloses all my desires, sometimes from the mountain, at other times across the river from the plain!

Dear Wilhelm, I have thought over many things concerning man's ambition to extend himself, to make new discoveries, to roam about; and, on the other hand, his inner urge voluntarily to submit to limitation, to jog along in the groove of habit without looking to right or left. It is strange how, when I came here and looked down from the mountain into the lovely valley, everything attracted me. There was the grove! Ah, could I but mingle with its shades! There was the mountaintop! Ah, could I but overlook from there the wide landscape! The interlocked hills and familiar valleys! Ah, could I but lose myself in them!—I hurried here and there and came back, not having found what I hoped to find. Oh, it is the same with the distance as with the future! A vast, twilit whole lies before our soul; our emotions lose themselves in it as do our eyes, and we long to surrender our entire being and let ourselves sink into one great well of blissful feeling. Alas, when we approach, when There has become Here, everything is as it was before, and we are left with our poverty, our narrowness, while our soul thirsts for comfort that slipped away.

So the most restless vagabond yearns in the end for his native land, and finds in his poor hut, in the arms of his wife, in the circle of his children, and in his labour to support them all, the happiness he searched the wide world for in vain.

When I walk in the morning at sunrise to my Wahlheim and pick my own dish of green peas in the garden of the inn, sit down and shell them while I read my Homer, and then choose a pan in the kitchen, cut off some butter and put the peas on the fire, covering the pan and sitting down so that I may shake them from time to time—I feel vividly how the wanton suitors of Penelope slaughtered oxen and swine, cut them up, and roasted them. There is nothing that fills me with more quiet, genuine emotion than those features of patriarchal life which

I can, thank God, weave without affectation into my own way
of living. How happy I am that my heart is open to the simple,
innocent delight of the man who brings a head of cabbage
to his table which he himself has grown, enjoying not only
the cabbage but all the fine days, the lovely mornings when
he planted it, the pleasant evenings when he watered it, so
that, after having experienced pleasure in its growth he may,
at the end, again enjoy in one single moment all that has gone
before.

29 June

The day before yesterday the physician came out here to
see the bailiff and found me on the floor among Lotte's
children, as some crawled over me, and others teased me,
while my tickling them brought on loud cries. The doctor,
very dogmatic and stiff as a puppet, who arranges the pleats
of his cuffs and pulls out the endless frills of his jabot as
he talks, thought all this to be beneath the dignity of an
intelligent person, as I saw from the way he turned up his
nose. I did not let him discourage me, however; and, while
he was discussing very rational matters, I rebuilt the houses
of cards that the children had knocked down. He later went all
over town complaining that the bailiff's children were naughty
enough but that Werther would now spoil them completely.

Yes, dear Wilhelm, children are nearer my heart than
anything else on earth. When I watch them and see in
these little creatures the seeds of all the virtues, all the
forces they will need one day so badly; when I see in
their obstinacy the future perseverance and firmness of
character, in their mischievousness the happy temper and
the facility needed to evade the world's dangers, all so natural
and innocent!—always, always I keep repeating the golden
words of the Teacher of mankind: Unless ye become even as
one of these! And yet, dearest friend, we treat them, who are
our equals whom we should look upon as our models, as our
subjects. We don't want them to have a will of their own!—Do
we not have one? And in what lies our privilege? Because we
are older and wiser!—Good Lord, from your Heaven you
look down on nothing but old children and young children;
and your Son has already long ago proclaimed in which age

you find greater joy. That people believe in Him and yet do not listen to His words—this also is an old story—and model their children upon themselves, and—farewell, Wilhelm! I do not wish to rave any longer.

1 July

What Lotte's presence must mean to a sick person I can feel in my own poor heart, which is worse off than many a one that pines on a sickbed. She is going to spend some days in the town with a good woman who, from what the doctors say, is nearing her end and wishes to have Lotte at her bedside in her last moments. A week ago I accompanied Lotte on her visit to the pastor of St. ——, a little village, about an hour away, in the mountains. We arrived there at about four in the afternoon. Lotte had brought her second sister with her. On entering the courtyard of the parsonage, shaded by two tall walnut trees, we found the good old man sitting on a bench in front of the house door; when he saw Lotte, he became very animated, forgot his knotty stick and tried to get up and meet her. She ran towards him, made him sit down again while she seated herself at his side, gave him her father's warmest greetings, and hugged his ugly, dirty youngest boy, the apple of his old father's eye. You should have seen her holding the old man's attention with her talk, raising her voice to reach his almost deaf ears; telling him about the healthy young people who had died unexpectedly, about the excellent effects of Karlsbad, and praising his resolution to go there next summer; and saying how she thought he looked much better and brisker than the last time she had seen him. Meanwhile, I was being polite to the pastor's wife. The old man became very cheerful. And as I could not help but admire the beautiful walnut trees that shaded us so pleasantly, he began to tell us, although with some difficulty, their history. 'We don't know,' he said, 'who planted the older one; some say this pastor, others that one. But the younger tree, behind there, is as old as my wife, fifty next October. Her father planted it the morning of the day she was born. He was my predecessor here, and I cannot tell you how much he loved that tree, and certainly it is no less dear to me. My wife was sitting under it on a log with her knitting when I first entered this courtyard as a poor student twenty-seven years ago.' Lotte inquired after his daughter and was told she had gone out to the labourers in the field with a Herr Schmidt, and the old man took up his story again: how his predecessor had grown fond of him, and his daughter as well; and how he had become first his curate and then his successor. He had hardly finished his story when his daughter came through the garden with Herr Schmidt. She welcomed Lotte with warm affection, and I confess that I found her very pleasing: a lively brunette with a shapely figure, who might have been an entertaining companion during a short stay in the country. Her suitor (for Herr Schmidt was obviously this) was an educated but reserved man who refused to join the conversation, although Lotte kept trying to draw him in. What most distressed me was that I gathered from the expression on his face that it was obstinacy and moodiness rather than limited intelligence that kept him from communication. This fact became gradually only too clear; for when Friederike, later on our walk, changed places with Lotte and, occasionally, with me, the gentleman's face, swarthy by nature, darkened so visibly that soon Lotte tugged my sleeve, giving me to understand that I had been too polite to Friederike. Now, nothing makes me more angry than people who torment one another, particularly if young people in the prime of their lives, when they should be most receptive of all pleasures, mutually spoil their few good days by putting on moody faces, realizing only when it is too late that they have wasted something irrecoverable. It greatly annoyed me; and when we had returned to the parsonage, toward evening, and were seated around the table drinking our milk, and the conversation turned toward the joys and sorrows of this world, I could not help but pick up the thread and fervently attack bad moods. 'We human beings often complain,' I began, 'that there are so few good days and so many bad ones; but I think we are generally wrong. If our hearts were always open to enjoy the good, which God gives us every day, then we should also have enough strength to bear the evil, whenever it comes.'—'But we cannot command our dispositions,' said the pastor's wife. 'How much depends on the body! If one does not feel well, everything seems wrong.'—I admitted that. 'Then,' I said, 'we'll look at moodiness as a

disease and see if there is a remedy for it.'—'That makes sense,'
said Lotte. 'I, for one, believe at least that much depends on
ourselves. I speak from my own experience. If something irritates me and is about to make me depressed, I jump up and
sing a few dance tunes up and down the garden, and immediately the mood is gone.'—'That is just what I wanted to say,' I
replied. 'Bad humour is exactly like laziness, because it is a
kind of laziness. Our nature has a strong inclination toward
both, and yet, if we are strong enough to pull ourselves
together, our work is quickly and easily done, and we find
real pleasure in activity.' Friederike listened very attentively,
but her young man made the objection that man is not
his own master, least of all master of his emotions. 'Here we
are speaking of an unpleasant emotion,' I rejoined, 'and
certainly everyone would like to elude it. No one knows the
extent of his powers unless he has tested them thoroughly.
A sick person will certainly consult all available doctors and
will not reject the greatest suffering or the bitterest medicine
if he can recover the good health he longs for.' I noticed
that the good old pastor was straining his ears to catch the
gist of our discussion, and I raised my voice and turned to
him. 'They preach against so many vices,' I said, 'but I never
heard anyone attacking bad humour from the pulpit.' 'The
pastors in towns should do just that,' he said. 'The peasants
are never ill-humoured; but a little preaching might do no
harm here sometimes, and it would at least be a lesson for
my wife and for the bailiff.' Everyone laughed, and he heartily
joined in, until he was seized by a fit of coughing that for a time
interrupted our conversation. Then the young man began to
speak once more: 'You call bad humour a vice; I think that an
exaggeration.'—'Not at all,' I retorted, 'if that which harms
oneself as well as one's neighbour deserves the name. Is it
not enough that we cannot make each other happy; should
we in addition deprive each other of that pleasure which every
heart may sometimes grant itself? And give me the name of the
man who is in a bad mood and yet gallant enough to hide it, to
bear it alone without blighting other people's happiness! Or is
it not perhaps an inner resentment at our own unworthiness, a
dissatisfaction with ourselves, which is always bound up with
some envy stirred up by foolish vanity? We see people happy

whom we have not made happy, and that is unbearable to us.'
Lotte gave me a smile, having noticed the emotion with which
I spoke, and a tear in the eye of Friederike spurred me on to
continue.—'Woe to them,' I said, 'who abuse their power over
the hearts of others and deprive them of any simple joy which
there has its source. All the gifts, all the favours in the world
cannot for a moment replace the inner happiness which the
envious moodiness of our tyrant has spoiled.'

My whole heart was full at this moment; the memory of past
events rushed into my mind, and my eyes filled with tears.

'If people would only warn themselves daily,' I exclaimed,
'that one cannot do anything for one's friends but leave them
their pleasure and add to their happiness by sharing it with
them. Are you able to give them one drop of comfort when
their souls are tormented by a violent passion or crushed by
grief?

'And when the last fatal sickness assails the beloved whom
you have worn out in the days of her youth, and she lies
prostrate in pitiable exhaustion, her unseeing eyes fixed on
Heaven, the cold sweat of death coming and going on her pale
forehead, and you stand at the bedside like a condemned man
with the desperate feeling that you can do nothing; and you
feel agony cramp your heart so that you wish to sacrifice all in
order to inspire the dying person with one invigorating drop,
one spark of courage . . .'

The memory of a similar scene at which I had been present
completely overwhelmed me as I said these words. I raised my
handkerchief to my eyes and left the company. Only the voice
of Lotte, who called out to me that it was time to leave, brought
me to myself. And how she scolded me on our way home for
my too warm sympathy with everything, saying it would be my
ruin and that I should spare myself! O angel, for your sake I
must live!

6 July

She stays with her dying friend and is ever the same active,
lovely creature whose presence soothes pain and makes
people happy wherever she goes. She went for a walk last
evening with Marianne and her youngest sister. I knew of
it, and went to meet them, and we walked together. After

an hour and a half we returned to the town and stopped at the fountain which is so dear to me, and now will be a thousand times dearer. Lotte sat down on the little wall above, and we stood near her. I looked around and alas! the time when my heart was so lonely returned vividly to my mind.—'Dear fountain,' I said, 'it is a long time since I rested near your coolness; I have sometimes even passed by in a hurry without giving you a glance.'—I looked down and saw the little girl coming up the steps, carefully carrying a glass of water. I looked at Lotte and felt deeply what she means to me. Meanwhile, the child approached with the glass, and Marianne wanted to take it from her, but 'No!' cried the little one with sweetest expression. 'No, you must drink first, Lotte!' I was so delighted with the candour, the goodness, with which these words were said, that I could not otherwise express my emotion but lifted the child in my arms and kissed her so fervently that she immediately began to scream and to weep. 'That was not right of you,' said Lotte.—I was puzzled.—'Come, darling,' she continued, taking the child by the hand and leading her down the steps. 'There, wash your face, quick, quick, in the clear spring water, and everything will be all right again.'—While I stood watching the little girl rub her cheeks with her wet little hands, so trustful that the miraculous spring water would wash away the defilement, and remove the chance of being disgraced by an ugly beard; and when I heard Lotte say: 'Now, that will do!' (but the child went on washing herself eagerly, as though Much would help more than Little)—I tell you, Wilhelm, never did I attend a ceremony of baptism with more reverence; and when Lotte came up the steps again, I would gladly have knelt before her, as before a prophet who has washed away with holy water the crimes of a nation.

That same evening, in the happiness of my heart, I could not help repeating the little incident to a man I thought to have common sense, as he is intelligent; but what was his reaction! He said that Lotte had been very thoughtless; that one should never deceive children; such deceit would give rise to innumerable misconceptions and superstitions from which children should be protected at an early age.—It came to my mind that there had been a christening in the man's family only a week ago; therefore I changed the subject but in my heart remained faithful to the truth: that we should deal with children as God deals with us; and He makes us happiest when He lets us stagger about under a benign delusion.

8 July

What children we are! How we crave for a noticing glance! We had gone to Wahlheim. The ladies were driving out, and during our walks together I thought I saw in Lotte's eyes—but I am a fool. Forgive me; you should see those eyes. I must be brief, for I am so sleepy that I can hardly keep my eyes open.—Well, the ladies were getting into the carriage and young W., Selstadt, Audran, and I were standing around it. There was a lively conversation going on through the carriage door with other young men, who were lighthearted and talkative enough. I tried to catch Lotte's glance. Alas, it wandered from one young man to the other, but it did not fall on me! Me! Me! Who stood there absorbed in her alone! My heart bade her a thousand farewells, and she did not notice me! The carriage drove off, and tears stood in my eyes. I looked after her, and saw Lotte's head-dress lean out of the carriage window as she turned to look back—ah, at me? Dear friend, I am torn by this uncertainty. My only consolation is: She may have turned to look back at me! Perhaps! Good night! Oh, what a child I am!

10 July

You should see what an absurd figure I cut when people talk about her in company! Even more so if they ask me how I like her—like! I hate the word like poison. What sort of a person is he who likes Lotte, whose heart and mind is not completely possessed by her! Like! The other day someone asked me if I 'liked' Ossian!

11 July

Frau M. is very ill indeed; I pray for her life because I suffer with Lotte. I rarely see her at my friend's, but today she told me a curious incident. Old M. is a hard, close-fisted man who has tormented and kept a tight rein on his wife all during her lifetime, but she has always succeeded in managing somehow. A few days ago, when the doctor had given up hope for her, she sent for her husband—Lotte was in the room—and said to him: 'I have to confess something that might cause confusion and annoyance after my death. Until lately I have managed the household as neatly and as economically as possible; but you will forgive me for having deceived you during the last thirty years. At the beginning of our married life you fixed a very small sum for the purchase of food and for other domestic expenses. When our household became larger and our business grew, you could not be persuaded to raise my weekly allowance in proportion; you very well know that when our expenses were heaviest, you required me to manage on seven florins a week. I accepted this money without protest, but I took the balance needed from the weekly receipts, as nobody suspected that your wife would steal from your till. I have not squandered the money, and I might have met Eternity with hope and confidence, even without confessing all this, if I had not thought of the woman who will have to keep house after me, and who may be at a loss how to make ends meet, as you will always insist then that your first wife managed with so little.'

I spoke to Lotte about the incredible delusion of a man who does not suspect that there must be something wrong when a person manages with seven guilders and expenses are obviously perhaps twice as much. But I have personally known people who would accept the presence of the prophet's 'unfailing cruse of oil' in their home without being surprised.

13 July

No, I do not deceive myself! In her dark eyes I have read a genuine sympathy for me and my destiny. Yes, I feel—and in this I can trust my heart—that she—oh, may I, can I express the Heaven that exists in these words?—that she loves me!

Loves me!—And how precious I become in my own eyes, how I—to you as an understanding person I may say it—how I admire myself since she loves me.

Is this presumption, or a sense of true proportion? I do not know the man whom I once feared as a rival in Lotte's heart. And yet, when she speaks of her fiancé with such warmth, such affection, I feel like one who has been deprived of all his honours and titles and who has had to yield his sword.

Oh, how my blood rushes through my veins when my fingers unintentionally brush hers or when our feet touch under the table. I shrink back as though from fire, but a secret force drives me forward again, although everything swims before my eyes. Her innocent, candid soul does not divine how tormenting such small intimacies can be. And when, while we talk, she puts her hand on mine and, animated by what we are saying, moves closer to me, so that the heavenly breath of her mouth reaches my lips, I am close to fainting, as if struck by lightning. And, Wilhelm, if I should ever dare—this heavenly confidence—you understand! No, my heart is not so depraved! Weak! Weak enough!—And is that not depravity?

She is sacred to me. Any desire is silenced in her presence. I never know what I feel when I am with her; it is as if my soul were spinning through every nerve. She plays a melody on her clavichord with the touch of an angel, so simple, so ethereal! It is her favourite tune, and I am cured of all pain, confusion, and melancholy the moment she strikes the first note.

Not one word about the magic power of music in antiquity seems to me improbable when I am under the spell of her simple melody. And how well she knows when to play it, at the moment when I feel like blowing out my brains. The confusion and darkness of my soul are then dispersed, and I can breathe more freely again.

Wilhelm, what would the world mean to our hearts without love! What is a magic lantern without its lamp! As soon as you insert the little lamp, then the most colourful pictures are thrown on your white wall. And even though they are nothing but fleeting phantoms, they make us happy as we stand before them like little boys, delighted at the miraculous visions. I have not been able to see Lotte today; a party which I could not refuse to attend prevented me from going. What should I do? I sent my servant to her, only so that I might have someone near me who had been in her presence today. How impatiently I waited for his return, how happy I was to see him back. I should have liked to take him by his shoulder and kiss him, if I had not been too embarrassed to do so.

It is said that the Bologna stone, when placed in the sun, absorbs the sun's rays and is luminous for a while in the dark. I felt the same with the boy. The consciousness that her eyes had rested on his face, his cheeks, the buttons of his jacket and the collar of his overcoat, made all these sacred and precious to me. At that moment I would not have parted with him for a thousand taler. I felt so happy in his presence. God forbid that you should laugh at me, Wilhelm. Are these delusions if they make us so happy?

19 July

'I am going to see her,' is my first cry in the morning when I rouse myself and gaze at the glorious sun in a perfectly serene mood. 'I am going to see her!' And thus I have no other wish for the rest of the day. Everything, everything is drowned in this prospect.

20 July

I cannot yet accept your suggestion that I should accompany the envoy to——. I am not very fond of a subordinate position; and we all know that the man is a disgusting fellow, besides. You write that my mother would like to see me doing some active work; it makes me laugh. Am I not now active? and does it make any real difference whether I count peas or lentils? As everything in the world amounts after all to nothing to speak of, a person who drudges for the sake of others, for money or honours or what not, without following his own ambition, his own need, is always a fool.

24 July

Since you are so concerned that I should not neglect my drawing, I would rather skip that subject than confess that I have not done much lately.

Never before have I been happier, never has my sensitiveness to Nature been richer or deeper, even to the smallest stone, the tiniest blade of grass, and yet—I do not know how to express myself, but my powers of perception are so weak that everything floats and fluctuates before my mind, so that I cannot seize any outline; but I imagine I could do better if I had some clay or wax. I shall get some clay if this state lasts much longer, and I shall knead away even if cakes should be the outcome.

Three times I have started Lotte's portrait, and three times I have bungled it, which makes me very cross, the more so because I was at one time quite successful in getting likenesses. Finally I gave up and cut her silhouette, and with that I shall be satisfied.

26 July

Yes, dear Lotte. I shall order and look after everything; please keep on giving me commissions, and frequent ones. But I ask you one favour: no more sand in the notes you write me. I took today's quickly to my lips, and something gritted between my teeth.

26 July

Many times I have made up my mind not to see her so often. If one could only stick to one's resolutions! Every day I succumb to temptation, and then promise myself most solemnly that I shall stay away tomorrow for once; but when tomorrow comes, I again find some irresistible reason to go, and, before I know it, I am with her. Either she has said the night before, 'You will come tomorrow, won't you?' and who could then stay away? Or she has given me some errand, and I think it is proper to bring her the answer in person; or the day is so very lovely that I walk to Wahlheim, and, when I am there, it is only half an hour to her!—I am so close to her aura—zut! and I am there. My grandmother knew a fairy tale about the Magnetic Mountain. Ships which sailed too close to it were suddenly deprived of all their iron; all the nails flew toward the mountain, and the poor sailors were shipwrecked among the collapsing planks.

30 July

Albert has arrived, and I shall go away. Even if he were the best, the most noble person, one to whom I would be willing to submit myself in every respect—it would still be

unbearable to see him before my eyes in possession of so much
perfection. Possession!—Enough, Wilhelm, the Bridegroom
is here! A worthy, agreeable man whom one cannot help
liking. Fortunately, I was not present when he was welcomed
back. That would have torn my heart. He has so much sense
of decorum that he has not once kissed Lotte in my presence.
God bless him! I must love him for the respect with which he
treats her. For me he has the kindest feelings, but I suspect
that this is Lotte's doing rather than an impulse of his own
spirit; for in these matters women have a delicate way, and
they are right; if they can keep two devoted admirers on
mutual good terms the advantage is always on their side,
although it is rarely achieved.

Meanwhile I cannot deny Albert my esteem. His outward
composure is in very strong contrast to the restlessness which
I cannot conceal of my own character. He feels deeply, and he
knows what he possesses in Lotte. He seems seldom to be in a
bad mood, a sin which, as you know, I hate more in human
beings than any other.

He thinks me a person of sensitive intelligence; and my
devotion to Lotte, my warm enthusiasm for everything she
does, increases his triumph, and he loves her all the more. I
am undecided whether he may not sometimes torment her
with petty jealously; were I in his place, I would not be entirely
free from that demon.

Be that as it may! My happiness with Lotte is gone. Shall
I call this folly or delusion? What are names! The situation
itself is evident. I knew everything I now know before Albert
returned; I knew that I could not make any claims upon her,
nor did I make any; so far, that is, as it is possible for one not
to feel desire in the presence of such sweetness. And yet the
idiot now stares with wide eyes because the other man really
arrives and carries off the girl.

I firmly set my teeth and mock at my misery: and I would
mock twice and thrice at anyone who might suggest that I
should resign myself, since nothing can be helped in any case.
Don't pester me with those empty-headed people!—I roam
about in the woods, and when I arrive at Lotte's house and
find Albert sitting with her in the arbour in her garden, and I
cannot then leave, I behave in a wild and boisterous way and

start all sorts of tomfooleries. 'For Heaven's sake,' said Lotte to me today, 'please don't make a scene, as you did last night! You are dreadful when you show off in that way.' Between ourselves, I wait for the time when Albert is busy; then zut! I am there; and I am always happy when I find her alone.

8 August

Please, dear Wilhelm, do not think that I had you in mind when I called those people intolerable who ask us to resign ourselves to an inevitable fate. I really never thought for a moment that you could hold such an opinion. And, fundamentally, you are right. I have only one objection: in this world we are seldom faced with an Either-Or; all emotions and modes of action show as many varieties of shape and shading as exist between a hooked nose and one that is turned up.

So you won't be angry with me when I grant your whole argument, and yet continue in my attempt to slip in between the Either and the Or.

'Either,' you say, 'you have some reason to hope, so far as Lotte is concerned, or you have none. Very well, in the first case, try to carry the matter through; try to reach the fulfilment of your wishes. Otherwise, pull yourself together and try to get rid of an unfortunate passion that is bound to burn up all your energy.' My dear friend! That is well said, and easily said.

But can you demand it of the unhappy man whose whole life is slowly and irremediably wasting away of a lingering disease; can you demand that he should make a definite end of his misery by the stab of a dagger? And does not the disease, at the very same time that it burns up his strength, also destroy the courage he needs to free himself from it?

In the evening

My diary, which I have neglected for some time, fell into my hands today, and I am amazed how I ran into this situation with full awareness, step by step. How clearly I have seen my condition, yet how childishly I have acted. How clearly I still see it, and yet show no sign of improvement.

10 August

If I were not an idiot, I could lead the best and happiest of lives. One cannot easily imagine the union of pleasanter circumstances for anyone than that in which I am now placed. Oh, how true it is that our heart alone creates its own happiness! To be a member of this charming family, to be loved by the father like a son, by the children like a father, and by Lotte!—And then there is that worthy Albert, who never disturbs my happiness by peevish bad manners; who meets me with warm friendship; for whom I am, next to Lotte, the most cherished being in the world. Wilhelm, it is a joy to hear us talk about Lotte on our walks together. There is nothing more ridiculous on this earth than our relationship; and yet I am often moved to tears when I think of it.

When he tells me of Lotte's kindly mother; how on her deathbed she entrusted Lotte with the care of her household and her children, and Lotte herself to Albert's care; how from that day on Lotte had been animated by an entirely new spirit; how she had conscientiously taken over the house and become a real mother to the children; how not one moment of her time had been spent without tasks and active love, and yet she kept her former cheerfulness and lightness of heart.—While he talks I walk along beside him and pick wayside flowers, arrange them carefully into a nosegay, and—throw them into the river which flows beside the path, and watch them float gently downstream.—I do not remember if I wrote you that Albert is going to remain here; he will receive a handsome salary from a position with the Court, where he is in great favour. I have seldom seen his equal in regard to order and diligence in handling affairs.

12 August

Albert is certainly the best man under the sun. Yesterday a remarkable scene took place between us. I went to take leave of him because I was suddenly seized by the desire to ride into the mountains, where I am now writing you. As I paced up and down his room I caught sight of a brace of pistols. 'Will you lend me your pistols for my trip?' I asked him. 'By all means,' he replied, 'if you will take the trouble to load them; I only keep them here *pro forma*.' I took one of them down, and he continued: 'Since the day that my precaution paid me a nasty trick, I do not want to have anything more to do with that sort of thing.' I was curious to hear the story.—'I was staying,' he said, 'for about three months with a friend in the country. I had taken along an unloaded pair of pistols, and I slept unconcerned. One rainy afternoon when I was sitting about, doing nothing, the thought crossed my mind—I do not know why—that we might be attacked and might need the pistols—you know how one sometimes imagines things. I gave them to the servant to clean and load. He was dallying with the maids and wanted to scare them, when, God knows how, the pistol went off. The ramrod was still in the barrel and struck the ball of the right thumb of one of the girls and smashed it. Of course, I had to pay for her tears as well as for the medical treatment; and since that day I have left all my firearms unloaded. But, dear friend, what is the use of caution? One never learns enough about danger! Although—' You already know that I am very fond of the fellow up to the point when he says 'although.' For does it not go without saying that any general statement has its exceptions? But he is so scrupulous that when he thinks he has said anything rash or commonplace or only partly true, he does not stop qualifying, modifying, adding and subtracting until, at last, there is nothing left of the subject. On this occasion he became so deeply entangled in the matter that I finally did not listen to him any longer. I suddenly became dejected, and, with a violent gesture, pressed the mouth of the pistol to my forehead above the right eye. 'Come, come,' Albert exclaimed, taking the pistol from me, 'what are you doing?'—'It is not loaded,' I said.—'Even so, what's the idea?' he retorted impatiently. 'I cannot imagine how a person can be so foolish as to shoot himself; the mere thought of it is repulsive.'

'Why must people like you,' I exclaimed, 'when you discuss any action, immediately say: "This is foolish, that is wise; this is good, that is bad!" And what does it all mean? Does it mean that you have really discovered the inner circumstances of an action? Do you know how to explain definitely the reason why it happened, why it had to happen? If you indeed knew, you would be less hasty in your judgements.'

'You will have to admit,' said Albert, 'that certain actions remain vicious, from whatever motives they may have risen.'

I shrugged my shoulders and granted him that. 'But, dear friend,' I continued, 'even in that general case, a few exceptions can exist. It is true that theft is a vice; but does the man who goes out to steal in order to save himself and his family from starvation—does he deserve pity or punishment? Who will be the first to cast a stone at the husband who sacrifices to his just indignation his unfaithful wife and her vile seducer? Or at the young girl who in one blissful hour loses herself in the irresistible joys of love? Even our laws themselves, those cold-blooded pedants, can be moved toward clemency, and refrain from punishing.'

'It is quite a different matter,' Albert replied, 'when a man is carried away by his passions and loses all power of reflection; he can then be considered a drunkard or a madman.'

'O you rational people,' I exclaimed, smiling. 'Passion! Drunkenness! Madness! You stand there so complacently, without any real sympathy, you moralists, condemning the drunkard, detesting the madman, passing by like the Levite, and thanking God that you are not made as one of these. I myself have been drunk more than once; my passions have never been very far removed from madness, and yet I do not feel any remorse. For I have learned in my own way that all unusual people who have accomplished something great or seemingly impossible have always been proclaimed to be drunk or mad.

'But even in everyday life it is unbearable to hear people say of almost anyone who acts in a rather free, noble or unexpected way: "That man is drunk, or he is crazy!" Shame on you sober ones! Shame on you sages!'

'Now, that is another of your whims,' said Albert. 'You exaggerate everything, and you are certainly wrong when you compare suicide, which we discuss here, to great actions, since no one can consider it as anything but a weakness. For it is certainly easier to die than bravely to bear a life of misery.'

I was about to break off, as no kind of argument upsets me more than when someone utters a trivial commonplace while I am speaking from the heart. But I kept my temper, because

I had heard this sort of talk only too often and had been annoyed by it many times before. Therefore I replied rather forcibly: 'You call that weakness? Please, don't be misled by appearances. Would you call a nation weak that groans under the intolerable yoke of a tyrant, when it at last rises and breaks its chains? A man, horrified that his house has caught fire, feels all his strength tighten and carries with ease burdens that he would scarcely be able to move in a calmer mood; or a man in the rage of having been insulted takes on single-handed half a dozen opponents and defeats them—can such people be called weak? If, my friend, exertion means strength, why should overexertion mean the opposite?'—Albert looked at me and said, 'Don't be offended if I say that the examples you give me are irrelevant to our subject.'—'That may be so,' I replied. 'People have often reproached me for my irrational way of associating things, a way which, they say, often verges on absurdity. Let us see if we have any other way of imagining how a person may feel when he has decided to throw off the ordinarily agreeable burden of life, for only insofar as we can enter into another's emotions have we the right to discuss such matters.

'Human nature,' I continued, 'has its limits; it can bear joy, suffering, and pain to a certain degree, but it collapses as soon as that degree is exceeded. The question, therefore, is not whether someone is weak or strong, but what degree of suffering he can actually endure, be it moral or physical; and I find it just as strange to call a man who takes his own life a coward as it would be improper to call a coward a man who is dying of a malignant fever.'

'Paradoxical! Very paradoxical!' Albert exclaimed.—'Not so much as you may think,' I replied. 'You admit that we call a disease fatal which attacks Nature so violently that her forces are partly consumed or so largely put out of action that they cannot recover and restore the ordinary course of life by some lucky turn.

'Now, my friend, let us apply this same sort of reasoning to the mind. Let us watch man in his limited sphere and see how impressions affect him, how he is obsessed by ideas, until finally a growing passion robs him of any possible calmness of mind and becomes his ruin.

'A composed, sensible person who has a clear view of the condition of the unfortunate man tries in vain to give advice; just as the healthy man, standing at the bedside of the sick, is unable to transfer to the latter the smallest fraction of his own strength.'

Albert thought all this too general in expression. I reminded him of a girl who had been found in the river, drowned some time before, and told him again her history.—She was a good-natured young creature who had grown up within a narrow circle of domestic tasks weekly laid out for her, with no other prospect of possible amusement than Sunday walks about town with her friends, dressed in her Sunday finery which she had gradually acquired; or perhaps once in a long while a dance; or an occasional lively chat with a neighbour interested in the source of a quarrel, or some slander—a girl whose passionate nature sooner or later feels urgent desires, which are fed by the flatteries of men. All her former pleasures little by little become stale; until she finally meets a man to whom she is irresistibly drawn by a strange, unfamiliar feeling, a man on whom she now stakes all her hopes, forgetting the world around her, hearing nothing, seeing nothing, feeling nothing but him alone, longing for him alone. Unspoiled by the shallow pleasures of an inconstant vanity, her desire draws her straight to one goal—she wants to be his, to find in a lasting union all the happiness she has missed, to experience all her yearned-for joy. His repeated promises give certainty to her hope; his bold caresses inflame her desire and hold her whole being in a state of suspense, in anticipation of some supreme delights. She works herself up to the highest pitch of excitement and finally, when she opens her arms to embrace all her wishes—her lover abandons her. Stunned, and almost out of her mind, she finds herself above an abyss; all around her is darkness; no way out, no consolation, no hope! The one person in whom she had found the centre of her existence has left her. She does not see the wide world spread out before her or the many others who might replace her loss; she feels herself alone, abandoned by all—and blindly hunted into a corner by the terrible agony of her heart, she throws herself into the depths to drown all her anguish in the embrace of death.—That, Albert, is the story of more than one; and now tell me, is not this a case like that of a disease? Nature is unable to find a way out from the maze of confused and contradictory forces, and the patient must die.

'Shame on him who looks on and says: "The foolish girl! If she had let time do its work, her despair would have lost its force, and very probably another man would have appeared willing to comfort her."—This is exactly as if someone should say: "The fool—to die of fever! If he had waited until he had recovered his strength, until the sap of life was improved, until the tumult in his blood had subsided, all would have been well, and he would still be alive today!" '

Albert, who had not quite grasped my comparison, had a few more objections to make, among them that, after all, I had only spoken of a simple girl. What he could not understand was how a person of intelligence, whose mind was not narrow, and who was capable of a larger view of things, could be exculpated.—'My friend,' I exclaimed, 'man is human, and the small amount of intelligence one may possess counts little or nothing against the rage of passion and the limits of human nature pressing upon him. Moreover—but of that another time,' I said, and took my hat. Oh, my heart was so full!—And we parted without having understood each other. How difficult it is to understand one another in this world.

15 August

It is certainly true that nothing in the world makes a person indispensable but love. I feel that Lotte would not like to lose me, and the children have no other idea than that I should appear every morning. I went out there today to tune Lotte's clavichord but I did not get around to this task, for the children followed me everywhere, asking to be told a fairy tale, and Lotte herself begged me to do as they wished. I cut the bread for their supper, which they now take from me as eagerly as from Lotte, and told them their favourite story of the princess who was served by ghostly hands. I am learning a good deal from all this, I assure you; and I am amazed what an impression I make. When I sometimes have to invent a small detail which I forget the next time, they at once tell me that the story was different at the previous telling;

so now I practise reciting it without alterations from beginning to end, like a chant. This has taught me what harm an author necessarily does to his book in a second revised edition, even though it may gain in poetic merit thereby. The very first impression finds us receptive; and we are so made that we can be convinced of the most incredible things; but these fix themselves immediately in our mind, and woe to him who would erase and eliminate them.

18 August

Must it so be that whatever makes man happy must later become the source of his misery?

That generous and warm feeling for living Nature which flooded my heart with such bliss, so that I saw the world around me as a Paradise, has now become an unbearable torment, a sort of demon that persecutes me wherever I go. When I formerly looked from the rock far across the river and the fertile valleys to the distant hills, and saw everything on all sides sprout and spring forth—the mountains covered with tall, thick trees from base to summit, the valleys winding between pleasant shading woods, the gently flowing river gliding among the whispering reeds and reflecting light clouds which sailed across the sky under the mild evening breeze; when I listened to the birds that bring the forest to life, while millions of midges danced in the red rays of a setting sun whose last flare roused the buzzing beetle from the grass; and all the whirring and weaving around me drew my attention to the ground underfoot where the moss, which wrests its nourishment from my hard rock, and the broom plant, which grows on the slope of the arid sand hill, revealed to me the inner, glowing, sacred life of Nature—how fervently did I take all this into my warm heart, feeling like a god in that overflowing abundance, while the beautiful forms of the infinite universe stirred and inspired my soul. Huge mountains surrounded me, precipices opened before me, and torrents gushed downward; the rivers streamed below, and wood and mountains sang; and I saw them at their mutual work of creation in the depths of the earth, all these unfathomable forces. And above the earth and below the sky swarms the variety of creatures, multifarious and multiform. Everything, everything populated with a thousand shapes; and mankind, huddled together in the security of its little houses, nesting throughout and dominating the wide world in its own way. Poor fool who belittles everything because you are yourself so small! From the inaccessible mountains, across the wasteland untrod by human foot, to the end of the unexplored seas breathes the spirit of the eternal Creator who rejoices in every atom of dust that divines Him and lives.—Oh, the times when I longed to fly on the crane's wings, as it passed overhead, to the shores of the illimitable ocean, in order to drink from the foaming cup of the Infinite an elating sensation of life, and to feel, if only for a moment, in the cramped forces of my being one drop of the bliss of that Being who creates everything in and through Himself.

My friend, only the memory of those hours eases my heart. Even the effort to recall and to express again in words those inexpressible sensations lifts my soul above itself, but also intensifies the anguish of my present state.

It is as if a curtain has been drawn away from my soul, and the scene of unending life is transformed before my eyes into the pit of the forever-open grave. Can you say: 'This is!' when everything passes, everything rolls past with the speed of lightning and so rarely exhausts the whole power of its existence, alas, before it is swept away by the current, drowned and smashed on the rocks? There is not one moment which does not consume you and yours, and not one moment when you yourself are not inevitably destructive; the most harmless walk costs the lives of thousands of poor, minute worms; *one* step of your foot annihilates the painstaking constructions of ants, and stamps a small world into its ignominious grave. Ha! It is not the notable catastrophes of the world, the floods that wash away our villages, the earthquakes that swallow up our town which move me; my heart is instead worn out by the consuming power latent in the whole of Nature which has formed nothing that will not destroy its neighbour and itself. So I stagger with anxiety, Heaven and Earth and their weaving powers around me! I see nothing but an eternally devouring and ruminating monster.

21 August

In vain do I stretch my arms out for her in the morning, when I try arouse myself from troubled dreams; in vain do I seek her at night in my bed, deluded by some happy and innocent dream in which I am sitting beside her in the meadow, holding her hand and covering it with a thousand kisses. And when, still heavy with sleep, I grope for her and suddenly find myself fully awake, a torrent of tears bursts from my oppressed heart, and I weep bitterly in view of a hopeless future.

22 August

It is disastrous, Wilhelm! All my energies are tuned to another pitch, have changed to a restless inactivity; I cannot be idle and yet at the same time cannot set to work at anything. My power of imagination fails me; I am insensible to Nature, and I am sick of books. If we fail ourselves, everything fails us. I swear that I should sometimes like to be a workman so that I could see, when I wake up in the morning, some prospect for the coming day, some impetus, some hope. I often envy Albert, whom I see buried up to his ears in documents; and I imagine that I should be better off were I in his place. Already more than once the thought of writing to you and to the Minister flashed through my mind, in order to apply for the post at the Legation which, you have assured me, I would not be refused. So I myself believe. The Minister has liked me for a long time, and has frequently urged me to devote myself to some work; and sometimes, for an hour or so, it seems the thing to do. But when I come to consider it a little later, I remember the fable of the horse which, tired of its freedom, let itself be saddled and harnessed and was ridden to death. I don't know what to do. And, my dear fellow, isn't my longing for a change in my situation an innate, uneasy impatience that will pursue me wherever I go?

28 August

One thing is certain; if my disease could be cured, these people would cure it. Today is my birthday, and very early in the morning I received a little parcel from Albert. When I opened it I saw immediately one of the bows of pink ribbon

Lotte had been wearing when I first met her and which I had often implored her to give me. The parcel also contained two books in duodecimo: the small Homer printed by Wetstein, which I had often wished to possess, so that I should not have to drag about with me on my walks the large volume edited by Ernesti. You see! that is how they anticipate my wishes, how well they select the small tokens of friendship which are a thousand times more precious than the dazzling presents which humiliate us, betraying the vanity of the giver. I kiss the ribbon over and over again and drink in with every breath the memory of the few blissful moments in those happy and irretrievable days. Wilhelm, so it is, and I do not complain—the blossoms of life are only phantoms. How many fade, leaving no trace behind; how few bear fruit, and how few of these fruits ripen! But still enough are left; but still—O my brother! should we neglect the ripe fruit, refuse to enjoy it, and let it rot?

Farewell! It is a glorious summer, and I often sit up in the trees of Lotte's orchard and take down with a long pole the pears from the highest branches. She stands below and catches them when I lower the pole.

30 August

Unhappy man! are you not a fool? Do you not deceive yourself? To what use is this endless raging passion? I have no prayers left except prayers to her; my imagination calls up no other image than hers, and I see everything in the world only in relation to her. And thus I spend many happy hours—until I must again tear myself from her. O Wilhelm, what things my heart urges me to do! After I have been with her for two or three hours, delighting in her form, her bearing, in the heavenly expressiveness of what she says, my nerves slowly become tense, my eyes grow dim, my ears no longer take in her words; and it seems as if an assassin had clutched me fast by the throat; if then my wildly beating heart tries to relieve my oppression but only succeeds in increasing my confusion—Wilhelm, in such moments I often do not know if I am indeed in this world. And if melancholy did not sometimes take hold of me, and Lotte grant me the poor comfort of crying my eyes out over her hand, I have to leave; I must get into the open air; I roam about in the fields. To climb a steep mountain is then my joy, working my way through pathless forest, through thickets which bruise me and thorns which tear me. Then I feel some relief. Some! And when I sink to the ground tired and thirsty, or sit on a fallen tree in the lonely forest, in the dead of night, when the full moon hangs over me, to give my wounded feet some relief, and then slip away in a calm sleep of exhaustion in the half-light—O Wilhelm! the solitude of a cell, the hairshirt and the spiked belt would be sweet comfort to my yearning heart. Adieu! I see no end to this misery except in the grave.

3 September

I must go! Thank you, Wilhelm, for having confirmed me in my wavering decision. For two weeks I have been constantly thinking of leaving her. I must go. She is again in the town, staying with a friend. And Albert—and—I must go!

10 September

What a night it has been, Wilhelm! And now I can endure anything. I shall not see her again. Oh, if I could only fall on your neck and describe with a thousand joyous tears all the emotions that are storming in my heart. Here I sit, gasping for breath, trying to calm down, and waiting for the morning to come; horses are ordered for sunrise.

And she sleeps peacefully and does not know that she will never see me again. I have torn myself away and was strong enough not to betray my intention while we talked together for two hours. Good God, what a conversation it was!

Albert had promised me to be in the garden with Lotte immediately after supper. I stood on the terrace under the tall chestnut trees and watched the sun, which was, for me, setting for the last time over the lovely valley and the gentle river. I had so often stood here with her, looking at the beautiful scene, and now—I paced up and down the avenue that was so dear to me. I had often been drawn to this place by a secret impulse before I even knew Lotte; and how delighted we had been when, at the beginning of our acquaintance, we discovered our mutual liking for the place, which is really one of the most romantic I have ever seen planned by art.

First you have the wide view between the chestnut trees—but, I remember having already written you a great deal about it, how one is soon closed in by high screens of beech trees, and how the avenue grows darker and darker, because of the adjoining shrubbery, until at last all ends in a secluded little circle, around which a thrilling solitude hovers. I can still feel the odd sensation which touched me when I first entered it at high noon; I had a faint presentiment of the kind of setting it would make for both happiness and pain.

I had indulged in these sweet and yearning thoughts of parting and reunion for almost half an hour, when I heard them coming up the terrace. I ran to meet them, took Lotte's hand and kissed it with deep emotion. We had just reached the top of the terrace when the moon rose behind the wooded hill; we talked of various things and approached, before we knew it, the sombre recess. Lotte entered and sat down, Albert beside her, as I did too, but my inner restlessness did not allow me to remain seated for long; I stood up, stood in front of them, paced to and fro, and again sat down: it was an agonizing situation. Lotte drew our attention to the beautiful effect of moonlight illuminating the whole length of the terrace before us, which opened where the screening beech trees ended: a lovely sight, the more striking because complete darkness closed us in on all sides. We were silent, until she said, after a time: 'I never take a moonlight walk, never, without thinking of my dear lost ones; without being overawed by the sense of death and of future life. We shall live,' she went on, her voice vibrating with the most beautiful emotion, 'but, Werther, shall we find one another again and know one another? What do you feel? What do you say?'

'Lotte,' I said, giving her my hand as my eyes filled with tears, 'we shall meet again, here and beyond.' My voice failed me. Wilhelm, did she have to ask me that when my heart was in anguish because of our coming separation!

'And I wonder if our dear lost ones know about us,' she continued, 'if they feel that we remember them with warm affection when everything goes well with us? Oh, the image of my mother is always with me when I sit among her children, my children, on a quiet evening, and they gather around me as they used to gather around her, and then I look up to

Heaven with longing and tears, and wish that she might for
a moment look in on us and see how I have kept my promise
given to her in the hour of her death: to be a mother to
her children. With what feeling I then cry out: "Forgive me,
dearest Mother, if I am not to them what you were. Oh, do
I not do everything I can; are they not dressed and fed and,
what is more, cared for and loved? Could you only see the
harmony among us, dear sainted Mother, you would thank
with fervent gratitude the God whom you implored with your
last bitter tears to protect your children." '

These were her words! O Wilhelm, who can repeat what she
said? How can dead cold written words convey the heavenly
flower of her soul? Albert gently interrupted her: 'Dear Lotte,
this affects you too much. I know that your soul is immersed
in these ideas, but I implore you—' 'O Albert!' she replied,
'I know you have not forgotten those evenings when we sat
together at the small round table, when Father was away on
a journey, and we had sent the little ones to bed. You often
had a good book with you, but you seldom had time to read.
Was not the association with her exquisite soul worth more
than anything else? The beautiful, gentle, cheerful and always
active woman! God alone knows how often, in my bed, I have
prayed in tears that He might make me her equal.'

'Lotte,' I cried, kneeling before her and taking her hand,
which I covered with tears, 'Lotte, the blessing of God rests
upon you, and the spirit of your mother.'—'If you had only
known her,' she said, and pressed my hand. 'She was worthy to
be known by you.' I almost fainted. Never had anything more
magnificent, more exalting, been said about me. She continued: 'And this woman had to die in the flower of her years,
when her youngest son was only six months old. Her illness
was not a long one; she was calm and resigned, and she worried only about her children, especially the youngest. When
her end drew near, she said to me: "Send them up to me!" and I
brought them into her room—the little one, who did not understand, and the older ones, who were very much upset; they
stood around her bed and she raised her hands and prayed
over them, then kissed one after the other and sent them
away, saying to me: "Be their mother!" I gave her my hand
and promised.—"You promise a great deal, my daughter,"

she said, "both the heart of a mother and the eye of a mother. I have often seen from your grateful tears that you feel what that means. Feel this for your sisters and brothers, and for your father the loyalty and obedience of a wife. You will comfort him." She asked to see him, but he had left the house to hide his unbearable grief—he was completely broken.

'Albert, you were in the room with us. She had heard someone walking about, and asked who it was, and called you to her side. How she looked at you and at me, her mind relieved and at rest, knowing that we would be happy, be happy together.' Albert took Lotte in his arms and kissed her, crying: 'We are! We shall be!' The usually imperturbable Albert was shaken, and I was beside myself.

'Werther,' she began, 'and this woman had to die! Dear God! When I sometimes think that the dearest thing in our lives was taken away, and that no one felt it as keenly as the children, who complained for a long time afterward that the black men had carried away their mother!'

She stood up, and I woke, shaken, from my trance, but remained seated, still holding her hand. 'We must go,' she said, 'it is late.' She tried to withdraw her hand, but I held it all the more firmly. 'We shall meet again,' I exclaimed, 'we shall find one another, and know one another under whatever form. I am going away,' I went on. 'I go voluntarily, but if I should have to say "Forever" I could not bear it. Farewell, Lotte! Farewell, Albert! We shall meet again.'—'Yes, tomorrow, I suppose,' she replied lightly. How I felt that word 'tomorrow'! Oh, she was unsuspecting, when she drew her hand away.—They walked down the avenue; I stood in the moonlight, looking after them; then I flung myself on the ground and wept until my tears were exhausted, sprang up again and ran out on the terrace, where I still could catch a glimpse of her white dress moving in the shadow of the tall linden trees near the garden gate. I stretched out my arms, and it disappeared.

BOOK TWO

WE arrived here yesterday. The envoy is indisposed and will, therefore, stay at home a few days. If he were not so disagreeable, all would be well. I feel that Destiny has some hard tests in store for me. But I won't lose courage! A light heart can bear anything! A light heart? I laugh when those words come from my pen. Oh, a little more lightheartedness would make me the happiest being under the sun. What! With others around me of scanty talent and ability, bragging in complacent self-content, should I despair of my abilities and gifts? Good Lord, you who presented me with all these, why did You not keep half, and give me instead self-confidence and contentment!

Patience! Patience! Things will improve. For, my dear friend, I admit that you were right. Since I have been seeing all sorts of people day in and day out, and have observed how they carry on, I am more lenient with myself. It is true that we are so made that we compare everything with ourselves and ourselves with everything. Therefore, our fortune or misfortune depends on the objects and persons to which we compare ourselves; and for that reason nothing is more dangerous than solitude. Our imagination, by its nature inclined to exalt itself, and nourished by the fantastic imagery of poetry, creates a series of beings of which we are the lowest, so that everything else appears more wonderful, everyone else more perfect. And that is completely natural. We so frequently feel that we are lacking in many qualities which another person apparently possesses; and we then furnish such a person with everything we ourselves possess and with a certain idealistic complacency in addition. And in this fashion a Happy Being is finished to perfection—the creature of our imagination.

If, on the other hand, we just continue to do our best in spite of weakness and hard work, we very often find that, with all our delaying and tacking about, we achieve more than others with their sailing and rowing—and—it gives us a true feeling of our worth if we keep pace with others or even overtake them.

26 November

I begin rather to enjoy myself. The best feature is that there is enough work to do, and that the variety of people, the many new characters, form a colourful drama for my spirit. I have made the acquaintance of Count C., a man I am forced to admire more every day; an intelligent, broad-minded man who has not become cold through his quickness of perception, but radiates a great feeling of friendship and affection. He showed an interest in me when I had to deliver a message; from my first words he saw that we understood each other and that he could talk with me as he could not with everyone. I cannot praise sufficiently his candid manner with me. Nothing in this world equals the warm pleasure we take in seeing a great mind opening to us.

24 December

The envoy annoys me greatly, as I knew he would. He is the most meticulous fool that ever lived, proceeding step by step and fussing like an old maid; a man who is never satisfied with his own work, and consequently never satisfied with another's. I do my work quickly and like to leave things written down as they come; but he is capable of returning my memorandum to me, saying: 'It is good, but better look through it once more; one is always able to find a better word, a more precise particle.' It's enough to drive one mad!—No 'and,' not the smallest conjunction, must be omitted; and he is a deadly enemy of the inversions that sometimes slip from my pen. If one does not reel off his periods to the traditional tune, he does not understand one word of them. It is a burden to have to work with such a man.

The confidence of Count C. is my only compensation. The other day he told me quite frankly how dissatisfied he is with the slowness and pedantry of the envoy. 'That type of person makes things difficult for himself as well as for others. But,' he added, 'one has to resign oneself like a traveller who has to cross a mountain; of course, if the mountain were not there, the journey would be much shorter and easier; but there it is, and one has to scale it!'

My old gentleman also sensed in a way that the Count

prefers me to him and that vexes and annoys him, so that he seizes any opportunity to disparage the Count in my presence. I, of course, contradict him and only make matters worse. Yesterday I even lost my temper, for his words were meant for me, as well, when he said: 'The Count is quite good at worldly affairs, because he works quickly and has a fluent pen, but, like all literary people, he lacks solid erudition.' He then grimaced, as though to say: 'Do you feel the prick?' But it had no effect on me; I felt only contempt for a man capable of so thinking and behaving. I held my ground and parried with considerable heat. I said that the Count was a man one had to respect for both his character and his knowledge. 'I have never met anyone,' I continued, 'whose range of interests is so wide, and who yet expends so much energy on matters of ordinary life.' This was all Greek to him, and I took leave, not wishing to be choked by more gall and having to listen to further nonsense.

And all this I owe to you, who talked me into assuming this yoke, and harped so much on activity. Activity! If it is true that the man who plants potatoes, or rides into town to sell his grain, is not doing more than I, then I shall slave for another ten years on this galley to which I am at present chained.

And the splendid misery, the boredom among the horrid people who are assembled here! Their social ambitions, the way they watch and spy on one another in order to gain another tiny step; their most contemptible passions flaunted without any reticence. One woman, for instance, tells everyone about her nobility and her native country, so that every stranger is forced to think: 'This woman is a fool to pride herself on that little bit of nobility and on her country's fame.' But, to make it worse, the woman is in reality the daughter of a district clerk from this very region. You see, I cannot understand the human race when it has so little judgement and prostitutes itself in such a vulgar way.

In fact, I realize each day more clearly, dear friend, how foolish it is to judge others by oneself. And as I am so preoccupied with myself, and since this heart of mine is so stormy, oh, how gladly would I let others go their way if they would only let me go mine!

What irritates me most of all are the disgraceful social

conditions. I know, of course, as well as anyone, how necessary class distinctions are, and how many advantages I myself gain from them; but they should not stand in my way just when I might enjoy some little pleasure, some gleam of joy on this earth. The other day, on a walk, I made the acquaintance of Fräulein von B., a charming creature, who has preserved a great naturalness in the midst of this stiff and conventional life. We were very congenial as we talked, and when we separated I asked permission to visit her. She consented so frankly that I could hardly wait for the proper moment to make my call. She does not come from these parts and lives in the house of an aunt. I thoroughly disliked the old lady's looks, but I showed her much attention and, for the most part, turned the conversation in her direction. In less than half an hour I guessed almost all that the girl later confirmed: namely, that her dear old aunt lacked everything, having neither a decent fortune nor wits, and no prop but her family tree, and was protected only by her noble rank, behind which she had entrenched herself and enjoyed the last pleasure left her: to look down from her height on the heads of the burghers. They say she was very beautiful in her youth and frittered away her life, at first by tormenting many a poor young man with her whims; but in middle age obediently submissive to the domination of an old officer who, in exchange for this submission and a moderate dowry, spent the Bronze Age with her, and died. She now finds herself alone in the Iron Age; and no one would pay any attention to her if her niece were not so charming.

8 January, 1772

What dreadful people there are, whose minds are completely absorbed in matters of etiquette, whose thoughts and aspirations all year long turn over the single problem how to push oneself one chair higher at table. And it is not as though they had nothing else to do. No, on the contrary, work continues to pile up because trivial annoyances hinder the dispatch of more important matters. Last week a quarrel started during a sleighing party and the whole fun was spoiled.

The fools, who do not understand that actual rank does not matter at all and that he who occupies the top very rarely plays the chief role. How often a king is ruled by a minister; how many ministers by their secretaries! And who is then the first? I believe it is the man who knows his fellow-men at a glance and has sufficient power or shrewdness to harness their forces and passions to the execution of his plans.

20 January

I must write you, dear Lotte, here in the taproom of a poor country inn, where I have taken refuge from a heavy storm. Since the time I have been a stranger wandering around in D., that depressing hole of a town, among strangers to my heart, there has not been one moment, not one, when my heart would have told me to write you; but now, in this hovel, this solitary narrow place, while snow and hail pelt on my little window, my first thought is of you. The moment I entered, your image, the memory of you, suddenly overwhelmed me, O Lotte, so sacred and so warm! Dear God, it was the first happy moment in a long time.

If you could see me, my dear, in the flood of distractions! How dried up my senses are getting to be; not for one minute does my heart overflow—not one blissful hour! Nothing! Nothing! I seem to be standing before a sort of raree show, watching the little men and little horses jerk before my eyes; and I often ask myself if everything is not an optical illusion. I join in the play or, rather, I am moved about like a marionette, and sometimes, when I grasp the wooden hand of my neighbour, I shrink back with a shudder. Every evening I plan to enjoy the sunrise, and each morning I fail to get up. During the day I look forward to the moonlight, but later I stay in my room. I do not even know why I get up or why I go to bed.

The leaven which set my life in motion is wanting; the charm which kept me awake far into the night and roused me from my sleep in the morning is gone.

I have found only one feminine friend here: a Fräulein von B., who resembles you, dear Lotte, if anyone can possibly resemble you. 'Well, well!' you will say, 'this fellow resorts to pretty compliments!' There is some truth in it, I have lately been very gallant, which is, after all, my nature to be. I have been very witty, and the ladies say that no one can flatter as well as I (or tell lies, you will add, because one cannot flatter without lying, you see). But I wanted to talk about Fräulein von B. She has a great deal of spirit, which shines out from her blue eyes. Her high rank is a burden to her, as it does not satisfy any of the desires of her heart. She longs to escape from the turmoil, and we spend hours with fantasies of country scenes filled with pure happiness; ah, and of you! How often must she do homage to you! She is not compelled to—she does it voluntarily, loves to hear about you, and loves you.

I wish that I could be sitting at your feet in the dear, familiar room, with our little ones dancing about us; and if they became too noisy, I could gather them around me and quiet them with a frightening fairy tale.

The sun is sinking in full glory over the dazzling snow-white countryside; the storm has passed, and I—must return to my cage. Adieu! Is Albert with you? And how—? God forgive me that question!

8 February

For a week we have had the most horrible weather, but for me it is a blessing. As long as I have been here, there has not been one fine day has not been spoiled or ruined for me by someone. Now, when it pours, and drizzles, and freezes, and thaws, I think—well, it cannot be worse inside than it is out of doors, or vice versa; and that is good. When the sun rises in the morning and promises a fine day, I can never resist exclaiming, 'Now they again have a heavenly gift which they can spoil for one another.' Nothing exists that these people cannot spoil for one another. Health, reputation, happiness, recreation! And all this largely through silliness, stupidity, and narrow-mindedness. Sometimes I feel like imploring them on my knees not to rage so violently against themselves.

17 February

I fear that my envoy and I will not be together much longer. That man is absolutely unbearable. His way of working and of handling affairs is so ridiculous that I cannot restrain myself from contradicting him; and I often handle some matter at my will and in my own way—a way, of course, which he always disapproves. For this reason he has recently complained of me at Court, and the Minister reproved me, although mildly; but still it was a reproof; and I was about to send in my resignation when I received a personal letter from him—a letter that brought me down on my knees in admiration of its generous, wise, and noble feeling. He puts my extreme sensitiveness in the right place, although he credits my exaggerated ideas of efficiency, of influence upon others, of more intelligent management of business, as youthful and praiseworthy courage; and he does not wish to eradicate these ideas but to temper them, and lead them into the right direction where they can be sure of producing a powerful effect. I am now fortified for a week, and have found my balance again. Peace of mind is a wonderful thing, as is pleasure in oneself. Dear friend, if only these treasures were not so fragile as they are precious and beautiful.

20 February

God bless you, dear friends, and give you all the happy days of which I am deprived.

Thank you, Albert, for having kept me in the dark. I was waiting for news about the day of your wedding and had intended on that day solemnly to take down Lotte's silhouette from my wall and bury it among other papers. Now you are a married couple, and her silhouette is still there. Well, it shall stay there! And why not? I know that I am still with you; that I remain in Lotte's heart without doing any harm to you; I have—yes, I have the second place in it, and will and must keep that place. Oh, I should go mad if she were able to forget—Albert, Hell lies in that thought. Albert, farewell! Farewell, angel from Heaven! Farewell, Lotte!

15 March

Something has so humiliated me that I shall be forced to leave this place, and I gnash my teeth! The Devil! The harm is done, and it is *your* fault alone—*you* spurred me on, pushed and tormented me into accepting a position that was not congenial to me. Well, here I am! and you have had your way! And in order to prevent you from telling me that it was my eccentric ideas which ruined everything, I here recount, dear sir, the story, plain and clear, as a chronicler would put it down.

Count C. is very fond of me and singles me out, as is

well known, and as I have written you many times. He had
invited me for dinner at his house yesterday, on the very
day when the whole aristocratic set, ladies and gentlemen,
are accustomed to meet there late in the evening. I had
completely forgotten this fact; and it also did not occur to me
that subordinate officials like myself are not welcome on such
occasions. Very well. I dined with the Count, and afterward
we walked up and down the great hall in conversation and
were joined later by Colonel B.; so the hour of the party
drew near. God knows, I did not suspect anything. Then the
more-than-gracious Lady S. entered with her spouse and her
nobly hatched little goose of a flat-bosomed and tight-laced
daughter. *En passant*, they opened their eyes wide and turned
up their noses in the traditional highly aristocratic manner.
As that clique is entirely repulsive to me, I had decided to
leave, only waiting until the Count could free himself from
trivial chatter, when Fräulein von B. entered the room. Since
I become always a little more cheerful when I see her, I stayed
on, took my place behind her chair, and noticed only after
some time had passed that she was not talking to me with
her usual frankness but with some embarrassment. This took
me by surprise. 'Is she really like the rest of these people?' I
asked myself and was piqued. I wanted to leave, but stayed
on, because I should have liked to free her from a blame I
did not believe, and still hoped for a kind word from her
and—whatever you wish. Meanwhile, more and more people
were filling the room. Baron F. all gotten up in a complete
outfit dating back to the coronation of Francis I, Hofrat R.
(but here *in qualitate* called Herr von N.) with his deaf wife,
not to mention the badly-reduced-in-circumstances J., who
had patched up the worn places in his old-fashioned clothes
with brand-new material—all these people kept arriving in
swarms; and I spoke to some of those I knew who were,
however, very laconic, I thought—and paid attention only
to my Fräulein von B. I did not notice that the dames at the
far end of the room were whispering into each other's ears or
that this whispering spread to the gentlemen; that Lady S. was
talking to the Count (Fräulein von B. recounted all this to me
afterward), until he finally came up to me and drew me into
a window recess. 'You know our strange social conventions,'

he said, 'and I notice that the company is displeased to see you here, although I should not want you, for anything in the world—' 'Your Excellency!' I interrupted, 'I apologise exceedingly; I should have thought of this before, and I know you will forgive me my inconsequence. I wanted to leave some time ago, but a malicious spirit held me back,' I added, smiling and bowing to him. The Count pressed my hand with a warmth that expressed everything. I turned my back on the illustrious company, slipped away and took a cabriolet to M., to see the sunset from the hill, while reading in Homer the magnificent passage which describes how Odysseus is entertained by the faithful swineherd. All this was perfect.

In the evening I returned to the inn for supper. There were only a few people in the taproom, playing at dice at the corner of a table, having turned back the tablecloth. The honest Adelin then came in, put down his hat when he saw me, and, coming up closer, said to me in a low voice: 'Did something annoy you?' 'Annoy me?' I said.—'The Count asked you to leave his party.'—'The Devil take it!' I said. 'I was glad to get out into the fresh air.'—'Good that you take it so lightly,' he said. 'The thing that worries me is that everyone is already talking.' Now for the first time the whole thing began to irritate me. I imagined that everyone who came in for supper glanced at me and seemed to know about the incident. My blood was up.

And today when everyone pities me wherever I go and when I hear that my triumphant rivals are saying, 'You see where arrogance leads, when proud people who boast of their little share of brains think they can ignore all conventions' (and whatever else these gossiping dogs may invent), one would like to take a knife and plunge it into one's heart; for, whatever one may say about independence, I should like to see the person who can allow rascals to slander him when they have the upper hand. When it is only empty talk, it is easy to ignore them.

16 March

Everything is against me. Today I met Fräulein von B. in the avenue. I could not keep myself from speaking to her;

to tell her, as soon as we were at some distance from her companions, how much she had hurt me the other day. 'O Werther,' she said with deep feeling, 'how could you, knowing my heart, interpret my confusion in such a way? How I suffered for you from the moment I entered the room! I foresaw everything, and a warning word was on the tip of my tongue a dozen times. I knew that Lady S. and Lady T. would leave with their husbands rather than remain while you were there; and I knew that the Count cannot risk their displeasure—and now all this scandal!'—'What do you mean?' I asked, concealing my alarm, because everything that Adelin had told me the previous day made me suddenly feel very uneasy.—'How much it has already cost me,' said the sweet creature with tears in her eyes.—I was no longer master of myself, and was ready to throw myself at her feet. 'Do tell me the truth,' I cried. The tears ran down her cheeks, and I was almost out my mind. She dried her tears without trying to conceal them. 'You know my aunt,' she began. 'She was at the party and with her keen eyes kept a close watch on everything. Werther, I had to suffer for it last night, and this morning I was given a lecture on my friendship with you, and was forced to listen to the degrading, discrediting things she said about you, and could not—was not allowed to—defend you half as much as I wished.'

Every word she spoke pierced my heart like a sword. She did not sense how charitable it would have been to keep all this from me; and she went on to say that more gossip would soon begin to run wild, and mentioned the sort of people who would gloat over it. How delighted they all would be about the punishment I had received for my arrogance and haughty contempt toward others, for which they had often blamed me. All this, Wilhelm, I had to hear from her, spoken in a tone of sincerest sympathy. I was completely crushed, and am still furious. I wish that someone would have the courage to blame me openly so that I could thrust my dagger through his body; if I saw blood, I should certainly feel better. Today I have taken up a knife a dozen times, intending to relieve with it my suffocating heart. I have been told that a noble breed of horses, when overheated and hunted almost to death, will by instinct bite open a vein and so recover their breath. I often feel the same. I should like to open one of my veins and gain eternal freedom for myself.

24 March

I have sent in my resignation to the Court, and I hope that it will be accepted. You will forgive me for not asking your permission first. It is absolutely necessary for me to leave; and everything you will say, to persuade me to stay, I myself know. And therefore—sugar the bitter pill for my mother. I cannot help myself, and she must put up with the fact that I cannot help her either. Of course, it is going to hurt her. To see the beginning brilliant career of her son, which might have mounted, perhaps, to the office of privy councillor and envoy, stop so suddenly, and the little horse brought back to its stable! Now think of the matter as you will and try to figure out the possible conditions under which I might and should have stayed. Enough, I am going. But that you may know where I am going, let me tell you that Prince ——, who likes my company extremely, when he heard of my intention, invited me to accompany him to his estates, and to spend the lovely springtime there. He has promised that I will be completely left alone, and as we understand one another very well, up to a certain point, I shall take my chance and go with him.

19 April

THANK you for both your letters. I have not answered them because I kept back the enclosed note until my resignation had been accepted by the Court. I was afraid that my mother would appeal to the Minister and frustrate my decision. But now everything has been settled, and my discharge has been signed. I can't tell you how reluctantly it was granted, and what the Minister wrote me; you would burst into fresh laments. The hereditary prince sent me twenty-five ducats as a farewell gift, with a note which moved me to tears. Therefore I do not need the money from my mother, for which I asked her the other day.

5 May

I leave here tomorrow, and, as my birthplace is only six miles away from my route, I want to visit it again and indulge in the memory of former happy days. I plan to enter the town by the same gate through which my mother drove out with me when she left the dear familiar place after the death of my father to shut herself in the unbearable town where she now lives. Adieu, Wilhelm; you are going to hear from me about my journey.

9 May

I have ended the pilgrimage to my native town with all the devotion of a pilgrim, and many unexpected emotions have taken hold of me. I asked the postilion to stop beside the tall linden tree, fifteen minutes from the town, on the road to S. There I got out and ordered him to drive on, as I wished to walk and to enjoy every memory in a new and vivid way to my heart's content. There I now stood under the linden tree which was once the goal and boundary of my walks as a boy. How different from the present moment! In those days, in my happy ignorance, my greatest desire had been to get away, out into the unknown world, where I hoped to find all the joy and all the satisfaction possible for my aspiring and yearning heart. Now I had come back from that wide world—oh, my friend, with so many shattered hopes, so many ruined plans. I saw before me the mountains which had so many times been the goal of my desires. I used to sit here for hours, longing to be beyond, completely absorbed, heart and soul, in those woods, those valleys which appeared to my eyes so pleasant and mysterious. If I knew that I had to return home at a certain hour, how I loathed leaving the beloved spot!—As I approached the town, I greeted all the familiar little garden houses, but heartily disliked the newer ones, as well as all the other changes that had been made. I entered by the town gate; and now I knew my way again at once. Dear friend, I'll not go into any details; for, delightful as they are, such a detailed description might be monotonous. I had planned to take a room overlooking the market place, next to our old house. As I walked in that direction I noticed that the school, wherein a conscientious old dame had penned up our childhood, had been turned into a shop. I vividly remembered the restlessness, the tears, the dullness of mind, the anxiety of heart, that I suffered in that hole. Every single step I took stirred up memories. No pilgrim in the Holy Land could come across so many places of religious memory, or have a soul more filled with pious emotion.—Another example among thousands: I went down along the river to a certain farm, where formerly I had often walked. This was the place where we boys used to compete, skimming flat stones which skipped along the surface of the water. I clearly remembered how often I stood there, following the river with my eyes, with strange presentiments in my heart; how colourfully my imagination painted the countries through which the river flowed, and how soon I discovered that my imagination had limits. Still I knew that the river ran on and on, and I completely lost myself in the vision of an unseen far country.—You see, dear friend, how limited and how happy were the glorious Ancients! how naïve their emotions and their poetry! When Ulysses speaks of the immeasurable sea and the infinite earth, everything is true, human, deeply felt, intimate, and mysterious. What is the use of my present knowledge, which I share with any schoolboy, that the earth is round? Man needs only a few clods of earth whereon to enjoy himself, and even fewer for his last rest.

Here I am in the Prince's hunting lodge. Life with this gentleman goes along very well, for he is simple and sincere. But he is surrounded by a strange crowd of people whom I cannot understand at all. They are evidently not bad fellows, but they do not have the look of honest ones. Sometimes they make an honest impression on me, but I cannot bring myself to trust them. Another thing I regret is that the Prince often talks about matters he has only heard or read, and he then takes a position that some other person may have presented to him.

Besides, he admires my intelligence and my talents more than my heart, which is, after all, my only pride, and the fountainhead of all—all strength, happiness and misery. Anyone can know what I know. My heart alone is my own.

25 May

I had something on my mind which I did not want to tell you until it was carried out; now that nothing has come of it, it does not matter. I wanted to go to the war; that is what I have long had at heart. It was my chief reason for coming here with the Prince, who is a general in the——service. During one of our walks I told him of my intention; he advised against it, and there would have had to be more passion in me than actually existed in my passing mood to have prevented me from listening to his arguments.

11 June

You can say what you will; I cannot stay here any longer. What is the use? Time hangs heavy on my hands. The Prince treats me very well, yet I do not feel on my own ground. Fundamentally, we have nothing in common. He is an intelligent man, but of the average kind; to talk to him is not too different from reading a well-written book. I shall stay another week and then take up my wandering again. My drawing is the best thing I have done here. The Prince has a feeling for art and might feel still more strongly in that direction if he were not limited by the pseudo-scientific approach and by trite terminology. I often get furious when I talk with him about Nature and Art with warmth and imagination, only to have him attempt to be clever as he stumbles in with some trite term.

16 June

It is true, I am only a wanderer, a pilgrim on this earth! But are you more?

18 June

Where do I want to go? I tell you in confidence that I must stay here another two weeks; and then I pretend to myself that I wish to visit the mines in——. But, to tell you the truth, there is nothing in that. I only want to be closer to Lotte once more; that is all. And I mock at my heart—and do what it demands.

29 July

No, it is good! Everything is good! I—her husband! O God, who made me, if you had given me that unspeakable happiness, my whole life would be one perpetual prayer. I will not protest—forgive my tears, forgive my hopeless wishes! She—my wife! If I could have closed in my arms the loveliest creature under the sun.—A shudder goes through my whole body, Wilhelm, when I see Albert put his arm around her slender waist.

And may I say it? Why not, Wilhelm? She would have been happier with me than with him. Oh, he is not the man to satisfy all the needs of her heart. A certain lack of sensitiveness, a certain lack of—call it as you will.—His heart does not beat in sympathy with, say, a passage in a favourite book, where my heart and Lotte's beat in the same rhythm; as on a hundred other occasions when our feelings about the action of a third person are in accord. Dear Wilhelm! It is true that he loves her with all his soul; and how much such a love deserves!

A most disagreeable person has interrupted me. My tears are dried. I am distracted. Adieu, dear friend.

4 August

I am not alone in suffering. The hopes of all men are shattered and their expectations betrayed. I went to see the good woman I met under the linden tree. Her older boy ran up to meet me; his joyful shouts brought her near; she looked very downcast. Her first words were, 'Kind sir, my little Hans is dead!' He was the youngest of her sons. I was silent. 'And my husband,' she went on, 'has returned from Switzerland with empty pockets. If some kind people had not helped him, he would have been forced to beg. He caught a fever on the way.' I did not know what to say. I gave something to the little one. She asked me to accept a few apples, which I did, and left this place of melancholy memory.

21 August

As quick as you turn your hand, so quickly everything has changed. Now and then a happier glimpse of life dawns for me, but, alas, only for a moment!—When I become lost in dreams I cannot avoid thinking, 'What if Albert should die? You would! she would—' And then I begin to run after the chimera until it leads me to abysses from which I shrink back in horror.

When I walk out of the town gate, along the road over which I first drove to fetch Lotte to the ball, how changed it all is! Everything, everything is over! No visible trace of the past, not a heartbeat of my former emotion. I feel like a ghost must feel who returns to the burned and destroyed castle which he built in the flower of his youth and filled with splendid objects, and on his deathbed hopefully bequeathed to his beloved son.

3 September

Sometimes I cannot understand how another *can*, how he *dare* love her, since I alone love her completely and devotedly, knowing only her, and having nothing in the world but her!

4 September

Yes, it is so. As Nature declines toward autumn, autumn is in me and around me. My leaves are turning yellow, and already the leaves of the trees nearby have fallen. Did I not once write you, soon after I arrived here, of a certain peasant lad? I inquired about him again in Wahlheim, and was told that he had been turned out of service; but no one seemed to know his whereabouts. Yesterday I met him by chance on my way to another village; I spoke to him, and he told me his story, which moved me more than I can say, as you will easily understand when I repeat it to you. But why repeat it? Why do I not keep my grief and my anxiety to myself? Why should I worry you? Why do I always give you reason to deplore and to reprove me? Never mind! This may also be part of my destiny!

With subdued sadness, mingled with shyness, the lad answered my questions at first; but soon, as if he suddenly recognized himself and myself once more, he confessed to me with more confidence the mistakes he had made, and mourned over his misfortunes. Dear friend, if I could only lay before your judgement every word of his story! He confessed, in fact he told me with a sort of joyful reminiscence, that his passion for the woman who employed him had daily grown on him, to the degree that he finally had not known what to do; had not known, as he expressed it, which way to turn his head. He had not been able to eat, to drink or to sleep; he had felt as if something was choking him. He did what he was not supposed to do, and forgot what he had been ordered to do; it was as if an evil spirit drove him on, until one day, knowing the woman to be in an upper room, he had followed her, or rather had been drawn after her by some magic power. When she resisted his demands, he was about to use force; he did not know what happened to him, and God was his witness that his intentions toward her had always been honest, that his most ardent wish was that she might marry him and spend the rest of her life with him.—After having talked for a while, he began to falter, like a person who has something more to say but lacks the courage to speak out. At last he confessed rather timidly that she had allowed him a few small familiarities and had not grudged him some intimacies. He checked himself two or three times, again and again protesting emphatically that he did not mention this to defame her, as he put it; he loved and respected her as much as formerly; he had never mentioned the matter before to anyone and now told it to me only to convince me that he was not unnatural and not insane. And now, dear friend, you will again hear my old song, which I am forever repeating: if you could have seen this man as he stood before me, as he still stands before my mind! Could I but describe to you every exact detail so that you could understand what a warm interest I take—must take—in his destiny. But enough of this; as you know my destiny as well, as you know me as well, you will understand only too clearly what attracts me to all unfortunate beings, and particularly to this one.

As I re-read this letter, I see that I have forgotten to finish the story which you can, however, easily imagine for yourself. The woman defended herself, and at this moment her brother came in. This brother had for a long time hated the lad and wished to have him out of the house, being afraid that his children would lose the inheritance of his childless sister if she should marry again (an inheritance they looked forward to with keen expectation). The woman's brother immediately showed him the door and raised such a hue and cry that the woman, even if she had wished to, could not well have taken him back into her service. She had now hired another farm hand; but this man, too, people said, had caused a definite break between the brother and herself; and she was expected almost certainly to marry this new man; but my lad said that he was determined to make an end of himself before that day.

What I recount to you here is not exaggerated or sentimentalized; indeed, I may say that I have told it poorly, very poorly, and vulgarized it, by telling it in our conventional moralizing phrases.

This kind of love, this fidelity, this passion, is, as you see, no poetic invention. It is alive; it exists in its purest form among those people whom we call uneducated and coarse. We educated people—miseducated into nothingness! Read this story with reverence, I beg you. Today I am calm while I write; you see from my handwriting that I do not scribble and scrawl as I usually do. Read, dearest friend, and bear in mind that you are reading the story of your friend as well. Yes, all this has happened to me, and will happen to me, and I am not as good-natured by half, or as determined as the poor wretch with whom I almost haven't the courage to compare myself.

5 September

She had written a little note to her husband, who was in the country attending to some business. It began: 'Best and dearest of men! Come back as soon as you can; I await you with the utmost joy.'—A friend came in and brought a message from Albert saying that he would be delayed because of some circumstance or other. Lotte's note was not sent; and I found it by chance in the evening. I read it and smiled; and she asked me why. 'What a divine gift is imagination!' I exclaimed. 'For a moment I could pretend to myself that this was written to me.'—She did not reply and seemed displeased; and I fell silent.

6 September

I struggled with myself before I decided to discard my plain blue dress coat, which I wore when I first danced with Lotte; but it had become very shabby. I have had a new one made, exactly like the first, down to collar and lapels; and also another yellow waistcoat and a pair of breeches.

But the effect is not quite the same. I don't know—it may be that in time I shall like it better.

12 September

She has been away for a few days to meet Albert and return with him. Today, when I came into her room, she was back and welcomed me; and I kissed her hand with great delight.

A canary flew down from the mirror and perched on her shoulder. 'A new friend,' she said, and called him to her hand. 'It is a present for my little ones. How sweetly he behaves! Look at him! When I give him a crumb of bread, he flutters his wings and pecks so daintily. He also kisses me. Look!'

When she offered her sweet lips to the little bird, he nestled closely to them, as though he could feel the happiness given to him.

'He shall kiss you, too,' she said, handing the bird over to me. The tiny beak made its way from her lips to mine, and the pecking touch was like a breath—a foretaste of the pleasures of love.

'His kiss is not without greed,' I said. 'He looks for food and flies back, not satisfied with an empty caress.'

'He also takes food from my mouth,' she said. She offered some crumbs to the bird with her lips, which smiled with the happiness of innocently sympathizing love.

I turned my eyes away. She should not do this! She should not inflame my imagination with these pictures of heavenly innocence and joy and arouse my heart from the sleep into which the monotony of life often lulls it. But why not? She trusts me so implicitly! She knows how much I love her!

15 September

It is enough to drive one mad, Wilhelm, to see people without any sense or feeling for the few remaining precious things in this world. You know of the walnut trees, where I sat with the good pastor of St. —— and Lotte—those noble walnut trees which, God knows, always filled me with a deep sense of joy! How friendly and cool they made the parsonage yard! How beautiful the branches were—and then the recollection of the good clergymen who had planted them so many years ago. The schoolmaster frequently mentioned the name of one of these, heard from his grandfather; he is said to have been such a good man, and his memory was ever sacred to me as I sat under the trees. I tell you, I saw tears in the schoolmaster's eyes when he spoke yesterday of their having been cut down. Cut down! I am furious and could kill the dog who struck the first blow with his axe. I would become utterly despondent if I should see only one such tree, standing in my courtyard, wither with age. Dearest friend, there is at least one redeeming feature in the situation. What a wonderful thing is human sympathy! The whole village grumbles; and I hope that the present pastor's wife will notice, in regard to butter, eggs, and other presents, how much she has hurt the feelings of the whole place. For it is *she*, the wife of the new pastor (our old one is dead), a thin and sickly creature who has every reason not to take any interest in the world, as no one takes any interest in her: a foolish woman who pretends to erudition, pokes her nose into an examination of the Canon, works a good deal at the new-fangled critico-moralist reformation of Christianity, and shrugs her shoulders at the excessive enthusiasm of Lavater. Her health is completely shattered, and for this reason she cannot find any pleasure in anything on God's earth. Only that sort of a creature could think of cutting down my walnut trees. You see, I cannot get over the shock! Just imagine, the falling leaves made her yard damp and dirty; the trees deprived her of sunlight; when the nuts were ripe, the boys pelted them with stones, and this made her nervous, this disturbed her profound meditations when she was weighing the merits of the differing arguments of Kennicot, Semler and Michaelis. When I saw how glum the villagers were, especially the old ones, I asked, 'Why did you let it happen?'—'When the magistrate wants it,' they answered, 'what can you do?' But justice has triumphed. The magistrate, and the pastor (who, after all, wanted to profit from his wife's whims which anyway did not flavour his soup), had thought of sharing the proceeds; but the Board of Revenue still had old claims to the ground where the trees had stood; and the Board sold them to the highest bidder. There they lie! Oh, if I were a prince! I would know what to do—with the pastor's wife, the magistrate, and the Board of Revenue!—Prince! Indeed, if I were a prince, would I really worry about the trees of my country?

10 October

If I only see her dark eyes, I feel happy! But it makes me angry that Albert does not seem as delighted as he—hoped—as I—thought to be, if—I am not fond of dashes, but it is the only way of expressing myself here—and I think I make myself sufficiently clear.

12 October

Ossian has taken the place of Homer in my heart. What a world this sublime poet has opened to me! I wander with him over the heath, where the gale howls on all sides and sweeps along with it the spirits of our ancestors in the flowing mist and in the darkling light of the moon. I hear from the mountains, and in the roar of the torrent the faint groan of spirits in their caverns, and the lament of the maiden who pines for death beside the four moss-covered and grass-grown stones that mark the grave of her fallen hero, her lover. I then come upon the wandering grey bard who searches for the foosteps of his fathers on the vast heath and finds alas! only their tombstones; and then laments as he gazes at the lovely evening star reflected in the rolling waves of the sea. And I see past ages glow into life in the soul of the hero, when the friendly beam shone on the adventures of the brave, and the moonlight illuminated their ships, homeward bound and hung with wreaths of victory. When I read deep sorrow on the bard's brow, and see the last and lonely great one stagger exhausted toward his grave, drinking in ever-fresh, agonizing joys among the helpless shades of his dead companions, and then look down upon the cold earth and the tall waving grass, crying out: 'The traveller will come, will come, who knew me in my beauty, and he will ask: "Where is the bard, Fingal's great son?" His footsteps tread on my grave, and he will seek for me on this earth in vain.'—O friend! I wish I could draw my sword like a noble paladin, and free my lord from the stabbing agony of a slowly ebbing life with one stroke; and then let my soul follow the liberated demigod.

19 October

Oh, this void, this terrifying void I feel in my breast! I often think: if you could once, only once, press her to your heart, this void would be filled.

26 October

Yes, dear friend, I feel more and more certain that the existence of any human being matters little, very little. A friend had come to visit Lotte, and I went into the next room and opened a book but could not read; then I took up a pen to write. I heard them speaking in low voices; they talked of unimportant matters and exchanged news of the town: how this girl would marry, how another was very ill. 'She has a dry cough; the bones show in her face, and she has fainting spells; I wouldn't give a penny for her life,' said the friend. 'N.N. is also in very poor health,' said Lotte.—'He is badly swollen,' said the other. And my lively imagination carried me to the bedside of these unfortunates; I saw them reluctantly turning their backs on life while my little ladies, Wilhelm, talked as one talks about a stranger who is dying. And when I look around the room and see on all sides Lotte's dresses and Albert's papers, and the furniture, everything so familiar to me, even this inkwell, I think to myself: 'See what you mean to this house! On the whole your friends respect you; you often make them happy, and it seems to your heart that it could not live without them; and yet—if you should go, if you should leave this circle, would they—how long would they feel the void which your loss will create in their destinies? how long?'—Oh, how transitory is man, that even in the place where he finds real confirmation of his existence, where he makes the one true impress of his personality in the memories, in the souls of those he loves, that even there he must fade and vanish, and how soon!

27 October

I often feel like tearing open my breast or knocking out my brains when I think how little human beings can do for one another. Oh, the love, the joy, the warmth and the delight which I do not feel myself, no other person will give me;

and, with a heart full of supreme happiness, I still cannot make another person happy who stands before me cold and impassive.

27 October, evening

I have so much in me, and the feeling for her absorbs it all; I have so much, and without her it all comes to nothing.

30 October

How many times have I been on the point of embracing her! God knows what a torture it is to see such loveliness moving about, and not to be permitted to stretch out one's hands to it; for this gesture is, after all, one of the most natural of human impulses. Do not children grasp at anything that comes their way?—And I?

3 November

I often lie down to sleep wishing—yes, sometimes hoping not to wake up again; and the next morning I open my eyes, again see the sun, and feel wretched. Oh, if I only could have moods, could shift the blame on the weather, a third person, or on an unsuccessful enterprise, then only half the weight of this unbearable burden of discontent would rest on me. Miserable me! I know only too well that the fault is with me alone—not fault! Enough, the source of all my misery is hidden in myself, as was formerly the source of all my happiness. Am I not the same who not long ago was intoxicated by the abundance of his emotions, and who stepped into a paradise wherever he went, with a heart ready longingly to embrace the whole world? And now this heart is dead, and thrills of delight radiate from it no longer; my eyes are dry, and my feelings, no longer refreshed by the relief of tears, contract my brow into anxious furrows. I suffer terribly because I have lost what was the one delight of my life—the holy, animating power that helped me to create worlds around me—it has gone! When I now look out of my window at the distant hill, and see how the early sun pierces the mist above it and lights up the peaceful meadows, and how the gentle river between its leafless willows winds toward me—oh, when this glorious Nature lies before me as immobile as on a little lacquered painting, and all this beauty cannot pump one single drop of happiness from my heart to my brain, and the whole man stands before the face of God like a dried-up well, like a broken pitcher—I have often thrown myself on the ground and implored God for tears, as a farmer prays for rain when the sky is leaden above him, and the ground around him is parched.

But alas! I feel that God does not send rain or sunshine because of our impetuous prayers; and those times that so torment me when I look back—why were they so blessed? Only because I patiently waited for His spirit, and embraced the joy that descended on me with an undivided, deeply grateful heart.

8 November

She has reproached me with my excesses! Oh, with what sweetness! My excesses: that now and then, when I allow myself a glass of wine, I drink the whole bottle. 'Don't do it,' she said. 'Think of Lotte.'—'Think!' I said, 'do you need to tell me that? I think or I do not think. You are always before my soul. Today I sat near the place where you got out of the carriage the other day—' She began to speak of other matters, to keep me from pursuing that subject too deeply. Dear friend, I am lost! She can do with me as she wishes.

15 November

Thank you, Wilhelm, for your warm sympathy and your well-meaning advice; and, please, do not worry. Let me suffer to the end; in spite of my listlessness I still have enough strength to see it through. I have a deep respect for religion, you know that; I feel that it is a support for many weary souls, a comfort for many who die of thirst. Only—can it, must it, be that for everyone? When you look at the great world, you see thousands for whom it has meant nothing, thousands for whom it will never mean anything, preached or not preached; and must it then mean something to me? Did not even the Son of God say that those would be about Him whom His Father had given Him? What if I should not have been given to Him? Suppose, as my heart tells me, God the Father wanted to keep me for Himself?—Please, do not interpret this wrongly; do not see any sarcasm in these innocent words; it is my whole soul which I lay open to you; otherwise I should prefer to have kept silence; for, as you know, I do not like to waste words concerning matters of which everyone else is an ignorant as myself. Is it not man's destiny to bear his lot patiently and to drain the cup to the dregs? Yet did not the cup become too bitter for the human lips of God's only Son? Why, then, should I brag and pretend that it tastes sweet to me? And why should I be ashamed at the terrible moment when my whole life trembles between being and not-being; when the past flashes like lightning over the gloomy abyss of the future and everything around me collapses, and the world is destroyed with me—is it not then the voice of a creature thrown completely on his own resources, who has failed himself and is resistlessly plunging into the abyss, that grinds out the cry, 'My God! My God! why hast Thou forsaken me?' And should I be ashamed to use those words; should I fear the moment not spared Him who rolls the heavens together like a scroll?

21 November

She does not see, she does not realize, that she is preparing a poison that will be the ruin of us both; and I voluptuously drain the cup she hands me for my destruction. What is the meaning of the friendly glance she often—often?—no, not often but still, at times, gives me, of the pleasure with which she accepts an involuntary expression of my emotion, of the compassion for my suffering which appears on her brow?

Yesterday, when I was leaving, she gave me her hand and said: 'Adieu, dear Werther!'—Dear Werther! It was the first time she had called me 'dear,' and the word went to the marrow of my bones. I have repeated it to myself a hundred times; and last night, before I went to bed, I talked all sorts of nonsense. I suddenly said, 'Good night, dear Werther!' and afterwards had to laugh at myself.

22 November

I cannot pray, 'Let her be mine!' And yet how often do I think of her as mine. I cannot pray, 'Give her to me!' because she belongs to another man. I go on joking at my suffering, and if I gave myself up to this game, it would bring on a whole litany of antitheses.

24 November

She feels how I am suffering. Today her glance went straight to my heart. I found her alone; I did not speak and she looked at me. And I no longer saw her lovable beauty, no longer the gentle light of her exquisite spirit; all that disappeared. I saw a far more wonderful look in her eyes: an expression of warmest sympathy, of the sweetest compassion. Why was I not allowed to throw myself at her feet? Why could I not take her in my arms and answer her with a thousand kisses? She took refuge at the clavichord, and her soft voice breathed out a melody to the accompaniment of her playing. Never have I seen her lips so charming; it was as if they opened thirstily, to drink in the sweet tones which welled up from the instrument; as if only a mysterious echo reverberated from her innocent mouth. If I could only describe it to you! I was resigned; I bowed my head and vowed: 'Never shall I dare to kiss those lips, on which heavenly spirits hover.' And yet—I shall—Ha! you see, it stands like a barrier before my soul—this supreme happiness—and then die to atone for my sin—sin?

26 November

Sometimes I say to myself: 'Your destiny is unique; call the others fortunate—no one has been so tormented as you.' Then I read an ancient poet, and it seems to me as though I look into my own heart. I have so much to endure! Oh, were there other men before me as miserable as I?

30 November

I cannot, I cannot regain my balance! Wherever I go I am faced with an apparition which completely upsets me. Today! O Destiny! O Mankind!

I was walking by the river at noon; I had no desire to eat. Everything was bleak; a cold and humid westerly wind blew from the mountains, and the grey rain clouds drifted into the valley. Some distance away I saw a man in a shabby green coat crawling among the rocks and evidently looking for herbs. When I came closer and the noise I made caused him to turn, I saw a very interesting face, whose main feature was a quiet melancholy and which otherwise expressed nothing but a frank good-natured disposition. Part of his long black hair was fastened into two rolls with pins, and the rest, braided into a thick queue, hung down his back. As his clothes indicated a man of the lower classes, I thought he would not resent my interest in what he was doing; so I asked him what he was looking for. 'I am looking for flowers,' he answered with a deep sigh, 'but I do not find any.'—'This is not the right season of the year,' I said, smiling.—'There are so many flowers,' he said, coming down toward me. 'In my garden are roses and honeysuckle of two kinds, one of which my father gave me; they grow like weeds; I have already looked for two days for them and cannot find them. There are always flowers out here, too, yellow and blue and red ones; and the thousand-guilder-plant has a lovely little flower. I cannot find any at all.' I noticed something queer about him and therefore asked cautiously, 'What will you do with the flowers?' A strange convulsive smile flashed over his face. 'If you won't betray me,' he said, pressing a finger on his mouth, 'I have promised my sweetheart a nosegay.'—'That is very nice of you,' I said.—'Oh,' he said, 'she has a lot of other things; she is rich.'—'And yet she will like your nosegay,' I said.—'Oh,' he rambled on, 'she has jewels and a crown.'—'What is her name?'—'If the States-General would only pay me,' he replied, 'I would be a different person! Yes, there was a time when I was well off. Now I am done for. Now I am—' A tearful look heavenward expressed everything. 'So you were happy?' I asked.—'Oh, I wish I were so again!' he answered. 'I felt as fine, as gay, as light as a fish in the water.'—'Heinrich!' an old woman who came toward us called. 'Heinrich, where are you? We have looked everywhere for you. Come and eat.'—'Is he your son?' I asked, going up to her.—'Yes, my poor son!' she replied. 'God has put a heavy cross on my shoulders.'—'How long has he been like this?' I asked.—'He has been quiet now for six months,' she said. 'Thank God he has improved; before then he was raving mad for a whole year and lay in chains in the madhouse. Now he wouldn't do harm to anyone, and he talks of nothing but kings and emperors. He was such a good-natured, quiet boy, who helped support me, and wrote a beautiful hand, and all of a sudden he became gloomy, fell into a violent fever, then into stark madness, and he is now as you see him. If I could tell you, sir—' I interrupted the flow of her words with the question, 'What did he mean when he spoke of a time when he was so happy and well off?'—'The foolish fellow!' she cried, with a compassionate smile, 'by that he means the time when he was out of his mind; he always praises those days; it was when he was at the asylum and did not know himself.' The last expression struck me like a thunderbolt; I pressed some money into her hand and left her in haste.

'When you were happy!' I cried aloud, while I hurried back to the town, 'when you felt as carefree as a fish in the water. God in Heaven! did you make it men's destiny only to be happy before they come to reason and after they have lost it again? Poor fellow!—and yet how I envy you your melancholy mind and the confusion of your senses in which you wander. Full of hope, you set out to pick flowers for your queen—in winter—and you are sad because you do not find any and do not understand why you cannot find any. And I—I set out without hope, without a purpose, and return home just as I came. You imagine what a person you would be if the States-General would pay you. Happy creature, who can blame an earthly impediment for his lack of happiness. You do not feel! You do not know that your misery lies in your ruined heart, in your ruined brain, and that all the kings and emperors of this world cannot help you.'

He should perish without comfort who mocks at a sick man for travelling to the remotest medicinal springs, even though these may only increase his sickness and make his final exit more painful! who feels superior to the oppressed heart that sets forth on a pilgrimage to the Holy Sepulchre to free itself from pangs of conscience and sufferings of the soul. Every footstep on an unbeaten path that bruises the feet is a drop of balm for an anguished spirit, and, at the end of a day's journey thus endured, that heart will lie down to rest, eased of many a sorrow. And can you call all this delusion, your armchair quibblers? Delusion! O God, you see my tears! Did You, who created man so poor, have to give him fellow creatures who deprive him of his little poverty, of his little confidence in You, You All-loving Father! For what is trust in a healing root, in the tears of the vine—what is it but trust in You, that You have endowed everything that surrounds us with the power of healing and soothing which we need every hour? Father, whom I do not know! Father, who once filled my whole soul and has now turned His face from me! Call me to You! Break Your silence! Your silence will not keep this soul from thirsting. And is it possible that a human father could be angry when his unexpectedly returning son embraces him, crying: 'I am back again, Father. Don't be angry that I interrupted my journey, which you wanted me to continue. The world is everywhere the same—trouble and work, reward and pleasure; but what is that to me? I am only happy where you are, and I want to suffer and to enjoy in your presence.'—And You, dear Heavenly Father, would You turn him away from You?

1 December

Wilhelm! the man I wrote you about, the happy unfortunate man, was a clerk in Lotte's father's office; and a desperate passion for her, which he fostered, concealed, confessed, and which finally cost him his position, has driven him mad. Try to imagine from these dry words how this story upset me when Albert told it as calmly as you will, perhaps, read it.

4 December

I beg you—you see, I am done for; I cannot bear it any longer. Today I sat near her as she played the clavichord, all sorts of tunes and with so much expression. So much! So much! What could I do? Her little sister sat on my knee and dressed her doll. Tears came into my eyes. I bowed my head and caught sight of her wedding ring. The tears ran down my cheeks—and suddenly Lotte began to play the heavenly old melody. All at once my soul was touched by a feeling of consolation, by a memory of the past, of the other occasions when I had heard the song, of the dark intervals of vexation between, of shattered hopes, and then—I walked up and down the room, my heart almost suffocated by the rush of emotions. 'For God's sake,' I said, in a vehement outburst, 'for God's sake, stop!' She paused and looked at me steadily. 'Werther,' she said with a smile that went deep to my heart, 'Werther, you are very sick. You dislike the things you once liked. Go! I beg you, calm yourself!' I tore myself from her sight, and—God! you see my misery and will put an end to it.

6 December

How her image haunts me! Awake or asleep, she fills my entire being. Here, when I close my eyes, here, in my forehead, at the focus of my inner vision, her dark eyes remain. Here! but I cannot put it into words. When I close my eyes, they are there; like an ocean, like an abyss, they lie before me, in me, taking hold of all my thoughts.

What is man, that celebrated demigod! Does he not lack powers just where he needs them most? And when he soars with joy, or sinks into suffering, is he not in both cases held back and restored to dull, cold consciousness at the very moment when he longs to lose himself in the fullness of the Infinite?

[THE EDITOR TO THE READER]

I should very much prefer that documents written in his own hand concerning the last remarkable days of our friend were at our disposal, and that it were not necessary for me to interrupt the sequence of his posthumous letters by direct narration.

I have taken great pains to collect exact facts by word of mouth from those who were well informed about his history; it is a simple story, and, apart from a few details, all evidence agrees. It is only with regard to the emotional attitude of the actors that opinions differ and judgement is divided.

Nothing remains for us but to relate conscientiously what we were able to gather after repeated efforts, to insert the letters found after our friend's death and to consider the smallest note valuable, for the particular reason that it is so difficult to uncover the true and real motives of even a single action by persons who are not of the usual type.

Depression and apathy had more and more rooted themselves in Werther's mind, had become tangled and gradually had taken hold of his whole being. The harmony of his spirit was totally destroyed; an inner heat and vehemence, unsettling all the forces of his nature, produced the most adverse effects and left him finally in an exhausted condition, out of which he struggled more desperately than when fighting against former troubles. The anguish of his heart consumed his spirit's remaining powers, his vivacity, and his bright intellect. He became a depressing companion, more and more unhappy and more unjust due to this unhappiness. So, at least, say Albert's friends; they maintain that Werther had been unable to judge a simple, quiet man to whom had been given a long-wished-for happiness which he hoped to preserve for the years to come, Werther himself being a person who squandered, as it were, every day all he had, and then suffered and was in need in the evening. Albert, they said, had not changed in so short a time; he was still the same person whom Werther had known, had respected and admired from the beginning of their acquaintance. Albert loved Lotte above everything; he was proud of her and wished that everyone recognize her as a woman above women. Can anyone, therefore, blame him for wishing to avoid even the shadow of suspicion, for not being inclined to share this treasure even in the most harmless way? His friends do not deny that Albert frequently left the room when Werther was with Lotte; but this was neither because of hate nor because of antipathy toward his friends, but only because of his feeling that Werther was depressed by his presence.

Lotte's father felt indisposed and could not leave the house. Therefore, he sent his carriage for her, and she drove out to see him. It was a lovely winter day; the first snow had fallen heavily and covered the whole countryside.

The next morning Werther went out to join her and, if Albert could not come, to accompany her home.

The clear weather had no effect on his gloomy mood; a dull weight pressed on his soul; the sad scenes he had recently witnessed were branded in his memory; and nothing but one painful thought after another crossed his brooding mind. Since he was in constant struggle with himself, the circumstances of others, too, seemed to him precarious and confused. He believed that he had destroyed the harmonious relationship between Albert and his wife, and he reproached himself, at the same time, that he mixed with this reproach a secret indignation against the husband.

His thoughts revolved the same questions while he walked along. 'Yes, yes,' he said to himself, grinding his teeth, 'so that is companionship—intimate, friendly, affectionate, sympathetic—a placid and constant loyalty! It is, as a matter of fact, satiety and indifference! Doesn't he take more interest in any trifling piece of business than in his dear, delightful wife? Does he appreciate his good fortune? Does he know how to respect her as she deserves? He has her—very well—he has her—I know that, as I know some other things too. I thought I had become used to it, but it is going to drive me mad; it is going to kill me. And has his friendship stood the test? Does he not already see in my devotion to Lotte a trespassing on his own rights, and in my attentions to her a mute reproach? I know well. I feel that he does not like my coming to the house; he wishes me away and cannot bear my presence.'

Werther often slowed his brisk pace and often, stopping short, seemed to consider going back; but again and again he directed his steps forward and, engaged in these thoughts and soliloquies, and almost against his will, eventually arrived at the hunting lodge.

He went into the house, asking for Lotte and her father, and found the whole family rather upset. The oldest boy told him that a calamity had occurred in Wahlheim; a peasant had been murdered. This piece of news did not make any special impression on Werther.—He entered the room and found Lotte trying to persuade her father not to go to Wahlheim, as he intended to do, in spite of his illness, in order to hold an inquest on the scene of the deed. The identity of the murderer was still unknown; the murdered man had been found that morning in front of his house. There was some suspicion:

the victim had been employed by a widow who formerly had another man in her service, and this former servant had left her house after some altercation.

When Werther heard this, he became very excited. 'Is it possible!' he exclaimed, 'I must go there at once; I could not have a quiet moment otherwise.' He rushed to Wahlheim, living over in his mind all he knew of the matter; he did not for one moment doubt that the murder had been committed by the man with whom he had so often talked and who had become so important to him. As Werther crossed under the linden trees to reach the inn where they had brought the dead man, he shuddered at the sight of this formerly beloved place. The threshold, where the children of the neighbours had so often played, was spattered with blood. Love and loyalty, the most beautiful of human emotions, had turned into violence and murder. The great trees were without foliage and rimmed with hoarfrost; the lovely hedges which arched over the low wall of the churchyard were bare; and the snow-covered gravestones could be seen through the gaps.

When he came nearer to the inn, in front of which the whole village had gathered, shouts were suddenly heard. A group of armed men could be seen in the distance, and everyone cried out that the murderer had been arrested. Werther looked in that direction and was no longer in doubt. Yes! it was the young farm hand who had loved the widow so ardently, and whom he had met not long ago roaming about in a state of suppressed rage and silent despair.

'What have you done, you unfortunate fellow!' exclaimed Werther, going up to the prisoner. The young man looked at him quietly and in silence, but said at last, with great calm: 'No one is going to have her; she will have no one!' They took the prisoner into the inn, and Werther left in haste. The horrible and violent meeting had shaken him through and through. For one short moment he had been torn from his melancholy, his gloom and his apathetic resignation; he was overcome by compassion and moved by an irresistible desire to save this man, whose predicament he felt deeply. He considered him, even as a criminal, to be free of real guilt, and identified himself so completely with him that he was certain to be able to also convince others. He could not wait to plead for him; the most persuasive arguments rose to his lips; he walked quickly back to the hunting lodge and could not keep himself from rehearsing, in an undertone, as he went along, the defence he wanted to present to the bailiff.

When he entered the house, he found that Albert had arrived; this dampened his spirits for a moment but he managed, after a while, to control himself and began to impress his opinions on the bailiff with much warmth. The latter shook his head repeatedly, and although Werther with the greatest brilliance, passion and truth put forward everything a human being could say to exculpate another human being, the bailiff remained unmoved, as one can easily understand. He did not even allow our friend to finish his discourse but eagerly contradicted him and reproached him for defending an assassin. He pointed out to him that in this way every law would be annulled, the whole security of the state endangered; and besides, he added, he himself would not be able to do anything in a case like this without taking upon himself the heaviest responsibility. Everything would have to be done in the legal way, and according to instructions.

Werther did not yet surrender, and implored the bailiff to look the other way if someone tried to help the man escape. This, too, the bailiff refused to do. Albert, who had finally joined in the discussion, sided with the older man. Werther was overruled and left in a terrible state of suffering after the bailiff had said to him several times: 'No, there is no help for him.'

How deeply these words must have struck him we can see from a note found among his papers, undoubtedly written that same day.

'There is no help for you, unfortunate man! I see only too well that there is no help for us!'

Albert's final words in the matter of the prisoner, spoken in the bailiff's presence, had disgusted Werther extremely: he thought he noticed in them a slight irritability toward himself. And though, on further reflection, he could not fail to see that both men were probably right, he still felt that he would sacrifice his integrity if he should confess, if he should admit that it was so. A note related to this conflict, which perhaps expresses his whole relation to Albert, has been found among his papers.

'What is the use of my saying to myself again and again: He is honest and good; but it still breaks my heart; I cannot be just.'

As the evening was mild and the snow had begun to melt, Lotte and Albert walked home. On the way Lotte now and then looked back, as though she missed Werther's company. Albert began to speak of Werther; he criticized him, although he did him full justice. He touched upon his unfortunate passion and expressed the wish that it might be possible to send him away. 'I wish this for your sake, as well,' he said; 'and,' he added, 'I implore you to try and turn his attentions to you in another direction and limit his frequent visits, which have already been generally noticed and have caused a certain amount of talk.' Lotte was silent, and Albert seems to have resented her silence, since from that time on he did not mention Werther again, and, whenever she spoke of him, stopped the conversation or changed the subject.

Werther's unsuccessful attempt to help the unfortunate man was the last flare of a fading light; after this he sank only deeper into his grief and apathy and became almost frantic when he heard that he might be called to testify against the man, who had, by now, taken to denying everything.

All the unpleasantnesses that he had ever faced during his official life, the humiliation at the Count's party, as well as every other situation in which he had failed, now came and went in his mind. Somehow he found in all this a justification for his present inactivity; he felt himself cut off from any prospects, incapable of grasping any of those chances by which one takes hold of the occupations of everyday life; and, completely absorbed in his curious emotional state, his way of thinking and his hopeless passion, in the unchanging monotony of a cheerless relationship with the lovable and beloved creature whose peace he disturbed, straining his powers to the utmost but wearing them out without purpose and prospect—he steadily advanced toward his tragic end.

A few posthumous letters are the most convincing evidence of his confused state of mind, of his passion, of his restless actions and efforts, and of his weariness of life; and we are therefore inserting them here.

12 December

Dear Wilhelm, my condition is one which those unfortunate people who were thought to be haunted by evil spirits must have experienced. I am sometimes gripped by something that is neither anxiety nor desire; it is an unfamiliar inner rage which threatens to tear open my breast, which clutches at my throat. Oh, it hurts, it hurts! And then I wander about in the dreadful night scenes of this inhuman time of year.

Last night something drove me out of the house. A thaw had suddenly set in, and I had heard that the river had overflowed and all the brooks were swollen, and that my dear valley, in its whole length, from Wahlheim down, was flooded. After eleven at night I hurried out. It was terrifying to see from the rock the churning waters whirling in the moonlight, gushing forth over meadows, fields, and hedges; and up and down the broad valley one tempestuous sea under the howling wind! And when the moon came out again and rested on a black cloud, and the flood rolled and roared before me in the terrible, magnificent light, I shuddered with awe and also with longing. Oh, with wide-open arms I faced the abyss and breathed: 'Down, down!' and was lost in an ecstatic wish to hurl down all my agonies, all my sufferings! to storm along with the waves! Yet I did not have the strength to lift my feet from the ground and end all my agony.—My hourglass has not yet run out, I feel it! Oh, Wilhelm, how gladly would I have surrendered my mortal existence, to tear the clouds apart with that gale and to embrace the floods. Ha! will not the prisoner some day be granted this bliss?—And when I looked down with nostalgic longing at the spot where I had once rested with Lotte, under a willow, after a long walk in the summer's heat, I saw that it was also flooded; I could hardly make out where the willow stood. Wilhelm! And I thought of her meadows, of the whole countryside around the hunting lodge, of our arbour, now shattered by the raving torrent. And a sun shaft of the past pierced through, as when a prisoner has a vision of flocks and herds, meadows and former dignities. I remained standing there! I do not blame myself, for I have the courage to die. I should have—Now I am sitting here like an old woman who gleans her firewood from the fences and begs her bread from door to door, so as to prolong and to ease her wasting and cheerless existence for another short space of time.

14 December

What is this, what has happened to me, dear friend? I am alarmed at myself. Is not my love for her the most sacred, the purest, the most brotherly love? Have I ever felt any culpable desire in my soul? But I will not protest!—And now—dreams! Oh, how right were the instincts of those peoples who attributed such contradictory effects to unknown powers! Last night—I tremble to confess it—I held her in my arms, close to my breast, and covered her love-murmuring lips with endless kisses; my eyes sank into the intoxication of hers. Dear God! Am I culpable that I even now feel a supreme happiness in again living through those glowing moments of joy in all their intensity? Lotte! Lotte!—And this is the end! My mind is in a daze; for a week I have not been able to concentrate, my eyes are full of tears. I feel nowhere at home, and everywhere at home. I have no wish; I make no demand. It would be better for me to leave.

It was about this time, and under these circumstances, that Werther gradually became confirmed in his resolution to leave this world. Since his return to Lotte, this resolution had been always his last straw, his last hope; but he had made up his mind that it should result in no headlong or rash act; that he would take this step with full premeditation and with the coolest possible determination.

His doubts, and his inner struggle, are evident from a note which was probably the beginning of a letter to Wilhelm and was found, without date, among his papers:

'Her presence, her destiny, and her sympathy with mine press the last tears from my ebbing mind.

'To lift the curtain and step behind it! That is all! And why with fear and trembling? Because no one knows what one may see there? or because one cannot return? Or because it is, after all, a peculiarity of our mind to apprehend that confusion and darkness exist in places of which we know nothing definite?'

Finally the tragic thought became more and more familiar to him, and his plan became firm and irrevocable, as witness the following ambiguous letter written to his friend.

20 December

'I owe it to your love, Wilhelm, that you understood my words as you did. Yes, you are right; it would be better for me to leave. Your suggestion that I return to you all does not quite satisfy me; at least I should like to come by a roundabout way, especially as we can expect continued frost and good roads. I am very glad that you intend to come and fetch me; if you will only wait another two weeks until I have written you a second letter with further details. No fruit should be picked before it is ripe. And two weeks more or less make a great difference. Please tell my mother that she should pray for her son, who asks forgiveness for all the trouble he has given her. It was my destiny to hurt those to whom I owed happiness. Farewell, dearest friend! May Heaven bless you. Farewell!'

What happened at this time in Lotte's heart, how she felt about her husband and about her unhappy friend, we hardly dare express in words, though, knowing her character, we can form for ourselves a faint idea; and the sensitive soul of a woman will be able to enter into her thought and feelings.

So much is certain—that she had firmly decided by herself to do everything that would keep Werther at a distance and that her hesitation was based on a warm feeling of pity for her friend, as she knew how difficult, yes, how almost impossible, the separation would be for him. She felt, however, at this time, a still greater pressure in herself to act; her husband had become completely silent about this relationship, and, as she herself had never touched the subject again, she now wished all the more to give actual proof that her feelings toward Albert were worthy of his toward her.

On the same day that Werther wrote the letter to his friend which we have given above—it was the Sunday before Christmas—he came to see Lotte in the evening and found her alone. She was busy arranging some toys she had made for her younger sisters and brothers. Werther spoke of the pleasure the children would have and of the times when the unexpected opening of a door and the sight of a Christmas tree trimmed with wax candles and hung with candies and apples made one speechless with delight. 'You also are going to get Christmas presents,' said Lotte, hiding her embarrassment under a sweet smile, 'if you are very good: a little roll of wax tapers and something more.'—'And what do you call good?' he cried. 'How shall I be? How can I be, dearest Lotte?'—'Thursday night is Christmas Eve,' she said, 'when the children will come here with my father, and everyone will receive his presents. Do come, too—but not before.' Werther was taken aback. 'Please,' she continued, 'that's how it is; I implore you, for the sake of my peace of mind. It cannot, cannot go on like this.' He turned away and paced up and down the room, muttering to himself that phrase, 'It cannot go on like this.' Lotte, who sensed the terrible state of mind into which her words had thrown him, tried to divert his thoughts with all sorts of questions, but in vain. 'No, Lotte,' he exclaimed, 'I shall not see you again!'—'Why not?' she asked. 'Werther! You can, you must see us again; only do be reasonable. Oh, why did you have to be born with this violent temper, this uncontrollable clinging passion for everything you touch! Please,' she said, taking his hand, 'be reasonable! Your intellect, your knowledge, your talents, should offer you such a variety of satisfactions! Be a man! Get rid of this hopeless attachment to one who can do nothing but pity you.' He gritted his teeth and gave her a dark look. She kept his hand in hers. 'Think it over calmly, if only for a moment, Werther!' she said. 'Do you not feel that you deceive yourself, that you deliberately ruin yourself? Why must it be I, Werther? Just I, who belong to another? Why must that be? I am afraid, very much afraid, that it is only the impossibility of possessing me that attracts you so much.'—He withdrew his hand, giving her a fixed and angry look. 'Clever!' he mocked, 'very clever. Did Albert perhaps make that remark? Diplomatic, very diplomatic!'—'Anyone might make it,' she retorted. 'And should there exist in the wide world no other girl who could satisfy the desires of your heart? Take your courage in both hands and look for her—I swear you will find her. I have been worried for a long time, for you and for us, about your self-banishment to this narrow circle. Make up your mind! Travel will and must distract you! Look around and find an object worthy of your love; then come back and enjoy with us the pure happiness of true friendship.'

'All that should be printed,' he said with a frozen smile, 'and we could recommend it to educators. Dear Lotte, give me a little time and everything will turn out well.'—'Only one thing more, Werther, do not return before Christmas Eve!' He was about to answer when Albert entered. They exchanged a rather frigid 'Good evening!' and walked up and down the room together in some embarrassment. Werther then began a conversation on unimportant matters, but it soon petered out. Albert did the same and then asked his wife about some errands he had wanted her to do for him. When he heard that they had not been done, he spoke some words to her which sounded to Werther cold and even harsh. Werther wanted to leave, but he did not have the power, and he delayed until eight o'clock. All this time he was becoming more and more irritated and angry; and, when the table was set, he took his hat and stick, although Albert invited him to stay for supper. Werther imagined this to be only a conventional gesture of politeness, thanked him coldly, and left.

He returned to his lodging, took the candle from the hand of his servant, who wanted to light him upstairs, and went alone to his room. There he burst into uncontrolled loud weeping, talked to himself in great agitation, pacing excitedly up and down, and finally flung himself on his bed, without taking off his clothes, where his servant found him when, plucking up courage, he went in about eleven o'clock to ask if his master wanted him to pull off his boots. Werther allowed him to do this but told him not to come into the room in the morning before he called.

On Monday morning, the twenty-first of December, he wrote the following letter to Lotte; it was found sealed on his writing desk after his death and was brought to her. I shall insert parts of it here at intervals, as it appears from later events that it was written in a fragmentary manner.

'It is decided, Lotte, that I shall die, and I am writing you this calmly, without any romantic exaltation, on the morning of the day when I shall see you for the last time. When you read this, my dearest, the cold grave will already cover the stiffened body of the restless, unfortunate man who does not know any sweeter way to pass the last moments of his life than to talk to you. I have had a terrible, but ah, what a wonderful night. It has strengthened and confirmed my resolution: to die! Yesterday, when I tore myself away from you, my whole nature in terrible revolt, everything rushing into my heart, and when my hopeless, cheerless existence so close to you overwhelmed me with a ghastly chill—I was hardly able to reach my room; almost beside myself, I fell on my knees, and, O God, you granted me a last consolation of bitter tears! A thousand plans, a thousand hopes raged in my soul, but finally it was there, firmly, wholly, the one last thought: to die! I lay down, and this morning, in the peace of awakening, it is still firm, still strong in my heart: to die!—It is not despair; it is the certainty that I have suffered enough, and that I am sacrificing myself for you. Yes, Lotte! Why should I hide it from you? One of us three must go, and I am to be that one! O my dearest, my wounded heart has been haunted by a terrible demon—often. To murder your husband! Or you! Or myself! Well, so be it! When you walk to the top of the mountain, on a fine summer evening, remember me; how I often came up there from the valley to meet you; and then look across to the churchyard and to my grave, where the wind gently sways the tall grass in the light of the setting sun.—I was calm when I began to write this letter and now, now I am weeping like a child, when all this comes so vividly to my mind.'

Shortly before ten o'clock Werther called his servant and, while dressing, told him that, since he would leave this place in a few days, he should clean his clothes and prepare everything for packing. He also gave him the order to ask everywhere for any bills to his account, to collect some books which he had loaned, and to pay the poor people to whom he had usually given some money every week, a sum covering two months.

He had his dinner served in his room and afterward rode out to the bailiff's house but did not find him at home. Lost in thought, he walked up and down in the garden, evidently overwhelmed in his mind with all his sad memories in these last months.

The children did not long leave him in peace but followed him and ran up to him, saying that when tomorrow had come, and again tomorrow, and another day after that, they would go to Lotte's and get their Christmas presents; and they told him about the marvels which their childish imagination promised them. 'Tomorrow,' he cried, 'and again tomorrow and still another day after that!' and kissed them all affectionately and was about to leave when the smallest boy tried to whisper something in his ear. He confided that his big brothers had written beautiful New Year's greetings, *so* big! one for Papa, one for Albert and Lotte, and one for Herr Werther, too! and that they would themselves deliver them early on New Year's Day. This almost broke Werther's heart. He gave something to each of the children, mounted his horse, sent his greetings to the old man, and rode away with tears in his eyes.

About five o'clock in the afternoon he arrived at his lodging and ordered the housemaid to see that the fire be kept burning until late that night. He told his servant to pack his books and his linen at the bottom of his trunk and to make a bundle of his clothes. It was probably then he wrote the following passage of his last letter to Lotte:

'You do not expect me! You think I shall obey you and not see you again until Christmas Eve. O Lotte! today or never again. On Christmas Eve you will hold this piece of paper in your hand, trembling and covering it with your sweet tears. I will, I must! Oh, how relieved I am now that I have made up my mind.'

Meanwhile, Lotte was in a peculiar frame of mind. After her last talk with Werther she had realized how hard it would be for her to be separated from him, and how he would suffer if he had to leave her.

She had mentioned almost casually in Albert's presence that Werther would not return until Christmas Eve; and Albert had ridden out to see an official in the neighbourhood with whom he had to settle some business, and where he would have to spend the night.

Now she sat at home alone—none of her family was with

her—and she gave herself up to her thoughts, which quietly moved over her circumstances. She saw herself united forever to the husband whose love and loyalty she knew, to whom she was deeply devoted and whose calmness of disposition and whose trustworthiness seemed to be intended by Providence for a good wife to build on it her life's happiness; she keenly realized how much he would always mean to her and to her children. On the other hand, Werther had become very dear to her heart; from the very beginning of their acquaintance the harmony of their minds had showed itself in the most pleasant way, and continued friendly relations with him as well as their many mutual experiences had made a lasting impression on her heart. She had become accustomed to share with him everything of interest she felt or thought; and his departure threatened to create a great gap in her existence which could not be filled again. Oh, if she only had the power to transform him this very moment into a brother, how happy she would be!—had she only been fortunate enough to marry him off to one of her friends, or could she be allowed to hope that his friendship with Albert might be completely restored!

She passed all her friends in review, one after the other, but found a flaw in each and could not think of one girl to whom she would not have begrudged Werther.

As she pondered on all this, she felt for the first time, keenly if subconsciously, that in her heart of hearts she secretly wished to keep him for herself, at the same time saying to herself that she could not, should not, keep him; her innocent, noble nature, usually so light and resourceful, felt the weight of a melancholy that sees all hope for happiness barred. Her heart was oppressed, and a dark mist lay upon her eyes.

It was half past six when she heard Werther coming up the stairs; she immediately recognized his step, and his voice as he asked for her. Her heart beat violently, we may say almost for the first time, at his arrival. She would have preferred to have had him told she was not at home; and when he came into the room, she received him in a kind of frantic confusion with the words, 'You have broken your promise!'—'I did not promise anything,' was his answer.—'But you could at least have respected my request,' she said. 'I asked you not to come, for my peace and yours!'

She did not quite know what she did or said as she sent a message to some friends because she did not wish to be alone with Werther. He had brought her some books and asked her about others while she wished, now, that her friends would arrive, now, that they would not. The maid returned, bringing a message that both girls were unable to come.

At first she thought of having her maid sit with her work in the adjoining room, but she then changed her mind. Werther paced up and down the room, and she went to the clavichord and began to play a minuet; but it did not go smoothly. She recovered herself and sat down quietly beside Werther, who had taken his customary place on the sofa.

'Don't you have anything to read to me?' she asked. He had nothing. 'In my drawer over there,' she began, 'is your translation of some of the songs of Ossian. I have not yet read them because I always hoped you would read them to me. But lately there has never been any time or occasion.' He smiled and took out the songs; a shudder ran through him as he took them in his hands, and his eyes filled with tears as he looked at the written pages. He sat down again and read:

'Star of descending night! fair is thy light in the west! Thou liftest thy unshorn head from thy cloud; thy steps are stately on thy hill. What dost thou behold in the plain? The stormy winds are laid. The murmur of the torrent comes from afar. Roaring waves climb the distant rock. The flies of evening are on their feeble wings; the hum of their course is on the field. What dost thou behold, fair light? But thou dost smile and depart. The waves come with joy around thee; they bathe thy lovely hair. Farewell, thou silent beam! Let the light of Ossian's soul arise!

'And it does arise in its strength! I behold my departed friends. Their gathering is on Lora, as in the days of other years. Fingal comes like a watery column of mist; his heroes are around, and, see! the bards of song—grey-haired Ullin! Stately Ryno! Alpin, with the tuneful voice! the soft complaint of Minona! How are you changed, my friends, since the days of Selma's feast, when we contended, like gales of spring as they fly along the hill, and bend by turns the feebly whistling grass.

'Minona came forth in her beauty, with downcast look and tearful eye. Her hair flew slowly on the blast that rushed unfrequent from the hill. The souls of the heroes were sad when she raised the tuneful voice. Often had they seen the grave of Salgar, the dark dwelling of white-bosomed Colma. Colma left alone on the hill, with all her voice of song! Salgar promised to come; but the night descended around. Hear the voice of Colma, when she sat alone on the hill!

'COLMA. It is night; I am alone, forlorn on the hill of storms. The wind is heard on the mountain. The torrent is howling down the rock. No hut receives me from the rain; forlorn on the hill of winds!

'Rise, moon, from behind thy clouds! Stars of the night, arise! Lead me, some light, to the place where my love rests from the chase alone! His bow near him unstrung, his dogs panting around him! But here I must sit alone by the rock of the mossy stream. The stream and the wind roar aloud. I hear not the voice of my love! Why delays my Salgar; why the chief of the hill his promise? Here is the rock, and here the tree; here is the roaring stream! Thou didst promise with night to be here. Ah, whither is my Salgar gone? With thee I would fly from my father, with thee from my brother of pride. Our race have long been foes: we are not foes, O Salgar!

'Cease a little while, O wind! stream, be thou silent awhile! Let my voice be heard around; let my wanderer hear me! Salgar! it is Colma who calls. Here is the tree and the rock. Salgar, my love, I am here! Why delayest thou thy coming? Lo! the calm moon comes forth. The flood is bright in the vale; the rocks are grey on the steep. I see him not on the brow. His dogs come not before him with tidings of his near approach. Here I must sit alone!

'Who lie on the heath beside me? Are they my love and my brother? Speak to me, O my friends! To Colma they give no reply. Speak to me: I am alone! My soul is tormented with fears. Ah, they are dead! Their swords are red from the fight. Oh, my brother! my brother! why hast thou slain my Salgar? Why, O Salgar! hast thou slain my brother? Dear were ye both to me! what shall I say in your praise? Thou wert fair on the hill among thousands! he was terrible in fight! Speak to me! hear my voice! hear me, sons of my love! They are silent,

silent forever! Cold, cold are their breasts of clay! Oh, from the rock on the hill, from the top of the windy steep, speak ye ghosts of the dead! Speak, I will not be afraid! Whither are ye gone to rest? In what cave of the hill shall I find the departed? No feeble voice is on the gale: no answer half drowned in the storm!

'I sit in my grief: I wait for morning in my tears! Rear the tomb, ye friends of the dead. Close it not till Colma comes. My life flies away like a dream. Why should I stay behind? Here shall I rest with my friends, by the stream of the sounding rock. When night comes on the hill—when the loud winds arise, my ghost shall stand in the blast, and mourn the death of my friends. The hunter shall hear from his booth; he shall fear, but love my voice! For sweet shall my voice be for my friends: pleasant were her friends to Colma.

'Such was thy song, Minona, softly blushing daughter of Torman. Our tears descended for Colma, and our souls were sad! Ullin came with his harp; he gave the song of Alpin. The voice of Alpin was pleasant; the soul of Ryno was a beam of fire! But they had rested in the narrow house; their voice had ceased in Selma! Ullin had returned one day from the chase before the heroes fell. He heard their strife on the hill; their song was soft, but sad. They mourned the fall of Morar, first of mortal men! His soul was like the soul of Fingal; his sword like the sword of Oscar. But he fell, and his father mourned; his sister's eyes were full of tears, the sister of car-borne Morar. She retired from the song of Ullin, like the moon in the west, when she foresees the shower, and hides her fair head in a cloud. I touched the harp with Ullin; the song of mourning rose!

'RYNO: The wind and the rain are past; calm is the noon of day. The clouds are divided in heaven. Over the green hills flies the inconstant sun. Red through the stony vale comes down the stream of the hill. Sweet are thy murmurs, O stream! but more sweet is the voice I hear. It is the voice of Alpin, the son of song, mourning for the dead! Bent is his head of age; red his tearful eye. Alpin, thou son of song, why alone on the silent hill? why complainest thou, as a blast in the wood, as a wave on the lonely shore?

'ALPIN: My tears, O Ryno! are for the dead—my voice for those that have passed away. Tall thou art on the hill; fair among the sons of the vale. But thou shalt fall like Morar; the mourner shall sit on thy tomb. The hills shall know thee no more; thy bow shall lie in thy hall unstrung!

'Thou wert swift, O Morar! as a roe on the desert; terrible as a meteor of fire. Thy wrath was as the storm; thy sword in battle as lightning in the field. Thy voice was a stream after rain, like thunder on distant hills. Many fell by thy arms: they were consumed in the flames of thy wrath. But when thou didst return from war, how peaceful was thy brow! Thy face was like the sun after rain, like the moon in the silence of night; calm as the breast of the lake when the loud wind is laid.

'Narrow is thy dwelling now! dark the place of thine abode! With three steps I compass thy grave, O thou who was so great before! Four stones, with their heads of moss, are the only memorial of thee. A tree with scarce a leaf, long grass which whistles in the wind, mark to the hunter's eye the grave of the mighty Morar. Morar! thou are low indeed. Thou hast no mother to mourn thee, no maid with her tears of love. Dead is she that brought thee forth. Fallen is the daughter of Morglan.

'Who on his staff is this? Who is this whose head is white with age, whose eyes are red with tears, who quakes at every step? It is thy father, O Morar! the father of no son but thee. He heard of thy fame in war, he heard of foes dispersed. He heard of Morar's renown; why did he not hear of his wound? Weep, thou father of Morar! Weep, but thy son heareth thee not. Deep is the sleep of the dead—low their pillow of dust. No more shall he hear thy voice—no more awake at thy call. When shall it be morn in the grave, to bid the slumberer awake? Farewell, thou bravest of men! thou conqueror in the field! But the field shall see thee no more, nor the dark wood be lightened with the splendour of thy steel. Thou hast left no son. The song shall preserve thy name. Future times shall hear of thee—they shall hear of the fallen Morar!

'The grief of all arose, but most the bursting sigh of Armin. He remembers the death of his son, who fell in the days of his youth. Carmor was near the hero, the chief of the echoing Galmal. Why burst the sigh of Armin? he said. Is there a cause to mourn? The song comes with its music to melt and please the soul. It is like soft mist that, rising from a lake, pours on the silent vale; the green flowers are filled with dew, but the sun returns in his strength, and the mist is gone. Why art thou sad, O Armin, chief of the sea-surrounded Gorma?

'Sad I am, nor small is my cause of woe! Carmor, thou hast lost no son, thou hast lost no daughter of beauty. Colgar the valiant lives, and Annira, fairest maid. The boughs of thy house ascend, O Carmor! But Armin is the last of his race. Dark is thy bed, O Daura! deep they sleep in the tomb! When shalt thou wake with thy songs—with all thy voice of music? Arise, winds of autumn, arise; blow along the heath! Streams of the mountains roar; roar, tempests in the groves of my oaks! Walk through broken clouds, O moon! show thy pale face at intervals; bring to my mind the night when all my children fell—when Arindal the mighty fell, when Daura the lovely failed. Daura, my daughter, thou wert fair—fair as the moon on Fura, white as the driven snow, sweet as the breathing gale. Arindal, thy bow was strong, thy spear was swift on the field, thy lock was like mist on the wave, thy shield a red cloud in a storm! Armar, renowned in war, came and sought Daura's love. He was not long refused: fair was the hope of their friends.

'Erath, son of Odgal, repined: his brother had been slain by Armar. He came disguised like a son of the sea; fair was his skiff on the wave, white his locks of age, calm his serious brow. Fairest of women, he said, lovely daughter of Armin! a rock not distant in the sea bears a tree on its side: red shines the fruit afar. There Armar waits for Daura. I come to carry his love! She went—she called on Armar. Naught answered but the son of the rock. Armar, my love, my love! why tormentest thou me with fear? Hear, son of Arnart, hear! it is Daura who calleth thee. Erath the traitor fled laughing to the land. She lifted up her voice—she called for her brother and her father. Arindal! Armin! none to relieve you, Daura.

'Her voice came over the sea. Arindal, my son, descended from the hill, rough in the spoils of the chase. His arrows rattled by his side; his bow was in his hand, five dark-grey dogs attended his steps. He saw fierce Erath on the shore; he seized and bound him to an oak. Thick wind the thongs of

the hide around his limbs; he loads the winds with his groans.
Arindal ascends the deep in his boat to bring Daura to land.
Armar came in his wrath, and let fly the grey-feathered shaft.
It sung, it sunk in thy heart. O Arindal, my son! for Erath the
traitor thou diest. The oar is stopped at once: he panted on
the rock and expired. What is thy grief, O Daura, when round
thy feet is poured thy brother's blood? The boat is broken in
twain. Armar plunges into the sea to rescue his Daura, or die.
Sudden a blast from a hill came over the waves; he sank, and
he rose no more.

'Alone, on the sea-beat rock, my daughter was heard to
complain; frequent and loud were her cries. What could her
father do? All night I stood on the shore: I saw her by the
faint beam of the moon. All night I heard her cries. Loud
was the wind; the rain beat hard on the hill. Before morning
appeared, her voice was weak; it died away like the evening
breeze among the grass of the rocks. Spent with grief, she
expired, and left thee, Armin, alone. Gone is my strength in
war, fallen my pride among women. When the storms aloft
arise, when the north lifts the wave on high, I sit by the
sounding shore, and look on the fatal rock. Often, by the
setting moon, I see the ghosts of my children; half viewless
they walked in mournful conference together.'

A flood of tears which rushed from Lotte's eyes, giving
relief to her oppressed heart, interrupted Werther's reading.
He threw down the paper, took her hand, and broke into
bitter sobs. Lotte rested her head on her arm and covered her
eyes with her handkerchief. Both were in a terrible emotional
state. They felt their own misery in the fate of the noble Gaels,
felt it together and their tears mingled. Werther's lips and
eyes burned on Lotte's arm, and a shudder ran through her
body. She wanted to escape, but grief and pity weighed upon
her with leaden force. She took a deep breath in order to
control herself and, sobbing, asked Werther, in a lovely voice,
to continue. Werther trembled; he thought his heart would
break, but he took up the paper and read, his voice shaking
with emotion:

'Why dost thou awake me, O breath of spring? Thou dost
woo me and say: I cover thee with the dew of Heaven! But the

time of my fading is near, near is the storm that will scatter my leaves! Tomorrow the wanderer shall come, he that saw me in my beauty shall come. His eyes will search me in the field around, and will not find me.'

The whole power of these words rushed upon the unhappy man. Completely desperate, he threw himself at Lotte's feet, seized her hands, pressed them upon his eyes and against his forehead; and an apprehension of his terrible intention seemed to brush against her soul. A tumult rose in her; she took his hands, pressed them against her breast and, bending toward him with a mournful gesture, their glowing cheeks touched. The world was lost to them. He clasped her in his arms, held her close against him, and covered her trembling lips with a shower of passionate kisses. 'Werther!' she cried with choking voice, turning away, 'Werther!' she pushed him away with a feeble hand. 'Werther!' she cried in a calmer tone, and with admirable dignity. He did not resist, released her from his embrace, and threw himself almost senseless on the floor at her feet. She quickly got up and said in a terrified confusion, torn between love and indignation, 'This was the last time, Werther! You will not see me again.' And with a look full of love for the unhappy man, she rushed into the next room and locked the door behind her. Werther stretched out his arms toward her but did not have the courage to hold her back. He lay on the floor, his head on the sofa, and remained in this position for more than half an hour, when a noise brought him to himself. It was the maid, who wanted to set the table. He walked up and down the room, and, when he saw that he was again alone, he went to the door of the next room and called gently, 'Lotte! Lotte! only one word more! a farewell!' There was no answer. He waited and implored and again waited; then he rushed away, calling, 'Farewell, Lotte! farewell forever!'

He came to the town gate. The watchman, who already knew him, opened it for him without a word. It drizzled between rain and snow; and a little before eleven he knocked at the gate again. His servant noticed, when Werther returned to his lodging, that his master had arrived hatless. He did not dare to mention this and helped him to undress; his clothes were wet through. His hat was later found on a steep bluff overlooking the valley, and it is hard to explain how he could have climbed to that height in the dark and wet night without falling to his death.

He went to bed and slept a long time. His servant found him writing when he brought the coffee he ordered the next morning. He was adding the following lines to his letter to Lotte:

'For the last time then, for the last time I open my eyes to this world. Alas, they shall not see the sun again, for today it is hidden behind a veil of mist. Now, Nature, mourn your son, your friend, your lover who nears his end. Lotte, this is a unique sensation, and yet it resembles a twilight dream, when one says to oneself: "This is the last morning. The last!" Lotte, these words mean nothing to me. Am I not standing here alive, in the possession of all my faculties, and yet tomorrow I shall lie prostrate and motionless on the ground. To die! What does that mean? Look, we are dreaming when we speak of death. I have seen many people die; but so limited is the human mind that it has no clear conception of the beginning and the end of our existence. At this moment I am still mine, yours! yours, my beloved! And the next moment—separated, divorced from you, perhaps forever?—No, Lotte, no! How can I *not* be? How can you *not* be? We *are* after all.—*Not* be! What does that mean? It is only a word, a mere sound which stirs nothing in me.—Dead, Lotte! thrown into the cold ground, so narrow, so dark!—I once had a friend who meant everything to me in my awkward youth; she died, and I followed the bier and stood beside her grave when they lowered the coffin, and the ropes that held it whirred as they were loosened and jerked up again; and then the first shovelful of earth fell with a thud, and the fearful chest gave back a hollow sound, more muffled every time, until it was completely covered with earth. I fell to the ground beside the grave—shocked, shaken, frightened, heartbroken; but I did not know what had happened to me—what will happen to me.—Death! The grave! I do not understand these words.

'Oh, forgive me! forgive me! Yesterday! It should have been the last moment of my life. O angel! for the first time, quite without doubt, I had in my heart of hearts the glowing thought: she loves me! she loves me! My lips are still burning with the sacred fire kindled by yours; there is a fresh warm feeling of happiness in my heart. Forgive me! forgive me!

'Oh, I knew that you loved me—knew it from the first warmhearted glance, from the first pressure of your hand; and yet, when I was not with you, when I saw Albert at your side, I was again tormented by feverish doubts.

'Do you remember the flowers you sent me when you had been unable to say one word to me or give me your hand at that hateful party? Oh, I was on my knees before them almost all night; and, for me, they put the seal on your love. But alas! these impressions faded, as the feeling of God's mercy gradually fades from the soul of the believer after it had been showered on him in holy and visible symbols.

'All this is transitory, but no Eternity shall extinguish the warm life that I drank yesterday from your lips and that I still feel within me. She loves me! This arm held her, these lips have trembled on her lips, this mouth has stammered against hers. She is mine! You are mine, Lotte, forever!

'And what does it mean that Albert is your husband? Husband! That may be for this world—and in this world it is sin that I love you, that I should like to snatch you from his arms into mine. Sin? Very well, and I am punishing myself for it; for this sin, which I have tasted in all its rapture, which gave me life-giving balm and strength. From now on you are mine! mine, Lotte! I go before you. I go to my Father, to your Father. I shall put my sorrow before Him, and He will comfort me until you come; and I shall fly to meet you and clasp you and stay with you before the Infinite Being in an eternal embrace.

'I do not dream; I am not deluded! So near to the grave, I see everything with great clearness. We shall be! we shall see one another again, see your mother. I shall see her, find her and ah! pour out all my heart to her, your mother, your very image.'

Shortly before eleven o'clock Werther asked his servant if he thought Albert had returned. The boy said, 'Yes, I saw his horse led into the stables.' Werther then gave him an unsealed note which contained the words:

'Will you be good enough to lend me your pistols for my intended journey. And goodbye.'

Lotte had slept little that night; everything she had feared had happened, in a manner which she had neither anticipated nor imagined. Her blood, that usually ran so innocently and lightly through her veins, was in a feverish tumult; a thousand emotions tormented her great soul. Was it the passion of Werther's embraces that reverberated in her heart? Was it indignation at his boldness? Was it a dissatisfied comparison of her present condition with those days of completely candid and frank innocence, when she had unclouded confidence in herself? How was she to face her husband? How to confess to him a scene which she might indeed describe without reserve, and yet of which she did not dare to make a clean breast? She and Albert had not talked to each other freely for so long. Should she now be the first to break silence and to give her husband such an unexpected disclosure just at the wrong time? She was afraid that even the mere mention of Werther's visit would make a disagreeable impression; and now this unexpected catastrophe! Was she allowed to hope that her husband would see the whole affair in the right light, would accept it entirely without prejudice? And could she wish him to read her heart? And yet, could she deceive the man in whose eyes she had always been like a crystal-clear glass—open and candid—and from whom she had been incapable of concealing any emotions, nor had wished to conceal any? All these questions worried her and made her uneasy; and all the while her thoughts kept returning to Werther, who was lost to her; whom she could not give up; whom she had, unfortunately, to leave to himself; and to whom, when he lost her, nothing was left.

How heavily the thought of the deadlock between Albert and herself weighed now on her heart, a deadlock which, at this moment, she could not explain. Even such sensible and good-natured people tend to become tongue-tied with each other, because of some latent differences of opinion; each of them thinking himself right and the other wrong; and the situation then becomes so complicated and exasperating that it is impossible to untie the knot at the critical moment on which all depends. If some happy intimacy had brought them together before this; if love and tolerance had mutually revived between them and opened their hearts—perhaps our friend might have been saved.

And yet, another strange circumstance played a part. Werther had never, as we know from his letters, kept his longing to depart from this world a secret. Albert had often argued with him on the subject; and this subject had several times been talked over by Lotte and her husband. The latter had not only felt a strong revulsion against such an act but also more than once said with a kind of irritability, which was otherwise quite incompatible with his character, that he believed he had sufficient reason to doubt the seriousness of any such intention on Werther's part; he had even sometimes allowed himself to ridicule the whole thing and mentioned his sceptical attitude to Lotte. This may have set her mind at rest for a time, whenever her thoughts presented to her the tragic picture—but it also prevented her from communicating to her husband the anxieties that tormented her at this moment.

Albert returned, and Lotte welcomed him with an embarrassed haste. He was not in a cheerful mood, as he had not been successful in settling his business, and the bailiff in the neighbourhood had been a rigid, a narrow-minded man. Besides, the roughness of the road had put him in a bad temper.

He asked if anything had happened, and she answered, much too quickly, 'Werther was here last night.' Then Albert asked if any letters had arrived, and was told that one letter and some packets had been put in his room. He went there, and Lotte was alone. The presence of the man whom she loved and respected had made a fresh impression upon her. She remembered his generosity, his love and his kindness, and felt more at ease. A secret impulse urged her to follow him; she took her needlework and went to his room as she often was in the habit of doing. She found him busy opening the packets and reading their contents. A few apparently contained rather unpleasant news. Lotte asked him several questions, which he answered curtly, and he then went to his high desk to write.

In this manner they passed an hour together, and Lotte's spirits were sinking lower and lower. She felt how difficult it would be for her to reveal to her husband, even if he were in the best of moods, all that weighed on her soul; and she lapsed into a sadness with distressed her only the more as she tried to hide it and choke down her tears.

When Werther's young servant appeared, she became very embarrassed. He handed the note to Albert, who calmly turned to his wife and said, 'Give him the pistols!'—'I wish him a pleasant journey,' he said to the youth. Lotte was thunderstruck; she staggered when she tried to get up, and almost fainted. Trembling, she walked slowly to the wall, took down the pistols, wiped off the dust, hesitated, and would have hesitated still longer if Albert's questioning glance had not urged her on. She gave the fatal weapons to the young man without saying a word; and when he had left the house, she gathered her work together and went to her room in a state of unspeakable anxiety. Her heart prophesied to her the most terrible possibilities. Her first thought was to throw herself at her husband's feet and to tell him the whole truth about last night's events, as well as her own guilt and her forebodings. But again she could not even hope to persuade her husband to go and see Werther. Meanwhile, the table had been set, and a good friend of Lotte's, who had stopped in for a moment to ask her something, said she would go immediately but stayed, making conversation during the meal more bearable. They pulled themselves together; they talked; they told stories, and were even able to forget.

The boy brought the pistols to Werther, who was delighted to hear that Lotte herself had handed them to him. He ordered bread and wine; then sent the boy out for his own supper, sat down and wrote:

'They have passed through your hands; you have wiped the dust from them. I kiss them a thousand times because you have touched them; and you, Heavenly Spirit, approve of my decision! And you, Lotte, offer me the weapon—you, from whose hands I wished to receive death, and ah! not receive it. Oh, how I questioned my servant! You trembled when you gave them to him, but you did not send me any farewell. Alas, alas! no farewell! Should you have closed your heart to me because of the moment that pledged me to you forever? Lotte, a thousand years cannot efface that memory!

And I feel that you cannot hate him who burns with love for you.'

After supper he told the boy to finish packing, tore up many papers, and went out to pay some small remaining debts. He returned and again went out, through the town gate, in spite of the rain, to the Count's garden. He wandered about the neighbouring countryside, came back at nightfall and again wrote:

'Wilhelm, I have seen the fields, the woods, and the sky for the last time. Farewell, you, too! Dear Mother, forgive me! Comfort her, Wilhelm! God bless you both! My affairs are all settled. Farewell! We shall meet again and with more joy.'

'Albert, I have repaid your kindness badly, and yet you will forgive me. I have disturbed the peace of your home; I have destroyed your confidence in each other. Farewell! I am about to make an end. Oh, if my death could make you happy again. Albert! Albert! Make the angel happy, and with this I implore God's blessing on you!'

In the evening he spent a great deal of time looking through his papers. He tore some up and threw them into the fire and sealed some packets addressed to Wilhelm. These contained short articles and fragmentary ideas, some of which I have read; and around ten o'clock, when he asked that the fire be replenished and that he be brought a bottle of wine, he sent his servant, whose room, like the other bedrooms of the house, was at the far end, to bed. The boy lay down without taking off his clothes so as to be ready at an early hour, for his master had told him that the post horses would be in front of the house before six o'clock the next morning.

'*After eleven*

'Everything is so quiet around me, and my soul is so calm. I thank you, God, who gives these last moments such warmth, such strength! I walk to the window, my dearest and see—still see—some stars in the eternal sky, shining through the stormy, fleeting clouds. No, you will not fall! The Eternal Father carries you near His heart, and me as well. I see the stars that make up the shaft of the Dipper, my favourite constellation. When I used to leave you at night and had passed your gate, these stars were just opposite me. How often have I looked up at them with rapture! How often have I raised my hands to them, regarding them as a symbol, a hallowed token of my happiness. And still now—O Lotte, does not everything remind me of you? Are you not always near me; and have I not, like a child, greedily snatched all sorts of trifles which you, dear saint, had touched!

'Precious silhouette! I return it to you, Lotte, and ask you to take good care of it. I have covered it with many, many kisses; I have greeted it a thousand times whenever I went out or came home.

'I have written your father a note and asked him to take care of my body. In the churchyard are two linden trees, in a far corner, next to the field; there I should like to rest. He can and will do this service to his friend. Do ask him, too. I do not like to hurt the feelings of devout Christians, who might not want to rest beside a poor, unhappy man. Oh, I wished you would bury me by the wayside or in a remote valley, where priest and Levite may pass by the marked stone, thankful that they are not as other men, and the Samaritan may shed a tear.

'Here, Lotte! I do not shudder to grasp the cold and dreadful cup from which I am about to drink the ecstasy of death. Your hand gave it to me, and I do not flinch. All, all the desires and hopes of my life are fulfilled! So cold, so rigid to knock at the iron gate of death.

'Had I been granted the happiness to die for *you!*, Lotte, to sacrifice myself for *you!* I would die bravely, I would die cheerfully, if I could restore to you the peace and happiness of your life. But alas! it is reserved for only a very few noble souls to shed their blood for those who are dear to them, and by their deaths to fan the flame of life of their friends to a new and wonderfully increased splendour.

'I want to be buried in these clothes I wear, Lotte! You have touched them and hallowed them. I have also asked your father to carry out this request. My soul hovers above the coffin. Do not let them look through my pockets. This rose-coloured ribbon which you wore on your breast the first time I saw you, surrounded by your children—oh, give them a thousand kisses, and tell them the fate of their unhappy friend. The darling children! they swarm around me. Ah, how quickly I grew fond of you; I could not keep away from you from the first moment.—Let this ribbon be buried with me; you gave it to me on my birthday. How eagerly I accepted all this!—Ah, I did not think the way would end here! Be calm! Please, be calm!

'They are loaded.—The clock strikes twelve.—So be it! Lotte! Lotte! Farewell! Farewell!'

A neighbour saw the flash of the powder and heard the shot; but, as everything remained quiet, he did not pay further attention to it.

Next morning, around six o'clock, the servant entered the room with a candle. He found his master lying on the floor, the pistol beside him, and blood everywhere. He called, he touched him; no answer came, only a rattling in the throat. He ran for a doctor and for Albert. Lotte heard the bell; a tremor seized all her limbs. She woke her husband; the got up, and the servant, sobbing and stammering, told her news. Lotte fainted and fell to the ground at Albert's feet.

When the doctor arrived, he found the unfortunate young man on the floor, past help; his pulse was still beating; all his limbs were paralysed. He had shot himself through the head above the right eye, and his brain was laid bare. They bled him needlessly; the blood flowed; he was still breathing.

From the blood on the back of the armchair they concluded that he had committed the act while sitting at his writing desk. He had then slid down and rolled around the chair in convulsions. He was lying on his back, facing the window, enfeebled, fully dressed, in his boots, his blue coat and yellow waistcoat.

The house, the neighbourhood, the town, was in a tumult. Albert came in. They had laid Werther on his bed and bandaged his forehead; his face was already the face of a dead man; he did not move. His lungs still gave forth a dreadful rattling sound, now weak, now stronger; they expected the end.

He had drunk only one glass of the wine. Lessing's *Emilia Galotti* lay open on his desk.

I cannot describe Albert's consternation, Lotte's distress.

On hearing the news, the old bailiff rode up to the house at full speed; he kissed his dying friend and wept bitter tears. His

older sons arrived soon afterward on foot; they knelt beside
the bed with expressions of uncontrollable grief and kissed
Werther's hands and mouth; the oldest, whom Werther had
always loved most, clung to him to the bitter end, when they
had to tear the boy away by force. Werther died at noon.
The presence of the bailiff and the arrangements he made
prevented a public disturbance. That night around eleven the
bailiff had Werther buried at the place he himself had chosen.
The old man and his sons followed the body to the grave;
Albert was unable to. Lotte's life was in danger. Workmen
carried the coffin. No clergyman attended.

William Beckford

VATHEK

1786

WILLIAM BECKFORD (1759–1844) was the son of William Beckford (1709–70), Lord Mayor of London and a controversial figure, especially celebrated for his strong defence of John Wilkes. Beckford *fils* was one of the strangest eccentrics that even England, a country fertile in producing such characters, can show. A good European in the eighteenth-century manner—he spent periods in Paris, in Lausanne, and in Cintra, thus familiarizing himself with the political and social systems of three countries—he became a Member of Parliament, but increasingly sought isolation in his family mansion of Fonthill Giffard in the West Country. Here he amassed (like Vathek) a large collection of curios, and spent such colossal sums on fantastic schemes of decoration and purchase of works of art that, in spite of his great wealth, he was obliged to sell the place in 1822. Stories of his strange behaviour and freaks of fancy, some reliable, others less so, have always abounded.

Beckford was a sceptic and ironist typical of that generation of Englishmen who were attracted to the French Enlightenment with its anti-Christian and anti-clerical programme. *Vathek* would not have been written, or at any rate would have been a different work, without the example of Voltaire's *Zadig* (1748). Not that anyone could have written such a book merely by imitating someone else. Its outrageous inventiveness, its extravagant humour, and its general air of satirical high spirits make it an entirely enjoyable *divertissement*, enormously popular in its day and never quite forgotten since.

Beckford wrote *Vathek* in French, perhaps feeling that it would appeal more to a French than to an English taste, but as it turned out an anonymous English translation was published (1786) before the French edition (1787), and it is this that we give here.

VATHEK, ninth Caliph of the race of the Abassides, was the son of Motassem, and the grandson of Haroun Al Raschid. From an early accession to the throne, and the talents he possessed to adorn it, his subjects were induced to expect that his reign would be long and happy. His figure was pleasing and majestic; but when he was angry one of his eyes became so terrible that no person could bear to behold it, and the wretch upon whom it was fixed instantly fell backward, and sometimes expired. For fear, however, of depopulating his dominions, and making his palace desolate, he but rarely gave way to his anger.

Being much addicted to women and the pleasures of the table, he sought by his affability to procure agreeable companions; and he succeeded the better as his generosity was unbounded, and his indulgences unrestrained, for he was by no means scrupulous, nor did he think with the Caliph Omar Ben Abdalaziz, that it was necessary to make a hell of this world to enjoy Paradise in the next.

He surpassed in magnificence all his predecessors. The palace of Alkoremmi, which his father Motassem had erected on the hill of Pied Horses, and which commanded the whole city of Samarah, was in his idea far too scanty; he added therefore five wings, or rather other palaces, which he designed for the particular gratification of each of his senses.

In the first of these were tables continually covered with the most exquisite dainties, which were supplied both by night and by day according to their constant consumption, whilst the most delicious wines and the choicest cordials flowed forth from a hundred fountains that were never exhausted. This palace was called 'The Eternal or Unsatiating Banquet.'

The second was styled 'The Temple of Melody, or the Nectar of the Soul.' It was inhabited by the most skilful musicians and admired poets of the time, who not only displayed their talents within, but, dispersing in bands without, caused every surrounding scene to reverberate their songs, which were continually varied in the most delightful succession.

The palace named 'The Delight of the Eyes, or the Support

of Memory,' was one entire enchantment. Rarities collected from every corner of the earth were there found in such profusion as to dazzle and confound, but for the order in which they were arranged. One gallery exhibited the pictures of the celebrated Mani, and statues that seemed to be alive. Here a well-managed perspective attracted the sight, there the magic of optics agreeably deceived it; whilst the naturalist on his part exhibited, in their several classes, the various gifts that Heaven had bestowed on our globe. In a word, Vathek omitted nothing in this palace that might gratify the curiosity of those who resorted to it, although he was not able to satisfy his own, for he was of all men the most curious.

'The Palace of Perfumes,' which was termed likewise 'The Incentive to Pleasure,' consisted of various halls where the different perfumes which the earth produces were kept perpetually burning in censers of gold. Flambeaux and aromatic lamps were here lighted in open day. But the too powerful effects of this agreeable delirium might be avoided by descending into an immense garden, where an assemblage of every fragrant flower diffused through the air the purest odours.

The fifth palace, denominated 'The Retreat of Joy, or the Dangerous,' was frequented by troops of young females beautiful as the houris and not less seducing, who never failed to receive with caresses all whom the Caliph allowed to approach them; for he was by no means disposed to be jealous, as his own women were secluded within the palace he inhabited himself.

Notwithstanding the sensuality in which Vathek indulged, he experienced no abatement in the love of his people, who thought that a sovereign immersed in pleasure was not less tolerable to his subjects than one that employed himself in creating them foes. But the unquiet and impetuous disposition of the Caliph would not allow him to rest there; he had studied so much for his amusement in the lifetime of his father as to acquire a great deal of knowledge, though not a sufficiency to satisfy himself; for he wished to know everything, even sciences that did not exist. He was fond of engaging in disputes with the learned, but liked them not to push their opposition with warmth; he stopped the mouths of those with presents whose mouths could be stopped, whilst others, whom his liberality was unable to subdue, he sent to prison to cool their blood; a remedy that often succeeded.

Vathek discovered also a predilection for theological controversy, but it was not with the orthodox that he usually held. By this means he induced the zealots to oppose him, and then persecuted them in return; for he resolved at any rate to have reason on his side.

The great prophet Mahomet, whose vicars the caliphs are, beheld with indignation from his abode in the seventh heaven the irreligious conduct of such a vicegerent. 'Let us leave him to himself,' said he to the Genii, who are always ready to receive his commands; 'Let us see to what lengths his folly and impiety will carry him; if he run into excess we shall know how to chastise him. Assist him, therefore, to complete the tower which, in imitation of Nimrod, he hath begun, not, like that great warrior, to escape being drowned, but from the insolent curiosity of penetrating the secrets of Heaven; he will not divine the fate that awaits him.'

The Genii obeyed, and when the workmen had raised their structure a cubit in the daytime, two cubits more were added in the night. The expedition with which the fabric arose was not a little flattering to the vanity of Vathek. He fancied that even insensible matter showed a forwardness to subserve his designs, not considering that the successes of the foolish and wicked form the first rod of their chastisement.

His pride arrived at its height when, having ascended for the first time the eleven thousand stairs of his tower, he cast his eyes below and beheld men not larger than pismires, mountains than shells, and cities than bee-hives.

The idea which such an elevation inspired of his own grandeur completely bewildered him; he was almost ready to adore himself, till, lifting his eyes upward, he saw the stars as high above him as they appeared when he stood on the surface of the earth. He consoled himself, however, for this transient perception of his littleness, with the thought of being great in the eyes of others, and flattered himself that the light of his mind would extend beyond the reach of his sight, and transfer to the stars the decrees of his destiny.

With this view the inquisitive Prince passed most of his

nights on the summit of his tower, till he became an adept in the mysteries of astrology, and imagined that the planets had disclosed to him the most marvellous adventures, which were to be accomplished by an extraordinary personage from a country altogether unknown.

Prompted by motives of curiosity he had always been courteous to strangers, but from this instant he redoubled his attention, and ordered it to be announced by sound of trumpet through all the streets of Samarah that no one of his subjects, on peril of displeasure, should either lodge or detain a traveller, but forthwith bring him to the palace.

Not long after this proclamation there arrived in his metropolis a man so hideous, that the very guards who arrested him were forced to shut their eyes as they led him along.

The Caliph himself appeared startled at so horrible a visage, but joy succeeded to this emotion of terror when the stranger displayed to his view such rarities as he had never before seen, and of which he had no conception.

In reality nothing was ever so extraordinary as the merchandise this stranger produced; most of his curiosities, which were not less admirable for their workmanship than splendour, had besides their several virtues described on a parchment fastened to each. There were slippers which enabled the feet to walk; knives that cut without the motion of a hand; sabres which dealt the blow at the person they were wished to strike, and the whole enriched with gems that were hitherto unknown.

The sabres, whose blades emitted a dazzling radiance, fixed more than all the Caliph's attention, who promised himself to decipher at his leisure the uncouth characters engraven on their sides. Without, therefore, demanding their price he ordered all the coined gold to be brought from his treasury, and commanded the merchant to take what he pleased. The stranger complied with modesty and silence.

Vathek, imagining that the merchant's taciturnity was occasioned by the awe which his presence inspired, encouraged him to advance, and asked him, with an air of condescension, 'Who he was? whence he came? and where he obtained such beautiful commodities?'

The man, or rather monster, instead of making a reply, thrice rubbed his forehead, which, as well as his body, was blacker than ebony; four times clapped his paunch, the projection of which was enormous; opened wide his huge eyes, which glowed like firebrands; began to laugh with a hideous noise, and discovered his long amber-coloured teeth bestreaked with green.

The Caliph, though a little startled, renewed his inquiries, but without being able to procure a reply; at which, beginning to be ruffled, he exclaimed:

'Knowest thou, varlet, who I am? and at whom thou art aiming thy gibes?' Then, addressing his guards:

'Have ye heard him speak? is he dumb?'

'He hath spoken,' they replied, 'though but little.'

'Let him speak again, then,' said Vathek, 'and tell me who he is, whence he came, and where he procured these singular curiosities, or I swear by the ass of Balaam that I will make him rue his pertinacity.'

The menace was accompanied by the Caliph with one of his angry and perilous glances, which the stranger sustained without the slightest emotion, although his eyes were fixed on the terrible eye of the Prince.

No words can describe the amazement of the courtiers when they beheld this rude merchant withstand the encounter unshocked. They all fell prostrate with their faces on the ground to avoid the risk of their lives, and continued in the same abject posture till the Caliph exclaimed in a furious tone:

'Up, cowards! seize the miscreant! see that he be committed to prison and guarded by the best of my soldiers! Let him, however, retain the money I gave him; it is not my intent to take from him his property, I only want him to speak.'

No sooner had he uttered these words than the stranger was surrounded, pinioned with strong fetters, and hurried away to the prison of the great tower, which was encompassed by seven empalements of iron bars, and armed with spikes in every direction longer and sharper than spits.

The Caliph, nevertheless, remained in the most violent agitation; he sat down indeed to eat, but of the three hundred covers that were daily placed before him could taste of no more than thirty-two. A diet to which he had been so little accustomed was sufficient of itself to prevent him from sleeping; what then must be its effect when joined to the anxiety that preyed upon his spirits? At the first glimpse of dawn he hastened to the prison, again to importune this intractable stranger; but the rage of Vathek exceeded all bounds on finding the prison empty, the gates burst asunder, and his guards lying lifeless around him. In the paroxysm of his passion he fell furiously on the poor carcasses, and kicked them till evening without intermission. His courtiers and viziers exerted their efforts to soothe his extravagance, but finding every expedient ineffectual they all united in one vociferation:

'The Caliph is gone mad! the Caliph is out of his senses!'

This outcry, which soon resounded through the streets of Samarah, at length reaching the ears of Carathis, his mother; she flew in the utmost consternation to try her ascendency on the mind of her son. Her tears and caresses called off his attention, and he was prevailed upon by her entreaties to be brought back to the palace.

Carathis, apprehensive of leaving Vathek to himself, caused him to be put to bed, and seating herself by him, endeavoured by her conversation to heal and compose him. Nor could anyone have attempted it with better success, for the Caliph not only loved her as a mother, but respected her as a person of superior genius; it was she who had induced him, being a Greek herself, to adopt all the sciences and systems of her country, which good Mussulmans hold in such thorough abhorrence. Judicial astrology was one of those systems in which Carathis was a perfect adept; she began, therefore, with reminding her son of the promise which the stars had made him, and intimated an intention of consulting them again.

'Alas!' sighed the Caliph, as soon as he could speak, 'what a fool have I been! not for the kicks bestowed on my guards who so tamely submitted to death, but for never considering that this extraordinary man was the same the planets had foretold, whom, instead of ill-treating, I should have conciliated by all the arts of persuasion.'

'The past,' said Carathis, 'cannot be recalled, but it behoves us to think of the future; perhaps you may again see the object you so much regret; it is possible the inscriptions on the sabres will afford information. Eat, therefore, and take thy repose, my dear son; we will consider to-morrow in what manner to act.'

Vathek yielded to her counsel as well as he could, and arose in the morning with a mind more at ease. The sabres he commanded to be instantly brought, and poring upon them through a green glass, that their glittering might not dazzle, he set himself in earnest to decipher the inscriptions; but his reiterated attempts were all of them nugatory; in vain did he beat his head and bite his nails, not a letter of the whole was he able to ascertain. So unlucky a disappointment would have undone him again had not Carathis by good fortune entered the apartment.

'Have patience, son!' said she; 'you certainly are possessed of every important science, but the knowledge of languages is a trifle at best, and the accomplishment of none but a pedant. Issue forth a proclamation that you will confer such rewards as become your greatness upon anyone that shall interpret what you do not understand, and what it is beneath you to learn; you will soon find your curiosity gratified.'

'That may be,' said the Caliph; 'but in the meantime I shall be horribly disgusted by a crowd of smatterers, who will come to the trial as much for the pleasure of retailing their jargon as from the hope of gaining the reward. To avoid this evil it will be proper to add that I will put every candidate to death who shall fail to give satisfaction; for, thank heaven! I have skill enough to distinguish between one that translates and one that invents.'

'Of that I have no doubt,' replied Carathis; 'but to put the ignorant to death is somewhat severe, and may be productive of dangerous effects; content yourself with commanding their beards to be burnt—beards in a state are not quite so essential as men.'

The Caliph submitted to the reasons of his mother, and sending for Morakanabad, his prime vizir, said:

'Let the common criers proclaim, not only in Samarah, but throughout every city in my empire, that whosoever will repair hither and decipher certain characters which appear to be inexplicable shall experience the liberality for which I am renowned; but that all who fail upon trial shall have their beards burnt off to the last hair. Let them add also that I will bestow fifty beautiful slaves and as many jars of apricots from the isle of Kirmith upon any man that shall bring me intelligence of the stranger.'

The subjects of the Caliph, like their sovereign, being great admirers of women and apricots from Kirmith, felt their mouths water at these promises, but were totally unable to gratify their hankering, for no one knew which way the stranger had gone.

As to the Caliph's other requisition, the result was different. The learned, the half-learned, and those who were neither, but fancied themselves equal to both, came boldly to hazard their beards, and all shamefully lost them.

The exaction of these forfeitures, which found sufficient employment for the eunuchs, gave them such a smell of singed hair as greatly to disgust the ladies of the seraglio, and make it necessary that this new occupation of their guardians should be transferred into other hands.

At length, however, an old man presented himself whose beard was a cubit and a half longer than any that had appeared before him. The officers of the palace whispered to each other, as they ushered him in, 'What a pity such a beard should be burnt!' Even the Caliph, when he saw it, concurred with them in opinion, but his concern was entirely needless. This venerable personage read the characters with facility, and explained them verbatim as follows: 'We were made where everything good is made; we are the least of the wonders of a place where all is wonderful, and deserving the sight of the first potentate on earth.'

'You translate admirably!' cried Vathek; 'I know to what these marvellous characters allude. Let him receive as many robes of honour and thousands of sequins of gold as he hath spoken words. I am in some measure relieved from the perplexity that embarrassed me!'

Vathek invited the old man to dine, and even to remain some days in the palace. Unluckily for him he accepted the offer, for the Caliph, having ordered him next morning to be called, said:

'Read again to me what you have read already; I cannot hear too often the promise that is made me, the completion of which I languish to obtain.'

The old man forthwith put on his green spectacles, but they instantly dropped from his nose on perceiving that the characters he had read the day preceding had given place to others of different import.

'What ails you?' asked the Caliph; 'and why these symptoms of wonder?'

'Sovereign of the world,' replied the old man, 'these sabres hold another language today from that they yesterday held.'

'How say you?' returned Vathek; 'but it matters not! tell me, if you can, what they mean.'

'It is this, my Lord,' rejoined the old man: 'Woe to the rash mortal who seeks to know that of which he should remain ignorant, and to undertake that which surpasseth his power!'

'And woe to thee!' cried the Caliph, in a burst of indignation; 'today thou art void of understanding; begone from my presence; they shall burn but the half of thy beard because thou wert yesterday fortunate in guessing; my gifts I never resume.'

The old man, wise enough to perceive he had luckily escaped, considering the folly of disclosing so disgusting a truth, immediately withdrew, and appeared not again.

But it was not long before Vathek discovered abundant reason to regret his precipitation; for though he could not decipher the characters himself, yet by constantly poring upon them he plainly perceived that they every day changed, and unfortunately no other candidate offered to explain them.

This perplexing occupation inflamed his blood, dazzled his sight, and brought on a giddiness and debility that he could not support. He failed not, however, though in so reduced a condition, to be often carried to his tower, as he flattered himself that he might there read in the stars which he went to consult something more congenial to his wishes; but in this his hopes were deluded, for his eyes, dimmed by the vapours of his head, began to subserve his curiosity so ill that he beheld nothing but a thick dun cloud, which he took for the most direful of omens.

Agitated with so much anxiety, Vathek entirely lost all firmness; a fever seized him, and his appetite failed. Instead of being one of the greatest eaters he became as distinguished for drinking. So insatiable was the thirst which tormented him that his mouth, like a funnel, was always open to receive the various liquors that might be poured into it, and especially cold water, which calmed him more than every other.

This unhappy prince, being thus incapacitated for the enjoyment of any pleasure, commanded the palaces of the five senses to be shut up; forbore to appear in public, either to display his magnificence or administer justice, and retired to the inmost apartment of his harem. As he had ever been an indulgent husband, his wives, overwhelmed with grief at his deplorable situation, incessantly offered their prayers for his health, and unremittingly supplied him with water.

In the meantime the Princess Carathis, whose affliction no words can describe, instead of restraining herself to sobbing and tears, was closeted daily with the Vizir Morakanabad, to find out some cure or mitigation of the Caliph's disease.

Under the persuasion that it was caused by enchantment, they turned over together, leaf by leaf, all the books of magic that might point out a remedy, and caused the horrible stranger, whom they accused as the enchanter, to be everywhere sought for with the strictest diligence.

At the distance of a few miles from Samarah stood a high mountain, whose sides were swarded with wild thyme and basil, and its summit overspread with so delightful a plain that it might be taken for the paradise destined for the faithful.

Upon it grew a hundred thickets of eglantine and other fragrant shrubs, a hundred arbours of roses, jessamine and honeysuckle, as many clumps of orange trees, cedar and citron, whose branches, interwoven with the palm, the pomegranate, and the vine, presented every luxury that could regale the eye or the taste.

The ground was strewed with violets, hare-bells, and pansies, in the midst of which sprung forth tufts of jonquils, hyacinths, and carnations, with every other perfume that impregnates the air. Four fountains, not less clear than deep, and so abundant as to slake the thirst of ten armies, seemed profusely placed here to make the scene more resemble the garden of Eden, which was watered by the four sacred rivers.

Here the nightingale sang the birth of the rose, her well-beloved, and at the same time lamented its short-lived beauty; whilst the turtle deplored the loss of more substantial pleasures, and the wakeful lark hailed the rising light that reanimates the whole creation.

Here more than anywhere the mingled melodies of birds expressed the various passions they inspired, as if the exquisite fruits which they pecked at pleasure had given them a double energy.

To this mountain Vathek was sometimes brought for the sake of breathing a purer air, and especially to drink at will of the four fountains, which were reputed in the highest degree salubrious and sacred to himself. His attendants were his mother, his wives, and some eunuchs, who assiduously employed themselves in filling capacious bowls of rock crystal, and emulously presenting them to him; but it frequently happened that his avidity exceeded their zeal, insomuch that he would prostrate himself upon the ground to lap up the water, of which he could never have enough.

One day, when this unhappy prince had been long lying in so debasing a posture, a voice, hoarse but strong, thus addressed him:

'Why assumest thou the function of a dog, O Caliph, so proud of thy dignity and power?'

At this apostrophe he raised his head and beheld the stranger that had caused him so much affliction. Inflamed with anger at the sight, he exclaimed:

'Accursed Giaour! what comest thou hither to do? Is it not enough to have transformed a prince remarkable for his agility into one of those leather barrels which the Bedouin Arabs carry on their camels when they traverse the deserts? Perceivest thou not that I may perish by drinking to excess no less than by a total abstinence?'

'Drink, then, this draught,' said the stranger, as he presented to him a phial of a red and yellow mixture; 'and, to satiate the thirst of thy soul as well as of thy body, know that I am an Indian, but from a region of India which is wholly unknown.'

The Caliph, delighted to see his desires accomplished in part, and flattering himself with the hope of obtaining their entire fulfilment, without a moment's hesitation swallowed the potion, and instantaneously found his health restored, his thirst appeased, and his limbs as agile as ever.

In the transports of his joy Vathek leaped upon the neck of the frightful Indian, and kissed his horrid mouth and hollow cheeks as though they had been the coral lips and the lilies and roses of his most beautiful wives; whilst they, less terrified than jealous at the sight, dropped their veils to hide the blush of mortification that suffused their foreheads.

Nor would the scene have closed here had not Carathis, with all the art of insinuation, a little repressed the raptures of her son. Having prevailed upon him to return to Samarah she caused a herald to precede him, whom she commanded to proclaim as loudly as possible: 'The wonderful stranger hath appeared again, he hath healed the Caliph, he hath spoken! he hath spoken!'

Forthwith all the inhabitants of this vast city quitted their habitations, and ran together in crowds to see the procession of Vathek and the Indian, whom they now blessed as much as they had before execrated, incessantly shouting:

'He hath healed our sovereign, he hath spoken! he hath spoken!' Nor were these words forgotten in the public festivals, which were celebrated the same evening, to testify the general joy; for the poets applied them as a chorus to all the songs they composed.

The Caliph in the meanwhile caused the palaces of the Senses to be again set open; and, as he found himself prompted to visit that of Taste in preference to the rest, immediately ordered a splendid entertainment, to which his great officers and favourite courtiers were all invited. The Indian, who was placed near the Prince, seemed to think that as a proper acknowledgement of so distinguished a privilege he could neither eat, drink, nor talk too much. The various dainties were no sooner served up than they vanished, to the great mortification of Vathek, who piqued himself on being the greatest eater alive, and at this time in particular had an excellent appetite.

The rest of the company looked round at each other in amazement; but the Indian, without appearing to observe it, quaffed large bumpers to the health of each of them, sung in a style altogether extravagant, related stories at which he laughed immoderately, and poured forth extemporaneous verses, which would not have been thought bad but for the strange grimaces with which they were uttered. In a word, his loquacity was equal to that of a hundred astrologers, he ate as much as a hundred porters, and caroused in proportion.

The Caliph, notwithstanding the table had been thirty times covered, found himself incommoded by the voraciousness of his guest, who was now considerably declined in the Prince's esteem. Vathek, however, being unwilling to betray the chagrin he could hardly disguise, said in a whisper to Bababalouk, the chief of his eunuchs, 'You see how enormous his performances in every way are, what would be the consequence should he get at my wives! Go! redouble your vigilance, and be sure look well to my Circassians, who would be more to his taste than all of the rest.'

The bird of the morning had thrice renewed his song when the hour of the Divan sounded. Vathek, in gratitude to his subjects having promised to attend, immediately rose from the table and repaired thither, leaning upon his vizir, who could scarcely support him, so disordered was the poor Prince by the wine he had drunk, and still more by the extravagant vagaries of his boisterous guest.

The vizirs, the officers of the crown and of the law, arranged themselves in a semicircle about their sovereign and preserved a respectful silence, whilst the Indian, who looked as cool as if come from a fast, sat down without ceremony on the step of the throne, laughing in his sleeve at the indignation with which his temerity had filled the spectators.

The Caliph, however, whose ideas were confused and his head embarrassed, went on administering justice at haphazard, till at length the prime vizir, perceiving his situation, hit upon a sudden expedient to interrupt the audience and rescue the honour of his master, to whom he said in a whisper:

'My Lord, the Princess Carathis, who hath passed the night in consulting the planets, informs you that they portend you evil, and the danger is urgent. Beware lest this stranger, whom you have so lavishly recompensed for his magical gewgaws, should make some attempt on your life; his liquor, which at first had the appearance of effecting your cure, may be no more than a poison of a sudden operation. Slight not this surmise, ask him at least of what it was compounded, whence he procured it, and mention the sabres which you seem to have forgotten.'

Vathek, to whom the insolent airs of the stranger became every moment less supportable, intimated to his vizir by a wink of acquiescence that he would adopt his advice, and at once turning towards the Indian said, 'Get up, and declare in full Divan of what drugs the liquor was compounded you enjoined me to take, for it is suspected to be poison; add also the explanation I have so earnestly desired concerning the sabres you sold me, and thus show your gratitude for the favours heaped on you.'

Having pronounced these words in as moderate a tone as a caliph well could, he waited in silent expectation for an answer. But the Indian, still keeping his seat, began to renew his loud shouts of laughter, and exhibit the same horrid grimaces he had shown them before, without vouchsafing a word in reply.

Vathek, no longer able to brook such insolence, immediately kicked him from the steps; instantly descending, repeated his blow, and persisted with such assiduity as incited all who were present to follow his example. Every foot was aimed at the Indian, and no sooner had anyone given him a kick than he felt himself constrained to reiterate the stroke.

The stranger afforded them no small entertainment; for, being both short and plump, he collected himself into a ball, and rolled round on all sides at the blows of his assailants, who pressed after him wherever he turned with an eagerness beyond conception, whilst their numbers were every moment increasing. The ball indeed, in passing from one apartment to another, drew every person after it that came in its way, insomuch that the whole palace was thrown into confusion, and resounded with a tremendous clamour. The women of the harem, amazed at the uproar, flew to their blinds to discover the cause; but no sooner did they catch a glimpse of the ball than, feeling themselves unable to refrain, they broke from the clutches of their eunuchs, who to stop their flight pinched them till they bled, but in vain; whilst themselves, though trembling with terror at the escape of their charge, were as incapable of resisting the attraction.

The Indian, after having traversed the halls, galleries,

chambers, kitchens, gardens, and stables of the palace, at last took his course through the courts; whilst the Caliph, pursuing him closer than the rest, bestowed as many kicks as he possibly could, yet not without receiving now and then one, which his competitors in their eagerness designed for the ball.

Carathis, Morakanabad, and two or three old vizirs, whose wisdom had hitherto withstood the attraction, wishing to prevent Vathek from exposing himself in the presence of his subjects, fell down in his way to impede the pursuit; but he, regardless of their obstruction, leaped over their heads and went on as before. They then ordered the Muezzins to call the people to prayers, both for the sake of getting them out of the way, and of endeavouring by their petitions to avert the calamity; but neither of these expedients was a whit more successful; the sight of this fatal ball was alone sufficient to draw after it every beholder. The Muezzins themselves, though they saw it but at a distance, hastened down from their minarets and mixed with the crowd, which continued to increase in so surprising a manner that scarce an inhabitant was left in Samarah, except the aged, the sick confined to their beds, and infants at the breast, whose nurses could run more nimbly without them. Even Carathis, Morakanabad, and the rest were all become of the party.

The shrill screams of the females, who had broken from their apartments and were unable to extricate themselves from the pressure of the crowd, together with those of the eunuchs jostling after them, terrified lest their charges should escape from their sight, increased by the execration of husbands urging forward and menacing both, kicks given and received, stumblings and overthrows at every step; in a word, the confusion that universally prevailed rendered Samarah like a city taken by storm and devoted to absolute plunder.

At last the cursed Indian, who still preserved his rotundity of figure, after passing through all the streets and public places and leaving them empty, rolled onwards to the plain of Catoul, and traversed the valley at the foot of the mountain of the Four Fountains.

As a continual fall of water had excavated an immense gulf in the valley, whose opposite side was closed in by a steep acclivity, the Caliph and his attendants were apprehensive lest the ball should bound into the chasm, and to prevent it redoubled their efforts, but in vain. The Indian persevered in his onward direction, and, as had been apprehended, glancing from the precipice with the rapidity of lightning, was lost in the gulf below.

Vathek would have followed the perfidious Giaour had not an invisible agency arrested his progress. The multitude that pressed after him were at once checked in the same manner, and a calm instantaneously ensued. They all gazed at each other with an air of astonishment, and, notwithstanding that the loss of veils and turbans, together with torn habits and dust blended with sweat, presented a most laughable spectacle, there was not one smile to be seen; on the contrary, all, with looks of confusion and sadness, returned in silence to Samarah and retired to their inmost apartments, without ever reflecting that they had been impelled by an invisible power into the extravagance for which they reproached themselves; for it is but just that men, who so often arrogate to their own merit the good of which they are but instruments, should attribute to themselves the absurdities which they could not prevent.

The Caliph was the only person that refused to leave the valley. He commanded his tents to be pitched there, and stationed himself on the very edge of the precipice, in spite of the representations of Carathis and Morakanabad, who pointed out the hazard of its brink giving way, and the vicinity to the Magician that had so severely tormented him. Vathek derided all their remonstrances, and, having ordered a thousand flambeaux to be lighted, and directed his attendants to proceed in lighting more, lay down on the slippery margin and attempted, by help of this artificial splendour, to look through that gloom which all the fires of the empyrean had been insufficient to pervade. One while he fancied to himself voices arising from the depth of the gulf; at another he seemed to distinguish the accents of the Indian, but all was no more than the hollow murmur of waters, and the din of the cataracts that rushed from steep to steep down the sides of the mountain.

Having passed the night in this cruel perturbation, the

Caliph at daybreak retired to his tent, where, without taking
the least sustenance, he continued to doze till the dusk of
evening began again to come on. He then resumed his
vigils as before, and persevered in observing them for many
nights together. At length, fatigued with so successless an
employment, he sought relief from change. To this end he
sometimes paced with hasty strides across the plain, and, as
he wildly gazed at the stars, reproached them with having
deceived him; but lo! on a sudden the clear, blue sky appeared
streaked over with streams of blood, which reached from the
valley even to the city of Samarah. As this awful phenomenon
seemed to touch his tower Vathek at first thought of repairing
thither to view it more distinctly, but feeling himself unable to
advance, and being overcome with apprehension, he muffled
up his face in his robe.

Terrifying as these prodigies were, this impression upon
him was no more than momentary, and served only to
stimulate his love of the marvellous. Instead therefore of
returning to his palace, he persisted in the resolution of
abiding where the Indian vanished from his view. One night,
however, while he was walking as usual on the plain, the moon
and the stars at once were eclipsed, and a total darkness
ensued; the earth trembled beneath him, and a voice came
forth, the voice of the Giaour, who, in accents more sonorous
than thunder, thus addressed him:

'Wouldest thou devote thyself to me? Adore then the
terrestrial influences, and abjure Mahomet. On these conditions I will bring thee to the palace of subterranean fire; there
shalt thou behold in immense depositories the treasures which
the stars have promised thee, and which will be conferred by
those Intelligences whom thou shalt thus render propitious.
It was thence I brought my sabres, and it is there that Soliman
Ben Daoud reposes, surrounded by the talismans that control
the world.'

The astonished Caliph trembled as he answered, yet in
a style that showed him to be no novice in preternatural
adventures:

'Where art thou? be present to my eyes; dissipate the
gloom that perplexes me, and of which I deem thee the
cause; after the many flambeaux I have burnt to discover

thee, thou mayest at least grant a glimpse of thy horrible visage.'

'Abjure, then, Mahomet,' replied the Indian, 'and promise me full proofs of thy sincerity, otherwise thou shalt never behold me again.'

The unhappy Caliph, instigated by insatiable curiosity, lavished his promises in the utmost profusion. The sky immediately brightened, and by the light of the planets, which seemed almost to blaze, Vathek beheld the earth open, and at the extremity of a vast black chasm a portal of ebony, before which stood the Indian, still blacker, holding in his hand a golden key that caused the lock to resound.

'How,' cried Vathek, 'can I descend to thee without the certainty of breaking my neck? Come, take me, and instantly open the portal.'

'Not so fast,' replied the Indian, 'impatient Caliph! Know that I am parched with thirst, and cannot open this door till my thirst be thoroughly appeased. I require the blood of fifty of the most beautiful sons of thy vizirs and great men, or neither can my thirst nor thy curiosity be satisfied. Return to Samarah, procure for me this necessary libation, come back hither, throw it thyself into this chasm, and then shalt thou see!'

Having thus spoken the Indian turned his back on the Caliph, who, incited by the suggestion of demons, resolved on the direful sacrifice. He now pretended to have regained his tranquillity, and set out for Samarah amidst the acclamations of a people who still loved him, and forbore not to rejoice when they believed him to have recovered his reason. So successfully did he conceal the emotion of his heart that even Carathis and Morakanabad were equally deceived with the rest. Nothing was heard of but festivals and rejoicings; the ball, which no tongue had hitherto ventured to mention, was again brought on the tapis; a general laugh went round, though many, still smarting under the hands of the surgeon from the hurts received in that memorable adventure, had no great reason for mirth.

The prevalence of this gay humour was not a little grateful to Vathek, as perceiving how much it conduced to his project. He put on the appearance of affability to everyone, but especially to his vizirs and the grandees of his court, whom he failed not to regale with a sumptuous banquet, during which he insensibly inclined the conversation to the children of his guests. Having asked with a good-natured air who of them were blessed with the handsomest boys, every father at once asserted the pretensions of his own, and the contest imperceptibly grew so warm that nothing could have withheld them from coming to blows but their profound reverence for the person of the Caliph. Under the pretence therefore of reconciling the disputants Vathek took upon him to decide, and with this view commanded the boys to be brought.

It was not long before a troop of these poor children made their appearance, all equipped by their fond mothers with such ornaments as might give the greatest relief to their beauty, or most advantageously display the graces of their age. But whilst this brilliant assemblage attracted the eyes and hearts of everyone besides, the Caliph scrutinized each in his turn with a malignant avidity that passed for attention, and selected from their number the fifty whom he judged the Giaour would prefer.

With an equal show of kindness as before he proposed to celebrate a festival on the plain for the entertainment of his young favourites, who, he said, ought to rejoice still more than all at the restoration of his health on account of the favours he intended for them.

The Caliph's proposal was received with the greatest delight, and soon published through Samarah; litters, camels, and horses were prepared. Women and children, old men and young, everyone placed himself in the station he chose. The cavalcade set forward, attended by all the confectioners in the city and its precincts; the populace following on foot composed an amazing crowd, and occasioned no little noise; all was joy, nor did anyone call to mind what most of them had suffered when they first travelled the road they were now passing so gaily.

The evening was serene, the air refreshing, the sky clear, and the flowers exhaled their fragrance; the beams of the declining sun, whose mild splendour reposed on the summit of the mountain, shed a glow of ruddy light over its green declivity and the white flocks sporting upon it; no sounds were audible, save the murmurs of the Four Fountains and

the reeds and voices of shepherds, calling to each other from
different eminences.

The lovely innocents proceeding to the destined sacrifice
added not a little to the hilarity of the scene; they approached
the plain full of sportiveness, some coursing butterflies, others
culling flowers, or picking up the shining little pebbles that
attracted their notice. At intervals they nimbly started from
each other, for the sake of being caught again and mutually
imparting a thousand caresses.

The dreadful chasm, at whose bottom the portal of ebony
was placed, began to appear at a distance; it looked like a
black streak that divided the plain. Morakanabad and his
companions took it for some work which the Caliph had
ordered; unhappy men! little did they surmise for what it
was destined.

Vathek, not liking they should examine it too nearly,
stopped the procession, and ordered a spacious circle to
be formed on this side, at some distance from the accursed
chasm. The body-guard of eunuchs was detached to measure
out the lists intended for the games, and prepare ringles
for the lines to keep off the crowd. The fifty competitors
were soon stripped, and presented to the admiration of the
spectators the suppleness and grace of their delicate limbs;
their eyes sparkled with a joy which those of their fond
parents reflected. Everyone offered wishes for the little
candidate nearest his heart, and doubted not of his being
victorious; a breathless suspense awaited the contest of these
amiable and innocent victims.

The Caliph, availing himself of the first moment to retire
from the crowd, advanced towards the chasm, and there
heard, yet not without shuddering, the voice of the Indian,
who, gnashing his teeth, eagerly demanded, 'Where are they?
where are they? perceivest thou not how my mouth waters?'

'Relentless Giaour!' answered Vathek with emotion, 'can
nothing content thee but the massacre of these lovely victims?
Ah! wert thou to behold their beauty it must certainly move
thy compassion.'

'Perdition on thy compassion, babbler!' cried the Indian.
'Give them me, instantly give them, or my portal shall be
closed against thee for ever!'

'Not so loudly,' replied the Caliph, blushing.

'I understand thee,' returned the Giaour with the grin of an ogre; 'thou wantest to summon up more presence of mind; I will for a moment forbear.'

During this exquisite dialogue the games went forward with all alacrity, and at length concluded just as the twilight began to overcast the mountains. Vathek, who was still standing on the edge of the chasm, called out with all his might: 'Let my fifty little favourites approach me separately, and let them come in the order of their success. To the first I will give my diamond bracelet, to the second my collar of emeralds, to the third my aigret of rubies, to the fourth my girdle of topazes, and to the rest each a part of my dress, even down to my slippers.'

This declaration was received with reiterated acclamations, and all extolled the liberality of a Prince who would thus strip himself for the amusement of his subjects and the encouragement of the rising generation.

The Caliph in the meanwhile undressed himself by degrees, and, raising his arm as high as he was able, made each of the prizes glitter in the air; but whilst he delivered it with one hand to the child, who sprung forward to receive it, he with the other pushed the poor innocent into the gulf, where the Giaour with a sullen muttering incessantly repeated, 'More! more!'

This dreadful device was executed with so much dexterity that the boy who was approaching him remained unconscious of the fate of his forerunner; and as to the spectators, the shades of evening, together with their distance, precluded them from perceiving any object distinctly. Vathek, having in this manner thrown in the last of the fifty, and expecting that the Giaour, on receiving them, would have presented the key, already fancied himself as great as Soliman, and consequently above being amenable for what he had done: when, to his utter amazement, the chasm closed, and the ground became as entire as the rest of the plain.

No language could express his rage and despair. He execrated the perfidy of the Indian, loaded him with the most infamous invectives, and stamped with his foot as resolving to be heard; he persisted in this demeanour till his strength failed him, and then fell on the earth like one void of sense. His vizirs and grandees, who were nearer than the rest, supposed him at first to be sitting on the grass at play with their amiable children; but at length, prompted by doubt, they advanced towards the spot and found the Caliph alone, who wildly demanded what they wanted?

'Our children! our children!' cried they.

'It is assuredly pleasant,' said he, 'to make me accountable for accidents; your children while at play fell from the precipice that was here, and I should have experienced their fate had I not been saved by a sudden start back.'

At these words the fathers of the fifty boys cried out aloud, the mothers repeated their exclamations an octave higher, whilst the rest, without knowing the cause, soon drowned the voices of both with still louder lamentations of their own.

'Our Caliph,' said they, and the report soon circulated, 'Our Caliph has played us this trick to gratify his accursed Giaour. Let us punish him for his perfidy! let us avenge ourselves! let us avenge the blood of the innocent! let us throw this cruel Prince into the gulf that is near, and let his name be mentioned no more!'

At this rumour and these menaces, Carathis, full of consternation, hastened to Morakanabad and said, 'Vizir, you have lost two beautiful boys, and must necessarily be the most afflicted of fathers, but you are virtuous, save your master.'

'I will brave every hazard,' replied the vizir, 'to rescue him from his present danger, but afterwards will abandon him to his fate. Bababalouk,' continued he, 'put yourself at the head of your eunuchs; disperse the mob, and, if possible, bring back this unhappy Prince to his palace.' Bababalouk and his fraternity, felicitating each other in a low voice on their disability of ever being fathers, obeyed the mandate of the vizir; who, seconding their exertions to the utmost of his power, at length accomplished his generous enterprise, and retired as he resolved to lament at his leisure.

No sooner had the Caliph re-entered his palace than Carathis commanded the doors to be fastened; but perceiving the tumult to be still violent, and hearing the imprecations which resounded from all quarters, she said to her son:

'Whether the populace be right or wrong, it behoves you to provide for your safety; let us retire to your own apartment, and thence through the subterranean passage, known only to ourselves, into your tower; there, with the assistance of the mutes who never leave it, we may be able to make some resistance. Bababalouk, supposing us to be still in the palace, will guard its avenues for his own sake; and we shall soon find, without the counsels of that blubberer Morakanabad, what expedient may be the best to adopt.

Vathek, without making the least reply, acquiesced in his mother's proposal, and repeated as he went: 'Nefarious Giaour! where art thou? Hast thou not yet devoured those poor children? Where are thy sabres? thy golden key? thy talismans?'

Carathis, who guessed from these interrogations a part of the truth, had no difficulty to apprehend in getting at the whole, as soon as he should be a little composed in his tower. This Princess was so far from being influenced by scruples that she was as wicked as woman could be, which is not saying a little, for the sex pique themselves on their superiority in every competition. The recital of the Caliph, therefore, occasioned neither terror nor surprise to his mother; she felt no emotion but from the promises of the Giaour, and said to her son:

'This Giaour, it must be confessed, is somewhat sanguinary in his taste, but the terrestrial powers are always terrible; nevertheless, what the one hath promised and the others can confer will prove a sufficient indemnification; no crimes should be thought too dear for such a reward; forbear then to revile the Indian, you have not fulfilled the conditions to which his services are annexed; for instance, is not a sacrifice to the subterranean Genii required? and should we not be prepared to offer it as soon as the tumult is subsided? This charge I will take on myself, and have no doubt of succeeding by means of your treasures, which, as there are now so many others in store, may without fear be exhausted.'

Accordingly the Princess, who possessed the most consummate skill in the art of persuasion, went immediately back through the subterranean passage; and, presenting herself to the populace from a window of the palace, began to harangue them with all the address of which she was mistress, whilst

Bababalouk showered money from both hands amongst the crowd, who by these united means were soon appeased; every person retired to his home, and Carathis returned to the tower.

Prayer at break of day was announced, when Carathis and Vathek ascended the steps which led to the summit of the tower, where they remained for some time, though the weather was lowering and wet. This impending gloom corresponded with their malignant dispositions; but when the sun began to break through the clouds they ordered a pavilion to be raised as a screen from the intrusion of his beams. The Caliph, overcome with fatigue, sought refreshment from repose, at the same time hoping that significant dreams might attend on his slumbers; whilst the indefatigable Carathis, followed by a party of her mutes, descended to prepare whatever she judged proper for the oblation of the approaching night.

By secret stairs, known only to herself and to her son, she first repaired to the mysterious recesses in which were deposited the mummies that had been brought from the catacombs of the ancient Pharaohs; of these she ordered several to be taken. Thence she resorted to a gallery where, under the guard of fifty female negroes, mute and blind of the right eye, were preserved the oil of the most venomous serpents, rhinoceros' horns, and woods of a subtile and penetrating odour procured from the interior of the Indies, together with a thousand other horrible rarities. This collection had been formed for a purpose like the present by Carathis herself, from a presentiment that she might one day enjoy some intercourse with the infernal powers to whom she had ever been passionately attached, and to whose taste she was no stranger.

To familiarize herself the better with the horrors in view the Princess remained in the company of her negresses, who squinted in the most amiable manner from the only eye they had, and leered with exquisite delight at the skulls and skeletons which Carathis had drawn forth from her cabinets, whose key she entrusted to no one, all of them making contortions and uttering a frightful jargon, but very amusing to the Princess, till at last, being stunned by their jibbering and suffocated by the potency of their exhalations, she was forced to quit the gallery, after stripping it of a part of its treasures.

Whilst she was thus occupied the Caliph, who instead of the visions he expected had acquired in these insubstantial regions a voracious appetite, was greatly provoked at the negresses, for, having totally forgotten their deafness, he had impatiently asked them for food, and seeing them regardless of his demand he began to cuff, pinch, and push them, till Carathis arrived to terminate a scene so indecent, to the great content of these miserable creatures, who, having been brought up by her, understood all her signs, and communicated in the same way their thoughts in return.

'Son! what means all this?' said she, panting for breath. 'I thought I heard as I came up the shrieks of a thousand bats tearing from their crannies in the recesses of a cavern, and it was the outcry only of these poor mutes whom you were so unmercifully abusing. In truth, you but ill deserve the admirable provision I have brought you.'

'Give it me instantly,' exclaimed the Caliph; 'I am perishing for hunger!'

'As to that,' answered she, 'you must have an excellent stomach, if it can digest what I have been preparing.'

'Be quick,' replied the Caliph; 'but, oh heavens! what horrors! what do you intend?'

'Come, come,' returned Carathis, 'be not so squeamish, but help me to arrange everything properly, and you shall see that what you reject with such symptoms of disgust will soon complete your felicity. Let us get ready the pile for the sacrifice of to-night, and think not of eating till that is performed; know you not that all solemn rites are preceded by a rigorous abstinence?'

The Caliph, not daring to object, abandoned himself to grief and the wind that ravaged his entrails, whilst his mother went forward with the requisite operations. Phials of serpents' oil, mummies and bones were soon set in order on the balustrade of the tower; the pile began to rise, and in three hours was as many cubits high. At length darkness approached, and Carathis, having stripped herself to her inmost garment, clapped her hands in an impulse of ecstasy and struck light with all her force. The mutes followed her example, but Vathek, extenuated with hunger and impatience, was unable to support himself, and fell down in a swoon. The sparks had already kindled the dry wood, the venomous oil burst into a thousand blue flames, the mummies dissolving emitted a thick dun vapour, and the rhinoceros' horns beginning to consume, all together diffused such a stench that the Caliph, recovering, started from his trance and gazed wildly on the scene in full blaze around him. The oil gushed forth in a plenitude of streams, and the negresses, who supplied it without intermission, united their cries to those of the Princess. At last the fire became so violent, and the flames reflected from the polished marble so dazzling, that the Caliph, unable to withstand the heat and the blaze, effected his escape, and clambered up the imperial standard.

In the meantime the inhabitants of Samarah, scared at the light which shone over the city, arose in haste, ascended their roofs, beheld the tower on fire, and hurried half naked to the square. Their love for their Sovereign immediately awoke, and, apprehending him in danger of perishing in his tower, their whole thoughts were occupied with the means of his safety. Morakanabad flew from his retirement, wiped away his tears, and cried out for water like the rest. Bababalouk, whose olfactory nerves were more familiarized to magical odours, readily conjecturing that Carathis was engaged in her favourite amusements, strenuously exhorted them not to be alarmed. Him, however, they treated as an old poltroon, and forbore not to style him a rascally traitor. The camels and dromedaries were advancing with water, but no one knew by which way to enter the tower. Whilst the populace was obstinate in forcing the doors a violent east wind drove such a volume of flame against them as at first forced them off, but afterwards rekindled their zeal; at the same time the stench of the horns and mummies increasing most of the crowd fell backward in a state of suffocation, those that kept their feet mutually wondered at the cause of the smell, and admonished each other to retire.

Morakanabad, more sick than the rest, remained in a piteous condition; holding his nose with one hand he persisted in his efforts with the other to burst open the doors and obtain admission. A hundred and forty of the strongest and most resolute at length accomplished their purpose; having gained the staircase by their violent exertions, they attained a great height in a quarter of an hour.

Carathis, alarmed at the signs of her mutes, advanced to the staircase, went down a few steps, and heard several voices calling out from below, 'You shall in a moment have water!' Being rather alert, considering her age, she presently regained the top of the tower, and bade her son suspend the sacrifice for some minutes, adding:

'We shall soon be enabled to render it more grateful; certain dolts of your subjects, imagining no doubt that we were on fire, have been rash enough to break through those doors which had hitherto remained inviolate for the sake of bringing up water; they are very kind, you must allow, so soon to forget the wrongs you have done them, but that is of little moment. Let us offer them to the Giaour; let them come up; our mutes who neither want strength nor experience, will soon despatch them, exhausted as they are with fatigue.'

'Be it so,' answered the Caliph, 'provided we finish and I dine.'

In fact, these good people, out of breath from ascending eleven thousand stairs in such haste, and chagrined at having spilt by the way the water they had taken, were no sooner arrived at the top than the blaze of the flames and the fumes of the mummies at once overpowered their senses. It was a pity, for they beheld not the agreeable smile with which the mutes and the negresses adjusted the cord to their necks; these amiable personages rejoiced, however, no less at the scene; never before had the ceremony of strangling been performed with so much facility; they all fell without the least resistance or struggle, so that Vathek, in the space of a few moments, found himself surrounded by the dead bodies of his faithfullest subjects, all which were thrown on the top of the pile.

Carathis, whose presence of mind never forsook her, perceiving that she had carcasses sufficient to complete her oblation, commanded the chains to be stretched across the staircase, and the iron doors barricaded, that no more might come up.

No sooner were these orders obeyed than the tower shook, the dead bodies vanished in the flames, which at once changed from a swarthy crimson to a bright rose colour; an ambient vapour emitted the most exquisite fragrance, the marble columns rang with harmonious sounds, and the liquefied horns diffused a delicious perfume. Carathis, in transports, anticipated the success of her enterprise, whilst her mutes and negresses, to whom these sweets had given the colic, retired to their cells grumbling.

Scarcely were they gone when, instead of the pile, horns, mummies, and ashes, the Caliph both saw and felt, with a degree of pleasure which he could not express, a table covered with the most magnificent repast—flagons of wine and vases of exquisite sherbet floating on snow. He availed himself without scruple of such an entertainment, and had already laid hands on a lamb stuffed with pistachios, whilst Carathis was privately drawing from a filigree urn a parchment that seemed to be endless, and which had escaped the notice of her son, totally occupied in gratifying an importunate, appetite; he left her to peruse it without interruption which having finished, she said to him in an authoritative tone:

'Put an end to your gluttony, and hear the splendid promises with which you are favoured!' She then read as follows: 'Vathek, my well-beloved, thou hast surpassed my hopes; my nostrils have been regaled by the savour of thy mummies, thy horns, and still more by the lives devoted on the pile. At the full of the moon cause the bands of thy musicians and thy tymbals to be heard; depart from thy palace surrounded by all the pageants of majesty; thy most faithful slaves, thy best-beloved wives, thy most magnificent litters, thy richest-laden camels, and set forward on thy way to Istakhar; there await I thy coming—that is the region of wonders; there shalt thou receive the diadem of Gian Ben Gian, the talismans of Soliman, and the treasures of the pre-Adamite Sultans; there shalt thou be solaced with all kinds of delight. But beware how thou enterest any dwelling on thy route, or thou shalt feel the effects of my anger.'

The Caliph, who, notwithstanding his habitual luxury, had never before dined with so much satisfaction, gave full scope to the joy of these golden tidings, and betook himself to drinking anew. Carathis, whose antipathy to wine was by no means insuperable, failed not to supply a reason for every bumper, which they ironically quaffed to the health of Mahomet. This infernal liquor completed their impious temerity, and prompted them to utter a profusion of blasphemies; they gave a loose to their wit at the expense of the ass of Balaam, the dog of the Seven Sleepers, and the other animals admitted into the paradise of Mahomet. In this sprightly humour they descended the eleven thousand stairs, diverting themselves as they went at the anxious faces they saw on the square through the oillets of the tower, and at length arrived at the royal apartments by the subterranean passage. Bababalouk was parading to and fro, and issuing his mandates with great pomp to the eunuchs, who were snuffing the lights and painting the eyes of the Circassians. No sooner did he catch sight of the Caliph and his mother than he exclaimed:

'Hah! you have then, I perceive, escaped from the flames; I was not, however, altogether out of doubt.'

'Of what moment is it to us what you thought, or think?' cried Carathis. 'Go, speed, tell Morakanabad that we immediately want him; and take care how you stop by the way to make your insipid reflections.'

Morakanabad delayed not to obey the summons, and was received by Vathek and his mother with great solemnity; they told him, with an air of composure and commiseration, that the fire at the top of the tower was extinguished; but that it had cost the lives of the brave people who sought to assist them.

'Still more misfortunes!' cried Morakanabad with a sigh. 'Ah, Commander of the faithful, our holy Prophet is certainly irritated against us! it behoves you to appease him.'

'We will appease him hereafter!' replied the Caliph, with a smile that augured nothing of good. 'You will have leisure sufficient for your supplications during my absence; for this country is the bane of my health. I am disgusted with the mountain of the Four Fountains, and am resolved to go and drink of the stream of Rocnabad; I long to refresh myself in the delightful valleys which it waters. Do you, with the advice of my mother, govern my dominions, and take care to supply whatever her experiments may demand; for you well know that our tower abounds in materials for the advancement of science.'

The tower but ill suited Morakanabad's taste. Immense treasures had been lavished upon it; and nothing had he ever seen carried thither but female negroes, mutes, and abominable drugs. Nor did he know well what to think of Carathis, who, like a chameleon, could assume all possible colours; her cursed eloquence had often driven the poor Mussulman to his last shifts. He considered, however, that if she possessed but few good qualities her son had still fewer, and that the alternative on the whole would be in her favour. Consoled, therefore, with this reflection, he went in good spirits to soothe the populace, and make the proper arrangements for his master's journey.

Vathek, to conciliate the Spirits of the subterranean palace, resolved that his expedition should be uncommonly splendid. With this view he confiscated on all sides the property of his subjects, whilst his worthy mother stripped the seraglios she visited of the gems they contained. She collected all the sempstresses and embroiderers of Samarah and other cities, to the distance of sixty leagues, to prepare pavilions, palanquins, sofas, canopies, and litters for the train of the monarch. There was not left in Masulipatan a single piece of chintz, and so much muslin had been bought up to dress out Bababalouk and the other black eunuchs that there remained not an ell in the whole Irak of Babylon.

During these preparations Carathis, who never lost sight of her great object, which was to obtain favour with the Powers of darkness, made select parties of the fairest and most delicate ladies of the city; but in the midst of their gaiety she contrived to introduce serpents amongst them, and to break pots of scorpions, under the table; they all bit to a wonder; and Carathis would have left them to bite were it not that, to fill up the time, she now and then amused herself in curing their wounds with an excellent anodyne of her own invention, for this good Princess abhorred being indolent.

Vathek, who was not altogether so active as his mother, devoted his time to the sole gratification of his senses in the palaces which were severally dedicated to them; he disgusted himself no more with the Divan or the Mosque. One half of Samarah followed his example, whilst the other lamented the progress of corruption.

In the midst of these transactions the embassy returned which had been sent in pious times to Mecca. It consisted of the most reverend Moullahs, who had fulfilled their commission and brought back one of those precious besoms which are used to sweep the sacred Caaba; a present truly worthy of the greatest potentate on earth!

The Caliph happened at this instant to be engaged in an apartment by no means adapted to the reception of embassies, though adorned with a certain magnificence, not only to render it agreeable, but also because he resorted to it frequently, and stayed a considerable time together. Whilst occupied in this retreat he heard the voice of Bababalouk calling out from between the door and the tapestry that hung before it:

'Here are the excellent Mahomet Ebn Edris al Shafei and the seraphic Al Mouhadethin, who have brought the besom from Mecca, and with tears of joy intreat they may present it to your Majesty in person.'

'Let them bring the besom hither; it may be of use,' said Vathek, who was still employed, not having quite racked off his wine.

'How!' answered Bababalouk, half aloud and amazed.

'Obey,' replied the Caliph, 'for it is my sovereign will; go instantly, vanish; for here will I receive the good folk, who have thus filled thee with joy.'

The eunuch departed muttering, and bade the venerable train attend him. A sacred rapture was diffused amongst these reverend old men. Though fatigued with the length of their expedition, they followed Bababalouk with an alertness almost miraculous, and felt themselves highly flattered, as they swept along the stately porticoes, that the Caliph would not receive them like ambassadors in ordinary in his hall of audience. Soon reaching the interior of the harem (where, through blinds of persian, they perceived large soft eyes, dark and blue, that went and came like lightning), penetrated with respect and wonder, and full of their celestial mission, they

advanced in procession towards the small corridors that
appeared to terminate in nothing, but nevertheless led to
the cell where the Caliph expected their coming.

'What! is the Commander of the faithful sick?' said Ebn
Edris al Shafei in a low voice to his companion.

'I rather think he is in his oratory,' answered Al
Mouhadethin.

Vathek, who heard the dialogue, cried out:

'What imports it you how I am employed? Approach
without delay.'

They advanced, and Bababalouk almost sunk with confusion, whilst the Caliph, without showing himself, put forth
his hand from behind the tapestry that hung before the
door, and demanded of them the besom. Having prostrated
themselves as well as the corridor would permit, and even in
a tolerable semicircle, the venerable Al Shafei, drawing forth
the besom from the embroidered and perfumed scarves in
which it had been enveloped, and secured from the profane
gaze of vulgar eyes, arose from his associates, and advanced
with an air of the most awful solemnity towards the supposed
oratory; but with what astonishment! with what horror was
he seized! Vathek, bursting out into a villainous laugh,
snatched the besom from his trembling hand, and, fixing
upon some cobwebs that hung suspended from the ceiling,
gravely brushed away till not a single one remained. The old
men, overpowered with amazement, were unable to lift their
beards from the ground, for as Vathek had carelessly left
the tapestry between them half drawn they were witnesses
to the whole transaction; their tears gushed forth on the
marble, Al Mouhadethin swooned through mortification and
fatigue, whilst the Caliph, throwing himself backward on his
seat, shouted and clapped his hands without mercy. At last,
addressing himself to Bababalouk:

'My dear black,' said he, 'go, regale these pious poor souls
with my good wine from Shiraz, and as they can boast of
having seen more of my palace than anyone besides, let them
also visit my office courts, and lead them out by the back steps
that go to my stables.' Having said this he threw the besom
in their face, and went to enjoy the laugh with Carathis.
Bababalouk did all in his power to console the ambassadors,

but the two most infirm expired on the spot; the rest were carried to their beds, whence, being heartbroken with sorrow and shame, they never arose.

The succeeding night Vathek, attended by his mother, ascended the tower to see if everything were ready for his journey, for he had great faith in the influence of the stars. The planets appeared in their most favourable aspects. The Caliph, to enjoy so flattering a sight, supped gaily on the roof, and fancied that he heard during his repast loud shouts of laughter resound through the sky in a manner that inspired the fullest assurance.

All was in motion at the palace; lights were kept burning through the whole of the night; the sound of implements and of artisans finishing their work, the voices of women and their guardians who sung at their embroidery, all conspired to interrupt the stillness of nature and infinitely delight the heart of Vathek, who imagined himself going in triumph to sit upon the throne of Soliman.

The people were not less satisfied than himself, all assisted to accelerate the moment which should rescue them from the wayward caprices of so extravagant a master.

The day preceding the departure of this infatuated Prince was employed by Carathis in repeating to him the decrees of the mysterious parchment, which she had thoroughly gotten by heart, and in recommending him not to enter the habitation of anyone by the way.

'For well thou knowest,' added she, 'how liquorish thy taste is after good dishes and young damsels; let me, therefore, enjoin thee to be content with thy old cooks, who are the best in the world, and not to forget that in thy ambulatory seraglio there are three dozen pretty faces which Bababalouk hath not yet unveiled. I myself have a great desire to watch over thy conduct and visit the subterranean palace, which no doubt contains whatever can interest persons like us; there is nothing so pleasing as retiring to caverns; my taste for dead bodies and everything mummy-like is decided, and I am confident thou wilt see the most exquisite of their kind. Forget me not then, but the moment thou art in possession of the talismans which are to open to thee the mineral kingdoms and the centre of the earth itself, fail not to despatch some trusty genius to take

me and my cabinet, for the oil of the serpents I have pinched
to death will be a pretty present to the Giaour, who cannot but
be charmed with such dainties.'

Scarcely had Carathis ended this edifying discourse when
the sun, setting behind the mountain of the Four Fountains,
gave place to the rising moon; this planet being that evening
at full appeared of unusual beauty and magnitude in the
eyes of the women, the eunuchs, and the pages, who were
all impatient to set forward. The city re-echoed with shouts
of joy and flourishing of trumpets; nothing was visible but
plumes nodding on pavilions, and aigrets shining in the
mild lustre of the moon; the spacious square resembled an
immense parterre, variegated with the most stately tulips of
the East.

Arrayed in the robes which were only worn at the most
distinguished ceremonials, and supported by his vizir and
Bababalouk, the Caliph descended the grand staircase of
the tower in the sight of all his people; he could not forbear
pausing at intervals to admire the superb appearance which
everywhere courted his view, whilst the whole multitude,
even to the camels with their sumptuous burthens, knelt
down before him. For some time a general stillness prevailed
which nothing happened to disturb but the shrill screams
of some eunuchs in the rear; these vigilant guards, having
remarked certain cages of the ladies swagging somewhat
awry, and discovered that a few adventurous gallants
had contrived to get in, soon dislodged the enraptured
culprits, and consigned them with good commendations to
the surgeons of the serail. The majesty of so magnificent a
spectacle was not, however, violated by incidents like these.
Vathek meanwhile saluted the moon with an idolatrous air
that neither pleased Morakanabad nor the doctors of the law,
any more than the vizirs and the grandees of his court, who
were all assembled to enjoy the last view of their Sovereign.

At length the clarions and trumpets from the top of
the tower announced the prelude of departure. Though
the instruments were in unison with each other, yet a
singular dissonance was blended with their sounds; this
proceeded from Carathis, who was singing her direful
orisons to the Giaour, whilst the negresses and mutes

supplied thorough-bass without articulating a word. The good Mussulmans fancied that they heard the sullen hum of those nocturnal insects which presage evil, and importuned Vathek to beware how he ventured his sacred person.

On a given signal the great standard of the Califat was displayed, twenty thousand lances shone around it, and the Caliph, treading loyally on the cloth of gold which had been spread for his feet, ascended his litter amidst the general awe that possessed his subjects.

The expedition commenced with the utmost order and so entire a silence that even the locusts were heard from the thickets on the plain of Catoul. Gaiety and good humour prevailing, six good leagues were past before the dawn; and the morning star was still glittering in the firmament when the whole of this numerous train had halted on the banks of the Tigris, where they encamped to repose for the rest of the day.

The three days that followed were spent in the same manner; but on the fourth the heavens looked angry, lightnings broke forth in frequent flashes, re-echoing peals of thunder succeeded, and the trembling Circassians clung with all their might to their ugly guardians. The Caliph himself was greatly inclined to take shelter in the large town of Gulchissar, the governor of which came forth to meet him, and tendered every kind of refreshment the place could supply; but, having examined his tablets, he suffered the rain to soak him almost to the bone, notwithstanding the importunity of his first favourites. Though he began to regret the palace of the senses, yet he lost not sight of his enterprise, and his sanguine expectations confirmed his resolution. His geographers were ordered to attend him, but the weather proved so terrible that these poor people exhibited a lamentable appearance; and as no long journeys had been undertaken since the time of Haroun al Raschid, their maps of the different countries were in a still worse plight than themselves. Everyone was ignorant which way to turn; for Vathek, though well versed in the course of the heavens, no longer knew his situation on earth; he thundered even louder than the elements, and muttered forth certain hints of the bow-string, which were not very soothing to literary ears.

Disgusted at the toilsome weariness of the way, he determined to cross over the craggy heights and follow the guidance of a peasant, who undertook to bring him in four days to Rocnabad. Remonstrances were all to no purpose; his resolution was fixed, and an invasion commenced on the province of the goats, who sped away in large troops before them. It was curious to view on these half-calcined rocks camels richly caparisoned, and pavilions of gold and silk waving on their summits, which till then had never been covered but with sapless thistles and fern.

The females and eunuchs uttered shrill wailings at the sight of the precipices below then, and the dreary prospects that opened in the vast gorges of the mountains. Before they could reach the ascent of the steepest rock night overtook them, and a boisterous tempest arose which, having rent the awnings of the palanquins and cages, exposed to the raw gusts the poor ladies within, who had never before felt so piercing a cold. The dark clouds that overcast the face of the sky deepened the horrors of this disastrous night, insomuch that nothing could be heard distinctly but the mewling of pages and lamentations of sultanas.

To increase the general misfortune the frightful uproar of wild beasts resounded at a distance, and there were soon perceived in the forest they were skirting the glaring of eyes which could belong only to devils or tigers. The pioneers, who as well as they could had marked out a track, and a part of the advanced guard were devoured before they had been in the least apprised of their danger. The confusion that prevailed was extreme; wolves, tigers, and other carnivorous animals, invited by the howling of their companions, flocked together from every quarter; the crashing of bones was heard on all sides, and a fearful rush of wings overhead, for now vultures also began to be of the party.

The terror at length reached the main body of the troops which surrounded the monarch and his harem, at the distance of two leagues from the scene. Vathek (voluptuously reposed in his capacious litter upon cushions of silk, with two little pages beside him of complexions more fair than the enamel of Franguestan, who were occupied in keeping off flies) was soundly asleep, and contemplating in his dreams the treasures of Soliman. The shrieks, however, of his wives awoke him with a start, and, instead of the Giaour with his key of gold, he beheld Bababalouk full of consternation.

'Sire,' exclaimed this good servant of the most potent of monarchs, 'misfortune is arrived at its height; wild beasts, who entertain no more reverence for your sacred person than for that of a dead ass, have beset your camels and their drivers; thirty of the richest laden are already become their prey, as well as your confectioners, your cooks, and purveyors; and, unless our holy Prophet should protect us, we all shall have eaten our last meal.'

At the mention of eating the Caliph lost all patience; he began to bellow and even beat himself (for there was no seeing in the dark). The rumour every instant increased, and Bababalouk, finding no good could be done with his master, stopped both his ears against the hurly-burly of the harem, and called out aloud:

'Come, ladies and brothers! all hands to work; strike light in a moment! never shall it be said that the Commander of the faithful served to regale these infidel brutes.'

Though there wanted not in this bevy of beauties a sufficient number capricious and wayward, yet on the present occasion they were all compliance; fires were visible in a twinkling in all their cages; ten thousand torches were lighted at once. The Caliph himself seized a large one of wax; every person followed his example, and by kindling ropes' ends dipped in oil, and fastened on poles an amazing blaze was spread. The rocks were covered with the splendour of sunshine; the trails of sparks wafted by the wind communicated to the dry fern, of which there was plenty. Serpents were observed to crawl forth from their retreats with amazement and hissings, whilst the horses snorted, stamped the ground, tossed their noses in the air, and plunged about without mercy.

One of the forests of cedar that bordered their way took fire, and the branches that overhung the path, extending their flames to the muslins and chintzes which covered the cages of the ladies, obliged them to jump out at the peril of their necks. Vathek, who vented on the occasion a thousand blasphemies, was himself compelled to touch with his sacred feet the naked earth.

Never had such an incident happened before. Full of mortification, shame, and despondence, and not knowing how to walk, the ladies fell into the dirt. 'Must I go on foot!' said one; 'Must I wet my feet!' cried another; 'Must I soil my dress! asked a third; 'Execrable Bababalouk!' exclaimed all; 'Outcast of hell! what hadst thou to do with torches? Better were it to be eaten by tigers than to fall into our present condition! we are for ever undone! Not a porter is there in the army, not a currier of camels, but hath seen some part of our bodies, and what is worse, our very faces!' On saying this the most bashful amongst them hid their foreheads on the ground, whilst such as had more boldness flew at Bababalouk; but he, well apprized of their humour and not wanting in shrewdness, betook himself to his heels along with his comrades, all dropping their torches and striking their tymbals.

It was not less light than in the brightest of the dog-days, and the weather was hot in proportion; but how degrading was the spectacle to behold the Caliph bespattered like an ordinary mortal! As the exercise of his faculties seemed to be suspended, one of his Ethiopian wives (for he delighted in variety) clasped him in her arms, threw him upon her shoulder like a sack of dates, and, finding that the fire was hemming them in, set off with no small expedition, considering the weight of her burden. The other ladies, who had just learnt the use of their feet, followed her; their guards galloped after, and the camel-drivers brought up the rear as fast as their charge would permit.

They soon reached the spot where the wild beasts had commenced the carnage, which they had too much spirit to leave, notwithstanding the approaching tumult and the luxurious supper they had made. Bababalouk, nevertheless, seized on a few of the plumpest, which were unable of budge from the place, and began to flay them with admirable adroitness. The cavalcade being got so far from the conflagration as that the heat felt rather grateful than violent, it was immediately resolved on to halt. The tattered chintzes were picked up, the scraps left by the wolves and tigers interred, and vengeance was taken on some dozens of vultures that were too much glutted to rise on the wing. The camels, which had been left unmolested to make sal ammoniac being numbered, and the ladies once more enclosed in their cages, the imperial tent was pitched on the levellest ground they could find.

Vathek, reposing upon a mattress of down, and tolerably recovered from the jolting of the Ethiopian, who to his feelings seemed the roughest trotting jade he had hitherto mounted, called out for something to eat. But alas! those delicate cakes which had been baked in silver ovens for his royal mouth, those rich manchets, amber comfits, flagons of Shiraz wine, porcelain vases of snow, and grapes from the banks of the Tigris, were all irremediably lost! And nothing had Bababalouk to present in their stead but a roasted wolf, vultures *à la daube,* aromatic herbs of the most acrid poignancy, rotten truffles, boiled thistles, and such other wild plants as must ulcerate the throat and parch up the tongue. Nor was he better provided in the article of drink, for he could procure nothing to accompany these irritating viands but a few vials of abominable brandy, which had been secreted by the scullions in their slippers.

Vathek made wry faces at so savage a repast, and Bababalouk answered them with shrugs and contortions; the Caliph, however, ate with tolerable appetite, and fell into a nap that lasted six hours. The splendour of the sun reflected from the white cliffs of the mountains, in spite of the curtains that enclosed him, at length disturbed his repose; he awoke terrified, and stung to the quick by those wormwood-colour flies, which emit from their wings a suffocating stench. The miserable monarch was perplexed how to act, though his wits were not idle in seeking expedients, whilst Bababalouk lay snoring amidst a swarm of those insects that busily thronged to pay court to his nose. The little pages, famished with hunger, had dropped their fans on the ground and exerted their dying voices in bitter reproaches against the Caliph, who now for the first time heard the language of truth.

Thus stimulated, he renewed his imprecations against the Giaour, and bestowed upon Mahomet some soothing expressions.

'Where am I?' cried he; 'what are these dreadful rocks? these valleys of darkness? Are we arrived at the horrible Kaf? Is the Simurgh coming to pluck out my eyes as a punishment for undertaking this impious enterprise?' Having said this he bellowed like a calf, and turned himself towards an outlet in the side of his pavilion; but alas! what objects occurred to his view? On one side a plain of black sand that appeared to be unbounded, and on the other perpendicular crags, bristled over with those abominable thistles which had so severely lacerated his tongue. He fancied, however, that he perceived, amongst the brambles and briers, some gigantic flowers, but was mistaken, for these were only the dangling palampores and variegated tatters of his gay retinue. As there were several clefts in the rock whence water seemed to have flowed, Vathek applied his ear with the hope of catching the sound of some latent runnel, but could only distinguish the low murmurs of his people, who were repining at their journey, and complaining for the want of water.

'To what purpose,' asked they, 'have we been brought hither? Hath our Caliph another tower to build? Or have the relentless Afrits, whom Carathis so much loves, fixed in this place their abode?'

At the name of Carathis Vathek recollected the tablets he had received from his mother, who assured him they were fraught with preternatural qualities, and advised him to consult them as emergencies might require. Whilst he was engaged in turning them over he heard a shout of joy and a loud clapping of hands; the curtains of his pavilion were soon drawn back, and he beheld Bababalouk, followed by a troop of his favourites, conducting two dwarfs, each a cubit high, who brought between them a large basket of melons, oranges, and pomegranates. They were singing in the sweetest tones the words that follow:

'We dwell on the top of these rocks in a cabin of rushes and canes; the eagles envy us our nest; a small spring supplies us with Abdest, and we daily repeat prayers which the Prophet approves.

'We love you, O Commander of the faithful! our master, the good Emir Fakreddin, loves you also; he reveres in your person the vicegerent of Mahomet.

'Little as we are, in us he confides; he knows our hearts to be good as our bodies are contemptible, and hath placed us here to aid those who are bewildered on these dreary mountains.

'Last night, whilst we were occupied within our cell in reading the holy Koran, a sudden hurricane blew out our lights and rocked our habitation; for two whole hours a palpable darkness prevailed, but we heard sounds at a distance which we conjectured to proceed from the bells of a cafila passing over the rocks; our ears were soon filled with deplorable shrieks, frightful roarings, and the sound of tymbals.

'Chilled with terror, we concluded that the Deggial, with his exterminating angels, had sent forth their plagues on the earth. In the midst of these melancholy reflections we perceived flames of the deepest red glow in the horizon, and found ourselves in a few moments covered with flakes of fire. Amazed at so strange an appearance, we took up the volume dictated by the blessed Intelligence, and, kneeling by the light of the fire that surrounded us, we recited the verse which says:

' "Put no trust in anything but the mercy of Heaven; there is no help save in the holy Prophet; the mountain of Kaf itself may tremble, it is the power of Alla only that cannot be moved."

'After having pronounced these words we felt consolation, and our minds were hushed into a sacred repose; silence ensued, and our ears clearly distinguished a voice in the air, saying:

' "Servants of my faithful servant! go down to the happy valley of Fakreddin; tell him that an illustrious opportunity now offers to satiate the thirst of his hospitable heart.

' "The Commander of true believers is this day bewildered amongst these mountains and stands in need of thy aid."

'We obeyed with joy the angelic mission, and our master, filled with pious zeal, hath culled with his own hands these melons, oranges, and pomegranates. He is following us with a hundred dromedaries laden with the purest waters of his fountains, and is coming to kiss the fringe of your consecrated robe, and implore you to enter his humble habitation, which, placed amidst these barren wilds, resembles an emerald set in lead.'

The dwarfs, having ended their address, remained still standing, and, with hands crossed upon their bosoms, preserved a respectful silence.

Vathek, in the midst of this curious harangue, seized the basket and long before it was finished the fruits had dissolved in his mouth. As he continued to eat his piety increased, and in the same breath which recited his prayers he called for the Koran and sugar.

Such was the state of his mind when the tablets, which were thrown by at the approach of the dwarfs, again attracted his eye. He took them up, but was ready to drop on the ground when he beheld, in large, red characters, these words inscribed by Carathis, which were indeed enough to make him tremble:

'Beware of thy old doctors, and their puny messengers of but one cubit high; distrust their pious frauds, and, instead of eating their melons, impale on a spit the bearers of them. Shouldst thou be such a fool as to visit them the portal of the subterranean palace will be shut in thy face, and with such force as shall shake thee asunder; thy body shall be spit upon, and bats will engender in thy belly.'

'To what tends this ominous rhapsody?' cries the Caliph; 'and must I then perish in these deserts with thirst, whilst I may refresh myself in the valley of melons and cucumbers? Accursed be the Giaour, with his portal of ebony! he hath made me dance attendance too long already. Besides, who shall prescribe laws to me? I forsooth must not enter anyone's habitation! Be it so; but what one can I enter that is not my own!'

Bababalouk, who lost not a syllable of this soliloquy, applauded it with all his heart, and the ladies for the first time agreed with him in opinion.

The dwarfs were entertained, caressed, and seated with great ceremony on little cushions of satin. The symmetry of their persons was the subject of criticism; not an inch of them was suffered to pass unexamined; knick-nacks and dainties were offered in profusion, but all were declined with respectful gravity. They clambered up the sides of the Caliph's seat, and, placing themselves each on one of his shoulders, began to whisper prayers in his ears; their tongues quivered like the leaves of a poplar, and the patience of Vathek was almost exhausted, when the acclamations of the troops announced the approach of Fakreddin, who was come with a hundred old greybeards and as many Korans and dromedaries. They instantly set about their ablutions, and began to repeat the Bismillah. Vathek, to get rid of these officious monitors, followed their example, for his hands were burning.

The good Emir, who was punctiliously religious and likewise a great dealer in compliments, made an harangue five times more prolix and insipid than his harbingers had already delivered. The Caliph, unable any longer to refrain, exclaimed:

'For the love of Mahomet, my dear Fakreddin, have done! let us proceed to your valley, and enjoy the fruits that heaven hath vouchsafed you.'

The hint of proceeding put all into motion. The venerable attendants of the Emir set forward somewhat slowly, but Vathek, having ordered his little pages in private to goad on the dromedaries, loud fits of laughter broke forth from the cages, for the unwieldy curveting of these poor beasts, and the ridiculous distress of their superannuated riders, afforded the ladies no small entertainment.

They descended, however, unhurt into the valley by the large steps which the Emir had cut in the rock, and already the murmuring of streams and the rustling of leaves began to catch their attention. The cavalcade soon entered a path which was skirted by flowering shrubs, and extended to a vast wood of palm trees, whose branches overspread a building of hewn stone. The edifice was crowned with nine domes, and adorned with as many portals of bronze, on which was engraven the following inscription:

'This is the asylum of pilgrims, the refuge of travellers, and the depository of secrets for all parts of the world.'

Nine pages, beautiful as the day, and clothed in robes of Egyptian linen, very long and very modest, were standing at each door. They received the whole retinue with an easy and inviting air. Four of the most amiable placed the Caliph on a magnificent taktrevan; four others, somewhat less graceful, took charge of Bababalouk, who capered for joy at the snug little cabin that fell to his share; the pages that remained waited on the rest of the train.

When everything masculine was gone out of sight the gate of a large enclosure on the right turned on its harmonious hinges, and a young female of a slender form came forth. Her light brown hair floated in the hazy breeze of the twilight; a troop of young maidens, like the Pleiades, attended her on tip-toe. They hastened to the pavilions that contained the sultanas, and the young lady, gracefully bending, said to them:

'Charming Princesses, everything is ready; we have pre-pared beds for your repose, and strewed your apartments with jasmine; no insects will keep off slumber from visiting your eyelids, we will dispel them with a thousand plumes; come then, amiable ladies! refresh your delicate feet and your ivory limbs in baths of rose-water; and, by the light of perfumed lamps, your servants shall amuse you with tales.'

The sultanas accepted with pleasure these obliging offers, and followed the young lady to the Emir's harem, where we must for a moment leave them and return to the Caliph.

Vathek found himself beneath a vast dome, illuminated by a thousand lamps of rock crystal; as many vases of the same material, filled with excellent sherbet, sparkled on a large table, where a profusion of viands were spread. Amongst others were sweetbreads stewed in milk of almonds, saffron soups, and lamb *à la crème*, of all which the Caliph was amazingly fond. He took of each as much as he was able, testified his sense of the Emir's friendship by the gaiety of his heart, and made the dwarfs dance against their will, for these little devotees durst not refuse the Commander of the faithful. At last he spread himself on the sofa, and slept sounder than he had ever slept before.

Beneath this dome a general silence prevailed, for there was nothing to disturb it but the jaws of Bababalouk, who had untrussed himself to eat with greater advantage being anxious to make amends for his fast in the mountains. As his spirits were too high to admit of his sleeping, and not loving to be idle, he proposed to himself to visit the harem, and repair to his charge of the ladies, to examine if they had been properly lubricated with the balm of Mecca, if their eyebrows and tresses were in order, and, in a word, to perform all the little offices they might need. He sought for the harem a long time, but without being able to find out the door; he durst not speak aloud for fear of disturbing the Caliph, and not a soul was stirring in the precincts of the palace; he almost despaired of effecting his purpose, when a low whispering just reached his ear. It came from the dwarfs, who were returned to their old occupation, and, for the nine hundred and ninety-ninth time in their lives, were reading over the Koran. They very politely invited Bababalouk to be of their party, but his head was full of other concerns. The dwarfs, though scandalised at his dissolute morals, directed him to the apartments he wanted to find. His way thither lay through a hundred dark corridors, along which he groped as he went, and at last began to catch, from the extremity of a passage, the charming gossiping of the women, which not a little delighted his heart.

'Ah, ha! what, not yet asleep?' cried he; and, taking long strides as he spoke, 'did you not suspect me of abjuring my charge? I stayed but to finish what my master had left.'

Two of the black eunuchs, on hearing a voice so loud, detached a party in haste, sabre in hand, to discover the cause; but presently was repeated on all sides:

"Tis only Bababalouk! no one but Bababalouk!'

This circumspect guardian, having gone up to a thin veil of carnation-coloured silk that hung before the doorway, distinguished, by means of the softened splendour that shone through it, an oval bath of dark porphyry, surrounded by curtains festooned in large folds. Through the apertures between them, as they were not drawn close, groups of young slaves were visible, amongst whom Bababalouk perceived his pupils, indulgingly expanding their arms, as if to embrace the perfumed water and refresh themselves after their fatigues. The looks of tender languor, their confidential whispers, and the enchanting smiles with which they were imparted, the exquisite fragrance of the roses, all combined to inspire a voluptuousness which even Bababalouk himself was scarce able to withstand.

He summoned up, however, his usual solemnity, and, in the peremptory tone of authority, commanded the ladies instantly to leave the bath. Whilst he was issuing these mandates the young Nouronihar daughter of the Emir, who was sprightly as an antelope, and full of wanton gaiety beckoned one of her slaves to let down the great swing, which was suspended to the ceiling by cords of silk, and whilst this was being done winked to her companions in the bath, who, chagrined to be forced from so soothing a state of indolence, began to twist it round Bababalouk, and tease him with a thousand vagaries.

When Nouronihar perceived that he was exhausted with fatigue she accosted him with an arch air of respectful concern and said:

'My lord! it is not by any means decent that the chief eunuch of the Caliph, our Sovereign, should thus continue standing; deign but to recline your graceful person upon this sofa, which will burst with vexation if it have not the honour to receive you.'

Caught by these flattering accents, Bababalouk gallantly replied:

'Delight of the apple of my eye! I accept the invitation of thy honeyed lips; and, to say truth, my senses are dazzled with the radiance that beams from thy charms.'

'Repose, then, at your ease,' replied the beauty, and placed him on the pretended sofa, which, quicker than lightning, gave way all at once. The rest of the women, having aptly conceived her design, sprang naked from the bath, and plied the swing with such unmerciful jerks that it swept through the whole compass of a very lofty dome, and took from the poor victim all power of respiration; sometimes his feet rased the surface of the water, and at others the skylight almost flattened his nose. In vain did he pierce the air with the cries of a voice that resembled the ringing of a cracked basin, for their peals of laughter were still more predominant.

Nouronihar, in the inebriety of youthful spirits, being used only to eunuchs of ordinary harems, and having never seen anything so royal and disgusting, was far more diverted than all of the rest. She began to parody some Persian verses, and sung with an accent most demurely piquant:

> O gentle white dove, as thou soar'st through the air,
> Vouchsafe one kind glance on the mate of thy love;
> Melodious Philomel, I am thy rose;
> Warble some couplet to ravish my heart!

The sultanas and their slaves, stimulated by these pleasantries, persevered at the swing with such unremitted assiduity that at length the cord which had secured it snapt suddenly asunder, and Bababalouk fell floundering like a turtle to the bottom of the bath. This accident occasioned a universal shout; twelve little doors, till now unobserved, flew open at once, and the ladies in an instant made their escape, after throwing all the towels on his head, and putting out the lights that remained.

The deplorable animal, in water to the chin, overwhelmed with darkness, and unable to extricate himself from the wrap that embarrassed him, was still doomed to hear for his further consolation the fresh bursts of merriment his disaster occasioned. He bustled, but in vain, to get from the bath, for the margin was become so slippery with the oil spilt in breaking the lamps that at every effort he slid back with a plunge, which resounded aloud through the hollow of the dome. These cursed peals of laughter at every relapse were redoubled; and he, who thought the place infested rather by devils than women, resolved to cease groping and abide in the bath, where he amused himself with soliloquies, interspersed with imprecations, of which his malicious neighbours reclining on down suffered not an accent to escape. In this delectable plight the morning surprised him. The Caliph, wondering at his absence, had caused him to be everywhere sought for. At last he was drawn forth, almost smothered from the wisp of linen, and wet even to the marrow. Limping and chattering his teeth, he appeared before his master, who inquired what was the matter, and how he came soused in so strange a pickle?

'And why did you enter this cursed lodge?' answered Bababalouk, gruffly. 'Ought a monarch like you to visit with his harem the abode of a grey-bearded Emir, who knows nothing of life? And with what gracious damsels doth the

place, too, abound! Fancy to yourself how they have soaked
me like a burnt crust, and made me dance like a jack-pudding
the live-long night through, on their damnable swing. What an
excellent lesson for your sultanas to follow, into whom I have
instilled such reserve and decorum!'

Vathek, comprehending not a syllable of all this invective,
obliged him to relate minutely the transaction; but, instead
of sympathizing with the miserable sufferer, he laughed
immoderately at the device of the swing, and the figure
of Bababalouk mounting upon it. The stung eunuch could
scarcely preserve the semblance of respect.

'Ay, laugh, my lord! laugh,' said he; 'but I wish this
Nouronihar would play some trick on you, she is too wicked
to spare even majesty itself.'

Those words made for the present but a slight impression
on the Caliph; but they not long after recurred to his mind.

This conversation was cut short by Fakreddin, who came to
request that Vathek would join in the prayers and ablutions to
be solemnized on a spacious meadow, watered by innumerable
streams. The Caliph found the waters refreshing, but the
prayers abominably irksome. He diverted himself, however,
with the multitude of Calenders, Santons, and Dervishes, who
were continually coming and going, but especially with the
Brahmins, Fakirs, and other enthusiasts, who had travelled
from the heart of India, and halted on their way with the Emir.
These latter had, each of them, some mummery peculiar
to himself. One dragged a huge chain wherever he went,
another an ouran-outang, whilst a third was furnished with
scourges, and all performed to a charm; some clambered up
trees, holding one foot in the air; others poised themselves
over a fire, and without mercy filliped their noses. There
were some amongst them that cherished vermin, which were
not ungrateful in requiting their caresses. These rambling
fanatics revolted the hearts of the Dervishes, the Calenders,
and Santons. However, the vehemence of their aversion soon
subsided, under the hope that the presence of the Caliph
would cure their folly, and convert them to the Mussulman
faith; but alas! how great was their disappointment! for
Vathek, instead of preaching to them, treated them as
buffoons, bade them present his compliments to Visnow

and Ixhora, and discovered a predilection for a squat old
man from the isle of Serendib, who was more ridiculous than
any of the rest.

'Come!' said he, 'for the love of your gods bestow a few slaps
on your chops to amuse me.'

The old fellow, offended at such an address, began loudly
to weep; but, as he betrayed a villainous drivelling in his tears,
the Caliph turned his back and listened to Bababalouk, who
whispered, whilst he held the umbrella over him:

'Your Majesty should be cautious of this odd assembly,
which hath been collected I know not for what. Is it
necessary to exhibit such spectacles to a mighty Potentate,
with interludes of Talapoins more mangy than dogs? Were
I you I would command a fire to be kindled, and at
once purge the earth of the Emir, his harem, and all his
menagerie.'

'Tush, dolt,' answered Vathek; 'and know that all this
infinitely charms me; nor shall I leave the meadow till I
have visited every hive of these pious mendicants.'

Wherever the Caliph directed his course objects of pity
were sure to swarm round him; the blind, the purblind,
dwarfs without noses, damsels without ears, each to extol
the munificence of Fakreddin, who, as well as his attendant
greybeards, dealt about gratis plasters and cataplasms to all
that applied. At noon a superb corps of cripples made its
appearance, and soon after advanced by platoons on the
plain, the completest association of invalids that had ever
been embodied till then. The blind went groping with the
blind, the lame limped on together, and the maimed made
gestures to each other with the only arm that remained; the
sides of a considerable waterfall were crowded by the deaf,
amongst whom were some from Pegû with ears uncommonly
handsome and large, but were still less able to hear than the
rest; nor were there wanting others in abundance with hump-
backs, wenny necks and even horns, of an exquisite polish.

The Emir, to aggrandize the solemnity of the festival in
honour of his illustrious visitant, ordered the turf to be spread
on all sides with skins and tablecloths, upon which were served
up for the good Mussulmans pilaus of every hue, with other
orthodox dishes; and, by the express order of Vathek, who

was shamefully tolerant, small plates of abominations for
regaling the rest. This Prince, on seeing so many mouths
put in motion, began to think it time for employing his
own. In spite, therefore, of every remonstrance from the
chief of his eunuchs, he resolved to have a dinner dressed
on the spot. The complaisant Emir immediately gave orders
for a table to be placed in the shade of the willows. The first
service consisted of fish, which they drew from a river flowing
over sands of gold at the foot of a lofty hill; these were broiled
as fast as taken, and served up with a sauce of vinegar, and
small herbs that grew on Mount Sinai; for everything with the
Emir was excellent and pious.

The dessert was not quite set on when the sound of lutes
from the hill was repeated by the echoes of the neighbouring
mountains. The Caliph, with an emotion of pleasure and
surprise, had no sooner raised up his head than a handful
of jasmine dropped on his face. An abundance of tittering
succeeded the frolic, and instantly appeared through the
bushes the elegant forms of several young females, skipping
and bounding like roes. The fragrance diffused from their
hair struck the sense of Vathek, who, in an ecstasy, suspending
his repast, said to Bababalouk:

'Are the Peries come down from their spheres? Note her
in particular whose form is so perfect, venturously running
on the brink of the precipice, and turning back her head,
as regardless of nothing but the graceful flow of her robe;
with what captivating impatience doth she contend with the
bushes for her veil! could it be she who threw the jasmine
at me?'

'Ay! she it was; and you too would she throw from the top
of the rock,' answered Bababalouk, 'for that is my good friend
Nouronihar, who so kindly lent me her swing; my dear lord
and master,' added he, twisting a twig that hung by the rind
from a willow, 'let me correct her for her want of respect; the
Emir will have no reason to complain, since (bating what I owe
to his piety) he is much to be censured for keeping a troop of
girls on the mountains whose sharp air gives their blood too
brisk a circulation.'

'Peace, blasphemer,' said the Caliph; 'speak not thus of her,
who over her mountains leads my heart a willing captive;

contrive rather that my eyes may be fixed upon hers, that I
may respire her sweet breath, as she bounds panting along
these delightful wilds!'

On saying these words Vathek extended his arms towards
the hill, and directing his eyes with an anxiety unknown to
him before, endeavoured to keep within view the object that
enthralled his soul; but her course was as difficult to follow
as the flight of one of those beautiful blue butterflies of
Cashmere, which are at once so volatile and rare.

The Caliph, not satisfied with seeing, wished also to hear
Nouronihar, and eagerly turned to catch the sound of her
voice; at last he distinguished her whispering to one of her
companions behind the thicket whence she had thrown the
jasmine:

'A Caliph, it must be owned, is a fine thing to see, but my
little Gulchenrouz is much more amiable; one lock of his
hair is of more value to me than the richest embroidery of
the Indies; I had rather that his teeth should mischievously
press my finger than the richest ring of the Imperial treasure;
where have you left him, Sutlememe? and why is he now not
here?'

The agitated Caliph still wished to hear more, but she
immediately retired with all her attendants; the fond monarch
pursued her with his eyes till she was gone out of sight, and
then continued like a bewildered and benighted traveller,
from whom the clouds had obscured the constellation that
guided his way; the curtain of night seemed dropped before
him; everything appeared discoloured; the falling waters
filled his soul with dejection, and his tears trickled down
the jasmines he had caught from Nouronihar, and placed
in his inflamed bosom. He snatched up a shining pebble,
to remind him of the scene where he felt the first tumults
of love.

Two hours were elapsed, and evening drew on before he
could resolve to depart from the place. He often, but in
vain, attempted to go; a soft languor enervated the powers
of his mind; extending himself on the brink of the stream he
turned his eyes towards the blue summits of the mountain and
exclaimed:

'What concealest thou behind thee? what is passing in thy

solitudes? Whither is she gone? O heaven! perhaps she is now wandering in thy grottos, with her happy Gulchenrouz!'

In the meantime the damps began to descend, and the Emir, solicitous for the health of the Caliph, ordered the imperial litter to be brought. Vathek, absorbed in his reveries, was imperceptibly removed and conveyed back to the saloon that received him the evening before.

But let us leave the Caliph, immersed in his new passion, and attend Nouronihar beyond the rocks, where she had again joined her beloved Gulchenrouz. This Gulchenrouz was the son of Ali Hassan, brother to the Emir, and the most delicate and lovely creature in the world. Ali Hassan, who had been absent ten years on a voyage to the unknown seas, committed at his departure this child, the only survivor of many, to the care and protection of his brother. Gulchenrouz could write in various characters with precision, and paint upon vellum the most elegant arabesques that fancy could devise; his sweet voice accompanied the lute in the most enchanting manner, and when he sung the loves of Megnoun and Leileh, or some unfortunate lovers of ancient days, tears insensibly overflowed the cheeks of his auditors; the verses he composed (for, like Megnoun, he too was a poet) inspired that unresisting languor so frequently fatal to the female heart; the women all doted upon him, for though he had passed his thirteenth year, they still detained him in the harem; his dancing was light as the gossamer waved by the zephyrs of spring, but his arms, which twined so gracefully with those of the young girls in the dance, could neither dart the lance in the chase, nor curb the steeds that pastured his uncle's domains. The bow, however, he drew with a certain aim, and would have excelled his competitors in the race could he have broken the ties that bound him to Nouronihar.

The two brothers had mutually engaged their children to each other, and Nouronihar loved her cousin more than her eyes; both had the same tastes and amusements, the same long, languishing looks, the same tresses, the same fair complexions, and when Gulchenrouz appeared in the dress of his cousin he seemed to be more feminine than even herself. If at any time he left the harem to visit Fakreddin it was with all the bashfulness of a fawn, that consciously ventures from the

lair of its dam. He was, however, wanton enough to mock the
solemn old greybeards to whom he was subject, though sure
to be rated without mercy in return; whenever this happened
he would plunge into the recesses of the harem, and, sobbing,
take refuge in the arms of Nouronihar, who loved even his
faults beyond the virtues of others.

It fell out this evening that, after leaving the Caliph in the
meadow, she ran with Gulchenrouz over the green sward of
the mountain that sheltered the vale where Fakreddin had
chosen to reside. The sun was dilated on the edge of the
horizon; and the young people, whose fancies were lively
and inventive, imagined they beheld in the gorgeous clouds
of the west the domes of Shadukiam and Ambreabad, where
the Peries have fixed their abode. Nouronihar, sitting on
the slope of the hill, supported on her knees the perfumed
head of Gulchenrouz; the air was calm, and no sound stirred
but the voices of other young girls, who were drawing cool
water from the streams below. The unexpected arrival of the
Caliph and the splendour that marked his appearance had
already filled with emotion the ardent soul of Nouronihar;
her vanity irresistibly prompted her to pique the Prince's
attention, and this she took good care to effect whilst he
picked up the jasmine she had thrown upon him. But when
Gulchenrouz asked after the flowers he had culled for her
bosom Nouronihar was all in confusion; she hastily kissed his
forehead, arose in a flutter, and walked with unequal steps
on the border of the precipice. Night advanced, and the pure
gold of the setting sun had yielded to a sanguine red, the glow
of which, like the reflection of a burning furnace, flushed
Nouronihar's animated countenance. Gulchenrouz, alarmed
at the agitation of his cousin, said to her with a supplicating
accent:

'Let us be gone; the sky looks portentous, the tamarisks
tremble more than common, and the raw wind chills my very
heart; come! let us be gone, 'tis a melancholy night!'

Then, taking hold of her hand, he drew it towards the path
he besought her to go. Nouronihar unconsciously followed
the attraction, for a thousand strange imaginations occupied
her spirit; she passed the large round of honeysuckles, her
favourite resort, without ever vouchsafing it a glance, yet

Gulchenrouz could not help snatching off a few shoots in his way, though he ran as if a wild beast were behind.

The young females seeing him approach in such haste, and according to custom expecting a dance, instantly assembled in a circle and took each other by the hand; but Gulchenrouz, coming up out of breath, fell down at once on the grass. This accident struck with consternation the whole of this frolicsome party; whilst Nouronihar, half distracted, and overcome, both by the violence of her exercise and the tumult of her thoughts, sunk feebly down at his side, cherished his cold hands in her bosom, and chafed his temples with a fragrant unguent. At length he came to himself, and, wrapping up his head in the robe of his cousin, entreated that she would not return to the harem; he was afraid of being snapped at by Shaban, his tutor, a wrinkled old eunuch of a surly disposition; for having interrupted the stated walk of Nouronihar, he dreaded lest the churl should take it amiss. The whole of this sprightly group, sitting round upon a mossy knoll, began to entertain themselves with various pastimes, whilst their superintendents the eunuchs were gravely conversing at a distance. The nurse of the Emir's daughter, observing her pupil sit ruminating with her eyes on the ground, endeavoured to amuse her with diverting tales, to which Gulchenrouz, who had already forgotten his inquietudes, listened with a breathless attention; he laughed, he clapped his hands, and passed a hundred little tricks on the whole of the company, without omitting the eunuchs, whom he provoked to run after him, in spite of their age and decrepitude.

During these occurrences the moon arose, the wind subsided, and the evening became so serene and inviting, that a resolution was taken to sup on the spot. Sutlememe, who excelled in dressing a salad, having filled large bowls of porcelain with eggs of small birds, curds turned with citron juice, slices of cucumber, and the inmost leaves of delicate herbs, handed it round from one to another, and gave each their shares in a large spoon of Cocknos. Gulchenrouz, nestling as usual in the bosom of Nouronihar, pouted out his vermilion little lips against the offer of Sutlememe, and would take it only from the hand of his cousin, on whose mouth he hung like a bee inebriated with the quintessence of flowers. One of the eunuchs ran to fetch melons, whilst others were employed in showering down almonds from the branches that overhung this amiable party.

In the midst of this festive scene there appeared a light on the top of the highest mountain, which attracted the notice of every eye; this light was not less bright than the moon when at full, and might have been taken for her had it not been that the moon was already risen. The phenomenon occasioned a general surprise, and no one could conjecture the cause; it could not be a fire, for the light was clear and bluish, nor had meteors ever been seen of that magnitude or splendour. This strange light faded for a moment, and immediately renewed its brightness; it first appeared motionless at the foot of the rock, whence it darted in an instant to sparkle in a thicket of palm trees; thence it glided along the torrent, and at last fixed in a glen that was narrow and dark. The moment it had taken its direction Gulchenrouz, whose heart always trembled at anything sudden or rare, drew Nouronihar by the robe, and anxiously requested her to return to the harem. The women were importunate in seconding the entreaty, but the curiosity of the Emir's daughter prevailed; she not only refused to go back, but resolved at all hazards to pursue the appearance. Whilst they were debating what was best to be done the light shone forth so dazzling a blaze that they all fled away shrieking. Nouronihar followed them a few steps, but, coming to the turn of a little by-path, stopped and went back alone. As she ran with an alertness peculiar to herself it was not long before she came to the place where they had just been supping. The globe of fire now appeared stationary in the glen, and burned in majestic stillness. Nouronihar, compressing her hands upon her bosom, hesitated for some moments to advance; the solitude of her situation was new, the silence of the night awful, and every object inspired sensations which till then she never had felt; the affright of Gulchenrouz recurred to her mind, and she a thousand times turned to go back, but this luminous appearance was always before her. Urged on by an irresistible impulse she continued to approach it, in defiance of every obstacle that opposed her progress.

At length she arrived at the opening of the glen; but, instead of coming up to the light, she found herself surrounded by darkness, excepting that at a considerable distance a faint spark glimmered by fits. She stopped a second time; the sound of waterfalls mingling their murmurs, the hollow rustlings amongst the palm branches, and the funereal screams of the birds from their rifted trunks, all conspired to fill her with terror; she imagined every moment that she trod on some venomous reptile. All the stories of malignant Dives and dismal Ghoules thronged into her memory; but her curiosity was, notwithstanding, more predominant than her fears. She therefore firmly entered a winding track that led towards the spark, but, being a stranger to the path, she had not gone far when she began to repent of her rashness.

'Alas!' said she, 'that I were but in those secure and illuminated apartments where my evenings glided on with Gulchenrouz! Dear child! how would thy heart flutter with terror wert thou wandering in these wild solitudes like me!' At the close of this apostrophe she regained her road, and, coming to steps hewn out in the rock, ascended them undismayed. The light, which was now gradually enlarging, appeared above her on the summit of the mountain. At length she distinguished a plaintive and melodious union of voices, proceeding from a sort of cavern, that resembled the dirges which are sung over tombs; a sound likewise, like that which arises from the filling of baths, at the same time struck her ear. She continued ascending, and discovered large wax torches in full blaze planted here and there in the fissures of the rock; this preparation filled her with fear, whilst the subtle and potent odour which the torches exhaled caused her to sink almost lifeless at the entrance of the grot.

Casting her eyes within in this kind of trance she beheld a large cistern of gold, filled with a water whose vapour distilled on her face a dew of the essence of roses; a soft symphony resounded through the grot. On the sides of the cistern she noticed appendages of royalty, diadems and feathers of the heron, all sparkling with carbuncles. Whilst her attention was fixed on this display of magnificence the music ceased, and a voice instantly demanded:

'For what monarch were these torches kindled, this bath prepared, and these habiliments, which belong not only to the sovereigns of the earth, but even to the Talismanic Powers?'

To which a second voice answered:

'They are for the charming daughter of the Emir Fakreddin.'

'What,' replied the first, 'for that trifler, who consumes her time with a giddy child, immersed in softness, and who at best can make but an enervated husband?'

'And can she,' rejoined the other voice, 'be amused at such empty trifles, whilst the Caliph, the Sovereign of the world, he who is destined to enjoy the treasures of the pre-Adamite Sultans, a prince six feet high, and whose eyes pervade the inmost soul of a female, is inflamed with the love of her? No! she will be wise enough to answer that passion alone that can aggrandize her glory; no doubt she will, and despise the puppet of her fancy. Then all the riches this place contains as well as the carbuncle of Giamschid, shall be hers.'

'You judge right,' returned the first voice, 'and I haste to Istakhar to prepare the palace of subterranean fire for the reception of the bridal pair.'

The voices ceased, the torches were extinguished, the most entire darkness succeeded, and Nouronihar, recovering with a start, found herself reclined on a sofa in the harem of her father. She clapped her hands, and immediately came together Gulchenrouz and her women, who, in despair at having lost her, had despatched eunuchs to seek her in every direction. Shaban appeared with the rest, and began to reprimand her with an air of consequence:

'Little impertinent,' said he, 'whence got you false keys? or are you beloved of some Genius that hath given you a pick-lock? I will try the extent of your power; come, to your chamber! through the two skylights; and expect not the company of Gulchenrouz; be expeditious! I will shut you up in the double tower.'

At these menaces Nouronihar indignantly raised her head, opened on Shaban her black eyes, which, since the important dialogue of the enchanted grot, were considerably enlarged, and said:

'Go, speak thus to slaves, but learn to reverence her who is born to give laws, and subject all to her power.'

She was proceeding in the same style, but was interrupted by a sudden exclamation of 'The Caliph! The Caliph!' The curtains at once were thrown open, and the slaves prostrate in double rows, whilst poor little Gulchenrouz hid himself beneath the elevation of a sofa. At first appeared a file of black eunuchs, trailing after them long trains of muslin embroidered with gold, and holding in their hands censers, which dispensed as they passed the grateful perfume of the wood of aloes; next marched Bababalouk with a solemn strut, and tossing his head as not overpleased at the visit; Vathek came close after, superbly robed, his gait was unembarrassed and noble, and his presence would have engaged admiration, though he had not been the Sovereign of the world. He approached Nouronihar with a throbbing heart, and seemed enraptured at the full effulgence of her radiant eyes, of which he had before caught but a few glimpses; but she instantly depressed them, and her confusion augmented her beauty.

Bababalouk, who was a thorough adept in coincidences of this nature, and knew that the worst game should be played with the best face, immediately made a signal for all to retire; and no sooner did he perceive beneath the sofa the little one's feet than he drew him forth without ceremony, set him upon his shoulders, and lavished on him as he went off a thousand odious caresses. Gulchenrouz cried out, and resisted till his cheeks became the colour of the blossom of the pomegranate, and the tears that started into his eyes shot forth a gleam of indignation. He cast a significant glance at Nouronihar, which the Caliph, noticing, asked:

'Is that, then, your Gulchenrouz?'

'Sovereign of the world!' answered she, 'spare my cousin, whose innocence and gentleness deserve not your anger!'

'Take comfort,' said Vathek, with a smile, 'he is in good hands; Bababalouk is fond of children, and never goes without sweetmeats and comfits.'

The daughter of Fakreddin was abashed, and suffered Gulchenrouz to be borne away without adding a word. The tumult of her bosom betrayed her confusion; and Vathek, becoming still more impassioned, gave a loose to his frenzy, which had only not subdued the last faint strugglings of reluctance when the Emir suddenly bursting in, threw in his face upon the ground at the feet of the Caliph, and said:

'Commander of the faithful! abase not yourself to the meanness of your slave.'

'No, Emir,' replied Vathek, 'I raise her to an equality with myself; I declare her my wife, and the glory of your race shall extend from one generation to another.'

'Alas! my lord,' said Fakreddin, as he plucked off the honours of his beard, 'cut short the days of your faithful servant rather than force him to depart from his word. Nouronihar, as her hands evince, is solemnly promised to Gulchenrouz, the son of my brother Ali Hassan; they are united also in heart, their faith is mutually plighted, and affiances so sacred cannot be broken.'

'What then!' replied the Caliph bluntly; 'would you surrender this divine beauty to a husband more womanish than herself? And can you imagine that I will suffer her charms to decay in hands so inefficient and nerveless? No! she is destined to live out her life within my embraces; such is my will; retire and disturb not the night I devote to the homage of her charms.'

The irritated Emir drew forth his sabre, presented it to Vathek, and, stretching out his neck, said in a firm tone of voice:

'Strike your unhappy host, my lord! he has lived long enough, since he hath seen the Prophet's Vicegerent violate the rites of hospitality.'

At his uttering these words Nouronihar, unable to support any longer the conflict of her passions, sunk down in a swoon. Vathek, both terrified for her life and furious at an opposition to his will, bade Fakreddin assist his daughter, and withdrew, darting his terrible look at the unfortunate Emir, who suddenly fell backward bathed in a sweat cold as the damp of death.

Gulchenrouz, who had escaped from the hands of Bababalouk, and was that instant returned, called out for help as loudly as he could, not having strength to afford it himself. Pale and panting, the poor child attempted to revive Nouronihar by caresses; and it happened that the thrilling warmth of his lips restored her to life. Fakreddin, beginning also to recover from the look of the Caliph, with difficulty tottered to a seat, and after warily casting round his eye to see if this dangerous Prince were gone sent for Shaban and Sutlememe, and said to them apart:

'My friends! violent evils require as violent remedies. The Caliph has brought desolation and horror into my family, and how shall we resist his power? another of his looks will send me to my grave. Fetch, then, that narcotic powder which the Dervish brought me from Aracan. A dose of it, the effect of which will continue three days, must be administered to each of these children. The Caliph will believe them to be dead, for they will have all the appearance of death. We shall go as if to inter them in the cave of Meimoune, at the entrance of the great desert of sand, and near the cabin of my dwarfs. When all the spectators shall be withdrawn, you, Shaban, and four select eunuchs, shall convey them to the lake, where provision shall be ready to support them a month, for one day allotted to the surprise this event will occasion, five to the tears, a fortnight to reflection, and the rest to prepare for renewing his progress, will, according to my calculation, fill up the whole time that Vathek will tarry, and I shall then be freed from his intrusion.'

'Your plan,' said Sutlememe, 'is a good one, if it can but be effected. I have remarked that Nouronihar is well able to support the glances of the Caliph and that he is far from being sparing of them to her. Be assured, therefore, notwithstanding her fondness for Gulchenrouz, she will never remain quiet while she knows him to be here, unless we can persuade her that both herself and Gulchenrouz are really dead, and that they were conveyed to those rocks for a limited season to expiate the little faults of which their love was the cause. We will add that we killed ourselves in despair, and that your dwarfs, whom they never yet saw, will preach to them delectable sermons. I will engage that everything shall succeed to the bent of your wishes.'

'Be it so!' said Fakreddin, 'I approve your proposal; let us lose not a moment to give it effect.'

They forthwith hastened to seek for the powder, which, being mixed in a sherbet, was immediately drunk by Gulchenrouz and Nouronihar. Within the space of an hour both were seized with violent palpitations, and a general numbness gradually ensued. They arose from the floor, where they had remained ever since the Caliph's departure, and, ascending to the sofa, reclined themselves at full length upon it, clasped in each other's embraces.

'Cherish me, my dear Nouronihar!' said Gulchenrouz; 'put thy hand upon my heart, for it feels as if it were frozen. Alas! thou art as cold as myself! Hath the Caliph murdered us both with his terrible look?'

'I am dying!' cried she in a faltering voice; 'press me closer, I am ready to expire!'

'Let us die then together,' answered the little Gulchenrouz, whilst his breast laboured with a convulsive sigh; 'let me at least breathe forth my soul on thy lips!' They spoke no more, and became as dead.

Immediately the most piercing cries were heard through the harem, whilst Shaban and Sutlememe personated with great adroitness the parts of persons in despair. The Emir, who was sufficiently mortified to be forced into such untoward expedients, and had now for the first time made a trial of his powder, was under no necessity of counterfeiting grief. The slaves, who had flocked together from all quarters, stood motionless at the spectacle before them; all lights were extinguished save two lamps, which shed a wan glimmering over the faces of these lovely flowers, that seemed to be faded in the spring-time of life; funeral vestments were prepared, their bodies were washed with rose-water, their beautiful tresses were braided and incensed, and they were wrapped in simars whiter than alabaster. At the moment that their attendants were placing two wreaths of their favourite jasmines on their brows, the Caliph, who had just heard of the tragical catastrophe, arrived. He looked not less pale and haggard than the Ghoules, that wander at night among graves. Forgetful of himself and everyone else he broke through the midst of the slaves, fell prostrate at the foot of the sofa, beat his bosom, called himself 'atrocious murderer!' and invoked upon his head a thousand imprecations. With a trembling hand he raised the veil that covered the countenance of Nouronihar, and, uttering a loud shriek, fell lifeless on the floor. The chief of the eunuchs dragged him off with horrible grimaces and repeated as he went:

'Ay, I foresaw she would play you some ungracious turn!'

No sooner was the Caliph gone than the Emir commanded biers to be brought and forbad that anyone should enter the harem. Every window was fastened, all instruments of music were broken, and the Imans began to recite their prayers. Towards the close of this melancholy day Vathek sobbed in silence, for they had been forced to compose with anodynes his convulsions of rage and desperation.

At the dawn of the succeeding morning the wide folding doors of the palace were set open, and the funeral procession moved forward for the mountain. The wailful cries of 'La Ilah illa Alla!' reached to the Caliph, who was eager to cicatrise himself and attend the ceremonial; nor could he have been dissuaded had not his excessive weakness disabled him from walking. At the first few steps he fell on the ground, and his people were obliged to lay him on a bed, where he remained many days in such a state of insensibility as excited compassion in the Emir himself.

When the procession was arrived at the grot of Meimoune, Shaban and Sutlememe dismissed the whole of the train, excepting the four confidential eunuchs who were appointed to remain. After resting some moments near the biers, which had been left in the open air, they caused them to be carried to the brink of a small lake, whose banks were overgrown with a hoary moss; this was the great resort of herons and storks, which preyed continually on little blue fishes. The dwarfs, instructed by the Emir, soon repaired thither, and, with the help of the eunuchs, began to construct cabins of rushes and reeds, a work in which they had admirable skill; a magazine also was contrived for provisions, with a small oratory for themselves, and a pyramid of wood neatly piled to furnish the necessary fuel, for the air was bleak in the hollows of the mountains.

At evening two fires were kindled on the brink of the lake, and the two lovely bodies, taken from their biers, were carefully deposited upon a bed of dried leaves within the same cabin. The dwarfs began to recite the Koran with their clear, shrill voices, and Shaban and Sutlememe stood at some distance, anxiously waiting the effects of the powder. At length Nouronihar and Gulchenrouz faintly stretched out their arms, and gradually opening their eyes began to survey with looks of increasing amazement every object around them; they even attempted to rise, but for want of strength fell back again. Sutlememe on this administered a cordial, which the Emir had taken care to provide.

Gulchenrouz, thoroughly aroused, sneezed out aloud, and raising himself with an effort that expressed his surprise left the cabin, and inhaled the fresh air with the greatest avidity.

'Yes,' said he, 'I breathe again! again do I exist! I hear sounds! I behold a firmament spangled over with stars!'

Nouronihar, catching these beloved accents, extricated herself from the leaves, and ran to clasp Gulchenrouz to her bosom. The first objects she remarked were their long simars, their garlands of flowers, and their naked feet; she hid her face in her hands to reflect. The vision of the enchanted bath, the despair of her father, and, more vividly than both, the majestic figure of Vathek recurred to her memory. She recollected also that herself and Gulchenrouz had been sick and dying, but all these images bewildered her mind.

Not knowing where she was she turned her eyes on all sides, as if to recognise the surrounding scene. This singular lake, those flames reflected from its glassy surface, the pale hues of its banks, the romantic cabins, the bulrushes that sadly waved their drooping heads, the storks whose melancholy cries blended with the shrill voices of the dwarfs, everything conspired to persuade them that the Angel of Death had opened the portal of some other world.

Gulchenrouz, on his part, lost in wonder, clung to the neck of his cousin; he believed himself in the region of phantoms, and was terrified at the silence she preserved. At length, addressing her:

'Speak,' said he, 'where are we? Do you not see those spectres that are stirring the burning coals? Are they Monker and Nakir, come to throw us into them? Does the fatal bridge cross this lake, whose solemn stillness perhaps conceals from us an abyss, in which for whole ages we shall be doomed incessantly to sink?'

'No, my children!' said Sutlememe, going towards them, 'take comfort! the exterminating Angel, who conducted our souls hither after yours, hath assured us that the chastisement of your indolent and voluptuous life shall be restricted to a certain series of years, which you must pass in this dreary abode, where the sun is scarcely visible and where the soil yields neither fruits nor flowers. These,' continued she, pointing to the dwarfs, 'will provide for our wants, for souls so mundane as ours retain too strong a tincture of their earthly extraction; instead of meats your food will be nothing but rice, and your bread shall be moistened in the fogs that brood over the surface of the lake.'

At this desolating prospect the poor children burst into tears, and prostrated themselves before the dwarfs, who perfectly supported their characters, and delivered an excellent discourse of a customary length upon the sacred camel, which after a thousand years was to convey them to the paradise of the faithful.

The sermon being ended, and ablutions performed, they praised Alla and the prophet, supped very indifferently, and retired to their withered leaves. Nouronihar and her little cousin consoled themselves on finding that, though dead, they yet lay in one cabin. Having slept well before, the remainder of the night was spent in conversation on what had befallen them, and both, from a dread of apparitions, betook themselves for protection to one another's arms.

In the morning, which was lowering and rainy, the dwarfs mounted high poles like minarets, and called them to prayers. The whole congregation, which consisted of Sutlememe, Shaban, the four eunuchs and some storks, were already assembled. The two children came forth from their cabin with a slow and dejected pace. As their minds were in a tender and melancholy mood their devotions were performed with fervour. No sooner were they finished than Gulchenrouz demanded of Sutlememe and the rest, 'how they happened to die so opportunely for his cousin and himself?'

'We killed ourselves,' returned Sutlememe, 'in despair at your death.'

On this, said Nouronihar, who, notwithstanding what was past, had not yet forgotten her vision:

'And the Caliph! is he also dead of his grief? and will he likewise come hither?'

The dwarfs, who were prepared with an answer, most demurely replied:

'Vathek is damned beyond all redemption!'

'I readily believe so,' said Gulchenrouz, 'and am glad from my heart to hear it, for I am convinced it was his horrible look that sent us hither to listen to sermons and mess upon rice.'

One week passed away on the side of the lake unmarked by any variety; Nouronihar ruminating on the grandeur of which death had deprived her, and Gulchenrouz applying to prayers and to panniers, along with the dwarfs, who infinitely pleased him.

Whilst this scene of innocence was exhibiting in the mountains, the Caliph presented himself to the Emir in a new light. The instant he recovered the use of his senses, with a voice that made Bababalouk quake, he thundered out:

'Perfidious Giaour! I renounce thee for ever! it is thou who hast slain my beloved Nouronihar! and I supplicate the pardon of Mahomet, who would have preserved her to me had I been more wise. Let water be brought to perform my ablutions, and let the pious Fakreddin be called to offer up his prayers with mine, and reconcile me to him; afterwards we will go together and visit the sepulchre of the unfortunate Nouronihar. I am resolved to become a hermit, and consume the residue of my days on this mountain, in hope of expiating my crimes.'

Nouronihar was not altogether so content, for though she felt a fondness for Gulchenrouz, who, to augment the attachment, had been left at full liberty with her, yet she still regarded him as but a bauble that bore no competition with the carbuncle of Giamschid. At times she indulged doubts on the mode of her being, and scarcely could believe that the dead had all the wants and whims of the living. To gain satisfaction, however, on so perplexing a topic she arose one morning whilst all were asleep, with a breathless caution, from the side of Gulchenrouz, and, after having given him a soft kiss, began to follow the windings of the lake till it terminated with a rock, whose top was accessible though lofty; this she clambered up with considerable toil, and, having reached the summit, set forward in a run, like a doe that unwittingly follows her hunter. Though she skipped along with the alertness of an antelope, yet at intervals she was forced to desist and rest beneath the tamarisks to recover her breath. Whilst she, thus reclined, was occupied with her little reflections on the apprehension that she had some knowledge of the place, Vathek, who finding himself that morning but ill at ease had gone forth before the dawn, presented himself on a sudden to her view. Motionless with surprise he durst not approach the figure before him, which lay shrouded up in a simar, extended on the ground, trembling and pale, but yet lovely to behold. At length Nouronihar, with a mixture of pleasure and affliction, raising her fine eyes to him, said:

'My lord! are you come hither to eat rice and hear sermons with me?'

'Beloved phantom!' cried Vathek, 'dost thou speak? hast thou the same graceful form? the same radiant features? art thou palpable likewise?' and, eagerly embracing her, added, 'Here are limbs and a bosom animated with a gentle warmth! What can such a prodigy mean?'

Nouronihar with diffidence answered, 'You know, my lord, that I died on the night you honoured me with your visit. My cousin maintains it was from one of your glances, but I cannot believe him, for to me they seem not so dreadful. Gulchenrouz died with me, and we were both brought in a region of desolation, where we are fed with a wretched diet. If you be dead also, and are come hither to join us, I pity your lot, for you will be stunned with the noise of the dwarfs and the storks. Besides, it is mortifying in the extreme that you, as well as myself, should have lost the treasures of the subterranean palace.'

At the mention of the subterranean palace the Caliph suspended his caresses, which, indeed, had proceeded pretty far, to seek from Nouronihar an explanation of her meaning. She then recapitulated her vision, what immediately followed, and the history of her pretended death, adding also a description of the place of expiation whence she had fled, and all in a manner that would have extorted his laughter, had not the thoughts of Vathek been too deeply engaged. No sooner, however, had she ended than he again clasped her to his bosom, and said:

'Light of my eyes! the mystery is unravelled; we both are alive! Your father is a cheat who, for the sake of dividing, hath deluded us both. And the Giaour, whose design, as far as

I can discover, is that we shall proceed together, seems scarce a whit better; it shall be some time at least before he find us in his palace of fire. Your lovely little person in my estimation is far more precious than all the treasures of the pre-Adamite Sultans, and I wish to possess it at pleasure, and in open day, for many a moon, before I go to burrow underground like a mole. Forget this little trifler, Gulchenrouz, and——'

'Ah! my lord!' interposed Nouronihar, 'let me entreat that you do him no evil.'

'No, no!' replied Vathek, 'I have already bid you forbear to alarm yourself for him. He has been brought up too much on milk and sugar to stimulate my jealousy. We will leave him with the dwarfs, who, by-the-by, are my old acquaintants; their company will suit him far better than yours. As to other matters, I will return no more to your father's. I want not to have my ears dinned by him and his dotards with the violation of the rites of hospitality, as if it were less an honour for you to espouse the Sovereign of the world than a girl dressed up like a boy!'

Nouronihar could find nothing to oppose in a discourse so eloquent; she only wished the amorous monarch had discovered more ardour for the carbuncle of Giamschid; but flattered herself it would gradually increase, and therefore yielded to his will with the most bewitching submission.

When the Caliph judged it proper he called for Bababalouk, who was asleep in the cave of Meimoune, and dreaming that the phantom of Nouronihar, having mounted him once more on her swing, had just given him such a jerk that he one moment soared above the mountains and the next sunk into the abyss. Starting from his sleep at the voice of his master, he ran gasping for breath, and had nearly fallen backward at the sight, as he believed, of the spectre by whom he had so lately been haunted in his dream.

'Ah, my lord!' cried he, recoiling ten steps, and covering his eyes with both hands, 'do you then perform the office of a ghoul? 'Tis true you have dug up the dead, yet hope not to make her your prey, for after all she hath caused me to suffer she is even wicked enough to prey upon you.'

'Cease thy folly,' said Vathek, 'and thou shalt soon be convinced that it is Nouronihar herself, alive and well, whom I clasp to my breast. Go only and pitch my tents in the neighbouring valley; there will I fix my abode with this beautiful tulip, whose colours I soon shall restore; there exert thy best endeavours to procure whatever can augment the enjoyments of life, till I shall disclose to thee more of my will.'

The news of so unlucky an event soon reached the ears of the Emir, who abandoned himself to grief and despair, and began, as did all his old greybeards, to begrime his visage with ashes. A total supineness ensued, travellers were no longer entertained, no more plasters were spread, and, instead of the charitable activity that had distinguished this asylum, the whole of its inhabitants exhibited only faces of a half-cubit long, and uttered groans that accorded with their forlorn situation.

Though Fakreddin bewailed his daughter as lost to him for ever, yet Gulchenrouz was not forgotten. He despatched immediate instruction to Sutlememe, Shaban, and the dwarfs, enjoining them not to undeceive the child in respect to his state, but, under some pretence, to convey him far from the lofty rock at the extremity of the lake, to a place which he should appoint, as safer from danger, for he suspected that Vathek intended him evil.

Gulchenrouz in the meanwhile was filled with amazement at not finding his cousin, nor were the dwarfs at all less surprised; but Sutlememe, who had more penetration, immediately guessed what had happened. Gulchenrouz was amused with the delusive hope of once more embracing Nouronihar in the interior recesses of the mountains, where the ground, strewed over with orange blossoms and jasmines, offered beds much more inviting than the withered leaves in their cabin, where they might accompany with their voices the sounds of their lutes, and chase butterflies in concert. Sutlememe was far gone in this sort of description when one of the four eunuchs beckoned her aside to apprise her of the arrival of a messenger from their fraternity, who had explained the secret of the flight of Nouronihar, and brought the commands of the Emir. A council with Shaban and the dwarfs was immediately held. Their baggage being stowed in consequence of it, they embarked in a shallop and quietly sailed with the little one, who acquiesced in all their proposals. Their voyage proceeded in the same manner till they came to the place where the lake sinks beneath the hollow of the rock; but as soon as the bark had entered it, and Gulchenrouz found himself surrounded with darkness, he was seized with a dreadful consternation, and incessantly uttered the most piercing outcries, for he now was persuaded he should actually be damned for having taken too many little freedoms in his lifetime with his cousin.

But let us return to the Caliph and her who ruled over his heart. Bababalouk had pitched the tents and closed up the extremities of the valley with magnificent screens of India cloth, which were guarded by Ethiopian slaves with their drawn sabres. To preserve the verdure of this beautiful enclosure in its natural freshness the white eunuchs went continually round it with their red water vessels. The waving of fans was heard near the imperial pavilion, where, by the voluptuous light that glowed through the muslins, the Caliph enjoyed at full view all the attractions of Nouronihar. Inebriated with delight he was all ear to her charming voice, which accompanied the lute, while she was not less captivated with his descriptions of Samarah and the tower full of wonders, but especially with his relation of the adventure of the ball, and the chasm of the Giaour with its ebony portal.

In this manner they conversed for a day and a night; they bathed together in a basin of black marble, which admirably relieved the fairness of Nouronihar. Bababalouk, whose good graces this beauty had regained, spared no attention that their repasts might be served up with the minutest exactness; some exquisite rarity was ever placed before them; and he sent even to Shiraz for that fragrant and delicious wine, which had been hoarded up in bottles prior to the birth of Mahomet. He had excavated little ovens in the rock to bake the nice manchets which were prepared by the hands of Nouronihar, whence they had derived a flavour so grateful to Vathek that he regarded the ragouts of his other wives as entirely maukish; whilst they would have died at the Emir's of chagrin at finding themselves so neglected, if Fakreddin, notwithstanding his resentment, had not taken pity upon them.

The Sultana Dilara, who till then had been the favourite,

took this dereliction of the Caliph to heart with a vehemence
natural to her character; for during her continuance in favour
she had imbibed from Vathek many of his extravagant fancies,
and was fired with impatience to behold the superb tombs of
Istakar, and the palace of forty columns; besides, having been
brought up amongst the Magi, she had fondly cherished the
idea of the Caliph's devoting himself to the worship of fire;
thus his voluptuous and desultory life with her rival was to
her a double source of affliction. The transient piety of Vathek
had occasioned her some serious alarms, but the present was
an evil of far greater magnitude; she resolved, therefore,
without hesitation, to write to Carathis, and acquaint her that
all things went ill; that they had eaten, slept, and revelled
at an old Emir's, whose sanctity was very formidable, and
that after all the prospect of possessing the treasures of the
pre-Adamite Sultans was no less remote than before. This
letter was entrusted to the care of two woodmen, who were
at work on one of the great forests of the mountains, and,
being acquainted with the shortest cuts, arrived in ten days
at Samarah.

The Princess Carathis was engaged at chess with Morakanabad, when the arrival of these wood-fellers was
announced. She, after some weeks of Vathek's absence, had
forsaken the upper regions of her tower, because everything
appeared in confusion among the stars, which she consulted
relative to the fate of her son. In vain did she renew her fumiga-
tions, and extend herself on the roof to obtain mystic visions.
Nothing more could she see in her dreams than pieces of
brocade, nosegays of flowers, and other unmeaning gewgaws.

These disappointments had thrown her into a state of
dejection, which no drug in her power was sufficient to
remove. Her only resource was in Morakanabad, who was a
good man, and endowed with a decent share of confidence,
yet whilst in her company he never thought himself on roses.

No person knew aught of Vathek, and a thousand ridiculous stories were propagated at his expense. The eagerness of
Carathis may be easily guessed at receiving the letter, as well
as her rage at reading the dissolute conduct of her son.

'Is it so?' said she; 'either I will perish, or Vathek shall
enter the palace of fire. Let me expire in flames, provided

he may reign on the throne of Soliman!' Having said this, and whirled herself round in a magical manner, which struck Morakanabad with such terror as caused him to recoil, she ordered her great camel Alboufaki to be brought, and the hideous Nerkes with the unrelenting Cafour to attend.

'I require no other retinue,' said she to Morakanabad; 'I am going on affairs of emergency, a truce therefore to parade! Take you care of the people, fleece them well in my absence; for we shall expend large sums, and one knows not what may betide.'

The night was uncommonly dark, and a pestilential blast ravaged the plain of Catoul that would have deterred any other traveller, however urgent the call; but Carathis enjoyed most whatever filled others with dread. Nerkes concurred in opinion with her, and Cafour had a particular predilection for a pestilence. In the morning this accomplished caravan, with the wood-fellers who directed their route, halted on the edge of an extensive marsh, whence so noxious a vapour arose as would have destroyed any animal but Alboufaki, who naturally inhaled these malignant fogs. The peasants entreated their convoy not to sleep in this place.

'To sleep,' cried Carathis, 'what an excellent thought! I never sleep but for visions; and, as to my attendants, their occupations are too many to close the only eye they each have.'

The poor peasants, who were not over-pleased with their party, remained open-mouthed with surprise.

Carathis alighted, as well as her negresses, and severally stripping off their outer garments they all ran in their drawers, to cull from those spots where the sun shone fiercest the venomous plants that grew on the marsh. This provision was made for the family of the Emir, and whoever might retard the expedition to Istakar. The woodmen were overcome with fear when they beheld these three horrible phantoms run, and, not much relishing the company of Alboufaki, stood aghast at the command of Carathis to set forward, notwithstanding it was noon, and the heat fierce enough to calcine even rocks. In spite, however, of every remonstrance, they were forced implicitly to submit.

Alboufaki, who delighted in solitude, constantly snorted

whenever he perceived himself near a habitation; and Carathis, who was apt to spoil him with indulgence, as constantly turned him aside, so that the peasants were precluded from procuring subsistence, for the milch goats and ewes, which Providence had sent towards the district they traversed to refresh travellers with their milk, all fled at the sight of the hideous animal and his strange riders. As to Carathis, she needed no common aliment, for her invention had previously furnished her with an opiate to stay her stomach, some of which she imparted to her mutes.

At the fall of night Alboufaki, making a sudden stop, stamped with his foot, which to Carathis, who understood his paces, was a certain indication that she was near the confines of some cemetery. The moon shed a bright light on the spot, which served to discover a long wall, with a large door in it standing ajar, and so high that Alboufaki might easily enter. The miserable guides, who perceived their end approaching, humbly implored Carathis, as she had now so good an opportunity, to inter them, and immediately gave up the ghost. Nerkes and Cafour, whose wit was of a style peculiar to themselves, were by no means parsimonious of it on the folly of these poor people, nor could anything have been found more suited to their tastes than the site of the burying-ground and the sepulchres which its precincts contained. There were at least two thousand of them on the declivity of a hill—some in the form of pyramids, others like columns, and, in short, the variety of their shapes was endless. Carathis was too much immersed in her sublime contemplations to stop at the view, charming as it appeared in her eyes. Pondering the advantages that might accrue from her present situation, she could not forbear to exclaim:

'So beautiful a cemetery must be haunted by ghouls! and they want not for intelligence. Having heedlessly suffered my guides to expire, I will apply for directions to them, and as an inducement will invite them to regale on these fresh corpses.'

After this short soliloquy she beckoned to Nerkes and Cafour, and made signs with her fingers, as much as to say:

'Go, knock against the sides of the tombs, and strike up your delightful warblings, that are so like to those of the guests whose company I wish to obtain.'

The negresses, full of joy at the behests of their mistress, and promising themselves much pleasure from the society of the ghouls, went with an air of conquest, and began their knockings at the tombs. As their strokes were repeated a hollow noise was heard in the earth, the surface hove up into heaps, and the ghouls on all sides protruded their noses, to inhale the effluvia which the carcasses of the woodmen began to emit.

They assembled before a sarcophagus of white marble, where Carathis was seated between the bodies of her miserable guides. The Princess received her visitants with distinguished politeness, and, when supper was ended, proceeded with them to business. Having soon learnt from them everything she wished to discover, it was her intention to set forward forthwith on her journey, but her negresses, who were forming tender connections with the ghouls, importuned her with all their fingers to wait at least till the dawn. Carathis, however, being chastity in the abstract, and an implacable enemy to love and repose, at once rejected their prayer, mounted Alboufaki, and commanded them to take their seats in a moment. Four days and four nights she continued her route, without turning to the right hand or left; on the fifth she traversed the mountains and half-burnt forests, and arrived on the sixth before the beautiful screens which concealed from all eyes the voluptuous wanderings of her son.

It was daybreak, and the guards were snoring on their posts in careless security, when the rough trot of Alboufaki awoke them in consternation. Imagining that a group of spectres ascended from the abyss was approaching, they all without ceremony took to their heels. Vathek was at that instant with Nouronihar in the bath, hearing tales and laughing at Bababalouk who related them; but no sooner did the outcry of his guards reach him than he flounced from the water like a carp, and as soon threw himself back at the sight of Carathis, who, advancing with her negresses upon Alboufaki, broke through the muslin awnings and veils of the pavilion. At this sudden apparition Nouronihar (for she was not at all times free from remorse) fancied that the moment of celestial vengeance was come, and clung about the Caliph in amorous despondence.

Carathis, still seated on her camel, foamed with indignation at the spectacle which obtruded itself on her chaste view. She thundered forth without check or mercy:

'Thou double-headed and four-legged monster! what means all this winding and writhing? Art thou not ashamed to be seen grasping this limber sapling, in preference to the sceptre of the pre-Adamite Sultans? Is it then for this paltry doxy that thou hast violated the conditions in the parchment of our Giaour? Is it on her thou hast lavished thy precious moments? Is this the fruit of the knowledge I have taught thee? Is this the end of thy journey? Tear thyself from the arms of this little simpleton, drown her in the water before me, and instantly follow my guidance.'

In the first ebullition of his fury Vathek resolved to make a skeleton of Alboufaki, and to stuff the skins of Carathis and her blacks; but the ideas of the Giaour, the palace of Istakar, the sabres and the talismans, flashing before his imagination with the simultaneousness of lightning, he became more moderate, and said to his mother, in a civil but decisive tone:

'Dread lady! you shall be obeyed, but I will not drown Nouronihar; she is sweeter to me than a Myrabolan comfit, and is enamoured of carbuncles, especially that of Giamschid, which hath also been promised to be conferred upon her; she, therefore, shall go along with us, for I intend to repose with her beneath the canopies of Soliman. I can sleep no more without her.'

'Be it so!' replied Carathis, alighting, and at the same time committing Alboufaki to the charge of her women.

Nouronihar, who had not yet quitted her hold, began to take courage, and said with an accent of fondness to the Caliph.

'Dear Sovereign of my soul! I will follow thee, if it be thy will, beyond the Kaf in the land of the Afrits. I will not hesitate to climb for thee the nest of the Simurgh, who, this lady excepted, is the most awful of created existences.'

'We have here then,' subjoined Carathis, 'a girl both of courage and science!'

Nouronihar had certainly both; but, notwithstanding all

her firmness, she could not help casting back a look of regret upon the graces of her little Gulchenrouz, and the days of tenderness she had participated with him. She even dropped a few tears, which Carathis observed, and inadvertently breathed out with a sigh:

'Alas! my gentle cousin! what will become of him?'

Vathek at this apostrophe knitted up his brows, and Carathis inquired what it could mean?

'She is preposterously sighing after a stripling with languishing eyes and soft hair, who loves her,' said the Caliph.

'Where is he?' asked Carathis. 'I must be acquainted with this pretty child, for,' added she, lowering her voice, 'I design before I depart to regain the favour of the Giaour. There is nothing so delicious in his estimation as the heart of a delicate boy, palpitating with the first tumults of love.'

Vathek, as he came from the bath, commanded Bababalouk to collect the women and other movables of his harem, embody his troops, and hold himself in readinesss to march in three days; whilst Carathis retired alone to a tent, where the Giaour solaced her with encouraging visions. But at length waking, she found at her feet Nerkes and Cafour, who informed her by their signs that having led Alboufaki to the borders of a lake, to browse on some moss that looked tolerably venomous, they had discovered certain blue fishes of the same kind with those in the reservoir on the top of the tower.

'Ah! ha!' said she, 'I will go thither to them. These fish are past doubt of a species that, by a small operation, I can render oracular; they may tell me where this little Gulchenrouz is whom I am bent upon sacrificing.' Having thus spoken, she immediately set out with her swarthy retinue.

It being but seldom that time is lost in the accomplishment of a wicked enterprise, Carathis and her negresses soon arrived at the lake, where, after burning the magical drugs with which they were always provided, they, stripping themselves naked, waded to their chins, Nerkes and Cafour waving torches around them, and Carathis pronouncing her barbarous incantations. The fishes with one accord thrust forth their heads from the water, which was violently rippled by the flutter of their fins, and at length finding themselves constrained by the potency of the charm, they opened their piteous mouths, and said:

'From gills to tail we are yours, what seek ye to know?'

'Fishes,' answered she, 'I conjure you, by your glittering scales, tell me where now is Gulchenrouz?'

'Beyond the rock,' replied the shoal in full chorus; 'will this content you?' for we do not delight in expanding our mouths.'

'It will,' returned the Princess; 'I am not to learn that you like not long conversations. I will leave you, therefore, to repose, though I had other questions to propound.' The instant she had spoken the water became smooth, and the fishes at once disappeared.

Carathis, inflated with the venom of her projects, strode hastily over the rock, and found the amiable Gulchenrouz asleep in an arbour, whilst the two dwarfs were watching at his side, and ruminating their accustomed prayers. These diminutive personages possessed the gift of divining whenever an enemy to good Mussulmans approached; thus they anticipated the arrival of Carathis, who, stopping short, said to herself:

'How placidly doth he recline his lovely little head! how pale and languishing are his looks! it is just the very child of my wishes!'

The dwarfs interrupted this delectable soliloquy by leaping instantly upon her, and scratching her face with their utmost zeal. But Nerkes and Cafour, betaking themselves to the succour of their mistress, pinched the dwarfs so severely in return that they both gave up the ghost, imploring Mahomet to inflict his sorest vengeance upon this wicked woman and all her household.

At the noise which this strange conflict occasioned in the valley Gulchenrouz awoke, and, bewildered with terror, sprung impetuously upon an old fig tree that rose against the acclivity of the rocks, thence gained their summits, and ran for two hours without once looking back. At last, exhausted with fatigue, he fell, as if dead, into the arms of a good old Genius, whose fondness for the company of children had made it his sole occupation to protect them, and who, whilst performing his wonted rounds, through the air, happening on the cruel

Giaour at the instant of his growling in the horrible chasm, rescued the fifty little victims which the impiety of Vathek had devoted to his maw. These the Genius brought up in nests still higher than the clouds, and himself fixed his abode in a nest more capacious than the rest, from which he had expelled the possessors that had built it.

These inviolable asylums were defended against the Dives and the Afrits by waving streamers, on which were inscribed in characters of gold, that flashed like lightning, the names of Alla and the Prophet. It was there that Gulchenrouz, who as yet remained undeceived with respect to his pretended death, thought himself in the mansions of eternal peace. He admitted without fear the congratulations of his little friends, who were all assembled in the nest of the venerable Genius, and vied with each other in kissing his serene forehead and beautiful eyelids. This he found to be the state congenial to his soul; remote from the inquietudes of earth, the impertinence of harems, the brutality of eunuchs, and the lubricity of women. In this peaceable society his days, months, and years glided on, nor was he less happy than the rest of his companions, for the Genius, instead of burthening his pupils with perishable riches and the vain sciences of the world, conferred upon them the boon on perpetual childhood.

Carathis, unaccustomed to the loss of her prey, vented a thousand execrations on her negresses for not seizing the child, instead of amusing themselves with pinching to death the dwarfs, from which they could gain no advantage. She returned into the valley murmuring, and finding that her son was not risen from the arms of Nouronihar, discharged her ill-humour upon both. The idea, however, of departing next day for Istakar, and cultivating, through the good offices of the Giaour, an intimacy with Eblis himself, at length consoled her chagrin. But fate had ordained it otherwise.

In the evening, as Carathis was conversing with Dilara, who, through her contrivance, had become of the party, and whose taste resembled her own, Bababalouk came to acquaint her 'that the sky towards Samarah looked of a fiery red, and seemed to portend some alarming disaster.' Immediately, recurring to her astrolabes and instruments of magic, she took the altitude of the planets, and discovered by her calculations, to her great mortification, that a formidable revolt had taken place at Samarah; that Motavakel, availing himself of the disgust which was inveterate against his brother, had incited commotions amongst the populace, made himself master of the palace, and actually invested the great tower, to which Morakanabad had retired, with a handful of the few that still remained faithful to Vathek.

'What!' exclaimed she; 'must I lose then my tower! my mutes! my negresses! my mummies! and, worse than all, the laboratory in which I have spent so many a night! without knowing at least if my hair-brained son will complete his adventure? No! I will not be the dupe! Immediately will I speed to support Morakanabad. By my formidable art the clouds shall sleet hailstones in the faces of the assailants, and shafts of red-hot iron on their heads. I will spring mines of serpents and torpedoes from beneath them and we shall soon see the stand they will make against such an explosion!'

Having thus spoken Carathis hastened to her son, who was tranquilly banqueting with Nouronihar in his superb carnation-coloured tent.

'Glutton that thou art!' cried she, 'were it not for me thou wouldst soon find thyself the commander only of pies. Thy faithful subjects have abjured the faith they swore to thee; Motavakel thy brother now reigns on the hill of pied horses, and had I not some slight resources in the tower would not be easily persuaded to abdicate. But, that time may not be lost, I shall only add four words: Strike tent to-night, set forward, and beware how thou loiterest again by the way. Though thou hast forfeited the conditions of the parchment, I am not yet without hope; for it cannot be denied that thou hast violated to admiration the laws of hospitality, by seducing the daughter of the Emir after having partaken of his bread and his salt. Such a conduct cannot but be delightful to the Giaour, and if on thy march thou canst signalise thyself by an additional crime all will still go well, and thou shalt enter the palace of Soliman in triumph. Adieu! Alboufaki and my negresses are waiting.'

The Caliph had nothing to offer in reply; he wished his mother a prosperous journey, and ate on till he had finished his supper. At midnight the camp broke up, amidst the flourishing of trumpets and other martial instruments; but loud indeed must have been the sound of the tymbals to overpower the blubbering of the Emir and his long-beards, who, by an excessive profusion of tears, had so far exhausted the radical moisture, that their eyes shrivelled up in their sockets, and their hairs dropped off by the roots. Nouronihar, to whom such a symphony was painful, did not grieve to get out of hearing; she accompanied the Caliph in the imperial litter, where they amused themselves with imagining the splendour which was soon to surround them. The other women, overcome with dejection, were dolefully rocked in their cages, whilst Dilara consoled herself with anticipating the joy of celebrating the rites of fire on the stately terraces of Istakar.

In four days they reached the spacious valley of Rocnabad. The season of spring was in all its vigour, and the grotesque branches of the almond trees in full blossom fantastically chequered the clear blue sky; the earth, variegated with hyacinths and jonquils, breathed forth a fragrance which diffused through the soul a divine repose; myriads of bees and scarce fewer of Santons had there taken up their abode; on the banks of the stream hives and oratories were alternately ranged, and their neatness and whiteness were set off by the deep green of the cypresses that spired up amongst them. These pious personages amused themselves with cultivating little gardens that abounded with flowers and fruits, especially musk-melons of the best flavour that Persia could boast; sometimes dispersed over the meadow, they entertained themselves with feeding peacocks whiter than snow, and turtles more blue that the sapphire. In this manner were they occupied when the harbingers of the imperial procession began to proclaim:

'Inhabitants of Rocnabad! prostrate yourselves on the brink of your pure waters, and tender your thanksgivings to heaven that vouchsafeth to show you a ray of its glory; for lo! the Commander of the faithful draws near.'

The poor Santons, filled with holy energy, having bustled to light up wax torches in their oratories and expand the Koran on their ebony desks, went forth to meet the Caliph with baskets of honey-comb, dates, and melons. But, whilst they were advancing in solemn procession and with measured steps, the horses, camels, and guards wantoned over their tulips and other flowers, and made a terrible havoc amongst them. The Santons could not help casting from one eye a look of pity on the ravages committing around them, whilst the other was fixed upon the Caliph and heaven. Nouronihar, enraptured with the scenery of a place which brought back to her remembrance the pleasing solitudes where her infancy had passed, entreated Vathek to stop; but he, suspecting that each oratory might be deemed by the Giaour a distinct habitation, commanded his pioneers to level them all. The Santons stood motionless with horror at the barbarous mandate, and at last broke out into lamentations; but these were uttered with so ill a grace that Vathek bade his eunuchs to kick them from his presence. He then descended from the litter with Nouronihar. They sauntered together in the meadow, and amused themselves with culling flowers and passing a thousand pleasantries on each other. But the bees, who were staunch Mussulmans, thinking it their duty to revenge the insult on their dear masters the Santons, assembled so zealously to do it with effect that the Caliph and Nouronihar were glad to find their tents prepared to receive them.

Bababalouk, who in capacity of purveyor had acquitted himself with applause as to peacocks and turtles, lost no time in consigning some dozens to the spit, and as many more to be fricasseed. Whilst they were feasting, laughing, carousing, and blaspheming at pleasure on the banquet so liberally furnished, the Moullahs, the Sheikhs, the Cadis, and Imans of Shiraz (who seemed not to have met the Santons) arrived, leading by bridles of riband inscribed from the Koran a train of asses, which were loaded with the choicest fruits the country could boast. Having presented their offerings to the Caliph they petitioned him to honour their city and mosques with his presence.

'Fancy not,' said Vathek, 'that you can detain me; your presents I condescend to accept, but beg you will let me be quiet, for I am not over-fond of resisting temptation. Retire then; yet, as it is not decent for personages so reverend to return on foot, and as you have not the appearance of expert riders, my eunuchs shall tie your asses, with the precaution that your backs be not turned towards me, for they understand etiquette.'

In this deputation were some high-stomached Sheikhs, who, taking Vathek for a fool, scrupled not to speak their opinion. These Bababalouk girded with double cords, and, having well disciplined their asses with nettles behind, they all started with a preternatural alertness, plunging, kicking, and running foul of each other in the most ludicrous manner imaginable.

Nouronihar and the Caliph mutually contended who should most enjoy so degrading a sight. They burst out in volleys of laughter to see the old men and their asses fall into the stream; the leg of one was fractured, the shoulder of another dislocated, the teeth of a third dashed out, and the rest suffered still worse.

Two days more, undisturbed by fresh embassies, having been devoted to the pleasures of Rocnabad, the expedition proceeded, leaving Shiraz on the right, and verging towards a large plain, whence were discernible on the edge of the horizon the dark summits of the mountains of Istakar.

At this prospect the Caliph and Nouronihar were unable to repress their transports. They bounded from their litter to the ground, and broke forth into such wild exclamations as amazed all within hearing. Interrogating each other they shouted, 'Are we not approaching the radiant palace of light? or gardens more delightful than those of Sheddad?' Infatuated mortals! they thus indulged delusive conjecture, unable to fathom the decrees of the Most High!

The good Genii, who had not totally relinquished the superintendence of Vathek, repairing to Mahomet in the seventh heaven, said:

'Merciful Prophet! stretch forth thy propitious arm towards thy Vicegerent, who is ready to fall irretrievably into the snare which his enemies, the Dives, have prepared to destroy him. The Giaour is awaiting his arrival in the abominable palace of fire, where, if he once set his foot, his perdition will be inevitable.'

Mahomet answered with an air of indignation:

'He hath too well deserved to be resigned to himself, but I permit you to try if one effort more will be effectual to divert him from pursuing his ruin.'

One of these beneficent Genii, assuming without delay the exterior of a shepherd, more renowned for his piety than all the Dervishes and Santons of the region, took his station near a flock of white sheep on the slope of a hill, and began to pour forth from his flute such airs of pathetic melody as subdued the very soul, and, awakening remorse, drove far from it every frivolous fancy. At these energetic sounds the sun hid himself beneath a gloomy cloud, and the waters of two little lakes, that were naturally clearer than crystal, became of a colour like blood. The whole of this superb assembly was involuntarily drawn towards the declivity of the hill. With downcast eyes they all stood abashed, each upbraiding himself with the evil he had done; the heart of Dilara palpitated, and the chief of the eunuchs with a sigh of contrition implored pardon of the women, whom for his own satisfaction he had so often tormented.

Vathek and Nouronihar turned pale in their litter and, regarding each other with haggard looks, reproached themselves—the one with a thousand of the blackest crimes, a thousand projects of impious ambition—the other with the desolation of her family and the perdition of the amiable Gulchenrouz. Nouronihar persuaded herself that she heard in the fatal music the groans of her dying father, and Vathek the sobs of the fifty children he had sacrificed to the Giaour. Amidst these complicated pangs of anguish they perceived themselves impelled towards the shepherd, whose countenance was so commanding that Vathek for the first time felt overawed, whilst Nouronihar concealed her face with her hands.

The music paused, and the Genius, addressing the Caliph, said:

'Deluded Prince! to whom Providence hath confided the care of innumerable subjects, is it thus that thou fulfillest thy mission? Thy crimes are already completed, and art thou now hastening towards thy punishment? Thou knowest that beyond these mountains Eblis and his accursed Dives hold their infernal empire; and, seduced by a malignant phantom, thou art proceeding to surrender thyself to them! This moment is the last of grace allowed thee; abandon thy atrocious purpose; return; give back Nouronihar to her father, who still retains a few sparks of life; destroy thy tower with all its abominations; drive Carathis from thy councils; be just to thy subjects; respect the ministers of the Prophet; compensate for thy impieties by an exemplary life; and, instead of squandering thy days in voluptuous indulgence, lament thy crimes on the sepulchres of thy ancestors. Thou beholdest the clouds that obscure the sun; at the instant he recovers his splendour, if thy heart be not changed, the time of mercy assigned thee will be past for ever.'

Vathek, depressed with fear, was on the point of prostrating himself at the feet of the shepherd, whom he perceived to be of a nature superior to man; but, his pride prevailing, he audaciously lifted his head, and, glancing at him one of his terrible looks, said:

'Whoever thou art, withhold thy useless admonitions; thou wouldst either delude me, or art thyself deceived. If what I have done be so criminal as thou pretendest, there remains not for me a moment of grace. I have traversed a sea of blood to acquire a power which will make thy equals tremble; deem not that I shall retire when in view of the port, or that I will relinquish her who is dearer to me than either my life or thy mercy. Let the sun appear! let him illumine my career! it matters not where it may end.'

On uttering these words, which made even the Genius shudder, Vathek threw himself into the arms of Nouronihar, and commanded that his horses should be forced back to the road.

There was no difficulty in obeying these orders, for the attraction had ceased. The sun shone forth in all his glory, and the shepherd vanished with a lamentable scream.

The fatal impression of the music of the Genius remained notwithstanding in the heart of Vathek's attendants. They viewed each other with looks of consternation. At the approach of night almost all of them escaped, and of this numerous assemblage there only remained the chief of the eunuchs, some idolatrous slaves, Dilara and a few other women, who, like herself, were votaries of the religion of the Magi.

The Caliph, fired with the ambition of prescribing laws to the Intelligences of Darkness, was but little embarrassed at this dereliction; the impetuosity of his blood prevented him from sleeping, nor did he encamp any more as before. Nouronihar, whose impatience, if possible, exceeded his own, importuned him to hasten his march, and lavished on him a thousand caresses to beguile all reflection. She fancied herself already more potent than Balkis, and pictured to her imagination the Genii falling prostrate at the foot of her throne. In this manner they advanced by moonlight, till they came within view of the two towering rocks that form a kind of portal to the valley, at whose extremity rose the vast ruins of Istakar. Aloft on the mountain glimmered the fronts of various royal mausoleums, the horror of which was deepened by the shadows of night. They passed through two villages almost deserted, the only inhabitants remaining being a few feeble old men, who, at the sight of horses and litters, fell upon their knees and cried out:

'O heaven! is it then by these phantoms that we have been for six months tormented? Alas! it was from the terror of these spectres and the noise beneath the mountains that our people have fled, and left us at the mercy of maleficent spirits!'

The Caliph, to whom these complaints were but unpromising auguries, drove over the bodies of these wretched old men, and at length arrived at the foot of the terrace of black marble. There he descended from his litter, handing down Nouronihar. Both with beating hearts stared wildly around them, and expected with an apprehensive shudder the approach of the Giaour; but nothing as yet announced his appearance.

A deathlike stillness reigned over the mountain and through the air; the moon dilated on a vast platform the shades of the lofty columns, which reached from the terrace almost to the clouds; the gloomy watch-towers, whose numbers could not be counted, were veiled by no roof, and their capitals, of an architecture unknown in the records of the earth, served as an asylum for the birds of darkness, which, alarmed at the approach of such visitants, fled away croaking.

The chief of the eunuchs, trembling with fear, besought
Vathek that a fire might be kindled.

'No!' replied he, 'there is no time left to think of such trifles.
Abide where thou art, and expect my commands.'

Having thus spoken he presented his hand to Nouronihar,
and, ascending the steps of a vast staircase, reached the
terrace, which was flagged with squares of marble, and
resembled a smooth expanse of water, upon whose surface
not a leaf ever dared to vegetate. On the right rose the watch-
towers, ranged before the ruins of an immense palace, whose
walls were embossed with various figures. In front stood forth
the colossal forms of four creatures, composed of the leopard
and the griffin; and, though but of stone, inspired emotions
of terror. Near these were distinguished by the splendour of
the moon, which streamed full on the place, characters like
those on the sabres of the Giaour, that possessed the same
virtue of changing every moment. These, after vacillating for
some time, at last fixed in Arabic letters, and prescribed to the
Caliph the following words:

'Vathek! thou hast violated the conditions of my parchment,
and deservest to be sent back; but, in favour to thy companion,
and as the meed for what thou hast done to obtain it, EBLIS
permitteth that the portal of his palace shall be opened, and
the subterranean fire will receive thee into the number of its
adorers.'

He scarcely had read these words before the mountain
against which the terrace was reared trembled, and the
watch-towers were ready to topple headlong upon them. The
rock yawned, and disclosed within it a staircase of polished
marble that seemed to approach the abyss. Upon each stair
were planted two large torches, like those Nouronihar had
seen in her vision, the camphorated vapour ascending from
which gathered into a cloud under the hollow of the vault.

This appearance, instead of terrifying, gave new courage
to the daughter of Fakreddin. Scarcely deigning to bid
adieu to the moon and the firmament, she abandoned
without hesitation the pure atmosphere to plunge into these
infernal exhalations. The gait of those impious personages
was haughty and determined. As they descended by the
effulgence of the torches they gazed on each other with

mutual admiration, and both appeared so resplendent that they already esteemed themselves spiritual Intelligences; the only circumstance that perplexed them was their not arriving at the bottom of the stairs. On hastening their descent with an ardent impetuosity they felt their steps accelerated to such a degree that they seemed not walking but falling from a precipice. Their progress, however, was at length impeded by a vast portal of ebony, which the Caliph without difficulty recognised. Here the Giaour awaited them with the key in his hand.

'Ye are welcome,' said he to them, with a ghastly smile, 'in spite of Mahomet and all his dependents. I will now admit you into that palace where you have so highly merited a place.'

Whilst he was uttering these words he touched the enamelled lock with his key, and the doors at once expanded, with a noise still louder than the thunder of mountains, and as suddenly recoiled the moment they had entered.

The Caliph and Nouronihar beheld each other with amazement at finding themselves in a place which, though roofed with a vaulted ceiling, was so spacious and lofty that at first they took it for an immeasurable plain. But their eyes at length growing familiar to the grandeur of the objects at hand, they extended their view to those at a distance, and discovered rows of columns and arcades, which gradually diminished till they terminated in a point, radiant as the sun when he darts his last beams athwart the ocean. The pavement, strewed over with gold dust and saffron, exhaled so subtle an odour as almost overpowered them. They, however, went on, and observed an infinity of censers, in which ambergris and the wood of aloes were continually burning. Between the several columns were placed tables, each spread with a profusion of viands, and wines of every species sparkling in vases of crystal. A throng of Genii and other fantastic spirits of each sex danced lasciviously in troops, at the sound of music which issued from beneath.

In the midst of this immense hall a vast multitude was incessantly passing, who severally kept their right hands on their hearts, without once regarding anything around them. They had all the livid paleness of death; their eyes, deep sunk in their sockets, resembled those phosphoric meteors that glimmer by night in places of interment. Some stalked slowly on, absorbed in profound reverie; some, shrieking with agony, ran furiously about, like tigers wounded with poisoned arrows; whilst others, grinding their teeth in rage, foamed along, more frantic than the wildest maniac. They all avoided each other, and, though surrounded by a multitude that no one could number, each wandered at random, unheedful of the rest, as if alone on a desert which no foot had trodden.

Vathek and Nouronihar, frozen with terror at a sight so baleful, demanded of the Giaour what these appearances might mean, and why these ambulating spectres never withdrew their hands from their hearts.

'Perplex not yourselves,' replied he bluntly, 'with so much at once, you will soon be acquainted with all; let us haste and present you to Eblis.'

They continued their way through the multitude; but, notwithstanding their confidence at first, they were not sufficiently composed to examine with attention the various perspectives of halls and of galleries that opened on the right hand and left, which were all illuminated by torches and braziers, whose flames rose in pyramids to the centre of the vault. At length they came to a place where long curtains, brocaded with crimson and gold, fell from all parts in striking confusion; here the choirs and dances were heard no longer, the light which glimmered came from afar.

After some time Vathek and Nouronihar perceived a gleam brightening through the drapery, and entered a vast tabernacle carpeted with the skins of leopards. An infinity of elders with streaming beards and Afrits in complete armour had prostrated themselves before the ascent of a lofty eminence, on the top of which, upon a globe of fire, sat the formidable Eblis. His person was that of a young man, whose noble and regular features seemed to have been tarnished by malignant vapours; in his large eyes appeared both pride and despair; his flowing hair retained some resemblance to that of an angel of light; in his hand, which thunder had blasted, he swayed the iron sceptre that causes the monster Ouranabad, the Afrits, and all the powers of the abyss to tremble. At his presence the heart of Caliph sunk within him, and for the first time he fell prostrate on his face. Nouronihar, however, though greatly dismayed, could not help admiring the person of Eblis, for she expected to have seen some stupendous Giant. Eblis, with a voice more mild than might be imagined, but such as transfused through the soul the deepest melancholy, said:

'Creatures of clay, I receive you into mine empire; ye are numbered amongst my adorers; enjoy whatever this palace affords; the treasures of the pre-Adamite Sultans, their bickering sabres, and those talismans that compel the Dives to open the subterranean expanses of the mountain of Kaf, which communicate with these; there, insatiable as your curiosity may be, shall you find sufficient to gratify it; you shall possess the exclusive privilege of entering the fortress of Aherman and the halls of Argenk, where are portrayed all creatures endowed with intelligence, and the various animals that inhabited the earth prior to the creation of that contemptible being, whom ye denominate the Father of Mankind.'

Vathek and Nouronihar, feeling themselves revived and encouraged by this harangue, eagerly said to the Giaour:

'Bring us instantly to the place which contains these precious talismans.'

'Come!' answered this wicked Dive, with his malignant grin, 'come! and possess all that my Sovereign hath promised, and more.'

He then conducted them into a long aisle adjoining the tabernacle, preceding them with hasty steps, and followed by his disciples with the utmost alacrity. They reached at length a hall of great extent, and covered with a lofty dome, around which appeared fifty portals of bronze, secured with as many fastenings of iron. A funereal gloom prevailed over the whole scene; here, upon two beds of incorruptible cedar, lay recumbent the fleshless forms of the pre-Adamite Kings, who had been monarchs of the whole earth. They still possessed enough of life to be conscious of their deplorable condition; their eyes retained a melancholy motion; they regarded each other with looks of the deepest dejection; each holding his right hand motionless on his heart; at their feet were inscribed the events of their several reigns, their power, their pride, and their crimes. Soliman Raad, Soliman Daki, and Soliman Di Gian Ben Gian, who, after having chained up the Dives in the dark caverns of Kaf, became so presumptuous as to doubt of the Supreme Power; all these maintained great state, though not to be compared with the eminence of Soliman Ben Daoud.

This king, so renowned for his wisdom, was on the loftiest elevation, and placed immediately under the dome. He appeared to possess more animation than the rest, though from time to time he laboured with profound sighs, and, like his companions, kept his right hand on his heart; yet his countenance was more composed, and he seemed to be listening to the sullen roar of a vast cataract, visible in part through the grated portals. This was the only sound that intruded on the silence of these doleful mansions. A range of brazen vases surrounded the elevation.

'Remove the covers from these cabalistic depositories,' said the Giaour to Vathek, 'and avail thyself of the talismans, which will break asunder all these gates of bronze; and not only render thee master of the treasures contained within them, but also of the spirits by which they are guarded.'

The Caliph, whom this ominous preliminary had entirely disconcerted, approached the vases with faltering footsteps, and was ready to sink with terror when he heard the groans of Soliman. As he proceeded a voice from the livid lips of the Prophet articulated these words:

'In my lifetime I filled a magnificent throne, having on my right hand twelve thousand seats of gold, where the patriarchs and the prophets heard my doctrines; on my left the sages and doctors, upon as many thrones of silver, were present at all my decisions.

'Whilst I thus administered justice to innumerable multitudes, the birds of the air librating over me served as a canopy from the rays of the sun; my people flourished, and my palace rose to the clouds.

'I erected a temple to the Most High, which was the wonder of the universe; but I basely suffered myself to be seduced by the love of women, and a curiosity that could not be restrained by sublunary things.

'I listened to the counsels of Aherman and the daughter of Pharaoh, and adored fire and the hosts of heaven. I forsook the holy city, and commanded the Genii to rear the stupendous palace of Istakar, and the terrace of the watch-towers, each of which was consecrated to a star.

'There for a while I enjoyed myself in the zenith of glory and pleasure; not only men, but supernatural existences, were subject also to my will.

'I began to think, as these unhappy monarchs around had already thought, that the vengeance of Heaven was asleep, when at once the thunder burst my structures asunder and precipitated me hither; where, however, I do not remain, like the other inhabitants, totally destitute of hope, for an angel of light hath revealed that, in consideration of the piety of my early youth, my woes shall come to an end when this cataract shall for ever cease to flow; till then I am in torments, ineffable torments! An unrelenting fire preys on my heart.'

Having uttered this exclamation Soliman raised his hands towards Heaven, in token of supplication, and the Caliph discerned through his bosom, which was transparent as crystal, his heart enveloped in flames. At a sight so full of horror Nouronihar fell back, like one petrified, into the arms of Vathek, who cried out with a convulsive sob:

'O Giaour! whither hast thou brought us? Allow us to depart, and I will relinquish all thou hast promised. O Mahomet! remains there no more mercy?'

'None! none!' replied the malicious Dive. 'Know, miserable Prince! thou art now in the abode of vengeance and despair. Thy heart also will be kindled, like those of the other votaries of Eblis. A few days are allotted thee previous to this fatal period. Employ them as thou wilt; recline on these heaps of gold; command the Infernal Potentates; range at thy pleasure through these immense subterranean domains; no barrier shall be shut against thee. As for me, I have fulfilled my mission; I now leave thee to thyself.'

At these words he vanished.

The Caliph and Nouronihar remained in the most abject affliction; their tears unable to flow, scarcely could they support themselves. At length, taking each other despondingly by the hand, they went faltering from this fatal hall, indifferent which way they turned their steps. Every portal opened at their approach; the Dives fell prostrate before them; every reservoir of riches was disclosed to their view; but they no longer felt the incentives of curiosity, pride, or avarice. With like apathy they heard the chorus of Genii, and saw of stately banquets prepared to regale them. They went wandering on from chamber to chamber, hall to hall, and gallery to gallery, all without bounds or limit, all distinguishable by the same lowering gloom, all adorned with the same awful grandeur, all traversed by persons in search of repose and consolation, but who sought them in vain, for everyone carried within him a heart tormented in flames.

Shunned by these various sufferers, who seemed by their looks to be upbraiding the partners of their guilt, they withdrew from them to wait in direful suspense the moment which should render them to each other the like objects of terror.

'What!' exclaimed Nouronihar; 'will the time come when I shall snatch my hand from thine?'

'Ah!' said Vathek; 'and shall my eyes ever cease to drink from thine long draughts of enjoyment! Shall the moments of our reciprocal ecstasies be reflected on with horror! It was not thou that broughtest me hither. The principles by which Carathis perverted my youth have been the sole cause of my perdition!' Having given vent to these painful expressions he called to an Afrit, who was stirring up one of the braziers, and bade him fetch the Princess Carathis from the palace of Samarah.

After issuing these orders, the Caliph and Nouronihar continued walking amidst the silent crowd, till they heard voices at the end of the gallery. Presuming them to proceed from some unhappy beings, who like themselves were awaiting their final doom, they followed the sound, and found it to come from a small square chamber, where they discovered sitting on sofas five young men of goodly figure, and a lovely female, who were all holding a melancholy conversation by the glimmering of a lonely lamp; each had a gloomy and forlorn air, and two of them were embracing each other with great tenderness. On seeing the Caliph and the daughter of Fakreddin enter they arose, saluted, and gave them place. Then he who appeared the most considerable of the group addressed himself thus to Vathek:

'Strangers! who doubtless are in the same state of suspense with ourselves, as you do not yet bear your hand on your heart, if you are come hither to pass the interval allotted previous to the infliction of our common punishment, condescend to relate the adventures that have brought you to this fatal place, and we in return will acquaint you with ours, which deserve but too well to be heard. We will trace back our crimes to their source, though we are not permitted to repent. This is the only employment suited to wretches like us!'

The Caliph and Nouronihar assented to the proposal, and Vathek began, not without tears and lamentations, a sincere recital of every circumstance that had passed. When the afflicting narrative was closed the young man entered on his own. Each person proceeded in order, and when the fourth prince had reached the midst of his adventures a sudden noise interrupted him, which caused the vault to tremble and to open.

Immediately a cloud descended, which, gradually dissipating, discovered Carathis on the back of an Afrit, who grievously complained of his burden. She, instantly springing to the ground, advanced towards her son and said:

'What dost thou here in this little square chamber? As the Dives are become subject to thy beck, I expected to have found thee on the throne of the pre-Adamite Kings.'

'Execrable woman!' answered the Caliph, 'cursed be the day thou gavest me birth! Go, follow this Afrit, let him conduct thee to the hall of the Prophet Soliman: there thou wilt learn to what these palaces are destined, and how much I ought to abhor the impious knowledge thou hast taught me.'

'Has the height of power, to which thou art arrived, turned thy brain?' answered Carathis: 'but I ask no more than permission to shew my respect for Soliman the Prophet. It is, however, proper thou shouldest know that (as the Afrit has informed me neither of us shall return to Samarah) I requested his permission to arrange my affairs; and he politely consented. Availing myself, therefore, of the few moments allowed me, I set fire to the tower, and consumed in it the mutes, negresses, and serpents, which have rendered me so much good service: nor should I have been less kind to Morakanabad, had he not prevented me, by deserting at last

to thy brother. As for Bababalouk, who had the folly to return
to Samarah, to provide husbands for thy wives, I undoubtedly
would have put him to the torture; but being in a hurry, I
only hung him, after having decoyed him in a snare, with thy
wives: whom I buried alive by the help of my negresses; who
thus spent their last moments greatly to their satisfaction. With
respect to Dilara, who ever stood high in my favour, she hath
evinced the greatness of her mind, by fixing herself near, in
the service of one of the magi; and, I think, will soon be one
of our society.'

Vathek, too much cast down to express the indignation
excited by such a discourse, ordered the Afrit to remove
Carathis from his presence, and continued immersed in
thoughts which his companions durst not disturb.

Carathis, however, eagerly entered the dome of Soliman,
and, without regarding in the least the groans of the Prophet,
undauntedly removed the covers of the vases, and violently
seized on the talismans. Then, with a voice more loud than
had hitherto been heard within these mansions, she compelled
the Dives to disclose to her the most secret treasures, the most
profound stores, which the Afrit himself had not seen; she
passed by rapid descents known only to Eblis and his most
favoured potentates, and thus penetrated the very entrails
of the earth, where breathes the Sansar, or icy wind of
death; nothing appalled her dauntless soul; she perceived,
however, in all the inmates who bore their hands on their
heart a little singularity not much to her taste. As she was
emerging from one of the abysses Eblis stood forth to her view,
but, notwithstanding he displayed the full effulgence of his
infernal majesty, she preserved her countenance unaltered,
and even paid her compliments with considerable firmness.

This superb monarch thus answered:

'Princess, whose knowledge and whose crimes have merited
a conspicuous rank in my empire, thou dost well to employ the
leisure that remains, for the flames and torments, which are
ready to seize on thy heart, will not fail to provide thee with
full employment.'

He said this, and was lost in the curtains of his tabernacle.

Carathis paused for a moment with surprise; but, resolved
to follow the advice of Eblis, she assembled all the choirs of

Genii and all the Dives to pay her homage. Thus marched she in triumph through a vapour of perfumes, amidst the acclamations of all the malignant spirits, with most of whom she had formed a previous acquaintance; she even attempted to dethrone one of the Solimans for the purpose of usurping his place, when a voice, proceeding from the abyss of Death, proclaimed:

'ALL IS ACCOMPLISHED!'

Instantaneously the haughty forehead of the intrepid Princess was corrugated with agony; she uttered a tremendous yell, and fixed, no more to be withdrawn, her right hand upon her heart, which was become a receptacle of eternal fire.

In this delirium, forgetting all ambitious projects and her thirst for that knowledge which should ever be hidden from mortals, she overturned the offerings of the Genii, and, having execrated the hour she was begotten and the womb that had borne her, glanced off in a whirl that rendered her invisible, and continued to revolve without intermission.

At almost the same instant the same voice announced to the Caliph, Nouronihar, the five princes, and the princess the awful and irrevocable decree. Their hearts immediately took fire, and they at once lost the most precious of the gifts of heaven—Hope. These unhappy beings recoiled with looks of the most furious distraction. Vathek beheld in the eyes of Nouronihar nothing but rage and vengeance, nor could she discern aught in his but aversion and despair. The two princes who were friends, and till that moment had preserved their attachment, shrunk back, gnashing their teeth with mutual and unchangeable hatred. Kalilah and his sister made reciprocal gestures of imprecation, whilst the two other princes testified their horror for each other by the most ghastly convulsions and screams that could not be smothered. All severally plunged themselves into the accursed multitude, there to wander in an eternity of unabating anguish.

Such was, and such should be, the punishment of unrestrained passions and atrocious actions! Such is, and such should be, the chastisement of blind ambition, that would transgress those bounds which the Creator hath prescribed to human knowledge; and, by aiming at discoveries reserved for pure Intelligence, acquire that infatuated pride which perceives not the condition appointed to man is to be ignorant and humble.

Thus the Caliph Vathek, who, for the sake of empty pomp and forbidden power, had sullied himself with a thousand crimes, became a prey to grief without end and remorse without mitigation, whilst the humble and despised Gulchenrouz passed whole ages in undisturbed tranquillity and the pure happiness of childhood.

Maria Edgeworth

CASTLE RACKRENT

An Hibernian Tale

Taken from Facts, and from the Manners of the Irish
Squires, before the Year 1782

1800

MARIA EDGEWORTH (1767–1849) was the daughter of
Richard Lovell Edgeworth, an Irish gentleman of many talents,
who combined an interest in technology with a concern for
education. He sat in the last Irish parliament, he persuaded
the Government, in 1804, to set up a telegraph between
Dublin and Galway; he was a member of a committee set
up to enquire into the state of education in Ireland. Maria
shared her father's intellectual curiosity and wide interests,
and had besides a literary gift which won the admiration of
Scott and Jane Austen. She collaborated with her father on
the two-volume *Practical Education* (1798), which adopts with
some modification the ideas put forward by Rousseau in *Émile*.
She stoutly defended education for women in *Letters To Literary
Women*, 1795; and altogether it can fairly be said that the two
driving motives of her life were the furtherance of justice for
women, particularly as regards educational opportunity, and
justice for the Irish people.

Castle Rackrent has a secure place in literary history as the
first regional novel, complete with a glossary of unfamiliar
words; but in its irony, its indignation, and the narrative skill
by which the honest Thady is made to convey an impression
of the family completely opposite from the one he imagines
himself to be conveying, it is far more than a statistical first.
It is a little masterpiece, which has never been quite forgotten,
but deserves to be much more widely known.

Maria Edgeworth lived to give succour to many of the
wretched victims of the Irish Famine in 1846. It is a pity that,
after all her efforts to alleviate their lot, she should have had to
witness them reduced to such appalling suffering in the closing
stage of her own life.

References to Maria Edgeworth's 'Glossary', at the end of the
text, are cued by superscript 'g'.

PREFACE

THE prevailing taste of the public for anecdote has been censured and ridiculed by critics, who aspire to the character of superior wisdom: but if we consider it in a proper point of view, this taste is an incontestible proof of the good sense and profoundly philosophic temper of the present times. Of the numbers who study, or at least who read history, how few derive any advantage from their labors! The heroes of history are so decked out by the fine fancy of the professed historian; they talk in such measured prose, and act from such sublime or such diabolical motives, that few have sufficient taste, wickedness or heroism, to sympathize in their fate. Besides, there is much uncertainty even in the best authenticated antient or modern histories; and that love of truth, which in some minds is innate and immutable, necessarily leads to a love of secret memoirs and private anecdotes. We cannot judge either of the feelings or of the characters of men with perfect accuracy from their actions or their appearance in public; it is from their careless conversations, their half finished sentences, that we may hope with the greatest probability of success to discover their real characters. The life of a great or of a little man written by himself, the familiar letters, the diary of any individual published by his friends, or by his enemies after his decease, are esteemed important literary curiosities. We are surely justified in this eager desire to collect the most minute facts relative to the domestic lives, not only of the great and good, but even of the worthless and insignificant, since it is only by a comparison of their actual happiness or misery in the privacy of domestic life, that we can form a just estimate of the real reward of virtue, or the real punishment of vice. That the great are not as happy as they seem, that the external circumstances of fortune and rank do not constitute felicity, is asserted by every moralist; the historian can seldom, consistently with his dignity, pause to illustrate this truth, it is therefore to the biographer we must have recourse. After we have beheld splendid characters playing their parts on the great theatre of the world, with all the advantages of stage effect and decoration, we anxiously beg to be admitted behind the scenes, that we may take a nearer view of the actors and actresses.

Some may perhaps imagine, that the value of biography depends upon the judgment and taste of the biographer; but on the contrary it may be maintained, that the merits of a biographer are inversely as the extent of his intellectual powers and of his literary talents. A plain unvarnished tale is preferable to the most highly ornamented narrative. Where we see that a man has the power, we may naturally suspect that he has the will to deceive us, and those who are used to literary manufacture know how much is often sacrificed to the rounding of a period or the pointing an antithesis.

That the ignorant may have their prejudices as well as the learned cannot be disputed, but we see and despise vulgar errors; we never bow to the authority of him who has no great name to sanction its absurdities. The partiality which blinds a biographer to the defects of his hero, in proportion as it is gross ceases to be dangerous; but if it be concealed by the appearance of candor, which men of great abilities best know how to assume, it endangers our judgment sometimes, and sometimes our morals. If her Grace the Duchess of Newcastle, instead of penning her lord's elaborate eulogium, had undertaken to write the life of Savage, we should not have been in any danger of mistaking an idle, ungrateful libertine, for a man of genius and virtue. The talents of a biographer are often fatal to his reader. For these reasons the public often judiciously countenances those, who without sagacity to discriminate character, without elegance of style to relieve the tediousness of narrative, without enlargement of mind to draw any conclusions from the facts they relate, simply pour forth anecdotes and retail conversations, with all the minute prolixity of a gossip in a country town.

The author of the following memoirs has upon these grounds fair claims to the public favor and attention: he was an illiterate old steward, whose partiality to *the family* in which he was bred and born must be obvious to the reader. He tells the history of the Rackrent family in his vernacular idiom, and in the full confidence that Sir Patrick, Sir Murtagh, Sir Kit, and Sir Condy Rackrent's affairs, will be as interesting to all the world as they were to himself. Those who were acquainted with the manners of a certain class of the gentry of Ireland some years ago, will want no evidence of the truth of honest Thady's narrative: to those who are totally unacquainted with Ireland, the following Memoirs will perhaps be scarcely intelligible, or probably they may appear perfectly incredible. For the information of the *ignorant* English reader a few notes have been subjoined by the editor, and he had it once in contemplation to translate the language of Thady into plain English; but Thady's idiom is incapable of translation, and besides, the authenticity of his story would have been more exposed to doubt if it were not told in his own characteristic manner. Several years ago he related to the editor the history of the Rackrent family, and it was with some difficulty that he was persuaded to have it committed to writing; however, his feelings for '*the honor of the family*,' as he expressed himself, prevailed over his habitual laziness, and he at length completed the narrative which is now laid before the public.

The Editor hopes his readers will observe, that these are 'tales of other times;' that the manners depicted in the following pages are not those of the present age: the race of the Rackrents has long since been extinct in Ireland, and the drunken Sir Patrick, the litigious Sir Murtagh, the fighting Sir Kit, and the slovenly Sir Condy, are characters which could no more be met with at present in Ireland, than Squire Western or Parson Trulliber in England. There is a time when individuals can bear to be rallied for their past follies and absurdities, after they have acquired new habits and a new consciousness. Nations as well as individuals gradually lose attachment to their identity, and the present generation is amused rather than offended by the ridicule that is thrown upon their ancestors.

Probably we shall soon have it in our power, in a hundred instances, to verify the truth of these observations.

When Ireland loses her identity by an union with Great Britain, she will look back with a smile of good-humoured complacency on the Sir Kits and Sir Condys of her former existence.

AN HIBERNIAN TALE

CASTLE RACKRENT

HAVING out of friendship for the family, upon whose estate, praised be Heaven! I and mine have lived rent free time out of mind, voluntarily undertaken to publish the Memoirs of the Rackrent Family, I think it my duty to say a few words, in the first place, concerning myself.—My real name is Thady Quirk, though in the family I have always been known by no other than '*honest Thady*'—afterwards, in the time of Sir Murtagh, deceased, I remember to hear them calling me '*old Thady*;' and now I'm come to 'poor Thady'—for I wear a long great coat* winter and summer, which is very handy, as I never put my arms into the sleeves, (they are as good as new,) though, come Holantide next, I've had it these seven years; it holds on by a single button round my neck, cloak fashion—to look at me, you would hardly think 'poor Thady' was the father of attorney Quirk; he is a high gentleman, and never minds what poor Thady says, and having better than 1500 a-year, landed estate, looks down upon honest Thady,

---

*The cloak, or mantle, as described by Thady, is of high antiquity.—Spencer, in his 'View of the State of Ireland,' proves that it is not, as some have imagined, peculiarly derived from the Scythians, but that 'most nations of the world antiently used the mantle; for the Jews used it, as you may read of Elias's mantle, &c.; the Chaldees also used it, as you may read in Diodorus; the Egyptians likewise used it, as you may read in Herodotus, and may be gathered by the description of Berenice, in the Greek Commentary upon Callimachus; the Greeks also used it anciently, as appeareth by Venus's mantle lined with stars, though afterwards they changed the form thereof into their cloaks, called Pallia, as some of the Irish also use: and the ancient Latins and Romans used it, as you may read in Virgil, who was a very great antiquary, that Evander, when Eneas came to him at his feast, did entertain and feast him, sitting on the ground, and lying on mantles; insomuch as he useth the very word mantile for a mantle,

——————Humi mantilia sternunt.

so that it seemeth that the mantle was a general habit to most nations, and not proper to the Scythians only.'

Spencer knew the convenience of the said mantle, as housing, bedding, and cloathing:

'Iren. Because the commodity doth not countervail the discommodity; for the but I wash my hands of his doings, and as I have lived so will I die, true and loyal to the family.—The family of the Rackrents is, I am proud to say, one of the most ancient in the kingdom.—Every body knows this is not the old family name, which was O'Shaughlin, related to the Kings of Ireland—but that was before my time.—My grandfather was driver to the great Sir Patrick O'Shaughlin, and I heard him, when I was a boy, telling how the Castle Rackrent estate came to Sir Patrick—Sir Tallyhoo Rackrent was cousin-german to him, and had a fine estate of his own, only never a gate upon it, it being his maxim, that a car was the best gate.—Poor gentleman! he lost a fine hunter and his life, at last, by it, all in one day's hunt.—But I ought to bless that day, for the estate came straight into *the* family, upon one condition, which Sir Patrick O'Shaughlin at the time took sadly to heart, they say, but thought better of it afterwards, seeing how large a stake depended upon it, that he should, by Act of Parliament, take and bear the surname and arms of Rackrent.

Now it was that the world was to see what was *in* Sir Patrick.—On coming into the estate, he gave the finest entertainment ever was heard of in the country—not a man could stand after supper but Sir Patrick himself, who could sit out the best man in Ireland, let alone the three kingdoms itself.ᵍ—He had his house, from one year's end to another, as full of company as ever it could hold, and fuller; for rather than be left out of the parties at Castle Rackrent, many gentlemen, and those men of the first consequence and landed estates in the country, such as the O'Neills of Ballynagrotty, and the Moneygawls of Mount Juliet's Town,

inconveniences which thereby do arise, are much more many; for it is a fit house for an outlaw, a meet bed for a rebel, and an apt cloak for a thief.—First, the outlaw being, for his many crimes and villainies, banished from the towns and houses of honest men, and wandering in waste places, far from danger of law, maketh his mantle his house, and under it covereth himself from the wrath of Heaven, from the offence of the earth, and from the sight of men. When it raineth, it is his pent-house; when it bloweth, it is his tent; when it freezeth, it is his tabernacle. In summer he can wear it loose; in winter he can wrap it close; at all times he can use it; never heavy, never cumbersome. Likewise for a rebel it is as serviceable; for in this war that he maketh (if at least it deserve the name of war), when he still flieth from his foe, and lurketh in the *thick woods, (this should be black bogs,)* and straight passages waiting for advantages; it is his bed, yea, and almost his household-stuff.'

and O'Shannons of New Town Tullyhog, made it their choice, often and often, when there was no moon to be had for love or money, in long winter nights, to sleep in the chicken house, which Sir Patrick had fitted up for the purpose of accommodating his friends and the public in general, who honoured him with their company unexpectedly at Castle Rackrent; and this went on, I can't tell you how long—the whole country rang with his praises—Long life to him!—I'm sure I love to look upon his picture, now opposite to me; though I never saw him, he must have been a portly gentleman—his neck something short, and remarkable for the largest pimple on his nose, which, by his particular desire, is still extant in his picture—said to be a striking likeness, though taken when young.—He is said also to be the inventor of raspberry whiskey, which is very likely, as nobody has ever appeared to dispute it with him, and as there still exists a broken punch-bowl at Castle-Stopgap, in the garret, with an inscription to that effect—a great curiosity.—A few days before his death he was very merry; it being his honour's birth-day, he called my great grandfather in, God bless him! to drink the company's health, and filled a bumper himself, but could not carry it to his head, on account of the great shake in his hand—on this he cast his joke, saying, 'What would my poor father say to me if he was to pop out of the grave, and see me now?—I remember, when I was a little boy, the first bumper of claret he gave me after dinner, how he praised me for carrying it so steady to my mouth—Here's my thanks to him—a bumper toast'—Then he fell to singing the favourite song he learned from his father—for the last time, poor gentleman—he sung it that night as loud and hearty as ever, with a chorus—

> He that goes to bed, and goes to bed sober,
> Falls as the leaves do, falls as the leaves do, and dies in October—
> But he that goes to bed, and goes to bed mellow,
> Lives as he ought to do, lives as he ought to do, and dies an honest
> fellow.

Sir Patrick died that night—just as the company rose to drink his health with three cheers, he fell down in a sort of a fit, and was carried off—they sat it out, and were surprised, on enquiry, in the morning, to find it was all over with poor Sir Patrick—Never did any gentleman live and die more beloved in the country by rich and poor—his funeral was such a one as was never known before nor since in the county!—All the gentlemen in the three countries were at it—far and near, how they flocked!—my great grandfather said, that to see all the women even in their red cloaks, you would have taken them for the army drawn out.—Then such a fine whillaluh![g] you might have heard it to the farthest end of the county, and happy the man who could get but a sight of the hearse!—But who'd have thought it? Just as all was going on right, through his own town they were passing, when the body was seized for debt—a rescue was apprehended from the mob—but the heir who attended the funeral was against that, for fear of consequences, seeing that those villains acted under the disguise of the law—So, to be sure, the law must take its course—and little gain had the creditors for their pains. First and foremost, they had the curses of the country; and Sir Murtagh Rackrent the new heir, in the next place, on account of this affront to the body, refused to pay a shilling of the debts, in which he was countenanced by all the best gentlemen of property, and others of his acquaintance, Sir Murtagh alledging in all companies, that he all along meant to pay his father's debts of honor; but the moment the law was taken of him, there was an end of honor to be sure. It was whispered, (but none but the enemies of the family believe it) that this was all a sham seizure to get quit of the debts, which he had bound himself to pay in honor.

It's a long time ago, there's no saying how it was, but this for certain, the new man did not take at all after the old gentleman—The cellars were never filled after his death—and no open house, or any thing as it used to be—the tenants even were sent away without their whiskey[g]—I was ashamed myself, and knew not what to say for the honor of the family—But I made the best of a bad case, and laid it all at my lady's door, for I did not like *her* any how, nor any body else—she was of the family of the Skinflints, and a widow—It was a strange match for Sir Murtagh; the people in the country thought he demeaned himself greatly[g]—but *I* said nothing—I knew how it was—Sir Murtagh was a great lawyer, and looked to the great Skinflint estate; there, however, he overshot himself; for though one of the co-heiresses, he was never the better for her, for she outlived him many's the long day—he could not foresee that, to be sure, when he married her. I must say for her, she made him the best of wives, being a very notable stirring woman, and looking close to every thing. But I always suspected she had Scotch blood in her veins, any thing else I could have looked over in her from a regard to the family. She was a strict observer for self and servants of Lent, and all Fast days, but not holidays. One of the maids having fainted three times the last day of Lent, to keep soul and body together we put a morsel of roast beef into her mouth, which came from Sir Murtagh's dinner, who never fasted, not he; but somehow or other it unfortunately reached my lady's ears, and the priest of the parish had a complaint made of it the next day, and the poor girl was forced as soon as she could walk to do penance for it, before she could get any peace or absolution in the house or out of it. However, my lady was very charitable in her own way. She had a charity school for poor children, where they were taught to read and write gratis, and where they were kept well to spinning gratis for my lady in return; for she had always heaps of duty yarn from the tenants, and got all her household linen out of the estate from first to last; for after the spinning, the weavers on the estate took it in hand for nothing, because of the looms my lady's interest could get from the Linen Board to distribute gratis. Then there was a bleach yard near us, and the tenant dare refuse my lady nothing, for fear of a law-suit Sir Murtagh kept hanging over him about the water course. With these ways of managing, 'tis surprising how cheap my lady got things done, and how proud she was of it. Her table the same way—kept for next to nothing—duty fowls, and duty turkies, and duty geese,^g came as fast as we could eat 'em, for my lady kept a sharp look out, and knew to a tub of butter every thing the tenants had, all round. They knew her way, and what with fear of driving for rent and Sir Murtagh's law-suits, they were kept in such good order, they never thought of coming near Castle Stopgap without a present of something or other—nothing too much

or too little for my lady—eggs—honey—butter—meal—fish
—game, growse, and herrings, fresh or salt—all went for
something. As for their young pigs; we had them, and the best
bacon and hams they could make up, with all young chickens
in spring; but they were a set of poor wretches, and we had
nothing but misfortunes with them, always breaking and
running away—This, Sir Murtagh and my lady said, was all
their former landlord Sir Patrick's fault, who let 'em all get
the half year's rent into arrear—there was something in that,
to be sure—But Sir Murtagh was as much the contrary way—
For let alone making English tenantsg of them, every soul—
he was always driving and driving, and pounding and pounding,
and cantingg and canting, and replevying and replevying,
and he made a good living of trespassing cattle—there was
always some tenant's pig, or horse, or cow, or calf, or goose,
trespassing, which was so great a gain to Sir Murtagh, that
he did not like to hear me talk of repairing fences. Then his
herriots and duty workg brought him in something—his turf
was cut—his potatoes set and dug—his hay brought home,
and in short all the work about his house done for nothing;
for in all our leases there were strict clauses with heavy
penalties, which Sir Murtagh knew well how to enforce—so
many days duty work of man and horse, from every tenant,
he was to have, and had, every year; and when a man vexed
him, why the finest day he could pitch on, when the cratur
was getting in his own harvest, or thatching his cabin, Sir
Murtagh made it a principle to call upon him and his horse—so
he taught 'em all, as he said, to know the law of landlord and
tenant. As for law, I believe no man, dead or alive, ever loved
it so well as Sir Murtagh. He had once sixteen suits pending
at a time, and I never saw him so much himself — roads —
lanes — bogs — wells — ponds — eel-wires — orchards —
trees — tythes — vagrants — gravel-pits — sandpits — dung-
hills and nuisances — every thing upon the face of the earth
furnished him good matter for a suit. He used to boast that he
had a law-suit for every letter in the alphabet. How I used
to wonder to see Sir Murtagh in the midst of the papers in
his office—why he could hardly turn about for them. I made
bold to shrug my shoulders once in his presence, and thanked
my stars I was not born a gentleman to so much toil and

trouble—but Sir Murtagh took me up short with his old proverb, 'learning is better than house or land.' Out of forty-nine suits which he had, he never lost one but seventeeng; the rest he gained with costs, double costs, treble costs sometimes—but even that did not pay. He was a very learned man in the law, and had the character of it; but how it was I can't tell, these suits that he carried cost him a power of money—in the end he sold some hundreds a year of the family estate—but he was a very learned man in the law, and I know nothing of the matter except having a great regard for the family. I could not help grieving when he sent me to post up notices of the sale of the fee simple of the lands and appurtenances of Timoleague.—'I know, honest Thady,' says he to comfort me, 'what I'm about better than you do; I'm only selling to get the ready money wanting, to carry on my suit with spirit with the Nugents of Carricka-shaughlin.'

He was very sanguine about that suit with the Nugents of Carrickashaughlin. He would have gained it, they say, for certain, had it pleased Heaven to have spared him to us, and it would have been at the least a plump two thousand a year in his way; but things were ordered otherwise, for the best to be sure. He dug up a fairy-mount* against my advice, and had no luck afterwards. Though a learned man in the law, he was a little too incredulous in other matters. I warned him that I heard the very Banshee† that my grandfather heard, before I was born long, under Sir Patrick's window a few days before his death. But Sir Murtagh thought nothing of the Banshee,

*These fairy-mountsg are called ant-hills in England. They are held in high reverence by the common people in Ireland. A gentleman, who in laying out his lawn had occasion to level one of these hillocks, could not prevail upon any of his labourers to begin the ominous work. He was obliged to take a *loy* from one of their reluctant hands, and began the attack himself. The labourers agreed, that the vengeance of the fairies would fall upon the head of the presumptuous mortal, who first disturbed them in their retreat.

†The Banshee is a species of aristocratic fairy, who in the shape of a little hideous old woman has been known to appear, and heard to sing in a mournful supernatural voice under the windows of great houses, to warn the family that some of them are soon to die. In the last century every great family in Ireland had a Banshee, who attended regularly, but latterly their visits and songs have been discontinued.

nor of his cough with a spitting of blood, brought on, I understand, by catching cold in attending the courts, and overstraining his chest with making himself heard in one of his favorite causes. He was a great speaker, with a powerful voice; but his last speech was not in the courts at all. He and my lady, though both of the same way of thinking in some things, and though she was as good a wife and great economist as you could see, and he the best of husbands, as to looking into his affairs, and making money for his family; yet I don't know how it was, they had a great deal of sparring and jarring between them.—My lady had her privy purse—and she had her weed ashes,g and her sealing moneyg upon the signing of all the leases, with something to buy gloves besides; and besides again often took money from the tenants, if offered properly, to speak for them to Sir Murtagh about abatements and renewals. Now the weed ashes and the glove money he allowed her clear perquisites; though once when he saw her in a new gown saved out of the weed ashes, he told her to my face, (for he could say a sharp thing) that she should not put on her weeds before her husband's death. But it grew more serious when they came to the renewal businesses. At last, in a dispute about an abatement, my lady would have the last word, and Sir Murtagh grew mad;g I was within hearing of the door, and now wish I had made bold to step in. He spoke so loud, the whole kitchen was out on the stairsg—All on a sudden he stopped, and my lady too. Something has surely happened, thought I—and so it was, for Sir Murtagh in his passion broke a blood-vessel, and all the law in the land could do nothing in that case. My lady sent for five physicians, but Sir Murtagh died, and was buried. She had a fine jointure settled upon her, and took herself away to the great joy of the tenantry. I never said any thing, one way or the other, whilst she was part of the family, but got up to see her go at three o'clock in the morning—'It's a fine morning, honest Thady, says she; good bye to ye'—and into the carriage she stept, without a word more, good or bad, or even half-a-crown; but I made my bow, and stood to see her safe out of sight for the sake of the family.

Then we were all bustle in the house, which made me keep out of the way, for I walk slow and hate a bustle, but the house was all hurry-skurry, preparing for my new master.—Sir Murtagh, I forgot to notice, had no childer,* so the Rackrent estate went to his younger brother—a young dashing officer—who came amongst us before I knew for the life of me whereabouts I was, in a gig or some of them things, with another spark along with him, and led horses, and servants, and dogs, and scarce a place to put any Christian of them into; for my late lady had sent all the feather-beds off before her, and blankets, and household linen, down to the very knife cloths, on the cars to Dublin, which were all her own, lawfully paid for out of her own money—So the house was quite bare, and my young master, the moment ever he set foot in it out of his gig, thought all those things must come of themselves, I believe, for he never looked after any thing at all, but harum-scarum called for every thing as if we were conjurers, or he in a public-house. For my part, I could not bestir myself any how; I had been so used to my late master and mistress, all was upside down with me, and the new servants in the servants' hall were quite out of my way; I had nobody to talk to, and if it had not been for my pipe and tobacco should, I verily believe, have broke my heart for poor Sir Murtagh.

But one morning my new master caught a glimpse of me as I was looking at his horse's heels, in hopes of a word from him—and is that old Thady! says he, as he got into his gig—I loved him from that day to this, his voice was so like the family—and he threw me a guinea out of his waistcoat pocket, as he drew up the reins with the other hand, his horse rearing too; I thought I never set my eyes on a finer figure of a man—quite another sort from Sir Murtagh, though withal *to me*, a family likeness—A fine life we should have led, had he stayed amongst us, God bless him!—he valued a guinea as little as any man—money to him was no more than dirt, and his gentleman and groom, and all belonging to him, the same—but the sporting season over, he grew tired of the place, and having got down a great architect for the house, and an improver for the grounds, and seen their plans and

---

Childer—this is the manner in which many of Thady's rank, and others in Ireland, *formerly* pronounced the word *children*.

elevations, he fixed a day for settling with the tenants, but went off in a whirlwind to town, just as some of them came into the yard in the morning. A circular letter came next post from the new agent, with news that the master was sailed for England, and he must remit 500l. to Bath for his use, before a fortnight was at an end—Bad news still for the poor tenants, no change still for the better with them—Sir Kit Stopgap, my young master, left all to the agent, and though he had the spirit of a Prince, and lived away to the honour of his country abroad, which I was proud to hear of, what were we the better for that at home? The agent was one of your middle men,* who grind the face of the poor, and can never bear a man with a hat upon his head—he ferretted the tenants out of their lives—not a week without a call for money—drafts upon drafts from Sir Kit—but I laid it all to the fault of the agent; for, says I, what can Sir Kit do with so much cash, and he a single man? but still it went.—Rents must be all paid up to the day, and afore—no allowance for improving tenants—no consideration for those who had built upon their farms—No sooner was a lease out, but the land was advertised to the highest bidder—all the old tenants turned out, when they had spent their substance in the hope and trust of a renewal from the landlord.—All was now set at the highest penny to a parcel of poor wretches who meant to run away, and did so, after taking two crops out of the ground.

Middle men.—There was a class of men termed middle men in Ireland, who took large farms on long leases from gentlemen of landed property, and set the land again in small portions to the poor, as under tenants, at exorbitant rents. The *head-landlord*, as he *was* called, seldom saw his *under tenants*, but if he could not get the *middle man* to pay him his rent punctually, he *went to the land, and drove for his rent*, that is to say, he sent his steward or bailiff, or driver, to the land, to seize the cattle, hay, corn, flax, oats or potatoes, belonging to the under-tenants, and proceeded to sell these for his rent; it sometimes happened that these unfortunate tennants paid their rent twice over, once to the *middle man*, and once to the *head landlord*.

The characteristics of a middle man *were*, servility to his superiors, and tyranny towards his inferiors—The poor detested this race of beings. In speaking to them, however, they always used the most abject language, and the most humble tone and posture—'*Please your honour,—and please your honour's honour*,' they knew must be repeated as a charm at the beginning and end of every equivocating, exculpatory, or supplicatory sentence—and they were much more alert in doffing their caps to these new men, than to those of what they call *good old families*.—A witty carpenter once termed these middle men *journeymen-gentlemen*.

Then fining down the year's rent^g came into fashion—any thing for the ready penny, and with all this, and presents to the agent and the driver,^{g} there was no such thing as standing it—I said nothing, for I had a regard for the family, but I walked about, thinking if his honour Sir Kit, (long may he live to reign over us!) knew all this, it would go hard with him, but he'd see us righted—not that I had any thing for my own share to complain of, for the agent was always very civil to me, when he came down into the country, and took a great deal of notice of my son Jason.—Jason Quirk, though he be my son, I must say, was a good scholar from his birth, and a very 'cute lad—I thought to make him a priest,^{g} but he did better for himself—Seeing how he was as good a clerk as any in the county, the agent gave him his rent accounts to copy, which he did first of all for the pleasure of obliging the gentleman, and would take nothing at all for his trouble, but was always proud to serve the family.—By and by, a good farm bounding us to the east fell into his honour's hands, and my son put in a proposal for it; why shouldn't he as well as another?—The proposals all went over too the master at the Bath, who knowing no more of the land than the child unborn, only having once been out a grousing on it before he went to England; and the value of lands as the agent informed him, falling every year in Ireland, his honour wrote over in all haste a bit of a letter, saying he left it all to the agent, and that he must set it as well as he could to the best bidder, to be sure, and send him over £200. by return of post: with this the agent gave me a hint, and I spoke a good word for my son, and gave out in the country, that nobody need bid against us.—So his proposal was just the thing, and he a good tenant; and he got a promise of an abatement in the rent, after the first year, for advancing the half year's rent at signing the lease, which was wanting to compleat the agent's £200, by the return of the post, with all which my master wrote back he was well satisfied.—About this time we learned from the agent, as a great secret, how the money went so fast, and the reason of the thick coming of the master's drafts: he was a little too fond of play, and Bath, they say, was no place for a young man of his fortune, where there were so many of his own countrymen too haunting him up and down, day and night, who had nothing to lose—at last, at Christmas, the agent wrote over to stop the drafts, for he could raise no more money on bond or mortgage, or from the tenants, or any how, nor had he any more to lend himself, and desired at the same time to decline the agency for the future, wishing Sir Kit his health and happiness, and the compliments of the season—for I saw the letter before ever it was sealed, when my son copied it.—When the answer came, there was a new turn in affairs, and the agent was turned out; and my son Jason, who had corresponded privately with his honor occasionally on business, was forthwith desired by his honor to take the accounts into his own hands, and look them over till further orders—It was a very spirited letter, to be sure: Sir Kit sent his service, and the compliments of the season, in return to the agent, and he would fight him with pleasure to-morrow, or any day, for sending him such a letter, if he was born a gentleman, which he was sorry (for both their sakes) to find (too late) he was not.—Then, in a private postscript, he condescended to tell us that all would be speedily settled to his satisfaction, and we should turn over a new leaf, for he was going to be married in a fortnight to the grandest heiress in England, and had only immediate occasion at present for £200, as he would not choose to touch his lady's fortune for travelling expences home to Castle Rackrent, where he intended to be, wind and weather permitting, early in the next month, and desired fires, and the house to be painted, and the new building to go on as fast as possible for the reception of him and his lady before that time—with several words besides in the letter, which we could not make out, because, God bless him! he wrote in such a flurry—My heart warmed to my new lady when I read this; I was almost afraid it was too good news to be true—but the girls fell to scouring, and it was well they did, for we soon saw his marriage in the paper to a lady with I don't know how many tens of thousand pounds to her fortune—then I watched the post-office for his landing, and the news came to my son of his and the bride being in Dublin, and on the way home to Rackrent Gap—We had bonfires all over the country, expecting him down the next day, and we had his coming of age still to celebrate, which he had not time to do properly before he left the country; therefore a great ball was expected, and great doings upon his coming, as it were, fresh to take possession of his ancestors' estate.—I never shall forget the day he came home—we had waited and waited all day long till eleven o'clock at night, and I was thinking of sending the boy to lock the gates, and giving them up for that night, when there come the carriages thundering up to the great hall door—I got the first sight of the bride; for when the carriage door opened, just as she had her foot on the steps, I held the flam^g full in her face to light her, at which she shuts her eyes, but I had a full view of the rest of her, and greatly shocked I was, for by that light she was little better than a blackamoor, and seemed crippled, but that was only sitting so long in the chariot—'You're kindly welcome to Castle Rackrent, my lady,' says I, (recollecting who she was)—'Did your honor hear of the bonfires?' His honor spoke never a word, nor so much as handed her up the steps; he looked to me no more like himself than nothing at all; I know I took him for the skeleton of his honor—I was not sure what to say next to one or t'other, but seeing she was a stranger in a foreign country, I thought it but right to speak chearful to her, so I went back again to the bonfires—'My lady (says I, as she crossed the hall) there would have been fifty times as many, but for fear of the horses and frightening your ladyship—Jason and I forbid them, please your honor.'—With that she looked at me a little bewildered—'Will I have a fire lighted in the state room to-night?' was the next question I put to her—but never a word she answered, so I concluded she could not speak a word of English, and was from foreign parts—The short and the long of it was, I couldn't tell what to make of her, so I left her to herself, and went straight down to the servants' hall to learn something for certain about her. Sir Kit's own man was tired, but the groom set him a talking at last, and we had it all out before ever I closed my eyes that night. The bride might well be a great fortune—she was a *Jewish* by all accounts, who are famous for their great riches. I had never seen any of that tribe or nation before, and could only gather that she spoke a strange kind of English of her own, that she could not abide pork or sausages, and went neither to church nor mass.—Mercy upon his honor's poor soul, thought I, what will become of him and his, and all of us, with this heretic blackamore at the head of the Castle Rackrent estate. I never slept a wink all night for thinking of it, but before the servants I put my pipe in my mouth and kept my mind to myself; for I had a great regard for the family, and after this when strange gentlemen's servants came to the house, and would begin to talk about the bride, I took care to put the best foot foremost, and passed her for a Nabob, in the kitchen, which accounted for her dark complexion, and every thing.

The very morning after they came home, however, I saw how things were, plain enough, between Sir Kit and my lady, though they were walking together arm in arm after breakfast, looking at the new buildings and the improvements. 'Old Thady, (said my master, just as he used to do) how do you do?'—'Very well, I thank your honor's honor,' said I, but I saw he was not well pleased, and my heart was in my mouth as I walked along after him—'Is the large room damp, Thady?' said his honor—'Oh, damp, your honor! how should it but be as dry as a bone, (says I) after all the fires we have kept in it day and night—It's the barrack room^g your honor's talking on'—'And what is a barrack room, pray, my dear'—were the first words I ever heard out of my lady's lips—'No matter, my dear,' said he, and went on talking to me, ashamed like I should witness her ignorance.—To be sure to hear her talk, one might have taken her for an innocent,^g for it was 'what's this, Sir Kit? and what's that, Sir Kit?' all the way we went—To be sure, Sir Kit had enough to do to answer her—'And what do you call that, Sir Kit? (said she) that, that looks like a pile of black bricks, pray Sir Kit?' 'My turf stack, my dear,' said my master, and bit his lip—Where have you lived, my lady, all your life, not to know a turf stack when you see it, thought I, but I said nothing. Then, by-and-by, she takes out her glass and begins spying over the country—'And what's all that black swamp out yonder, Sir Kit?' says she—'My bog, my dear,' says he, and went on whistling—It's a very ugly prospect, my dear,' says she—'You don't see it, my dear, (says he) for we've planted it out, when the trees grow up, in summer time,' says he—'Where are the trees, (said she) my dear,' still looking through her glass—'You are blind, my dear, (says he) what are these under your eyes?'—'These shrubs?'

said she—'Trees,' said he—'May be they are what you call trees in Ireland, my dear, (says she) but they are not a yard high, are they?'—'They were planted out but last year, my lady' says I, to soften matters between them, for I saw she was going the way to make his honor mad with her—'they are very well grown for their age, and you'll not see the bog of Allyballycarricko'shaughlin at all at all through the skreen, when once the leaves come out—But, my lady, you must not quarrel with any part or parcel of Allyballycarricko'shaughlin, for you don't know how many hundred years that same bit of bog has been in the family, we would not part with the bog of Allyballycarricko'shaughlin upon no account at all; it cost the late Sir Murtagh two hundred good pounds to defend his title to it, and boundaries, against the O'Learys, who cut a road through it.'—Now one would have thought this would have been hint enough for my lady, but she fell to laughing like one out of their right mind, and made me say the name of the bog over for her to get it by heart a dozen times—then she must ask me how to spell it, and what was the meaning of it in English—Sir Kit standing by whistling all the while—I verily believe she laid the corner stone of all her future misfortunes at that very instant—but I said no more, only looked at Sir Kit.

There were no balls, no dinners, no doings, the country was all disappointed—Sir Kit's gentleman said, in a whisper to me, it was all my lady's own fault, because she was so obstinate about the cross—'What cross? (says I) is it about her being a heretic?'—'Oh, no such matter, (says he) my master does not mind her heresies, but her diamond cross, it's worth I can't tell you how much, and she has thousands of English pounds concealed in diamonds about her, which she as good as promised to give up to my master before he married, but now she won't part with any of them, and she must take the consequences.'

Her honey-moon, at least her Irish honey-moon, was scarcely well over, when his honour one morning said to me—'Thady, buy me a pig!'—and then the sausages were ordered, and here was the first open breaking out of my lady's troubles—my lady came down herself into the kitchen to speak to the cook about the sausages, and desired never to

see them more at her table.—Now my master had ordered
them, and my lady knew that—the cook took my lady's part,
because she never came down into the kitchen, and was young
and innocent in housekeeping, which raised her pity; besides,
said she, at her own table, surely, my lady should order and
disorder what she pleases—but the cook soon changed her
note, for my master made it a principle to have the sausages,
and swore at her for a Jew herself, till he drove her fairly out
of the kitchen—then for fear of her place, and because he
threatened that my lady should give her no discharge without
the sausages, she gave up, and from that day forward always
sausages or bacon, or pig meat, in some shape or other, went
up to table; upon which my lady shut herself up in her own
room, and my master said she might stay there, with an oath;
and to make sure of her, he turned the key in the door, and
kept it ever after in his pocket—We none of us ever saw
or heard her speak for seven years after that*—he carried

*This part of the history of the Rackrent family can scarcely be thought credible;
but in justice to honest Thady, it is hoped the reader will recollect the history
of the celebrated Lady Cathcart's conjugal imprisonment.—The Editor was
acquainted with Colonel M'Guire, Lady Cathcart's husband; he has lately seen
and questioned the maid-servant who lived with Colonel M'Guire during the
time of Lady Cathcart's imprisonment.—Her Ladyship was locked up in her
own house for many years; during which period her husband was visited by
the neighbouring gentry, and it was his regular custom at dinner to send
his compliments to Lady Cathcart, informing her that the company had the
honor to drink her ladyship's health, and begging to know whether there was
any thing at table that she would like to eat? the answer was always—'Lady
Cathcart's compliments, and she has every thing she wants'—An instance of
honesty in a poor Irishwoman deserves to be recorded.—Lady Cathcart had
some remarkably fine diamonds, which she had concealed from her husband,
and which she was anxious to get out of the house, lest he should discover them:
she had neither servant nor friend to whom she could entrust them; but she
had observed a poor beggar-woman who used to come to the house—she spoke
to her from the window of the room in which she was confined—the woman
promised to do what she desired, and Lady Cathcart threw a parcel, containing
the jewels, to her.—The poor woman carried them to the person to whom they
were directed; and several years afterwards, when Lady Cathcart recovered her
liberty, she received her diamonds safely.

At Colonel M'Guire's death, her ladyship was released.—The Editor, within
this year, saw the gentleman who accompanied her to England after her husband's
death.—When she first was told of his death, she imagined that the news was not
true, and that it was told only with an intention of deceiving her.—At his death she
had scarcely cloaths sufficient to cover her; she wore a red wig, looked scared, and
her understanding seemed stupified; she said that she scarcely knew one human

her dinner himself—then his honour had a great deal of company to dine with him, and balls in the house, and was as gay and gallant, and as much himself as before he was married—and at dinner he always drank my lady Rackrent's good health, and so did the company, and he sent out always a servant, with his compliments to my Lady Rackrent, and the company was drinking her ladyship's health, and begged to know if there was any thing at table he might send her; and the man came back, after the sham errand, with my lady Rackrent's compliments, and she was very much obliged to Sir Kit—she did not wish for any thing, but drank the company's health.—The country, to be sure, talked and wondered at my lady's being shut up, but nobody chose to interfere or ask any impertinent questions, for they knew my master was a man very apt to give a short answer himself, and likely to call a man out for it afterwards—he was a famous shot—had killed his man before he came of age, and nobody scarce dare look at him whilst at Bath.—Sir Kit's character was so well known in the county, that he lived in peace and quietness ever after, and was a great favorite with the ladies, especially when in process of time, in the fifth year of her confinement, my lady Stopgap fell ill, and took entirely to her bed, and he gave out that she was now skin and bone, and could not last through the winter.—In this he had two physicians' opinions to back him (for now he called in two physicians for her), and tried all his arts to get the diamond cross from her on her death bed, and to get her to make a will in his favour of her separate possessions—but she was there too tough for him—He used to swear at her behind her back, after kneeling to her to her face, and call her, in the presence of his gentleman, his stiff-necked Israelite, though before he married her, that same gentleman told me he used to call her (how he could bring it out I don't know!) 'my pretty Jessica'—To be sure, it must have been hard for her to guess what sort of a husband he

creature from another: her imprisonment lasted above twenty years.—These circumstances may appear strange to an English reader; but there is no danger in the present times, that any individual should exercise such tyranny as Colonel M'Guire's with impunity, the power being now all in the hands of government, and there being no possibility of obtaining from Parliament an act of indemnity for any cruelties.

reckoned to make her—when she was lying, to all expectation, on her death-bed, of a broken heart, I could not but pity her, though she was a Jewish; and considering too it was no fault of her's to be taken with my master so young as she was at the Bath, and so fine a gentleman as Sir Kit was when he courted her—and considering too, after all they had heard and seen of him as a husband, there were now no less than three ladies in our county talked of for his second wife, all at daggers drawing with each other, as his gentleman swore, at the balls, for Sir Kit for their partner—I could not but think them bewitched, but they all reasoned with themselves, that Sir Kit would make a good husband to any Christian, but a Jewish, I suppose, and especially as he was now a reformed rake; and it was not known how my lady's fortune was settled in her will, nor how the Castle Rackrent estate was all mortgaged, and bonds out against him, for he was never cured of his gaming tricks—but that was the only fault he had, God bless him!

My lady had a sort of fit, and it was given out she was dead, by mistake; this brought things to a sad crisis for my poor master—one of the three ladies shewed his letters to her brother, and claimed his promises, whilst another did the same. I don't mention names—Sir Kit, in his defence, said he would meet any man who dared question his conduct, and as to the ladies, they must settle it amongst them who was to be his second, and his third, and his fourth, whilst his first was still alive, to his mortification and theirs. Upon this, as upon all former occasions, he had the voice of the country with him, on account of the great spirit and propriety he acted with.—He met and shot the first lady's brother—the next day he called out the second, who had a wooden leg, and their place of meeting by appointment being in a new ploughed field, the wooden leg man stuck fast in it.—Sir Kit seeing his situation, with great candour fired his pistol over his head, upon which the seconds interposed, and convinced the parties there had been a slight misunderstanding between them; thereupon they shook hands cordially, and went home to dinner together.—This gentleman, to shew the world how they stood together, and by the advice of the friends of both parties to re-establish his sister's injured reputation, went out with Sir Kit as his second, and carried his message next day to the last of his adversaries.—I never saw him in such fine spirits as that day he went out—sure enough he was within aims-ace of getting quit handsomely of all his enemies; but unluckily, after hitting the toothpick out of his adversary's finger and thumb, he received a ball in a vital part, and was brought home, in little better than an hour after the affair, speechless, on a hand-barrow, to my lady; we got the key out of his pocket the first thing we did, and my son Jason ran to unlock the barrack-room, where my lady had been shut up for seven years, to acquaint her with the fatal accident.—The surprize bereaved her of her senses at first, nor would she believe but we were putting some new trick upon her, to entrap her out of her jewels, for a great while, till Jason bethought himself of taking her to the window, and shewed her the men bringing Sir Kit up the avenue upon the hand-barrow, which had immediately the desired effect; for directly she burst into tears, and pulling her cross from her bosom, she kissed it with as great devotion as ever I witnessed, and lifting up her eyes to Heaven, uttered some ejaculation, which none present heard—but I take the sense of it to be, she returned thanks for this unexpected interposition in her favour, when she had least reason to expect it.—My master was greatly lamented—there was no life in him when we lifted him off the barrow, so he was laid out immediately, and *waked* the same night.—The country was all in an uproar about him, and not a soul but cried shame upon his murderer, who would have been hanged surely, if he could have been brought to his trial whilst the gentlemen in the county were up about it, but he very prudently withdrew himself to the continent before the affair was made public.—As for the young lady who was the immediate cause of the fatal accident, however innocently, she could never shew her head after at the balls in the county or any place, and by the advice of her friends and physicians she was ordered soon after to Bath, where it was expected, if any where on this side of the grave, she would meet with the recovery of her health and lost peace of mind.—As a proof of his great popularity, I need only add, that there was a song made upon my master's untimely death in the newspapers, which was in everybody's mouth, singing up and down through the country, even down to the mountains, only three days after his unhappy exit.—He was also greatly bemoaned at the Curragh,g where his cattle were well known, and all who had taken up his bets formerly were particularly inconsolable for his loss to society.—His stud sold at the cantg at the greatest price ever known in the country; his favourite horses were chiefly disposed of amongst his particular friends, who would give any price for them for his sake; but no ready money was required by the new heir, who wished not to displease any of the gentlemen of the neighbourhood just upon his coming to settle amongst them; so a long credit was given where requisite, and the cash has never been gathered in from that day to this.

But to return to my lady—She got surprisingly well after my master's decease. No sooner was it known for certain that he was dead, than all the gentlemen within twenty miles of us came in a body as it were, to set my lady at liberty, and to protest against her confinement, which they now for the first time understood was against her own consent. The ladies too were as attentive as possible, striving who should be foremost with their morning visits; and they that saw the diamonds spoke very handsomely of them, but thought it a pity they were not bestowed, if it had so pleased God, upon a lady who would have become them better. All these civilities wrought little with my lady, for she had taken an unaccountable prejudice against the country and every thing belonging to it, and was so partial to her native land, that after parting with the cook, which she did immediately upon my master's decease, I never knew her easy one instant, night or day, but when she was packing up to leave us. Had she meant to make any stay in Ireland, I stood a great chance of being a great favorite with her, for when she found I understood the weather-cock, she was always finding some pretence to be talking to me, and asking me which way the wind blew, and was it likely, did I think, to continue fair for England.—But when I saw she had made up her mind to spend the rest of her days upon her own income and jewels in England, I considered her quite as a foreigner, and not at all any longer as part of the family.—She gave no vails to the servants at Castle Rackrent at parting, notwithstanding the old proverb of '*as rich as a Jew*,' which, she being a Jewish, they built upon with reason—But from first to last she brought nothing but misfortunes amongst us; and if it had not been all along with her, his honor Sir Kit would have been now alive in all appearance.—Her diamond cross was, they say, at the bottom of it all; and it was a shame for her, being his wife, not to show more duty, and to have given it up when he condescended to ask so often for such a bit of a trifle in his distresses, especially when he all along made it no secret he married for money.—But we will not bestow another thought upon her—This much I thought it lay upon my conscience to say, in justice to my poor master's memory.

'Tis an ill wind that blows nobody no good—the same wind that took the Jew Lady Rackrent over to England brought over the new heir to Castle Rackrent.

Here let me pause for breath in my story, for though I had a great regard for every member of the family, yet without compare Sir Conolly, commonly called for short amongst his friends Sir Condy Rackrent, was ever my great favorite, and indeed the most universally beloved man I had ever seen or heard of, not excepting his great ancestor Sir Patrick, to whose memory he, amongst other instances of generosity, erected a handsome marble stone in the church of Castle Rackrent, setting forth in large letters his age, birth, parentage, and many other virtues, concluding with the compliment so justly due, that 'Sir Patrick Rackrent lived and died a monument of old Irish hospitality.'

CONTINUATION OF THE MEMOIRS
OF THE
RACKRENT FAMILY

HISTORY OF SIR CONOLLY RACKRENT

SIR CONDY RACKRENT, by the grace of God heir at law to the Castle Rackrent estate, was a remote branch of the family: born to little or no fortune of his own, he was bred to the bar, at which having many friends to push him, and no mean natural abilities of his own, he doubtless would in process of time, if he could have borne the drudgery of that study, have been rapidly made king's counsel at the least—But things were disposed of otherwise, and he never went circuit but twice, and then made no figure for want of a fee, and being unable to speak in public. He received his education chiefly in the college of Dublin; but before he came to years of discretion, lived in the country in a small but slated house, within view of the end of the avenue. I remember him barefooted and headed, running through the street of O'Shaughlin's town, and playing at pitch and toss, ball, marbles, and what not, with the boys of the town, amongst whom my son Jason was a great favourite with him. As for me, he was ever my white-headed boy*—often's the time when I would call in at his father's, where I was always made welcome, he would slip down to me in the kitchen, and love to sit on my knee whilst I told him stories of the family and the blood from which he was sprung, and how he might look forward, if the *then* present man should die without childer, to being at the head of the Castle Rackrent estate.—This was then spoke quite and clear at random to please the child, but it pleased Heaven to accomplish my prophecy afterwards, which gave him a great opinion of my judgment in business. He went to a little grammar school with many others, and my son amongst the rest, who was in his class, and not a little useful to him in his book learning, which he acknowledged with gratitude ever after. These rudiments of his education thus completed, he got a horseback, to which exercise he was ever addicted, and used to gallop over the country whilst yet but a slip of a boy, under the care of Sir Kit's huntsman, who was very fond of him, and often lent him his gun and took him out a shooting under his own eye. By these means he became well acquainted and popular amongst the poor in the neighbourhood early, for there was not a cabin at which he had not stopped some morning or other along with the huntsman, to drink a glass of burnt whiskey out of an egg-shell, to do him good, and warm his heart, and drive the cold out of his stomach.—The old people always told him he was a great likeness of Sir Patrick,

---

White-headed boy—is used by the Irish as an expression of fondness.—It is upon a par with the English term *crony*.—We are at a loss for the derivation of this term.

which made him first have an ambition to take after him, as
far as his fortune should allow. He left us when of an age
to enter the college, and there completed his education and
nineteenth year; for as he was not born to an estate, his
friends thought it incumbent on them to give him the best
education which could be had for love or money, and a great
deal of money consequently was spent upon him at college and
Temple—He was very little altered for the worse, by what he
saw there of the great world, for when he came down into the
country to pay us a visit we thought him just the same man as
ever, hand and glove with every one, and as far from high,
though not without his own proper share of family pride, as
any man ever you see. Latterly, seeing how Sir Kit and the
Jewish lived together, and that there was no one between him
and the Castle Rackrent estate, he neglected to apply to the
law as much as was expected of him, and secretly many of
the tenants, and others, advanced him cash upon his note of
hand value received, promising bargains of leases and lawful
interest should he ever come into the estate.—All this was
kept a great secret, for fear the present man hearing of it
should take it into his head to take it ill of poor Condy,
and so should cut him off for ever by levying a fine, and
suffering a recovery to dock the entail—Sir Murtagh would
have been the man for that, but Sir Kit was too much taken
up philandering to consider the law in this case—or any
other.—These practices I have mentioned account for the
state of his affairs, I mean Sir Condy's, upon his coming into
the Castle Rackrent estate.—He could not command a penny
of his first year's income, which, and keeping no accounts, and
the great sight of company he did, with many other causes too
numerous to mention, was the origin of his distresses.—My
son Jason, who was now established agent, and knew every
thing, explained matters out of the face to Sir Conolly, and
made him sensible of his embarrassed situation. With a great
nominal rent-roll, it was almost all paid away in interest, which
being for convenience suffered to run on, soon doubled the
principal, and Sir Condy was obligated to pass new bonds
for the interest, now grown principal, and so on. Whilst this
was going on, my son requiring to be paid for his trouble,
and many years service in the family gratis, and Sir Condy

not willing to take his affairs into his own hands, or to look them even in the face, he gave my son a bargain of some acres which fell out of lease at a reasonable rent; Jason set the land as soon as his lease was sealed to under-tenants, to make the rent, and got two hundred a year profit rent, which was little enough, considering his long agency.—He bought the land at twelve years purchase two years afterwards, when Sir Condy was pushed for money on an execution, and was at the same time allowed for his improvements thereon. There was a sort of hunting lodge upon the estate convenient to my son Jason's land, which he had his eye upon about this time; and he was a little jealous of Sir Condy, who talked of setting it to a stranger, who was just come into the country—Captain Moneygawl was the man; he was son and heir to the Moneygawls of Mount Juliet's town, who had a great estate in the next county to ours, and my master was loth to disoblige the young gentleman, whose heart was set upon the lodge; so he wrote him back that the lodge was at his service, and if he would honor him with his company at Castle Rackrent, they could ride over together some morning and look at it before signing the lease.—Accordingly the Captain came over to us, and he and Sir Condy grew the greatest friends ever you see, and were for ever out a shooting or a hunting together, and were very merry in the evenings, and Sir Condy was invited of course to Mount Juliet's town, and the family intimacy that had been in Sir Patrick's time was now recollected, and nothing would serve Sir Condy but he must be three times a week at the least with his new friends—which grieved me, who knew by the Captain's groom and gentleman how they talked of him at Mount Juliet's town, making him quite, as one may say, a laughing stock and a butt for the whole company: but they were soon cured of *that* by an accident that surprised 'em not a little, as it did me.—There was a bit of a scrawl found upon the waiting maid of old Mr. Moneygawl's youngest daughter Miss Isabella, that laid open the whole; and her father, they say, was like one out of his right mind, and swore it was the last thing he ever should have thought of when he invited my master to his house, that his daughter should think of such a match.—But their talk signified not a straw; for as Miss

Isabella's maid reported, her young mistress was fallen over head and ears in love with Sir Condy, from the first time that ever her brother brought him into the house to dinner: the servant who waited that day behind my master's chair was the first who knew it, as he says; though it's hard to believe him, for he did not tell till a great while afterwards; but however, it's likely enough as the thing turned out that he was not far out of the way; for towards the middle of dinner, as he says, they were talking of stage plays, having a play-house, and being great play actors at Mount Juliet's town, and Miss Isabella turns short to my master and says— 'Have you seen the play-bill, Sir Condy?'—'No, I have not,' said he.—'Then more shame for you, (said the Captain her brother) not to know that my sister is to play Juliet to-night, who plays it better than any woman on or off the stage in all Ireland.'—'I am very happy to hear it,' said Sir Condy, and there the matter dropped for the present; but Sir Condy all this time, and a great while afterwards, was at a terrible nonplus, for he had no liking not he to stage plays, nor to Miss Isabella either; to his mind, as it came out over a bowl of whiskey punch at home, his little Judy M'Quirk, who was daughter to a sister's son of mine, was worth twenty of Miss Isabella—He had seen her often when he stopped at her father's cabin to drink whiskey out of the egg-shell, out of hunting, before he came to the estate, and as she gave out was under something like a promise of marriage to her—Any how I could not but pity my poor master, who was so bothered between them, and he an easy-hearted man that could not disoblige nobody, God bless him. To be sure it was not his place to behave ungenerous to Miss Isabella, who had disobliged all her relations for his sake, as he remarked; and then she was locked up in her chamber and forbid to think of him any more, which raised his spirit, because his family was, as he observed, as good as theirs at any rate, and the Rackrents a suitable match for the Moneygawls any day in the year; all which was true enough; but it grieved me to see that upon the strength of all this Sir Condy was growing more in the mind to carry off Miss Isabella to Scotland, in spite of her relations, as she desired.

'It's all over with our poor Judy!' said I, with a heavy sigh, making bold to speak to him one night when he was a little

cheerful, and standing in the servants' hall all alone with me,
as was often his custom—'Not at all (said he) I never was
fonder of Judy than at this present speaking, and to prove it to
you, (said he, and he took from my hand a halfpenny, change
that I had just got along with my tobacco); and to prove it to
you, Thady, says he, it's a toss up with me which I shall marry
this minute, her or Mr. Moneygawl of Mount Juliet's Town's
daughter—so it is'—'Oh, boo! boo*! (says I, making light of it,
to see what he would go on to next)—your honor's joking, to
be sure, there's no compare between our poor Judy and Miss
Isabella, who has a great fortune, they say.'—'I'm not a man
to mind a fortune, nor never was, (said Sir Condy proudly,)
whatever her friends may say; and to make short of it, (says
he) I'm come to a determination upon the spot;' with that he
swore such a terrible oath, as made me cross myself†—'and by
this book, (said he, snatching up my ballad book, mistaking it
for my prayer-book, which lay in the window)—and by this
book, (said he) and by all the books that ever were shut and
opened—it's come to a toss up with me, and I'll stand or fall
by the toss, and so, Thady, hand me over that *pin*‡ out of the
ink-horn,' and he makes a cross on the smooth side of the
halfpenny—'Judy M'Quirk, (said he) her mark,**' God bless
him! his hand was a little unsteadied by all the whiskey punch
he had taken, but it was plain to see his heart was for poor
Judy.—My heart was all as one as in my mouth, when I saw
the halfpenny up in the air, but I said nothing at all, and when
it came down, I was glad I had kept myself to myself, for to be
sure now it was all over with poor Judy.—'Judy's out a luck,'
said I, striving to laugh—'I'm out a luck,' said he, and I never

---

* *Boo! Boo!* an exclamation equivalent to *Pshaw!* or *Nonsense.*
† *As made me cross myself*—The Roman Catholics.
‡ *Pin* read *pen*—it formerly was vulgarly pronounced *pin* in Ireland.
** *Her mark*—It *was* the custom in Ireland for those who could not write, to
make a cross to stand for their signature, as was formerly the practice of our
English monarchs.—The Editor inserts the facsimile of an Irish *mark*, which may
hereafter be valuable to a judicious antiquary—

Her
Judy × M'Quirk
Mark.

In bonds or notes, signed in this manner, a witness is requisite, as the name is
frequently written by him or her.

saw a man look so cast down; he took up the halfpenny off the flag, and walked away quite sobered like by the shock.—Now though as easy a man you would think as any in the wide world, there was no such thing as making him unsay one of these sort of vows,* which he had learned to reverence when young, as I well remember teaching him to toss up for bog berries on my knee.—So I saw the affair was as good as settled between him and Miss Isabella, and I had no more to say but to wish her joy, which I did the week afterwards upon her return from Scotland with my poor master.

My new lady was young, as might be supposed of a lady that had been carried off by her own consent to Scotland, but I could only see her at the first through her veil, which, from bashfulness or fashion, she kept over her face—'And am I to walk through all this crowd of people, my dearest love?' said she to Sir Condy, meaning us servants and tenants, who had gathered at the back gate—'My dear (said Sir Condy) there's nothing for it but to walk, or to let me carry you as far as the house, for you see the back road's too narrow for a carriage, and the great piers have tumbled down across the front approach, so there's no driving the right way by reason of the ruins'—'Plato, thou reasonest well!' said she, or words to that effect, which I could no ways understand; and again, when her foot stumbled against a broken bit of a car wheel, she cried out—'Angels and ministers of grace, defend us!'—Well, thought I, to be sure if she's no Jewish like the last, she is a mad woman for certain, which is as bad: it would have been as well for my poor master to have taken up with poor Judy, who is in her right mind any how.

She was dressed like a mad woman, moreover, more than like any one I ever saw afore or since, and I could not take my eyes off her, but still followed behind her, and her feathers on

---

*Vows—It has been maliciously and unjustly hinted, that the lower classes of the people in Ireland pay but little regard to oaths; yet it is certain that some oaths or vows have great power over their minds.—Sometimes they swear they will be revenged on some of their neighbours; this is an oath they never are known to break.—But what is infinitely more extraordinary and unaccountable, they sometimes make a vow against whiskey; these vows are usually limited to a short time.—A woman who has a drunken husband is most fortunate if she can prevail upon him to go to the priest, and make a vow against whiskey for a year, or a month, or a week, or a day.

the top of her hat were broke going in at the low back door, and she pulled out her little bottle out of her pocket to smell to when she found herself in the kitchen, and said, 'I shall faint with the heat of this odious, odious place'—'My dear, it's only three steps across the kitchen, and there's a fine air if your veil was up,' said Sir Condy, and with that threw back her veil, so that I had then a full sight of her face; she had not at all the colour of one going to faint, but a fine complexion of her own, as I then took it to be, though her maid told me after it was all put on; but even complexion and all taken in, she was no way, in point of good looks, to compare to poor Judy; and with all she had a quality toss with her; but may be it was my over partiality to Judy, into whose place I may say she stept, that made me notice all this.—To do her justice, however, she was, when we came to know her better, very liberal in her house-keeping, nothing at all of the Skin-flint in her; she left every thing to the housekeeper, and her own maid, Mrs. Jane, who went with her to Scotland, gave her the best of characters for generosity; she seldom or ever wore a thing twice the same way, Mrs. Jane told us, and was always pulling her things to pieces, and giving them away, never being used in her father's house to think of expence in any thing—and she reckoned, to be sure, to go on the same way at Castle Rackrent; but when I came to enquire, I learned that her father was so mad with her for running off after his locking her up, and forbidding her to think any more of Sir Condy, that he would not give her a farthing; and it was lucky for her she had a few thousands of her own, which had been left to her by a good grandmother, and these were very convenient to begin with. My master and my lady set out in great style; they had the finest coach and chariot, and horses and liveries, and cut the greatest dash in the county, returning their wedding visits!—and it was immediately reported that her father had undertaken to pay all my master's debts, and of course all his tradesmen gave him a new credit, and every thing went on smack smooth, and I could not but admire my lady's spirit, and was proud to see Castle Rackrent again in all its glory.—My lady had a fine taste for building and furniture, and play-houses, and she turned every thing topsy-turvy, and made the barrack-room into a theatre, as she called it, and she went on as if she had a mint of money at her elbow; and to be sure I thought she knew best, especially as Sir Condy said nothing to it one way or the other. All he asked, God bless him! was to live in peace and quietness, and have his bottle, or his whiskey punch at night to himself.—Now this was little enough, to be sure, for any gentleman, but my lady couldn't abide the smell of the whiskey punch.—'My dear, (says he) you liked it well enough before we were married, and why not now?'—'My dear, (said she) I never smelt it, or I assure you I should never have prevailed upon myself to marry you.'—'My dear, I am sorry you did not smell it, but we can't help that now, (returned my master, without putting himself in a passion, or going out of his way, but just fair and easy helped himself to another glass, and drank it off to her good health). All this the butler told me, who was going backwards and forwards unnoticed with the jug, and hot water, and sugar, and all he thought wanting.—Upon my master's swallowing the last glass of whiskey punch, my lady burst into tears, calling him an ungrateful, base, barbarous wretch! and went off into a fit of hysterics, as I think Mrs. Jane called it, and my poor master was greatly frighted, this being the first thing of the kind he had seen; and he fell straight on his knees before her, and, like a good-hearted cratur as he was, ordered the whiskey punch out of the room, and bid 'em throw open all the windows, and cursed himself, and then my lady came to herself again, and when she saw him kneeling there, bid him get up, and not forswear himself any more, for that she was sure he did not love her, nor never had: this we learnt from Mrs. Jane, who was the only person left present at all this—'My dear, (returns my master, thinking to be sure of Judy, as well he might) whoever told you so is an incendiary, and I'll have 'em turned out of the house this minute, if you'll only let me know which of them it was.'—'Told me what?' says my lady, starting upright in her chair.—'Nothing, nothing at all,' said my master, seeing he had overshot himself, and that my lady spoke at random; 'but what you said just now that I did not love you, Bella, who told you that?'—'My own sense,' said she, and she put her handkerchief to her face, and leant back upon Mrs. Jane, and fell to sobbing as if her heart would break.—'Why now Bella, this is very strange of you, (said my poor master) if nobody has told you nothing, what is it you are taking on for at this rate, and exposing yourself and me for this way?'—'Oh say no more, say no more, every word you say kills me, (cried my lady, and she ran on like one, as Mrs. Jane says, raving)—Oh Sir Condy, Sir Condy! I that had hoped to find in you "my father, brother, husband, friend".'—'Why now faith this is a little too much; do Bella, try to recollect yourself, my dear; am not I your husband, and of your own chusing, and is not that enough?'—'Oh too much! too much!' cried my lady, wringing her hands.—'Why, my dear, come to your right senses for the love of heaven—see is not the whiskey punch, jug and bowl and all, gone out of the room long ago? what is it in the wide world you have to complain of?'—But still my lady sobbed and sobbed, and called herself the most wretched of women; and among other out of the way provoking things, asked my master, was he fit company for her, and he drinking all night. This nettling him, which it was hard to do, he replied, that as to drinking all night, he was then as sober as she was herself, and that it was no matter how much a man drank, provided it did no ways affect or stagger him—that as to being fit company for her, he thought himself of a family to be fit company for any lord or lady in the land, but that he never prevented her from seeing and keeping what company she pleased, and that he had done his best to make Castle Rackrent pleasing to her since her marriage, having always had the house full of visitors, and if her own relations were not amongst them, he said, that was their own fault and their pride's fault, of which he was sorry to find her ladyship had so unbecoming a share—So concluding, he took his candle and walked off to his room, and my lady was in her tantarums for three days after, and would have been so much longer, no doubt, but some of her friends, young ladies and cousins and second cousins, came to Castle Rackrent, by my poor master's express invitation, to see her, and she was in a hurry to get up, as Mrs. Jane called it, a play for them, and so got well, and was as finely dressed and as happy to look at as ever, and all the young ladies who used to be in her room dressing of her said in Mrs. Jane's hearing, that my lady was the happiest bride ever they had seen, and that to be sure a love match was the only thing for happiness, where the parties could any way afford it.

As to affording it, God knows it was little they knew of the matter; my lady's few thousands could not last for ever, especially the way she went on with them, and letters from tradesfolk came every post thick and threefold, with bills as long as my arm of years and years standing; my son Jason had 'em all handed over to him, and the pressing letters were all unread by Sir Condy, who hated trouble and could never be brought to hear talk of business, but still put it off and put it off, saying—settle it any how, or bid 'em call again to-morrow, or speak to me about it some other time.—Now it was hard to find the right time to speak, for in the mornings he was a-bed and in the evenings over his bottle, where no gentleman chuses to be disturbed.—Things in a twelve-month or so came to such a pass, there was no making a shift to go on any longer, though we were all of us well enough used to live from hand to mouth at Castle Rackrent. One day, I remember, when there was a power of company, all sitting after dinner in the dusk, not to say dark, in the drawing-room, my lady having rung five times for candles and none to go up, the housekeeper sent up the footman, who went to my mistress and whispered behind her chair how it was.—'My lady, (says he) there are no candles in the house.'—'Bless me, (says she) then take a horse, and gallop off as fast as you can to Carrick O'Fungus and get some.'—'And in the mean time tell them to step into the play-house, and try if there are not some bits left,' added Sir Condy, who happened to be within hearing. The man was sent up again to my lady, to let her know there was no horse to go but one that wanted a shoe.—'Go to Sir Condy, then, I know nothing at all about the horses, (said my lady) why do you plague me with these things?'—How it was settled I really forget, but to the best of my remembrance, the boy was sent down to my son Jason's to borrow candles for the night. Another time in the winter, and on a desperate cold day, there was no turf in for the parlour and above stairs, and scarce enough for the cook in the kitchen, the little *gossoon** was sent off to the neighbours to see and beg or

---

* *Gossoon*—a little boy—from the French word *Garçon*.—In most Irish families

borrow some, but none could he bring back with him for love or money; so as needs must we were forced to trouble Sir Condy—'Well, and if there's no turf to be had in the town or country, why what signifies talking any more about it, can't ye go and cut down a tree?'—'Which tree, please your honor?' I made bold to say.—'Any tree at all that's good to burn, (said Sir Condy); send off smart, and get one down and the fires lighted before my lady gets up to breakfast, or the house will be to too hot to hold us.'—He was always very considerate in all things about my lady, and she wanted for nothing whilst he had it to give.—Well, when things were tight with them about this time, my son Jason put in a word again about the lodge, and made a genteel offer to lay down the purchase money to relieve Sir Condy's distresses.—Now Sir Condy had it from the best authority, that there were two writs come down to the Sheriff against his person, and the Sheriff, as ill luck would have it, was no friend of his, and talked how he must do his duty, and how he would do it, if it was against the first man in the county, or even his own brother, let alone one who had voted against him at the last election, as Sir Condy had done.—So Sir Condy was fain to take the purchase money of the lodge from my son Jason to settle matters; and sure enough it was a good bargain for both parties, for my son bought the fee simple of a good house for him and his heirs for ever for little or nothing, and by selling of it for that same my master saved himself from a gaol. Every way it turned out fortunate for Sir Condy; for before the money was all gone there came a general election, and he being so well beloved in the county, and one of the oldest families, no one had a better right to stand candidate for the vacancy; and he was called upon by all his friends, and the whole county I may say, to declare himself against the old member, who had little thought of a contest. My master did not relish the thoughts of a troublesome canvas, and all the ill will he might bring upon himself by

there *used* to be a bare-footed Gossoon, who was slave to the cook and the butler, and who in fact, without wages, did all the hard work of the house.—Gossoons were always employed as messengers.—The Editor has known a gossoon to go on foot, without shoes or stockings, fifty-one English miles between sun-rise and sun-set.

disturbing the peace of the county, besides the expence, which was no trifle; but all his friends called upon one another to subscribe, and formed themselves into a committee, and wrote all his circular letters for him, and engaged all his agents, and did all the business unknown to him, and he was well pleased that it should be so at last, and my lady herself was very sanguine about the election, and there was open house kept night and day at Castle Rackrent, and I thought I never saw my lady look so well in her life as she did at that time; there were grand dinners, and all the gentlemen drinking success to Sir Condy till they were carried off; and then dances and balls, and the ladies all finishing with a raking pot of tea[g] in the morning. Indeed it was well the company made it their choice to sit up all nights, for there was not half beds enough for the sights of people that were in it, though there were shake downs in the drawing-room always made up before sun-rise, for those that liked it. For my part, when I saw the doings that were going on, and the loads of claret that went down the throats of them that had no right to be asking for it, and the sights of meat that went up to table and never came down, besides what was carried off to one or t'other below stairs, I couldn't but pity my poor master who was to pay for all, but I said nothing for fear of gaining myself ill will. The day of election will come some time or other, says I to myself, and all will be over—and so it did, and a glorious day it was as any I ever had the happiness to see; huzza! huzza! Sir Condy Rackrent for ever, was the first thing I hears in the morning, and the same and nothing else all day, and not a soul sober only just when polling, enough to give their votes as became 'em, and to stand the brow-beating of the lawyers who came tight enough upon us; and many of our freeholders were knocked off, having never a freehold that they could safely swear to, and Sir Condy was not willing to have any man perjure himself for his sake, as was done on the other side, God knows, but no matter for that.—Some of our friends were dumb-founded, by the lawyers asking them—had they ever been upon the ground where their freeholds lay?—Now Sir Condy being tender of the consciences of them that had not been on the ground, and so could not swear to a freehold when cross-examined by them lawyers, sent out for a couple of cleaves-full of the sods of his farm of Gulteeshinnagh: and as soon as the sods came into town he set each man upon his sod, and so then ever after, you know, they could fairly swear they had been upon the ground*.—We gained the day by this piece of honesty. I thought I should have died in the streets for joy when I seed my poor master chaired, and he bare-headed and it raining as hard as it could pour; but all the crowds following him up and down, and he bowing and shaking hands with the whole town.—Is that Sir Condy Rackrent in the chair?' says a stranger man in the crowd—'The same,' says I—who else should it be? God bless him!'—'And I take it then you belong to him,' says he.—'Not at all,' (says I) 'but I live under him, and have done so these two hundred years and upwards, me and mine.'—'It's lucky for you, then,' rejoins he, 'that he is where he is, for was he any where else but in the chair this minute he'd be in a worse place, for I was sent down on purpose to put him up†, and here's my order for so doing in my pocket.'—It was a writ that villain the wine merchant had marked against my poor master, for some hundreds of an old debt which it was a shame to be talking of at such a time as this.—'Put it in your pocket again, and think no more of it any ways for seven years to come, my honest friend, (says I), he's a member a Parliament now, praised be God, and such as you can't touch him; and if you'll take a fool's advice, I'd have ye keep out of the way this day, or you'll run a good chance of getting your deserts amongst my master's friends, unless you chuse to drink his health like every body else.'—'I've no objection to that in life,' said he; so we went into one of the public houses kept open for my master, and we had a great deal of talk about this thing and that, and 'how is it (says he) your master keeps on so well upon his legs; I heard say he was off Holantide twelve-month past.'—'Never was better or heartier in his life,' said I.—'It's not that I'm after speaking of, (said he) but there was a great report of his being ruined.'—'No matter, (says I) the Sheriffs two years running were his particular friends, and the Sub-sheriffs were

---

* This was actually done at an election in Ireland.
† *To put him up*—to put him in gaol.

both of them gentlemen, and were properly spoken to; and so the writs lay snug with them, and they, as I understand by my son Jason the custom in them cases is, returned the writs as they came to them to those that sent 'em, much good may it do them, with word in Latin that no such person as Sir Condy Rackrent, Bart. was to be found in those parts.'—'Oh, I understand all those ways better, no offence, than you,' says he, laughing, and at the same time filling his glass to my master's good health, which convinced me he was a warm friend in his heart after all, though appearances were a little suspicious or so at first.—'To be sure, (says he, still cutting his joke) when a man's over head and shoulders in debt, he may live the faster for it and the better if he goes the right way about it—or else how is it so many live on so well, as we see every day, after they are ruined?'—'How is it, (says I, being a little merry at the time) how is it but just as you see the ducks in the kitchen yard just after their heads are cut off by the cook, running round and round faster than when alive.'—At which conceit he fell a laughing, and remarked he had never had the happiness yet to see the chicken yard at Castle Rackrent.—'It won't be long so, I hope, (says I) you'll be kindly welcome there, as every body is made by my master; there is not a freer spoken gentleman or a better beloved, high or low, in all Ireland.'—And of what passed after this I'm not sensible, for we drank Sir Condy's good health and the downfall of his enemies till we could stand no longer ourselves—And little did I think at the time, or till long after, how I was harbouring my poor master's greatest of enemies myself. This fellow had the impudence, after coming to see the chicken-yard, to get me to introduce him to my son Jason—little more than the man that never was born did I guess at his meaning by this visit; he gets him a correct list fairly drawn out from my son Jason of all my master's debts, and goes straight round to the creditors and buys them all up, which he did easy enough, seeing the half of them never expected to see their money out of Sir Condy's hands. Then when this base-minded limb of the law, as I afterwards detected him in being, grew to be sole creditor over all, he takes him out a custodiam on all the denominations and sub-denominations, and every carton and half cartong upon

the estate—and not content with that, must have an execution
against the master's goods and down to the furniture, though
little worth, of Castle Rackrent itself.—But this is a part of my
story I'm not come to yet, and it's bad to be forestalling—ill
news flies fast enough all the world over. To go back to
the day of the election, which I never think of but with
pleasure and tears of gratitude for those good times; after
the election was quite and clean over, there comes shoals of
people from all parts, claiming to have obliged my master
with their votes, and putting him in mind of promises which
he could never remember himself to have made—one was
to have a freehold for each of his four sons—another was
to have a renewal of a lease—another an abatement—one
came to be paid ten guineas for a pair of silver buckles sold
my master on the hustings, which turned out to be no better
than copper gilt—another had a long bill for oats, the half of
which never went into the granary to my certain knowledge,
and the other half were not fit for the cattle to touch; but
the bargain was made the week before the election, and
the coach and saddle horses were got into order for the
day, besides a vote fairly got by them oats—so no more
reasoning on that head—but then there was no end to them
that were telling Sir Condy he had engaged to make their
sons excisemen, or high constables, or the like; and as for
them that had bills to give in for liquor, and beds, and straw,
and ribbons, and horses, and post-chaises for the gentlemen
freeholders that came from all parts and other counties to
vote for my master, and were not, to be sure, to be at any
charges, there was no standing against all these; and worse
than all the gentlemen of my master's committee, who managed all for him, and talked how they'd bring him in without
costing him a penny, and subscribed by hundreds very
genteelly, forgot to pay their subscriptions, and had laid
out in agents and lawyers, fees and secret service money,
the Lord knows how much, and my master could never ask
one of them for their subscription, you are sensible, nor for
the price of a fine horse he had sold one of them, so it all
was left at his door. He could never, God bless him again, I
say, bring himself to ask a gentleman for money, despising
such sort of conversation himself; but others, who were not

gentlemen born, behaved very uncivil in pressing him at this very time, and all he could do to content 'em all was to take himself out of the way as fast as possible to Dublin, where my lady had taken a house as fitting for him, a Member of Parliament, to attend his duty in there all the winters.—I was very lonely when the whole family was gone, and all the things they had ordered to go and forgot sent after them by the stage. There was then a great silence in Castle Rackrent, and I went moping from room to room, hearing the doors clap for want of right locks, and the wind through the broken windows that the glazier never would come to mend, and the rain coming through the roof and best ceilings all over the house, for want of the slater whose bill was not paid; besides our having no slates or shingles for that part of the old building which was shingled, and burnt when the chimney took fire, and had been open to the weather ever since. I took myself to the servants' hall in the evening to smoke my pipe as usual, but missed the bit of talk we used to have there sadly, and ever after was content to stay in the kitchen and boil my little potatoes*, and put up my bed there; and every post day I looked in the newspaper, but no news of my master in the house.—He never spoke good or bad—but, as the butler wrote down word to my son Jason, was very ill used by the government about a place that was promised him and never given, after his supporting them against his conscience very honorably, and being greatly abused for it, which hurt him greatly, he having the name of a great patriot in the country before. The house and living in Dublin too was not to be had for nothing, and my son Jason said Sir Condy must soon be looking out for a new agent, for I've done my part and can do no more—if my lady had the bank of Ireland to spend, it would go all in one winter, and Sir Condy would never gainsay her, though he does not care the rind of a lemon for her all the while.

Now I could not bear to hear Jason giving out after this manner against the family, and twenty people standing by

---

* *My little potatoes*—Thady does not mean by this expression that his potatoes were less than other people's, or less than the usual size—*little* is here used only as an Italian diminutive, expressive of fondness.

in the street. Ever since he had lived at the Lodge of his own he looked down, howsomever, upon poor old Thady, and was grown quite a great gentleman, and had none of his relations near him—no wonder he was no kinder to poor Sir Condy than to his own kith and kin*.—In the spring it was the villain that got the list of the debts from him brought down the custodiam, Sir Condy still attending his duty in Parliament; and I could scarcely believe my own old eyes, or the spectacles with which I read it, when I was shewn my son Jason's name joined in the custodiam; but he told me it was only for form's sake, and to make things easier, than if all the land was under the power of a total stranger.—Well, I did not know what to think—it was hard to be talking ill of my own, and I could not but grieve for my poor master's fine estate, all torn by these vultures of the law; so I said nothing, but just looked on to see how it would all end.

It was not till the month of June that he and my lady came down to the country.—My master was pleased to take me aside with him to the brewhouse that same evening, to complain to me of my son and other matters, in which he said he was confident I had neither art nor part: he said a great deal more to me, to whom he had been fond to talk ever since he was my white-headed boy before he came to the estate, and all that he said about poor Judy I can never forget, but scorn to repeat.—He did not say an unkind word of my lady, but wondered, as well he might, her relations would do nothing for him or her, and they in all this great distress.—He did not take any thing long to heart, let it be as it would, and had no more malice or thought of the like in him than the child that can't speak; this night it was all out of his head before he went to his bed.—He took his jug of whiskey punch—My lady was grown quite easy about the whiskey punch by this time, and so I did suppose all was going on right betwixt them, till I learnt the truth through Mrs. Jane, who talked over their affairs to the housekeeper, and I within hearing. The night my master came home, thinking of nothing at all, but just making merry, he drank his bumper toast 'to the deserts

* *Kith and kin*—family or relations—*Kin* from *kind*—*Kith* from—we know not what.

of that old curmudgeon my father-in-law, and all enemies at Mount Juliet's town.'—Now my lady was no longer in the mind she formerly was, and did no ways relish hearing her own friends abused in her presence, she said.—'Then why don't they shew themselves your friends, (said my master,) and oblige me with the loan of the money I condescended, by your advice, my dear, to ask?—It's now three posts since I sent off my letter, desiring in the postscript a speedy answer by the return of the post, and no account at all from them yet.'—'I expect they'll write to *me* next post,' says my lady, and that was all that passed then; but it was easy from this to guess there was a coolness betwixt them, and with good cause.

The next morning being post day, I sent off the gossoon early to the post-office to see was there any letter likely to set matters to rights, and he brought back one with the proper post-mark upon it, sure enough, and I had no time to examine, or make any conjecture more about it, for into the servants' hall pops Mrs. Jane with a blue bandbox in her hand, quite entirely mad.—'Dear Ma'am, and what's the matter?' says I.—'Matter enough, (says she) don't you see my band-box is wet through, and my best bonnet here spoiled, besides my lady's, and all by the rain coming in through that gallery window, that you might have got mended if you'd had any sense, Thady, all the time we were in town in the winter.'—'Sure I could not get the glazier, Ma'am,' says I.—'You might have stopped it up any how,' says she.—'So I did, Ma'am, to the best of my ability, one of the panes with the old pillow-case, and the other with a piece of the old stage green curtain—sure I was as careful as possible all the time you were away, and not a drop of rain came in at that window of all the windows in the house, all winter, Ma'am, when under my care; and now the family's come home, and it's summer time, I never thought no more about it to be sure—but dear, it's a pity to think of your bonnet, Ma'am—but here's what will please you, Ma'am, a letter from Mount Juliet's town for my lady.' With that she snatches it from me without a word more, and runs up the back stairs to my mistress; I follows with a slate to make up the window—this window was in the long passage, or gallery, as my lady gave out orders to have it called, in the gallery leading to my master's bed-chamber and

her's, and when I went up with the slate, the door having no
lock, and the bolt spoilt, was a-jar after Mrs. Jane, and as I was
busy with the window, I heard all that was saying within.

'Well, what's in your letter, Bella, my dear? (says he) you're
a long time spelling it over.'—'Won't you shave this morning,
Sir Condy,' says she, and put the letter in her pocket.—'I
shaved the day before yesterday, (says he) my dear, and that's
not what I'm thinking of now—but anything to oblige you,
and to have peace and quietness, my dear'—and presently I
had a glimpse of him at the cracked glass over the chimney-
piece, standing up shaving himself to please my lady.—But
she took no notice, but went on reading her book, and
Mrs. Jane doing her hair behind.—'What is it you're reading
there, my dear?—phoo, I've cut myself with this razor; the
man's a cheat that sold it me, but I have not paid him for
it yet—What is it you're reading there? did you hear my
asking you, my dear?' 'The sorrows of Werter,' replies by
lady, as well as I could hear.—'I think more of the sorrows
of Sir Condy, (says my master, joking like).—What news from
Mount Juliet's town?'—'No news, (says she) but the old story
over again; my friends all reproaching me still for what I
can't help now.'—'Is it for marrying me, (said my master,
still shaving); what signifies, as you say, talking of that when
it can't be helped now.'

With that she heaved a great sigh, that I heard plain enough
in the passage.—'And did not you use me basely, Sir Condy,
(says she) not to tell me you were ruined before I married
you?'—'Tell you, my dear, (said he) did you ever ask me one
word about it? and had not you friends enough of your own,
that were telling you nothing else from morning to night,
if you'd have listened to them slanders.'—'No slanders, nor
are my friends slanderers; and I can't bear to hear them
treated with disrespect as I do, (says my lady, and took out
her pocket handkerchief)—they are the best of friends, and
if I had taken their advice—But my father was wrong to lock
me up, I own; that was the only unkind thing I can charge him
with; for if he had not locked me up, I should never have had
a serious thought of running away as I did.'—'Well, my dear,
(said my master) don't cry and make yourself uneasy about it
now, when it's all over, and you have the man of your own

choice in spite of 'em all.'—'I was too young, I know, to make
a choice at the time you ran away with me, I'm sure,' says my
lady, and another sigh, which made my master, half shaved
as he was, turn round upon her in surprise—'Why Bella,
(says he) you can't deny what you know as well as I do,
that it was at own particular desire, and that twice under
your own hand and seal expressed, that I should carry you
off as I did to Scotland, and marry you there.'—'Well, say
no more about it, Sir Condy, (said my lady, pettish like)—I
was a child then, you know.'—'And as far as I know, you're
little better now, my dear Bella, to be talking in this manner
to your husband's *face*; but I won't take it ill of you, for I know
it's something in that letter you put in your pocket just now,
that has set you against me all on a sudden, and imposed
upon your understanding.'—'It is not so very easy as you
think it, Sir Condy, to impose upon *my* understanding', (said
my lady)—'My dear, (says he) I have, and with reason, the best
opinion of your understanding of any man now breathing,
and you know I have never set my own in competition with
it; till now, my dear Bella, (says he, taking her hand from her
book as kind as could be,) till now—when I have the great
advantage of being quite cool, and you not; so don't believe
one word your friends say against your own Sir Condy, and
lend me the letter out of your pocket, till I see what it is they
can have to say.'—'Take it then, (says she,) and as you are
quite cool, I hope it is a proper time to request you'll allow me
to comply with the wishes of all my own friends, and return to
live with my father and family, during the remainder of my
wretched existence, at Mount Juliet's Town.'

At this my poor master fell back a few paces, like one that
had been shot—'You're not serious, Bella, (says he) and could
you find it in your heart to leave me this way in the very
middle of my distresses, all alone?'—But recollecting himself
after his first surprise, and a moment's time for reflection, he
said, with a great deal of consideration for my lady—'Well,
Bella, my dear, I believe you are right; for what could you
do at Castle Rackrent, and an execution against the goods
coming down, and the furniture to be canted, and an auction
in the house all next week—so you have my full consent to
go, since that is your desire, only you must not think of my

accompanying you, which I could not in honour do upon the terms I always have been since our marriage with your friends; besides I have business to transact at home—so in the mean time, if we are to have any breakfast this morning, let us go down and have it for the last time in peace and comfort, Bella.'

Then as I heard my master coming to the passage door, I finished fastening up my slate against the broken pane, and when he came out, I wiped down the window seat with my wig*, bade him a good morrow as kindly as I could, seeing he was in trouble, though he strove and thought to hide it from me.—'This window is all racked and tattered, (says I,) and it's what I'm striving to mend.' 'It *is* all racked and tattered plain enough, (says he) and never mind mending it, honest old Thady, says he, it will do well enough for you and I, and that's all the company we shall have left in the house by-and-bye.'—'I'm sorry to see your honour so low this morning, (says I,) but you'll be better after taking your breakfast.'—'Step down to the servants' hall, (says he) and bring me up the pen and ink into the parlour, and get a sheet of paper from Mrs. Jane, for I have business that can't brook to be delayed, and come into the parlour with the pen and ink yourself, Thady, for I must have you to witness my signing a paper I have to execute in a hurry.'—Well, while I was getting of the pen and ink-horn, and the sheet of paper, I ransacked my brains to think what could be the papers my poor master could have to execute in such a hurry, he that never thought of such a thing as doing business afore breakfast in the whole course of his life for any man living—but this was for my lady, as I afterwards found, and the more genteel of him after all her treatment.

* Wigs were formerly used instead of brooms in Ireland, for sweeping or dusting tables, stairs, &c. The Editor doubted the fact, till he saw a labourer of the old school sweep down a flight of stairs with his wig; he afterwards put it on his head again with the utmost composure, and said, 'Oh please your honour, it's never a bit the worse.'

It must be acknowledged that these men are not in any danger of catching cold by taking off their wigs occasionally, because they usually have fine crops of hair growing under their wigs.—The wigs are often yellow, and the hair which appears from beneath them black; the wigs are usually too small, and are raised up by the hair beneath, or by the ears of the wearers.

I was just witnessing the paper that he had scrawled over, and was shaking the ink out of my pen upon the carpet, when my lady came in to breakfast, and she started as if it had been a ghost, as well she might, when she saw Sir Condy writing at this unseasonable hour.—'That will do very well, Thady,' says he to me, and took the paper I had signed to, without knowing what upon the earth it might be, out of my hands, and walked, folding it up, to my lady—

'You are concerned in this, my lady Rackrent, (says he, putting it into her hands,) and I beg you'll keep this memorandum safe, and shew it to your friends the first thing you do when you get home, but put it in your pocket now, my dear, and let us eat our breakfast, in God's name.'—'What is all this?' said my lady, opening the paper in great curiosity—'It's only a bit of a memorandum of what I think becomes me to do whenever I am able, (says my master); you know my situation, tied hand and foot at the present time being, but that can't last always, and when I'm dead and gone, the land will be to the good, Thady, you know; and take notice it's my intention your lady should have a clear five hundred a year jointure off the estate, afore any of my debts are paid.'—'Oh, please your honour, says I, I can't expect to live to see that time, being now upwards of fourscore and ten years of age, and you a young man, and likely to continue so, by the help of God.'—I was vexed to see my lady so insensible too, for all she said was—'This is very genteel of you, Sir Condy—You need not wait any longer, Thady'—so I just picked up the pen and ink that had tumbled on the floor, and heard my master finish with saying—'You behaved very genteel to me, my dear, when you threw all the little you had in your own power, along with yourself, into my hands; and as I don't deny but what you may have had some things to complain of, (to be sure he was thinking then of Judy, or of the whiskey punch, one or t'other, or both); and as I don't deny but you may have had something to complain of, my dear, it is but fair you should have something in the form of compensation to look forward too agreeably in future; besides it's an act of justice to myself, that none of your friends, my dear, may ever have it to say against me I married for money, and not for love.'—'That is the last thing I should ever have thought of saying of you,

Sir Condy,' said my lady, looking very gracious.—'Then, my dear, (said Sir Condy) we shall part as good friends as we met, so, all's right.'

I was greatly rejoiced to hear this, and went out of the parlour to report it all to the kitchen.—The next morning my lady and Mrs. Jane set out for Mount Juliet's town in the jaunting car; many wondered at my lady's chusing to go away, considering all things, upon the jaunting car, as if it was only a party of pleasure; but they did not know till I told them, that the coach was all broke in the journey down, and no other vehicle but the car to be had; besides, my lady's friends were to send their coach to meet her at the cross roads—so it was all done very proper.

My poor master was in great trouble after my lady left us.—The execution came down, and every thing at Castle Rackrent was seized by the gripers, and my son Jason, to his shame be it spoken, amongst them—I wondered, for the life of me, how he could harden himself to do it, but then he had been studying the law, and had made himself attorney Quirk; so he brought down at once a heap of accounts upon my master's head—To Cash lent, and to ditto, and to ditto, and to ditto, and oats, and bills paid at the milliner's and linen-draper's, and many dresses for the fancy balls in Dublin for my lady, and all the bills to the workmen and tradesmen for the scenery of the theatre, and the chandler's and grocer's bills, and taylor's, besides butcher's and baker's, and worse than all, the old one of that base wine-merchant's, that wanted to arrest my poor master for the amount on the election day, for which amount Sir Condy afterwards passed his note of hand, bearing lawful interest from the date thereof; and the interest and compound interest was now mounted to a terrible deal on many other notes and bonds for money borrowed, and there was besides hush-money to the sub-sheriffs, and sheets upon sheets of old and new attornies' bills, with heavy balances, *as per former account furnished*, brought forward with interest thereon; then there was a powerful deal due to the Crown for sixteen years arrear of quit-rent of the town lands of Carrickshaughlin, with drivers' fees, and a compliment to the receiver every year for letting the quit-rent run on, to oblige Sir Condy and Sir Kit afore him.—Then there was bills for spirits, and ribbons at the election time, and the gentlemen of the Committee's accounts unsettled, and their subscriptions never gathered; and there was cows to be paid for, with the smith and farrier's bills to be set against the rent of the demesne, with calf and hay-money: then there was all the servants' wages, since I don't know when, coming due to them, and sums advanced for them by my son Jason for clothes, and boots, and whips and odd monies for sundries expended by them in journies to town and elsewhere, and pocket-money for the master continually, and messengers and postage before his being a parliament man—I can't myself tell you what besides; but this I know, that when the evening came on the which Sir Condy had appointed to settle all with my son Jason; and when he comes into the parlour, and sees the sight of bills and load of papers all gathered on the great dining table for him, he puts his hands before both his eyes, and cries out—'Merciful Jasus! what is it I see before me!'—Then I sets an arm chair at the table for him, and with a deal of difficulty he sits him down, and my son Jason hands him over the pen and ink to sign to this man's bill and t'other man's bill, all which he did without making the least objections; indeed, to give him his due, I never seen a man more fair, and honest, and easy in all his dealings, from first to last, as Sir Condy, or more willing to pay every man his own as far as he was able, which is as much as any one can do.—'Well, (says he, joking like with Jason) I wish we could settle it all with a stroke of my grey-goose-quill.—What signifies making me wade through all this ocean of papers here; can't you now, who understand drawing out an account, Debtor and Creditor, just sit down here at the corner of the table, and get it done out for me, that I may have a clear view of the balance, which is all I need be talking about, you know?'—'Very true, Sir Condy, nobody understands business better than yourself,' says Jason.—'So I've a right to do, being born and bred to the bar, (says Sir Condy)—Thady, do step out and see are they bringing in the tings for the punch, for we've just done all we have to do this evening.'—I goes out accordingly, and when I came back, Jason was pointing to the balance, which was a terrible sight to my poor master.—'Pooh! pooh! pooh! (says he) here's so many noughts they dazzle my eyes, so they do, and put me in mind of all I suffered, larning of my numeration table, when I was a boy, at the day-school along with you, Jason—Units, tens, hundreds, tens of hundreds.—Is the punch ready, Thady?' says he, seeing me—'Immediately, the boy has the jug in his hand; it's coming up stairs, please your honour, as fast as possible,' says I, for I saw his honour was tired out of his life, but Jason, very short and cruel, cuts me off with—'Don't be talking of punch yet a while, it's no time for punch yet a bit—Units, tens, hundreds, goes he on, counting over the master's shoulder—units, tens, hundreds, thousands'—'A-a-agh! hold your hand, (cries my master,) where in this wide world am I to find hundreds, or units itself, let alone thousands?'—'The balance has been running on too long, (says Jason, sticking to him as I could not have done at the time if you'd have given both the Indies and Cork to boot); the balance has been running on too long, and I'm distressed myself on your account, Sir Condy, for money, and the thing must be settled now on the spot, and the balance cleared off,' says Jason. 'I'll thank you, if you'll only shew me how,' says Sir Condy.—'There's but one way, (says Jason) and that's ready enough; when there's no cash, what can a gentleman do but go to the land?'—'How can you go to the land, and it under custodiam to yourself already, (says Sir Condy) and another custodiam hanging over it? and no one at all can touch it, you know, but the custodees.'—'Sure can't you sell, though at a loss?—sure you can sell, and I've a purchaser ready for you,' says Jason.—'Have ye so? (said Sir Condy) that's a great point gained; but there's a thing now beyond all, that perhaps you don't know yet, barring Thady has let you into the secret.'—'Sarrah bit of a sacret, or any thing at all of the kind has he learned from me these fifteen weeks come St. John's eve, (says I) for we have scarce been upon speaking terms of late—but what is it your honor means of a secret?'—'Why the secret of the little keepsake I gave my lady Rackrent the morning she left us, that she might not go back empty-handed to her friends.'—'My lady Rackrent, I'm sure, has baubles and keepsakes enough, as those bills on the table will shew, (says Jason); but whatever it is, (says he, taking up his pen) we must add it to the balance, for to be sure it can't be paid for.'—'No, nor can't till after my decease, (said

Sir Condy) that's one good thing.'—Then coloring up a good deal, he tells Jason of the memorandum of the five hundred a year jointure he had settled upon my lady; at which Jason was indeed mad, and said a great deal in very high words, that it was using a gentleman who had the management of his affairs, and was moreover his principal creditor, extremely ill, to do such a thing without consulting him, and against his knowledge and consent. To all which Sir Condy had nothing to reply, but that, upon his conscience, it was in a hurry, and without a moment's thought on his part, and he was very sorry for it, but if it was to do over again he would do the same; and he appealed to me, and I was ready to give my evidence, if that would do, to the truth of all he said.

So Jason with much ado was brought to agree to a compromise.—'The purchaser that I have ready (says he) will be much displeased to be sure at the incumbrance on the land, but I must see and manage him—here's a deed ready drawn up—we have nothing to do but to put in the consideration money and our names to it.—And how much am I going to sell?—the lands of O'Shaughlin's-town, and the lands of Gruneaghoolaghan, and the lands of Crookaghnawaturgh, (says he, just reading to himself)—and—'Oh, murder, Jason! — sure you won't put this in'—the castle, stable, and appurtenances of Castle Rackrent—Oh, murder! (says I, clapping my hands) this is too bad, Jason.'—'Why so? (said Jason) when it's all, and a great deal more to the back of it, lawfully mine was I to push for it.' 'Look at him (says I, pointing to Sir Condy, who was just leaning back in his arm chair, with his arms falling beside him like one stupefied) is it you, Jason, that can stand in his presence and recollect all he has been to us, and all we have been to him, and yet use him so at the last?'—'Who will he find to use him better, I ask you? (said Jason)—If he can get a better purchaser, I'm content; I only offer to purchase to make things easy and oblige him—though I don't see what compliment I am under, if you come to that; I have never had, asked, or charged more than sixpence in the pound receiver's fees, and where would he have got an agent for a penny less?' 'Oh Jason! Jason! how will you stand to this in the face of the county, and all who know you, (says I); and what will people think and say, when they see you living here in Castle Rackrent, and the lawful owner turned out of the seat of his ancestors, without a cabin to put his head into, or so much as a potatoe to eat?'—Jason, whilst I was saying this and a great deal more, made me signs, and winks, and frowns; but I took no heed, for I was grieved and sick at heart for my poor master, and couldn't but speak.

'Here's the punch! (says Jason, for the door opened)— here's the punch!'—Hearing that, my master starts up in his chair and recollects himself, and Jason uncorks the whiskey—'Set down the jug here,' says he, making room for it beside the papers opposite to Sir Condy, but still not stirring the deed that was to make over all. Well, I was in great hopes he had some touch of mercy about him, when I saw him making the punch, and my master took a glass; but Jason put it back as he was going to fill again, saying, 'No, Sir Condy, it shan't be said of me, I got your signature to this deed when you were half-seas over; you know, your name and hand-writing in that condition would not, if brought before the courts, benefit me a straw, wherefore let us settle all before we go deeper in the punch-bowl.'—'Settle all as you will, (said Sir Condy, clapping his hands to his ears) but let me hear no more, I'm bothered to death this night.'—'You've only to sign,' said Jason, putting the pen to him.—'Take all and be content,' said my master—So he signed—and the man who brought in the punch witnessed it, for I was not able, but crying like a child; and besides, Jason said, which I was glad of, that I was no fit witness, being so old and doating. It was so bad with me, I could not taste a drop of the punch itself, though my master himself, God bless him! in the midst of his trouble, poured out a glass for me and brought it up to my lips.—'Not a drop, I thank your honor's honor as much as if I took it though,' and I just set down the glass as it was and went out; and when I got to the street door, the neighbour's childer who were playing at marbles there, seeing me in great trouble, left their play, and gathered about me to know what ailed me; and I told them all, for it was a great relief to me to speak to these poor childer, that seemed to have some natural feeling left in them: and when they were made sensible that Sir Condy was going to leave Castle Rackrent for good and all, they set up a whillalu that could be heard to the farthest end of

the street; and one fine boy he was, that my master had given
an apple to that morning, cried the loudest, but they all were
the same sorry, for Sir Condy was greatly beloved amongst
the childer* for letting them go a nutting in the demesne
without saying a word to them, though my lady objected to
them.—The people in the town who were the most of them
standing at their doors, hearing the childer cry, would know
the reason of it; and when the report was made known, the
people one and all gathered in great anger against my son
Jason, and terror at the notion of his coming to be landlord
over them, and they cried, No Jason! No Jason!—Sir Condy!
Sir Condy! Sir Condy Rackrent for ever! and the mob grew
so great and so loud I was frighted, and made my way back to
the house to warn my son to make his escape, or hide himself
for fear of the consequences.—Jason would not believe me,
till they came all round the house and to the windows with
great shouts—then he grew quite pale, and asked Sir Condy
what had he best do?—'I'll tell you what you'd best do, (said
Sir Condy, who was laughing to see his fright) finish your glass
first, then let's go to the window and shew ourselves, and I'll
tell 'em, or you shall if you please, that I'm going to the Lodge
for change of air for my health, and by my own desire, for
the rest of my days.'—'Do so,' said Jason, who never meant
it should have been so, but could not refuse him the Lodge
at this unseasonable time. Accordingly Sir Condy threw up
the sash and explained matters, and thanked all his friends,
and bid 'em look in at the punch bowl, and observe that Jason
and he had been sitting over it very good friends; so the mob
was content, and he sent 'em out some whiskey to drink his
health, and that was the last time his honor's health was ever
drank at Castle Rackrent.

The very next day, being too proud, as he said to me, to stay
an hour longer in a house that did not belong to him, he sets
off to the Lodge, and I along with him not many hours after.
And there was great bemoaning through all O'Shauglin's
town, which I stayed to witness, and gave my poor master
a full account of when I got to the Lodge.—He was very low
and in his bed when I got there, and complained of a great

---

* This is the invariable pronunciation of the lower Irish.

pain about his heart, but I guessed it was only trouble, and all
the business, let alone vexation, he had gone through of late;
and knowing the nature of him from a boy, I took my pipe,
and while smoking it by the chimney, began telling him how he
was beloved and regretted in the county, and it did him a deal
of good to hear it.—'Your honor has a great many friends yet
that you don't know of, rich and poor, in the county (says I);
for as I was coming along on the road I met two gentlemen
in their own carriages, who asked after you, knowing me, and
wanted to know where you was, and all about you, and even
how old I was—think of that.'—Then he wakened out of his
doze, and began questioning me who the gentlemen were.
And the next morning it came into my head to go, unknown
to any body, with my master's compliments round to many of
the gentlemen's houses where he and my lady used to visit,
and people that I knew were his great friends, and would go
to Cork to serve him any day in the year, and I made bold to
try to borrow a trifle of cash from them.—They all treated me
very civil for the most part, and asked a great many questions
very kind about my lady and Sir Condy and all the family, and
were greatly surprised to learn from me Castle Rackrent was
sold, and my master at the Lodge for his health; and they all
pitied him greatly, and he had their good wishes if that would
do, but money was a thing they unfortunately had not any of
them at this time to spare. I had my journey for my pains, and
I, not used to walking, nor supple as formerly, was greatly
tired, but had the satisfaction of telling my master when I
got to the Lodge all the civil things said by high and low.

'Thady, (says he) all you've been telling me brings a strange
thought into my head; I've a notion I shall not be long for this
world any how, and I've a great fancy to see my own funeral
afore I die.' I was greatly shocked at the first speaking to hear
him speak so light about his funeral, and he to all appearance
in good health, but recollecting myself, answered—'To be
sure it would be a fine sight as one could see, I dared to say,
and one I should be proud to witness, and I did not doubt
his honor's would be as great a funeral as ever Sir Patrick
O'Shaughlin's was, and such a one as that had never been
known in the county afore or since.' But I never thought he
was in earnest about seeing his own funeral himself, till the

next day he returns to it again.—'Thady, (says he) as far as the wake* goes, sure I might without any great trouble have the satisfaction of seeing a bit of my own funeral.'—'Well, since your honour's honour's so bent upon it, (says I, not willing to cross him, and he in trouble) we must see what we can do.'—So he fell into a sort of a sham disorder, which was easy done, as he kept his bed and no one to see him; and I got my shister, who was an old woman very handy about the sick, and very skilful, to come up to the Lodge to nurse him; and we gave out, she knowing no better, that he was just at his latter end, and it answered beyond any thing; and there was a great throng of people, men, women and childer, and there being only two rooms at the Lodge, except what was locked up full of Jason's furniture and things, the house was soon as full and fuller than it could hold, and the heat, and smoke, and noise wonderful great; and standing amongst them that were near the bed, but not thinking at all of the dead, I was started by the sound of my master's voice from under the great coats that had been thrown all at top, and I went close up, no one noticing.—'Thady, (says he) I've had enough of this, I'm smothering, and I can't hear a word of all they're saying of the deceased.'—'God bless you, and lie still quiet (says I) a bit longer, for my shister's afraid of ghosts, and would die on the spot with the fright, was she to see you come to life all on a sudden this way without the least preparation.'—So he lays him still, though well nigh stifled, and I made all haste to tell the secret of the joke, whispering to one and t'other, and there was a great surprise, but not so great as we had laid out it would.—'And aren't we to have the pipes and tobacco, after coming so far to-night?' says some; but they were all well enough pleased when his honor got up to drink with them, and sent for more spirits from a shebean-house†, where they very civilly let him have it upon credit—so the night passed off very merrily, but to my mind Sir Condy was rather upon the sad order in the midst of it all, not finding there had been

---

* A wake^g in England is a meeting avowedly for merriment—in Ireland, it is a nocturnal meeting avowedly for the purpose of watching and bewailing the dead; but in reality for gossipping and debauchery.

† *Shebean-house*, a hedge alehouse.—Shebean properly means weak small-beer, taplash.

such a great talk about himself after his death as he had always expected to hear.

The next morning when the house was cleared of them, and none but my shister and myself left in the kitchen with Sir Condy, one opens the door and walks in, and who should it be but Judy M'Quirk herself.—I forgot to notice that she had been married long since, whilst young Captain Moneygawl lived at the Lodge, to the Captain's huntsman, who after a while listed and left her, and was killed in the wars. Poor Judy fell off greatly in her good looks after her being married a year or two, and being smoke-dried in the cabin and neglecting herself like, it was hard for Sir Condy himself to know her again till she spoke; but when she says, 'It's Judy M'Quirk, please your honor, don't you remember her?'—'Oh, Judy, is it you? (says his honor)—yes, sure I remember you very well—but you're greatly altered, Judy.'—'Sure it's time for me, (says she) and I think your honor since I *seen* you last, but that's a great while ago, is altered too.'—'And with reason, Judy, (says Sir Condy, fetching a sort of sigh)—but how's this, Judy, (he goes on) I take it a little amiss of you that you were not at my wake last night?' 'Ah, don't be being jealous of that, (says she) I didn't hear a sentence of your honor's wake till it was all over, or it would have gone hard with me but I would have been at it sure—but I was forced to go ten miles up the country three days ago to a wedding of a relation of my own's, and didn't get home till after the wake was over; but (says she) it won't be so, I hope, the next time*, please your honor.'—'That we shall see, Judy, (says his honor) and may be sooner than you think for, for I've been very unwell this while past, and don't reckon any way I'm long for this world.' At this Judy takes up the corner of her apron, and puts it first to one eye and then to t'other, being to all appearance in great trouble; and my shister put in her word, and bid his honor have a good heart, for she was sure it was only the gout that Sir Patrick used to have flying about him, and that he ought to drink a glass or a bottle extraordinary to keep it out of his

---

* At the coronation of one of our monarchs, the king complained of the confusion which happened in the procession—The great officer who presided told his majesty, 'That it should not be so next time.'

stomach, and he promised to take her advice, and sent out for
more spirits immediately; and Judy made a sign to me, and I
went over to the door to her, and she said—'I wonder to see
Sir Condy so low!—Has he heard the news?' 'What news?'
says I.—'Didn't ye hear it, then? (says she) my lady Rackrent
that was is kilt^g and lying for dead, and I don't doubt but
it's all over her with by this time.'—'Mercy on us all, (says
I) how was it?—'The jaunting car it was that ran away with
her, (says Judy).—I was coming home that same time from
Biddy M'Guggin's marriage, and a great crowd of people too
upon the road coming from the fair of Crookaghnawatur,
and I sees a jaunting car standing in the middle of the road,
and with the two wheels off and all tattered.—What's this?
says I.'—'Didn't ye hear of it? (says they that were looking
on) it's my lady Rackrent's car that was running away from
her husband, and the horse took fright at a carrion that lay
across the road, and so ran away with the jaunting car, and
my lady Rackrent and her maid screaming, and the horse
ran with them against a car that was coming from the fair,
with the boy asleep on it, and the lady's petticoat hanging
out of the jaunting car caught, and she was dragged I can't
tell you how far upon the road, and it all broken up with
the stones just going to be pounded, and one of the road
makers with his sledge hammer in his hand stops the horse
at the last; but my lady Rackrent was all kilt* and smashed,
and they lifted her into a cabin hard by, and the maid was
found after, where she had been thrown, in the gripe of the
ditch, her cap and bonnet all full of bog water—and they say
my lady can't live any way. Thady, pray now is it true what
I'm told for sartain, that Sir Condy has made over all to your
son Jason?'—'All,' says I.—'All entirely,' says she again.—'All
entirely,' says I.—'Then (says she) that's a great shame, but
don't be telling Jason what I say.'—'And what is it you say?

---

* *Kilt and smashed*—Our author is not here guilty of an anticlimax.—The mere
English reader, from a similarity of sound between the words *kilt* and *killed*, might
be induced to suppose that their meanings are similar, yet they are not by any
means in Ireland synonymous terms. Thus you may hear a man exclaim—'I'm
kilt and murdered!'—but he frequently means only that he has received a black
eye, or a slight contusion.—*I'm kilt all over*—means that he is in a worse state than
being simply *kilt*—Thus—*I'm kilt with the cold*—is nothing to—*I'm kilt all over with
the rheumatism.*^g

(cries Sir Condy, leaning over betwixt us, which made Judy start greatly)—I know the time when Judy M'Quirk would never have stayed so long talking at the door, and I in the house.' 'Oh, (says Judy) for shame, Sir Condy, times are altered since then, and it's my lady Rackrent you ought to be thinking of.'—'And why should I be thinking of her, that's not thinking of me now?' says Sir Condy.—'No matter for that, (says Judy, very properly) it's time you should be thinking of her if ever you mean to do it at all, for don't you know she's lying for death?'—'My lady Rackrent! (says Sir Condy in a surprise) why it's but two days since we parted, as you very well know, Thady, in her full health and spirits, and she and her maid along with her going to Mount Juliet's town on her jaunting car.'—'She'll never ride no more on her jaunting car, (said Judy) for it has been the death of her sure enough.'—'And is she dead then?' says his honor.—'As good as dead, I hear, (says Judy) but there's Thady here has just learnt the whole truth of the story as I had it, and it is fitter he or any body else should be telling it you than I, Sir Condy—I must be going home to the childer.'—But he stops her, but rather from civility in him, as I could see very plainly, than any thing else, for Judy was, as his honor remarked, at her first coming in, greatly changed, and little likely, as far as I could see—though she did not seem to be clear of it herself—little likely to be my lady Rackrent now, should there be a second toss-up to be made.—But I told him the whole story out of the face, just as Judy had told it to me, and he sent off a messenger with his compliments to Mount Juliet's town that evening to learn the truth of the report, and Judy bid the boy that was going call in at Tim M'Enerney's shop in O'Shaughlin's town and buy her a new shawl.—'Do so, (says Sir Condy) and tell Tim to take no money from you, for I must pay him for the shawl myself.'—At this my shister throws me over a look, and I says nothing, but turned the tobacco in my mouth, whilst Judy began making a many words about it, and saying how she could not be beholden for shawls to any gentleman. I left her there to consult with my shister, did she think there was any thing in it, and my shister thought I was blind to be asking her the question, and I thought my shister must see more into it than I did, and recollecting all past times and every thing, I changed my mind, and came over to her way of thinking, and we settled it that Judy was very like to be my lady Rackrent after all, if a vacancy should have happened.

The next day, before his honor was up, somebody comes with a double knock at the door, and I was greatly surprised to see it was my son Jason.—'Jason, is it you? (says I) what brings you to the Lodge? (says I) is it my lady Rackrent? we know that already since yesterday.' 'May be so, (says he) but I must see Sir Condy about it.'—'You can't see him yet, (says I) sure he is not awake.' 'What then, (says he) can't he be wakened? and I standing at the door.—'I'll not be disturbing his honor for you, Jason (says I); many's the hour you've waited in your time, and been proud to do it, till his honor was at leisure to speak to you.—His honor,' says I, raising my voice—at which his honor wakens of his own accord, and calls to me from the room to know who it was I was speaking to. Jason made no more ceremony, but follows me into the room.—'How are you, Sir Condy, (says he) I'm happy to see you looking so well; I came up to know how you did to-day, and to see did you want for any thing at the Lodge.'—'Nothing at all, Mr. Jason, I thank you, (says he, for his honor had his own share of pride, and did not chuse, after all that had passed, to be beholden, I suppose, to my son)—but pray take a chair and be seated, Mr. Jason.'—Jason sat him down upon the chest, for chair there was none, and after he had sat there some time, and a silence on all sides—'What news is there stirring in the country, Mr. Jason M'Quirk?' says Sir Condy, very easy, yet high like.—'None that's news to you, Sir Condy, I hear (says Jason). I am sorry to hear of my lady Rackrent's accident.'—'I am much obliged to you, and so is her ladyship, I'm sure,' answers Sir Condy, still stiff; and there was another sort of a silence, which seemed to lie the heaviest on my son Jason.

'Sir Condy, (says he at last, seeing Sir Condy disposing himself to go to sleep again) Sir Condy, I dare say you recollect mentioning to me the little memorandum you gave to lady Rackrent about the £500 a year jointure.'—'Very true, (said Sir Condy) it is all in my recollection.'—'But if my lady Rackrent dies there's an end of all jointure,' says Jason. 'Of course,' says Sir Condy.—'But it's not a matter of certainty

that my lady Rackrent won't recover,' says Jason.—'Very true,
Sir,' says my master.—'It's a fair speculation then, for you to
consider what the chance of the jointure on those lands when
out of custodiam will be to you.'—'Just five hundred a year, I
take it, without any speculation at all,' said Sir Condy.—'That's
supposing the life dropt and the custodiam off, you know,
begging your pardon, Sir Condy, who understand business,
that is a wrong calculation.'—'Very likely so, (said Sir Condy)
but Mr. Jason, if you have any thing to say to me this morning
about it, I'd be obliged to you to say it, for I had an indifferent
night's rest last night, and wouldn't be sorry to sleep a little this
morning.'—'I have only three words to say, and those more
of consequence to you, Sir Condy, than me. You are a little
cool, I observe, but I hope you will not be offended at what
I have brought here in my pocket,'—and he pulls out two
long rolls, and showers down golden guineas upon the bed.
'What's this? (said Sir Condy) it's long since'—but his pride
stops him—'All these are your lawful property this minute, Sir
Condy, if you please,' said Jason.—'Not for nothing, I'm sure,
(said Sir Condy, and laughs a little)—nothing for nothing, or
I'm under a mistake with you, Jason.'—'Oh, Sir Condy, we'll
not be indulging ourselves in any unpleasant retrospects, (says
Jason) it's my present intention to behave, as I'm sure you will,
like a gentleman in this affair.—Here's two hundred guineas,
and a third I mean to add, if you should think proper to make
over to me all your right and title to those lands that you know
of.'—'I'll consider of it,' said my master; and a great deal more,
that I was tired listening to, was said by Jason, and all that,
and the sight of the ready cash upon the bed worked with
his honor; and the short and the long of it was, Sir Condy
gathered up the golden guineas and tied up in a handkerchief,
and signed some paper Jason brought with him as usual, and
there was an end of the business; Jason took himself away, and
my master turned himself round and fell asleep again.

I soon found what had put Jason in such a hurry to conclude
this business. The little gossoon we had sent off the day before
with my master's compliments to Mount Juliet's town, and
to know how my lady did after her accident, was stopped
early this morning, coming back with his answer through
O'Shaughlin's town, at Castle Rackrent by my son Jason,

and questioned of all he knew of my lady from the servants at Mount Juliet's town; and the gossoon told him my lady Rackrent was not expected to live over night, so Jason thought it high time to be moving to the Lodge, to make his bargain with my master about the jointure afore it should be too late, and afore the little gossoon should reach us with the news. My master was greatly vexed, that is, I may say, as much as ever I seen him, when he found how he had been taken in; but it was some comfort to have the ready cash for immediate consumption in the house any way.

And when Judy came up that evening, and brought the childer to see his honor, he unties the handkerchief, and God bless him! whether it was little or much he had, 'twas all the same with him, he gives 'em all round guineas a-piece.—'Hold up your head, (says my shister to Judy, as Sir Condy was busy filling out a glass of punch for her eldest boy)—Hold up your head, Judy, for who knows but we may live to see you yet at the head of the Castle Rackrent estate.'—'May be so, (says she) but not the way you are thinking of.'—I did not rightly understand which way Judy was looking when she makes this speech, till a while after.—'Why Thady, you were telling me yesterday that Sir Condy had sold all entirely to Jason, and where then does all them guineas in the handkerchief come from?' 'They are the purchase money of my lady's jointure,' says I.—Judy looks a little bit puzzled at this.—'A penny for your thoughts, Judy, (says my shister)—hark, sure Sir Condy is drinking her health.'—He was at the table in *the room*,* drinking with the exciseman and the gauger, who came up to see his honor, and we were standing over the fire in the kitchen.—'I don't much care is he drinking my health or not (says Judy), and it is not Sir Condy I'm thinking of, with all your jokes, whatever he is of me.' 'Sure you wouldn't refuse to be my lady Rackrent, Judy, if you had the offer?' says I.—'But if I could do better?' says she. 'How better?' says I and my shister both at once.—'How better! (says she) why what signifies it to be my lady Rackrent and no Castle? sure what good is the car and no horse to draw it?'—'And where will ye get the horse, Judy?' says I.—'Never

---

* *The room*—the principal room in the house.

you mind that, (says she)—may be it is your own son Jason
might find that.'—'Jason! (says I) don't be trusting to him,
Judy. Sir Condy, as I have good reason to know, spoke well of
you, when Jason spoke very indifferently of you, Judy.'—No
matter (says Judy), it's often men speak the contrary just to
what they think of us.'—'And you the same way of them, no
doubt, (answers I).—Nay don't be denying it, Judy, for I think
the better of ye for it, and shouldn't be proud to call ye the
daughter of a shister's son of mine, if I was to hear ye talk
ungrateful, and any way disrespectful of his honor.'—'What
disrespect, (says she) to say I'd rather, if it was my luck, be the
wife of another man?' 'You'll have no luck, mind my words,
Judy,' says I; and all I remembered about my poor master's
goodness in tossing up for her afore he married at all came
across me, and I had a choaking in my throat that hindered
me to say more.—'Better luck, any how, Thady, (says she)
than to be like some folk, following the fortunes of them that
have none left.' 'Oh King of Glory! (says I) hear the pride
and ungratitude of her, and he giving his last guineas but a
minute ago to her childer, and she with the fine shawl on her
he made a present of but yesterday!'—'Oh troth, Judy, you're
wrong now,' says my shister, looking at the shawl.—'And was
not he wrong yesterday then, (says she) to be telling me I was
greatly altered, to affront me?'—'But Judy, (says I) what is it
brings you here then at all in the mind you are in—is it to
make Jason think the better of you?'—'I'll tell you no more
of my secrets, Thady, (says she) nor would have told you this
much, had I taken you for such an unnatural fader as I find
you are, not to wish your own son prefarred to another.'—'Oh
troth, *you* are wrong, now, Thady,' says my shister.—Well, I
was never so put to it in my life between these womens, and my
son and my master, and all I felt and thought just now, I could
not upon my conscience tell which was the wrong from the
right.—So I said not a word more, but was only glad his honor
had not the luck to hear all Judy had been saying of him, for I
reckoned it would have gone nigh to break his heart, not that I
was of opinion he cared for her as much as she and my shister
fancied, but the ungratitude of the whole from Judy might not
plase him, and he could never stand the notion of not being
well spoken of or beloved like behind his back. Fortunately

for all parties concerned, he was so much elevated at this time, there was no danger of his understanding any thing, even if it had reached his ears. There was a great horn at the Lodge, ever since my master and Captain Moneygawl was in together, that used to belong originally to the celebrated Sir Patrick, his ancestor, and his honor was fond often of telling the story that he larned from me when a child, how Sir Patrick drank the full of this horn without stopping, and this was what no other man afore or since could without drawing breath.—Now Sir Condy challenged the gauger, who seemed to think little of the horn, to swallow the contents, and it filled to the brim, with punch; and the gauger said it was what he could not do for nothing, but he'd hold Sir Condy a hundred guineas he'd do it.—'Done, (says my master) I'll lay you a hundred golden guineas to a tester* you don't.'—'Done,' says the gauger, and done and done's enough between two gentlemen. The gauger was cast, and my master won the bet, and thought he'd won a hundred guineas, but by the wording it was adjudged to be only a tester that was his due, by the exciseman. It was all one to him, he was as well pleased, and I was glad to see him in such spirits again.

The gauger, bad luck to him! was the man that next proposed to my master to try himself could he take at a draught the contents of the great horn.—'Sir Patrick's horn! (said his honor) hand it to me—I'll hold you your own bet over again I'll swallow it.'—'Done, (says the gauger) I'll lay ye any thing at all you do no such thing.'—'A hundred guineas to sixpence I do, (says he) bring me the handkerchief.'—I was loth, knowing he meant the handkerchief with the gold in it, to bring it out in such company, and his honor not very well able to reckon it. 'Bring me the handkerchief then, Thady,' says he, and stamps with his foot; so with that I pulls it out of my great coat pocket, where I had put it for safety.—Oh, how it grieved me to see the guineas counting upon the table, and they the last my master had. Says Sir Condy to me—'Your hand is steadier than mine to-night, Old Thady, and that's

* *Tester*—Sixpence—from the French word tête, a head. A piece of silver stamped with a head, which in old French was called, 'un testion,' and which was about the value of an old English sixpence.—Tester is used in Shakspeare.

a wonder; fill you the horn for me.'—And so wishing his honor success, I did—but I filled it, little thinking of what would befall him.—He swallows it down, and drops like one shot.—We lifts him up, and he was speechless and quite black in the face. We put him to bed, and in a short time he wakened raving with a fever on his brain. He was shocking either to see or hear.—'Judy! Judy! have ye no touch of feeling? won't you stay to help us nurse him?' says I to her, and she putting on her shawl to go out of the house.—'I'm frighted to see him, (says she) and wouldn't, nor couldn't stay in it—and what use?—he can't last till the morning.' With that she ran off.—There was none but my shister and myself left near him of all the many friends he had. The fever came and went, and came and went, and lasted five days, and the sixth he was sensible for a few minutes, and said to me, knowing me very well—'I'm in burning pain all within side of me, Thady,'—I could not speak, but my shister asked him, would he have this thing or t'other to do him good?—'No, (says he) nothing will do me good no more'—and he gave a terrible screech with the torture he was in—then again a minute's ease—'brought to this by drink (says he)—where are all the friends?—where's Judy?—Gone, hey?—Aye, Sir Condy has been a fool all his days'—said he, and there was the last word he spoke, and died. He had but a very poor funeral, after all.

If you want to know any more, I'm not very well able to tell you; but my lady Rackrent did not die as was expected of her, but was only disfigured in the face ever after by the fall and bruises she got; and she and Jason, immediately after my poor master's death, set about going to law about that jointure; the memorandum not being on stamped paper, some say it is worth nothing, others again it may do; others say, Jason won't have the lands at any rate—many wishes it so—for my part, I'm tired wishing for any thing in this world, after all I've seen in it—but I'll say nothing; it would be a folly to be getting myself ill will in my old age. Jason did not marry, nor think of marrying Judy, as I prophesied, and I am not sorry for it—who is?—As for all I have here set down from memory and hearsay of the family, there's nothing but truth in it from beginning to end, that you may depend upon, for where's the use of telling lies about the things which every body knows as well as I do?

The Editor could have readily made the catastrophe of Sir Condy's history more dramatic and more pathetic, if he thought it allowable to varnish the plain round tale of faithful Thady. He lays it before the English reader as a specimen of manners and characters, which are perhaps unknown in England. Indeed the domestic habits of no nation in Europe were less known to the English than those of their sister country, till within these few years.

Mr. Young's picture of Ireland, in his tour through that country, was the first faithful portrait of its inhabitants. All the features in the foregoing sketch were taken from the life, and they are characteristic of that mixture of quickness, simplicity, cunning, carelessness, dissipation, disinterestedness, shrewdness and blunder, which in different forms, and with various success, has been brought upon the stage or delineated in novels.

It is a problem of difficult solution to determine, whether an Union will hasten or retard the amelioration of this country. The few gentlemen of education who now reside in this country will resort to England: they are few, but they are in nothing inferior to men of the same rank in Great Britain. The best that can happen will be the introduction of British manufacturers in their places.

Did the Warwickshire militia, who were chiefly artisans, teach the Irish to drink beer, or did they learn from the Irish to drink whiskey?

ADVERTISEMENT
TO THE
ENGLISH READER

SOME friends who have seen Thady's history since it has been printed have suggested to the Editor, that many of the terms and idiomatic phrases with which it abounds could not be intelligible to the English reader without farther explanation. The Editor has therefore furnished the following Glossary.

GLOSSARY

Page 211. *Monday morning*] Thady begins his Memoirs of the Rackrent
Family by dating *Monday morning*, because no great undertaking can
be auspiciously commenced in Ireland on any morning but *Monday
morning*.—'Oh, please God we live till Monday morning, we'll set the
slater to mend the roof of the house—On Monday morning we'll fall to
and cut the turf—On Monday morning we'll see and begin mowing—On
Monday morning, please your honor, we'll begin and dig the potatoes,'
&c.

All the intermediate days between the making of such speeches and
the ensuing Monday are wasted, and when Monday morning comes it is
ten to one that the business is deferred to *the next* Monday morning. The
Editor knew a gentleman who, to counteract this prejudice, made his
workmen and laborers begin all new pieces of work upon a Saturday.

Page 212. Let alone the three kingdoms itself] *Let alone*, in this sentence,
means *put out of the consideration*. This phrase *let alone*, which is now used
as the imperative of a verb, may in time become a conjunction, and
may exercise the ingenuity of some future etymologist. The celebrated
Horne Tooke has proved most satisfactorily, that the conjunction *but*
comes from the imperative of the Anglo-Saxon verb *(beonutan) to be out*;
also that *if* comes from *gif*, the imperative of the Anglo-Saxon verb which
signifies *to give*, &c. &c.

Page 214. Whillaluh] Ullaloo, Gol, or lamentation over the dead—

'Magnoque ululante tumultu.' VIRGIL.
'Ululatibus omne
Implevere nemus.' OVID.

A full account of the Irish Gol or Ullaloo, and of the Caoinan or Irish
funeral song, with its first semichorus, second semichorus, full chorus
of sighs and groans, together with the Irish words and music, may be
found in the fourth volume of the Transactions of the Royal Irish
Academy. For the advantage of *lazy* readers, who would rather read
a page than walk a yard, and from compassion, not to say sympathy
with their infirmity, the Editor transcribes the following passages.

'The Irish have been always remarkable for their funeral lamentations, and this peculiarity has been noticed by almost every traveller
who visited them. And it seems derived from their Celtic ancestors, the
primaeval inhabitants of this isle. . . .'

'It has been affirmed of the Irish, that to cry was more natural to
them than to any other nation, and at length the Irish cry became
proverbial. . . .'

'Cambrensis in the twelfth century says, the Irish then musically expressed their griefs; that is, they applied the musical art, in which they excelled all others, to the orderly celebration of funeral obsequies, by dividing the mourners into two bodies, each alternately singing their part, and the whole at times joining in full chorus. . . . The body of the deceased, dressed in grave clothes and ornamented with flowers, was placed on a bier or some elevated spot. The relations and Keeners (*singing mourners*) ranged themselves in two divisions, one at the head and the other at the feet of the corpse. The bards and croteries had before prepared the funeral Caoinan. The chief bard of the head chorus began by singing the first stanza in a low, doleful tone, which was softly accompanied by the harp: at the conclusion the foot semichorus began the lamentation, or Ullaloo, from the final note of the preceding stanza, in which they were answered by the head semichorus; then both united in one general chorus. The chorus of the first stanza being ended, the chief bard of the foot semichorus began the second Gol or lamentation, in which they were answered by that of the head; and then as before both united in the general full chorus. Thus alternately were the song and chorusses performed during the night. The genealogy, rank, possessions, the virtues and vices of the dead were rehearsed, and a number of interrogations were addressed to the deceased: as, Why did he die? If married, whether his wife was faithful to him, his sons dutiful, or good hunters or warriors? If a woman, whether her daughters were fair or chaste? If a young man, whether he had been crossed in love? or if the blue-eyed maids of Erin treated him with scorn?'

We are told that formerly the feet (the metrical feet) of the Caoinan were much attended to, but on the decline of the Irish bards these feet were gradually neglected, the Caoinan fell into a sort of slip-shod metre amongst women. Each province had different Caoinans, or at least different imitations of the original. There was the Munster cry, the Ulster cry, &c. It became an extempore performance, and every set of Keeners varied the melody according to their own fancy.

It is curious to observe how customs and ceremonies degenerate. The present Irish cry or howl cannot boast of much melody, nor is the funeral procession conducted with much dignity. The crowd of people who assembled at these funerals sometimes amounts to a thousand, often to four or five hundred. They gather as the bearers of the hearse proceed on their way, and when they pass through any village, or when they come near any houses, they begin to cry—Oh! Oh! Oh! Oh! Oh! Agh! Agh! raising their notes from the first *Oh!* to the last *Agh!* in a kind of mournful howl. This gives notice to the inhabitants of the village that a *funeral is passing*, and immediately they flock out to follow it. In the province of Munster it is a common thing for the women to follow a funeral, to join in the universal cry with all their might and main for some time, and then to turn and ask—'Arrah! who is it that's dead?—who is it we're crying for?'—Even the poorest people have their own burying-places, that is, spots of ground in the church-yards, where they say that their ancestors have been buried ever since the wars of Ireland: and if these burial-places are ten miles from the place where a man dies, his friends and neighbours take care to carry his corpse thither. Always one priest, often five or six priests, attend these funerals; each priest repeats a mass, for which he is paid sometimes a shilling, sometimes half a crown, sometimes half a guinea, or a guinea, according to the circumstances, or as they say, according to the *ability* of the deceased. After the burial of any very poor man who has left a widow or children, the priest makes what is called *a collection* for the widow; he goes round to every person present, and each contributes sixpence or a shilling, or what they please. The reader will find in the note upon the word *Wake* more particulars respecting the conclusion of the Irish funerals.

Certain old women, who cry particularly loud and well, are in great request, and, as a man said to the Editor, 'Every one would wish and be proud to have such at his funeral, or at that of his friends.' The lower Irish are wonderfully eager to attend the funerals of their friends and relations, and they make their relationships branch out to a great extent. The proof that a poor man has been well beloved during his life, is his having a crowded funeral. To attend a neighbour's funeral is a cheap proof of humanity, but it does not, as some imagine, cost nothing. The time spent in attending funerals may be safely valued at half a million to the Irish nation: the Editor thinks that double that sum would not be too high an estimate. The habits of profligacy and drunkenness which are acquired at *wakes* are here put out of the question. When a labourer, a carpenter, or a smith is not at his work, which frequently happens, ask where he is gone, and ten to one the answer is—'Oh faith, please your honor, he couldn't do a stroke to-day, for he's gone to *the* funeral.'

Even beggars, when they grow old, go about begging *for their own funerals*; that is, begging for money to buy a coffin, candles, pipes and tobacco.—For the use of the candles, pipes and tobacco, see *Wake*.

Those who value customs in proportion to their antiquity, and nations in proportion to their adherence to antient customs, will doubtless admire the Irish *Ullaloo*, and the Irish nation, for persevering in this usage from time immemorial. The Editor, however, has observed some alarming symptoms, which seem to prognosticate the declining taste for the Ullaloo in Ireland. In a comic theatrical entertainment represented not long since on the Dublin stage, a chorus of old women was introduced, who set up the Irish howl round the relics of a physician, who is supposed to have fallen under the wooden sword of Harlequin. After the old women have continued their Ullaloo for a decent time, with all the necessary accompaniments of wringing their hands, wiping or rubbing their eyes with the corners of their gowns or aprons, &c. one of the mourners suddenly suspends her lamentable cries, and turning to her neighbour, asks—'Arrah now, honey, who is it we're crying for?'

Page 214. The tenants even were sent away without their whiskey] It is usual with some landlords to give their inferior tenants a glass of whiskey when they pay their rents. Thady calls it *their* whiskey; not that the whiskey is actually the property of the tenants, but that it becomes their *right*, after it has been often given to them. In this general mode of reasoning respecting *rights*, the lower Irish are not singular, but they are peculiarly quick and tenacious in claiming these rights.—'Last year your honor gave me some straw for the roof of my house, and I *expect* your honor will be after doing the same this year.'—In this manner gifts are frequently turned into tributes. The high and low are not always dissimilar in their habits. It is said that the Sublime Ottoman Porte is very apt to claim gifts as tributes: thus it is dangerous to send the Grand Seignor a fine horse on his birth-day one year, lest on his next birth-day he should expect a similar present, and should proceed to demonstrate the reasonableness of his expectations.

Page 214. He demeaned himself greatly] Means, he lowered, or disgraced himself much.

Page 215. Duty fowls, and duty turkies, and duty geese] In many leases in Ireland, tenants were *formerly* bound to supply an inordinate quantity of poultry to their landlords. The Editor knew of sixty turkies being reserved in one lease of a small farm.

Page 216. English tenants] An English tenant does not mean a tenant who is an Englishman, but a tenant who pays his rent the day that it is due. It is a common prejudice in Ireland, amongst the poorer classes of people, to believe that all tenants in England pay their rents on the very day when they become due. An Irishman, when he goes to take a farm, if he wants to prove to his landlord that he is a substantial man, offers to become an *English tenant*. If a tenant disobliges his landlord by voting against him, or against his opinion, at an election, the tenant is immediately informed by the agent that he must become *an English tenant*. This threat does not imply that he is to change his language or his country, but that he must pay all the arrear of rent which he owes, and that he must thenceforward pay his rent on the day when it becomes due.

Page 216. Canting] Does not mean talking or writing hypocritical nonsense, but selling substantially by auction.

Page 216. Duty work] It was formerly common in Ireland to insert clauses in leases, binding tenants to furnish their landlords with laborers and horses for several days in the year. Much petty tyranny and oppression have resulted from this feudal custom. Whenever a poor man disobliged his landlord, the agent sent to him for his duty work, and Thady does not exaggerate when he says, that the tenants were often called from their own work to do that of their landlord. Thus the very means of earning their rent were taken from them: whilst they were getting home their landlord's harvest, their own was often ruined, and yet their rents were expected to be paid as punctually as if their time had been at their own disposal. This appears the height of absurd injustice.

In Esthonia, amongst the poor Sclavonian race of peasant slaves, they pay tributes to their lords, not under the name of duty work, duty geese, duty turkies, &c. but under the name of *righteousnesses*. The following ballad is a curious specimen of Estonian poetry:

This is the cause that the country is ruined,
And the straw of the thatch is eaten away,
The gentry are come to live in the land—
Chimneys between the village,
And the proprietor upon the white floor!
The sheep brings forth a lamb with a white forehead;
This is paid to the lord for a *righteousness sheep*.
The sow farrows pigs,
They go to the spit of the lord.
The hen lays eggs,
They go into the lord's frying-pan.
The cow drops a male calf,
That goes into the lord's herd as a bull.
The mare foals a horse foal,
That must be for my lord's nag.
The boor's wife has sons,
They must go to look after my lord's poultry.

Page 217. Out of forty-nine suits which he had, he never lost one—but seventeen] Thady's language in this instance is a specimen of a mode of rhetoric common in Ireland. An astonishing assertion is made in the beginning of a sentence, which ceases to be in the least surprizing when you hear the qualifying explanation that follows. Thus a man who is in the last stage of staggering drunkenness will, if he can articulate, swear to you—'Upon his conscience now (and may he never stir from the spot alive if he is telling a lie) upon his conscience he has not tasted a drop of any thing, good or bad, since morning at-all-at-all—but half a pint of whiskey, please your honor.'

Page 217. Fairy-mounts] Barrows. It is said that these high mounts were of great service to the natives of Ireland, when Ireland was invaded by the Danes. Watch was always kept on them, and upon the approach of an enemy a fire was lighted to give notice to the next watch, and thus the intelligence was quickly communicated through the country. *Some years ago*, the common people believed that these Barrows were inhabited by fairies, or as they call them, by the *good people*.—'Oh troth, to the best of my belief, and to the best of my judgment and opinion, (said an elderly man to the Editor) it was only the old people that had nothing to do, and got together and were telling stories about them fairies, but to the best of my judgment there's nothing in it.—Only this I heard myself not very many years back, from a decent kind of a man, a grazier, that as he was coming just *fair and easy (quietly)* from the fair, with some cattle and sheep that he had not sold, just at the church of——, at an angle of the road like, he was met by a good looking man, who asked him where was he going? And he answered, "Oh, far enough, I must be going all night."—"No, that you mustn't nor won't (says the man), you'll sleep with me the night, and you'll want for nothing, nor your cattle nor sheep neither, nor your *beast (horse)*; so come along with me."—With that the grazier *lit* (alighted) from his horse, and it was dark night; but presently he finds himself, he does not know in the wide world how, in a fine house, and plenty of everything to eat and drink— nothing at all wanting that he could wish for or think of—And he does not *mind* *(recollect,* or *know)* how at last he falls asleep; and in the morning he finds himself lying, not in ever a bed or a house at all, but just in the angle of the road where first he met the strange man: there he finds himself lying on his back on the grass, and all his sheep feeding as quiet as ever all round about him, and his horse the same way, and the bridle of the beast over his wrist. And I asked him what he thought of it, and from first to last he could think of nothing but for certain sure it must have been the fairies that entertained him so well. For there was no house to see any where nigh hand, or any building, or barn, or place at all, but only the church and the *mote (barrow)*. There's another odd thing enough that they tell about this same church, that if any person's corpse, that had not a right to be buried in that church-yard, went to be burying there in it, no not all the men, women, or childer in all Ireland could get the corpse any way into the church-yard; but as they would be trying to go into the church-yard, their feet would seem to be going backwards instead of forwards; aye, continually backwards the whole funeral would seem to go; and they would never set foot with the corpse in the church-yard. Now they say, that it is the fairies do all this; but it is my opinion it is all idle talk, and people are after being wiser now.'

The country people in Ireland certainly *had* great admiration mixed with reverence, if not dread of fairies. They believed, that beneath these fairy mounts were spacious subterraneous palaces inhabited by *the good people,* who must not on any account be disturbed. When the wind raises a little eddy of dust upon the road, the poor people believe that it is raised by the fairies, that it is a sign that they are journeying from one of the fairy mounts to another, and they say to the fairies, or to the dust as it passes—'God speed ye, gentlemen, God speed ye.' This averts any evil that *the good people* might be inclined to do them. There are innumerable stories told of the friendly and unfriendly feats of these busy fairies; some of these tales are ludicrous, and some romantic enough for poetry. It is a pity that poets should lose such convenient, though diminutive machinery.—By the by, Parnell, who shewed himself so deeply 'skilled of faerie lore,' was an Irishman; and though he has presented his faeries to the world in the ancient English dress of 'Britain's Isle, and Arthur's days,' it is probable that his first acquaintance with them began in his native country.

Some remote origin for the most superstitious or romantic popular illusions or vulgar errors may often be discovered. In Ireland, the old churches and church-yards have been usually fixed upon as the scenes of wonders. Now the antiquarians tell us, that near the ancient churches in that kingdom caves of various constructions have from time to time been discovered, which were formerly used as granaries or magazines by the ancient inhabitants, and as places to which they retreated in time of danger. There is (p. 84 of the R. I. A. Transactions for 1789) a particular account of a number of these artificial caves at the West end of the church of Killossy, in the county of Kildare. Under a rising ground, in a dry sandy soil, these subterraneous dwellings were found: they have pediment roofs, and they communicate with each other by small apertures. In the Brehon laws these are mentioned, and there are finds inflicted by those laws upon persons who steal from the subterraneous granaries. All these things shew, that there was a real foundation for the stories which were told of the appearance of lights and of sounds of voices near these places. The persons who had property concealed there very willingly countenanced every wonderful relation that tended to make these places objects of sacred awe or superstitious terror.

Page 218. Weed ashes] By antient usage in Ireland, all the weeds on a farm belonged to the farmer's wife, or to the wife of the squire who holds the ground in his own hands. The great demand for alkaline salts in bleaching rendered these ashes no inconsiderable perquisite.

Page 218. Sealing money] Formerly it was the custom in Ireland for tenants to give the squire's lady from two to fifty guineas as a perquisite upon the sealing of their leases. The Editor not very long since knew of a baronet's lady accepting fifty guineas as sealing money, upon closing a bargain for a considerable farm.

Page 218. Sir Murtagh grew mad] Sir Murtagh grew angry.

Page 218. The whole kitchen was out on the stairs] Means that all the inhabitants of the kitchen came out of the kitchen and stood upon the stairs. These, and similar expressions, shew how much the Irish are disposed to metaphor and amplification.

Page 221. Fining down the yearly rent] When an Irish gentleman, like Sir Kit Rackrent, has lived beyond his income, and finds himself distressed for want of ready money, tenants obligingly offer to take his land at a rent far below the value, and to pay him a small sum of money in hand, which they call fining down the yearly rent. The temptation of this ready cash often blinds the landlord to his future interest.

Page 221. Driver] A man who is employed to drive tenants for rent; that is, to drive the cattle belonging to tenants to pound. The office of driver is by no means a sinecure.

Page 221. I thought to make him a priest] It was customary amongst those of Thady's rank, in Ireland, whenever they could get a little money, to send their sons abroad to St. Omer's, or to Spain, to be educated as priests. Now they are educated at Maynooth. The Editor has lately known a young lad, who began by being a post-boy, afterwards turn into a carpenter; then quit his plane and work-bench to study his *Humanities*, as he said, at the college of Maynooth: but after he had gone through his course of Humanities, he determined to be a soldier instead of a priest.

Page 223. Flam] Short for flambeau.

Page 224. Barrack room] Formerly it was customary, in gentlemen's houses in Ireland, to fit up one large bedchamber with a number of beds for the reception of occasional visitors. These rooms were called Barrack rooms.

Page 224. An innocent] in Ireland, means a simpleton, an idiot.

Page 230. The Curragh] is the Newmarket of Ireland.

Page 230. The Cant] The auction.

Page 233. And so should cut him off for ever, by levying a fine, and suffering a recovery to dock the entail] The English reader may perhaps be surprised at the extent of Thady's legal knowledge, and at the fluency with which he pours forth law terms; but almost every poor man in Ireland, be he farmer, weaver, shopkeeper, or steward, is, beside his other occupations, occasionally a lawyer. The nature of processes, ejectments, custodiams, injunctions, replevins, &c. &c. are perfectly known to them, and the terms are as familiar to them as to any attorney. They all love law. It is a kind of lottery, in which every man, staking his own wit or cunning against his richer neighbour's property, feels that he has little to lose and much to gain.

'I'll have the law of you, so I will!'—is the saying of an Englishman who expects justice. 'I'll have you before his honor'—is the threat of an Irishman who hopes for partiality. Miserable is the life of a justice of the peace in Ireland the day after a fair, especially if he resides near a small town. The multitude of the *kilt* (*kilt* does not mean *killed*, but hurt) and wounded who came before his honor with black eyes or bloody heads is astonishing, but more astonishing is the number of those, who, though they are scarcely able by daily labour to procure daily food, will nevertheless, without the least reluctance, waste six or seven hours of the day lounging in the yard or hall of a justice of the peace, waiting to make some complaint about—nothing. It is impossible to convince them that *time is money*. They do not set any value upon their own time, and they think that others estimate theirs at less than nothing. Hence they make no scruple of telling a justice of the peace a story of an hour long about a *tester* (sixpence): and if he grow impatient, they attribute it to some secret prejudice which he entertains against them.

Their method is to get a story completely by heart, and to tell it, as they call it, *out of the face*, that is, from the beginning to the end, without interruption.

'Well, my good friend, I have seen you lounging about these three hours in the yard; what is your business?'

'Please your honor, it is what I want to speak one word to your honor.'

'Speak then, but be quick—What is the matter?'

'Nothing strange—The matter, please your honor, is nothing at-all-at-all, only just about the grazing of a horse, please your honor, that this man here sold me at the fair of Gurtishannon last Shrove fair, which lay down three times with myself, please your honor, and *kilt* me; not to be telling your honor of how, no later back than yesterday night, he lay down in the house there within, and all the childer standing round, and it was God's mercy he did not fall a'-top of them, or into the fire to burn himself. So please your honor, to-day I took him back to this man, which owned him, and after a great deal to do I got the mare again I *swopped* (*exchanged*) him for; but he wont't pay the grazing of the horse for the time I had him, though he promised to pay the grazing in case

the horse didn't answer; and he never did a day's work, good or bad,
please your honor, all the time he was with me, and I had the doctor to
him five times, any how. And so, please your honor, it is what I expect
your honor will stand my friend, for I'd sooner come to your honor for
justice than to any other in all Ireland. And so I brought him here before
your honor, and expect your honor will make him pay me the grazing, or
tell me, can I process him for it at the next assizes, please your honor?'

The defendant now, turning a quid of tobacco with his tongue into
some secret cavern in his mouth, begins his defence with—

'Please your honor, under favor, and saving your honor's presence,
there's not a word of truth in all this man has been saying from beginning
to end, upon my conscience, and I wouldn't for the value of the horse
itself, grazing and all, be after telling your honor a lie. For please your
honor, I have a dependance upon your honor that you'll do me justice,
and not be listening to him or the like of him. Please your honor, it's what
he has brought me before your honor, because he had a spite against me
about some oats I sold your honor, which he was jealous of, and a shawl
his wife got at my shister's shop there without, and never paid for; so I
offered to set the shawl against the grazing, and give him a receipt in
full of all demands, but he wouldn't out of spite, please your honor; so
he brought me before your honor, expecting your honor was mad with
me for cutting down the tree in the horse park, which was none of my
doing, please your honor—ill luck to them that went and belied me to
your honor behind my back!—So if your honor is pleasing, I'll tell you
the whole truth about the horse that he swopped against my mare, out
of the face.—Last Shrove fair I met this man, Jemmy Duffy, please your
honor, just at the corner of the road where the bridge is broke down that
your honor is to have the presentment for this year—long life to you for
it!—And he was at that time coming from the fair of Gurtishannon, and
I the same way. 'How are you, Jemmy?' says I.—'Very well, I thank ye
kindly, Bryan,' says he; 'shall we turn back to Paddy Salmon's, and take
a naggin of whiskey to our better acquaintance?'—'I don't care if I did,
Jemmy,' says I; 'only it is what I can't take the whiskey, because I'm
under an oath against it for a month.' Ever since, please your honor,
the day your honor met me on the road, and observed to me I could
hardly stand I had taken so much—though upon my conscience your
honor wronged me greatly that same time—ill luck to them that belied
me behind my back to your honor!—Well, please your honor, as I was
telling you, as he was taking the whiskey, and we talking of one thing or
t'other, he makes me an offer to swop his mare that he couldn't sell at
the fair of Gurtishannon, because nobody would be troubled with the
beast, please your honor, against my horse, and to oblige him I took the
mare—sorrow take her! and him along with her!—She kicked me a new
car, that was worth three pounds ten, to tatters the first time ever I put
her into it, and I expect your honor will make him pay me the price of
the car, any how, before I pay the grazing, which I've no right to pay
at-all-at-all, only to oblige him.—But I leave it all to your honour—and
the whole grazing he ought to be charging for the beast is but two and

eight-pence half-penny, any how, please your honour. So I'll abide by what your honor says, good or bad. I'll leave it all to your honor.'

I'll leave *it* all to your honor—literally means, I'll leave all the trouble to your honor.

The Editor knew a justice of the peace in Ireland, who had such a dread of *having it all left to his honor*, that he frequently gave the complainants the sum about which they were disputing to make peace between them, and to get rid of the trouble of hearing their stories *out of the face*. But he was soon cured of this method of buying off disputes, by the increasing multitude of those who, out of pure regard to his honor, came 'to get justice from him, because they would sooner come before him than before any man in all Ireland.'

Page 243. A raking pot of tea] We should observe, that this custom has long since been banished from the higher orders of Irish gentry. The mysteries of a raking pot of tea, like those of the Bona Dea, are supposed to be sacred to females, but now and then it has happened that some of the male species, who were either more audacious or more highly favored than the rest of their sex, have been admitted by stealth to these orgies. The time when the festive ceremony begins varies according to circumstances, but it is never earlier than twelve o'clock at night; the joys of a raking pot of tea depending on its being made in secret, and at an unseasonable hour. After a ball, when the more discreet part of the company had departed to rest, a few chosen female spirits, who have footed it till they can foot it no longer, and till the sleepy notes expire under the slurring hand of the musician, retire to a bed-chamber, call the favorite maid, who alone is admitted, bid her *put down the kettle*, lock the door, and amidst as much giggling and scrambling as possible, they get round a tea-table, on which all manner of things are huddled together. Then begin mutual railleries and mutual confidences amongst the young ladies, and the faint scream and the loud laugh is heard, and the romping for letters and pocket-books begins, and gentlemen are called by their surnames, or by the general name of fellows—pleasant fellows! charming fellows! odious fellows! abominable fellows!—and then all prudish decorums are forgotten, and then we might be convinced how much the satyrical poet was mistaken when he said,

'There is no woman where there's no reserve.'

The merit of the original idea of a raking pot of tea evidently belongs to the washerwoman and the laundry-maid. But why should not we have *Low life above stairs*, as well as *High life below stairs*?

Page 245. Carton, or half Carton] Thady means cartron or half cartron. 'According to the old record in the black book of Dublin, a *cantred* is said to contain 30 *villatas terras*, which are also called *quarters* of land (quarterons, *cartrons*); every one of which quarters must contain so much ground as will pasture 400 cows and 17 plough-lands. A knight's fee was composed of 8 hydes, which amount to 160 acres, and that is generally deemed about a *ploughland*.'

The Editor was favored by a learned friend with the above Extract, from a MS. of Lord Totness's in the Lambeth library.

Page 261. Wake] A wake, in England, means a festival held upon the anniversary of the Saint of the parish. At these wakes rustic games, rustic conviviality, and rustic courtship, are pursued with all the ardour and all the appetite, which accompany such pleasures as occur but seldom.—In Ireland a wake is a midnight meeting, held professedly for the indulgence of holy sorrow, but usually it is converted into orgies of unholy joy. When an Irish man or woman of the lower order dies, the straw which composed his bed, whether it has been contained in a bag to form a mattress, or simply spread upon the earthen floor, is immediately taken out of the house, and burned before the cabin door, the family at the same time setting up the death howl. The ears and eyes of the neighbours being thus alarmed, they flock to the house of the deceased, and by their vociferous sympathy excite and at the same time sooth the sorrows of the family.

It is curious to observe how good and bad are mingled in human institutions. In countries which were thinly inhabited, this custom prevented private attempts against the lives of individuals, and formed a kind of Coroner's inquest upon the body which had recently expired, and burning the straw upon which the sick man lay became a simple preservative against infection. At night the dead body is waked, that it to say, all the friends and neighbours of the deceased collect in a barn or stable, where the corpse is laid upon some boards, or an unhinged door supported upon stools, the face exposed, the rest of the body covered with a white sheet. Round the body are stuck in brass candlesticks, which have been borrowed perhaps at five miles distance, as many candles as the poor person can beg or borrow, observing always to have an odd number. Pipes and tobacco are first distributed, and then according to the *ability* of the deceased, cakes and ale, and sometimes whiskey, are *dealt* to the company.

> 'Deal on, deal on, my merry men all,
> Deal on your cakes and your wine,
> For whatever is dealt at her funeral to-day
> Shall be dealt to-morrow at mine.'

After a fit of universal sorrow, and the comfort of a universal dram, the scandal of the neighbourhood, as in higher circles, occupy the company. The young lads and lasses romp with one another, and when the fathers and mothers are at last overcome with sleep and whiskey, (*vino & somno*) the youth become more enterprizing and are frequently successful. It is said that more matches are made at wakes than at weddings.

Page 263. Kilt] This word frequently occurs in the following pages, where it means not *killed*, but much *hurt*. In Ireland, not only cowards, but the brave 'die many times before their death'. There *Killing is no murder*.

Elizabeth Gaskell

MR HARRISON'S CONFESSIONS
1851

LORD DAVID CECIL made a good common-sense point when in *Early Victorian Novelists* he began the chapter on Elizabeth Gaskell (1810–65) with the words, 'Charlotte Brontë's admirers do not think of her as Mrs Nichols; George Eliot's admirers would wonder whom we meant if one referred to her as Mrs Cross. But Elizabeth Cleghorn Stevenson is known to the world as Mrs Gaskell. This is just as it should be. There is a great difference between her and her famous rivals: and this difference is fitly symbolized in the different form of name under which she elected to write.' Cecil was writing in 1934, when it was still customary to differentiate the sex of women writers, but even in our dour epoch when they are unceremoniously lumped in as 'Austen', 'Woolf', 'Plath', the sex lost in the shirt-sleeved abruptness that is felt to be what women want or at any rate must be given, one still feels a persistent wish to give Mrs Gaskell her 'Mrs'. A Cheshire girl, at the age of twenty-two she married a Unitarian minister in Manchester and seems never to have regretted it. She was perfectly content with marriage and with her husband, and altogether seems to have been as convinced of the superiority of domestic harmony and family devotion over all other forms of happiness as Queen Victoria herself. She sees life as a minister's wife in the provinces sees it, and her achievement is that because it seems wonderfully fresh and interesting to her, it seems the same to us, her readers.

Even the occasion of her plunge into authorship was domestic and maternal; her only son, William, died at a year old, and to distract her mind from the grief this caused her she wrote *Mary Barton* (1848), which attracted the attention of Dickens. He had not yet launched the phenomenally successful periodical *Household Words*, but after it began in 1851 he made Mrs Gaskell a regular contributor, notably with the first episode of *Cranford* in 1851 and the whole of *North and South* in 1854–5.

Warm-hearted, observant of detail, a natural story-teller, endowed with humour and insight, Mrs Gaskell was the ideal contributor to the magazines of her day; *Mr Harrison's Confessions* appeared in *The Lady's Companion* in 1851, the central date of the mid-Victorian era, the year of the Great Exhibition, when the values of Victoria and her consort Albert dominated England and England dominated the world. It is a good-humoured story of the misunderstanding and gossip that surround a young doctor trying to establish himself both professionally and personally in a North

Midland country town, and in the unselfconsciousness both of its humour and its pathos it has all the perfect confidence of its epoch. The ladies, of marriageable and not-so-marriageable age, are just as much on the *qui vive* for husbands as the early heroines of Jane Austen, and the society Mrs Gaskell describes is not unlike that of Jane Austen, though slightly lower in the social scale; but her writing is less spare and astringent and her judgements softer; Jane Austen has matchless wit, but Mrs Gaskell has companionable humour.

The success of her work brought her some modest wealth, enough to travel to France, Germany, and Italy, and to buy property when she needed it; and also the friendship of other writers, including some of the most famous (Charlotte Brontë, the Carlyles, Ruskin, and, up to a point, Dickens, though they tended to remain editor and contributor). But she never became oblivious of the industrial workers in the Manchester area, or their equally poor counterparts in the countryside, and tried in every way she could to alleviate their frequent sufferings. Mid-Victorian England needed a novelist like Mrs Gaskell, and the *nouvelle* reprinted here, though an early work and not one of her peaks, is a pleasant reminder of her likeable qualities.

I

THE fire was burning gaily. My wife had just gone upstairs to put baby to bed. Charles sat opposite to me, looking very brown and handsome. It was pleasant enough that we should feel sure of spending some weeks under the same roof, a thing which we had never done since we were mere boys. I felt too lazy to talk, so I ate walnuts and looked into the fire. But Charles grew restless.

'Now that your wife is gone upstairs, Will, you must tell me what I've wanted to ask you ever since I saw her this morning. Tell me all about the wooing and winning. I want to have the receipt for getting such a charming little wife of my own. Your letters only gave the barest details. So set to, man, and tell me every particular.'

'If I tell you all, it will be a long story.'

'Never fear. If I get tired, I can go to sleep, and dream that I am back again, a lonely bachelor, in Ceylon, and I can waken up when you have done, to know that I am under your roof. Dash away, man! "Once upon a time, a gallant young bachelor"——There's a beginning for you!'

'Well, then, "Once upon a time, a gallant young bachelor" was sorely puzzled where to settle, when he had completed his education as a surgeon—I must speak in the first person; I cannot go on as a gallant young bachelor. I had just finished walking the hospitals when you went to Ceylon, and, if you remember, I wanted to go abroad like you, and thought of offering myself as a ship-surgeon; but I found I should rather lose caste in my profession; so I hesitated, and while I was hesitating, I received a letter from my father's cousin, Mr. Morgan—that old gentleman who used to write such long letters of good advice to my mother, and who tipped me a five-pound note when I agreed to be bound apprentice to Mr. Howard, instead of going to sea. Well, it seems the old gentleman had all along thought of taking me as his partner, if I turned out pretty well; and as he heard a good account of me from an old friend of his, who was a surgeon at Guy's, he wrote to propose this arrangement: I was to have a third of the profits for five years; after that, half; and eventually I was to succeed to the whole. It was no bad offer for a penniless man like me, as Mr. Morgan had a capital country practice, and, though I did not know him personally, I had formed a pretty good idea of him, as an honourable, kind-hearted, fidgety, meddlesome old bachelor; and a very correct notion it was, as I found out in the very first half-hour of seeing him. I had had some idea that I was to live in his house, as he was a bachelor and a kind of family friend; and I think he was afraid that I should expect this arrangement, for when I walked up to his door, with the porter carrying my portmanteau, he met me on the steps, and while he held my hand and shook it, he said to the porter, "Jerry, if you'll wait a moment, Mr. Harrison will be ready to go with you to his lodgings, at Jocelyn's, you know"; and then turning to me, he addressed his first words of welcome. I was a little inclined to think him inhospitable, but I got to understand him better afterwards. "Jocelyn's", said he, "is the best place I have been able to hit upon in a hurry, and there is a good deal of fever about, which made me desirous that you should come this month—a low kind of typhoid, in the oldest part of the town. I think you'll be comfortable there for a week or two. I have taken the liberty of desiring my housekeeper to send down one or two things which give the place a little more of a home aspect—an easy-chair, a beautiful case of preparations, and one or two little matters in the way of eatables; but if you'll take my advice, I've a plan in my head which we will talk about to-morrow morning. At present, I don't like to keep you standing out on the steps here, so I'll not detain you from your lodgings, where I rather think my housekeeper is gone to get tea ready for you."

'I thought I understood the old gentleman's anxiety for his own health, which he put upon care for mine, for he had on a kind of loose grey coat, and no hat on his head. But I wondered that he did not ask me indoors, instead of keeping me on the steps. I believe, after all, I made a mistake in supposing he was afraid of taking cold; he was only afraid of being seen in deshabille. And for his apparent inhospitality, I had not been long in Duncombe before I understood the comfort of having one's house considered as a castle into which no one might intrude, and saw good reason for the practice Mr. Morgan had established of coming to his door to speak to every one. It was only the effect of habit that made him receive me so. Before long, I had the free run of his house.

'There was every sign of kind attention and forethought on the part of some one, whom I could not doubt to be Mr. Morgan, in my lodgings. I was too lazy to do much that evening, and sat in the little bow-window which projected over Jocelyn's shop, looking up and down the street. Duncombe calls itself a town, but I should call it a village. Really, looking from Jocelyn's, it is a very picturesque place. The houses are anything but regular; they may be mean in their details; but altogether they look well; they have not that flat, unrelieved front, which many towns of far more pretensions present. Here and there a bow-window—every now and then a gable, cutting up against the sky—occasionally a projecting upper storey—throws good effect of light and shadow along the street; and they have a queer fashion of their own of colouring the whitewash of some of the houses with a sort of pink blotting-paper tinge, more like the stone of which Mayence is built than anything else. It may be very bad taste, but to my mind it gives a rich warmth to the colouring. Then, here and there a dwelling-house has a court in front, with a grass-plot on each side of the flagged walk, and a large tree or two—limes or horse chestnuts—which send their great, projecting upper branches over into the street, making round dry places of shelter on the pavement in the times of summer showers.

'While I was sitting in the bow-window, thinking of the contrast between this place and the lodgings in the heart of London, which I had left only twelve hours before—the window open here, and, although in the centre of the town, admitting only scents from the mignonette boxes on the sill, instead of the dust and smoke of —— Street—the only sound heard in this, the principal street, being the voices of mothers calling their playing children home to bed, and the eight o'clock bell of the old parish church bim-bomming in remembrance of the curfew; while I was sitting thus idly, the door opened, and the little maid-servant, dropping a curtsy, said—

' "Please, sir, Mrs. Munton's compliments, and she would be glad to know how you are after your journey."

'There! was not that hearty and kind? Would you even the dearest chum I had at Guy's have thought of doing such a thing? while Mrs. Munton, whose name I had never heard of before, was doubtless suffering anxiety till I could relieve her mind by sending back word that I was pretty well.

' "My compliments to Mrs. Munton, and I am pretty well: much obliged to her." It was as well to say only "pretty well", for "very well" would have destroyed the interest Mrs. Munton evidently felt in me. Good Mrs. Munton! Kind Mrs. Munton! Perhaps, also, young—handsome—rich—widowed Mrs. Munton! I rubbed my hands with delight and amusement, and, resuming my post of observation, began to wonder at which house Mrs. Munton lived.

'Again the little tap, and the little maid-servant—

' "Please, sir, the Miss Tomkinsons' compliments, and they would be glad to know how you feel yourself after your journey."

'I don't know why, but the Miss Tomkinsons' name had not such a halo about it as Mrs. Munton's. Still it was very pretty in the Miss Tomkinsons to send and inquire. I only wished I did not feel so perfectly robust. I was almost ashamed that I could not send word I was quite exhausted by fatigue, and had fainted twice since my arrival. If I had but had a headache, at least! I heaved a deep breath: my chest was in perfect order; I had caught no cold; so I answered again—

' "Much obliged to the Miss Tomkinsons; I am not much fatigued; tolerably well: my compliments."

'Little Sally could hardly have got downstairs, before she returned, bright and breathless—

' "Mr. and Mrs. Bullock's compliments, sir, and they hope you are pretty well after your journey."

'Who would have expected such kindness from such an unpromising name? Mr. and Mrs. Bullock were less interesting, it is true, than their predecessors; but I graciously replied—

' "My compliments; a night's rest will perfectly recruit me."

'The same message was presently brought up from one or two more unknown kind hearts. I really wished I were not so ruddy-looking. I was afraid I should disappoint the tender-hearted town when they saw what a hale young fellow I was. And I was almost ashamed of confessing to a great appetite for supper when Sally came up to inquire what I would have. Beefsteaks were so tempting; but perhaps I ought rather to have water-gruel, and go to bed. The beefsteak carried the day, however. I need not have felt such a gentle elation of spirits, as this mark of the town's attention is paid to every one when they arrive after a journey. Many of the same people have sent to inquire after you—great, hulking, brown fellow as you are—only Sally spared you the infliction of devising interesting answers.

II

'THE next morning Mr. Morgan came before I had finished breakfast. He was the most dapper little man I ever met. I see the affection with which people cling to the style of dress that was in vogue when they were beaux and belles, and received the most admiration. They are unwilling to believe that their youth and beauty are gone, and think that the prevailing mode is unbecoming. Mr. Morgan will inveigh by the hour together against frock-coats, for instance, and whiskers. He keeps his chin close shaven, wears a black dress-coat, and dark-grey pantaloons; and in his morning round to his town patients, he invariably wears the brightest and blackest of Hessian boots, with dangling silk tassels on each side. When he goes home, about ten o'clock, to prepare for his ride to see his country patients, he puts on the most dandy top-boots I ever saw, which he gets from some wonderful bootmaker a hundred miles off. His appearance is what one calls "jemmy"; there is no other word that will do for it. He was evidently a little discomfited when he saw me in my breakfast costume, with the habits which I brought with me from the fellows at Guy's; my feet against the fireplace, my chair balanced on its hind legs (a habit of sitting which I afterwards discovered he particularly abhorred); slippers on my feet (which, also, he considered a most ungentlemanly piece of untidiness "out of a bedroom"); in short, from what I afterwards learned, every prejudice he had was outraged by my appearance on this first visit of his. I put my book down, and sprang up to receive him. He stood, hat and cane in hand.

' "I came to inquire if it would be convenient for you to accompany me on my morning's round, and to be introduced to a few of our friends." I quite detected the little tone of coldness, induced by his disappointment at my appearance, though he never imagined that it was in any way perceptible. "I will be ready directly, sir," said I; and bolted into my bedroom, only too happy to escape his scrutinizing eye.

'When I returned, I was made aware, by sundry indescribable little coughs and hesitating noises, that my dress did not satisfy him. I stood ready, hat and gloves in hand; but still he did not offer to set off on our round. I grew very red and hot. At length he said—

' "Excuse me, my dear young friend, but may I ask if you have no other coat besides that—'cut-away', I believe you call them? We are rather sticklers for propriety, I believe, in Duncombe; and much depends on a first impression. Let it be professional, my dear sir. Black is the garb of our profession. Forgive my speaking so plainly, but I consider myself *in loco parentis*."

'He was so kind, so bland, and, in truth, so friendly, that I felt it would be most childish to take offence; but I had a little resentment in my heart at this way of being treated. However, I mumbled, "Oh, certainly, sir, if you wish it"; and returned once more to change my coat—my poor cut-away.

' "Those coats, sir, give a man rather too much of a sporting appearance, not quite befitting the learned professions; more as if you came down here to hunt than to be the Galen or Hippocrates of the neighbourhood." He smiled graciously, so I smothered a sigh; for, to tell you the truth, I had rather anticipated—and, in fact, had boasted at Guy's of—the runs I hoped to have with the hounds; for Duncombe was in a famous hunting district. But all these ideas were quite dispersed when Mr. Morgan led me to the inn-yard, where there was a horse-dealer on his way to a neighbouring fair, and "strongly advised me"—which in our relative circumstances was equivalent to an injunction—to purchase a little, useful, fast-trotting, brown cob, instead of a fine, showy horse, "who would take any fence I put him to," as the horse-dealer assured me. Mr. Morgan was evidently pleased when I bowed to his decision, and gave up all hopes of an occasional hunt.

He opened out a great deal more after this purchase. He told me his plan of establishing me in a house of my own, which looked more respectable, not to say professional, than being in

lodgings; and then he went on to say that he had lately lost a
friend, a brother surgeon in a neighbouring town, who had left a
widow with a small income, who would be very glad to live with
me, and act as mistress to my establishment; thus lessening the
expense.

‘ "She is a lady-like woman," said Mr. Morgan, "to judge from
the little I have seen of her; about forty-five or so; and may really
be of some help to you in the little etiquettes of our profession;
the slight, delicate attentions which every man has to learn, if
he wishes to get on in life. This is Mrs. Munton's, sir," said he,
stopping short at a very unromantic-looking green door, with a
brass knocker.

'I had no time to say, "Who is Mrs. Munton?" before we had
heard Mrs. Munton was at home, and were following the tidy
elderly servant up the narrow carpeted stairs into the drawing-
room. Mrs. Munton was the widow of a former vicar, upwards of
sixty, rather deaf; but, like all the deaf people I have ever seen,
very fond of talking; perhaps because she then knew the subject,
which passed out of her grasp when another began to speak. She
was ill of a chronic complaint, which often incapacitated her from
going out; and the kind people of the town were in the habit of
coming to see her and sit with her, and of bringing her the
newest, freshest, tit-bits of news; so that her room was the centre
of the gossip of Duncombe—not of scandal, mind; for I make
a distinction between gossip and scandal. Now you can fancy
the discrepancy between the ideal and the real Mrs. Munton.
Instead of any foolish notion of a beautiful, blooming widow,
tenderly anxious about the health of the stranger, I saw a
homely, talkative, elderly person, with a keen, observant eye,
and marks of suffering on her face; plain in manner and dress,
but still unmistakably a lady. She talked to Mr. Morgan, but she
looked at me; and I saw that nothing I did escaped her notice.
Mr. Morgan annoyed me by his anxiety to show me off; but he
was kindly anxious to bring out every circumstance to my credit
in Mrs. Munton's hearing, knowing well that the town-crier had
not more opportunities to publish all about me than she had.

‘ "What was that remark you repeated to me of Sir Astley
Cooper's?" asked he. It had been the most trivial speech in
the world that I had named as we walked along, and I felt
ashamed of having to repeat it: but it answered Mr. Morgan's

purpose, and before night all the town had heard that I was a favourite pupil of Sir Astley's (I had never seen him but twice in my life); and Mr. Morgan was afraid that as soon as he knew my full value I should be retained by Sir Astley to assist him in his duties as surgeon to the Royal Family. Every little circumstance was pressed into the conversation which could add to my importance.

' "As I once heard Sir Robert Peel remark to Mr. Harrison, the father of our young friend here—The moons in August are remarkably full and bright."—If you remember, Charles, my father was always proud of having sold a pair of gloves to Sir Robert, when he was staying at the Grange, near Biddicombe, and I suppose good Mr. Morgan had paid his only visit to my father at the time; but Mrs. Munton evidently looked at me with double respect after this incidental remark, which I was amused to meet with, a few months afterwards, disguised in the statement that my father was an intimate friend of the Premier's, and had, in fact, been the adviser of most of the measures taken by him in public life. I sat by, half indignant and half amused. Mr. Morgan looked so complacently pleased at the whole effect of the conversation, that I did not care to mar it by explanations; and, indeed, I had little idea at the time how small sayings were the seeds of great events in the town of Duncombe. When we left Mrs. Munton's, he was in a blandly communicative mood.

' "You will find it a curious statistical fact, but five-sixths of our householders of a certain rank in Duncombe are women. We have widows and old maids in rich abundance. In fact, my dear sir, I believe that you and I are almost the only gentlemen in the place—Mr. Bullock, of course, excepted. By gentlemen, I mean professional men. It behoves us to remember, sir, that so many of the female sex rely upon us for the kindness and protection which every man who is worthy of the name is always so happy to render."

'Miss Tomkinson, on whom we next called, did not strike me as remarkably requiring protection from any man. She was a tall, gaunt, masculine-looking woman, with an air of defiance about her, naturally; this, however, she softened and mitigated, as far as she was able, in favour of Mr. Morgan. He, it seemed to me, stood a little in awe of the lady, who was very *brusque* and plain-spoken, and evidently piqued herself on her decision of character and sincerity of speech.

' "So, this is the Mr. Harrison we have heard so much of from you, Mr. Morgan? I must say, from what I had heard, that I had expected something a little more—hum—hum! But he's young yet; he's young. We have been all anticipating an Apollo, Mr. Harrison, from Mr. Morgan's description, and an Aesculapius combined in one; or, perhaps, I might confine myself to saying Apollo, as he, I believe, was the god of medicine!"

'How could Mr. Morgan have described me without seeing me? I asked myself.

'Miss Tomkinson put on her spectacles, and adjusted them on her Roman nose. Suddenly relaxing from her severity of inspection, she said to Mr. Morgan—"But you must see Caroline. I had nearly forgotten it; she is busy with the girls, but I will send for her. She had a bad headache yesterday, and looked very pale; it made me very uncomfortable."

'She rang the bell, and desired the servant to fetch Miss Caroline.

'Miss Caroline was the younger sister—younger by twenty years; and so considered as a child by Miss Tomkinson, who was fifty-five, at the very least. If she was considered as a child, she was also petted and caressed, and cared for as a child; for she had been left as a baby to the charge of her elder sister; and when the father died, and they had to set up a school, Miss Tomkinson took upon herself every difficult arrangement, and denied herself every pleasure, and made every sacrifice in order that "Carry" might not feel the change in their circumstances. My wife tells me she once knew the sisters purchase a piece of silk, enough, with management, to have made two gowns; but Carry wished for flounces, or some such fal-lals; and, without a word, Miss Tomkinson gave up her gown to have the whole made up as Carry wished, into one handsome one; and wore an old, shabby affair herself as cheerfully as if it were Genoa velvet. That tells the sort of relationship between the sisters as well as anything, and I consider myself very good to name it thus early, for it was long before I found out Miss Tomkinson's real goodness; and we had a great quarrel first. Miss Caroline looked very delicate and die-away when she came in; she was as soft and sentimental as Miss Tomkinson was hard and masculine; and had a way of saying, "Oh, sister, how can you?" at Miss Tomkinson's startling speeches, which I never liked—especially as it was accompanied by a sort of protesting look at the company present, as if she wished to have it understood that she was shocked at her sister's *outré* manners. Now, that was not faithful between sisters. A remonstrance in private might have done good—though, for my own part, I have grown to like Miss Tomkinson's speeches and ways; but I don't like the way some people have of separating themselves from what may be unpopular in their relations. I know I spoke rather shortly to Miss Caroline when she asked me whether I could bear the change from "the great metropolis" to a little country village. In the first place, why could not she call it "London", or "town", and have done with it? And in the next place, why should she not love the place that was her home well enough to fancy that every one would like it when they came to know it as well as she did?

'I was conscious I was rather abrupt in my conversation with her, and I saw that Mr. Morgan was watching me, though he pretended to be listening to Miss Tomkinson's whispered account of her sister's symptoms. But when we were once more in the street, he began, "My dear young friend"——

'I winced; for all the morning I had noticed that when he was going to give a little unpalatable advice, he always began with "My dear young friend". He had done so about the horse.

' "My dear young friend, there are one or two hints I should like to give you about your manner. The great Sir Everard Home used to say, 'A general practitioner should either have a very good manner, or a very bad one.' Now, in the latter case, he must be possessed of talents and acquirements sufficient to ensure his being sought after, whatever his manner might be. But the rudeness will give notoriety to these qualifications. Abernethy is a case in point. I rather, myself, question the taste of bad manners. I, therefore, have studied to acquire an attentive, anxious politeness, which combines ease and grace with a tender regard and interest. I am not aware whether I have succeeded (few men do) in coming up to my ideal; but I recommend you to strive after this manner, peculiarly befitting our profession. Identify yourself with your patients, my dear sir. You have sympathy in your good heart, I am sure, to really feel pain when listening to their account of their sufferings, and it soothes them to see the expression of this feeling in your manner. It is, in fact, sir, manners that make the man in our profession. I don't set myself up as an example—far from it; but—— This is Mr. Hutton's, our vicar; one of the servants is indisposed, and I shall be glad of the opportunity of introducing you. We can resume our conversation at another time."

'I had not been aware that we had been holding a conversation, in which, I believe, the assistance of two persons is required. Why had not Mr. Hutton sent to ask after my health the evening before, according to the custom of the place? I felt rather offended.

III

'THE vicarage was on the north side of the street, at the end opening towards the hills. It was a long low house, receding behind its neighbours; a court was between the door and the street, with a flag-walk and an old stone cistern on the right-hand side of the door; Solomon's seal growing under the windows. Some one was watching from behind the window-curtain; for the door opened, as if by magic, as soon as we reached it; and we entered a low room, which served as hall, and was matted all over, with deep, old-fashioned window-seats, and Dutch tiles in the fireplace; altogether it was very cool and refreshing, after the hot sun in the white and red street.

' "Bessie is not so well, Mr. Morgan," said the sweet little girl of eleven or so, who had opened the door. "Sophy wanted to send for you; but papa said he was sure you would come soon this morning, and we were to remember that there were other sick people wanting you."

' "Here's Mr. Morgan, Sophy," said she, opening the door into an inner room, to which we descended a step, as I remember well; for I was nearly falling down it, I was so caught by the picture within. It was like a picture—at least, seen through the door-frame. A sort of mixture of crimson and sea-green in the room, and a sunny garden beyond, a very low casement window, open to the amber air; clusters of white roses peeping in, and Sophy sitting on a cushion on the ground, the light coming from above on her head, and a little, sturdy, round-eyed brother kneeling by her, to whom she was teaching the alphabet. It was a mighty relief to him when we came in, as I could see; and I am much mistaken if he was easily caught again to say his lesson, when he was once sent off to find papa. Sophy rose quietly, and of course we were just introduced, and that was all, before she took Mr. Morgan upstairs to see her sick servant. I was left to myself in the room. It looked so like a home, that it at once made me know the full charm of the word. There were books and work about, and tokens of employment; there was a child's plaything on the floor; and against the sea-green walls there hung a likeness or two, done in water-colours; one, I was sure, was that of Sophy's mother. The chairs and sofa were covered with chintz, the same as the curtains—a little pretty red rose on a white ground. I don't know where the crimson came from, but I am sure there was crimson somewhere; perhaps in the carpet. There was a glass door beside the window, and you went up a step into the garden. This was, first, a grass plot, just under the windows, and beyond that, straight gravel walks, with box-borders and narrow flower-beds on each side, most brilliant and gay at the end of August, as it was then; and behind the flower-borders were fruit-trees trained over woodwork, so as to shut out the beds of kitchen-garden within.

'While I was looking round, a gentleman came in, who, I was sure, was the Vicar. It was rather awkward, for I had to account for my presence there.

' "I came with Mr. Morgan; my name is Harrison," said I, bowing. I could see he was not much enlightened by this explanation, but we sat down and talked about the time of year, or some such matter, till Sophy and Mr. Morgan came back. Then I saw Mr. Morgan to advantage. With a man whom he respected, as he did the Vicar, he lost the prim, artificial manner he had in general, and was calm and dignified; but not so dignified as the Vicar. I never saw any one like him. He was very quiet and reserved, almost absent at times; his personal appearance was not striking; but he was altogether a man you would talk to with your hat off whenever you met him. It was his character that produced this effect—character that he never thought about, but that appeared in every word, and look, and motion.

' "Sophy," said he, "Mr. Morgan looks very warm; could you not gather a few jargonelle pears off the south wall? I fancy there are some ripe there. Our jargonelle pears are remarkably early this year."

'Sophy went into the sunny garden, and I saw her take a rake and tilt at the pears, which were above her reach, apparently. The parlour had become chilly (I found out afterwards it had a flag floor, which accounts for its coldness), and I thought I should like to go into the warm sun. I said I would go and help the young lady; and without waiting for an answer, I went into the warm, scented garden, where the bees were rifling the flowers, and making a continual, busy sound. I think Sophy had begun to despair of getting the fruit, and was glad of my assistance. I thought I was very senseless to have knocked them down so soon, when I found we were to go in as soon as they were gathered. I should have liked to have walked round the garden, but Sophy walked straight off with the pears, and I could do nothing but follow her. She took up her needlework while we ate them: they were very soon finished, and when the Vicar had ended his conversation with Mr. Morgan about some poor people, we rose up to come away. I was thankful that Mr. Morgan had said so little about me. I could not have endured that he should have introduced Sir Astley Cooper or Sir Robert Peel at the vicarage; nor yet could I have brooked much mention of my "great opportunities for acquiring a thorough knowledge of my profession", which I had heard him describe to Miss Tomkinson', while her sister was talking to me. Luckily, however, he spared me all this at the Vicar's. When we left, it was time to mount our horses and go the country rounds, and I was glad of it.

IV

'BY and by the inhabitants of Duncombe began to have parties in my honour. Mr. Morgan told me it was on my account, or I don't think I should have found it out. But he was pleased at every fresh invitation, and rubbed his hands, and chuckled, as if it was a compliment to himself, as in truth it was.

'Meanwhile, the arrangement with Mrs. Rose had been brought to a conclusion. She was to bring her furniture, and place it in a house, of which I was to pay the rent. She was to be the mistress, and, in return, she was not to pay anything for her board. Mr. Morgan took the house, and delighted in advising and settling all my affairs. I was partly indolent, and partly amused, and was altogether passive. The house he took for me was near his own: it had two sitting-rooms downstairs, opening into each other by folding-doors, which were, however, kept shut in general. The back room was my consulting room ("the library," he advised me to call it), and he gave me a skull to put on the top of my bookcase, in which the medical books were all ranged on the conspicuous shelves; while Miss Austen, Dickens, and Thackeray were, by Mr. Morgan himself, skilfully placed in a careless way, upside down or with their backs turned to the wall. The front parlour was to be the dining-room, and the room above was furnished with Mrs. Rose's drawing-room chairs and table, though I found she preferred sitting downstairs in the dining-room close to the window, where, between every stitch, she could look up and see what was going on in the street. I felt rather queer to be the master of this house, filled with another person's furniture, before I had even seen the lady whose property it was.

'Presently she arrived. Mr. Morgan met her at the inn where the coach stopped, and accompanied her to my house. I could see them out of the drawing-room window, the little gentleman stepping daintily along, flourishing his cane, and evidently talking away. She was a little taller than he was, and in deep widow's mourning; such veils and falls, and capes and cloaks, that she looked like a black crape haycock. When we were introduced, she put up her thick veil, and looked around and sighed.

' "Your appearance and circumstances, Mr. Harrison, remind me forcibly of the time when I was married to my dear husband, now at rest. He was then, like you, commencing practice as a surgeon. For twenty years I sympathized with him, and assisted him by every means in my power, even to making up pills when the young man was out. May we live together in like harmony for an equal length of time! May the regard between us be equally sincere, although, instead of being conjugal, it is to be maternal and filial!"

'I am sure she had been concocting this speech in the coach, for she afterwards told me she was the only passenger. When she had ended, I felt as if I ought to have had a glass of wine in my hand, to drink, after the manner of toasts. And yet I doubt if I should have done it heartily, for I did not hope to live with her for twenty years; it had rather a dreary sound. However, I only bowed and kept my thoughts to myself. I asked Mr. Morgan, while Mrs. Rose was upstairs taking off her things, to stay to tea; to which he agreed, and kept rubbing his hands with satisfaction, saying—

' "Very fine woman, sir; very fine woman! And what a manner! How she will receive patients, who may wish to leave a message during your absence. Such a flow of words to be sure!"

'Mr. Morgan could not stay long after tea, as there were one or two cases to be seen. I would willingly have gone, and had my hat on, indeed, for the purpose, when he said it would not be respectful, "not the thing," to leave Mrs. Rose the first evening of her arrival.

' "Tender deference to the sex—to a widow in the first months of her loneliness—requires a little consideration, my dear sir. I will leave that case at Miss Tomkinson's for you; you will perhaps call early to-morrow morning. Miss Tomkinson is rather particular, and is apt to speak plainly if she does not think herself properly attended to."

'I had often noticed that he shuffled off the visits to Miss Tomkinson's on me, and I suspect he was a little afraid of the lady.

'It was rather a long evening with Mrs. Rose. She had nothing to do, thinking it civil, I suppose, to stop in the parlour, and not go upstairs and unpack. I begged I might be no restraint upon her if she wished to do so; but (rather to my disappointment) she smiled in a measured, subdued way, and said it would be a pleasure to her to become better acquainted with me. She went upstairs once, and my heart misgave me when I saw her come down with a clean folded pocket-handkerchief. Oh, my prophetic soul!—she was no sooner seated, than she began to give me an account of her late husband's illness, and symptoms, and death. It was a very common case, but she evidently seemed to think it had been peculiar. She had just a smattering of medical knowledge, and used the technical terms so very malapropos that I could hardly keep from smiling; but I would not have done it for the world, she was evidently in such deep and sincere distress. At last she said—

' "I have the 'dognoses' of my dear husband's complaint in my desk, Mr. Harrison, if you would like to draw up the case for the

Lancet. I think he would have felt gratified, poor fellow, if he had been told such a compliment would be paid to his remains, and that his case should appear in those distinguished columns."

'It was rather awkward; for the case was of the very commonest, as I said before. However, I had not been even this short time in practice without having learnt a few of those noises which do not compromise one, and yet may bear a very significant construction if the listener chooses to exert a little imagination.

'Before the end of the evening, we were such friends that she brought me down the late Mr. Rose's picture to look at. She told me she could not bear herself to gaze upon the beloved features; but that if I would look upon the miniature, she would avert her face. I offered to take it into my own hands, but she seemed wounded at the proposal, and said she never, never could trust such a treasure out of her own possession; so she turned her head very much over her left shoulder, while I examined the likeness held by her extended right arm.

'The late Mr. Rose must have been rather a good-looking, jolly man; and the artist had given him such a broad smile, and such a twinkle about the eyes, that it really was hard to help smiling back at him. However, I restrained myself.

'At first Mrs. Rose objected to accepting any of the invitations which were sent her to accompany me to the tea-parties in the town. She was so good and simple, that I was sure she had no other reason than the one which she alleged—the short time that had elapsed since her husband's death; or else, now that I had had some experience of the entertainments which she declined so pertinaciously, I might have suspected that she was glad of the excuse. I used sometimes to wish that I was a widow. I came home tired from a hard day's riding, and if I had but felt sure that Mr. Morgan would not come in, I should certainly have put on my slippers and my loose morning coat, and have indulged in a cigar in the garden. It seemed a cruel sacrifice to society to dress myself in tight boots, and a stiff coat, and go to a five-o'clock tea. But Mr. Morgan read me such lectures upon the necessity of cultivating the goodwill of the people among whom I was settled, and seemed so sorry, and almost hurt, when I once complained of the dullness of these parties, that I felt I could not be so selfish as to decline more than one out of three. Mr. Morgan, if he found that I had an invitation for the evening, would often take the longer round, and the more distant visits. I suspected him at first of the design, which I confess I often entertained, of shirking the parties; but I soon found out he was really making a sacrifice of his inclinations for what he considered to be my advantage.

V

'THERE was one invitation which seemed to promise a good deal of pleasure. Mr. Bullock (who is the attorney of Duncombe) was married a second time to a lady from a large provincial town; she wished to lead the fashion—a thing very easy to do, for every one was willing to follow her. So instead of giving a tea-party in my honour, she proposed a picnic to some old hall in the neighbourhood; and really the arrangements sounded tempting enough. Every patient we had seemed full of the subject; both those who were invited and those who were not. There was a moat round the house, with a boat on it; and there was a gallery in the hall, from which music sounded delightfully. The family to whom the place belonged were abroad, and lived at a newer and grander mansion when they were at home; there were only a farmer and his wife in the old hall, and they were to have the charge of the preparations. The little, kind-hearted town was delighted when the sun shone bright on the October morning of our picnic; the shopkeepers and cottagers all looked pleased as they saw the cavalcade gathering at Mr. Bullock's door. We were somewhere about twenty in number; a "silent few", she called us; but I thought we were quite enough. There were the Miss Tomkinsons, and two of their young ladies—one of them belonged to a "county family", Mrs. Bullock told me in a whisper; then came Mr. and Mrs. and Miss Bullock, and a tribe of little children, the offspring of the present wife. Miss Bullock was only a step-daughter. Mrs. Munton had accepted the invitation to join our party, which was rather unexpected by the host and hostess, I imagine, from little remarks that I overheard; but they made her very welcome. Miss Horsman (a maiden lady who had been on a visit from home till last week) was another. And last, there were the Vicar and his children.

These, with Mr. Morgan and myself, made up the party. I was very much pleased to see something more of the Vicar's family. He had come in occasionally to the evening parties, it is true; and spoken kindly to us all; but it was not his habit to stay very long at them. And his daughter was, he said, too young to visit. She had had the charge of her little sisters and brother since her mother's death, which took up a good deal of her time, and she was glad of the evenings to pursue her own studies. But to-day the case was different; and Sophy, and Helen, and Lizzie, and even little Walter, were all there, standing at Mrs. Bullock's door; for we none of us could be patient enough to sit still in the parlour with Mrs. Munton and the elder ones, quietly waiting for the two chaises and the spring-cart, which were to have been there by two o'clock, and now it was nearly a quarter past. "Shameful! the brightness of the day would be gone." The sympathetic shopkeepers, standing at their respective doors with their hands in their pockets, had, one and all, their heads turned in the direction from which the carriages (as Mrs. Bullock called them) were to come. There was a rumble along the paved street; and the shopkeepers turned and smiled, and bowed their heads congratulatingly to us; all the mothers and all the little children of the place stood clustering round the door to see us set off. I had my horse waiting; and, meanwhile, I assisted people into their vehicles. One sees a good deal of management on such occasions. Mrs. Munton was handed first into one of the chaises; then there was a little hanging back, for most of the young people wished to go in the cart—I don't know why. Miss Horsman, however, came forward, and as she was known to be the intimate friend of Mrs. Munton, so far was satisfactory. But who was to be third—bodkin with two old ladies, who liked the windows shut? I saw Sophy speaking to Helen; and then she came forward and offered to be the third. The two old ladies looked pleased and glad (as every one did near Sophy); so that chaise-full was arranged. Just as it was going off, however, the servant from the vicarage came running with a note for her master. When he had read it, he went to the chaise door, and I suppose told Sophy, what I afterwards heard him say to Mrs. Bullock, that the clergyman of a neighbouring parish was ill, and unable to read the funeral service for one of his parishioners, who was to be buried that afternoon. The Vicar was, of course, obliged to go, and said he should not return home that night. It seemed a relief to some, I perceived, to be without the little restraint of his dignified presence. Mr. Morgan came up just at the moment, having ridden hard all the morning to be in time to join our party; so we were resigned, on the whole, to the Vicar's absence. His own family regretted him the most, I noticed, and I liked them all the better for it. I believe that I came next in being sorry for his departure; but I respected and admired him, and felt always the better for having been in his company. Miss Tomkinson, Mrs. Bullock, and the "county" young lady, were in the next chaise. I think the last would rather have been in the cart with the younger and merrier set, but I imagine that was considered *infra dig*. The remainder of the party were to ride and tie; and a most riotous, laughing set they were. Mr. Morgan and I were on horseback; at least I led my horse, with little Walter riding on him; his fat, sturdy legs standing stiff out on each side of my cob's broad back. He was a little darling, and chattered all the way, his sister Sophy being the heroine of all his stories. I found he owed this day's excursion entirely to her begging papa to let him come; nurse was strongly against it—"cross old nurse!" he called her once, and then said, "No, not cross; kind nurse; Sophy tells Walter not to say cross nurse." I never saw so young a child so brave. The horse shied at a log of wood. Walter looked very red, and grasped the mane, but sat upright like a little man, and never spoke all the time the horse was dancing. When it was over he looked at me, and smiled—

' "You would not let me be hurt, Mr. Harrison, would you?" He was the most winning little fellow I ever saw.

'There were frequent cries to me from the cart, "Oh, Mr. Harrison! do get us that branch of blackberries; you can reach it with your whip handle." "Oh, Mr. Harrison! there were such splendid nuts on the other side of that hedge; would you just turn back for them?" Miss Caroline Tomkinson was once or twice rather faint with the motion of the cart, and asked me for my smelling bottle, as she had forgotten hers. I was amused at the idea of my carrying such articles about with me. Then she thought she should like to walk, and got out, and came on my side of the road; but I found little Walter the pleasanter companion, and soon set the horse off into a trot, with which pace her tender constitution could not keep up.

'The road to the old hall was along a sandy lane, with high hedge-banks; the wych-elms almost met overhead. "Shocking farming!" Mr. Bullock called out; and so it might be, but it was very pleasant and picturesque-looking. The trees were gorgeous, in their orange and crimson hues, varied by great, dark-green holly-bushes, glistening in the autumn sun. I should have thought the colours too vivid, if I had seen them in a picture, especially when we wound up the brow, after crossing the little bridge over the brook (what laughing and screaming there was as the cart splashed through the sparkling water!)—and I caught the purple hills beyond. We could see the old hall, too, from that point, with its warm rich woods billowing up behind, and the blue waters of the moat lying still under the sunlight.

'Laughing and talking is very hungry work, and there was a universal petition for dinner when we arrived at the lawn before the hall, where it had been arranged that we were to dine. I saw Miss Carry take Miss Tomkinson aside, and whisper to her; and presently the elder sister came up to me, where I was busy, rather apart, making a seat of hay, which I had fetched from the farmer's loft for my little friend Walter, who, I had noticed, was rather hoarse, and for whom I was afraid of a seat on the grass, dry as it appeared to be.

' "Mr. Harrison, Caroline tells me she has been feeling very faint, and she is afraid of a return of one of her attacks. She says she has more confidence in your medical powers than in Mr. Morgan's. I should not be sincere if I did not say that I differ from her; but as it is so, may I beg you to keep an eye upon her? I tell her she had better not have come if she did not feel well; but, poor girl, she had set her heart upon this day's pleasure. I have offered to go home with her; but she says, if she can only feel sure you are at hand, she would rather stay."

'Of course, I bowed, and promised all due attendance on Miss Caroline; and in the meantime, until she did require my services, I thought I might as well go and help the Vicar's daughter, who looked so fresh and pretty in her white muslin dress, here, there, and everywhere, now in the sunshine, now in the green shade, helping every one to be comfortable, and thinking of every one but herself.

'Presently, Mr. Morgan came up.

' "Miss Caroline does not feel quite well. I have promised your services to her sister."

' "So have I, sir. But Miss Sophy cannot carry this heavy basket."

'I did not mean her to have heard this excuse; but she caught it up and said—

' "Oh, yes, I can! I can take the things out one by one. Go to poor Miss Caroline, pray, Mr. Harrison."

'I went; but very unwillingly, I must say. When I had once seated myself by her, I think she must have felt better. It was, probably, only a nervous fear, which was relieved when she knew she had assistance near at hand; for she made a capital dinner. I thought she would never end her modest requests for "just a little more pigeon-pie, or a merry-thought of chicken". Such a hearty meal would, I hope, effectually revive her; and so it did; for she told me she thought she could manage to walk round the garden, and see the old peacock yews, if I would kindly give her my arm. It was very provoking; I had so set my heart upon being with the Vicar's children. I advised Miss Caroline strongly to lie down a little, and rest before tea, on the sofa in the farmer's kitchen; you cannot think how persuasively I begged her to take care of herself. At last she consented, thanking me for my tender interest; she should never forget my kind attention to her. She little knew what was in my mind at the time. However, she was safely consigned to the farmer's wife, and I was rushing out in search of a white gown and a waving figure, when I encountered Mrs. Bullock at the door of the hall. She was a fine, fierce-looking woman. I thought she had appeared a little displeased at my (unwilling) attentions to Miss Caroline at dinner-time; but now, seeing me alone, she was all smiles.

' "Oh, Mr. Harrison, all alone! How is that? What are the young ladies about to allow such churlishness? And, by the way, I have left a young lady who will be very glad of your assistance, I am sure—my daughter, Jemima" (her step-daughter, she meant). "Mr. Bullock is so particular, and so tender a father, that he would be frightened to death at the idea of her going into the boat on the moat unless she was with some one who could swim. He is gone to discuss the new wheel-plough with the farmer (you know agriculture is his hobby, although law, horrid law, is his business). But the poor girl is pining on the bank, longing for my permission to join the others, which I dare not give unless you will kindly accompany her, and promise, if any accident happens, to preserve her safe."

'Oh, Sophy, why was no one anxious about you?

VI

'MISS BULLOCK was standing by the waterside, looking wistfully, as I thought, at the water party; the sound of whose merry laughter came pleasantly enough from the boat, which lay off (for, indeed, no one knew how to row, and she was of a clumsy, flat-bottomed build) about a hundred yards, "weatherbound," as they shouted out, among the long stalks of the water-lilies.

'Miss Bullock did not look up till I came close to her; and then, when I told her my errand, she lifted up her great, heavy, sad eyes, and looked at me for a moment. It struck me, at the time, that she expected to find some expression on my face which was not there, and that its absence was a relief to her. She was a very pale, unhappy-looking girl, but very quiet, and, if not agreeable in manner, at any rate not forward or offensive. I called to the party in the boat, and they came slowly enough through the large, cool, green lily-leaves towards us. When they got near, we saw there was no room for us, and Miss Bullock said she would rather stay in the meadow and saunter about, if I would go into the boat; and I am certain from the look on her countenance that she spoke the truth; but Miss Horsman called out, in a sharp voice, while she smiled in a very disagreeable, knowing way—

' "Oh, mamma will be displeased if you don't come in, Miss Bullock, after all her trouble in making such a nice arrangement."

'At this speech the poor girl hesitated, and at last, in an undecided way, as if she was not sure whether she was doing right, she took Sophy's place in the boat. Helen and Lizzie landed with their sister, so that there was plenty of room for

Miss Tomkinson, Miss Horsman, and all the little Bullocks; and the three vicarage girls went off strolling along the meadow side, and playing with Walter, who was in a high state of excitement. The sun was getting low, but the declining light was beautiful upon the water; and, to add to the charm of the time, Sophy and her sisters, standing on the green lawn in front of the hall, struck up the little German canon, which I had never heard before—

Oh wie wohl ist mir am abend, &c.

At last we were summoned to tug the boat to the landing-steps on the lawn, tea and a blazing wood fire being ready for us in the hall. I was offering my arm to Miss Horsman, as she was a little lame, when she said again, in her peculiar disagreeable way, "Had you not better take Miss Bullock, Mr. Harrison? It will be more satisfactory."

'I helped Miss Horsman up the steps, however, and then she repeated her advice; so, remembering that Miss Bullock was in fact the daughter of my entertainers, I went to her; but though she accepted my arm, I could perceive she was sorry that I had offered it.

'The hall was lighted by the glorious wood fire in the wide old grate; the daylight was dying away in the west; and the large windows admitted but little of what was left, through their small leaded frames, with coats of arms emblazoned upon them. The farmer's wife had set out a great long table, which was piled with good things; and a huge black kettle sang on the glowing fire, which sent a cheerful warmth through the room as it crackled and blazed. Mr. Morgan (who I found had been taking a little round in the neighbourhood among his patients) was there, smiling and rubbing his hands as usual. Mr. Bullock was holding a conversation with the farmer at the garden-door on the nature of different manures, in which it struck me that if Mr. Bullock had the fine names and the theories on his side, the farmer had all the practical knowledge and the experience, and I know which I would have trusted. I think Mr. Bullock rather liked to talk about Liebig in my hearing; it sounded well, and was knowing. Mrs. Bullock was not particularly placid in her mood. In the first place, I wanted to sit by the Vicar's

daughter, and Miss Caroline as decidedly wanted to sit on
my other side, being afraid of her fainting fits, I imagine. But
Mrs. Bullock called me to a place near her daughter. Now I
thought I had done enough civility to a girl who was evidently
annoyed rather than pleased by my attentions, and I pretended
to be busy stooping under the table for Miss Caroline's gloves,
which were missing; but it was of no avail; Mrs. Bullock's fine,
severe eyes were awaiting my reappearance, and she summoned
me again.

' "I am keeping this place on my right hand for you, Mr.
Harrison. Jemima, sit still!"

'I went up to the post of honour and tried to busy myself
with pouring out coffee to hide my chagrin; but after forgetting
to empty the water put in ("to warm the cups", Mrs. Bullock
said), and omitting to add any sugar, the lady told me she would
dispense with my services, and turn me over to my neighbour
on the other side.

' "Talking to the younger lady was, no doubt, more Mr.
Harrison's vocation than assisting the elder one." I dare say
it was only the manner that made the words seem offensive.
Miss Horsman sat opposite to me, smiling away. Miss Bullock
did not speak, but seemed more depressed than ever. At length,
Miss Horsman and Mrs. Bullock got to a war of innuendoes,
which were completely unintelligible to me, and I was very
much displeased with my situation; while, at the bottom of the
table, Mr. Morgan and Mr. Bullock were making the young
ones laugh most heartily. Part of the joke was Mr. Morgan
insisting upon making tea at that end; and Sophy and Helen
were busy contriving every possible mistake for him. I thought
honour was a very good thing, but merriment a better. Here
was I in the place of distinction, hearing nothing but cross
words. At last the time came for us to go home. As the evening
was damp, the seats in the chaises were the best and most to
be desired. And now Sophy offered to go in the cart; only she
seemed anxious, and so was I, that Walter should be secured
from the effects of the white wreaths of fog rolling up from the
valley; but the little violent affectionate fellow would not be
separated from Sophy. She made a nest for him on her knee
in one corner of the cart, and covered him with her own shawl;
and I hoped that he would take no harm. Miss Tomkinson,

Mr. Bullock, and some of the young ones walked; but I seemed chained to the windows of the chaise, for Miss Caroline begged me not to leave her, as she was dreadfully afraid of robbers; and Mrs. Bullock implored me to see that the man did not overturn them in the bad roads, as he had certainly had too much to drink.

'I became so irritable before I reached home, that I thought it was the most disagreeable day of pleasure I had ever had, and could hardly bear to answer Mrs. Rose's never-ending questions. She told me, however, that from my account the day was so charming that she thought she should relax in the rigour of her seclusion, and mingle a little more in the society of which I gave so tempting a description. She really thought her dear Mr. Rose would have wished it; and his will should be law to her after his death, as it had ever been during his life. In compliance, therefore, with his wishes, she would even do a little violence to her own feelings.

'She was very good and kind; not merely attentive to everything which she thought could conduce to my comfort, but willing to take any trouble in providing the broths and nourishing food which I often found it convenient to order, under the name of kitchen-physic, for my poorer patients; and I really did not see the use of her shutting herself up, in mere compliance with an etiquette, when she began to wish to mix in the little quiet society of Duncombe. Accordingly I urged her to begin to visit, and even when applied to as to what I imagined the late Mr. Rose's wishes on that subject would have been, answered for that worthy gentleman, and assured his widow that I was convinced he would have regretted deeply her giving way to immoderate grief, and would have been rather grateful than otherwise at seeing her endeavour to divert her thoughts by a few quiet visits. She cheered up, and said, "As I really thought so, she would sacrifice her own inclinations, and accept the very next invitation that came."

VII

'I WAS roused from my sleep in the middle of the night by a messenger from the vicarage. Little Walter had got the croup, and Mr. Morgan had been sent for into the country. I dressed myself hastily, and went through the quiet little street. There was a light burning upstairs at the vicarage. It was in the nursery. The servant, who opened the door the instant I knocked, was crying sadly, and could hardly answer my inquiries as I went upstairs, two steps at a time, to see my little favourite.

'The nursery was a great large room. At the farther end it was lighted by a common candle, which left the other end, where the door was, in shade, so I suppose the nurse did not see me come in, for she was speaking very crossly.

' "Miss Sophy!" said she, "I told you over and over again it was not fit for him to go, with the hoarseness that he had, and you would take him. It will break your papa's heart, I know; but it's none of my doing."

'Whatever Sophy felt, she did not speak in answer to this. She was on her knees by the warm bath, in which the little fellow was struggling to get his breath, with a look of terror on his face that I have often noticed in young children when smitten by a sudden and violent illness. It seems as if they recognized something infinite and invisible, at whose bidding the pain and the anguish come, from which no love can shield them. It is a very heart-rending look to observe, because it comes on the faces of those who are too young to receive comfort from the words of faith, or the promises of religion. Walter had his arms tight round Sophy's neck, as if she, hitherto his paradise-angel, could save him from the dread shadow of Death. Yes! of Death! I knelt down by him on the other side, and examined him. The very robustness of his little frame gave violence to the disease, which is always one of the most fearful by which children of his age can be attacked.

' "Don't tremble, Watty," said Sophy, in a soothing tone; "it's Mr. Harrison, darling, who let you ride on his horse." I could detect the quivering in the voice, which she tried to make so calm and soft to quiet the little fellow's fears. We took him out of the bath, and I went for leeches. While I was away,

Mr. Morgan came. He loved the vicarage children as if he were their uncle; but he stood still and aghast at the sight of Walter—so lately bright and strong—and now hurrying alone to the awful change—to the silent mysterious land, where, tended and cared for as he had been on earth, he must go—alone. The little fellow! the darling!

'We applied the leeches to his throat. He resisted at first; but Sophy, God bless her! put the agony of her grief on one side, and thought only of him, and began to sing the little songs he loved. We were all still. The gardener had gone to fetch the Vicar; but he was twelve miles off, and we doubted if he would come in time. I don't know if they had any hope; but the first moment Mr. Morgan's eyes met mine, I saw that he, like me, had none. The ticking of the house-clock sounded through the dark, quiet house. Walter was sleeping now, with the black leeches yet hanging to his fair, white throat. Still Sophy went on singing little lullabies, which she had sung under far different and happier circumstances. I remember one verse, because it struck me at the time as strangely applicable.

> Sleep, baby, sleep!
> Thy rest shall angels keep;
> While on the grass the lamb shall feed,
> And never suffer want or need.
>
> Sleep, baby, sleep.

The tears were in Mr. Morgan's eyes. I do not think either he or I could have spoken in our natural tones; but the brave girl went on, clear though low. She stopped at last, and looked up.

' "He is better, is he not, Mr. Morgan?"

' "No, my dear. He is—ahem"—he could not speak all at once. Then he said—"My dear! he will be better soon. Think of your mamma, my dear Miss Sophy. She will be very thankful to have one of her darlings safe with her, where she is."

'Still she did not cry. But she bent her head down on the little face, and kissed it long and tenderly.

' "I will go for Helen and Lizzie. They will be sorry not to see him again." She rose up and went for them. Poor girls, they came in, in their dressing-gowns, with eyes dilated with sudden emotion, pale with terror, stealing softly along, as if sound could disturb him. Sophy comforted them by gentle caresses. It was over soon.

'Mr. Morgan was fairly crying like a child. But he thought it necessary to apologize to me, for what I honoured him for. "I am a little overdone by yesterday's work, sir. I have had one or two bad nights, and they rather upset me. When I was your age I was as strong and manly as any one, and would have scorned to shed tears."

'Sophy came up to where we stood.

' "Mr. Morgan! I am so sorry for papa. How shall I tell him?" She was struggling against her own grief for her father's sake. Mr. Morgan offered to await his coming home; and she seemed thankful for the proposal. I, new friend, almost stranger, might stay no longer. The street was as quiet as ever; not a shadow was changed; for it was not yet four o'clock. But during the night a soul had departed.

'From all I could see, and all I could learn, the Vicar and his daughter strove which should comfort the other the most. Each thought of the other's grief—each prayed for the other rather than for themselves. We saw them walking out, countrywards; and we heard of them in the cottages of the poor. But it was some time before I happened to meet either of them again. And then I felt, from something indescribable in their manner towards me, that I was one of the

Peculiar people, whom Death had made dear.

That one day at the old hall had done this. I was, perhaps, the last person who had given the little fellow any unusual pleasure. Poor Walter! I wish I could have done more to make his short life happy!

VIII

'THERE was a little lull, out of respect to the Vicar's grief, in the visiting. It gave time to Mrs. Rose to soften down the anguish of her weeds.

'At Christmas, Miss Tomkinson sent out invitations for a party. Miss Caroline had once or twice apologized to me because such an event had not taken place before; but, as she said, "the avocations of their daily life prevented their having such little *réunions* except in the vacations." And, sure enough, as soon as the holidays began, came the civil little note—

' "The Misses Tomkinson request the pleasure of Mrs. Rose's and Mr. Harrison's company at tea, on the evening of Monday, the 23rd inst. Tea at five o'clock."

'Mrs. Rose's spirit roused, like a war-horse at the sound of the trumpet, at this. She was not of a repining disposition, but I do think she believed the party-giving population of Duncombe had given up inviting her, as soon as she had determined to relent, and accept the invitations, in compliance with the late Mr. Rose's wishes.

'Such snippings of white love-ribbon as I found everywhere, making the carpet untidy! One day, too, unluckily, a small box was brought to me by mistake. I did not look at the direction, for I never doubted it was some hyoscyamus which I was expecting from London; so I tore it open, and saw inside a piece of paper, with "No more grey hair", in large letters, upon it. I folded it up in a hurry, and sealed it afresh, and gave it to Mrs. Rose; but I could not refrain from asking her, soon after, if she could recommend me anything to keep my hair from turning grey, adding that I thought prevention was better than cure. I think she made out the impression of my seal on the paper after that; for I learned that she had been crying, and that she talked about there being no sympathy left in the world for her since Mr. Rose's death; and that she counted the days until she could rejoin him in the better world. I think she counted the days to Miss Tomkinson's party, too; she talked so much about it.

'The covers were taken off Miss Tomkinson's chairs, and curtains, and sofas; and a great jar full of artificial flowers was placed in the centre of the table, which, as Miss Caroline told me, was all her doing, as she doted on the beautiful and artistic in life. Miss Tomkinson stood, erect as a grenadier, close to the door, receiving her friends, and heartily shaking them by the hands as they entered: she said she was truly glad to see them. And so she really was.

'We had just finished tea, and Miss Caroline had brought out a little pack of conversation cards—sheaves of slips of cardboard, with intellectual or sentimental questions on one set, and equally intellectual and sentimental answers on the other; and as the answers were fit to any and all the questions, you may think they were a characterless and "wersh" set of things. I had just been asked by Miss Caroline—

' "*Can you tell what those dearest to you think of you at this present time?*" and had answered—

' "*How can you expect me to reveal such a secret to the present company!*" when the servant announced that a gentleman, a friend of mine, wished to speak to me downstairs.

' "Oh, show him up, Martha; show him up!" said Miss Tomkinson, in her hospitality.

' "Any friend of our friend's is welcome," said Miss Caroline, in an insinuating tone.

'I jumped up, however, thinking it might be some one on business; but I was so penned in by the spider-legged tables, stuck out on every side, that I could not make the haste I wished; and before I could prevent it, Martha had shown up Jack Marshland, who was on his road home for a day or two at Christmas.

'He came up in a hearty way, bowing to Miss Tomkinson, and explaining that he had found himself in my neighbourhood, and had come over to pass a night with me, and that my servant had directed him where I was.

'His voice, loud at all times, sounded like Stentor's in that little room, where we all spoke in a kind of purring way. He had no swell in his tones; they were *forte* from the beginning. At first it seemed like the days of my youth come back again, to hear full, manly speaking; I felt proud of my friend, as he thanked Miss Tomkinson for her kindness in asking him to stay the evening. By and by he came up to me, and I dare say he thought he had lowered his voice, for he looked as if speaking confidentially, while in fact the whole room might have heard him.

' "Frank, my boy, when shall we have dinner at this good old lady's? I'm deuced hungry."

'Dinner! Why, we had had tea an hour ago. While he yet spoke, Martha came in with a little tray, on which was a single cup of coffee and three slices of wafer bread-and-butter. His dismay, and his evident submission to the decrees of Fate, tickled me so much, that I thought he should have a further taste of the life I led from month's end to month's end, and I gave up my plan of taking him home at once, and enjoyed the anticipation of the hearty laugh we should have together at the end of the evening. I was famously punished for my determination.

' "Shall we continue our game?" asked Miss Caroline, who had never relinquished her sheaf of questions.

'We went on questioning and answering with little gain of information to either party.

' "No such thing as heavy betting in this game, eh, Frank?" ' asked Jack, who had been watching us. "You don't lose ten pounds at a sitting, I guess, as you used to do at Short's. Playing for love, I suppose you call it?"

'Miss Caroline simpered, and looked down. Jack was not thinking of her. He was thinking of the days we had had at the "Mermaid". Suddenly he said, "Where were you this day last year, Frank?"

' "I don't remember!" said I.

' "Then I'll tell you. It's the 23rd—the day you were taken up for knocking down the fellow in Long Acre, and that I had to bail you out ready for Christmas Day. You are in more agreeable quarters to-night."

'He did not intend this reminiscence to be heard, but was not in the least put out when Miss Tomkinson, with a face of dire surprise, asked—

' "Mr. Harrison taken up, sir?"

' "Oh, yes, ma'am; and you see it was so common an affair with him to be locked up that he can't remember the dates of his different imprisonments."

'He laughed heartily; and so should I, but that I saw the impression it made. The thing was, in fact, simple enough, and capable of easy explanation. I had been made angry by seeing a great hulking fellow, out of mere wantonness, break the crutch from under a cripple; and I struck the man more violently than I intended, and down he went, yelling out for the police, and I had to go before the magistrate to be released. I disdained giving this explanation at the time. It was no business of theirs what I had been doing a year ago; but still Jack might have held his tongue. However, that unruly member of his was set a-going, and he told me afterwards he was resolved to let the old ladies into a little of life; and accordingly he remembered every practical joke we had ever had, and talked and laughed, and roared again. I tried to converse with Miss Caroline—Mrs. Munton—any one; but Jack was the hero of the evening, and every one was listening to him.

' "Then he has never sent any hoaxing letters since he came here, has he? Good boy! He has turned over a new leaf. He was the deepest dog at that I ever met with. Such anonymous letters as he used to send! Do you remember that to Mrs. Walbrook, eh, Frank? That was too bad!" (the wretch was laughing all the time). "No; I won't tell about it—don't be afraid. Such a shameful hoax!" (laughing again).

' "Pray do tell," I called out; for he made it seem far worse than it was.

' "Oh no, no; you've established a better character—I would not for the world nip your budding efforts. We'll bury the past in oblivion."

'I tried to tell my neighbours the story to which he alluded; but they were attracted by the merriment of Jack's manner, and did not care to hear the plain matter of fact.

'Then came a pause; Jack was talking almost quietly to Miss Horsman. Suddenly he called across the room—"How many times have you been out with the hounds? The hedges were blind very late this year, but you must have had some good mild days since."

' "I have never been out," said I shortly.

' "Never!—whew!——Why, I thought that was the great attraction to Duncombe."

'Now was not he provoking? He would condole with me, and fixed the subject in the minds of every one present.

'The supper trays were brought in, and there was a shuffling of situations. He and I were close together again.

' "I say, Frank, what will you lay me that I don't clear that tray before people are ready for their second helping? I'm as hungry as a hound."

' "You shall have a round of beef and a raw leg of mutton when you get home. Only do behave yourself here."

' "Well, for your sake; but keep me away from those trays, or I'll not answer for myself. 'Hould me, or I'll fight,' as the Irishman said. I'll go and talk to that little old lady in blue, and sit with my back to those ghosts of eatables."

'He sat down by Miss Caroline, who would not have liked his description of her; and began an earnest, tolerably quiet conversation. I tried to be as agreeable as I could, to do away with the impression he had given of me; but I found that every one drew up a little stiffly at my approach, and did not encourage me to make any remarks.

'In the middle of my attempts, I heard Miss Caroline beg Jack to take a glass of wine, and I saw him help himself to what appeared to be port; but in an instant he set it down from his lips, exclaiming, "Vinegar, by Jove!" He made the most horribly wry face: and Miss Tomkinson came up in a severe hurry to investigate the affair. It turned out it was some black-currant wine, on which she particularly piqued herself; I drank two glasses of it to ingratiate myself with her, and can testify to its sourness. I don't think she noticed my exertions, she was so much engrossed in listening to Jack's excuses for his malapropos observation. He told her, with the gravest face, that he had been a teetotaller so long that he had but a confused recollection of the distinction between wine and vinegar, particularly eschewing the latter, because it had been twice fermented; and that he had imagined Miss Caroline had asked him to take toast-and-water, or he should never have touched the decanter.

IX

'AS we were walking home, Jack said, "Lord, Frank! I've had such fun with the little lady in blue. I told her you wrote to me every Saturday, telling me the events of the week. She took all in." He stopped to laugh; for he bubbled and chuckled so that he could not laugh and walk. "And I told her you were deeply in love" (another laugh); "and that I could not get you to tell me the name of the lady, but that she had light brown hair—in short, I drew from life, and gave her an exact description of herself; and that I was most anxious to see her, and implore her to be merciful to you, for that you were a most timid, faint-hearted fellow with women." He laughed till I thought he would have fallen down. "I begged her, if she could guess who it was from my description—I'll answer for it she did—I took care of that; for I said you described a mole on the left cheek in the most poetical way, saying Venus had pinched it out of envy at seeing any one more lovely—oh, hold me up, or I shall fall—laughing and hunger make me so weak;—well, I say, I begged her, if she knew who your fair one could be, to implore her to save you. I said I knew one of your lungs had gone after a former unfortunate love-affair, and that I could not answer for the other if the lady here were cruel. She spoke of a respirator; but I told her that might do very well for the odd lung; but would it minister to a heart diseased? I really did talk fine. I have found out the secret of eloquence—it's believing what you've got to say; and I worked myself well up with fancying you married to the little lady in blue."

'I got to laughing at last, angry as I had been; his impudence was irresistible. Mrs. Rose had come home in the sedan, and gone to bed; and he and I sat up over the round of beef and brandy-and-water till two o'clock in the morning.

'He told me I had got quite into the professional way of mousing about a room, and mewing and purring according as my patients were ill or well. He mimicked me, and made me laugh at myself. He left early the next morning.

'Mr. Morgan came at his usual hour; he and Marshland would never have agreed, and I should have been uncomfortable to see two friends of mine disliking and despising each other.

'Mr. Morgan was ruffled; but with his deferential manner to women, he smoothed himself down before Mrs. Rose — regretted that he had not been able to come to Miss Tomkinson's the evening before, and consequently had not seen her in the society she was so well calculated to adorn. But when we were by ourselves, he said—

' "I was sent for to Mrs. Munton's this morning—the old spasms. May I ask what is this story she tells me about—about prison, in fact? I trust, sir, she has made some little mistake, and that you never were;—that it is an unfounded report."

He could not get it out—"that you were in Newgate for three months!" I burst out laughing; the story had grown like a mushroom indeed. Mr. Morgan looked grave. I told him the truth. Still he looked grave. "I've no doubt, sir, that you acted rightly; but it has an awkward sound. I imagined from your hilarity just now that there was no foundation whatever for the story. Unfortunately, there is."

' "I was only a night at the police-station. I would go there again for the same cause, sir."

' "Very fine spirit, sir—quite like Don Quixote; but don't you see you might as well have been to the hulks at once?"

' "No, sir; I don't."

' "Take my word, before long the story will have grown to that. However, we won't anticipate evil. *Mens conscia recti,* you remember, is the great thing. The part I regret is, that it may require some short time to overcome a little prejudice which the story may excite against you. However, we won't dwell on it. *Mens conscia recti!* Don't think about it, sir."

'It was clear he was thinking a good deal about it.

X

'TWO or three days before this time, I had had an invitation from the Bullocks to dine with them on Christmas Day. Mrs. Rose was going to spend the week with friends in the town where she formerly lived; and I had been pleased at the notion of being received into a family, and of being a little with Mr. Bullock, who struck me as a bluff, good-hearted fellow.

'But this Tuesday before Christmas Day, there came an invitation from the Vicar to dine there; there were to be only their own family and Mr. Morgan. "Only their own family." It was getting to be all the world to me. I was in a passion with myself for having been so ready to accept Mr. Bullock's invitation—coarse and ungentlemanly as he was; with his wife's airs of pretension and Miss Bullock's stupidity. I turned it over in my mind. No! I could not have a bad headache, which should prevent me going to the place I did not care for, and yet leave me at liberty to go where I wished. All I could do was to join the vicarage girls after church, and walk by their side in a long country ramble. They were quiet; not sad, exactly; but it was evident that the thought of Walter was in their minds on this day. We went through a copse where there were a good number of evergreens planted as covers for game. The snow was on the ground; but the sky was clear and bright, and the sun glittered on the smooth holly-leaves. Lizzie asked me to gather her some of the very bright red berries, and she was beginning a sentence with—

' "Do you remember,"—when Helen said "*Hush*", and looked towards Sophy, who was walking a little apart, and crying softly to herself. There was evidently some connexion between Walter and the holly-berries, for Lizzie threw them away at once when she saw Sophy's tears. Soon we came to a stile which led to an open, breezy common, half covered with gorse. I helped the little girls over it, and set them to run down the slope; but I took Sophy's arm in mine, and though I could not speak, I think she knew how I was feeling for her. I could hardly bear to bid her good-bye at the vicarage gate; it seemed as if I ought to go in and spend the day with her.

XI

'I VENTED my ill humour in being late for the Bullocks' dinner. There were one or two clerks, towards whom Mr. Bullock was patronizing and pressing. Mrs. Bullock was decked out in extraordinary finery. Miss Bullock looked plainer than ever; but she had on some old gown or other, I think, for I heard Mrs. Bullock tell her she was always making a figure of herself. I began to-day to suspect that the mother would not be sorry if I took a fancy to the step-daughter. I was again placed near her at dinner, and when the little ones came in to dessert I was made to notice how fond of children she was, and indeed when one of them nestled to her, her face did brighten; but the moment she caught this loud-whispered remark the gloom came back again, with something even of anger in her look; and she was quite sullen and obstinate when urged to sing in the drawing-room. Mrs. Bullock turned to me—

' "Some young ladies won't sing unless they are asked by gentlemen." She spoke very crossly. "If you ask Jemima, she will probably sing. To oblige me, it is evident she will not."

'I thought the singing, when we got it, would probably be a great bore; however, I did as I was bid, and went with my request to the young lady, who was sitting a little apart. She looked up at me with eyes full of tears, and said, in a decided tone (which, if I had not seen her eyes, I should have said was as cross as her mamma's), "No, sir, I will not." She got up, and left the room. I expected to hear Mrs. Bullock abuse her for her obstinacy. Instead of that, she began to tell me of the money that had been spent on her education; of what each separate accomplishment had cost. "She was timid," she said, "but very musical. Wherever her future home might be, there would be no want of music." She went on praising her till I hated her. If they thought I was going to marry that great lubberly girl, they were mistaken. Mr. Bullock and the clerks came up. He brought out Liebig, and called me to him.

' "I can understand a good deal of this agricultural chemistry," said he, "and have put it in practice—without much success, hitherto, I confess. But these unconnected letters puzzle me a little. I suppose they have some meaning, or else I should say it was mere book-making to put them in."

' "I think they give the page a very ragged appearance," said Mrs. Bullock, who had joined us. "I inherit a little of my late father's taste for books, and must say I like to see a good type, a broad margin, and an elegant binding. My father despised variety; how he would have held up his hands aghast at the cheap literature of these times! He did not require many books, but he would have twenty editions of those that he had; and he paid more for binding than he did for the books themselves. But elegance was everything with him. He would not have admitted your Liebig, Mr. Bullock; neither the nature of the subject, nor the common type, nor the common way in which your book is got up, would have suited him."

' "Go and make tea, my dear, and leave Mr. Harrison and me to talk over a few of these manures."

'We settled to it; I explained the meaning of the symbols, and the doctrine of chemical equivalents. At last he said, "Doctor! you're giving me too strong a dose of it at one time. Let's have a small quantity taken 'hodie'; that's professional, as Mr. Morgan would call it. Come in and call when you have leisure, and give me a lesson in my alphabet. Of all you've been telling me I can only remember that C means carbon and O oxygen; and I see one must know the meaning of all these confounded letters before one can do much good with Liebig."

' "We dine at three," said Mrs. Bullock. "There will always be a knife and fork for Mr. Harrison. Bullock! don't confine your invitation to the evening!' "

' "Why, you see, I've a nap always after dinner, so I could not be learning chemistry then."

' "Don't be so selfish, Mr. B. Think of the pleasure Jemima and I shall have in Mr. Harrison's society."

'I put a stop to the discussion by saying I would come in in the evenings occasionally, and give Mr. Bullock a lesson, but that my professional duties occupied me invariably until that time.

'I liked Mr. Bullock. He was simple, and shrewd; and to be with a man was a relief, after all the feminine society I went through every day.

XII

'THE next morning I met Miss Horsman.

' "So you dined at Mr. Bullock's yesterday, Mr. Harrison? Quite a family party, I hear. They are quite charmed with you, and your knowledge of chemistry. Mr. Bullock told me so, in Hodgson's shop, just now. Miss Bullock is a nice girl, eh, Mr. Harrison?" She looked sharply at me. Of course, whatever I thought, I could do nothing but assent. "A nice little fortune, too—three thousand pounds, consols, from her own mother."

'What did I care? She might have three millions for me. I had begun to think a good deal about money, though, but not in connexion with her. I had been doing up our books ready to

send out our Christmas bills, and had been wondering how far
the Vicar would consider three hundred a year, with a prospect
of increase, would justify me in thinking of Sophy. Think of her
I could not help; and the more I thought of how good, and
sweet, and pretty she was, the more I felt that she ought to
have far more than I could offer. Besides, my father was a
shopkeeper, and I saw the Vicar had a sort of respect for family.
I determined to try and be very attentive to my profession. I
was as civil as could be to every one; and wore the nap off the
brim of my hat by taking it off so often.

'I had my eyes open to every glimpse of Sophy. I am
overstocked with gloves now that I bought at that time, by
way of making errands into the shops where I saw her black
gown. I bought pounds upon pounds of arrowroot, till I was
tired of the eternal arrowroot puddings Mrs. Rose gave me. I
asked her if she could not make bread of it, but she seemed
to think that would be expensive; so I took to soap as a safe
purchase. I believe soap improves by keeping.

XIII

'THE more I knew of Mrs. Rose, the better I liked her. She was
sweet, and kind, and motherly, and we never had any rubs. I
hurt her once or twice, I think, by cutting her short in her
long stories about Mr. Rose. But I found out that when she
had plenty to do she did not think of him quite so much; so
I expressed a wish for Corazza shirts, and in the puzzle of
devising how they were to be cut out she forgot Mr. Rose for
some time. I was still more pleased by her way about some
legacy her elder brother left her. I don't know the amount,
but it was something handsome, and she might have set up
housekeeping for herself: but, instead, she told Mr. Morgan
(who repeated it to me), that she should continue with me, as
she had quite an elder sister's interest in me.

'The "county young lady", Miss Tyrrell, returned to Miss
Tomkinson's after the holidays. She had an enlargement of the
tonsils, which required to be frequently touched with caustic,
so I often called to see her. Miss Caroline always received

me, and kept me talking in her washed-out style, after I had seen my patient. One day she told me she thought she had a weakness about the heart, and would be glad if I would bring my stethoscope the next time, which I accordingly did; and while I was on my knees listening to the pulsations, one of the young ladies came in. She said—

' "Oh, dear! I never! I beg your pardon, ma'am," and scuttled out. There was not much the matter with Miss Caroline's heart: a little feeble in action or so, a mere matter of weakness and general languor. When I went down I saw two or three of the girls peeping out of the half-closed schoolroom door, but they shut it immediately, and I heard them laughing. The next time I called, Miss Tomkinson was sitting in state to receive me.

' "Miss Tyrrell's throat does not seem to make much progress. Do you understand the case, Mr. Harrison, or should we have further advice? I think Mr. Morgan would probably know more about it."

'I assured her it was the simplest thing in the world; that it always implied a little torpor in the constitution, and that we preferred working through the system, which of course was a slow process, and that the medicine the young lady was taking (iodide of iron) was sure to be successful, although the progress would not be rapid. She bent her head and said, "It might be so; but she confessed she had more confidence in medicines which had some effect."

'She seemed to expect me to tell her something; but I had nothing to say, and accordingly I bade goodbye. Somehow, Miss Tomkinson always managed to make me feel very small, by a succession of snubbings; and whenever I left her I had always to comfort myself under her contradictions by saying to myself, "Her saying it is so, does not make it so." Or I invented good retorts which I might have made to her brusque speeches if I had but thought of them at the right time. But it was provoking that I had not had the presence of mind to recollect them just when they were wanted.

XIV

'ON the whole, things went on smoothly. Mr. Holden's legacy
came in just about this time; and I felt quite rich. Five hundred
pounds would furnish the house, I thought, when Mrs. Rose left
and Sophy came. I was delighted, too, to imagine that Sophy
perceived the difference of my manner to her from what it
was to any one else, and that she was embarrassed and shy
in consequence, but not displeased with me for it. All was so
flourishing that I went about on wings instead of feet. We were
very busy, without having anxious cares. My legacy was paid
into Mr. Bullock's hands, who united a little banking business to
his profession of law. In return for his advice about investments
(which I never meant to take, having a more charming, if less
profitable, mode in my head), I went pretty frequently to teach
him his agricultural chemistry. I was so happy in Sophy's
blushes that I was universally benevolent, and desirous of
giving pleasure to every one. I went, at Mrs. Bullock's general
invitation, to dinner there one day unexpectedly: but there was
such a fuss of ill-concealed preparation consequent upon my
coming, that I never went again. Her little boy came in, with
an audibly given message from the cook, to ask—

' "If this was the gentleman as she was to send in the best
dinner-service and dessert for?"

'I looked deaf, but determined never to go again.

'Miss Bullock and I, meanwhile, became rather friendly. We
found out that we mutually disliked each other; and were
contented with the discovery. If people are worth anything, this
sort of non-liking is a very good beginning of friendship. Every
good quality is revealed naturally and slowly, and is a pleasant
surprise. I found out that Miss Bullock was sensible, and
even sweet-tempered, when not irritated by her stepmother's
endeavours to show her off. But she would sulk for hours after
Mrs. Bullock's offensive praise of her good points. And I never
saw such a black passion as she went into when she suddenly
came into the room when Mrs. Bullock was telling me of all the
offers she had had.

'My legacy made me feel up to extravagance. I scoured the
country for a glorious nosegay of camellias, which I sent to
Sophy on Valentine's Day. I durst not add a line, but I

wished the flowers could speak, and tell her how I loved her.

'I called on Miss Tyrrell that day. Miss Caroline was more simpering and affected than ever; and full of allusions to the day.

' "Do you affix much sincerity of meaning to the little gallantries of this day, Mr. Harrison?" asked she, in a languishing tone. I thought of my camellias, and how my heart had gone with them into Sophy's keeping; and I told her I thought one might often take advantage of such a time to hint at feelings one dared not fully express.

'I remembered afterwards the forced display she made, after Miss Tyrrell left the room, of a valentine. But I took no notice at the time; my head was full of Sophy.

'It was on that very day that John Brouncker, the gardener to all of us who had small gardens to keep in order, fell down and injured his wrist severely (I don't give you the details of the case, because they would not interest you, being too technical; if you've any curiosity, you will find them in the *Lancet* of August in that year). We all liked John, and this accident was felt like a town's misfortune. The gardens, too, just wanted doing up. Both Mr. Morgan and I went directly to him. It was a very awkward case, and his wife and children were crying sadly. He himself was in great distress at being thrown out of work. He begged us to do something that would cure him speedily, as he could not afford to be laid up, with six children depending on him for bread. We did not say much before him, but we both thought the arm would have to come off, and it was his right arm. We talked it over when we came out of the cottage. Mr. Morgan had no doubt of the necessity. I went back at dinner-time to see the poor fellow. He was feverish and anxious. He had caught up some expression of Mr. Morgan's in the morning, and had guessed the measure we had in contemplation. He bade his wife leave the room, and spoke to me by myself.

' "If you please, sir, I'd rather be done for at once than have my arm taken off, and be a burden to my family. I'm not afraid of dying, but I could not stand being a cripple for life, eating bread, and not able to earn it."

'The tears were in his eyes with earnestness. I had all along been more doubtful about the necessity of the amputation than

Mr. Morgan. I knew the improved treatment in such cases. In his days there was much more of the rough and ready in surgical practice; so I gave the poor fellow some hope.

'In the afternoon I met Mr. Bullock.

' "So you're to try your hand at an amputation tomorrow, I hear. Poor John Brouncker! I used to tell him he was not careful enough about his ladders. Mr. Morgan is quite excited about it. He asked me to be present, and see how well a man from Guy's could operate; he says he is sure you'll do it beautifully. Pah! no such sights for me, thank you."

'Ruddy Mr. Bullock went a shade or two paler at the thought.

' "Curious! how professionally a man views these things. Here's Mr. Morgan, who has been all along as proud of you as if you were his own son, absolutely rubbing his hands at the idea of this crowning glory, this feather in your cap! He told me just now he knew he had always been too nervous to be a good operator; and had therefore preferred sending for White from Chesterton. But now any one might have a serious accident who liked, for you would be always at hand."

'I told Mr. Bullock, I really thought we might avoid the amputation; but his mind was preoccupied with the idea of it, and he did not care to listen to me. The whole town was full of it. That is a charm in a little town, everybody is so sympathetically full of the same events. Even Miss Horsman stopped me to ask after John Brouncker with interest; but she threw cold water upon my intention of saving the arm.

' "As for the wife and family, we'll take care of them. Think what a fine opportunity you have of showing off, Mr. Harrison!"

'That was just like her. Always ready with her suggestions of ill-natured or interested motives.

'Mr. Morgan heard my proposal of a mode of treatment by which I thought it possible that the arm might be saved.

' "I differ from you, Mr. Harrison," said he. "I regret it, but I differ *in toto* from you. Your kind heart deceives you in this instance. There is no doubt that amputation must take place—not later than tomorrow morning, I should say. I have made myself at liberty to attend upon you, sir; I shall be happy to officiate as your assistant. Time was when I should have been proud to be principal, but a little trembling in my arm incapacitates me."

'I urged my reasons upon him again; but he was obstinate. He had, in fact, boasted so much of my acquirements as an operator, that he was unwilling I should lose this opportunity of displaying my skill. He could not see that there would be greater skill evinced in saving the arm; nor did I think of this at the time. I grew angry at his old-fashioned narrow-mindedness, as I thought it; and I became dogged in my resolution to adhere to my own course. We parted very coolly; and I went straight off to John Brouncker to tell him I believed that I could save the arm, if he would refuse to have it amputated. When I calmed myself a little, before going in and speaking to him, I could not help acknowledging that we should run some risk of locked jaw; but, on the whole, and after giving most earnest, conscientious thought to the case, I was sure that my mode of treatment would be best.

'He was a sensible man. I told him the difference of opinion that existed between Mr. Morgan and myself. I said that there might be some little risk attending the non-amputation; but that I should guard against it, and I trusted that I should be able to preserve his arm.

' "Under God's blessing," said he reverently. I bowed my head. I don't like to talk too frequently of the dependence which I always felt on that holy blessing, as to the result of my efforts; but I was glad to hear that speech of John's, because it showed a calm and faithful heart; and I had almost certain hopes of him from that time.

'We agreed that he should tell Mr. Morgan the reason of his objections to the amputation, and his reliance on my opinion. I determined to recur to every book I had relating to such cases, and to convince Mr. Morgan, if I could, of my wisdom. Unluckily, I found out afterwards that he had met Miss Horsman in the time that intervened before I saw him again at his own house that evening; and she had more than hinted that I shrank from performing the operation, "for very good reasons, no doubt. She had heard that the medical students in London were a bad set, and were not remarkable for regular attendance in the hospitals. She might be mistaken; but she thought it was, perhaps, quite as well poor John Brouncker had not his arm cut off by—— Was there not such a thing as mortification coming on after a clumsy operation? It was, perhaps, only a choice of deaths!"

'Mr. Morgan had been stung at all this. Perhaps I did not speak quite respectfully enough; I was a good deal excited. We only got more and more angry with each other; though he, to do him justice, was as civil as could be all the time, thinking that thereby he concealed his vexation and disappointment. He did not try to conceal his anxiety about poor John. I went home weary and dispirited. I made up and took the necessary applications to John; and, promising to return with the dawn of day (I would fain have stayed, but I did not wish him to be alarmed about himself). I went home, and resolved to sit up and study the treatment of similar cases.

'Mrs. Rose knocked at the door.

' "Come in!" said I sharply.

'She said she had seen I had something on my mind all day, and she could not go to bed without asking if there was nothing she could do. She was good and kind; and I could not help telling her a little of the truth. She listened pleasantly; and I shook her warmly by the hand, thinking that though she might not be very wise, her good heart made her worth a dozen keen, sharp, hard people, like Miss Horsman.

'When I went at daybreak, I saw John's wife for a few minutes outside of the door. She seemed to wish her husband had been in Mr. Morgan's hands rather than mine; but she gave me as good an account as I dared to hope for of the manner in which her husband had passed the night. This was confirmed by my own examination.

'When Mr. Morgan and I visited him together later on in the day, John said what we had agreed upon the day before; and I told Mr. Morgan openly that it was by my advice that amputation was declined. He did not speak to me till we had left the house. Then he said—"Now, sir, from this time, I consider this case entirely in your hands. Only remember the poor fellow has a wife and six children. In case you come round to my opinion, remember that Mr. White could come over, as he has done before, for the operation."

'So! Mr. Morgan believed I declined operating because I felt myself incapable. Very well! I was much mortified.

'An hour after we parted, I received a note to this effect—

' "DEAR SIR,—I will take the long round to-day, to leave you at liberty to attend to Brouncker's case, which I feel to be a very responsible one.

' "J. MORGAN."

'This was kindly done. I went back, as soon as I could, to John's cottage. While I was in the inner room with him, I heard the Miss Tomkinsons' voices outside. They had called to inquire. Miss Tomkinson came in, and evidently was poking and snuffing about. (Mrs. Brouncker told her that I was within; and within I resolved to be till they had gone.)

' "What is this close smell?" asked she. "I am afraid you are not cleanly. Cheese!—cheese in this cupboard! No wonder there is an unpleasant smell. Don't you know how particular you should be about being clean when there is illness about?"

'Mrs. Brouncker was exquisitely clean in general, and was piqued at these remarks.

' "If you please, ma'am, I could not leave John yesterday to do any house-work, and Jenny put the dinner-things away. She is but eight years old."

'But this did not satisfy Miss Tomkinson, who was evidently pursuing the course of her observations.

' "Fresh butter, I declare! Well now, Mrs. Brouncker, do you know I don't allow myself fresh butter at this time of the year? How can you save, indeed, with such extravagance!"

' "Please, ma'am," answered Mrs. Brouncker, "you'd think it strange, if I was to take such liberties in your house as you're taking here."

'I expected to hear a sharp answer. No! Miss Tomkinson liked true plain-speaking. The only person in whom she would tolerate round-about ways of talking was her sister.

' "Well, that's true," she said. "Still, you must not be above taking advice. Fresh butter is extravagant at this time of the year. However, you're a good kind of woman, and I've a great respect for John. Send Jenny for some broth as soon as he can take it. Come, Caroline, we have got to go on to Williams's."

'But Miss Caroline said that she was tired, and would rest where she was till Miss Tomkinson came back. I was a prisoner for some time, I found. When she was alone with Mrs. Brouncker, she said—

' "You must not be hurt by my sister's abrupt manner. She means well. She has not much imagination or sympathy, and cannot understand the distraction of mind produced by the illness of a worshipped husband." I could hear the loud sigh of commiseration which followed this speech. Mrs. Brouncker said—

' "Please, ma'am, I don't worship my husband. I would not be so wicked."

' "Goodness! You don't think it wicked, do you? For my part, if . . . I should worship, I should adore him." I thought she need not imagine such improbable cases. But sturdy Mrs. Brouncker said again—

' "I hope I know my duty better. I've not learned my Commandments for nothing. I know whom I ought to worship."

'Just then the children came in, dirty and unwashed, I have no doubt. And now Miss Caroline's real nature peeped out. She spoke sharply to them, and asked them if they had no manners, little pigs as they were, to come brushing against her silk gown in that way? She sweetened herself again, and was as sugary as love when Miss Tomkinson returned for her, accompanied by one whose voice, "like winds in summer sighing," I knew to be my dear Sophy's.

'She did not say much; but what she did say, and the manner in which she spoke, was tender and compassionate in the highest degree; and she came to take the four little ones back with her to the Vicarage, in order that they might be out of their mother's way; the older two might help at home. She offered to wash their hands and faces; and when I emerged from my inner chamber, after the Miss Tomkinsons had left, I found her with a chubby child on her knees, bubbling and spluttering against her white wet hand, with a face bright, rosy, and merry under the operation. Just as I came in, she said to him, "There, Jemmy, now I can kiss you with this nice clean face."

'She coloured when she saw me. I liked her speaking, and I liked her silence. She was silent now, and I "lo'ed her a' the better." I gave my directions to Mrs. Brouncker, and hastened to overtake Sophy and the children; but they had gone round by the lanes, I suppose, for I saw nothing of them.

'I was very anxious about the case. At night I went again. Miss Horsman had been there; I believe she was really kind among the poor, but she could not help leaving a sting behind her everywhere. She had been frightening Mrs. Brouncker about her husband; and been, I have no doubt, expressing her doubts of my skill; for Mrs. Brouncker began—

' "Oh, please, sir, if you'll only let Mr. Morgan take off his arm, I will never think the worse of you for not being able to do it."

'I told her it was from no doubt of my own competency to perform the operation that I wished to save the arm; but that he himself was anxious to have it spared.

' "Aye, bless him! he frets about not earning enough to keep us, if he's crippled; but, sir, I don't care about that. I would work my fingers to the bone, and so would the children; I'm sure we'd be proud to do for him, and keep him; God bless him! it would be far better to have him only with one arm, than to have him in the churchyard, Miss Horsman says"——

' "Confound Miss Horsman!" said I.

' "Thank you, Mr. Harrison," said her well-known voice behind me. She had come out, dark as it was, to bring some old linen to Mrs. Brouncker; for, as I said before, she was very kind to all the poor people of Duncombe.

' "I beg your pardon;" for I really was sorry for my speech, or rather, that she had heard it.

' "There is no occasion for any apology," she replied, drawing herself up, and pinching her lips into a very venomous shape.

'John was doing pretty well; but of course the danger of locked jaw was not over. Before I left, his wife entreated me to take off the arm; she wrung her hands in her passionate entreaty. "Spare him to me, Mr. Harrison," she implored. Miss Horsman stood by. It was mortifying enough; but I thought of the power which was in my hands, as I firmly believed, of saving the limb; and I was inflexible.

'You cannot think how pleasantly Mrs. Rose's sympathy came in on my return. To be sure, she did not understand one word of the case, which I detailed to her; but she listened with interest, and as long as she held her tongue I thought she was really taking it in; but her first remark was as malapropos as could be.

' "You are anxious to save the tibia—I see completely how difficult that will be. My late husband had a case exactly similar, and I remember his anxiety; but you must not distress yourself too much, my dear Mr. Harrison; I have no doubt it will end well."

'I knew she had no grounds for this assurance, and yet it comforted me.

'However, as it happened, John did fully as well as I could hope; of course, he was long in rallying his strength: and, indeed, sea-air was evidently so necessary for his complete restoration, that I accepted with gratitude Mrs. Rose's proposal of sending him to Highport for a fortnight or three weeks. Her kind generosity in this matter made me more desirous than ever of paying her every mark of respect and attention.

XV

'ABOUT this time there was a sale at Ashmeadow, a pretty house in the neighbourhood of Duncombe. It was likewise an easy walk, and the spring days tempted many people thither who had no intention of buying anything, but who liked the idea of rambling through the woods, gay with early primroses and wild daffodils, and of seeing the gardens and house, which till now had been shut up from the ingress of the townspeople. Mrs. Rose had planned to go, but an unlucky cold prevented her. She begged me to bring her a very particular account, saying she delighted in details, and always questioned the late Mr. Rose as to the side dishes of the dinners to which he went. The late Mr. Rose's conduct was always held up as a model to me, by the way. I walked to Ashmeadow, pausing or loitering with different parties of townspeople, all bound in the same direction. At last I found the Vicar and Sophy, and with them I stayed. I sat by Sophy and talked and listened. A sale is a very pleasant gathering after all. The auctioneer, in a country place, is privileged to joke from his rostrum; and having a personal knowledge of most of the people, can sometimes make a very keen hit at their circumstances, and turn the laugh against them. For instance, on the present occasion, there was a farmer present, with his wife, who was notoriously the grey mare. The auctioneer was selling some horse-cloths, and called out to recommend the article to her, telling her, with a knowing look at the company, that they would make her a dashing pair of trousers, if she was in want of such an article. She drew herself up with dignity, and said. "Come, John, we've had enough of these." Whereupon there was a burst of laughter, and in the midst of it John meekly followed his wife out of the place. The furniture in the sitting-rooms was, I believe, very beautiful, but I did not notice it much. Suddenly I heard the auctioneer speaking to me, "Mr. Harrison, won't you give me a bid for this table?"

'It was a very pretty little table of walnut-wood. I thought it would go into my study very well, so I gave him a bid. I saw Miss Horsman bidding against me, so I went off with full force, and at last it was knocked down to me. The auctioneer smiled, and congratulated me.

' "A most useful present for Mrs. Harrison, when that lady comes."

'Everybody laughed. They like a joke about marriage; it is so easy of comprehension. But the table which I had thought was for writing, turned out to be a work-table, scissors and thimble complete. No wonder I looked foolish. Sophy was not looking at me, that was one comfort. She was busy arranging a nosegay of wood-anemone and wild sorrel.

'Miss Horsman came up, with her curious eyes.

' "I had no idea things were far enough advanced for you to be purchasing a work-table, Mr. Harrison."

'I laughed off my awkwardness.

' "Did not you, Miss Horsman? You are very much behind-hand. You have not heard of my piano, then?"

' "No, indeed," she said, half uncertain whether I was serious or not. "Then it seems there is nothing wanting but the lady."

' "Perhaps she may not be wanting either," said I, for I wished to perplex her keen curiosity.

XVI

'WHEN I got home from my round, I found Mrs. Rose in some sorrow.

' "Miss Horsman called after you left," said she. "Have you heard how John Brouncker is at Highport?"

' "Very well," replied I. "I called on his wife just now, and she had just got a letter from him. She had been anxious about him, for she had not heard for a week. However, all's right now; and she has pretty well of work, at Mrs. Munton's, as her servant is ill. Oh, they'll do, never fear."

' "At Mrs. Munton's? Oh, that accounts for it, then. She is so deaf, and makes such blunders."

' "Accounts for what?" asked I.

' "Oh, perhaps I had better not tell you," hesitated Mrs. Rose.

' "Yes, tell me at once. I beg your pardon, but I hate mysteries."

' "You are so like my poor dear Mr. Rose. He used to speak to me just in that sharp, cross way. It is only that Miss Horsman called. She had been making a collection for John Brouncker's widow and"——

' "But the man's alive! said I.

' "So it seems. But Mrs. Munton had told her that he was dead. And she has got Mr. Morgan's name down at the head of the list, and Mr. Bullock's."

'Mr. Morgan and I had got into a short, cool way of speaking to each other ever since we had differed so much about the treatment of Brouncker's arm; and I had heard once or twice of his shakes of the head over John's case. He would not have spoken against my method for the world, and fancied that he concealed his fears.

' "Miss Horsman is very ill-natured, I think," sighed forth Mrs. Rose.

'I saw that something had been said of which I had not heard, for the mere fact of collecting money for the widow was good-natured, whoever did it; so I asked, quietly, what she had said.

' "Oh, I don't know if I should tell you. I only know she made me cry; for I'm not well, and I can't bear to hear any one that I live with abused."

'Come! this was pretty plain.

' "What did Miss Horsman say of me?" asked I, half laughing, for I knew there was no love lost between us.

' "Oh, she only said she wondered you could go to sales, and spend your money there, when your ignorance had made Jane Brouncker a widow, and her children fatherless."

' "Pooh! pooh! John's alive, and likely to live as long as you or I, thanks to you, Mrs. Rose."

'When my work-table came home, Mrs. Rose was so struck with its beauty and completeness, and I was so much obliged to her for her identification of my interests with hers, and the kindness of her whole conduct about John, that I begged her to accept of it. She seemed very much pleased; and, after a few apologies, she consented to take it, and placed it in the most conspicuous part of the front parlour, where she usually sat. There was a good deal of morning calling in Duncombe after the sale, and during this time the fact of John's being alive was established to the conviction of all except Miss Horsman, who, I believe, still doubted. I myself told Mr. Morgan, who immediately went to reclaim his money; saying to me, that he was thankful of the information; he was truly glad to hear it; and he shook me warmly by the hand for the first time for a month.

XVII

'A FEW days after the sale, I was in the consulting-room. The servant must have left the folding-doors a little ajar, I think. Mrs. Munton came to call on Mrs. Rose; and the former being deaf, I heard all the speeches of the latter lady, as she was obliged to speak very loud in order to be heard. She began—

' "This is a great pleasure, Mrs. Munton, so seldom as you are well enough to go out."

'Mumble, mumble, mumble, through the door.

' "Oh, very well, thank you. Take this seat, and then you can admire my new work-table, ma'am; a present from Mr. Harrison."

'Mumble, mumble.

' "Who could have told you, ma'am? Miss Horsman? Oh, yes, I showed it Miss Horsman."

'Mumble, mumble.

' "I don't quite understand you, ma'am." '

'Mumble, mumble.

' "I'm not blushing, I believe. I really am quite in the dark as to what you mean."

'Mumble, mumble.

' "Oh, yes, Mr. Harrison and I are most comfortable together. He reminds me so of my dear Mr. Rose—just as fidgety and anxious in his profession."

'Mumble, mumble.

' "I'm sure you are joking now, ma'am." Then I heard a pretty loud—

' "Oh, no"; mumble, mumble, mumble, for a long time.

' "Did he really? Well, I'm sure I don't know. I should be sorry to think he was doomed to be unfortunate in so serious an affair; but you know my undying regard for the late Mr. Rose."

'Another long mumble.

' "You're very kind, I'm sure. Mr. Rose always thought more of my happiness than his own"—a little crying—"but the turtle-dove has always been my ideal, ma'am."

'Mumble, mumble.

' "No one could have been happier than I. As you say, it is a compliment to matrimony."

'Mumble.

' "Oh, but you must not repeat such a thing. Mr. Harrison would not like it. He can't bear to have his affairs spoken about."

'Then there was a change of subject; an inquiry after some poor person, I imagine. I heard Mrs. Rose say—

' "She has got a mucous membrane, I'm afraid, ma'am."

'A commiserating mumble.

' "Not always fatal. I believe Mr. Rose knew some cases that lived for years after it was discovered that they had a mucous membrane." A pause. Then Mrs. Rose spoke in a different tone.

' "Are you sure, ma'am, there is no mistake about what he said?"

'Mumble.

' "Pray don't be so observant, Mrs. Munton; you find out too much. One can have no little secrets."

'The call broke up; and I heard Mrs. Munton say in the passage, "I wish you joy, ma'am, with all my heart. There's no use denying it; for I've seen all along what would happen."

'When I went in to dinner, I said to Mrs. Rose—

' "You've had Mrs. Munton here, I think. Did she bring any news?" To my surprise, she bridled and simpered, and replied, "Oh, you must not ask, Mr. Harrison: such foolish reports."

'I did not ask, as she seemed to wish me not, and I knew there were silly reports always about. Then I think she was vexed that I did not ask. Altogether she went on so strangely that I could not help looking at her; and then she took up a hand-screen, and held it between me and her. I really felt rather anxious.

' "Are you not feeling well?" said I innocently.

' "Oh, thank you, I believe I'm quite well; only the room is rather warm, is it not?"

' "Let me put the blinds down for you? the sun begins to have a good deal of power." I drew down the blinds.

' "You are so attentive, Mr. Harrison. Mr. Rose himself never did more for my little wishes than you do."

' "I wish I could do more—I wish I could show you how much I feel"——her kindness to John Brouncker, I was going on to say; but I was just then called out to a patient. Before I went I turned back, and said——

' "Take care of yourself, my dear Mrs. Rose; you had better rest a little."

' "For your sake, I will," said she tenderly.

'I did not care for whose sake she did it. Only I really thought she was not quite well, and required rest. I thought she was more affected than usual at tea-time; and could have been angry with her nonsensical ways once or twice, but that I knew the real goodness of her heart. She said she wished she had the power to sweeten my life as she could my tea. I told her what a comfort she had been all during my late time of anxiety, and then I stole out to try if I could hear the evening singing at the Vicarage, by standing close to the garden-wall.

XVIII

'THE next morning I met Mr. Bullock by appointment, to talk a little about the legacy which was paid into his hands. As I was leaving his office, feeling full of my riches, I met Miss Horsman. She smiled rather grimly, and said—

' "Oh! Mr. Harrison, I must congratulate I believe. I don't know whether I ought to have known, but as I do, I must wish you joy. A very nice little sum, too. I always said you would have money."

'So she had found out my legacy, had she? Well, it was no secret, and one likes the reputation of being a person of property. Accordingly I smiled, and said I was much obliged to her, and if I could alter the figures to my liking, she might congratulate me still more.

'She said, "Oh, Mr. Harrison, you can't have everything. It would be better the other way, certainly. Money is the great thing, as you've found out. The relation died most opportunely, I must say."

' "He was no relative," said I; "only an intimate friend."

' "Dear-ah-me! I thought it had been a brother! Well, at any rate, the legacy is safe."

'I wished her good morning, and passed on. Before long I was sent for to Miss Tomkinson's.

'Miss Tomkinson sat in severe state to receive me. I went in with an air of ease, because I always felt so uncomfortable.

' "Is this true that I hear?" asked she, in an inquisitorial manner.

'I thought she alluded to my five hundred pounds; so I smiled, and said that I believed it was.

' "Can money be so great an object with you, Mr. Harrison?" she asked again.

'I said I had never cared much for money, except as an assistance to any plan of settling in life; and then, as I did not like her severe way of treating the subject, I said that I hoped every one was well; though of course I expected some one was ill, or I should not have been sent for.

'Miss Tomkinson looked very grave and sad. Then she

answered: "Caroline is very poorly—the old palpitations at the heart; but of course that is nothing to you."

'I said I was very sorry. She had a weakness there, I knew. Could I see her? I might be able to order something for her.

'I thought I heard Miss Tomkinson say something in a low voice about my being a heartless deceiver. Then she spoke up. "I was always distrustful of you, Mr. Harrison. I never liked your looks. I begged Caroline again and again not to confide in you. I foresaw how it would end. And now I fear her precious life will be a sacrifice."

'I begged her not to distress herself, for in all probability there was very little the matter with her sister. Might I see her?

' "No!" she said shortly, standing up as if to dismiss me. "There has been too much of this seeing and calling. By my consent, you shall never see her again."

'I bowed. I was annoyed, of course. Such a dismissal might injure my practice just when I was most anxious to increase it.

' "Have you no apology, no excuse to offer?"

'I said I had done my best; I did not feel that there was any reason to offer an apology. I wished her good morning. Suddenly she came forwards.

' "Oh, Mr. Harrison," said she, "if you have really loved Caroline, do not let a little paltry money make you desert her for another."

'I was struck dumb. Loved Miss Caroline! I loved Miss Tomkinson a great deal better, and yet I disliked her. She went on—

' "I have saved nearly three thousand pounds. If you think you are too poor to marry without money, I will give it all to Caroline. I am strong, and can go on working; but she is weak, and this disappointment will kill her." She sat down suddenly, and covered her face with her hands. Then she looked up.

' "You are unwilling, I see. Don't suppose I would have urged you if it had been for myself; but she has had so much sorrow." And now she fairly cried aloud. I tried to explain; but she would not listen, but kept saying. "Leave the house, sir! leave the house!" But I would be heard.

' "I have never had any feeling warmer than respect for Miss Caroline, and I have never shown any different feeling. I never for an instant thought of making her my wife, and she has had no cause in my behaviour to imagine I entertained any such intention."

' "This is adding insult to injury," said she. "Leave the house, sir, this instant!"

XIX

'I WENT, and sadly enough. In a small town such an occurrence is sure to be talked about, and to make a great deal of mischief. When I went home to dinner I was so full of it, and foresaw so clearly that I should need some advocate soon to set the case in its right light, that I determined on making a confidante of good Mrs. Rose. I could not eat. She watched me tenderly, and sighed when she saw my want of appetite.

' "I am sure you have something on your mind, Mr. Harrison. Would it be—would it not be—a relief to impart it to some sympathizing friend?"

'It was just what I wanted to do.

' "My dear kind Mrs. Rose," said I, "I must tell you, if you will listen."

'She took up the fire-screen, and held it, as yesterday, between me and her.

' "The most unfortunate misunderstanding has taken place. Miss Tomkinson thinks that I have been paying attentions to Miss Caroline; when, in fact—may I tell you, Mrs. Rose?—my affections are placed elsewhere. Perhaps you have found it out already?" for indeed I thought I had been too much in love to conceal my attachment to Sophy from any one who knew my movements as well as Mrs. Rose.

'She hung down her head, and said she believed she had found out my secret.

' "Then only think how miserably I am situated. If I have any hope—oh, Mrs. Rose, do you think I have any hope"——

'She put the hand-screen still more before her face, and after some hesitation she said she thought "if I persevered—in time—I might have hope". And then she suddenly got up and left the room.

XX

'THAT afternoon I met Mr. Bullock in the street. My mind was so full of the affair with Miss Tomkinson that I should have passed him without notice, if he had not stopped me short, and said that he must speak to me; about my wonderful five hundred pounds, I supposed. But I did not care for that now.

' "What is this I hear," said he severely, "about your engagement with Mrs. Rose?"

' "With Mrs. Rose!" said I, almost laughing, although my heart was heavy enough.

' "Yes! with Mrs. Rose!" said he sternly.

' "I'm not engaged to Mrs. Rose," I replied. "There is some mistake."

' "I'm glad to hear it, sir," he answered, "very glad. It requires some explanation, however. Mrs. Rose has been congratulated, and has acknowledged the truth of the report. It is confirmed by many facts. The work-table you bought, confessing your intention of giving it to your future wife, is given to her. How do you account for these things, sir?"

'I said I did not pretend to account for them. At present, a good deal was inexplicable; and when I could give an explanation, I did not think that I should feel myself called upon to give it to him.

' "Very well, sir; very well," replied he, growing very red. "I shall take care and let Mr. Morgan know the opinion I entertain of you. What do you think that man deserves to be called who enters a family under the plea of friendship, and takes advantage of his intimacy to win the affections of the daughter, and then engages himself to another woman?"

'I thought he referred to Miss Caroline. I simply said I could only say that I was not engaged; and that Miss Tomkinson had been quite mistaken in supposing I had been paying any attentions to her sister beyond those dictated by mere civility.

' "Miss Tomkinson! Miss Caroline! I don't understand to what you refer. Is there another victim to your perfidy? What I allude to are the attentions you have paid to my daughter, Miss Bullock."

'Another! I could but disclaim, as I had done in the case of Miss Caroline; but I began to be in despair. Would Miss Horsman, too, come forward as a victim to my tender affections? It was all Mr. Morgan's doing, who had lectured me into this tenderly deferential manner. But on the score of Miss Bullock, I was brave in my innocence. I had positively disliked her; and so I told her father, though in more civil and measured terms, adding that I was sure the feeling was reciprocal.

'He looked as if he would like to horsewhip me. I longed to call him out.

' "I hope my daughter has had sense enough to despise you; I hope she has, that's all. I trust my wife may be mistaken as to her feelings."

'So, he had heard all through the medium of his wife. That explained something, and rather calmed me. I begged he would ask Miss Bullock if she had ever thought I had any ulterior object in my intercourse with her, beyond mere friendliness (and not so much of that, I might have added) I would refer it to her.

' "Girls," said Mr. Bullock, a little more quietly, "do not like to acknowledge that they have been deceived and disappointed. I consider my wife's testimony as likely to be nearer the truth than my daughter's, for that reason. And she tells me she never doubted but that, if not absolutely engaged, you understood each other perfectly. She is sure Jemima is deeply wounded by your engagement to Mrs. Rose."

' "Once for all, I am not engaged to anybody. Till you have seen your daughter, and learnt the truth from her, I will wish you farewell."

'I bowed in a stiff, haughty manner, and walked off homewards. But when I got to my own door, I remembered Mrs. Rose, and all that Mr. Bullock had said about her acknowledging the truth of the report of my engagement to her. Where could I go to be safe? Mrs. Rose, Miss Bullock, Miss Caroline—they lived as it were at the three points of an equilateral triangle; here was I in the centre. I would go to Mr. Morgan's, and drink tea with him. There, at any rate, I was secure from any one wanting to marry me; and I might be as professionally bland as I liked, without being misunderstood. But there, too, a *contretemps* awaited me.

XXI

'MR. MORGAN was looking grave. After a minute or two of humming and hawing, he said—

' "I have been sent for to Miss Caroline Tomkinson, Mr. Harrison. I am sorry to hear of this. I am grieved to find that there seems to have been some trifling with the affections of a very worthy lady. Miss Tomkinson, who is in sad distress, tells me that they had every reason to believe that you were attached to her sister. May I ask if you do not intend to marry her?" '

'I said, nothing was farther from my thoughts.

' "My dear sir," said Mr. Morgan, rather agitated, "do not express yourself so strongly and vehemently. It is derogatory to the sex to speak so. It is more respectful to say, in these cases, that you do not venture to entertain a hope; such a manner is generally understood, and does not sound like such positive objection."

' "I cannot help it, sir; I must talk in my own natural manner. I would not speak disrespectfully of any woman; but nothing should induce me to marry Miss Caroline Tomkinson; not if she were Venus herself, and Queen of England into the bargain. I cannot understand what has given rise to the ideas."

' "Indeed, sir; I think that is very plain. You have a trifling case to attend to in the house, and you invariably make it a pretext for seeing and conversing with the lady."

' "That was her doing, not mine!" said I vehemently.

' "Allow me to go on. You are discovered on your knees before her—a positive injury to the establishment, as Miss Tomkinson observes; a most passionate valentine is sent; and when questioned, you acknowledge the sincerity of meaning which you affix to such things." He stopped, for in his earnestness he had been talking more quickly than usual, and was out of breath. I burst in with my explanations—

' "The valentine I know nothing about."

' "It is in your handwriting," said he coldly. "I should be most deeply grieved to—in fact, I will not think it possible of your father's son. But I must say, it is in your handwriting."

'I tried again, and at last succeeded in convincing him that I had been only unfortunate, not intentionally guilty of winning Miss Caroline's affections. I said that I had been endeavouring, it was true, to practise the manner he had recommended, of universal sympathy, and recalled to his mind some of the advice he had given me. He was a good deal hurried.

' "But, my dear sir, I had no idea that you would carry it out to such consequences. 'Philandering,' Miss Tomkinson called it. That is a hard word, sir. My manner has been always tender and sympathetic; but I am not aware that I ever excited any hopes; there never was any report about me. I believe no lady was ever attached to me. You must strive after this happy medium, sir."

'I was still distressed. Mr. Morgan had only heard of one, but there were three ladies (including Miss Bullock) hoping to marry me. He saw my annoyance.

' "Don't be too much distressed about it, my dear sir; I was sure you were too honourable a man, from the first. With a conscience like yours, I would defy the world."

'He became anxious to console me, and I was hesitating whether I would not tell him all my three dilemmas, when a note was brought in to him. It was from Mrs. Munton. He threw it to me, with a face of dismay.

' "MY DEAR MR. MORGAN,—I most sincerely congratulate you on the happy matrimonial engagement I hear you have formed with Miss Tomkinson. All previous circumstances, as I have just been remarking to Miss Horsman, combine to promise you felicity. And I wish that every blessing may attend your married life.—Most sincerely yours,

' "JANE MUNTON."

'I could not help laughing, he had been so lately congratulating himself that no report of the kind had ever been circulated about himself. He said—

' "Sir! this is no laughing matter; I assure you it is not."

'I could not resist asking, if I was to conclude that there was no truth in the report.

' "Truth, sir! it's a lie from beginning to end. I don't like to speak too decidedly about any lady; and I've a great respect for Miss Tomkinson; but I do assure you, sir, I'd as soon marry one of Her Majesty's Life Guards. I would rather; it would be more suitable. Miss Tomkinson is a very worthy lady; but she's a perfect grenadier."

'He grew very nervous. He was evidently insecure. He thought it not impossible that Miss Tomkinson might come and marry him, *vi et armis*. I am sure he had some dim idea of abduction in his mind. Still, he was better off than I was; for he was in his own house, and report had only engaged him to one lady; while I stood, like Paris, among three contending beauties. Truly, an apple of discord had been thrown into our little town. I suspected at the time, what I know now, that it was Miss Horsman's doing; not intentionally, I will do her the justice to say. But she had shouted out the story of my behaviour to Miss Caroline up Mrs. Munton's trumpet; and that lady, possessed with the idea that I was engaged to Mrs. Rose, had imagined the masculine pronoun to relate to Mr. Morgan, whom she had seen only that afternoon *tête à tête* with Miss Tomkinson, condoling with her in some tender deferential manner, I'll be bound.

XXII

'I WAS very cowardly. I positively dared not go home; but at length I was obliged to. I had done all I could to console Mr. Morgan, but he refused to be comforted. I went at last. I rang at the bell. I don't know who opened the door, but I think it was Mrs. Rose. I kept a handkerchief to my face, and muttering something about having a dreadful toothache, I flew up to my room and bolted the door. I had no candle; but what did that signify. I was safe. I could not sleep; and when I did fall into a sort of doze, it was ten times worse wakening up. I could not remember whether I was engaged or not. If I was engaged, who was the lady? I had always considered myself as rather plain than otherwise; but surely I had made a mistake. Fascinating I certainly must be; but perhaps I was handsome.

As soon as day dawned, I got up to ascertain the fact at the looking-glass. Even with the best disposition to be convinced, I could not see any striking beauty in my round face, with an unshaven beard and a nightcap like a fool's cap at the top. No! I must be content to be plain, but agreeable. All this I tell you in confidence. I would not have my little bit of vanity known for the world. I fell asleep towards morning. I was awakened by a tap at my door. It was Peggy: she put in a hand with a note. I took it.

' "It is not from Miss Horsman?" said I, half in joke, half in very earnest fright.

' "No, sir; Mr. Morgan's man brought it."

'I opened it. It ran thus—

' "MY DEAR SIR,—It is now nearly twenty years since I have had a little relaxation, and I find that my health requires it. I have also the utmost confidence in you, and I am sure this feeling is shared by our patients. I have, therefore, no scruple in putting in execution a hastily formed plan, and going to Chesterton to catch the early train on my way to Paris. If your accounts are good, I shall remain away probably a fortnight. Direct to Meurice's.—Yours, most truly,

"'J. MORGAN.

' "PS—Perhaps it may be as well not to name where I am gone, especially to Miss Tomkinson."

'He had deserted me. He—with only one report—had left me to stand my ground with three.

' "Mrs. Rose's kind regards, sir, and it's nearly nine o'clock. Breakfast has been ready this hour, sir."

' "Tell Mrs. Rose I don't want any breakfast. Or stay" (for I was very hungry), "I will take a cup of tea and some toast up here."

'Peggy brought the tray to the door.

' "I hope you're not ill, sir?" said she kindly.

' "Not very. I shall be better when I get into the air."

' "Mrs. Rose seems sadly put about," said she; "she seems so grieved like."

'I watched my opportunity, and went out by the side door in the garden.

XXIII

'I HAD intended to ask Mr. Morgan to call at the vicarage, and give his parting explanation before they could hear the report. Now, I thought that if I could see Sophy, I would speak to her myself; but I did not wish to encounter the Vicar. I went along the lane at the back of the vicarage, and came suddenly upon Miss Bullock. She coloured, and asked me if I would allow her to speak to me. I could only be resigned; but I thought I could probably set one report at rest by this conversation.

'She was almost crying.

' "I must tell you, Mr. Harrison, I have watched you here in order to speak to you. I heard with the greatest regret of papa's conversation with you yesterday." She was fairly crying. "I believe Mrs. Bullock finds me in her way, and wants to have me married. It is the only way in which I can account for such a complete misrepresentation as she had told papa. I don't care for you in the least, sir. You never paid me any attentions. You've been almost rude to me; and I have liked you the better. That's to say, I never have liked you."

' "I am truly glad to hear what you say," answered I. "Don't distress yourself. I was sure there was some mistake."

'But she cried bitterly.

' "It is so hard to feel that my marriage—my absence—is desired so earnestly at home. I dread every new acquaintance we form with any gentleman. It is sure to be the beginning of a series of attacks on him, of which everybody must be aware, and to which they may think I am a willing party. But I should not much mind if it were not for the conviction that she wishes me so earnestly away. Oh, my own dear mamma, you would never"——

'She cried more than ever. I was truly sorry for her, and had just taken her hand, and began—"My dear Miss Bullock"——when the door in the wall of the vicarage garden opened. It was the Vicar letting out Miss Tomkinson, whose face was all swelled with crying. He saw me; but he did not bow, or make any sign. On the contrary, he looked down as from a severe eminence, and shut the door hastily. I turned to Miss Bullock.

' "I am afraid the Vicar has been hearing something to my disadvantage from Miss Tomkinson, and it is very awkward"—— She finished my sentence—"To have found us here together. Yes, but as long as we understand that we do not care for each other, it does not signify what people say."

' "Oh, but to me it does," said I. "I may, perhaps, tell you—but do not mention it to a creature—I am attached to Miss Hutton."

' "To Sophy! Oh, Mr. Harrison, I am so glad; she is such a sweet creature. Oh, I wish you joy."

' "Not yet; I have never spoken about it."

' "Oh, but it is certain to happen." She jumped with a woman's rapidity to a conclusion. And then she began to praise Sophy. Never was a man yet who did not like to hear the praises of his mistress. I walked by her side; we came past the front of the vicarage together. I looked up, and saw Sophy there, and she saw me.

'That afternoon she was sent away; sent to visit her aunt ostensibly; in reality, because of the reports of my conduct, which were showered down upon the Vicar, and one of which he saw confirmed by his own eyes.

XXIV

'I HEARD of Sophy's departure as one heard of everything, soon after it had taken place. I did not care for the awkwardness of my situation, which had so perplexed and amused me in the morning. I felt that something was wrong; that Sophy was taken away from me. I sank into despair. If anybody liked to marry me they might. I was willing to be sacrificed. I did not speak to Mrs. Rose. She wondered at me, and grieved over my coldness, I saw; but I had left off feeling anything. Miss Tomkinson cut me in the street; and it did not break my heart. Sophy was gone away; that was all I cared for. Where had they sent her to? Who was her aunt, that she should go and visit her? One day I met

Lizzie, who looked as though she had been told not to speak to me, but could not help doing so.

' "Have you heard from your sister?" said I.

' "Yes."

' "Where is she? I hope she is well."

' "She is at the Leoms"—I was not much wiser. "Oh yes, she is very well. Fanny says she was at the Assembly last Wednesday, and danced all night with the officers."

'I thought I would enter myself a member of the Peace Society at once. She was a little flirt, and a hard-hearted creature. I don't think I wished Lizzie good-bye.

XXV

'WHAT most people would have considered a more serious evil than Sophy's absence, befell me. I found that my practice was falling off. The prejudice of the town ran strongly against me. Mrs. Munton told me all that was said. She heard it through Miss Horsman. It was said—cruel little town—that my negligence or ignorance had been the cause of Walter's death; that Miss Tyrrell had become worse under my treatment; and that John Brouncker was all but dead, if he was not quite, from my mismanagement. All Jack Marshland's jokes and revelations, which had, I thought, gone to oblivion, were raked up to my discredit. He himself, formerly, to my astonishment, rather a favourite with the good people of Duncombe, was spoken of as one of my disreputable friends.

'In short, so prejudiced were the good people of Duncombe that I believe a very little would have made them suspect me of a brutal highway robbery, which took place in the neighbourhood about this time. Mrs. Munton told me, apropos of the robbery, that she had never yet understood the cause of my year's imprisonment in Newgate; she had no doubt, from what Mr. Morgan had told her, there was some good reason for it; but if I would tell her the particulars, she should like to know them.

'Miss Tomkinson sent for Mr. White, from Chesterton, to see Miss Caroline; and, as he was coming over, all our old patients seemed to take advantage of it, and send for him too.

'But the worst of all was the Vicar's manner to me. If he had cut me, I could have asked him why he did so. But the freezing change in his behaviour was indescribable, though bitterly felt. I heard of Sophy's gaiety from Lizzie. I thought of writing to her. Just then Mr. Morgan's fortnight of absence expired. I was wearied out by Mrs. Rose's tender vagaries, and took no comfort from her sympathy, which indeed I rather avoided. Her tears irritated, instead of grieving me. I wished I could tell her at once that I had no intention of marrying her.

XXVI

'MR. MORGAN had not been at home above two hours before he was sent for to the Vicarage. Sophy had come back, and I had never heard of it. She had come home ill and weary, and longing for rest: and the *rest* seemed approaching with awful strides. Mr. Morgan forgot all his Parisian adventures, and all his terror of Miss Tomkinson, when he was sent for to see her. She was ill of a fever, which made fearful progress. When he told me, I wished to force the Vicarage door, if I might but see her. But I controlled myself; and only cursed my weak indecision, which had prevented my writing to her. It was well I had no patients: they would have had but a poor chance of attention. I hung about Mr. Morgan, who might see her, and did see her. But from what he told me, I perceived that the measures he was adopting were powerless to check so sudden and violent an illness. Oh! if they would but let me see her. But that was out of the question. It was not merely that the Vicar had heard of my character as a gay Lothario, but that doubts had been thrown out of my medical skill. The accounts grew worse. Suddenly my resolution was taken. Mr. Morgan's very regard for Sophy made him more than usually timid in his practice. I had my horse saddled, and galloped to Chesterton. I took the express train to town. I went to Dr. ——. I told him every particular of the case. He listened; but shook his head. He wrote down a prescription; and recommended a new preparation, not yet in full use; a preparation of a poison, in fact.

' "It may save her," said he. "It is a chance, in such a state of things as you describe. It must be given on the fifth day, if the pulse will bear it. Crabbe makes up the preparation most skilfully. Let me hear from you, I beg."

'I went to Crabbe's; I begged to make it up myself; but my hands trembled, so that I could not weigh the quantities. I asked the young man to do it for me. I went, without touching food, to the station, with my medicine and my prescription in my pocket. Back we flew through the country. I sprang on Bay Maldon, which my groom had in waiting, and galloped across the country to Duncombe.

'But I drew bridle when I came to the top of the hill—the hill above the old hall, from which we catch the first glimpse of the town, for I thought within myself that she might be dead; and I dreaded to come near certainty. The hawthorns were out in the woods, the young lambs were in the meadows, the song of the thrushes filled the air; but it only made the thought the more terrible.

' "What, if in this world of hope and life she lies dead!" I heard the church bells soft and clear. I sickened to listen. Was it the passing bell? No! it was ringing eight o'clock. I put spurs to my horse, down hill as it was. We dashed into the town. I turned him, saddle and bridle, into the stable-yard, and went off to Mr. Morgan's.

' "Is she ——?" said I. "How is she?"

' "Very ill. My poor fellow, I see how it is with you. She may live—but I fear. My dear sir, I am very much afraid."

'I told him of my journey and consultation with Dr. ——, and showed him the prescription. His hands trembled as he put on his spectacles to read it.

' "This is a very dangerous medicine, sir," said he, with his finger under the name of the poison.

' "It is a new preparation," said I. "Dr. —— relies much upon it."

' "I dare not administer it," he replied. "I have never tried it. It must be very powerful. I dare not play tricks in this case."

'I believe I stamped with impatience; but it was all of no use. My journey had been in vain. The more I urged the imminent danger of the case requiring some powerful remedy, the more nervous he became.

'I told him I would throw up the partnership. I threatened him with that, though, in fact, it was only what I felt I ought to do, and had resolved upon before Sophy's illness, as I had lost the confidence of his patients. He only said—

' "I cannot help it, sir. I shall regret it for your father's sake; but I must do my duty. I dare not run the risk of giving Miss Sophy this violent medicine—a preparation of a deadly poison."

'I left him without a word. He was quite right in adhering to his own views, as I can see now; but at the time I thought him brutal and obstinate.

XXVII

'I WENT home. I spoke rudely to Mrs. Rose, who awaited my return at the door. I rushed past, and locked myself in my room. I could not go to bed.

'The morning sun came pouring in, and enraged me, as everything did since Mr. Morgan refused. I pulled the blind down so violently that the string broke. What did it signify? The light might come in. What was the sun to me? And then I remembered that that sun might be shining on her—dead.

'I sat down and covered my face. Mrs. Rose knocked at the door. I opened it. She had never been in bed, and had been crying too.

' "Mr. Morgan wants to speak to you, sir."

'I rushed back for my medicine, and went to him. He stood at the door, pale and anxious.

' "She's alive, sir," said he, "but that's all. We have sent for Dr. Hamilton. I'm afraid he will not come in time. Do you know, sir, I think we should venture—with Dr. ——'s sanction—to give her that medicine. It is but a chance; but it is the only one, I'm afraid." He fairly cried before he had ended.

' "I've got it here," said I, setting off to walk; but he could not go so fast.

' "I beg your pardon, sir," said he, "for my abrupt refusal last night."

' "Indeed, sir," said I; "I ought much rather to beg your pardon. I was very violent."

' "Oh! never mind! never mind! Will you repeat what Dr. —— said?"

'I did so; and then I asked, with a meekness that astonished myself, if I might not go in and administer it.

' "No, sir," said he, "I'm afraid not. I am sure your good heart would not wish to give pain. Besides, it might agitate her, if she has any consciousness before death. In her delirium she has often mentioned your name; and, sir, I'm sure you won't name it again, as it may, in fact, be considered a professional secret; but I did hear our good Vicar speak a little strongly about you; in fact, sir, I did hear him curse you. You see the mischief it might make in the parish, I'm sure, if this were known."

'I gave him the medicine, and watched him in, and saw the door shut. I hung about the place all day. Poor and rich all came to inquire. The county people drove up in their carriages—the halt and the lame came on their crutches. Their anxiety did my heart good. Mr. Morgan told me that she slept, and I watched Dr. Hamilton into the house. The night came on. She slept. I watched round the house. I saw the light high up, burning still and steady. Then I saw it moved. It was the crisis, in one way or other.

XXVIII

'MR. MORGAN came out. Good old man! The tears were running down his cheeks: he could not speak; but kept shaking my hands. I did not want words. I understood that she was better.

' "Dr. Hamilton says, it was the only medicine that could have saved her. I was an old fool, sir. I beg your pardon. The Vicar shall know all. I beg your pardon, sir, if I was abrupt."

'Everything went on brilliantly from this time.

'Mr. Bullock called to apologize for his mistake, and consequent upbraiding. John Brouncker came home, brave and well.

'There was still Miss Tomkinson in the ranks of the enemy; and Mrs. Rose too much, I feared, in the ranks of the friends.

XXIX

'ONE night she had gone to bed, and I was thinking of going. I had been studying in the back room, where I went for refuge from her in the present position of affairs (I read a good number of surgical books about this time, and also *Vanity Fair*)—when I heard a loud, long-continued knocking at the door, enough to waken the whole street. Before I could get to open it, I heard that well-known bass of Jack Marshland's, once heard never to be forgotten, pipe up the negro song—

Who's dat knocking at de door?

'Though it was raining hard at the time, and I stood waiting to let him in, he would finish his melody in the open air; loud and clear along the street it sounded. I saw Miss Tomkinson's night-capped head emerge from a window. She called out "Police! police!"

'Now there were no police, only a rheumatic constable in the town; but it was the custom of the ladies, when alarmed at night, to call an imaginary police, which had, they thought, an intimidating effect; but as every one knew the real state of the unwatched town, we did not much mind it in general. Just now, however, I wanted to regain my character. So I pulled Jack in quavering as he entered.

' "You've spoilt a good shake," said he, "that's what you have. I'm nearly up to Jenny Lind; and you see I'm a nightingale, like her."

'We sat up late; and I don't know how it was, but I told him all my matrimonial misadventures.

' "I thought I could imitate your hand pretty well," said he. "My word! it was a flaming valentine! No wonder she thought you loved her!"

' "So that was your doing, was it? Now I'll tell you what you shall do to make up for it. You shall write me a letter confessing your hoax—a letter that I can show."

' "Give me pen and paper, my boy! you shall dictate. 'With a deeply penitent heart'—— Will that do for a beginning?"

'I told him what to write; a simple, straightforward confession of his practical joke. I enclosed it in a few lines of regret that, unknown to me, any of my friends should have so acted.

XXX

'ALL this time I knew that Sophy was slowly recovering. One day I met Miss Bullock, who had seen her.

' "We have been talking about you," said she, with a bright smile; for since she knew I disliked her, she felt quite at her ease, and could smile very pleasantly. I understood that she had been explaining the misunderstanding about herself to Sophy; so that when Jack Marshland's note had been sent to Miss Tomkinson's, I thought myself in a fair way to have my character established in two quarters. But the third was my dilemma. Mrs. Rose had really so much of my true regard for her good qualities, that I disliked the idea of a formal explanation, in which a good deal must be said on my side to wound her. We had become very much estranged ever since I had heard of this report of my engagement to her. I saw that she grieved over it. While Jack Marshland stayed with us, I felt at my ease in the presence of a third person. But he told me confidentially he durst not stay long, for fear some of the ladies should snap him up, and marry him. Indeed I myself did not think it unlikely that he would snap one of them up if he could. For when we met Miss Bullock one day, and heard her hopeful, joyous account of Sophy's progress (to whom she was a daily visitor), he asked me who that bright-looking girl was? And when I told him she was the Miss Bullock of whom I had spoken to him, he was pleased to observe that he thought I had been a great fool, and asked me if Sophy had anything like such splendid eyes. He made me repeat about Miss Bullock's unhappy circumstances at home, and then became very thoughtful—a most unusual and morbid symptom in his case.

'Soon after he went, by Mr. Morgan's kind offices and explanations, I was permitted to see Sophy. I might not speak much; it was prohibited, for fear of agitating her. We talked of the weather and the flowers; and we were silent. But her little white thin hand lay in mine; and we understood each other without words. I had a long interview with the Vicar afterwards; and came away glad and satisfied.

'Mr. Morgan called in the afternoon, evidently anxious, though he made no direct inquiries (he was too polite for that), to hear the result of my visit at the Vicarage. I told him to give me joy. He shook me warmly by the hand; and then rubbed his own together. I thought I would consult him about my dilemma with Mrs. Rose, who, I was afraid, would be deeply affected by my engagement.

' "There is only one awkward circumstance," said I—"about Mrs. Rose." I hesitated how to word the fact of her having received congratulations on her supposed engagement with me, and her manifest attachment; but, before I could speak, he broke in—

' "My dear sir, you need not trouble yourself about that; she will have a home. In fact, sir," said he, reddening a little, "I thought it would, perhaps, put a stop to those reports connecting my name with Miss Tomkinson's, if I married some one else. I hoped it might prove an efficacious contradiction. And I was struck with admiration for Mrs. Rose's undying memory of her late husband. Not to be prolix, I have this morning obtained Mrs. Rose's consent to—to marry her, in fact, sir!" said he, jerking out the climax.

'Here was an event! Then Mr. Morgan had never heard the report about Mrs. Rose and me. (To this day, I think she would have taken me, if I had proposed.) So much the better.

'Marriages were in the fashion that year. Mr. Bullock met me one morning, as I was going to ride with Sophy. He and I had quite got over our misunderstanding, thanks to Jemima, and were as friendly as ever. This morning he was chuckling aloud as he walked.

' "Stop, Mr. Harrison!" he said, as I went quickly past. "Have you heard the news? Miss Horsman has just told me Miss Caroline has eloped with young Hoggins! She is ten years older than he is! How can her gentility like being married to a tallow-chandler? It is a very good thing for her, though," he added, in a more serious manner; "old Hoggins is very rich; and though he's angry just now, he will soon be reconciled."

'Any vanity I might have entertained on the score of the three ladies who were, at one time, said to be captivated by my charms, was being rapidly dispersed. Soon after Mr. Hoggins's marriage, I met Miss Tomkinson face to face, for the first time since our memorable conversation. She stopped me, and said—

' "Don't refuse to receive my congratulations, Mr. Harrison, on your most happy engagement to Miss Hutton. I owe you an apology, too, for my behaviour when I last saw you at our house. I really did think Caroline was attached to you then; and it irritated me, I confess, in a very wrong and unjustifiable way. But I heard her telling Mr. Hoggins only yesterday that she had been attached to him for years; ever since he was in pinafores, she dated it from; and when I asked her afterwards how she could say so, after her distress on hearing that false report about you and Mrs. Rose, she cried, and said I never had understood her; and that the hysterics which alarmed me so much were simply caused by eating pickled cucumber. I am very sorry for my stupidity, and improper way of speaking; but I hope we are friends now, Mr. Harrison, for I should wish to be liked by Sophy's husband."

'Good Miss Tomkinson! to believe the substitution of indigestion for disappointed affection. I shook her warmly by the hand; and we have been all right ever since. I think I told you she is baby's godmother.

XXXI

'I HAD some difficulty in persuading Jack Marshland to be groomsman; but when he heard all the arrangements, he came. Miss Bullock was bridesmaid. He liked us all so well, that he came again at Christmas, and was far better behaved than he had been the year before. He won golden opinions indeed. Miss Tomkinson said he was a reformed young man. We dined all together at Mr. Morgan's (the Vicar wanted us to go there; but, from what Sophy told me, Helen was not confident of the mincemeat, and rather dreaded so large a party). We had a jolly day of it. Mrs. Morgan was as kind and motherly as ever; Miss Horsman certainly did set out a story that the Vicar was thinking of Miss Tomkinson for his second; or else, I think, we had no other report circulated in consequence of our happy, merry Christmas Day; and it is a wonder, considering how Jack Marshland went on with Jemima.'

Here Sophy came back from putting baby to bed; and Charles wakened up.

Count Lev Nikolayevich Tolstoy

THE DEATH OF
IVAN ILYCH

1886

COUNT LEV NIKOLAYEVICH TOLSTOY was born in
1828 at Yasnaya Polyana, an estate in the country not far from
Moscow. He was born to the position of an hereditary landowner
and also, since this was before Emancipation, an owner of serfs.
In youth Tolstoy was attached as a volunteer to the Russian army
in the Caucasus; he described his early formative experiences
brilliantly in *Childhood* (1852), *Boyhood* (1854), and *Youth* (1857),
issued in one volume in the latter year. It was natural for a young
man of good family to spend a few years in military pursuits, but
Tolstoy later joined the Army as a serving officer and took part in
the Crimean War, a very different experience that is reflected in his
first mature masterpiece, *War and Peace* (1852), though 'reflected' is
not the same thing as 'reported'; what Tolstoy the writer learnt from
Tolstoy the soldier was the essential nature of war and battle, not its
concrete events, since of course *War and Peace* is an epic narrative of
the Napoleonic invasion. His second venture into large-scale fiction,
Anna Karenina, followed in 1875–6; it is, in fact, the more perfect
book of the two, but both are undisputed masterpieces and placed
Tolstoy on a pinnacle of literary reputation which subsequently
became something of an embarrassment to him, after he underwent
a religious conversion that caused him to become impatient with art
as a frivolous pursuit, something that belonged with the vanities of
this world.

After describing this conversion in *Confession* (1882), Tolstoy
became concerned with moral and spiritual truth rather than with
imaginative insight as traditionally understood; his art became
didactic, he freed his serfs, renounced his copyrights, did his best
to live the life of a peasant, and in *What Is Art?* (1895) rejected the
bulk of his work. Such fiction as he wrote in his later years tends
to consist of short, concentrated parables such as *How Much Land
Does a Man Require?* and essays such as *What Then Must We Do?* In
The Death of Ivan Ilych he achieved a work that satisfied his austere
moral and spiritual demands while being of the highest possible
artistic quality, since the 'art' of this story resides in its economy,
its concentration of mood, and the fierce honesty which forbids any
blurring or softening of the issues. The colour and sweep of the two

great mature novels has gone, but such is the power of this story that we do not miss them.

The strength, intensity, moral commitment, and depth of Tolstoy's work caused him to be accepted internationally as a sage and prophet as well as a great artist. Although his later teachings were anarchistic, and his attitude towards government therefore such as would have landed anyone else in prison or at the very least in exile, the Tsarist Government never dared interfere with him, a remarkable state of affairs which had to wait for any kind of historical parallel until *l'affaire Pasternak* in the 1950s.

It is the more to be regretted that Tolstoy's heroic acts of self-abnegation did not bring him inward peace. His domestic relationships were inharmonious, his household torn by dissension, and in 1910, after a wild flight through the wintry landscape that itself reads like some extravagant episode in a novel of *Sturm und Drang*, he died in the upper room of a country railway station, mourned and wondered at by the entire civilized world.

I

DURING an interval in the Melvinski trial in the large building of the Law Courts the members and public prosecutor met in Ivan Egorovich Shebek's private room, where the conversation turned on the celebrated Krasovski case. Fedor Vasilievich warmly maintained that it was not subject to their jurisdiction, Ivan Egorovich maintained the contrary, while Peter Ivanovich, not having entered into the discussion at the start, took no part in it but looked through the *Gazette* which had just been handed in.

'Gentlemen,' he said, 'Ivan Ilych has died!'

'You don't say so!'

'Here, read it yourself,' replied Peter Ivanovich, handing Fedor Vasilievich the paper still damp from the press. Surrounded by a black border were the words: 'Praskovya Fedorovna Golovina, with profound sorrow, informs relatives and friends of the demise of her beloved husband Ivan Ilych Golovin, Member of the Court of Justice, which occurred on February the 4th of this year 1882. The funeral will take place on Friday at one o'clock in the afternoon.'

Ivan Ilych had been a colleague of the gentlemen present and was liked by them all. He had been ill for some weeks with an illness said to be incurable. His post had been kept open for him, but there had been conjectures that in case of his death Alexeev might receive his appointment, and that either Vinnikov or Shtabel would succeed Alexeev. So on receiving the news of Ivan Ilych's death the first thought of each of the gentlemen in that private room was of the changes and promotions it might occasion among themselves or their acquaintances.

'I shall be sure to get Shtabel's place or Vinnikov's' thought Fedor Vasilievich. 'I was promised that long ago, and the promotion means an extra eight hundred rubles a year for me besides the allowance.'

'Now I must apply for my brother-in-law's transfer from Kaluga,' thought Peter Ivanovich. 'My wife will be very glad, and then she won't be able to say that I never do anything for her relations.'

'I thought he would never leave his bed again,' said Peter Ivanovich aloud. 'It's very sad.'

'But what really was the matter with him?'

'The doctors couldn't say—at least they could, but each of them said something different. When last I saw him I thought he was getting better.'

'And I haven't been to see him since the holidays. I always meant to go.'

'Had he any property?'

'I think his wife had a little—but something quite trifling.'

'We shall have to go to see her, but they live so terribly far away.'

'Far away from you, you mean. Everything's far away from your place.'

'You see, he never can forgive my living on the other side of the river,' said Peter Ivanovich, smiling at Shebek. Then, still talking of the distances between different parts of the city, they returned to the Court.

Besides considerations as to the possible transfers and promotions likely to result from Ivan Ilych's death, the mere fact of the death of a near acquaintance aroused, as usual, in all who heard of it the complacent feeling that, 'it is he who is dead and not I'.

Each one thought or felt, 'Well, he's dead but I'm alive!' But the more intimate of Ivan Ilych's acquaintances, his so-called friends, could not help thinking also that they would now have to fulfil the very tiresome demands of propriety by attending the funeral service and paying a visit of condolence to the widow.

Fedor Vasilievich and Peter Ivanovich had been his nearest acquaintances. Peter Ivanovich had studied law with Ivan Ilych and had considered himself to be under obligations to him.

Having told his wife at dinner-time of Ivan Ilych's death, and of his conjecture that it might be possible to get her brother transferred to their circuit, Peter Ivanovich sacrificed his usual nap, put on his evening clothes, and drove to Ivan Ilych's house.

At the entrance stood a carriage and two cabs. Leaning against the wall in the hall downstairs near the cloak-stand was a coffin-lid covered with cloth of gold, ornamented with gold cord and tassels, that had been polished up with metal powder. Two ladies in black were taking off their fur cloaks. Peter Ivanovich recognized one of them as Ivan Ilych's sister, but the other was a stranger to him. His colleague Schwartz was just coming downstairs, but on seeing Peter Ivanovich enter he stopped and winked at him, as if to say: 'Ivan Ilych has made a mess of things—not like you and me.'

Schwartz's face with his Piccadilly whiskers, and his slim figure in evening dress, had as usual an air of elegant solemnity which contrasted with the playfulness of his character and had a special piquancy here, or so it seemed to Peter Ivanovich.

Peter Ivanovich allowed the ladies to precede him and slowly followed them upstairs. Schwartz did not come down but remained where he was, and Peter Ivanovich understood that he wanted to arrange where they should play bridge that evening. The ladies went upstairs to the widow's room, and Schwartz with seriously compressed lips but a playful look in his eyes, indicated by a twist of his eyebrows the room to the right where the body lay.

Peter Ivanovich, like everyone else on such occasions, entered feeling uncertain what he would have to do. All he knew was that at such times it is always safe to cross oneself. But he was not quite sure whether one should make obeisances while doing so. He therefore adopted a middle course. On entering the room he began crossing himself and made a slight movement resembling a bow. At the same time, as far as the motion of his head and arm allowed, he surveyed the room. Two young men—apparently nephews, one of whom was a high-school pupil—were leaving the room, crossing themselves as they did so. An old woman was standing motionless, and a lady with strangely arched eyebrows was saying something to her in a whisper. A vigorous, resolute Church Reader, in a frock-coat, was reading something in a loud voice with an expression that precluded any contradiction. The butler's assistant, Gerasim, stepping lightly in front of Peter Ivanovich, was strewing something on the floor. Noticing this, Peter Ivanovich was immediately aware of a faint odour of a decomposing body.

The last time he called on Ivan Ilych, Peter Ivanovich had seen Gerasim in the study. Ivan Ilych had been particularly

fond of him and he was performing the duty of a sick
nurse.

Peter Ivanovich continued to make the sign of the cross,
slightly inclining his head in an intermediate direction between
the coffin, the Reader, and the icons on the table in a corner of the
room. Afterwards, when it seemed to him that this movement of
his arm in crossing himself had gone on too long, he stopped and
began to look at the corpse.

The dead man lay, as dead men always lie, in a specially heavy
way, his rigid limbs sunk in the soft cushions of the coffin, with
the head forever bowed on his pillow. His yellow waxen brow
with bald patches over his sunken temples was thrust up in
the way peculiar to the dead, the protruding nose seeming to
press on the upper lip. He was much changed and had grown
even thinner since Peter Ivanovich had last seen him, but, as is
always the case with the dead, his face was handsomer and above
all more dignified than when he was alive. The expression on the
face said that what was necessary had been accomplished, and
accomplished rightly. Besides this there was in that expression
a reproach and a warning to the living. This warning seemed to
Peter Ivanovich out of place, or at least not applicable to him.
He felt a certain discomfort and so he hurriedly crossed himself
once more and turned and went out of the door—too hurriedly
and too regardless of propriety, as he himself was aware.

Schwartz was waiting for him in the adjoining room with legs
spread wide apart and both hands toying with his top-hat behind
his back. The mere sight of that playful, well-groomed, and
elegant figure refreshed Peter Ivanovich. He felt that Schwartz
was above all these happenings and would not surrender to any
depressing influences. His very look said that this incident of a
church service for Ivan Ilych could not be a sufficient reason
for infringing the order of the session—in other words, that
it would certainly not prevent his unwrapping a new pack of
cards and shuffling them that evening while a footman placed
four fresh candles on the table: in fact, that there was no reason
for supposing that this incident would hinder their spending the
evening agreeably. Indeed he said this in a whisper as Peter
Ivanovich passed him, proposing that they should meet for a
game at Fedor Vasilievich's. But apparently Peter Ivanovich was
not destined to play bridge that evening. Praskovya Fedorovna

(a short, fat woman who despite all efforts to the contrary had continued to broaden steadily from her shoulders downwards and who had the same extraordinarily arched eyebrows as the lady who had been standing by the coffin), dressed all in black, her head covered with lace, came out of her own room with some other ladies, conducted them to the room where the dead body lay, and said: 'The service will begin immediately. Please go in.'

Schwartz, making an indefinite bow, stood still, evidently neither accepting nor declining this invitation. Praskovya Fedorovna, recognizing Peter Ivanovich, sighed, went close up to him, took his hand and said: 'I know you were a true friend to Ivan Ilych . . .' and looked at him awaiting some suitable response. And Peter Ivanovich knew that, just as it had been the right thing to cross himself in that room, so what he had to do here was to press her hand, sigh, and say, 'Believe me . . .'. So he did all this and as he did it felt that the desired result had been achieved: that both he and she were touched.

'Come with me. I want to speak to you before it begins,' said the widow. 'Give me your arm.'

Peter Ivanovich gave her his arm and they went to the inner rooms, passing Schwartz who winked at Peter Ivanovich compassionately.

'That does for our bridge! Don't object if we find another player. Perhaps you can cut in when you do escape,' said his playful look.

Peter Ivanovich sighed still more deeply and despondently, and Praskovya Fedorovna pressed his arm gratefully. When they reached the drawing-room, upholstered in pink cretonne and lighted by a dim lamp, they sat down at the table—she on a sofa and Peter Ivanovich on a low pouffe, the springs of which yielded spasmodically under his weight. Praskovya Fedorovna had been on the point of warning him to take another seat, but felt that such a warning was out of keeping with her present condition and so changed her mind. As he sat down on the pouffe Peter Ivanovich recalled how Ivan Ilych had arranged this room and had consulted him regarding this pink cretonne with green leaves. The whole room was full of furniture and knick-knacks, and on her way to the sofa the lace of the widow's black shawl caught on the carved edge of the table. Peter Ivanovich rose to detach it, and the springs of the pouffe, relieved of his weight, rose also and gave him a push. The widow began detaching her shawl herself, and Peter Ivanovich again sat down, suppressing the rebellious springs of the pouffe under him. But the widow had not quite freed herself and Peter Ivanovich got up again, and again the pouffe rebelled and even creaked. When this was all over she took out a clean cambric handkerchief and began to weep. The episode with the shawl and the struggle with the pouffe had cooled Peter Ivanovich's emotions and he sat there with a sullen look on his face. This awkward situation was interrupted by Sokolov, Ivan Ilych's butler, who came to report that the plot in the cemetery that Praskovya Fedorovna had chosen would cost two hundred rubles. She stopped weeping and, looking at Peter Ivanovich with the air of a victim, remarked in French that it was very hard for her. Peter Ivanovich made a silent gesture signifying his full conviction that it must indeed be so.

'Please smoke,' she said in a magnanimous yet crushed voice, and turned to discuss with Sokolov the price of the plot for the grave.

Peter Ivanovich while lighting his cigarette heard her inquiring very circumstantially into the prices of different plots in the cemetery and finally decide which she would take. When this was done she gave instructions about engaging the choir. Sokolov then left the room.

'I look after everything myself,' she told Peter Ivanovich, shifting the albums that lay on the table; and noticing that the table was endangered by his cigarette-ash, she immediately passed him an ashtray, saying as she did so: 'I consider it an affectation to say that my grief prevents my attending to practical affairs. On the contrary, if anything can—I won't say console me, but—distract me, it is seeing to everything concerning him.' She again took out her handkerchief as if preparing to cry, but suddenly, as if mastering her feeling, she shook herself and began to speak calmly. 'But there is something I want to talk to you about.'

Peter Ivanovich bowed, keeping control of the springs of the pouffe, which immediately began quivering under him.

'He suffered terribly the last few days.'

'Did he?' said Peter Ivanovich.

'Oh, terribly! He screamed unceasingly, not for minutes but for hours. For the last three days he screamed incessantly. It was unendurable. I cannot understand how I bore it; you could hear him three rooms off. Oh, what I have suffered!'

'Is it possible that he was conscious all that time?' asked Peter Ivanovich.

'Yes,' she whispered. 'To the last moment. He took leave of us a quarter of an hour before he died, and asked us to take Volodya away.'

The thought of the sufferings of this man he had known so intimately, first as a merry little boy, then as a school-mate, and later as a grown-up colleague, suddenly struck Peter Ivanovich with horror, despite an unpleasant consciousness of his own and this woman's dissimulation. He again saw that brow, and that nose pressing down on the lip, and felt afraid for himself.

'Three days of frightful suffering and then death! Why, that might suddenly, at any time, happen to me,' he thought, and for a moment felt terrified. But—he did not himself know how—the customary reflection at once occurred to him that this had happened to Ivan Ilych and not to him, and that it should not and could not happen to him, and that to think that it could would be yielding to depression which he ought not to do, as Schwartz's expression plainly showed. After which reflection Peter Ivanovich felt reassured, and began to ask with interest about the details of Ivan Ilych's death, as though death was an accident natural to Ivan Ilych but certainly not to himself.

After many details of the really dreadful physical sufferings Ivan Ilych had endured (which details he learnt only from the effect those sufferings had produced on Praskovya Fedorovna's nerves) the widow apparently found it necessary to get to business.

'Oh, Peter Ivanovich, how hard it is! How terribly, terribly hard!' and she again began to weep.

Peter Ivanovich sighed and waited for her to finish blowing her nose. When she had done so he said, 'Believe me . . .', and she again began talking and brought out what was evidently her chief concern with him—namely, to question him as to how she could obtain a grant of money from the government on the occasion of her husband's death. She made it appear that she was asking Peter Ivanovich's advice about her pension, but he soon saw that she already knew about that to the minutest detail, more even than he did himself. She knew how much could be got out of the government in consequence of her husband's death, but wanted to find out whether she could not possibly extract something more. Peter Ivanovich tried to think of some means of doing so, but after reflecting for a while and, out of propriety, condemning the government for its niggardliness, he said he thought that nothing more could be got. Then she sighed and evidently began to devise means of getting rid of her visitor. Noticing this, he put out his cigarette, rose, pressed her hand, and went out into the ante-room.

In the dining-room where the clock stood that Ivan Ilych had liked so much and had bought at an antique shop, Peter Ivanovich met a priest and a few acquaintances who had come to attend the service, and he recognized Ivan Ilych's daughter, a handsome young woman. She was in black and her slim figure appeared slimmer than ever. She had a gloomy, determined, almost angry expression, and bowed to Peter Ivanovich as though he were in some way to blame. Behind her, with the same offended look, stood a wealthy young man, an examining magistrate, whom Peter Ivanovich also knew and who was her fiancé, as he had heard. He bowed mournfully to them and was about to pass into the death-chamber, when from under the stairs appeared the figure of Ivan Ilych's schoolboy son, who was extremely like his father. He seemed a little Ivan Ilych, such as Peter Ivanovich remembered when they studied law together. His tear-stained eyes had in them the look that is seen in the eyes of boys of thirteen or fourteen who are not pure-minded. When he saw Peter Ivanovich he scowled morosely and shamefacedly. Peter Ivanovich nodded to him and entered the death-chamber. The service began: candles, groans, incense, tears, and sobs. Peter Ivanovich stood looking gloomily down at his feet. He did not look once at the dead man, did not yield to any depressing influence, and was one of the first to leave the room. There was no one in the ante-room, but Gerasim darted out of the dead man's room, rummaged with his strong hands among the fur coats to find Peter Ivanovich's and helped him on with it.

'Well, friend Gerasim,' said Peter Ivanovich, so as to say something. 'It's a sad affair, isn't it?'

'It's God's will. We shall all come to it some day,' said Gerasim, displaying his teeth—the even, white teeth of a healthy peasant—and, like a man in the thick of urgent work, he briskly opened the front door, called the coachman, helped Peter Ivanovich into the sledge, and sprang back to the porch as if in readiness for what he had to do next.

Peter Ivanovich found the fresh air particularly pleasant after the smell of incense, the dead body, and carbolic acid.

'Where to, sir?' asked the coachman.

'It's not too late even now. . . . I'll call round on Fedor Vasilievich.'

He accordingly drove there and found them just finishing the first rubber, so that it was quite convenient for him to cut in.

II

IVAN ILYCH'S life had been simple and most ordinary and therefore most terrible.

He had been a member of the Court of Justice, and died at the age of forty-five. His father had been an official who after serving in various ministries and departments in Petersburg had made the sort of career which brings men to positions from which by reason of their long service they cannot be dismissed, though they are obviously unfit to hold any responsible position, and for whom therefore posts are specially created, which though fictitious carry salaries of from six to ten thousand rubles that are not fictitious, and in receipt of which they live on to a great age.

Such was the Privy Councillor and superfluous member of various superfluous institutions, Ilya Epimovich Golovin.

He had three sons, of whom Ivan Ilych was the second. The eldest son was following in his father's footsteps only in another department, and was already approaching that stage in the service at which a similar sinecure would be reached. The third son was a failure. He had ruined his prospects in a number of positions and was now serving in the railway department. His father and brothers, and still more their wives, not merely dislike meeting him, but avoided remembering his existence unless compelled to do so. His sister had married Baron Greff, a Petersburg official of her father's type. Ivan Ilych was *le phénix de la famille* as people said. He was neither as cold and formal as his elder brother nor as wild as the younger, but was a happy mean between them—an intelligent, polished, lively and agreeable man. He had studied with his younger brother at the School of Law, but the latter had failed to complete the course and was expelled when he was in the fifth class. Ivan Ilych finished the course well. Even when he was at the School of Law he was just what he remained for the rest of his life: a capable, cheerful, good-natured, and sociable man, though strict in the fulfilment of what he considered to be his duty: and he considered his duty to be what was so considered by those in authority. Neither as a boy nor as a man was he a toady, but from early youth was by nature attracted to people of high station as a fly is drawn to the light, assimilating their ways and views of life and establishing friendly relations with them. All the enthusiasms of childhood and youth passed without leaving much trace on him; he succumbed to sensuality, to vanity, and latterly among the highest classes to liberalism, but always within limits which his instinct unfailingly indicated to him as correct.

At school he had done things which had formerly seemed to him very horrid and made him feel disgusted with himself when he did them; but when later on he saw that such actions were done by people of good position and that they did not regard them as wrong, he was able not exactly to regard them as right, but to forget about them entirely or not be at all troubled at remembering them.

Having graduated from the School of Law and qualified for the tenth rank of the civil service, and having received money from his father for his equipment, Ivan Ilych ordered himself clothes at Scharmer's, the fashionable tailor, hung a medallion inscribed *respice finem* on his watch-chain, took leave of his professor and the prince who was patron of the school, had a farewell dinner with his comrades at Donon's first-class restaurant, and with his new and fashionable portmanteau, linen, clothes, shaving and other toilet appliances, and a travelling rug, all purchased at the best shops, he set off for one of the provinces where, through his father's influence, he had been attached to the Governor as an official for special service.

In the province Ivan Ilych soon arranged as easy and agreeable a position for himself as he had had at the School of Law. He performed his official tasks, made his career, and at the same time amused himself pleasantly and decorously. Occasionally he paid official visits to country districts, where he behaved with dignity both to his superiors and inferiors, and performed the duties entrusted to him, which related chiefly to the sectarians, with an exactness and incorruptible honesty of which he could not but feel proud.

In official matters, despite his youth and taste for frivolous gaiety, he was exceedingly reserved, punctilious, and even severe; but in society he was often amusing and witty, and always good-natured, correct in his manner, and *bon enfant,* as the governor and his wife—with whom he was like one of the family—used to say of him.

In the province he had an affair with a lady who made advances to the elegant young lawyer, and there was also a milliner; and there were carousals with aides-de-camp who visited the district, and after-supper visits to a certain outlying street of doubtful reputation; and there was too some obsequiousness to his chief and even to his chief's wife, but all this was done with such a tone of good breeding that no hard names could be applied to it. It all came under the heading of the French saying: '*Il faut que jeunesse se passe.*' It was all done with clean hands, in clean linen, with French phrases, and above all among people of the best society and consequently with the approval of people of rank.

So Ivan Ilych served for five years and then came a change in his official life. The new and reformed judicial institutions were introduced, and new men were needed. Ivan Ilych became such a new man. He was offered the post of examining magistrate, and he accepted it though the post was in another province and obliged him to give up the connexions he had formed and to make new ones. His friends met to give him a send-off; they had a group-photograph taken and presented him with a silver cigarette-case, and he set off to his new post.

As examining magistrate Ivan Ilych was just as *comme il faut* and decorous a man, inspiring general respect and capable of separating his official duties from his private life, as he had been when acting as an official on special service. His duties now as examining magistrate were far more interesting and attractive than before. In his former position it had been pleasant to wear an undress uniform made by Scharmer, and to pass through the crowd of petitioners and officials who were timorously awaiting an audience with the Governor, and who envied him as with free and easy gait he went straight into his chief's private room to have a cup of tea and a cigarette with him. But not many people had then been directly dependent on him—only police officials and the sectarians when he went on special missions—and he liked to treat them politely, almost as comrades, as if he were letting them feel that he who had the power to crush them was treating them in this simple, friendly way. There were then but few such people. But now, as an examining magistrate, Ivan Ilych felt that everyone without exception, even the most important and self-satisfied, was in his power, and that he need only write a few words on a sheet of paper with a certain heading, and this or that important, self-satisfied person would be brought before him in the role of an accused person or a witness, and if he did not choose to allow him to sit down, would have to stand before him and answer his questions. Ivan Ilych never abused his power; he tried on the contrary to soften its expression, but the consciousness of it and of the possibility of softening its effect, supplied the chief interest and attraction of his office. In his work itself, especially in his examinations, he very soon acquired a method of eliminating all considerations irrelevant to the legal aspect of the case, and reducing even the most complicated case to a form in which it would be presented on paper only in its externals, completely excluding his personal opinion of the matter, while above all observing every prescribed formality. The work was new and Ivan Ilych was one of the first men to apply the new Code of 1864.

On taking up the post of examining magistrate in a new town, he made new acquaintances and connexions, placed himself on a new footing, and assumed a somewhat different tone. He took up an attitude of rather dignified aloofness towards the provincial authorities, but picked out the best circle of legal gentlemen and wealthy gentry living in the town and assumed a tone of slight dissatisfaction with the government, of moderate liberalism, and of enlightened citizenship. At the same time, without at all altering the elegance of his toilet, he ceased shaving his chin and allowed his beard to grow as it pleased.

Ivan Ilych settled down very pleasantly in this new town. The society there, which inclined towards opposition to the Governor, was friendly, his salary was larger, and he began to play whist which he found added not a little to the pleasure of life, for he had a capacity for cards, played good-humouredly, and calculated rapidly and astutely, so that he usually won.

After living there for two years he met his future wife, Praskovya Fedorovna Mikhel, who was the most attractive, clever, and brilliant girl of the set in which he moved, and among other amusements and relaxations from his labours as examining magistrate, Ivan Ilych established light and playful relations with her.

While he had been an official on special service he had been accustomed to dance, but now as an examining magistrate it was exceptional for him to do so. If he danced now, he did it as if to show that though he served under the reformed order of things, and had reached the fifth official rank, yet when it came to dancing he could do it better than most people. So at the end of an evening he sometimes danced with Praskovya Fedorovna, and it was chiefly during these dances that he captivated her. She fell in love with him. Ivan Ilych had at first no definite intention of marrying, but when the girl fell in love with him he said to himself: 'Really, why shouldn't I marry?'

Praskovya Fedorovna came of a good family, was not bad looking, and had some little property. Ivan Ilych might have aspired to a more brilliant match, but even this was good. He had his salary, and she, he hoped, would have an equal income. She was well connected, and was a sweet, pretty, and thoroughly correct young woman. To say that Ivan Ilych married because be fell in love with Praskovya Fedorovna and found that she sympathized with his view of life would be as incorrect as to say that he married because his social circle approved of the match. He was swayed by both these considerations: the marriage gave him personal satisfaction, and at the same time it was considered the right thing by the most highly placed of his associates.

So Ivan Ilych got married.

The preparations for marriage and the beginning of married life, with its conjugal caresses, the new furniture, new crockery, and new linen, were very pleasant until his wife became pregnant—so that Ivan Ilych had begun to think that marriage would not impair the easy, agreeable, gay and always decorous character of his life, approved of by society and regarded by himself as natural, but would even improve it. But from the first months of his wife's pregnancy, something new, unpleasant, depressing, and unseemly, and from which there was no way of escape, unexpectedly showed itself.

His wife, without any reason—*de gaieté de cœur* as Ivan Ilych expressed it to himself—began to disturb the pleasure and propriety of their life. She began to be jealous without any cause, expected him to devote his whole attention to her, found fault with everything, and made coarse and ill-mannered scenes.

At first Ivan Ilych hoped to escape from the unpleasantness of this state of affairs by the same easy and decorous relation to life that had served him heretofore: he tried to ignore his wife's disagreeable moods, continued to live in his usual easy and pleasant way, invited friends to his house for a game of cards, and also tried going out to his club or spending his evenings with friends. But one day his wife began upbraiding him so vigorously, using such coarse words, and continued to abuse him every time he did not fulfil her demands, so resolutely and with such evident determination not to give way till he submitted—that is, till he stayed at home and was bored just as she was—that he became alarmed. He now realized that matrimony—at any rate with Praskovya Fedorovna—was not always conducive to the pleasures and amenities of life but on the contrary often infringed both comfort and propriety, and that he must therefore entrench himself against such infringement. And Ivan Ilych began to seek for means of doing so. His official duties were the one thing that imposed upon Praskovya Fedorovna, and by means of his official work and the duties attached to it he began struggling with his wife to secure his own independence.

With the birth of their child, the attempts to feed it and the various failures in doing so, and with the real and imaginary illnesses of mother and child, in which Ivan Ilych's sympathy was demanded but about which he understood nothing, the need of securing for himself an existence outside his family life became still more imperative.

As his wife grew more irritable and exacting and Ivan Ilych transferred the centre of gravity of his life more and more to his official work, so did he grow to like his work better and became more ambitious than before.

Very soon, within a year of his wedding, Ivan Ilych had realized that marriage, though it may add some comforts to life, is in fact a very intricate and difficult affair towards which in order to perform one's duty, that is, to lead a decorous life approved of by society, one must adopt a definite attitude just as towards one's official duties.

And Ivan Ilych evolved such an attitude towards married life. He only required of it those conveniences—dinner at home, housewife, and bed—which it could give him, and above all that propriety of external forms required by public opinion. For the rest he looked for light-hearted pleasure and propriety, and was very thankful when he found them, but if he met with antagonism and querulousness he at once retired into his separate fenced-off world of official duties, where he found satisfaction.

Ivan Ilych was esteemed a good official, and after three years was made Assistant Public Prosecutor. His new duties, their importance, the possibility of indicting and imprisoning anyone he chose, the publicity his speeches received, and the success he had in all these things, made his work still more attractive.

More children came. His wife became more and more querulous and ill-tempered, but the attitude Ivan Ilych had adopted towards his home life rendered him almost impervious to her grumbling.

After seven years' service in that town he was transferred to another province as Public Prosecutor. They moved, but were short of money and his wife did not like the place they moved to. Though the salary was higher the cost of living was greater, besides which two of their children died and family life became still more unpleasant for him.

Praskovya Fedorovna blamed her husband for every inconvenience they encountered in their new home. Most of the conversations between husband and wife, especially as to the children's education, led to topics which recalled former disputes, and those disputes were apt to flare up again at any moment. There remained only those rare periods of amorousness which still came to them at times but did not last long. These were islets at which they anchored for a while and then again set out upon that ocean of veiled hostility which showed itself in their aloofness from one another. This aloofness might have grieved Ivan Ilych had he considered that it ought not to exist, but he now regarded the position as normal, and even made it the goal at which he aimed in family life. His aim was to free himself more and more from those unpleasantnesses and to give them a semblance of harmlessness and propriety. He attained this by spending less and less time with his family, and when obliged to be at home he tried to safeguard his position by the presence of outsiders. The chief thing however was that he had his official duties. The whole interest of his life now centred in the official world and that interest absorbed him. The consciousness of his power, being able to ruin anybody he wished to ruin, the importance, even the external dignity of his entry into court, or meetings with his subordinates, his success with superiors and inferiors, and above all his masterly handling of cases, of which he was conscious—all this gave him pleasure and filled his life, together with chats with his colleagues, dinners, and bridge. So that on the whole Ivan Ilych's life continued to flow as he considered it should do—pleasantly and properly.

So things continued for another seven years. His eldest daughter was already sixteen, another child had died, and only one son was left, a schoolboy and a subject of dissension. Ivan Ilych wanted to put him in the School of Law, but to spite him Praskovya Fedorovna entered him at the High School. The daughter had been educated at home and had turned out well: the boy did not learn badly either.

III

SO Ivan Ilych lived for seventeen years after his marriage. He was already a Public Prosecutor of long standing, and had declined several proposed transfers while awaiting a more desirable post, when an unanticipated and unpleasant occurrence quite upset the peaceful course of his life. He was expecting to be offered the post of presiding judge in a university town, but Happe somehow came to the front and obtained the appointment instead. Ivan Ilych became irritable, reproached Happe, and quarrelled both with him and with his immediate superiors—who became colder to him and again passed him over when other appointments were made.

This was in 1880, the hardest year of Ivan Ilych's life. It was then that it became evident on the one hand that his salary was insufficient for them to live on, and on the other that he had been forgotten, and not only this, but that what was for him the greatest and most cruel injustice appeared to others a quite ordinary occurrence. Even his father did not consider it his duty to help him. Ivan Ilych felt himself abandoned by everyone, and that they regarded his position with a salary of 3,500 rubles as quite normal and even fortunate. He alone knew that with the consciousness of the injustices done him, with his wife's incessant nagging, and with the debts he had contracted by living beyond his means, his position was far from normal.

In order to save money that summer he obtained leave of absence and went with his wife to live in the country at her brother's place.

In the country, without his work, he experienced *ennui* for the first time in his life, and not only *ennui* but intolerable depression, and he decided that it was impossible to go on living like that, and that it was necessary to take energetic measures.

Having passed a sleepless night pacing up and down the veranda, he decided to go to Petersburg and bestir himself, in order to punish those who had failed to appreciate him and to get transferred to another ministry.

Next day, despite many protests from his wife and her brother, he started for Petersburg with the sole object of obtaining a post with a salary of five thousand rubles a year. He was no longer bent on any particular department, or tendency, or kind of activity. All he now wanted was an appointment to another post with a salary of five thousand rubles, either in the administration, in the banks, with the railways, in one of the Empress Marya's Institutions, or even in the customs—but it had to carry with it a salary of five thousand rubles and be in a ministry other than that in which they had failed to appreciate him.

And this quest of Ivan Ilych's was crowned with remarkable and unexpected success. At Kursk an acquaintance of his, F. I. Ilyin, got into the first-class carriage, sat down beside

Ivan Ilych, and told him of a telegram just received by the
Governor of Kursk announcing that a change was about to take
place in the ministry: Peter Ivanovich was to be superseded by
Ivan Semenovich.

The proposed change, apart from its significance for Russia,
had a special significance for Ivan Ilych, because by bringing
forward a new man, Peter Petrovich, and consequently his friend
Zakhar Ivanovich, it was highly favourable for Ivan Ilych, since
Zakhar Ivanovich was a friend and colleague of his.

In Moscow this news was confirmed, and on reaching Petersburg Ivan Ilych found Zakhar Ivanovich and received a definite
promise of an appointment in his former department of Justice.

A week later he telegraphed to his wife: 'Zakhar in Miller's
place. I shall receive appointment on presentation of report.'

Thanks to this change of personnel, Ivan Ilych had unexpectedly obtained an appointment in his former ministry
which placed him two stages above his former colleagues besides
giving him five thousand rubles salary and three thousand five
hundred rubles for expenses connected with his removal. All
his ill humour towards his former enemies and the whole
department vanished, and Ivan Ilych was completely happy.

He returned to the country more cheerful and contented than
he had been for a long time. Praskovya Fedorovna also cheered
up and a truce was arranged between them. Ivan Ilych told of
how he had been fêted by everybody in Petersburg, how all those
who had been his enemies were put to shame and now fawned on
him, how envious they were of his appointment, and how much
everybody in Petersburg had liked him.

Praskovya Fedorovna listened to all this and appeared to
believe it. She did not contradict anything, but only made plans
for their life in the town to which they were going. Ivan Ilych
saw with delight that these plans were his plans, that he and
his wife agreed, and that, after a stumble, his life was regaining
its due and natural character of pleasant lightheartedness and
decorum.

Ivan Ilych had come back for a short time only, for he had
to take up his new duties on the 10th of September. Moreover,
he needed time to settle into the new place, to move all his
belongings from the province, and to buy and order many
additional things: in a word, to make such arrangements as

he had resolved on, which were almost exactly what Praskovya Fedorovna too had decided on.

Now that everything had happened so fortunately, and that he and his wife were at one in their aims and moreover saw so little of one another, they got on together better than they had done since the first years of marriage. Ivan Ilych had thought of taking his family away with him at once, but the insistence of his wife's brother and her sister-in-law, who had suddenly become particularly amiable and friendly to him and his family, induced him to depart alone.

So he departed, and the cheerful state of mind induced by his success and by the harmony between his wife and himself, the one intensifying the other, did not leave him. He found a delightful house, just the thing both he and his wife had dreamt of. Spacious, lofty reception rooms in the old style, a convenient and dignified study, rooms for his wife and daughter, a study for his son—it might have been specially built for them. Ivan Ilych himself superintended the arrangements, chose the wallpapers, supplemented the furniture (preferably with antiques which he considered particularly *comme il faut*), and supervised the upholstering. Everything progressed and progressed and approached the ideal he had set himself: even when things were only half completed they exceeded his expectations. He saw what a refined and elegant character, free from vulgarity, it would all have when it was ready. On falling asleep he pictured to himself how the reception-room would look. Looking at the yet unfinished drawing-room he could see the fireplace, the screen, the what-not, the little chairs dotted here and there, the dishes and plates on the walls, and the bronzes, as they would be when everything was in place. He was pleased by the thought of how his wife and daughter, who shared his taste in this matter, would be impressed by it. They were certainly not expecting as much. He had been particularly successful in finding, and buying cheaply, antiques which gave a particularly aristocratic character to the whole place. But in his letters he intentionally understated everything in order to be able to surprise them. All this so absorbed him that his new duties—though he liked his official work—interested him less than he had expected. Sometimes he even had moments of absent-mindedness during the Court Sessions, and would consider whether he should have straight or curved cornices for his curtains. He was so interested in it all that he often did things himself, rearranging the furniture, or rehanging the curtains. Once when mounting a step-ladder to show the upholsterer, who did not understand, how he wanted the hangings draped, he made a false step and slipped, but being a strong and agile man he clung on and only knocked his side against the knob of the window frame. The bruised place was painful but the pain soon passed, and he felt particularly bright and well just then. He wrote: 'I feel fifteen years younger.' He thought he would have everything ready by September, but it dragged on till mid-October. But the result was charming not only in his eyes but to everyone who saw it.

In reality it was just what is usually seen in the houses of people of moderate means who want to appear rich, and therefore succeed only in resembling others like themselves: there were damasks, dark wood, plants, rugs, and dull and polished bronzes—all the things people of a certain class have in order to resemble other people of that class. His house was so like the others that it would never have been noticed, but to him it all seemed to be quite exceptional. He was very happy when he met his family at the station and brought them to the newly furnished house all lit up, where a footman in a white tie opened the door into the hall decorated with plants, and when they went on into the drawing-room and the study uttering exclamations of delight. He conducted them everywhere, drank in their praises eagerly, and beamed with pleasure. At tea that evening, when Praskovya Fedorovna among other things asked him about his fall, he laughed, and showed them how he had gone flying and had frightened the upholsterer.

'It's a good thing I'm a bit of an athlete. Another man might have been killed, but I merely knocked myself, just here; it hurts when it's touched, but it's passing off already—it's only a bruise.'

So they began living in their new home—in which, as always happens, when they got thoroughly settled in they found they were just one room short—and with the increased income, which as always was just a little (some five hundred rubles) too little, but it was all very nice.

Things went particularly well at first, before everything was finally arranged and while something had still to be done: this thing bought, that thing ordered, another thing moved, and something else adjusted. Though there were some disputes between husband and wife, they were both so well satisfied and had so much to do that it all passed off without any serious quarrels. When nothing was left to arrange it became rather dull and something seemed to be lacking, but they were then making acquaintances, forming habits, and life was growing fuller.

Ivan Ilych spent his mornings at the law court and came home to dinner, and at first he was generally in a good humour, though he occasionally became irritable just on account of his house. (Every spot on the tablecloth or the upholstery, and every broken window-blind string, irritated him. He had devoted so much trouble to arranging it all that every disturbance of it distressed him.) But on the whole his life ran its course as he believed life should do: easily, pleasantly, and decorously.

He got up at nine, drank his coffee, read the paper, and then put on his undress uniform and went to the law courts. There the harness in which he worked had already been stretched to fit him and he donned it without a hitch: petitioners, inquiries at the chancery, the chancery itself, and the sittings public and administrative. In all this the thing was to exclude everything fresh and vital, which always disturbs the regular course of official business, and to admit only official relations with people, and then only on official grounds. A man would come, for instance, wanting some information. Ivan Ilych, as one in whose sphere the matter did not lie, would have nothing to do with him: but if the man had some business with him in his official capacity, something that could be expressed on officially stamped paper, he would do everything, positively everything he could within the limits of such relations, and in doing so would maintain the semblance of friendly human relations, that is, would observe the courtesies of life. As soon as the official relations ended, so did everything else. Ivan Ilych possessed this capacity to separate his real life from the official side of affairs and not mix the two, in the highest degree, and by long practice and natural aptitude had brought it to such a pitch that sometimes, in the manner of a virtuoso, he would even allow himself to let the human and official relations mingle. He let himself do this just because he felt that he could at any time he chose resume the strictly official attitude again and drop the human relation. And he did it, all easily, pleasantly, correctly, and even artistically. In the intervals between the sessions he smoked, drank tea, chatted a little about politics, a little about general topics, a little about cards, but most of all about official appointments. Tired, but with the feelings of a virtuoso—one of the first violins who has played his part in an orchestra with precision—he would return home to find that his wife and daughter had been out paying calls, or had a visitor, and that his son had been to school, had done his homework with his tutor, and was duly learning what is taught at high schools. Everything was as it should be. After dinner, if they had no visitors, Ivan Ilych sometimes read a book that was being much discussed at the time, and in the evening settled down to work, that is, read official papers, compared the depositions of witnesses, and noted paragraphs of the Code applying to them. This was neither dull nor amusing. It was dull when he might have been playing bridge, but if no bridge was available it was at any rate better than doing nothing or sitting with his wife. Ivan Ilych's chief pleasure was giving little dinners to which he invited men and women of good social position, and just as his drawing-room resembled all other drawing-rooms so did his enjoyable little parties resemble all other such parties.

Once they even gave a dance. Ivan Ilych enjoyed it and everything went off well, except that it led to a violent quarrel with his wife about the cakes and sweets. Praskovya Fedorovna had made her own plans, but Ivan Ilych insisted on getting everything from an expensive confectioner and ordered too many cakes, and the quarrel occurred because some of those cakes were left over and the confectioner's bill came to forty-five rubles. It was a great and disagreeable quarrel. Praskovya Fedorovna called him 'a fool and an imbecile', and he clutched at his head and made angry allusions to divorce.

But the dance itself had been enjoyable. The best people were there, and Ivan Ilych had danced with Princess Trufonova, a sister of the distinguished founder of the society 'Bear my Burden'.

The pleasures connected with his work were pleasures of ambition; his social pleasures were those of vanity; but Ivan Ilych's greatest pleasure was playing bridge. He acknowledged that whatever disagreeable incident happened in his life, the pleasure that beamed like a ray of light above everything else was to sit down to bridge with good players, not noisy partners, and of course to four-handed bridge (with five players it was annoying to have to stand out, though one pretended not to mind), to play a clever and serious game (when the cards allowed it) and then to have supper and drink a glass of wine. After a game of bridge, especially if he had won a little (to win a large sum was unpleasant), Ivan Ilych went to bed in specially good humour.

So they lived. They formed a circle of acquaintances among the best people and were visited by people of importance and by young folk. In their views as to their acquaintances, husband, wife and daughter were entirely agreed, and tacitly and unanimously kept at arm's length and shook off the various shabby friends and relations who, with much show of affection, gushed into the drawing-room with its Japanese plates on the walls. Soon these shabby friends ceased to obtrude themselves and only the best people remained in the Golovins' set.

Young men made up to Lisa, and Petrishchev, an examining magistrate and Dmitri Ivanovich Petrishchev's son and sole heir, began to be so attentive to her that Ivan Ilych had already spoken to Praskovya Fedorovna about it, and considered whether they should not arrange a party for them, or get up some private theatricals.

So they lived, and all went well, without change, and life flowed pleasantly.

IV

THEY were all in good health. It could not be called ill health if Ivan Ilych sometimes said that he had a queer taste in his mouth and felt some discomfort in his left side.

But this discomfort increased and, though not exactly painful, grew into a sense of pressure in his side accompanied by ill humour. And his irritability became worse and worse and began to mar the agreeable, easy, and correct life that had established itself in the Golovin family. Quarrels between husband and wife became more and more frequent, and soon the ease and amenity disappeared and even the decorum was barely maintained. Scenes again became frequent, and very few of those islets remained on which husband and wife could meet without an explosion. Praskovya Fedorovna now had good reason to say that her husband's temper was trying. With characteristic exaggeration she said he had always had a dreadful temper, and that it had needed all her good nature to put up with it for twenty years. It was true that now the quarrels were started by him. His burst of temper always came just before dinner, often just as he began to eat his soup. Sometimes he noticed that a plate or dish was chipped, or the food was not right, or his son put his elbow on the table, or his daughter's hair was not done as he liked it, and for all this he blamed Praskovya Fedorovna. At first she retorted and said disagreeable things to him, but once or twice he fell into such a rage at the beginning of dinner that she realized it was due to some physical derangement brought on by taking food, and so she restrained herself and did not answer, but only hurried to get the dinner over. She regarded this self-restraint as highly praiseworthy. Having come to the conclusion that her husband had a dreadful temper and made her life miserable, she began to feel sorry for herself, and the more she pitied herself the more she hated her husband. She began to wish he would die; yet she did not want him to die because then his salary would cease. And this irritated her against him still more. She considered herself dreadfully unhappy just because not even his death could save her, and though she concealed her exasperation, that hidden exasperation of hers increased his irritation also.

After one scene in which Ivan Ilych had been particularly unfair and after which he had said in explanation that he certainly was irritable but that it was due to his not being well, she said that if he was ill it should be attended to, and insisted on his going to see a celebrated doctor.

He went. Everything took place as he had expected and as it always does. There was the usual waiting and the important air assumed by the doctor, with which he was so familiar (resembling that which he himself assumed in court), and the sounding and listening, and the questions which called for answers that were foregone conclusions and were evidently unnecessary, and the look of importance which implied that 'if only you put yourself in our hands we will arrange everything—we know indubitably how it has to be done, always in the same way for everybody alike.' It was all just as it was in the law courts. The doctor put on just the same air towards him as he himself put on towards an accused person.

The doctor said that so-and-so indicated that there was so-and-so inside the patient, but if the investigation of so-and-so did not confirm this, then he must assume that and that. If he assumed that and that, then . . . and so on. To Ivan Ilych only one question was important: was his case serious or not? But the doctor ignored that inappropriate question. From his point of view it was not the one under consideration, the real question was to decide between a floating kidney, chronic catarrh, or appendicitis. It was not a question of Ivan Ilych's life or death, but one between a floating kidney and appendicitis. And that question the doctor solved brilliantly, as it seemed to Ivan Ilych, in favour of the appendix, with the reservation that should an examination of the urine give fresh indications the matter would be reconsidered. All this was just what Ivan Ilych had himself brilliantly accomplished a thousand times in dealing with men on trial. The doctor summed up just as brilliantly, looking over his spectacles triumphantly and even gaily at the accused. From the doctor's summing up Ivan Ilych concluded that things were bad, but that for the doctor, and perhaps for everybody else, it was a matter of indifference, though for him it was bad. And this conclusion struck him painfully, arousing in him a great feeling of pity for himself and of bitterness towards the doctor's indifference to a matter of such importance.

He said nothing of this, but rose, placed the doctor's fee on the table, and remarked with a sigh: 'We sick people probably often put inappropriate questions. But tell me, in general, is this complaint dangerous, or not? . . .'

The doctor looked at him sternly over his spectacles with one eye, as if to say: 'Prisoner, if you will not keep to the questions put to you, I shall be obliged to have you removed from the court.'

'I have already told you what I consider necessary and proper. The analysis may show something more.' And the doctor bowed.

Ivan Ilych went out slowly, seated himself disconsolately in his sledge, and drove home. All the way home he was going over what the doctor had said, trying to translate those complicated, obscure, scientific phrases into plain language and find in them an answer to the question: 'Is my condition bad? Is it very bad?

Or is there as yet nothing much wrong?' And it seemed to him that the meaning of what the doctor had said was that it was very bad. Everything in the streets seemed depressing. The cabmen, the houses, the passers-by, and the shops, were dismal. His ache, this dull gnawing ache that never ceased for a moment, seemed to have acquired a new and more serious significance from the doctor's dubious remarks. Ivan Ilych now watched it with a new and oppressive feeling.

He reached home and began to tell his wife about it. She listened, but in the middle of his account his daughter came in with her hat on, ready to go out with her mother. She sat down reluctantly to listen to this tedious story, but could not stand it long, and her mother too did not hear him to the end.

'Well, I am very glad,' she said. 'Mind now to take your medicine regularly. Give me the prescription and I'll send Gerasim to the chemist's.' And she went to get ready to go out.

While she was in the room Ivan Ilych had hardly taken time to breathe, but he sighed deeply when she left it.

'Well,' he thought, 'perhaps it isn't so bad after all.'

He began taking his medicine and following the doctor's directions, which had been altered after the examination of the urine. But then it happened that there was a contradiction between the indications drawn from the examination of the urine and the symptoms that showed themselves. It turned out that what was happening differed from what the doctor had told him, and that he had either forgotten, or blundered, or hidden something from him. He could not, however, be blamed for that, and Ivan Ilych still obeyed his orders implicitly and at first derived some comfort from doing so.

From the time of his visit to the doctor, Ivan Ilych's chief occupation was the exact fulfilment of the doctor's instructions regarding hygiene and the taking of medicine, and the observation of his pain and his excretions. His chief interests came to be people's ailments and people's health. When sickness, deaths, or recoveries were mentioned in his presence, especially when the illness resembled his own, he listened with agitation which he tried to hide, asked questions, and applied what he heard to his own case.

The pain did not grow less, but Ivan Ilych made efforts to force himself to think that he was better. And he could do this so long as nothing agitated him. But as soon as he had any unpleasantness with his wife, any lack of success in his official work, or held bad cards at bridge, he was at once acutely sensible of his disease. He had formerly borne such mischances, hoping soon to adjust what was wrong, to master it and attain success, or make a grand slam. But now every mischance upset him and plunged him into despair. He would say to himself: 'There now, just as I was beginning to get better and the medicine had begun to take effect, comes this accursed misfortune, or unpleasantness . . .' And he was furious with the mishap, or with the people who were causing the unpleasantness and killing him, for he felt that this fury was killing him but could not restrain it. One would have thought that it should have been clear to him that this exasperation with circumstances and people aggravated his illness, and that he ought therefore to ignore unpleasant occurrences. But he drew the very opposite conclusion: he said that he needed peace, and he watched for everything that might disturb it and became irritable at the slightest infringement of it. His condition was rendered worse by the fact that he read medical books and consulted doctors. The progress of his disease was so gradual that he could deceive himself when comparing one day with another—the difference was so slight. But when he consulted the doctors it seemed to him that he was getting worse, and even very rapidly. Yet despite this he was continually consulting them.

That month he went to see another celebrity, who told him almost the same as the first had done but put his questions rather differently, and the interview with this celebrity only increased Ivan Ilych's doubts and fears. A friend of a friend of his, a very good doctor, diagnosed his illness again quite differently from the others, and though he predicted recovery, his questions and suppositions bewildered Ivan Ilych still more and increased his doubts. A homoeopathist diagnosed the disease in yet another way, and prescribed medicine which Ivan Ilych took secretly for a week. But after a week, not feeling any improvement and having lost confidence both in the former doctor's treatment and in this one's, he became still more despondent. One day a lady acquaintance mentioned a cure effected by a wonder-working icon. Ivan Ilych caught himself listening attentively and beginning to believe that it had occurred. This incident alarmed him. 'Has my mind really weakened to such an extent?' he asked himself. 'Nonsense! It's all rubbish. I mustn't give way to nervous fears but having chosen a doctor must keep strictly to his treatment. That is what I will do. Now it's all settled. I won't think about it, but will follow the treatment seriously till summer, and then we shall see. From now there must be no more of this wavering!' This was easy to say but impossible to carry out. The pain in his side oppressed him and seemed to grow worse and more incessant, while the taste in his mouth grew stranger and stranger. It seemed to him that his breath had a disgusting smell, and he was conscious of a loss of appetite and strength. There was no deceiving himself: something terrible, new, and more important than anything before in his life, was taking place within him of which he alone was aware. Those about him did not understand or would not understand it, but thought everything in the world was going on as usual. Tl at tormented Ivan Ilych more than anything. He saw that his household, especially his wife and daughter who were in a perfect whirl of visiting, did not understand anything of it and were annoyed that he was so depressed and so exacting, as if he were to blame for it. Though they tried to disguise it he saw that he was an obstacle in their path, and that his wife had adopted a definite line in regard to his illness and kept to it regardless of anything he said or did. Her attitude was this: 'You know,' she would say to her friends, 'Ivan Ilych can't do as other people do, and keep to the treatment prescribed for him. One day he'll take his drops and keep strictly to his diet and go to bed in good time, but the next day unless I watch him he'll suddenly forget his medicine, eat sturgeon—which is forbidden—and sit up playing cards till one o'clock in the morning.'

'Oh, come, when was that?' Ivan Ilych would ask in vexation. 'Only once at Peter Ivanovich's.'

'And yesterday with Shebek.'

'Well even if I hadn't stayed up, this pain would have kept me awake.'

'Be that as it may you'll never get well like that, but will always make us wretched.'

Praskovya Fedorovna's attitude to Ivan Ilych's illness, as she expressed it both to others and to him, was that it was his own fault and was another of the annoyances he caused her. Ivan

Ilych felt that this opinion escaped her involuntarily—but that did not make it easier for him.

At the law courts too, Ivan Ilych noticed, or thought he noticed, a strange attitude towards himself. It sometimes seemed to him that people were watching him inquisitively as a man whose place might soon be vacant. Then again, his friends would suddenly begin to chaff him in a friendly way about his low spirits, as if the awful, horrible, and unheard-of-thing that was going on within him, incessantly gnawing at him and irresistibly drawing him away, was a very agreeable subject for jests. Schwartz in particular irritated him by his jocularity, vivacity, and *savoir-faire*, which reminded him of what he himself had been ten years ago.

Friends came to make up a set and they sat down to cards. They dealt, bending the new cards to soften them, and he sorted the diamonds in his hand and found he had seven. His partner said 'No trumps' and supported him with two diamonds. What more could be wished for? It ought to be jolly and lively. They would make a grand slam. But suddenly Ivan Ilych was conscious of that gnawing pain, that taste in his mouth, and it seemed ridiculous that in such circumstances he should be pleased to make a grand slam.

He looked at his partner Michael Mikhaylovich, who rapped the table with his strong hand and instead of snatching up the tricks pushed the cards courteously and indulgently towards Ivan Ilych that he might have the pleasure of gathering them up without the trouble of stretching out his hand for them. 'Does he think I am too weak to stretch out my arm?' thought Ivan Ilych, and forgetting what he was doing he over-trumped his partner, missing the grand slam by three tricks. And what was most awful of all was that he saw how upset Michael Mikhaylovich was about it but did not himself care. And it was dreadful to realise why he did not care.

They all saw that he was suffering, and said: 'We can stop if you are tired. Take a rest.' Lie down? No, he was not at all tired, and he finished the rubber. All were gloomy and silent. Ivan Ilych felt that he had diffused this gloom over them and could not dispel it. They had supper and went away, and Ivan Ilych was left alone with the consciousness that his life was poisoned and was poisoning the lives of others, and that this poison did not weaken but penetrated more and more deeply into his whole being.

With this consciousness, and with physical pain besides the terror, he must go to bed, often to lie awake the greater part of the night. Next morning he had to get up again, dress, go to the law courts, speak, and write; or if he did not go out, spend at home those twenty-four hours a day each of which was a torture. And he had to live thus all alone on the brink of an abyss, with no one who understood or pitied him.

V

SO one month passed and then another. Just before the New Year his brother-in-law came to town and stayed at their house. Ivan Ilych was at the law courts and Praskovya Fedorovna had gone shopping. When Ivan Ilych came home and entered his study he found his brother-in-law there—a healthy, florid man—unpacking his portmanteau himself. He raised his head on hearing Ivan Ilych's footsteps and looked up at him for a moment without a word. That stare told Ivan Ilych everything. His brother-in-law opened his mouth to utter an exclamation of surprise but checked himself, and that action confirmed it all.

'I have changed, eh?'

'Yes, there is a change.'

And after that, try as he would to get his brother-in-law to return to the subject of his looks, the latter would say nothing about it. Praskovya Fedorovna came home and her brother went out to her. Ivan Ilych locked the door and began to examine himself in the glass, first full face, then in profile. He took up a portrait of himself taken with his wife, and compared it with what he saw in the glass. The change in him was immense. Then he bared his arms to the elbow, looked at them, drew the sleeves down again, sat down on an ottoman, and grew blacker than night.

'No, no, this won't do!' he said to himself, and jumped up, went to the table, took up some law papers and began to read them, but could not continue. He unlocked the door and went into the reception-room. The door leading to the drawing-room was shut. He approached it on tiptoe and listened.

'No, you are exaggerating!' Praskovya Fedorovna was saying.

'Exaggerating! Don't you see it? Why, he's a dead man! Look at his eyes—there's no light in them. But what is it that is wrong with him?'

'No one knows. Nikolaevich [that was another doctor] said something, but I don't know what. And Leshchetitsky [this was the celebrated specialist] said quite the contrary . . .'

Ivan Ilych walked away, went to his own room, lay down, and began musing: 'The kidney, a floating kidney.' He recalled all the doctors had told him of how it detached itself and swayed about. And by an effort of imagination he tried to catch that kidney and arrest it and support it. So little was needed for this, it seemed to him. 'No, I'll go to see Peter Ivanovich again.' (That was the friend whose friend was a doctor.) He rang, ordered the carriage, and got ready to go.

'Where are you going, Jean? asked his wife, with a specially sad and exceptionally kind look.

This exceptionally kind look irritated him. He looked morosely at her.

'I must go to see Peter Ivanovich.'

He went to see Peter Ivanovich, and together they went to see his friend, the doctor. He was in, and Ivan Ilych had a long talk with him.

Reviewing the anatomical and physiological details of what in the doctor's opinion was going on inside him, he understood it all.

There was something, a small thing, in the vermiform appendix. It might all come right. Only stimulate the energy of one organ and check the activity of another, then absorption would take place and everything would come right. He got home rather late for dinner, ate his dinner, and conversed cheerfully, but could not for a long time bring himself to go back to work in his room. At last, however, he went to his study and did what was necessary, but the consciousness that he had put something aside—an important, intimate matter which he would revert to when his work was done—never left him. When he had finished his work he remembered that this intimate matter was the thought of his vermiform appendix. But he did not give himself up to it, and went to the drawing-room for tea. There were callers there, including the examining magistrate who was a desirable match for his daughter, and they were conversing, playing the piano, and singing. Ivan Ilych, as Praskovya Fedorovna remarked, spent that evening more cheerfully than usual, but he never for a moment forgot that he had postponed the important matter of the appendix. At eleven o'clock he said goodnight and went to his bedroom. Since his illness he had slept alone in a small room next to his study. He undressed and took up a novel by Zola, but instead of reading it he fell into thought, and in his imagination that desired improvement in the vermiform appendix occurred. There was the absorption and evacuation and the re-establishment of normal activity. 'Yes, that's it!' he said to himself. 'One need only assist nature, that's all.' He remembered his medicine, rose, took it, and lay down on his back watching for the beneficent action of the medicine and for it to lessen the pain. 'I need only take it regularly and avoid all injurious influences. I am already feeling better, much better.' He began touching his side: it was not painful to the touch. 'There, I really don't feel it. It's much better already.' He put out the light and turned on his side . . . 'The appendix is getting better, absorption is occurring.' Suddenly he felt the old, familiar, dull, gnawing pain, stubborn and serious. There was the same familiar loathsome taste in his mouth. His heart sank and he felt dazed. 'My God! My God!' he muttered. 'Again, again! And it will never cease.' And suddenly the matter presented itself in a quite different aspect. 'Vermiform appendix! Kidney!' he said to himself. 'It's not a question of appendix or kidney, but of life and . . . death. Yes, life was there and now it is going, going and I cannot stop it. Yes. Why deceive myself? Isn't it obvious to everyone but me that I'm dying, and that it's only a question of weeks, days . . . it may happen this moment. There was light and now there is darkness. I was here and now I'm going there! Where?' A chill came over him, his breathing ceased, and he felt only the throbbing of his heart.

'When I am not, what will there be? There will be nothing. Then where shall I be when I am no more? Can this be dying? No, I don't want to!' He jumped up and tried to light the candle, felt for it with trembling hands, dropped candle and candlestick on the floor, and fell back on his pillow.

'What's the use? It makes no difference,' he said to himself, staring with wide-open eyes into the darkness. 'Death. Yes, death. And none of them know or wish to know it, and they have no pity for me. Now they are playing.' (He heard through the door the distant sound of a song and its accompaniment.) 'It's all the same to them, but they will die too! Fools! I first, and they later, but it will be the same for them. And now they are merry . . . the beasts!'

Anger choked him and he was agonizingly, unbearably miserable. 'It is impossible that all men have been doomed to suffer this awful horror!' He raised himself.

'Something must be wrong. I must calm myself—must think it all over from the beginning.' And he again began thinking. 'Yes, the beginning of my illness: I knocked my side, but I was still quite well that day and the next. It hurt a little, then rather more. I saw the doctors, then followed despondency and anguish, more doctors, and I drew nearer to the abyss. My strength grew less and I kept coming nearer and nearer, and now I have wasted away and there is no light in my eyes. I think of the appendix—but this is death! I think of mending the appendix, and all the while here is death! Can it really be death?' Again terror seized him and he gasped for breath. He leant down and began feeling for the matches, pressing with his elbow on the stand beside the bed. It was in his way and hurt him, he grew furious with it, pressed on it still harder, and upset it. Breathless and in despair he fell on his back, expecting death to come immediately.

Meanwhile the visitors were leaving. Praskovya Fedorovna was seeing them off. She heard something fall and came in.

'What has happened?'

'Nothing. I knocked it over accidentally.'

She went out and returned with a candle. He lay there panting heavily, like a man who has run a thousand yards, and stared upwards at her with a fixed look.

'What is it, Jean?'

'No . . . o . . . thing. I upset it.' ('Why speak of it? She won't understand,' he thought.)

And in truth she did not understand. She picked up the stand, lit his candle, and hurried away to see another visitor off. When she came back he still lay on his back, looking upwards.

'What is it? Do you feel worse?'

'Yes.'

She shook her head and sat down.

'Do you know, Jean, I think we must ask Leshchetitsky to come and see you here.'

This meant calling in the famous specialist, regardless of expense. He smiled malignantly and said 'No'. She remained a little longer and then went up to him and kissed his forehead.

While she was kissing him he hated her from the bottom of his soul and with difficulty refrained from pushing her away.

'Goodnight. Please God you'll sleep.'

'Yes.'

VI

IVAN ILYCH saw that he was dying, and he was in continual despair.

In the depth of his heart he knew he was dying, but not only was he not accustomed to the thought, he simply did not and could not grasp it.

The syllogism he had learnt from Kiezewetter's Logic: 'Caius is a man, men are mortal, therefore Caius is mortal', had always seemed to him correct as applied to Caius, but certainly not as applied to himself. That Caius—man in the abstract—was mortal, was perfectly correct, but he was not Caius, not an abstract man, but a creature quite separate from all others. He had been little Vanya, with a mamma and a papa, with Mitya and Volodya, with toys, a coachman and a nurse, afterwards with Katenka and with all the joys, griefs, and delights of childhood, boyhood, and youth. What did Caius know of the smell of that striped leather ball Vanya had been so fond of? Had Caius kissed his mother's hand like that, and did the silk of her dress rustle so for Caius? Had he rioted like that at school when the pastry was bad? Had Caius been in love like that? Could Caius preside at a session as he did? 'Caius really was mortal, and it was right for him to die; but for me, little Vanya, Ivan Ilych, with all my thoughts and emotions, it's altogether a different matter. It cannot be that I ought to die. That would be too terrible.'

Such was his feeling.

'If I had to die like Caius I should have known it was so. An inner voice would have told me so, but there was nothing of the sort in me and I and all my friends felt that our case was quite different from that of Caius. And now here it is!' he said to himself. 'It can't be. It's impossible! But here it is. How is this? How is one to understand it?'

He could not understand it, and tried to drive this false, incorrect, morbid thought away and to replace it by other proper and healthy thoughts. But that thought, and not the thought only but the reality itself, seemed to come and confront him.

And to replace that thought he called up a succession of others, hoping to find in them some support. He tried to get back into the former current of thoughts that had once screened the thought of death from him. But strange to say, all that had formerly shut off, hidden, and destroyed, his consciousness of death, no longer had that effect. Ivan Ilych now spent most of his time in attempting to re-establish that old current. He would say to himself: 'I will take up my duties again—after all I used to live by them.' And banishing all doubts he would go to the law courts, enter into conversation with his colleagues, and sit carelessly as was his wont, scanning the crowd with a thoughtful look and leaning both his emaciated arms on the arms of his oak chair; bending over as usual to a colleague and drawing his papers nearer he would interchange whispers with him, and then suddenly raising his eyes and sitting erect would pronounce certain words and open the proceedings. But suddenly in the midst of those proceedings the pain in his side, regardless of the stage the proceedings had reached, would begin its own gnawing work. Ivan Ilych would turn his attention to it and try to drive the thought of it away, but without success. *It* would come and stand before him and look at him, and he would be petrified and the light would die out of his eyes, and he would again begin asking himself whether *It* alone was true. And his colleagues and subordinates would see with surprise and distress that he, the brilliant and subtle judge, was becoming confused and making mistakes. He would shake himself, try to pull himself together, manage somehow to bring the sitting to a close, and return home with the sorrowful consciousness that his judicial labours could not as formerly hide from him what he wanted them to hide, and could not deliver him from *It*. And what was worst of all was that *It* drew his attention to itself not in order to make him take some action but only that he should look at *It*, look it straight in the face: look at it and without doing anything, suffer inexpressibly.

And to save himself from this condition Ivan Ilych looked for consolations—new screens—and new screens were found and for a while seemed to save him, but then they immediately fell to pieces or rather became transparent, as if *It* penetrated them and nothing could veil *It*.

In these latter days he would go into the drawing-room he had arranged—that drawing-room where he had fallen and for the sake of which (how bitterly ridiculous it seemed) he had sacrificed his life—for he knew that his illness originated with that knock. He would enter and see that something had scratched the polished table. He would look for the cause of this and find that it was the bronze ornamentation of an album, that had got bent. He would take up the expensive album which he had lovingly arranged, and feel vexed with his daughter and her friends for their untidiness—for the album was torn here and there and some of the photographs turned upside down. He would put it carefully in order and bend the ornamentation back into position. Then it would occur to him to place all those things in another corner of the room, near the plants. He would call the footman, but his daughter or wife would come to help him. They would not agree, and his wife would contradict him, and he would dispute and grow angry. But that was all right, for then he did not think about *It*. *It* was invisible.

But then, when he was moving something himself, his wife would say: 'Let the servants do it. You will hurt yourself again.' And suddenly *It* would flash through the screen and he would see it. It was just a flash, and he hoped it would disappear, but he would involuntarily pay attention to his side. 'It sits there as before, gnawing just the same!' And he could no longer forget *It*, but could distinctly see it looking at him from behind the flowers. 'What is it all for?'

'It really is so! I lost my life over that curtain as I might have done when storming a fort. Is that possible? How terrible and how stupid. It can't be true! It can't, but it is.'

He would go to his study, lie down, and again be alone with *It*: face to face with *It*. And nothing could be done with *It* except to look at it and shudder.

VII

HOW it happened it is impossible to say because it came about step by step, unnoticed, but in the third month of Ivan Ilych's illness, his wife, his daughter, his son, his acquaintances, the doctors, the servants, and above all he himself, were aware that the whole interest he had for other people was whether he would soon vacate his place, and at last release the living from the discomfort caused by his presence and be himself released from his sufferings.

He slept less and less. He was given opium and hypodermic injections of morphine, but this did not relieve him. The dull depression he experienced in a somnolent condition at first gave him a little relief, but only as something new, afterwards it became as distressing as the pain itself or even more so.

Special foods were prepared for him by the doctors' orders, but all those foods became increasingly distasteful and disgusting to him.

For his excretions also special arrangements had to be made, and this was a torment to him every time—a torment from the uncleanliness, the unseemliness, and the smell, and from knowing that another person had to take part in it.

But just through this most unpleasant matter, Ivan Ilych obtained comfort. Gerasim, the butler's young assistant, always came in to carry the things out. Gerasim was a clean, fresh peasant lad, grown stout on town food and always cheerful and bright. At first the sight of him, in his clean Russian peasant costume, engaged on that disgusting task embarrassed Ivan Ilych.

Once when he got up from the commode too weak to draw up his trousers, he dropped into a soft arm-chair and looked with horror at his bare, enfeebled thighs with the muscles so sharply marked on them.

Gerasim with a firm light tread, his heavy boots emitting a pleasant smell of tar and fresh winter air, came in wearing a clean Hessian apron, the sleeves of his print shirt tucked up over his strong bare young arms; and refraining from looking at his sick master out of consideration for his feelings, and restraining the joy of life that beamed from his face, he went up to the commode.

'Gerasim!' said Ivan Ilych in a weak voice.

Gerasim started, evidently afraid he might have committed some blunder, and with a rapid movement turned his fresh, kind, simple young face which just showed the first downy signs of a beard.

'Yes, sir?'

'That must be very unpleasant for you. You must forgive me. I am helpless.'

'Oh, why, sir,' and Gerasim's eyes beamed and he showed his glistening white teeth, 'what's a little trouble? It's a case of illness with you, sir.'

And his deft strong hands did their accustomed task, and he went out of the room stepping lightly. Five minutes later he as lightly returned.

Ivan Ilych was still sitting in the same position in the arm-chair.

'Gerasim,' he said when the latter had replaced the freshly-washed utensil. 'Please come here and help me.' Gerasim went up to him. 'Lift me up. It is hard for me to get up, and I have sent Dmitri away.'

Gerasim went up to him, grasped his master with his strong arms deftly but gently, in the same way that he stepped—lifted him, supported him with one hand, and with the other drew up his trousers and would have set him down again, but Ivan Ilych asked to be led to the sofa. Gerasim, without an effort and without apparent pressure, led him, almost lifting him, to the sofa and placed him on it.

'Thank you. How easily and well you do it all!'

Gerasim smiled again and turned to leave the room. But Ivan Ilych felt his presence such a comfort that he did not want to let him go.

'One thing more, please move up that chair. No, the other one—under my feet. It is easier for me when my feet are raised.'

Gerasim brought the chair, set it down gently in place, and raised Ivan Ilych's legs on to it. It seemed to Ivan Ilych that he felt better while Gerasim was holding up his legs.

'It's better when my legs are higher,' he said. 'Place that cushion under them.'

Gerasim did so. He again lifted the legs and placed them, and again Ivan Ilych felt better while Gerasim held his legs. When he set them down Ivan Ilych fancied he felt worse.

'Gerasim,' he said. 'Are you busy now?'

'Not at all, sir,' said Gerasim, who had learnt from the townsfolk how to speak to gentlefolk.

'What have you still to do?'

'What have I to do? I've done everything except chopping the logs for tomorrow.'

'Then put my legs up a bit higher, can you?'

'Of course I can. Why not?' And Gerasim raised his master's legs higher and Ivan Ilych thought that in that position he did not feel any pain at all.

'And how about the logs?'

'Don't trouble about that, sir. There's plenty of time.'

Ivan Ilych told Gerasim to sit down and hold his legs, and began to talk to him. And strange to say it seemed to him that he felt better while Gerasim held his legs up.

After that Ivan Ilych would sometimes call Gerasim and get him to hold his legs on his shoulders, and he liked talking to him. Gerasim did it all easily, willingly, simply, and with a good nature that touched Ivan Ilych. Health, strength, and vitality in other people were offensive to him, but Gerasim's strength and vitality did not mortify but soothed him.

What tormented Ivan Ilych most was the deception, the lie, which for some reason they all accepted, that he was not dying but was simply ill, and that he only need keep quiet and undergo a treatment and then something very good would result. He however knew that do what they would nothing would come of it, only still more agonizing suffering and death. This deception tortured him—their not wishing to admit what they all knew and what he knew, but wanting to lie to him concerning his terrible condition, and wishing and forcing him to participate in that lie. Those lies—lies enacted over him on the eve of his death and destined to degrade this awful, solemn act to the level of their visitings, their curtains, their sturgeon for dinner—were a terrible agony for Ivan Ilych. And strangely enough, many times when they were going through their antics over him he had been within a hairbreadth of calling out to them: 'Stop lying! You know and I know that I am dying. Then at least stop lying about it!' But he had never had the spirit to do it. The awful, terrible act of his dying was, he could see, reduced by those about him to the level of a casual, unpleasant, and almost indecorous incident (as if someone entered a drawing-room diffusing an unpleasant odour) and this was done by that very decorum which he had served all his life long. He saw that no one felt for him, because no one even wished to grasp his position. Only Gerasim recognized it and pitied him. And so Ivan Ilych felt at ease only with him. He felt comforted when Gerasim supported his legs (sometimes all night long) and refused to go to bed, saying: 'Don't you worry, Ivan Ilych. I'll get sleep enough later on,' or when he suddenly became familiar and exclaimed: 'If you weren't sick it would be another matter, but as it is, why should I grudge a little trouble?' Gerasim alone did not lie; everything showed that he alone understood the facts of the case and did not consider it necessary to disguise them, but simply felt sorry for his emaciated and enfeebled master. Once when Ivan Ilych was sending him away he even said straight out: 'We shall all of us die, so why should I grudge a little trouble?'—expressing the fact that he did not think his work burdensome, because he was doing it for a dying man and hoped someone would do the same for him when his time came.

Apart from this lying, or because of it, what most tormented Ivan Ilych was that no one pitied him as he wished to be pitied. At certain moments after prolonged suffering he wished most of all (though he would have been ashamed to confess it) for someone to pity him as a sick child is pitied. He longed to be petted and comforted. He knew he was an important functionary, that he had a beard turning grey, and that therefore what he longed for was impossible, but still he longed for it. And in Gerasim's attitude towards him there was something akin to what he wished for, and so that attitude comforted him. Ivan Ilych wanted to weep, wanted to be petted and cried over, and then his colleague Shebek would come, and instead of weeping and being petted, Ivan Ilych would assume a serious, severe, and profound air, and by force of habit would express his opinion on a decision of the Court of Cassation and would stubbornly insist on that view. This falsity around him and within him did more than anything else to poison his last days.

VIII

IT was morning. He knew it was morning because Gerasim had gone, and Peter the footman had come and put out the candles, drawn back one of the curtains, and begun quietly to tidy up. Whether it was morning or evening, Friday or Sunday, made no difference, it was all just the same: the gnawing, unmitigated, agonizing pain, never ceasing for an instant, the consciousness of life inexorably waning but not yet extinguished, the approach of that ever dreaded and hateful death which was the only reality, and always the same falsity. What were days, weeks, hours, in such a case?

'Will you have some tea, sir?'

'He wants things to be regular, and wishes the gentlefolk to drink tea in the morning,' thought Ivan Ilych, and only said 'No'.

'Wouldn't you like to move on to the sofa, sir?'

'He wants to tidy up the room, and I'm in the way. I am uncleanliness and disorder,' he thought, and said only:

'No, leave me alone.'

The man went on bustling about. Ivan Ilych stretched out his hand. Peter came up, ready to help.

'What is it, sir?'

'My watch.'

Peter took the watch which was close at hand and gave it to his master.

'Half-past eight. Are they up?'

'No sir, except Vladimir Ivanich' (the son) 'who has gone to school. Praskovya Fedorovna ordered me to wake her if you asked for her. Shall I do so?'

'No, there's no need to.' 'Perhaps I'd better have some tea,' he thought, and added aloud: 'Yes, bring me some tea.'

Peter went to the door but Ivan Ilych dreaded being left alone. 'How can I keep him here? Oh, yes, my medicine.' 'Peter, give me my medicine.' 'Why not? Perhaps it may still do me some good.' He took a spoonful and swallowed it. 'No, it won't help. It's all tomfoolery, all deception,' he decided as soon as he became aware of the familiar, sickly, hopeless taste. 'No, I can't believe in it any longer. But the pain, why this pain? If it would only cease just for a moment!' And he moaned. Peter turned towards him. 'It's all right. Go and fetch me some tea.'

Peter went out. Left alone Ivan Ilych groaned not so much with pain, terrible though that was, as from mental anguish. Always and for ever the same, always these endless days and nights. If only it would come quicker! If only *what* would come quicker? Death, darkness? . . . No, no! Anything rather than death!

When Peter returned with the tea on a tray, Ivan Ilych stared at him for a time in perplexity, not realizing who and what he was. Peter was disconcerted by that look and his embarrassment brought Ivan Ilych to himself.

'Oh, tea! All right, put it down. Only help me to wash and put on a clean shirt.'

And Ivan Ilych began to wash. With pauses for rest, he washed his hands and then his face, cleaned his teeth, brushed his hair, and looked in the glass. He was terrified by what he saw, especially by the limp way in which his hair clung to his pallid forehead.

While his shirt was being changed he knew that he would be still more frightened at the sight of his body, so he avoided looking at it. Finally he was ready. He drew on a dressing-gown, wrapped himself in a plaid, and sat down in the armchair to take his tea. For a moment he felt refreshed, but as soon as he began to drink the tea he was again aware of the same taste, and the pain also returned. He finished it with an effort, and then lay down stretching out his legs, and dismissed Peter.

Always the same. Now a spark of hope flashes up, then a sea of despair rages, and always pain; always pain, always despair, and always the same. When alone he had a dreadful and distressing desire to call someone, but he knew beforehand that with others present it would be still worse. 'Another dose of morphine—to lose consciousness. I will tell him, the doctor, that he must think of something else. It's impossible, impossible, to go on like this.'

An hour and another pass like that. But now there is a ring at the door bell. Perhaps it's the doctor? It is. He comes in fresh, hearty, plump, and cheerful, with that look on his face that seems to say: 'There now, you're in a panic about something, but we'll arrange it all for you directly!' The doctor knows this expression is out of place here, but he has put it on once for all and can't take it off—like a man who has put on a frock-coat in the morning to pay a round of calls.

The doctor rubs his hands vigorously and reassuringly.

'Brr! How cold it is! There's such a sharp frost; just let me warm myself!' he says, as if it were only a matter of waiting till he was warm, and then he would put everything right.

'Well now, how are you?'

Ivan Ilych feels that the doctor would like to say: 'Well, how are our affairs?' but that even he feels that this would not do, and says instead: 'What sort of a night have you had?'

Ivan Ilych looks at him as much as to say: 'Are you really never ashamed of lying?' But the doctor does not wish to understand this question, and Ivan Ilych says: 'Just as terrible as ever. The pain never leaves me and never subsides. If only something . . .'

'Yes, you sick people are always like that. . . . There, now I think I am warm enough. Even Praskovya Fedorovna, who is so particular, could find no fault with my temperature. Well, now I can say good-morning,' and the doctor presses his patient's hand.

Then, dropping his former playfulness, he begins with a most serious face to examine the patient, feeling his pulse and taking his temperature, and then begins the sounding and auscultation.

Ivan Ilych knows quite well and definitely that all this is nonsense and pure deception, but when the doctor, getting down on his knee, leans over him, putting his ear first higher then lower, and performs various gymnastic movements over him with a significant expression on his face, Ivan Ilych submits to it all as he used to submit to the speeches of the lawyers, though he knew very well that they were all lying and why they were lying.

The doctor, kneeling on the sofa, is still sounding him when Praskovya Fedorovna's silk dress rustles at the door and she is heard scolding Peter for not having let her know of the doctor's arrival.

She comes in, kisses her husband, and at once proceeds to prove that she has been up a long time already, and only owing to a misunderstanding failed to be there when the doctor arrived.

Ivan Ilych looks at her, scans her all over, sets against her the whiteness and plumpness and cleanness of her hands and neck, the gloss of her hair, and the sparkle of her vivacious eyes. He hates her with his whole soul. And the thrill of hatred he feels for her makes him suffer from her touch.

Her attitude towards him and his disease is still the same. Just as the doctor had adopted a certain relation to his patient which he could not abandon, so had she formed one towards him—that he was not doing something he ought to do and was himself to blame, and that she reproached him lovingly for this—and she could not now change that attitude.

'You see he doesn't listen to me and doesn't take his medicine at the proper time. And above all he lies in a position that is no doubt bad for him—with his legs up.'

She described how he made Gerasim hold his legs up.

The doctor smiled with a contemptuous affability that said: 'What's to be done? These sick people do have foolish fancies of that kind, but we must forgive them.'

When the examination was over the doctor looked at his watch, and then Praskovya Fedorovna announced to Ivan Ilych that it was of course as he pleased, but she had sent today for a celebrated specialist who would examine him and have a consultation with Michael Danilovich (their regular doctor).

'Please don't raise any objections. I am doing this for my own sake,' she said ironically, letting it be felt that she was doing it all for his sake and only said this to leave him no right to refuse. He remained silent, knitting his brows. He felt that he was so surrounded and involved in a mesh of falsity that it was hard to unravel anything.

Everything she did for him was entirely for her own sake, and she told him she was doing for herself what she actually was doing for herself, as if that was so incredible that he must understand the opposite.

At half-past eleven the celebrated specialist arrived. Again the sounding began and the significant conversations in his presence and in another room, about the kidneys and the appendix, and the questions and answers, with such an air of importance that again, instead of the real question of life and death which now alone confronted him, the question arose of the kidney and appendix which were not behaving as they ought to and would now be attacked by Michael Danilovich and the specialist and forced to amend their ways.

The celebrated specialist took leave of him with a serious though not hopeless look, and in reply to the timid question Ivan Ilych, with eyes glistening with fear and hope, put to him as to whether there was a chance of recovery, said that he could not vouch for it but there was a possibility. The look of hope with which Ivan Ilych watched the doctor out was so pathetic that Praskovya Fedorovna, seeing it, even wept as she left the room to hand the doctor his fee.

The gleam of hope kindled by the doctor's encouragement did not last long. The same room, the same pictures, curtains, wallpaper, medicine bottles, were all there, and the same aching suffering body, and Ivan Ilych began to moan. They gave him a subcutaneous injection and he sank into oblivion.

It was twilight when he came to. They brought him his dinner and he swallowed some beef tea with difficulty, and then everything was the same again and night was coming on.

After dinner, at seven o'clock, Praskovya Fedorovna came into the room in evening dress, her full bosom pushed up by her corset, and with traces of powder on her face. She had reminded him in the morning that they were going to the theatre. Sarah Bernhardt was visiting the town and they had a box, which he had insisted on their taking. Now he had forgotten about it and her toilet offended him, but he concealed his vexation when he remembered that he had himself insisted on their securing a box and going because it would be an instructive and aesthetic pleasure for the children.

Praskovya Fedorovna came in, self-satisfied but yet with a rather guilty air. She sat down and asked how he was but, as he saw, only for the sake of asking and not in order to learn about it, knowing that there was nothing to learn—and then went on to what she really wanted to say: that she would not on any account have gone but that the box had been taken and Helen and their daughter were going, as well as Petrishchev (the examining magistrate, their daughter's fiancé) and that it was out of the question to let them go alone; but that she would have much preferred to sit with him for a while; and he must be sure to follow the doctor's orders while she was away.

'Oh, and Fedor Petrovich' (the fiancé) 'would like to come in. May he? And Lisa?'

'All right.'

Their daughter came in in full evening dress, her fresh young flesh exposed (making a show of that very flesh which in his own case caused so much suffering), strong, healthy, evidently in love, and impatient with illness, suffering, and death, because they interfered with her happiness.

Fedor Petrovich came in too, in evening dress, his hair curled *à la Capoul*, a tight stiff collar round his long sinewy neck, an enormous white shirt-front and narrow black trousers tightly stretched over his strong thighs. He had one white glove tightly drawn on, and was holding his opera hat in his hand.

Following him the schoolboy crept in unnoticed, in a new uniform, poor little fellow, and wearing gloves. Terribly dark shadows showed under his eyes, the meaning of which Ivan Ilych knew well.

His son had always seemed pathetic to him, and now it was dreadful to see the boy's frightened look of pity. It seemed to Ivan Ilych that Vasya was the only one besides Gerasim who understood and pitied him.

They all sat down and again asked how he was. A silence followed. Lisa asked her mother about the opera-glasses, and there was an altercation between mother and daughter as to who had taken them and where they had been put. This occasioned some unpleasantness.

Fedor Petrovich inquired of Ivan Ilych whether he had ever seen Sarah Bernhardt. Ivan Ilych did not at first catch the question, but then replied: 'No, have you seen her before?'

'Yes, in *Adrienne Lecouvreur*.'

Praskovya Fedorovna mentioned some rôles in which Sarah Bernhardt was particularly good. Her daughter disagreed. Conversation sprang up as to the elegance and realism of her acting—the sort of conversation that is always repeated and is always the same.

In the midst of the conversation Fedor Petrovich glanced at Ivan Ilych and became silent. The others also looked at him and grew silent. Ivan Ilych was staring with glittering eyes straight before him, evidently indignant with them. This had to be rectified, but it was impossible to do so. The silence had to be broken, but for a time no one dared to break it and they all became afraid that the conventional deception would suddenly become obvious and the truth become plain to all. Lisa was the first to pluck up courage and break that silence, but by trying to hide what everybody was feeling, she betrayed it.

'Well, if we are going it's time to start,' she said, looking at her watch, a present from her father, and with a faint and significant smile at Fedor Petrovich relating to something known only to them. She got up with a rustle of her dress.

They all rose, said goodnight, and went away.

When they had gone it seemed to Ivan Ilych that he felt better; the falsity had gone with them. But the pain remained—that same pain and that same fear that made everything monotonously alike, nothing harder and nothing easier. Everything was worse.

Again minute followed minute and hour followed hour. Everything remained the same and there was no cessation. And the inevitable end of it all became more and more terrible.

'Yes, send Gerasim here,' he replied to a question Peter asked.

IX

HIS wife returned late at night. She came in on tiptoe, but he heard her, opened his eyes, and made haste to close them again. She wished to send Gerasim away and to sit with him herself, but he opened his eyes and said: 'No, go away.'

'Are you in great pain?'

'Always the same.'

'Take some opium.'

He agreed and took some. She went away.

Till about three in the morning he was in a state of stupefied misery. It seemed to him that he and his pain were being thrust into a narrow, deep black sack, but though they were pushed

further and further in they could not be pushed to the bottom.
And this, terrible enough in itself, was accompanied by suffering.
He was frightened yet wanted to fall through the sack, he
struggled but yet co-operated. And suddenly he broke through,
fell, and regained consciousness. Gerasim was sitting at the foot
of the bed dozing quietly and patiently, while he himself lay with
his emaciated stockinged legs resting on Gerasim's shoulders; the
same shaded candle was there and the same unceasing pain.

'Go away, Gerasim,' he whispered.

'It's all right, sir. I'll stay a while.'

'No. Go away.'

He removed his legs from Gerasim's shoulders, turned side-
ways onto his arm, and felt sorry for himself. He only waited
till Gerasim had gone into the next room and then restrained
himself no longer but wept like a child. He wept on account of
his helplessness, his terrible loneliness, the cruelty of man, the
cruelty of God, and the absence of God.

'Why hast Thou done all this? Why hast Thou brought me
here? Why, why dost Thou torment me so terribly?'

He did not expect an answer and yet wept because there was
no answer and could be none. The pain again grew more acute,
but he did not stir and did not call. He said to himself: 'Go on!
Strike me! But what is it for? What have I done to Thee? What
is it for?'

Then he grew quiet and not only ceased weeping but even held
his breath and became all attention. It was as though he were
listening not to an audible voice but to the voice of his soul, to
the current of thoughts arising within him.

'What is it you want?' was the first clear conception capable of
expression in words, that he heard.

'What do you want? What do you want?' he repeated to
himself.

'What do I want? To live and not to suffer,' he answered.

And again he listened with such concentrated attention that
even his pain did not distract him.

'To live? How?' asked his inner voice.

'Why, to live as I used to—well and pleasantly.'

'As you lived before, well and pleasantly?' the voice repeated.

And in imagination he began to recall the best moments
of his pleasant life. But strange to say none of those best

moments of his pleasant life now seemed at all what they had then seemed—none of them except the first recollections of childhood. There, in childhood, there had been something really pleasant with which it would be possible to live if it could return. But the child who had experienced that happiness existed no longer, it was like a reminiscence of somebody else.

As soon as the period began which had produced the present Ivan Ilych, all that had then seemed joys now melted before his sight and turned into something trivial and often nasty.

And the further he departed from childhood and the nearer he came to the present the more worthless and doubtful were the joys. This began with the School of Law. A little that was really good was still found there—there was light-heartedness, friendship, and hope. But in the upper classes there had already been fewer of such good moments. Then during the first years of his official career, when he was in the service of the Governor, some pleasant moments again occurred: they were the memories of love for a woman. Then all became confused and there was still less of what was good; later on again there was still less that was good, and the further he went the less there was. His marriage, a mere accident, then the disenchantment that followed it, his wife's bad breath and the sensuality and hypocrisy: then that deadly official life and those preoccupations about money, a year of it, and two, and ten, and twenty, and always the same thing. And the longer it lasted the more deadly it became. 'It is as if I had been going downhill while I imagined I was going up. And that is really what it was. I was going up in public opinion, but to the same extent life was ebbing away from me. And now it is all done and there is only death.'

'Then what does it mean? Why? It can't be that life is so senseless and horrible. But if it really has been so horrible and senseless, why must I die and die in agony? There is something wrong!'

'Maybe I did not live as I ought to have done,' it suddenly occurred to him. 'But how could that be, when I did everything properly?' he replied, and immediately dismissed from his mind this, the sole solution of all the riddles of life and death, as something quite impossible.

'Then what do you want now? To live? Live how? Live as you lived in the law courts when the usher proclaimed "The judge is coming!" The judge is coming, the judge!' he repeated to himself. 'Here he is, the judge. But I am not guilty!' he exclaimed angrily. 'What is it for?' And he ceased crying, but turning his face to the wall continued to ponder on the same questions: Why, and for what purpose, is there all this horror? But however much he pondered he found no answer. And whenever the thought occurred to him, as it often did, that it all resulted from his not having lived as he ought to have done, he at once recalled the correctness of his whole life and dismissed so strange an idea.

X

ANOTHER fortnight passed. Ivan Ilych now no longer left his sofa. He would not lie in bed but lay on the sofa, facing the wall nearly all the time. He suffered ever the same unceasing agonies and in his loneliness pondered always on the same insoluble question: 'What is this? Can it be that it is Death?' And the inner voice answered: 'Yes, it is Death.'

'Why these sufferings?' And the voice answered, 'For no reason—they just are so.' Beyond and besides this there was nothing.

From the very beginning of his illness, ever since he had first been to see the doctor, Ivan Ilych's life had been divided between two contrary and alternating moods: now it was despair and the expectation of this uncomprehended and terrible death, and now hope and an intently interested observation of the functioning of his organs. Now before his eyes there was only a kidney or an intestine that temporarily evaded its duty, and now only that incomprehensible and dreadful death from which it was impossible to escape.

These two states of mind had alternated from the very beginning of his illness, but the further it progressed the more doubtful and fantastic became the conception of the kidney, and the more real the sense of impending death.

He had but to call to mind what he had been three months before and what he was now, to call to mind with what regularity he had been going downhill, for every possibility of hope to be shattered.

Latterly during that loneliness in which he found himself as he lay facing the back of the sofa, a loneliness in the midst of a populous town and surrounded by numerous acquaintances and relations but that yet could not have been more complete anywhere—either at the bottom of the sea or under the earth— during that terrible loneliness Ivan Ilych had lived only in memories of the past. Pictures of his past rose before him one after another. They always began with what was nearest in time and then went back to what was most remote—to his childhood—and rested there. If he thought of the stewed prunes that had been offered him that day, his mind went back to the raw shrivelled French plums of his childhood, their peculiar flavour and the flow of saliva when he sucked their stones, and along with the memory of that taste came a whole series of memories of those days: his nurse, his brother, and their toys. 'No, I mustn't think of that. . . . It is too painful,' Ivan Ilych said to himself, and brought himself back to the present—to the button on the back of the sofa and the creases in its morocco. 'Morocco is expensive, but it does not wear well: there had been a quarrel about it. It was a different kind of quarrel and a different kind of morocco that time when we tore father's portfolio and were punished, and mamma brought us some tarts. . . .' And again his thoughts dwelt on his childhood, and again it was painful and he tried to banish them and fix his mind on something else.

Then again together with that chain of memories another series passed through his mind—of how his illness had pro- gressed and grown worse. There also the further back he looked the more life there had been. There had been more of what was good in life and more of life itself. The two merged together. 'Just as the pain went on getting worse and worse so my life grew worse and worse,' he thought. 'There is one bright spot there at the back, at the beginning of life, and afterwards all becomes blacker and blacker and proceeds more and more rapidly—in inverse ratio to the square of the distance from death,' thought Ivan Ilych. And the example of a stone falling downwards with increasing velocity entered his mind. Life, a series of increasing sufferings, flies further and further towards its end—the most terrible suffering. 'I am flying. . . .' He shuddered, shifted himself, and tried to resist, but was already aware that resistance was impossible, and again with eyes weary of gazing but unable to cease seeing what was before them, he stared at the back of the sofa and waited—awaiting that dreadful fall and shock and destruction.

'Resistance is impossible!' he said to himself. 'If I could only understand what it is all for! But that too is impossible. An explanation would be possible if it could be said that I have not lived as I ought to. But it is impossible to say that,' and he remembered all the legality, correctitude, and propriety of his life. 'That at any rate can certainly not be admitted,' he thought, and his lips smiled ironically as if someone could see that smile and be taken in by it. 'There is no explanation! Agony, death. . . . What for?'

XI

ANOTHER two weeks went by in this way and during that fortnight an event occurred that Ivan Ilych and his wife had desired. Petrishchev formally proposed. It happened in the evening. The next day Praskovya Fedorovna came into her husband's room considering how best to inform him of it, but that very night there had been a fresh change for the worse in his condition. She found him still lying on the sofa but in a different position. He lay on his back, groaning and staring fixedly straight in front of him.

She began to remind him of his medicines, but he turned his eyes towards her with such a look that she did not finish what she was saying; so great an animosity, to her in particular, did that look express.

'For Christ's sake let me die in peace!' he said.

She would have gone away, but just then their daughter came in and went up to say good morning. He looked at her as he had done at his wife, and in reply to her inquiry about his health said dryly that he would soon free them all of himself. They were both silent and after sitting with him for a while went away.

'Is it our fault?' Lisa said to her mother. 'It's as if we were to blame! I am sorry for papa, but why should we be tortured?'

The doctor came at his usual time. Ivan Ilych answered 'Yes' and 'No', never taking his angry eyes from him, and at last said: 'You know you can do nothing for me, so leave me alone.'

'We can ease your sufferings.'

'You can't even do that. Let me be.'

The doctor went into the drawing-room and told Praskovya Fedorovna that the case was very serious and that the only resource left was opium to allay her husband's sufferings, which must be terrible.

It was true, as the doctor said, that Ivan Ilych's physical sufferings were terrible, but worse than the physical sufferings were his mental sufferings which were his chief torture.

His mental sufferings were due to the fact that that night, as he looked at Gerasim's sleepy, goodnatured face with its prominent cheek-bones, the question suddenly occurred to him: 'What if my whole life has really been wrong?'

It occurred to him that what had appeared perfectly impossible before, namely that he had not spent his life as he should have done, might after all be true. It occurred to him that his scarcely perceptible attempts to struggle against what was considered good by the most highly placed people, those scarcely noticeable impulses which he had immediately suppressed, might have been the real thing, and all the rest false. And his professional duties and the whole arrangement of his life and of his family, and all his social and official interests, might all have been false. He tried to defend all those things to himself and suddenly felt the weakness of what he was defending. There was nothing to defend.

'But if that is so,' he said to himself, 'and I am leaving this life with the consciousness that I have lost all that was given me and it is impossible to rectify it—what then?'

He lay on his back and began to pass his life in review in quite a new way. In the morning when he saw first his footman, then his wife, then his daughter, and then the doctor, their every word and movement confirmed to him the awful truth that had been revealed to him during the night. In them he saw himself—all that for which he had lived—and saw clearly that it was not real at all, but a terrible and huge deception which had hidden both life and death. This consciousness intensified his physical suffering tenfold. He groaned and tossed about, and pulled at his clothing which choked and stifled him. And he hated them on that account.

He was given a large dose of opium and became unconscious, but at noon his sufferings began again. He drove everybody away and tossed from side to side.

His wife came to him and said:

'Jean, my dear, do this for me. It can't do any harm and often helps. Healthy people often do it.'

He opened his eyes wide.

'What? Take communion? Why? It's unnecessary! However. . . .'

She began to cry.

'Yes, do, my dear. I'll send for our priest. He is such a nice man.'

'All right. Very well,' he muttered.

When the priest came and heard his confession, Ivan Ilych was softened and seemed to feel a relief from his doubts and consequently from his sufferings, and for a moment there came a ray of hope. He again began to think of the vermiform appendix and the possibility of correcting it. He received the sacrament with tears in his eyes.

When they laid him down again afterwards he felt a moment's ease, and the hope that he might live awoke in him again. He began to think of the operation that had been suggested to him. 'To live! I want to live!' he said to himself.

His wife came in to congratulate him after his communion, and when uttering the usual conventional words she added:

'You feel better, don't you?'

Without looking at her he said 'Yes'.

Her dress, her figure, the expression of her face, the tone of her voice, all revealed the same thing. 'This is wrong, it is not as it should be. All you have lived for and still live for is falsehood and deception, hiding life and death from you.' And as soon as he admitted that thought, his hatred and his agonizing physical suffering again sprang up, and with that suffering a consciousness of the unavoidable, approaching end. And to this was added a new sensation of grinding shooting pain and a feeling of suffocation.

The expression of his face when he uttered that 'yes' was dreadful. Having uttered it, he looked her straight in the eyes, turned on his face with a rapidity extraordinary in his weak state and shouted:

'Go away! Go away and leave me alone!'

XII

FROM that moment the screaming began that continued for three days, and was so terrible that one could not hear it through two closed doors without horror. At the moment he answered his wife he realized that he was lost, that there was no return, that the end had come, the very end, and his doubts were still unsolved and remained doubts.

'Oh! Oh! Oh!' he cried in various intonations. He had begun by screaming 'I won't!' and continued screaming on the letter 'o'.

For three whole days, during which time did not exist for him, he struggled in that black sack into which he was being thrust by an invisible, resistless force. He struggled as a man condemned to death struggles in the hands of the executioner, knowing that he cannot save himself. And every moment he felt that despite all his efforts he was drawing nearer and nearer to what terrified him. He felt that his agony was due to his being thrust into that black hole and still more to his not being able to get right into it. He was hindered from getting into it by his conviction that his life had been a good one. That very justification of his life held him fast and prevented his moving forward, and it caused him most torment of all.

Suddenly some force struck him in the chest and side, making it still harder to breathe, and he fell through the hole and there at the bottom was a light. What had happened to him was like the sensation one sometimes experiences in a railway carriage when one thinks one is going backwards while one is really going forwards and suddenly becomes aware of the real direction.

'Yes, it was all not the right thing,' he said to himself, 'but that's no matter. It can be done. But what *is* the right thing?' he asked himself, and suddenly grew quiet.

This occurred at the end of the third day, two hours before his death. Just then his schoolboy son had crept softly in and gone up to the bedside. The dying man was still screaming desperately and waving his arms. His hand fell on the boy's head, and the boy caught it, pressed it to his lips, and began to cry.

At that very moment Ivan Ilych fell through and caught sight of the light, and it was revealed to him that though his life had not been what it should have been, this could still be rectified. He asked himself, 'What *is* the right thing?' and grew still, listening. Then he felt that someone was kissing his hand. He opened his eyes, looked at his son, and felt sorry for him. His wife came up to him and he glanced at her. She was gazing at him open-mouthed, with undried tears on her nose and cheek and a despairing look on her face. He felt sorry for her too.

'Yes, I am making them wretched,' he thought. 'They are sorry, but it will be better for them when I die.' He wished to say this but had not the strength to utter it. 'Besides, why speak? I must act,' he thought. With a look at his wife he indicated his son and said: 'Take him away . . . sorry for him . . . sorry for you too. . . .' He tried to add, 'forgive me', but said 'forgo' and waved his hand, knowing that He whose understanding mattered would understand.

And suddenly it grew clear to him that what had been oppressing him and would not leave him was all dropping away at once from two sides, from ten sides, and from all sides. He was sorry for them, he must act so as not to hurt them: release them and free himself from these sufferings. 'How good and how simple!' he thought. 'And the pain?' he asked himself. 'What has become of it? Where are you, pain?'

He turned his attention to it.

'Yes, here it is. Well, what of it? Let the pain be.'

'And death . . . where is it?'

He sought his former accustomed fear of death and did not find it. 'Where is it? What death?' There was no fear because there was no death.

In place of death there was light.

'So that's what it is!' he suddenly exclaimed aloud. 'What joy!'

To him all this happened in a single instant, and the meaning of that instant did not change. For those present his agony continued for another two hours. Something rattled in his throat, his emaciated body twitched, then the gasping and rattle became less and less frequent.

'It is finished!' said someone near him.

He heard these words and repeated them in his soul.

'Death is finished,' he said to himself. 'It is no more!'

He drew in a breath, stopped in the midst of a sigh, stretched out, and died.

Robert Louis Stevenson

THE STRANGE CASE OF DR JEKYLL
AND MR HYDE

1886

ROBERT LOUIS STEVENSON (1850–94) was born in Edinburgh, the son of an engineer who had special responsibility
for lighthouses. He entered Edinburgh University at the age of
seventeen, thinking first to become an engineer and then a lawyer,
but an early affection of the lungs made it difficult for him to be
well in what Tennyson calls

> The bitter east, the misty summer
> And grey metropolis of the North

and he began to take frequent journeys in search of health,
his able and restless pen describing the places and events he
passed through, so that at first he became known to the public
as a travel writer. A canoe trip through Belgium and France
furnished material for *An Inland Voyage*, 1878; a journey on foot,
materials for *Travels with a Donkey in the Cévennes* in 1879. In 1881
he published, in the magazine *Young Folles*, a serial story, *The Sea
Cook or Treasure Island*, which attracted a large following and was
an instant success when it was published in book form as *Treasure
Island* in 1883. Other romances followed, the best being *Kidnapped*
(1886), a stirring historical story which is also a shrewd study of the
Scottish character and the difference between the Highland and the
Lowland temperament.

Stevenson was an admirable craftsman of letters; everything he
did was first-rate of its kind, and classic English prose, at its
highest point of perfection, before the distorting and disintegrating
pressures of the twentieth century got to work on it, can be seen
in him. The least thing he wrote is always worth reading, and, to
anyone who would like to know how to write good English, worth
reading carefully.

His travels continued; he went to the west of America, by
immigrant ship and train, and found a wife there, a Mrs Osbourne,
whose son Lloyd collaborated with him in some successful books,
notably *The Wrong Box* (1889). *The Strange Case of Doctor Jekyll and
Mr Hyde*, a masterly fable so famous that it has added an expression
to the language, appeared in 1885. Stevenson's lungs now became
definitely tubercular, and he set out in 1888 for the South Seas,
buying property in Samoa, where his health briefly returned before
his sudden death from a brain tumour in 1894.

STORY OF THE DOOR

MR. UTTERSON the lawyer was a man of a rugged countenance, that was never lighted by a smile; cold, scanty and
embarrassed in discourse; backward in sentiment; lean, long,
dusty, dreary, and yet somehow lovable. At friendly meetings,
and when the wine was to his taste, something eminently human
beaconed from his eye; something indeed which never found its
way into his talk, but which spoke not only in these silent symbols
of the after-dinner face, but more often and loudly in the acts of his
life. He was austere with himself; drank gin when he was alone,
to mortify a taste for vintages; and though he enjoyed the theatre,
had not crossed the doors of one for twenty years. But he had an
approved tolerance for others; sometimes wondering almost with
envy, at the high pressure of spirits involved in their misdeeds; and
in any extremity inclined to help rather than to reprove. 'I incline
to Cain's heresy,' he used to say quaintly: 'I let my brother go to
the devil in his own way.' In this character, it was frequently his
fortune to be the last reputable acquaintance and the last good
influence in the lives of down-going men. And to such as these, so
long as they came about his chambers, he never marked a shade
of change in his demeanour.

No doubt the feat was easy to Mr. Utterson; for he was
undemonstrative at the best, and even his friendships seemed
to be founded in a similar catholicity of good-nature. It is the
mark of a modest man to accept his friendly circle ready-made
from the hands of opportunity; and that was the lawyer's way.
His friends were those of his own blood, or those whom he had
known the longest; his affections, like ivy, were the growth of time,
they implied no aptness in the object. Hence, no doubt, the bond
that united him to Mr. Richard Enfield, his distant kinsman, the
well-known man about town. It was a nut to crack for many, what
these two could see in each other or what subject they could find
in common. It was reported by those who encountered them in
their Sunday walks that they said nothing, looked singularly dull,
and would hail with obvious relief the appearance of a friend. For
all that, the two men put the greatest store by these excursions,

counted them the chief jewel of each week, and not only set aside occasions of pleasure, but even resisted the calls of business, that they might enjoy them uninterrupted.

It chanced on one of these rambles that their way led them down a by-street in a busy quarter of London. The street was small, and what is called quiet, but it drove a thriving trade on the week-days. The inhabitants were all doing well, it seemed, and all emulously hoping to do better still, and laying out the surplus of their gains in coquetry; so that the shop-fronts stood along that thoroughfare with an air of invitation, like rows of smiling saleswomen. Even on Sunday, when it veiled its more florid charms and lay comparatively empty of passage, the street shone out in contrast to its dingy neighbourhood, like a fire in a forest; and with its freshly painted shutters, well-polished brasses, and general cleanliness and gaiety of note, instantly caught and pleased the eye of the passenger.

Two doors from one corner on the left hand going east, the line was broken by the entry of a court; and just at that point a certain sinister block of building thrust forward its gable on the street. It was two stories high; showed no window, nothing but a door on the lower story and a blind forehead of discoloured wall on the upper; and bore in every feature the marks of prolonged and sordid negligence. The door, which was equipped with neither bell nor knocker, was blistered and distained. Tramps slouched into the recess and struck matches on the panels; children kept shop upon the steps; the schoolboy had tried his knife on the moulding; and for close on a generation no one had appeared to drive away these random visitors or to repair their ravages.

Mr. Enfield and the lawyer were on the other side of the by-street, but when they came abreast of the entry, the former lifted up his cane and pointed.

'Did you ever remark that door?' he asked; and when his companion had replied in the affirmative, 'it is connected in my mind,' added he, 'with a very odd story.'

'Indeed?' said Mr. Utterson, with a slight change of voice, 'and what was that?'

'Well, it was this way,' returned Mr. Enfield: 'I was coming home from some place at the end of the world, about three o'clock of a black winter morning, and my way lay through a part of town where there was literally nothing to be seen but lamps. Street after street, and all the folks asleep—street after street, all lighted up as if for a procession and all as empty as a church—till at last I got into that state of mind when a man listens and listens and begins to long for the sight of a policeman. All at once I saw two figures: one a little man who was stumping along eastward at a good walk, and the other a girl of maybe eight or ten, who was running as hard as she was able down a cross street. Well, sir, the two ran into one another naturally enough at the corner; and then came the horrible part of the thing; for the man trampled calmly over the child's body and left her screaming on the ground. It sounds nothing to hear, but it was hellish to see. It wasn't like a man; it was like some damned Juggernaut. I gave a view-holloa, took to my heels, collared my gentleman, and brought him back to where there was already quite a group about the screaming child. He was perfectly cool, and made no resistance, but gave me one look, so ugly that it brought out the sweat on me like running. The people who had turned out were the girl's own family; and pretty soon, the doctor, for whom she had been sent, put in his appearance. Well, the child was not much the worse, more frightened, according to the Sawbones; and there you might have supposed would be an end to it. But there was one curious circumstance. I had taken a loathing to my gentleman at first sight. So had the child's family, which was only natural. But the doctor's case was what struck me. He was the usual cut-and-dry apothecary, of no particular age and colour, with a strong Edinburgh accent, and about as emotional as a bagpipe. Well, sir, he was like the rest of us; every time he looked at my prisoner, I saw that Sawbones turn sick and white with the desire to kill him. I knew what was in his mind, just as he knew what was in mine; and killing being out of the question, we did the next best. We told the man we could and would make such a scandal out of this as should make his name stink from one end of London to the other. If he had any friends or any credit, we undertook that he should lose them. And all the time, as we were pitching it in red-hot, we were keeping the women off him as best we could, for they were as wild as harpies. I never saw a circle of such hateful faces; and there was the man in the middle, with a kind of black, sneering coolness—frightened, too, I could see that—but carrying it off, sir, really like Satan. "If you choose to make capital out of this accident," said he, "I am naturally helpless. No gentleman but wishes to avoid a scene," says he. "Name your figure." Well, we screwed him up to a hundred pounds for the child's family; he would have clearly liked to stick out; but there was something about the lot of us that meant mischief, and at last he struck. The next thing was to get the money; and where do you think he carried us but to that place with the door?—whipped out a key, went in, and presently came back with the matter of ten pounds in gold and a cheque for the balance on Coutts's, drawn payable to bearer and signed with a name that I can't mention, though it's one of the points of my story, but it was a name at least very well known and often printed. The figure was stiff; but the signature was good for more than that, if it was only genuine. I took the liberty of pointing out to my gentleman that the whole business looked apocryphal, and that a man does not, in real life, walk into a cellar-door at four in the morning and come out of it with another man's cheque for close upon a hundred pounds. But he was quite easy and sneering. "Set your mind at rest," says he, "I will stay with you till the banks open and cash the cheque myself." So we all set off, the doctor, and the child's father, and our friend and myself, and passed the rest of the night in my chambers; and next day, when we had breakfasted, went in a body to the bank. I gave in the cheque myself, and said I had every reason to believe it was a forgery. Not a bit of it. The cheque was genuine.'

'Tut-tut,' said Mr. Utterson.

'I see you feel as I do,' said Mr. Enfield. 'Yes, it's a bad story. For my man was a fellow that nobody could have to do with, a really damnable man; and the person that drew the cheque is the very pink of the proprieties, celebrated too, and (what makes it worse) one of your fellows who do what they call good. Blackmail, I suppose; an honest man paying through the nose for some of the capers of his youth. Black Mail House is what I call that place with the door, in consequence. Though even that, you know, is far from explaining all,' he added, and with the words fell into a vein of musing.

From this he was recalled by Mr. Utterson asking rather suddenly: 'And you don't know if the drawer of the cheque lives there?'

'A likely place, isn't it?' returned Mr. Enfield. 'But I happened to have noticed his address; he lives in some square or other.'

'And you never asked about—the place with the door?' said Mr. Utterson.

'No, sir: I had a delicacy,' was the reply. 'I feel very strongly about putting questions; it partakes too much of the style of the day of judgment. You start a question, and it's like starting a stone. You sit quietly on the top of a hill; and away the stone goes, starting others; and presently some bland old bird (the last you would have thought of) is knocked on the head in his own back-garden and the family have to change their name. No, sir, I make it a rule of mine: the more it looks like Queer Street, the less I ask.'

'A very good rule too,' said the lawyer.

'But I have studied the place for myself,' continued Mr. Enfield. 'It seems scarcely a house. There is no other door, and nobody goes in or out of that one but, once in a great while, the gentleman of my adventure. There are three windows looking on the court on the first floor; none below; the windows are always shut, but they're clean. And then there is a chimney which is generally smoking; so somebody must live there. And yet it's not so sure; for the buildings are so packed together about that court that it's hard to say where one ends and another begins.'

The pair walked on again for a while in silence; and then, 'Enfield,' said Mr. Utterson, 'that's a good rule of yours.'

'Yes, I think it is,' returned Enfield.

'But for all that,' continued the lawyer, 'there's one point I want to ask: I want to ask the name of that man who walked over the child.'

'Well,' said Mr. Enfield, 'I can't see what harm it would do. He was a man of the name of Hyde.'

'H'm,' said Mr. Utterson. 'What sort of a man is he to see?'

'He is not easy to describe. There is something wrong with his appearance; something displeasing, something downright detestable. I never saw a man I so disliked, and yet I scarce know why. He must be deformed somewhere; he gives a strong feeling of deformity, although I couldn't specify the point. He's an extraordinary-looking man, and yet I really can name nothing out of the way. No, sir; I can make no hand of it; I can't describe him. And it's not want of memory; for I declare I can see him this moment.'

Mr. Utterson again walked some way in silence and obviously

under a weight of consideration. 'You are sure he used a key?' he inquired at last.

'My dear sir——' began Enfield, surprised out of himself.

'Yes, I know,' said Utterson; 'I know it must seem strange. The fact is, if I do not ask you the name of the other party it is because I know it already. You see, Richard, your tale has gone home. If you have been inexact in any point, you had better correct it.'

'I think you might have warned me,' returned the other with a touch of sullenness. 'But I have been pedantically exact, as you call it. The fellow had a key; and what's more, he has it still. I saw him use it not a week ago.'

Mr. Utterson sighed deeply but said never a word; and the young man presently resumed. 'Here is another lesson to say nothing,' said her. 'I am ashamed of my long tongue. Let us make a bargain never to refer to this again.'

'With all my heart,' said the lawyer. 'I shake hands on that, Richard.'

SEARCH FOR MR. HYDE

THAT evening Mr. Utterson came home to his bachelor house in sombre spirits and sat down to dinner without relish. It was his custom of a Sunday, when this meal was over, to sit close by the fire, a volume of some dry divinity on his reading-desk, until the clock of the neighbouring church rang out the hour of twelve, when he would go soberly and gratefully to bed. On this night, however, as soon as the cloth was taken away, he took up a candle and went into his business-room. There he opened his safe, took from the most private part of it a document endorsed on the envelope as Dr. Jekyll's Will, and sat down with a clouded brow to study its contents. The will was holograph, from Mr. Utterson, though he took charge of it now that it was made, had refused to lend the least assistance in the making of it; it provided not only that, in case of the decease of Henry Jekyll, M.D., D.C.L., LL.D., F.R.S., &c., all his possessions were to pass into the hands of his 'friend and benefactor Edward Hyde,' but that in case of Dr. Jekyll's 'disappearance or unexplained absence for any period exceeding three calendar months,' the said Edward Hyde should step into the said Henry Jekyll's shoes without further delay and free from any burthen or obligation, beyond the payment of a few small sums to the members of the doctor's household. This document had long been the lawyer's eyesore. It offended him both as a lawyer and as a lover of the sane and customary sides of life, to whom the fanciful was the immodest. And hitherto it was his ignorance of Mr. Hyde that had swelled his indignation; now, by a sudden turn, it was his knowledge. It was already bad enough when the name was but a name of which he could learn no more. It was worse when it began to be clothed upon with detestable attributes; and out of the shifting, insubstantial mists that had so long baffled his eye, there leaped up the sudden, definite presentment of a fiend.

'I thought it was madness,' he said, as he replaced the obnoxious paper in the safe, 'and now I begin to fear it is disgrace.'

With that he blew out his candle, put on a greatcoat, and set forth in the direction of Cavendish Square, that citadel of medicine, where his friend, the great Dr. Lanyon, had his house and received his crowding patients. 'If any one knows, it will be Lanyon,' he had thought.

The solemn butler knew and welcomed him; he was subjected to no stage of delay, but ushered direct from the door to the dining-room, where Dr. Lanyon sat alone over his wine. This was a hearty, healthy, dapper, red-faced gentleman, with a shock of hair prematurely white, and a boisterous and decided manner. At sight of Mr. Utterson, he sprang up from his chair and welcomed him with both hands. The geniality, as was the way of the man, was somewhat theatrical to the eye; but it reposed on genuine feeling. For these two were old friends, old mates both at school and college, both thorough respecters of themselves and of each other, and, what does not always follow, men who thoroughly enjoyed each other's company.

After a little rambling talk, the lawyer led up to the subject which so disagreeably preoccupied his mind.

'I suppose, Lanyon,' said her, 'you and I must be the two oldest friends that Henry Jekyll has?'

'I wish the friends were younger,' chuckled Dr. Lanyon. 'But I suppose we are. And what of that? I see little of him now.'

'Indeed?' said Utterson. 'I thought you had a bond of common interest.'

'We had,' was the reply. 'But it is more than ten years since Henry Jekyll became too fanciful for me. He began to go wrong, wrong in mind; and though of course I continue to take an interest in him for old sake's sake, as they say, I see and I have seen devilish little of the man. Such unscientific balderdash,' added the doctor, flushing suddenly purple, 'would have estranged Damon and Pythias.'

This little spirt of temper was somewhat of a relief to Mr. Utterson. 'They have only differed on some point of science,' he thought; and being a man of no scientific passions (except in the matter of conveyancing) he even added: 'It is nothing worse than that!' He gave his friend a few seconds to recover his composure, and then approached the question he had come to put. 'Did you ever come across a protégé of his—one Hyde?' he asked.

'Hyde,' repeated Lanyon. 'No. Never heard of him. Since my time.'

That was the amount of information that the lawyer carried back with him to the great, dark bed on which he tossed to and fro, until the small hours of the morning began to grow large. It was a night of little ease to his toiling mind, toiling in mere darkness and besieged by questions.

Six o'clock struck on the bells of the church that was so conveniently near to Mr. Utterson's dwelling, and still he was digging at the problem. Hitherto it had touched him on the intellectual side alone; but now his imagination also was engaged, or rather enslaved; and as he lay and tossed in the gross darkness of the night and the curtained room, Mr. Enfield's tale went by before his mind in a scroll of lighted pictures. He would be aware of the great field of lamps of a nocturnal city; then of the figure of a man walking swiftly; then of a child running from the doctor's; and then these met, and that human Juggernaut trod the child down and passed on regardless of her screams. Or else he would see a room in a rich house, where his friend lay asleep, dreaming and smiling at his dreams; and then the door of that room would be opened, the curtains of the bed plucked apart, the sleeper recalled, and lo! there would stand by his side a figure to whom power was given, and even at that dead hour he must rise and do its bidding. The figure in these two phases haunted the lawyer all night; and if any time he dozed over, it was but to see it glide more stealthily through sleeping houses, or move the more swiftly and still the more swiftly, even to dizziness, through wider labyrinths of lamplighted city, and at every street-corner crush a child and leave her screaming. And still the figure had no face by which he might know it; even in his dreams, it had no face, or one that baffled him and melted before his eyes; and thus it was that there sprang up and grew apace in the lawyer's mind a singularly strong, almost an inordinate, curiosity to behold the features of the real Mr. Hyde. If he could but once set eyes on him, he thought the mystery would lighten and perhaps roll altogether away, as was the habit of mysterious things when well examined. He might see a reason for his friend's strange preference or bondage (call it which you please) and even for the startling clauses of the will. And at least it would be a face worth seeing: the face of a man who was without bowels of mercy: a face which had but to show itself to raise up, in the mind of the unimpressionable Enfield, a spirit of enduring hatred.

From that time forward, Mr. Utterson began to haunt the door in the by-street of shops. In the morning before office hours, at noon when business was plenty and time scarce, at night under the face of the fogged city moon, by all lights and at all hours of solitude or concourse, the lawyer was to be found on his chosen post.

'If he be Mr. Hyde,' he had thought, 'I shall be Mr. Seek.'

And at last his patience was rewarded. It was a fine dry night; frost in the air; the streets as clean as a ballroom floor; the lamps, unshaken by any wind, drawing a regular pattern of light and shadow. By ten o'clock, when the shops were closed, the by-street was very solitary and, in spite of the low growl of London from all round, very silent. Small sounds carried far; domestic sounds out of the houses were clearly audible on either side of the roadway; and the rumour of the approach of any passenger preceded him by a long time. Mr. Utterson had been some minutes at his post, when he was aware of an odd, light footstep drawing near. In the course of his nightly patrols he had long grown accustomed to the quaint effect with which the footfalls of a single person, while he is still a great way off, suddenly spring out distinct from the vast hum and clatter of the city. Yet his attention had never before been so sharply and decisively arrested; and it was with a strong, superstitious prevision of success that he withdrew into the entry of the court.

The steps drew swiftly nearer, and swelled out suddenly louder as they turned the end of the street. The lawyer, looking forth from the entry, could soon see what manner of man he had to deal with. He was small and very plainly dressed, and the look of him, even at that distance, went somehow strongly against the watcher's inclination. But he made straight for the door, crossing the roadway to save time; and as he came, he drew a key from his pocket like one approaching home.

Mr. Utterson stepped out and touched him on the shoulder as he passed. 'Mr. Hyde, I think?'

Mr. Hyde shrank back with a hissing intake of the breath. But his fear was only momentary; and though he did not look the lawyer in the face, he answered coolly enough: 'That is my name. What do you want?'

'I see you are going in,' returned the lawyer. 'I am an old friend of Dr. Jekyll's—Mr. Utterson of Gaunt Street—you must have heard my name; and meeting you so conveniently, I thought you might admit me.'

'You will not find Dr. Jekyll; he is from home,' replied Mr. Hyde, blowing in the key. And then suddenly, but still without looking up, 'How did you know me?' he asked.

'On your side,' said Mr. Utterson, 'will you do me a favour?'

'With pleasure,' replied the other. 'What shall it be?'

'Will you let me see your face?' asked the lawyer.

Mr. Hyde appeared to hesitate, and then, as if upon some sudden reflection, fronted about with an air of defiance; and the pair stared at each other pretty fixedly for a few seconds. 'Now I shall know you again,' said Mr. Utterson. 'It may be useful.'

'Yes,' returned Mr. Hyde, 'it is as well we have met; and *à propos*, you should have my address.' And he gave a number of a street in Soho.

'Good God!' thought Mr. Utterson, 'can he too have been thinking of the will?' But he kept his feelings to himself and only grunted in acknowledgement of the address.

'And now,' said the other, 'how did you know me?'

'By description,' was the reply.

'Whose description?'

'We have common friends,' said Mr. Utterson.

'Common friends?' echoed Mr. Hyde, a little hoarsely. 'Who are they?'

'Jekyll, for instance,' said the lawyer.

'He never told you,' cried Hyde, with a flush of anger. 'I did not think you would have lied.'

'Come,' said Mr. Utterson, 'that is not fitting language.'

The other snarled aloud into a savage laugh; and the next moment, with extraordinary quickness, he had unlocked the door and disappeared into the house.

The lawyer stood awhile when Mr. Hyde had left him, the picture of disquietude. Then he began slowly to mount the street, pausing every step or two and putting his hand to his brow like a man in mental perplexity. The problem he was thus debating as he walked was one of a class that is rarely solved. Mr. Hyde was pale and dwarfish. He gave an impression of deformity without any nameable malformation, he had a displeasing smile, he had borne himself to the lawyer with a sort of murderous mixture of timidity and boldness, and he spoke with a husky, whispering and somewhat broken voice; all these were points against him, but not all of these together could explain the hitherto unknown disgust, loathing, and fear with which Mr. Utterson regarded him. 'There must be something else,' said the perplexed gentleman. 'There *is* something more, if I could find a name for it. God bless me, the man seems hardly human! Something troglodytic, shall we say? or can it be the old story of Dr. Fell? or is it the mere radiance of a foul soul that thus transpires through, and transfigures, its clay continent? The last, I think; for O my poor old Harry Jekyll, if ever I read Satan's signature upon a face, it is on that of your new friend.'

Round the corner from the by-street there was a square of ancient, handsome houses, now for the most part decayed from their high estate and let in flats and chambers to all sorts and conditions of men: map-engravers, architects, shady lawyers, and the agents of obscure enterprises. One house, however, second from the corner, was still occupied entire; and at the door of this, which wore a great air of wealth and comfort, though it was now plunged in darkness except for the fan-light, Mr. Utterson stopped and knocked. A well-dressed elderly servant opened the door.

'Is Dr. Jekyll at home, Poole?' asked the lawyer.

'I will see, Mr. Utterson,' said Poole, admitting the visitor, as he spoke, into a large, low-roofed, comfortable hall, paved with flags, warmed (after the fashion of a country house) by a bright, open fire, and furnished with costly cabinets of oak. 'Will you wait here by the fire, sir? or shall I give you a light in the dining-room?'

'Here, thank you,' said the lawyer, and he drew near and leaned on the tall fender. This hall, in which he was now left alone, was a pet fancy of his friend the doctor's; and Utterson himself was wont to speak of it as the pleasantest room in London. But to-night there was a shudder in his blood; the face of Hyde sat heavy on his memory; he felt (what was rare with him) a nausea and distaste of life; and in the gloom of his spirits, he seemed to read a menace in the flickering of the firelight on the polished cabinets and the uneasy starting of the shadow on the roof. He was ashamed of his relief, when Poole presently returned to announce that Dr. Jekyll was gone out.

'I saw Mr. Hyde go in by the old dissecting-room door, Poole,' he said. 'Is that right, when Dr. Jekyll is from home?'

'Quite right, Mr. Utterson, sir,' replied the servant. 'Mr. Hyde has a key.'

'Your master seems to repose a great deal of trust in that young man, Poole,' resumed the other musingly.

'Yes, sir, he do indeed,' said Poole. 'We have all orders to obey him.'

'I do not think I ever met Mr. Hyde?' asked Utterson.

'O dear no, sir. He never *dines* here,' replied the butler. 'Indeed, we see very little of him on this side of the house; he mostly comes and goes by the laboratory.'

'Well, good-night, Poole.'

'Good-night, Mr. Utterson.'

And the lawyer set out homeward with a very heavy heart. 'Poor Harry Jekyll,' he thought, 'my mind misgives me he is in deep waters! He was wild when he was young; a long while ago, to be sure; but in the law of God there is no statute of limitations. Ay, it must be that; the ghost of some old sin, the cancer of some concealed disgrace: punishment coming, *pede claudo,* years after memory has forgotten and self-love condoned the fault.' And the lawyer, scared by the thought, brooded awhile on his own past, groping in all the corners of memory, lest by chance some Jack-in-the-Box of an old iniquity should leap to light there. His past was fairly blameless; few men could read the rolls of their life with less apprehension; yet he was humbled to the dust by the many ill things he had done, and raised up again into a sober and fearful gratitude by the many that he had come so near to doing, yet avoided. And then, by a return on his former subject, he conceived a spark of hope. 'This Master Hyde, if he were studied,' thought he, 'must have secrets of his own: black secrets, by the look of him; secrets compared to which poor Jekyll's worst would be like sunshine. Things cannot continue as they are. It turns me cold to think of this creature stealing like a thief to Harry's bedside; poor Harry, what a wakening! And the danger of it; for if this Hyde suspects the existence of the will, he may grow impatient to inherit. Ay, I must put my shoulder to the wheel—if Jekyll will but let me,' he added, 'if Jekyll will only let me.' For once more he saw before his mind's eye, as clear as a transparency, the strange clauses of the will.

DR. JEKYLL WAS QUITE AT EASE

A FORTNIGHT later, by excellent good fortune, the doctor gave one of his pleasant dinners to some five or six old cronies, all intelligent, reputable men, and all judges of good wine; and Mr. Utterson so contrived that he remained behind after the others had departed. This was no new arrangement, but a thing that had befallen many scores of times. Where Utterson was liked, he was liked well. Hosts loved to detain the dry lawyer, when the light-hearted and the loose-tongued had already their foot on the threshold; they liked to sit awhile in his unobtrusive company, practising for solitude, sobering their minds in the man's rich silence after the expense and strain of gaiety. To this rule Dr. Jekyll was no exception; and as he now sat on the opposite side of the fire—a large, well-made, smooth-faced man of fifty, with something of a slyish cast perhaps, but every mark of capacity and kindness—you could see by his looks that he cherished for Mr. Utterson a sincere and warm affection.

'I have been wanting to speak to you, Jekyll,' began the latter. 'You know that will of yours?'

A close observer might have gathered that the topic was distasteful; but the doctor carried it off gaily. 'My poor Utterson,' said he, 'your are unfortunate in such a client. I never saw a man so distressed as you were by my will; unless it were that hidebound pedant, Lanyon, at what he called my scientific heresies. Oh, I know he's a good fellow—you needn't frown—an excellent fellow, and I always mean to see more of him; but a hidebound pedant for all that; an ignorant, blatant pedant. I was never more disappointed in any man than Lanyon.'

'You know I never approved of it,' pursued Utterson, ruthlessly disregarding the fresh topic.

'My will? Yes, certainly, I know that,' said the doctor, a trifle sharply. 'You have told me so.'

'Well, I tell you so again,' continued the lawyer. 'I have been learning something of young Hyde.'

The large handsome face of Dr. Jekyll grew pale to the very lips, and there came a blackness about his eyes. 'I do not care to hear more,' said he. 'This is a matter I thought we had agreed to drop.'

'What I heard was abominable,' said Utterson.

'It can make no change. You do not understand my position,' returned the doctor, with a certain incoherency of manner. 'I am painfully situated, Utterson; my position is a very strange—a very strange one. It is one of those affairs that cannot be mended by talking.'

'Jekyll,' said Utterson, 'you know me: I am a man to be trusted. Make a clean breast of this in confidence; and I make no doubt I can get you out of it.'

'My good Utterson,' said the doctor, 'this is very good of you, this is downright good of you, and I cannot find words to thank you in. I believe you fully; I would trust you before any man alive—ay, before myself, if I could make the choice; but indeed it isn't what you fancy; it is not so bad as that; and just to put your good heart at rest, I will tell you one thing: the moment I choose, I can be rid of Mr. Hyde. I give you my hand upon that; and I thank you again and again; and I will just add one little word, Utterson, that I'm sure you'll take in good part: this is a private matter, and I beg of you to let it sleep.'

Utterson reflected a little, looking in the fire.

'I have no doubt you are perfectly right,' he said at last, getting to his feet.

'Well, but since we have touched upon this business, and for the last time I hope,' continued the doctor, 'there is one point I should like you to understand. I have really a very great interest in poor Hyde. I know you have seen him; he told me so; and I fear he was rude. But I do sincerely take a great, a very great interest in that young man; and if I am taken away, Utterson, I wish you to promise me that you will bear with him and get his rights for him. I think you would, if you knew all; and it would be a weight off my mind if you would promise.'

'I can't pretend that I shall ever like him,' said the lawyer.

'I don't ask that,' pleaded Jekyll, laying his hand upon the other's arm; 'I only ask for justice; I only ask you to help him for my sake, when I am no longer here.'

Utterson heaved an irrepressible sigh. 'Well,' said he, 'I promise.'

THE CAREW MURDER CASE

NEARLY a year later, in the month of October 18—, London was startled by a crime of singular ferocity, rendered all the more notable by the high position of the victim. The details were few and startling. A maid-servant living alone in a house not far from the river had gone upstairs to bed about eleven. Although a fog rolled over the city in the small hours, the early part of the night was cloudless, and the lane, which the maid's window overlooked, was brilliantly lit by the full moon. It seems she was romantically given, for she sat down upon her box, which stood immediately under the window, and fell into a dream of musing. Never (she used to say, with streaming tears, when she narrated that experience), never had she felt more at peace with all men or thought more kindly of the world. And as she so sat she became aware of an aged and beautiful gentleman with white hair drawing near along the lane: and advancing to meet him another and very small gentleman, to whom at first she paid less attention. When they had come within speech (which was just under the maid's eyes) the older man bowed and accosted the other with a very pretty manner of politeness. It did not seem as if the subject of his address were of great importance; indeed, from his pointing, it sometimes appeared as if he were only inquiring his way; but the moon shone on his face as he spoke, and the girl was pleased to watch it, it seemed to breathe such an innocent and old-world kindness of disposition, yet with something high too, as of a well-founded self-content. Presently her eye wandered to the other, and she was surprised to recognise in him a certain Mr. Hyde, who had once visited her master, and for whom she had conceived a dislike. He had in his hand a heavy cane, with which he was trifling; but he answered never a word, and seemed to listen with an ill-contained impatience. And then all of a sudden he broke out in a great flame of anger, stamping with his foot, brandishing the cane, and carrying on (as the maid described it) like a madman. The old gentleman took a step back, with the air of one very much surprised and a trifle hurt; and at that Mr. Hyde broke out of all bounds and clubbed him to the earth. And next moment, with ape-like fury, he was trampling his victim under foot, and hailing down a storm of blows, under which the bones were audibly shattered and the body jumped upon the roadway. At the horror of these sights and sounds the maid fainted.

It was two o'clock when she came to herself and called for the police. The murderer was gone long ago; but there lay his victim in the middle of the lane, incredibly mangled. The stick with which the deed had been done, although it was of some rare and very tough and heavy wood, had broken in the middle under the stress of this insensate cruelty; and one splintered half had rolled in the neighbouring gutter—the other, without doubt, had been carried away by the murderer. A purse and a gold watch were found upon the victim; but no cards or papers, except a sealed and stamped envelope, which he had been probably carrying to the post, and which bore the name and address of Mr. Utterson.

This was brought to the lawyer the next morning before he was out of bed; and he had no sooner seen it, and been told the circumstances, than he shot out a solemn lip. 'I shall say nothing till I have seen the body,' said he; 'this may be very serious. Have the kindness to wait while I dress.' And with the same grave countenance he hurried through his breakfast and drove to the police station, whither the body had been carried. As soon as he came into the cell he nodded.

'Yes,' said he, 'I recognise him. I am sorry to say that this is Sir Danvers Carew.'

'Good God, sir,' exclaimed the officer, 'is it possible?' And the next moment his eye lighted up with professional ambition. 'This will make a deal of noise,' he said. 'And perhaps you can help us to the man.' And he briefly narrated what the maid had seen, and showed the broken stick.

Mr. Utterson had already quailed at the name of Hyde; but when the stick was laid before him he could doubt no longer; broken and battered as it was, he recognised it for one that he had himself presented many years before to Henry Jekyll.

'Is this Mr. Hyde a person of small stature?' he inquired.

'Particularly small and particularly wicked-looking, is what the maid calls him,' said the officer.

Mr. Utterson reflected; and then, raising his head, 'If you will come with me in my cab,' he said, 'I think I can take you to his house.'

It was by this time about nine in the morning, and the first fog of the season. A great chocolate-coloured pall lowered over heaven, but the wind was continually charging and routing these embattled vapours; so that as the cab crawled from street to street, Mr. Utterson beheld a marvellous number of degrees and hues of twilight; for here it would be dark like the back-end of evening; and there would be a glow of a rich, lurid brown, like the light of some strange conflagration; and here, for a moment, the fog would be quite broken up, and a haggard shaft of daylight would glance in between the swirling wreaths. The dismal quarter of Soho seen under these changing glimpses, with its muddy ways, and slatternly passengers, and its lamps, which had never been extinguished or had been kindled afresh to combat this mournful re-invasion of darkness, seemed, in the lawyer's eyes, like a district of some city in a nightmare.

The thoughts of his mind, besides, were of the gloomiest dye; and when he glanced at the companion of his drive, he was conscious of some touch of that terror of the law and the law's officers which may at times assail the most honest.

As the cab drew up before the address indicated, the fog lifted a little, and showed him a dingy street, a gin-palace, a low French eating-house, a shop for the retail of penny numbers and twopenny salads, many ragged children huddled in the doorways, and many women of many different nationalities passing out, key in hand, to have a morning glass; and the next moment the fog settled down again upon that part, as brown as umber, and cut him off from his blackguardly surroundings. This was the home of Henry Jekyll's favourite; of a man who was heir to a quarter of a million sterling.

An ivory-faced and silvery-haired old woman opened the door. She had an evil face, smoothed by hypocrisy; but her manners were excellent. Yes, she said, this was Mr. Hyde's, but he was not at home; he had been in that night very late, but had gone away again in less than an hour; there was nothing strange in that; his habits were very irregular, and he was often absent; for instance, it was nearly two months since she had seen him till yesterday.

'Very well then, we wish to see his rooms,' said the lawyer; and when the woman began to declare it was impossible, 'I had better tell you who this person is,' he added. 'This is Inspector Newcomen of Scotland Yard.'

A flash of odious joy appeared upon the woman's face. 'Ah!' said she, 'he is in trouble! What has he done?'

Mr. Utterson and the inspector exchanged glances. 'He don't seem a very popular character,' observed the latter. 'And now, my good woman, just let me and this gentleman have a look about us.'

In the whole extent of the house, which but for the old woman remained otherwise empty, Mr. Hyde had only used a couple of rooms; but these were furnished with luxury and good taste. A closet was filled with wine; the plate was of silver, the napery elegant; a good picture hung upon the walls, a gift (as Utterson supposed) from Henry Jekyll, who was much of a connoisseur; and the carpets were of many plies and agreeable in colour. At this moment, however, the rooms bore every mark of having been recently and hurriedly ransacked; clothes lay about the floor, with their pockets inside out; lockfast drawers stood open; and on the hearth there lay a pile of grey ashes, as though many papers had been burned. From these embers the inspector disinterred the butt-end of a green cheque-book, which had resisted the action of the fire; the other half of the stick was found behind the door; and as this clinched his suspicions, the officer declared himself delighted. A visit to the bank, where several thousand pounds were found to be lying to the murderer's credit, completed his gratification.

'You may depend upon it, sir,' he told Mr. Utterson: 'I have him in my hand. He must have lost his head, or he never would have left the stick or, above all, burned the cheque-book. Why, money's life to the man. We have nothing to do but wait for him at the bank, and get out the handbills.'

This last, however, was not so easy of accomplishment; for Mr. Hyde had numbered few familiars—even the master of the servant-maid had only seen him twice; his family could nowhere be traced; he had never been photographed; and the few who could describe him differed widely, as common observers will. Only on one point were they agreed; and that was the haunting sense of unexpressed deformity with which the fugitive impressed his beholders.

INCIDENT OF THE LETTER

IT was late in the afternoon when Mr. Utterson found his way to Dr. Jekyll's door, where he was at once admitted by Poole, and carried down by the kitchen offices and across a yard which had once been a garden to the building which was indifferently known as the laboratory or the dissecting-rooms. The doctor had bought the house from the heirs of a celebrated surgeon; and, his own tastes being rather chemical than anatomical, had changed the destination of the block at the bottom of the garden. It was the first time that the lawyer had been received in that part of his friend's quarters; and he eyed the dingy windowless structure with curiosity, and gazed round with a distasteful sense of strangeness as he crossed the theatre, once crowded with eager students and now lying gaunt and silent, the tables laden with chemical apparatus, the floor strewn with crates and littered with packing straw, and the light falling dimly through the foggy cupola. At the farther end, a flight of stairs mounted to a door covered with red baize; and through this, Mr. Utterson was at last received into the doctor's cabinet. It was a large room, fitted round with glass presses, furnished, among other things, with a cheval-glass and a business-table, and looking out upon the court by three dusty windows barred with iron. The fire burned in the grate; a lamp was set lighted on the chimney shelf, for even in the houses the fog began to lie thickly; and there, close up to the warmth, sat Dr. Jekyll, looking deadly sick; he did not rise to meet his visitor, but held out a cold hand and bade him welcome in a changed voice.

'And now,' said Mr. Utterson, as soon as Poole had left them, 'you have heard the news?'

The doctor shuddered. 'They were crying it in the square,' he said. 'I heard them in my dining-room.'

'One word,' said the lawyer. 'Carew was my client, but so are you, and I want to know what I am doing. You have not been mad enough to hide this fellow?'

'Utterson, I swear to God,' cried the doctor, 'I swear to God I will never set eyes on him again. I bind my honour to you that I am done with him in this world. It is all at an end. And indeed he does not want my help; you do not know him as I do; he is safe, he is quite safe; mark my words, he will never more be heard of.'

The lawyer listened gloomily; he did not like his friend's feverish manner. 'You seem pretty sure of him,' said he; 'and for your sake, I hope you may be right. If it came to a trial your name might appear.'

'I am quite sure of him,' replied Jekyll; 'I have grounds for certainty that I cannot share with any one. But there is one thing on which you may advise me. I have—I have received a letter; and I am at a loss whether I should show it to the police. I should like to leave it in your hands, Utterson; you would judge wisely, I am sure; I have so great a trust in you.'

'You fear, I suppose, that it might lead to his detection?' asked the lawyer.

'No,' said the other, 'I cannot say that I care what becomes of Hyde; I am quite done with him. I was thinking of my own character, which this hateful business has rather exposed.'

Utterson ruminated awhile; he was surprised at his friend's selfishness, and yet relieved by it. 'Well,' said he at last, 'let me see the letter.'

The letter was written in an odd, upright hand and signed 'Edward Hyde': and it signified, briefly enough, that the writer's benefactor, Dr. Jekyll, whom he had long so unworthily repaid for a thousand generosities, need labour under no alarm for his safety, as he had means of escape on which he placed a sure dependence. The lawyer liked this letter well enough; it put a better colour on the intimacy than he had looked for; and he blamed himself for some of his past suspicions.

'Have you the envelope?' he asked.

'I burned it,' replied Jekyll, 'before I thought what I was about. But it bore no postmark. The note was handed in.'

'Shall I keep this and sleep upon it?' asked Utterson.

'I wish you to judge for me entirely,' was the reply. 'I have lost confidence in myself.'

'Well, I shall consider,' returned the lawyer.—'And now one word more: it was Hyde who dictated the terms in your will about that disappearance?'

The doctor seemed seized with a qualm of faintness; he shut his mouth tight and nodded.

'I knew it,' said Utterson. 'He meant to murder you. You have had a fine escape.'

'I have had what is far more to the purpose,' returned the doctor solemnly: 'I have had a lesson—O God, Utterson, what a lesson I have had!' And he covered his face for a moment with his hands.

On his way out, the lawyer stopped and had a word or two with Poole. 'By the by,' said he, 'there was a letter handed in to-day: what was the messenger like?' But Poole was positive nothing had come except by post; 'and only circulars by that,' he added.

This news sent off the visitor with his fears renewed. Plainly the letter had come by the laboratory door; possibly, indeed, it had been written in the cabinet; and if that were so, it must be differently judged, and handled with the more caution. The newsboys, as he went, were crying themselves hoarse along the footways: 'Special edition. Shocking murder of an M.P.' That was the funeral oration of one friend and client; and he could not help a certain apprehension lest the good name of another should be sucked down in the eddy of the scandal. It was, at least, a ticklish decision that he had to make; and, self-reliant as he was by habit, he began to cherish a longing for advice. It was not to be had directly; but perhaps, he thought, it might be fished for.

Presently after, he sat on one side of his own hearth, with Mr. Guest, his head clerk, upon the other, and midway between, at a nicely calculated distance from the fire, a bottle of a particular old wine that had long dwelt unsunned in the foundations of his house. The fog still slept on the wing above the drowned city, where the lamps glimmered like carbuncles; and through the muffle and smother of these fallen clouds, the procession of the town's life was still rolling on through the great arteries with a sound as of a mighty wind. But the room was gay with firelight. In the bottle the acids were long ago resolved; the imperial dye had softened with time, as the colour grows richer in stained windows; and the glow of hot autumn afternoons on hillside vineyards was ready to be set free and to disperse the fogs of London. Insensibly the lawyer melted. There was no man from whom he kept fewer secrets than Mr. Guest; and he was not always sure that he kept as many as he meant. Guest had often been on business to the doctor's; he knew Poole; he could scarce have failed to hear of Mr. Hyde's familiarity about the house; he might draw conclusions: was it not as well, then, that he should see a letter which put that mystery to rights? and above all since Guest, being a great student and critic of handwriting, would consider the step natural and obliging? The clerk, besides, was a man of counsel; he would scarce read so strange a document without dropping a remark; and by that remark Mr. Utterson might shape his future course.

'This is a sad business about Sir Danvers,' he said.

'Yes, sir, indeed. It has elicited a great deal of public feeling,' returned Guest. 'The man, of course, was mad.'

'I should like to hear your views on that,' replied Utterson. 'I have a document here in his handwriting; it is between ourselves, for I scarce know what to do about it; it is an ugly business at the best. But there it is; quite in your way: a murderer's autograph.'

Guest's eyes brightened, and he sat down at once and studied it with passion. 'No, sir,' he said; 'not mad; but it is an odd hand.'

'And by all accounts a very odd writer,' added the lawyer.

Just then the servant entered with a note.

'Is that from Dr. Jekyll, sir?' inquired the clerk. 'I thought I knew the writing. Anything private, Mr. Utterson?'

'Only an invitation to dinner. Why? do you want to see it?'

'One moment. I thank you, sir'; and the clerk laid the two sheets of paper alongside and sedulously compared their contents. 'Thank you, sir,' he said at last, returning both; 'it's a very interesting autograph.'

There was a pause, during which Mr. Utterson struggled with himself. 'Why did you compare them, Guest?' he inquired suddenly.

'Well, sir,' returned the clerk, 'there's a rather singular resemblance; the two hands are in many points identical: only differently sloped.'

'Rather quaint,' said Utterson.

'It is, as you say, rather quaint,' returned Guest.

'I wouldn't speak of this note, you know,' said the master.

'No, sir,' said the clerk. 'I understand.'

But no sooner was Mr. Utterson alone that night than he locked the note into his safe, where it reposed from that time forward. 'What!' he thought. 'Henry Jekyll forge for a murderer!' And his blood ran cold in his veins.

REMARKABLE INCIDENT OF DR. LANYON

TIME ran on; thousands of pounds were offered in reward, for the death of Sir Danvers was resented as a public injury; but Mr. Hyde had disappeared out of the ken of the police as though he had never existed. Much of his past was unearthed, indeed, and all disreputable: tales came out of the man's cruelty, at once so callous and violent, of his vile life, of his strange associates, of the hatred that seemed to have surrounded his career; but of his present whereabouts, not a whisper. From the time he had left the house in Soho on the morning of the murder, he was simply blotted out; and gradually, as time drew on, Mr. Utterson began to recover from the hotness of his alarm, and to grow more at quiet with himself. The death of Sir Danvers was, to his way of thinking, more than paid for by the disappearance of Mr. Hyde. Now that that evil influence had been withdrawn, a new life began for Dr. Jekyll. He came out of his seclusion, renewed relations with his friends, became once more their familiar guest and entertainer; and whilst he had always been known for charities, he was now no less distinguished for religion. He was busy, he was much in the open air, he did good; his face seemed to open and brighten, as if with an inward consciousness of service; and for more than two months the doctor was at peace.

On the 8th of January Utterson had dined at the doctor's with a small party; Lanyon had been there; and the face of the host had looked from one to the other as in the old days when the trio were inseparable friends. On the 12th, and again on the 14th, the door was shut against the lawyer. 'The doctor was confined to the house,' Poole said, 'and saw no one.' On the 15th he tried again, and was again refused; and having now been used for the last two months to see his friend almost daily, he found this return of solitude to weigh upon his spirits. The fifth night he had in Guest to dine with him; and the sixth he betook himself to Dr. Lanyon's.

There at least he was not denied admittance; but when he came in, he was shocked at the change which had taken place in the doctor's appearance. He had his death-warrant written legibly upon his face. The rosy man had grown pale; his flesh had fallen away; he was visibly balder and older; and yet it was not so much these tokens of a swift physical decay that arrested the lawyer's notice, as a look in the eye and quality of manner that seemed to testify to some deep-seated terror of the mind. It was unlikely that the doctor should fear death; and yet that was what Utterson was tempted to suspect. 'Yes,' he thought; 'he is a doctor, he must know his own state and that his days are counted; and the knowledge is more than he can bear.' And yet when Utterson remarked on his ill-looks, it was with an air of great firmness that Lanyon declared himself a doomed man.

'I have had a shock,' he said, 'and I shall never recover. It is a question of weeks. Well, life has been pleasant; I liked it; yes, sir, I used to like it. I sometimes think if we knew all we should be more glad to get away.'

'Jekyll is ill too,' observed Utterson. 'Have you seen him?'

But Lanyon's face changed, and he held up a trembling hand. 'I wish to see or hear no more of Dr. Jekyll,' he said in a loud, unsteady voice. 'I am quite done with that person; and I beg that you will spare me any allusion to one whom I regard as dead.'

'Tut-tut,' said Mr. Utterson; and then, after a considerable pause, 'Can't I do anything?' he inquired. 'We are three very old friends, Lanyon; we shall not live to make others.'

'Nothing can be done,' returned Lanyon; 'ask himself.'

'He will not see me,' said the lawyer.

'I am not surprised at that,' was the reply. 'Some day, Utterson, after I am dead, you may perhaps come to learn the right and wrong of this. I cannot tell you. And in the meantime, if you can sit and talk with me of other things, for God's sake, stay and do so;

but if you cannot keep clear of this accursed topic, then, in God's name, go, for I cannot bear it.'

As soon as he got home, Utterson sat down and wrote to Jekyll, complaining of his exclusion from the house, and asking the cause of this unhappy break with Lanyon; and the next day brought him a long answer, often very pathetically worded, and sometimes darkly mysterious in drift. The quarrel with Lanyon was incurable. 'I do not blame our old friend,' Jekyll wrote, 'but I share his view that we must never meet. I mean from henceforth to lead a life of extreme seclusion; you must not be surprised, nor must you doubt my friendship, if my door is often shut even to you. You must suffer me to go my own dark way. I have brought on myself a punishment and a danger that I cannot name. If I am the chief of sinners, I am the chief of sufferers also. I could not think that this earth contained a place for sufferings and terrors so unmanning; and you can do but one thing, Utterson, to lighten this destiny, and that is to respect my silence.' Utterson was amazed; the dark influence of Hyde had been withdrawn, the doctor had returned to his old tasks and amities; a week ago, the prospect had smiled with every promise of a cheerful and an honoured age; and now in a moment, friendship and peace of mind and the whole tenor of his life were wrecked. So great and unprepared a change pointed to madness; but in view of Lanyon's manner and words, there must lie for it some deeper ground.

A week afterwards Dr. Lanyon took to his bed, and in something less than a fortnight he was dead. The night after the funeral, at which he had been sadly affected, Utterson locked the door of his business-room, and sitting there by the light of a melancholy candle, drew out and set before him an envelope addressed by the hand and sealed with the seal of his dead friend. 'PRIVATE: for the hands of G. J. Utterson ALONE, and in case of his predecease *to be destroyed unread,*' so it was emphatically superscribed; and the lawyer dreaded to behold the contents. 'I have buried one friend to-day,' he thought: 'what if this should cost me another?' And then he condemned the fear as a disloyalty, and broke the seal. Within there was another enclosure, likewise sealed, and marked upon the cover as 'not to be opened till the death or disappearance of Dr. Henry Jekyll.' Utterson could not trust his eyes. Yes, it was disappearance; here again, as in the mad will which he had long ago restored to its author, here again were the idea of a disappearance and the name of Henry Jekyll bracketed. But in the will that idea had sprung from the sinister suggestion of the man Hyde; it was set there with a purpose all too plain and horrible. Written by the hand of Lanyon, what should it mean? A great curiosity came on the trustee, to disregard the prohibition and dive at once to the bottom of these mysteries; but professional honour and faith to his dead friend were stringent obligations; and the packet slept in the inmost corner of his private safe.

It is one thing to mortify curiosity, another to conquer it; and it may be doubted if, from that day forth, Utterson desired the society of his surviving friend with the same eagerness. He thought of him kindly; but his thoughts were disquieted and fearful. He went to call indeed; but he was perhaps relieved to be denied admittance; perhaps, in his heart, he preferred to speak with Poole upon the doorstep and surrounded by the air and sounds of the open city, rather than to be admitted into that house of voluntary bondage, and to sit and speak with its inscrutable recluse. Poole had, indeed, no very pleasant news to communicate. The doctor, it appeared, now more than ever confined himself to the cabinet over the laboratory, where he would sometimes even sleep; he was out of spirits, he had grown very silent, he did not read; it seemed as if he had something on his mind. Utterson became so used to the unvarying character of these reports, that he fell off little by little in the frequency of his visits.

INCIDENT AT THE WINDOW

It chanced on Sunday, when Mr. Utterson was on his usual walk with Mr. Enfield, that their way lay once again through the by-street; and that when they came in front of the door, both stopped to gaze on it.

'Well,' said Enfield, 'that story's at an end at least. We shall never see more of Mr. Hyde.'

'I hope not,' said Utterson. 'Did I ever tell you that I once saw him, and shared your feeling of repulsion?'

'It was impossible to do the one without the other,' returned Enfield. 'And by the way, what an ass you must have thought me, not to know that this was a back way to Dr. Jekyll's! It was partly your own fault that I found it out, even when I did.'

'So you found it out, did you?' said Utterson. 'But if that be so, we may step into the court and take a look at the windows. To tell you the truth, I am uneasy about poor Jekyll; and even outside, I feel as if the presence of a friend might do him good.'

The court was very cool and a little damp, and full of premature twilight, although the sky, high up overhead, was still bright with sunset. The middle one of the three windows was half-way open; and sitting close beside it, taking the air with an infinite sadness of mien, like some disconsolate prisoner, Utterson saw Dr. Jekyll.

'What! Jekyll!' he cried. 'I trust you are better.'

'I am very low, Utterson,' replied the doctor drearily, 'very low. It will not last long, thank God.'

'You stay too much indoors,' said the lawyer. 'You should be out, whipping up the circulation like Mr. Enfield and me. (This is my cousin—Mr. Enfield—Dr. Jekyll.) Come now; get your hat and take a quick turn with us.'

'You are very good,' sighed the other. 'I should like to very much; but no, no, no, it is quite impossible; I dare not. But indeed, Utterson, I am very glad to see you; this is really a great pleasure; I would ask you and Mr. Enfield up, but the place is really not fit.'

'Why then,' said the lawyer good-naturedly, 'the best thing we can do is to stay down here and speak with you from where we are.'

'That is just what I was about to venture to propose,' returned the doctor, with a smile. But the words were hardly uttered, before the smile was struck out of his face and succeeded by an expression of such abject terror and despair as froze the very blood of the two gentlemen below. They saw it but for a glimpse, for the window was instantly thrust down; but that glimpse had been sufficient, and they turned and left the court without a word. In silence, too, they traversed the by-street; and it was not until they had come into a neighbouring thoroughfare, where even upon a Sunday there were still some stirrings of life, that Mr. Utterson at last turned and looked at his companion. They were both pale; and there was an answering horror in their eyes.

'God forgive us, God forgive us!' said Mr. Utterson.

But Mr. Enfield only nodded his head very seriously, and walked on once more in silence.

THE LAST NIGHT

MR. UTTERSON was sitting by his fireside one evening after dinner, when he was surprised to receive a visit from Poole.

'Bless me, Poole, what brings you here?' he cried; and then, taking a second look at him, 'What ails you?' he added, 'is the doctor ill?'

'Mr. Utterson,' said the man, 'there is something wrong.'

'Take a seat, and here is a glass of wine for you,' said the lawyer. 'Now, take your time, and tell me plainly what you want.'

'You know the doctor's ways, sir,' replied Poole, 'and how he shuts himself up. Well, he's shut up again in the cabinet; and I don't like it, sir—I wish I may die if I like it. Mr. Utterson, sir, I'm afraid.'

'Now, my good man,' said the lawyer, 'be explicit. What are you afraid of?'

'I've been afraid for about a week,' returned Poole, doggedly disregarding the question, 'and I can bear it no more.'

The man's appearance amply bore out his words; his manner was altered for the worse; and except for the moment when he had first announced his terror, he had not once looked the lawyer in the face. Even now, he sat with the glass of wine untasted on his knee, and his eyes directed to a corner of the floor. 'I can bear it no more,' he repeated.

'Come,' said the lawyer, 'I see you have some good reason, Poole; I see there is something seriously amiss. Try to tell me what it is.'

'I think there's been foul play,' said Poole hoarsely.

'Foul play!' cried the lawyer, a good deal frightened, and rather inclined to be irritated in consequence. 'What foul play? What does the man mean?'

I daren't say, sir,' was the answer; 'but will you come along with me and see for yourself?'

Mr. Utterson's only answer was to rise and get his hat and greatcoat; but he observed with wonder the greatness of the relief that appeared upon the butler's face, and perhaps with no less, that the wine was still untasted when he set it down to follow.

It was a wild, cold, seasonable night of March, with a pale moon, lying on her back as though the wind had tilted her, and a flying wrack of the most diaphanous and lawny texture. The wind made talking difficult, and flecked the blood into the face. It seemed to have swept the streets unusually bare of passengers, besides; for Mr. Utterson thought he had never seen that part of London so deserted. He could have wished it otherwise; never in his life had he been conscious of so sharp a wish to see and touch his fellow-creatures; for, struggle as he might, there was borne in upon his mind a crushing anticipation of calamity. The square, when they got there, was all full of wind and dust, and the thin trees in the garden were lashing themselves along the railing. Poole, who had kept all the way a pace or two ahead, now pulled up in the middle of the pavement, and, in spite of the biting weather, took off his hat and mopped his brow with a red pocket-handkerchief. But for all the hurry of his coming, these were not the dews of exertion that he wiped away, but the moisture of some strangling anguish; for his face was white, and his voice, when he spoke, harsh and broken.

'Well, sir,' he said, 'here we are, and God grant there be nothing wrong.'

'Amen, Poole,' said the lawyer.

Thereupon the servant knocked in a very guarded manner; the door was opened on the chain; and a voice asked from within, 'Is that you, Poole?'

'It's all right,' said Poole. 'Open the door.'

The hall, when they entered it, was brightly lighted up; the fire was built high; and about the hearth the whole of the servants, men and women, stood huddled together like a flock of sheep. At the sight of Mr. Utterson, the housemaid broke into hysterical whimpering; and the cook, crying out 'Bless God! it's Mr. Utterson,' ran forward as if to take him in her arms.

'What, what? Are you all here?' said the lawyer peevishly. 'Very irregular, very unseemly; your master would be far from pleased.'

'They're all afraid,' said Poole.

Blank silence followed, no one protesting; only the maid lifted up her voice and now wept loudly.

'Hold your tongue!' Poole said to her, with a ferocity of accent that testified to his own jangled nerves; and indeed, when the girl had so suddenly raised the note of her lamentation, they had all started and turned towards the inner door with faces of dreadful expectation. 'And now,' continued the butler, addressing the knife-boy, 'reach me a candle, and we'll get this through hands at once.' And then he begged Mr. Utterson to follow him, and led the way to the back-garden.

'Now, sir,' said he, 'you come as gently as you can. I want you to hear, and I don't want you to be heard. And see here, sir, if by any chance he was to ask you in, don't go.'

Mr. Utterson's nerves, at this unlooked-for termination, gave a jerk that nearly threw him from his balance; but he re-collected his courage and followed the butler into the laboratory building and through the surgical theatre, with its lumber of crates and bottles, to the foot of the stair. Here Poole motioned him to stand on one side and listen; while he himself, setting down the candle and making a great and obvious call on his resolution, mounted the steps and knocked with a somewhat uncertain hand on the red baize of the cabinet door.

'Mr. Utterson, sir, asking to see you,' he called; and, even as he did so, once more violently signed to the lawyer to give ear.

A voice answered from within: 'Tell him I cannot see any one,' it said complainingly.

'Thank you, sir,' said Poole, with a note of something like triumph in his voice; and taking up his candle, he led Mr. Utterson back across the yard and into the great kitchen, where the fire was out and the beetles were leaping on the floor.

'Sir,' he said, looking Mr. Utterson in the eyes, 'was that my master's voice?'

'It seems much changed,' replied the lawyer, very pale, but giving look for look.

'Changed? Well, yes, I think so,' said the butler. 'Have I been twenty years in this man's house, to be deceived about his voice? No, sir; master's made away with; he was made away with eight days ago, when we heard him cry out upon the name of God; and *who's* in there instead of him, and *why* it stays there, is a thing that cries to Heaven, Mr. Utterson!'

'This is a very strange tale, Poole; this is rather a wild tale, my man,' said Mr. Utterson, biting his finger. 'Suppose it were as you suppose, supposing Dr. Jekyll to have been—well, murdered, what could induce the murderer to stay? That won't hold water; it doesn't commend itself to reason.'

'Well, Mr. Utterson, you are a hard man to satisfy, but I'll do it yet,' said Poole. 'All this last week (you must know) him, or it, or whatever it is that lives in that cabinet, has been crying night and day for some sort of medicine and cannot get it to his mind. It was sometimes his way—the master's, that is—to write his orders on a sheet of paper and throw it on the stair. We've had nothing else this week back; nothing but papers, and a closed door, and the very meals left there to be smuggled in when nobody was looking. Well, sir, every day, ay, and twice and thrice in the same day, there have been orders and complaints, and I have been sent flying to all the wholesale chemists in town. Every time I brought the stuff back, there would be another paper telling me to return it, because it was not pure, and another order to a different firm. This drug is wanted bitter bad, sir, whatever for.'

'Have you any of these papers?' asked Mr. Utterson.

Poole felt in his pocket and handed out a crumpled note, which the lawyer, bending nearer to the candle, carefully examined. Its contents ran thus: 'Dr. Jekyll presents his compliments to Messrs. Maw. He assures them that their last sample is impure, and quite useless for his present purpose. In the year 18—, Dr. J. purchased a somewhat large quantity from Messrs. M. He now begs them to search with the most sedulous care, and should any of the same quality be left, to forward it to him at once. Expense is no consideration. The importance of this to Dr. J. can hardly be exaggerated.' So far the letter had run composedly enough, but here, with a sudden splutter of the pen, the writer's emotion had broken loose. 'For God's sake,' he had added, 'find me some of the old.'

'This is a strange note,' said Mr. Utterson; and then sharply, 'How do you come to have it open?'

'The man at Maw's was main angry, sir, and he threw it back to me like so much dirt,' returned Poole.

'This is unquestionably the doctor's hand, do you know?' resumed the lawyer.

'I thought it looked like it,' said the servant rather sulkily; and then, with another voice, 'But what matters hand-of-write?' he said. 'I've seen him!'

'Seen him?' repeated Mr. Utterson. 'Well?'

'That's it!' said Poole. 'It was this way. I came suddenly into the theatre from the garden. It seems he had slipped out to look for this drug, or whatever it is; for the cabinet door was open, and there he was at the far end of the room digging among the crates. He looked up when I came in, gave a kind of cry, and whipped upstairs into the cabinet. It was but for one minute that I saw him, but the hair stood up on my head like quills. Sir, if that was my master, why had he a mask upon his face? If it was my master, why did he cry out like a rat, and run from me? I have served him long enough. And then . . .' the man paused and passed his hand over his face.

'These are all very strange circumstances,' said Mr. Utterson, 'but I think I begin to see daylight. Your master, Poole, is plainly seized with one of those maladies that both torture and deform the sufferer; hence, for aught I know, the alteration of his voice; hence the mask and his avoidance of his friends; hence his eagerness to find this drug, by means of which the poor soul retains some hope of ultimate recovery—God grant that he be not deceived! There is my explanation; it is sad enough, Poole, ay, and appalling to consider; but it is plain and natural, hangs well together, and delivers us from all exorbitant alarms.'

'Sir,' said the butler, turning to a sort of mottled pallor, 'that thing was not my master, and there's the truth. My master'—here he looked round him and began to whisper—'is a tall, fine build of a man, and this was more of a dwarf.' Utterson attempted to protest. 'O sir,' cried Poole, 'do you think I do not know my master after twenty years? do you think I do not know where his head comes to in the cabinet door, where I saw him every morning of my life? No, sir, that thing in the mask was never Dr. Jekyll—God knows what it was, but it was never Dr. Jekyll; and it is the belief of my heart that there was murder done.'

'Poole,' replied the lawyer, 'if you say that, it will become my duty to make certain. Much as I desire to spare your master's feelings, much as I am puzzled by this note which seems to prove him to be still alive, I shall consider it my duty to break in that door.'

'Ah, Mr. Utterson, that's talking!' cried the butler.

'And now comes the second question,' resumed Utterson: 'Who is going to do it?'

'Why, you and me, sir,' was the undaunted reply.

'That is very well said,' returned the lawyer; 'and whatever comes of it, I shall make it my business to see you are no loser.'

'There is an axe in the theatre,' continued Poole; 'and you might take the kitchen poker for yourself.'

The lawyer took that rude but weighty instrument into his hand, and balanced it. 'Do you know, Poole,' he said, looking up, 'that you and I are about to place ourselves in a position of some peril?'

'You may say so, sir, indeed,' returned the butler.

'It is well, then, that we should be frank,' said the other. 'We both think more than we have said; let us make a clean breast. This masked figure that you saw, did you recognise it?'

'Well, sir, it went so quick, and the creature was so doubled up, that I could hardly swear to that,' was the answer. 'But if you mean, was it Mr. Hyde?—why, yes, I think it was! You see, it was much of the same bigness; and it had the same quick light way with it; and then who else could have got in by the laboratory door? You have not forgot, sir, that at the time of the murder he had still the key with him? But that's not all. I don't know, Mr. Utterson, if ever you met this Mr. Hyde?'

'Yes,' said the lawyer, 'I once spoke with him.'

'Then you must know as well as the rest of us that there was something queer about that gentleman—something that gave a man a turn—I don't know rightly how to say it, sir, beyond this: that you felt it in your marrow kind of cold and thin.'

'I own I felt something of what you describe,' said Mr. Utterson.

'Quite so, sir,' returned Poole. 'Well, when that masked thing like a monkey jumped from among the chemicals and whipped into the cabinet, it went down my spine like ice. Oh, I know it's not evidence, Mr. Utterson; I'm book-learned enough for that; but a man has his feelings, and I give you my Bible-word it was Mr. Hyde!'

'Ay, ay,' said the lawyer. 'My fears incline to the same point. Evil, I fear, founded—evil was sure to come—of that connection. Ay, truly, I believe you; I believe poor Harry is killed; and I believe his murderer (for what purpose, God alone can tell) is still lurking in his victim's room. Well, let our name be vengeance. Call Bradshaw.'

The footman came at the summons, very white and nervous.

'Pull yourself together, Bradshaw,' said the lawyer. 'This suspense, I know, is telling upon all of you; but it is now our intention to make an end of it. Poole, here, and I are going to force our way into the cabinet. If all is well, my shoulders are broad enough to bear the blame. Meanwhile, lest anything should really be amiss, or any malefactor seek to escape by the back, you and the boy must go round the corner with a pair of good sticks, and take your post at the laboratory door. We give you ten minutes to get to your stations.'

As Bradshaw left, the lawyer looked at his watch. 'And now, Poole, let us get to ours,' he said; and taking the poker under his arm, he led the way into the yard. The scud had banked over the moon, and it was now quite dark. The wind, which only broke in puffs and draughts into that deep well of building, tossed the light of the candle to and fro about their steps, until they came into the shelter of the theatre, where they sat down silently to wait. London hummed solemnly all around; but nearer at hand, the stillness was only broken by the sound of a footfall moving to and fro along the cabinet floor.

'So it will walk all day, sir,' whispered Poole; 'ay, and the better part of the night. Only when a new sample comes from the chemist, there's a bit of a break. Ah, it's an ill-conscience that's such an enemy to rest! Ah, sir, there's blood foully shed in every step of it! But hark again, a little closer—put your heart in your ears, Mr. Utterson, and tell me, is that the doctor's foot?'

The steps fell lightly and oddly, with a certain swing, for all they went so slowly; it was different indeed from the heavy creaking tread of Henry Jekyll. Utterson sighed. 'Is there never anything else?' he asked.

Poole nodded. 'Once,' he said. 'Once I heard it weeping!'

'Weeping? how that?' said the lawyer, conscious of a sudden chill of horror.

'Weeping like a woman or a lost soul,' said the butler. 'I came away with that upon my heart that I could have wept too.'

But now the ten minutes drew to an end. Poole disinterred the axe from under a stack of packing straw; the candle was set upon the nearest table to light them to the attack; and they drew near with bated breath to where that patient foot was still going up and down, up and down, in the quiet of the night.

'Jekyll,' cried Utterson, with a loud voice, 'I demand to see you.' He paused a moment, but there came no reply. 'I give you fair warning, our suspicions are aroused, and I must and shall see you,' he resumed; 'if not by fair means, then by foul—if not of your consent, then by brute force!'

'Utterson,' said the voice, 'for God's sake have mercy!'

'Ah, that's not Jekyll's voice—it's Hyde's!' cried Utterson. 'Down with the door, Poole.'

Poole swung the axe over his shoulder; the blow shook the building, and the red baize door leaped against the lock and hinges. A dismal screech, as of mere animal terror, rang from the cabinet. Up went the axe again, and again the panels crashed and the frame bounded; four times the blow fell; but the wood was tough and the fittings were of excellent workmanship; and it was not until the fifth, that the lock burst in sunder and the wreck of the door fell inwards on the carpet.

The besiegers, appalled by their own riot and the stillness that had succeeded, stood back a little and peered in. There lay the cabinet before their eyes in the quiet lamplight, a good fire glowing and chattering on the hearth, the kettle singing its thin strain, a drawer or two open, papers neatly set forth on the business-table, and, nearer the fire, the things laid out for tea: the quietest room, you would have said, and, but for the glazed presses full of chemicals, the most commonplace that night in London.

Right in the midst there lay the body of a man sorely contorted, and still twitching. They drew near on tiptoe, turned it on its back, and beheld the face of Edward Hyde. He was dressed in clothes far too large for him, clothes of the doctor's bigness; the cords of his face still moved with a semblance of life, but life was quite gone; and by the crushed phial in the hand and the strong smell of kernels that hung upon the air, Utterson knew that he was looking on the body of a self-destroyer.

'We have come too late,' he said sternly, ' whether to save or punish. Hyde is gone to his account; and it only remains for us to find the body of your master.'

The far greater proportion of the building was occupied by the theatre, which filled almost the whole ground story and was lighted from above, and by the cabinet, which formed an upper story at one end and looked upon the court. A corridor joined the theatre to the door on the by-street; and with this, the cabinet communicated separately by a second flight of stairs. There were besides a few dark closets and a spacious cellar. All these they now thoroughly examined. Each closet needed but a glance, for all were empty, and all, by the dust that fell from their doors, had stood long unopened. The cellar, indeed, was filled with crazy lumber, mostly dating from the times of the surgeon who was Jekyll's predecessor; but even as they opened the door, they were advertised of the uselessness of further search, by the fall of a perfect mat of cobweb which had for years sealed up the entrance. Nowhere was there any trace of Henry Jekyll, dead or alive.

Poole stamped on the flags of the corridor. 'He must be buried here,' he said, hearkening to the sound.

'Or he may have fled,' said Utterson, and he turned to examine the door in the by-street. It was locked; and lying near by on the flags, they found the key, already stained with rust.

'This does not look like use,' observed the lawyer.

'Use!' echoed Poole. 'Do you not see, sir, it is broken? much as if a man had stamped on it.'

'Ay,' continued Utterson, 'and the fractures, too, are rusty.' The two men looked at each other with a scare. 'This is beyond me, Poole,' said the lawyer. 'Let us go back to the cabinet.'

They mounted the stair in silence, and, still with an occasional awe-struck glance at the dead body, proceeded more thoroughly to examine the contents of the cabinet. At one table there were traces of chemical work, various measured heaps of some white salt being laid on glass saucers, as though for an experiment in which the unhappy man had been prevented.

'That is the same drug that I was always bringing him,' said Poole; and even as he spoke, the kettle with a startling noise boiled over.

This brought them to the fireside, where the easy-chair was drawn cosily up, and the tea-things stood ready to the sitter's elbow, the very sugar in the cup. There were several books on a shelf; one lay beside the tea-things open, and Utterson was amazed to find it a copy of a pious work, for which Jekyll had several times expressed a great esteem, annotated, in his own hand, with startling blasphemies.

Next, in the course of their review of the chamber, the searchers came to the cheval-glass, into whose depths they looked with an involuntary horror. But it was so turned as to show them nothing but the rosy glow playing on the roof, the fire sparkling in a hundred repetitions along the glazed front of the presses, and their own pale and fearful countenances stooping to look in.

'This glass have seen some strange things, sir,' whispered Poole.

'And surely none stranger than itself,' echoed the lawyer in the same tones. 'For what did Jekyll'—he caught himself up at the word with a start, and then conquering the weakness: 'what could Jekyll want with it?' he said.

'You may say that!' said Poole.

Next they turned to the business-table. On the desk, among the neat array of papers, a large envelope was uppermost, and bore, in the doctor's hand, the name of Mr. Utterson. The lawyer unsealed it, and several enclosures fell to the floor. The first was a will, drawn in the same eccentric terms as the one which he had returned six months before, to serve as a testament in case of death and as a deed of gift in case of disappearance; but, in place of the name of Edward Hyde, the lawyer, with indescribable amazement, read the name of Gabriel John Utterson. He looked at Poole, and then back at the paper, and last of all at the dead malefactor stretched upon the carpet.

'My head goes round,' he said. 'He has been all these days in possession; he had no cause to like me; he must have raged to see himself displaced; and he has not destroyed this document.'

He caught up the next paper; it was a brief note in the doctor's hand, and dated at the top. 'O Poole!' the lawyer cried, 'he was alive and here this day. He cannot have been disposed of in so short a space, he must be still alive, he must have fled! And then, why fled? and how? and in that case, can we venture to declare this suicide? Oh, we must be careful. I foresee that we may yet involve your master in some dire catastrophe.'

'Why don't you read it, sir?' asked Poole.

'Because I fear,' replied the lawyer solemnly. 'God grant I have no cause for it!' and with that he brought the paper to his eyes and read as follows:

'My dear Utterson,—When this shall fall into your hands, I shall have disappeared, under what circumstances I have not the penetration to foresee, but my instinct and all the circumstances of my nameless situation tell me that the end is sure, and must be early. Go then, and first read the narrative which Lanyon warned me he was to place in your hands; and if you care to hear more, turn to the confession of

Your unworthy and unhappy friend,

'HENRY JEKYLL.'

'There was a third enclosure?' asked Utterson.

'Here, sir,' said Poole, and gave into his hands a considerable packet sealed in several places.

The lawyer put it in his pocket. 'I would say nothing of this paper. If your master has fled or is dead, we may at least save his credit. It is now ten; I must go home and read these documents in quiet; but I shall be back before midnight, when we shall send for the police.'

They went out, locking the door of the theatre behind them; and Utterson, once more leaving the servants gathered about the fire in the hall, trudged back to his office to read the two narratives in which this mystery was now to be explained.

DR. LANYON'S NARRATIVE

ON the ninth of January, now four days ago, I received by the evening delivery a registered envelope, addressed in the hand of my colleague and old school-companion, Henry Jekyll. I was a good deal surprised by this; for we were by no means in the habit of correspondence; I had seen the man, dined with him, indeed, the night before; and I could imagine nothing in our intercourse that should justify the formality of registration. The contents increased my wonder; for this is how the letter ran:

10th December, 18—

'Dear Lanyon,—You are one of my oldest friends; and although we may have differed at times on scientific questions, I cannot remember, at least on my side, any break in our affection. There was never a day when, if you had said to me, "Jekyll, my life, my honour, my reason, depend upon you," I would not have sacrificed my fortune or my left hand to help you. Lanyon, my life, my honour, my reason, are all at your mercy; if you fail me to-night, I am lost. You might suppose, after this preface, that I am going to ask you for something dishonourable to grant. Judge for yourself.

'I want you to postpone all other engagements for to-night—ay, even if you were summoned to the bedside of an emperor; to take a cab, unless your carriage should be actually at the door; and with this letter in your hand for consultation, to drive straight to my house. Poole, my butler, has his orders; you will find him waiting your arrival with a locksmith. The door of my cabinet is then to be forced; and you are to go in alone; to open the glazed press (letter E) on the left hand, breaking the lock if it be shut; and to draw out, *with all its contents as they stand*, the fourth drawer from the top or (which is the same thing) the third from the bottom. In my extreme distress of mind I have a morbid fear of misdirecting you; but even if I am in error, you may know the right drawer by its contents: some powders, a phial, and a paper book. This drawer I beg of you to carry back with you to Cavendish Square exactly as it stands.

'That is the first part of the service: now for the second. You should be back, if you set out at once on the receipt of this, long before midnight; but I will leave you that amount of margin, not only in the fear of one of those obstacles that can neither be prevented nor foreseen, but because an hour when your servants are in bed is to be preferred for what will then remain to do. At midnight, then, I have to ask you to be alone in your consulting-room, to admit with your own hand into the house a man who will present himself in my name, and to place in his hands the drawer that you will have brought with you from my cabinet. Then you will have played your part and earned my gratitude completely. Five minutes afterwards, if you insist upon an explanation, you will have understood that these arrangements are of capital importance; and that by the neglect of one of them, fantastic as they must appear, you might have charged your conscience with my death or the shipwreck of my reason.

'Confident as I am that you will not trifle with this appeal, my heart sinks and my hand trembles at the bare thought of such a possibility. Think of me at this hour, in a strange place, labouring under a blackness of distress that no fancy can exaggerate, and yet well aware that, if you will but punctually serve me, my troubles will roll away like a story that is told. Serve me, my dear Lanyon, and save

'Your friend,

'H. J.

'*PS*—I had already sealed this up when a fresh terror struck upon my soul. It is possible that the post office may fail me, and this letter not come into your hands until to-morrow morning. In that case, dear Lanyon, do my errand when it shall be most convenient for you in the course of the day; and once more expect my messenger at midnight. It may then already be too late; and if that night passes without event, you will know that you have seen the last of Henry Jekyll.'

Upon the reading of this letter I made sure my colleague was insane; but till that was proved beyond the possibility of doubt, I felt bound to do as he requested. The less I understood of this farrago, the less I was in a position to judge of its importance; and an appeal so worded could not be set aside without a grave responsibility. I rose accordingly from table, got into a hansom, and drove straight to Jekyll's house. The butler was awaiting my arrival; he had received by the same post as mine a registered letter of instruction, and had sent at once for a locksmith and a carpenter. The tradesmen came while we were yet speaking; and we moved in a body to old Dr. Denman's surgical theatre, from which (as you are doubtless aware) Jekyll's private cabinet is most conveniently entered. The door was very strong, the lock excellent; the carpenter avowed he would have great trouble and have to do much damage, if force were to be used; and the locksmith was near despair. But this last was a handy fellow, and after two hours' work the door stood open. The press marked E was unlocked; and I took out the drawer, had it filled up with straw and tied in a sheet, and returned with it to Cavendish Square.

Here I proceeded to examine its contents. The powders were neatly enough made up, but not with the nicety of the dispensing chemist; so that it was plain they were of Jekyll's private manufacture; and when I opened one of the wrappers, I found what seemed to me a simple, crystalline salt of a white colour. The phial, to which I next turned my attention, might have been about half-full of a blood-red liquor, which was highly pungent to the sense of smell and seemed to me to contain phosphorus and some volatile ether. At the other ingredients I could make no guess. The book was an ordinary version-book, and contained little but a series of dates. These covered a period of many years, but I observed that the entries ceased nearly a year ago, and quite abruptly. Here and there a brief remark was appended to a date, usually no more than a single word: 'double' occurring perhaps six times in a total of several hundred entries; and once very early in the list, and followed by several marks of exclamation, 'total failure!!!' All this, though it whetted my curiosity, told me little that was definite. Here was a phial of some tincture, a paper of some salt, and a record of a series of experiments that had led (like too many of Jekyll's investigations) to no end of practical usefulness. How could the presence of these articles in my house affect either the honour, the sanity, or the life of my flighty colleague? If his messenger could go to one place, why could he not go to another? And even granting some impediment, why was this gentleman to be received by me in secret? The more I reflected, the more convinced I grew that I was dealing with a case of cerebral disease; and though I dismissed my servants to bed, I loaded an old revolver that I might be found in some posture of self-defence.

Twelve o'clock had scarce rung out over London, ere the knocker sounded very gently on the door. I went myself at the summons, and found a small man crouching against the pillars of the portico.

'Are you come from Dr. Jekyll?' I asked.

He told me 'yes' by a constrained gesture; and when I had bidden him enter, he did not obey me without a searching backward glance into the darkness of the square. There was a policeman not far off, advancing with his bull's-eye open; and at the sight I thought my visitor started and made greater haste.

These particulars struck me, I confess, disagreeably; and as I followed him into the bright light of the consulting-room, I kept my hand ready on my weapon. Here, at last, I had a chance of clearly seeing him. I had never set eyes on him before, so much was certain. He was small, as I have said; I was struck besides with the shocking expression of his face, with his remarkable combination of great muscular activity and great apparent debility of constitution, and—last but not least—with the odd, subjective disturbance caused by his neighbourhood. This bore some resemblance to incipient rigor, and was accompanied by a marked sinking of the pulse. At the time, I set it down to some idiosyncratic, personal distaste, and merely wondered at the acuteness of the symptoms; but I have since had reason to believe the cause to lie much deeper in the nature of man, and to turn on some nobler hinge than the principle of hatred.

This person (who had thus, from the first moment of his entrance, struck in me what I can only describe as a disgustful curiosity) was dressed in a fashion that would have made an ordinary person laughable: his clothes, that is to say, although they were of rich and sober fabric, were enormously too large for him in every measurement—the trousers hanging on his legs and rolled up to keep them from the ground, the waist of the coat below his haunches, and the collar sprawling wide upon his shoulders. Strange to relate, this ludicrous accoutrement was far from moving me to laughter. Rather, as there was something abnormal and misbegotten in the very essence of the creature that now faced me—something seizing, surprising, and revolting—this fresh disparity seemed but to fit in with and to reinforce it; so that to my interest in the man's nature and character there was added a curiosity as to his origin, his life, his fortune and status in the world.

These observations, though they have taken so great a space to be set down in, were yet the work of a few seconds. My visitor was, indeed, on fire with sombre excitement.

'Have you got it?' he cried. 'Have you got it?' And so lively was his impatience that he even laid his hand upon my arm and sought to shake me.

I put him back, conscious at his touch of a certain icy pang along my blood. 'Come, sir,' said I. 'You forget that I have not yet the pleasure of your acquaintance. Be seated, if you please.' And I showed him an example, and sat down myself in my customary seat and with as fair an imitation of my ordinary manner to a patient as the lateness of the hour, the nature of my pre-occupations, and the horror I had of my visitor, would suffer me to muster.

'I beg your pardon, Dr. Lanyon,' he replied civilly enough. 'What you say is very well founded; and my impatience has shown its heels to my politeness. I come here at the instance of your colleague, Dr. Henry Jekyll, on a piece of business of some moment; and I understood . . .' he paused and put his hand to his throat, and I could see, in spite of his collected manner, that he was wrestling against the approaches of the hysteria—'I understood, a drawer . . .'

But here I took pity on my visitor's suspense, and some perhaps on my own growing curiosity.

'There it is, sir,' said I, pointing to the drawer, where it lay on the floor behind a table and still covered with the sheet.

He sprang to it, and then paused, and laid his hand upon his heart; I could hear his teeth grate with the convulsive action of his jaws; and his face was so ghastly to see that I grew alarmed both for his life and reason.

'Compose yourself,' said I.

He turned a dreadful smile to me, and as if with the decision of despair, plucked away the sheet. At sight of the contents he uttered one loud sob of such immense relief that I sat petrified. And the next moment, in a voice that was already fairly well under control, 'Have you a graduated glass?' he asked.

I rose from my place with something of an effort and gave him what he asked.

He thanked me with a smiling nod, measured out a few minims of the red tincture and added one of the powders. The mixture, which was at first of a reddish hue, began, in proportion as the crystals melted, to brighten in colour, to effervesce audibly, and to throw off small fumes of vapour. Suddenly and at the same moment, the ebullition ceased and the compound changed to a dark purple, which faded again more slowly to a watery green. My visitor, who had watched these metamorphoses with a keen eye, smiled, set down the glass upon the table, and then turned and looked upon me with an air of scrutiny.

'And now,' said he, 'to settle what remains. Will you be wise? will you be guided? will you suffer me to take this glass in my hand and to go forth from your house without further parley? or has the greed of curiosity too much command of you? Think before you answer, for it shall be done as you decide. As you decide, you shall be left as you were before, and neither richer nor wiser, unless the sense of service rendered to a man in mortal distress may be counted as a kind of riches of the soul. Or, if you shall so prefer to choose, a new province of knowledge and new avenues to fame and power shall be laid open to you, here, in this room, upon the instant; and your sight shall be blasted by a prodigy to stagger the unbelief of Satan.'

'Sir,' said I, affecting a coolness that I was far from truly possessing, 'you speak enigmas, and you will perhaps not wonder that I hear you with no very strong impression of belief. But I have gone too far in the way of inexplicable services to pause before I see the end.'

'It is well,' replied my visitor. 'Lanyon, you remember your vows: what follows is under the seal of our profession. And now, you who have so long been bound to the most narrow and material views, you who have denied the virtue of transcendental medicine, you who have derided your superiors— behold!'

He put the glass to his lips and drank at one gulp. A cry followed; he reeled, staggered, clutched at the table and held on, staring with injected eyes, gasping with open mouth; and as I looked there came, I thought, a change—he seemed to swell—his face became suddenly black and the features seemed to melt and alter—and the next moment I had sprung to my feet and leaped back against the wall, my arm raised to shield me from that prodigy, my mind submerged in terror.

'O God!' I screamed, and 'O God!' again and again; for there before my eyes—pale and shaken, and half fainting, and groping before him with his hands, like a man restored from death—there stood Henry Jekyll!

What he told me in the next hour I cannot bring my mind to set on paper. I saw what I saw, I heard what I heard, and my soul sickened at it; and yet now when that sight has faded from my eyes, I ask myself if I believe it, and I cannot answer. My life is shaken to its roots; sleep has left me; the deadliest terror sits by me at all hours of the day and night; I feel that my days are numbered, and that I must die; and yet I shall die incredulous. As for the moral turpitude that man unveiled to me, even with tears of penitence, I cannot, even in memory, dwell on it without a start of horror. I will say but one thing, Utterson, and that (if you can bring your mind to credit it) will be more than enough. The creature who crept into my house that night was, on Jekyll's own confession, known by the name of Hyde, and hunted for in every corner of the land as the murderer of Carew.

HASTIE LANYON.

HENRY JEKYLL'S FULL STATEMENT OF THE CASE

I WAS born in the year 18— to a large fortune, endowed besides with excellent parts, inclined by nature to industry, fond of the respect of the wise and good among my fellow-men, and thus, as might have been supposed, with every guarantee of an honourable and distinguished future. And indeed the worst of my faults was a certain impatient gaiety of disposition such as has made the happiness of many, but such as I found it hard to reconcile with my imperious desire to carry my head high, and wear a more than commonly grave countenance before the public. Hence it came about that I concealed my pleasures; and that when I reached years of reflection, and began to look round me and take stock of my progress and position in the world, I stood already committed to a profound duplicity of life. Many a man would have even blazoned such irregularities as I was guilty of; but from the high views that I had set before me, I regarded and hid them with an almost morbid sense of shame. It was thus rather the exacting nature of my aspirations than any particular degradation in my faults, that made me what I was, and, with even a deeper trench than in the majority of men, severed in me those provinces of good and ill which divide and compound man's dual nature. In this case, I was driven to reflect deeply and inveterately on that hard law of life, which lies at the root of religion and is one of the most plentiful springs of distress. Though so profound a double-dealer, I was in no sense a hypocrite; both sides of me were in dead earnest; I was no more myself when I laid aside restraint and plunged in shame, than when I laboured, in the eye of day, at the furtherance of knowledge or the relief of sorrow and suffering. And it chanced that the direction of my scientific studies, which led wholly towards the mystic and the transcendental, reacted and shed a strong light on this consciousness of the perennial war among my members. With every day, and from both sides of my intelligence, the moral and the intellectual, I thus drew steadily nearer to that truth, by whose partial discovery I have been doomed to such a dreadful shipwreck: that man is not truly one, but truly two. I say two, because the state of my own knowledge does not pass beyond that point. Others will follow, others will outstrip me on the same lines; and I hazard the guess that man will be ultimately known for a mere polity of multifarious, incongruous and independent denizens. I for my part, from the nature of my life, advanced infallibly in one direction, and in one direction only. It was on the moral side, and in my own person, that I learned to recognise the thorough and primitive duality of man; I saw that of the two natures that contended in the field of my consciousness, even if I could rightly be said to be either, it was only because I was radically both; and from an early date, even before the course of my scientific discoveries had begun to suggest the most naked possibility of such a miracle, I had learned to dwell with pleasure, as a beloved day-dream on the thought of the separation of these elements. If each, I told myself, could but be housed in separate identities, life would be relieved of all that was unbearable; the unjust might go his way, delivered from the aspirations and remorse of his more upright twin; and the just could walk steadfastly and securely on his upward path, doing the good things in which he found his pleasure, and no longer exposed to disgrace and penitence by the hands of this extraneous evil. It was the curse of mankind that these incongruous fagots were thus bound together—that in the agonised womb of consciousness these polar twins should be continuously struggling. How, then, were they dissociated?

I was so far in my reflections when, as I have said, a side-light began to shine upon the subject from the laboratory table. I began to perceive more deeply than it has ever yet been stated, the trembling immateriality, the mist-like transience, of this seemingly so solid body in which we walk attired. Certain agents I found to have the power to shake and to pluck back that fleshy vestment, even as a wind might toss the curtains of a pavilion. For two good reasons, I will not enter deeply into this scientific branch of my confession. First, because I have been made to learn that the doom and burthen of our life is bound for ever on man's shoulders, and when the attempt is made to cast it off, it but returns upon us with more unfamiliar and more awful pressure. Second, because as my narrative will make, alas! too evident, my discoveries were incomplete. Enough, then, that I not only recognised my natural body for the mere aura and effulgence of certain of the powers that made up my spirit, but managed to compound a drug by which these powers should be dethroned from their supremacy, and a second form and countenance substituted, none the less natural to me because they were the expression, and bore the stamp, of lower elements in my soul.

I hesitated long before I put this theory to the test of practice. I knew well that I risked death; for any drug that so potently controlled and shook the very fortress of identity, might by the least scruple of an overdose or at the least inopportunity in the moment of exhibition, utterly blot out that immaterial tabernacle which I looked to it to change. But the temptation of a discovery so singular and profound at last overcame the suggestions of alarm. I had long since prepared my tincture; I purchased at once, from a firm of wholesale chemists, a large quantity of a particular salt which I knew, from my experiments, to be the last ingredient required; and late one accursed night, I compounded the elements, watched them boil and smoke together in the glass, and when the ebullition had subsided, with a strong glow of courage drank off the potion.

The most racking pangs succeeded; a grinding in the bones, deadly nausea, and a horror of the spirit that cannot be exceeded at the hour of birth or death. Then these agonies began swiftly to subside, and I came to myself as if out of a great sickness. There was something strange in my sensations, something indescribably new and, from its very novelty, incredibly sweet. I felt younger, lighter, happier in body; within I was conscious of a heady recklessness, a current of disordered sensual images running like a mill-race in my fancy, a solution of the bonds of obligation, an unknown but not an innocent freedom of the soul. I knew myself, at the first breath of this new life, to be more wicked, tenfold more wicked, sold a slave to my original evil; and the thought, in that moment, braced and delighted me like wine. I stretched out my hands, exulting in the freshness of these sensations; and in the act I was suddenly aware that I had lost in stature.

There was no mirror, at that date, in my room; that which

stands beside me as I write was brought there later on, and for the very purpose of these transformations. The night, however, was far gone into the morning—the morning, black as it was, was nearly ripe for the conception of the day—the inmates of my house were locked in the most rigorous hours of slumber; and I determined, flushed as I was with hope and triumph, to venture in my new shape as far as to my bedroom. I crossed the yard, wherein the constellations looked down upon me, I could have thought, with wonder, the first creature of that sort that their unsleeping vigilance had yet disclosed to them; I stole through the corridors, a stranger in my own house; and, coming to my room, I saw for the first time the appearance of Edward Hyde.

I must here speak by theory alone, saying not that which I know, but that which I suppose to be most probable. The evil side of my nature, to which I had now transferred the stamping efficacy, was less robust and less developed than the good which I had just deposed. Again, in the course of my life, which had been, after all, nine-tenths a life of effort, virtue, and control, it had been much less exercised and much less exhausted. And hence, as I think, it came about that Edward Hyde was so much smaller, slighter, and younger than Henry Jekyll. Even as good shone upon the countenance of the one, evil was written broadly and plainly on the face of the other. Evil besides (which I must still believe to be the lethal side of man) had left on that body an imprint of deformity and decay. And yet when I looked upon that ugly idol in the glass, I was conscious of no repugnance, rather of a leap of welcome. This, too, was myself. It seemed natural and human. In my eyes it bore a livelier image of the spirit, it seemed more express and single, than the imperfect and divided countenance I had been hitherto accustomed to call mine. And in so far I was doubtless right. I have observed that when I bore the semblance of Edward Hyde, none could come near to me at first without a visible misgiving of the flesh. This, as I take it, was because all human beings, as we meet them, are commingled out of good and evil: and Edward Hyde, alone in the ranks of mankind, was pure evil.

I lingered but a moment at the mirror: the second and conclusive experiment had yet to be attempted; it yet remained to be seen if I had lost my identity beyond redemption and must flee before daylight from a house that was no longer mine; and, hurrying back to my cabinet, I once more prepared and drank the cup, once more suffered the pangs of dissolution, and came to myself once more with the character, the stature, and the face of Henry Jekyll.

That night I had come to the fatal cross roads. Had I approached my discovery in a more noble spirit, had I risked the experiment while under the empire of generous or pious aspirations, all must have been otherwise, and from these agonies of death and birth I had come forth an angel instead of a fiend. The drug had no discriminating action; it was neither diabolical nor divine; it but shook the doors of the prison-house of my disposition; and like the captives of Philippi, that which stood within ran forth. At that time my virtue slumbered; my evil, kept awake by ambition, was alert and swift to seize the occasion; and the thing that was projected was Edward Hyde. Hence, although I had now two characters as well as two appearances, one was wholly evil, and the other was still the old Henry Jekyll, that incongruous compound of whose reformation and improvement I had already learned to despair. The movement was thus wholly toward the worse.

Even at that time I had not yet conquered my aversion to the dryness of a life of study. I would still be merrily disposed at times; and as my pleasures were (to say the least) undignified, and I was not only well known and highly considered, but growing towards the elderly man, this incoherency of my life was daily growing more unwelcome. It was on this side that my new power tempted me until I fell in slavery. I had but to drink the cup, to doff at once the body of the noted professor, and to assume, like a thick cloak, that of Edward Hyde. I smiled at the notion; it seemed to me at the time to be humorous; and I made my preparations with the most studious care. I took and furnished that house in Soho, to which Hyde was tracked by the police; and engaged as housekeeper a creature whom I well knew to be silent and unscrupulous. On the other side, I announced to my servants that a Mr. Hyde (whom I described) was to have full liberty and power about my house in the square; and to parry mishaps, I even called and made myself a familiar object, in my second character. I next drew up that will to which you so much objected; so that if anything befell me in the person of Doctor Jekyll, I could enter on that of Edward Hyde without pecuniary loss. And thus fortified, as I supposed, on every side, I began to profit by the strange immunities of my position.

Men have before hired bravos to transact their crimes, while their own person and reputation sat under shelter. I was the first that ever did so for his pleasures. I was the first that could thus plod in the public eye with a load of genial respectability, and in a moment, like a schoolboy, strip off these lendings and spring headlong into the sea of liberty. But for me, in my impenetrable mantle, the safety was complete. Think of it—I did not even exist! Let me but escape into my laboratory-door, give me but a second or two to mix and swallow the draught that I had always standing ready; and whatever he had done, Edward Hyde would pass away like the stain of breath upon a mirror; and there in his stead, quietly at home, trimming the midnight lamp in his study, a man who could afford to laugh at suspicion, would be Henry Jekyll.

The pleasures which I made haste to seek in my disguise were, as I have said, undignified; I would scarce use a harder term. But in the hands of Edward Hyde they soon began to turn towards the monstrous. When I would come back from these excursions, I was often plunged into a kind of wonder at my vicarious depravity. This familiar that I called out of my own soul, and sent forth alone to do his good pleasure, was a being inherently malign and villainous; his every act and thought centred on self; drinking pleasure with bestial avidity from any degree of torture to another; relentless like a man of stone. Henry Jekyll stood at times aghast before the acts of Edward Hyde; but the situation was apart from ordinary laws, and insidiously relaxed the grasp of conscience. It was Hyde, after all, and Hyde alone, that was guilty. Jekyll was no worse; he woke again to his good qualities seemingly unimpaired; he would even make haste, where it was possible, to undo the evil done by Hyde. And thus his conscience slumbered.

Into the details of the infamy at which I thus connived (for even now I can scarce grant that I committed it) I have no design of entering; I mean but to point out the warnings and the successive steps with which my chastisement approached. I met with one accident which, as it brought on no consequence, I shall no more than mention. An act of cruelty to a child aroused against me the anger of a passer-by, whom I recognised the other day in the person of your kinsman; the doctor and the child's family joined him; there were moments when I feared for my life; and at last, in order to pacify their too just resentment, Edward Hyde had to bring them to the door, and pay them in a cheque drawn in the name of Henry Jekyll. But this danger was easily eliminated from the future, by opening an account at another bank in the name of Edward Hyde himself; and when, by sloping my own hand backward, I had supplied my double with a signature, I thought I sat beyond the reach of fate.

Some two months before the murder of Sir Danvers, I had been out for one of my adventures, had returned at a late hour, and woke the next day in bed with somewhat odd sensations. It was in vain I looked about me; in vain I saw the decent furniture and tall proportions of my room in the square; in vain that I recognised the pattern of the bed-curtains and the design of the mahogany frame; something still kept insisting that I was not where I was, that I had not wakened where I seemed to be, but in the little room in Soho where I was accustomed to sleep in the body of Edward Hyde. I smiled to myself, and, in my psychological way, began lazily to inquire into the elements of this illusion, occasionally, even as I did so, dropping back into a comfortable morning doze. I was still so engaged when, in one of my more wakeful moments, my eye fell upon my hand. Now the hand of Henry Jekyll (as you have often remarked) was professional in shape and size: it was large, firm, white, and comely. But the hand which I now saw, clearly enough, in the yellow light of a mid-London morning, lying half shut on the bed-clothes, was lean, corded, knuckly, of a dusky pallor, and thickly shaded with a swart growth of hair. It was the hand of Edward Hyde.

I must have stared upon it for near half a minute, sunk as I was in the mere stupidity of wonder, before terror woke up in my breast as sudden and startling as the crash of cymbals; and bounding from my bed, I rushed to the mirror. At the sight that met my eyes my blood was changed into something exquisitely thin and icy. Yes, I had gone to bed Henry Jekyll, I had awakened Edward Hyde. How was this to be explained? I asked myself; and then, with another bound of terror—how was it to be remedied? It was well on in the morning; the servants were up; all my drugs were in the cabinet—a long journey, down two pairs of stairs, through the back passage, across the open court and through the anatomical theatre, from where I was then standing horror-struck. It might indeed be possible to cover my face; but of what use was that, when I was unable to conceal the alteration in my stature? And then, with an overpowering sweetness of relief, it came back upon my mind that the servants were already used to the coming and going of my second self. I had soon dressed, as well as I was able, in clothes of my own size: had soon passed through the house, where Bradshaw stared and drew back at seeing Mr. Hyde at such an hour and in such a strange array; and ten minutes later Dr. Jekyll had returned to his own shape, and was sitting down, with a darkened brow, to make a feint of breakfasting.

Small indeed was my appetite. This inexplicable incident, this reversal of my previous experience, seemed, like the Babylonian finger on the wall, to be spelling out the letters of my judgment; and I began to reflect more seriously than ever before on the issues and possibilities of my double existence. That part of me which I had the power of projecting had lately been much exercised and nourished; it had seemed to me of late as though the body of Edward Hyde had grown in stature, as though (when I wore that form) I were conscious of a more generous tide of blood; and I began to spy a danger that, if this were much prolonged, the balance of my nature might be permanently overthrown, the power of voluntary change be forfeited, and the character of Edward Hyde become irrevocably mine. The power of the drug had not been always equally displayed. Once, very early in my career, it had totally failed me; since then I had been obliged on more than one occasion to double, and once, with infinite risk of death, to treble the amount; and these rare uncertainties had cast hitherto the sole shadow on my contentment. Now, however, and in the light of that morning's accident, I was led to remark that whereas, in the beginning, the difficulty had been to throw off the body of Jekyll, it had of late gradually but decidedly transferred itself to the other side. All things therefore seemed to point to this: that I was slowly losing hold of my original and better self, and becoming slowly incorporated with my second and worse.

Between these two, I now felt I had to choose. My two natures had memory in common, but all other faculties were most unequally shared between them. Jekyll (who was composite) now with the most sensitive apprehensions, now with a greedy gusto, projected and shared in the pleasures and adventures of

Hyde; but Hyde was indifferent to Jekyll, or but remembered him as the mountain bandit remembers the cavern in which he conceals himself from pursuit. Jekyll had more than a father's interest; Hyde had more than a son's indifference. To cast in my lot with Jekyll was to die to those appetites which I had long secretly indulged, and had of late begun to pamper. To cast it in with Hyde was to die to a thousand interests and aspirations, and to become, at a blow and for ever, despised and friendless. The bargain might appear unequal; but there was still another consideration in the scales; for while Jekyll would suffer smartingly in the fires of abstinence, Hyde would be not even conscious of all that he had lost. Strange as my circumstances were, the terms of this debate are as old and commonplace as man; much the same inducements and alarms cast the die for any tempted and trembling sinner; and it fell out with me, as it falls with so vast a majority of my fellows, that I chose the better part, and was found wanting in the strength to keep to it.

Yes, I preferred the elderly and discontented doctor, surrounded by friends and cherishing honest hopes; and bade a resolute farewell to the liberty, the comparative youth, the light step, leaping pulses, and secret pleasures, that I had enjoyed in the disguise of Hyde. I made this choice perhaps with some unconscious reservation, for I neither gave up the house in Soho, nor destroyed the clothes of Edward Hyde, which still lay ready in my cabinet. For two months, however, I was true to my determination; for two months I led a life of such severity as I had never before attained to, and enjoyed the compensations of an approving conscience. But time began at last to obliterate the freshness of my alarm; the praises of conscience began to grow into a thing of course; I began to be tortured with throes and longings, as of Hyde struggling after freedom; and at last, in an hour of moral weakness, I once again compounded and swallowed the transforming draught.

I do not suppose that, when a drunkard reasons with himself upon his vice, he is once out of five hundred times affected by the dangers that he runs through his brutish, physical insensibility; neither had I, long as I had considered my position, made enough allowance for the complete moral insensibility and insensate readiness to evil, which were the leading characters of Edward Hyde. Yet it was by these that I was punished. My devil had been long caged, he came out roaring. I was conscious, even when I took the draught, of a more unbridled, a more furious propensity to ill. It must have been this, I suppose, that stirred in my soul that tempest of impatience with which I listened to the civilities of my unhappy victim; I declare at least, before God, no man morally sane could have been guilty of that crime upon so pitiful a provocation; and that I struck in no more reasonable spirit than that in which a sick child may break a plaything. But I had voluntarily stripped myself of all those balancing instincts, by which even the worst of us continues to walk with some degree of steadiness among temptations; and in my case, to be tempted, however slightly, was to fall.

Instantly the spirit of hell awoke in me and raged. With a transport of glee I mauled the unresisting body, tasting delight from every blow; and it was not till weariness had begun to succeed, that I was suddenly, in the top fit of my delirium, struck through the heart by a cold thrill of terror. A mist dispersed; I saw my life to be forfeit; and fled from the scene of these excesses, at once glorying and trembling, my lust of evil gratified and stimulated, my love of life screwed to the topmost peg. I ran to the house in Soho, and (to make assurance doubly sure) destroyed my papers; thence I set out through the lamplit streets, in the same divided ecstasy of mind, gloating on my crime, light-headedly devising others in the future, and yet still hastening and still hearkening in my wake for the steps of the avenger. Hyde had a song upon his lips as he compounded the draught, and as he drank it, pledged the dead man. The pangs of transformation had not done tearing him, before Henry Jekyll, with streaming tears of gratitude and remorse, had fallen upon his knees and lifted his clasped hands to God. The veil of self-indulgence was rent from head to foot, I saw my life as a whole: I followed it up from the days of childhood, when I had walked with my father's hand, and through the self-denying toils of my professional life, to arrive again and again, with the same sense of unreality, at the damned horrors of the evening. I could have screamed aloud; I sought with tears and prayers to smother down the crowd of hideous images and sounds with which my memory swarmed against me; and still, between the petitions, the ugly face of my iniquity stared into my soul. As the acuteness of this remorse began to die away, it was succeeded by a sense of joy. The problem of my conduct was solved. Hyde was thenceforth impossible; whether I would or not, I was now confined to the better part of my existence; and oh how I rejoiced to think it! with what willing humility I embraced anew the restrictions of natural life! with what sincere renunciation I locked the door by which I had so often gone and come, and ground the key under my heel!

The next day came the news that the murder had been overlooked, that the guilt of Hyde was patent to the world, and that the victim was a man high in public estimation. It was not only a crime, it had been a tragic folly. I think I was glad to know it; I think I was glad to have my better impulses thus buttressed and guarded by the terrors of the scaffold. Jekyll was now my city of refuge; let but Hyde peep out an instant, and the hands of all men would be raised to take and slay him.

I resolved in my future conduct to redeem the past; and I can say with honesty that my resolve was fruitful of some good. You know yourself how earnestly in the last months of last year, I laboured to relieve suffering; you know that much was done for others, and that the days passed quietly, almost happily for myself. Nor can I truly say that I wearied of this beneficent and innocent life; I think instead that I daily enjoyed it more completely; but I was still cursed with my duality of purpose and as the first edge of my penitence wore off, the lower side of me, so long indulged, so recently chained down, began to growl for licence. Not that I dreamed of resuscitating Hyde; the bare idea of that would startle me to frenzy: no, it was in my own person that I was once more tempted to trifle with my conscience; and it was as an ordinary secret sinner that I at last fell before the assaults of temptation.

There comes an end to all things; the most capacious measure is filled at last; and this brief condescension to evil finally destroyed the balance of my soul. And yet I was not alarmed; the fall seemed natural, like a return to the old days before I had made my discovery. It was a fine, clear, January day, wet under foot where the frost had melted, but cloudless overhead; and the Regent's Park was full of winter chirrupings and sweet with spring odours. I sat in the sun on a bench; the animal within me licking the chops of memory; the spiritual side a little drowsed, promising subsequent penitence, but not yet moved to begin. After all, I reflected, I was like my neighbours; and then I smiled, comparing myself with other men, comparing my active goodwill with the lazy cruelty of their neglect. And at the very moment of that vainglorious thought a qualm came over me, a horrid nausea and the most deadly shuddering. These passed away, and left me faint; and then, as in its turn the faintness subsided, I began to be aware of a change in the temper of my thoughts, a greater boldness, a contempt of danger, a solution of the bonds of obligation. I looked down; my clothes hung formlessly on my shrunken limbs; the hand that lay on my knee was corded and hairy. I was once more Edward Hyde. A moment before I had been safe of all men's respect, wealthy, beloved—the cloth laying for me in the dining-room at home; and now I was the common quarry of mankind, hunted, houseless, a known murderer, thrall to the gallows.

My reason wavered, but it did not fail me utterly. I have more than once observed that, in my second character, my faculties seemed sharpened to a point and my spirits more tensely elastic; thus it came about that, where Jekyll perhaps might have succumbed, Hyde rose to the importance of the moment. My drugs were in one of the presses of my cabinet; how was I to reach them? That was the problem that (crushing my temples in my hands) I set myself to solve. The laboratory door I had closed. If I sought to enter by the house, my own servants would consign me to the gallows. I saw I must employ another hand, and thought of Lanyon. How was he to be reached? how persuaded? Supposing that I escaped capture in the streets, how was I to make my way into his presence? and how should I, an unknown and displeasing visitor, prevail on the famous physician to rifle the study of his colleague, Dr. Jekyll? Then I remembered that of my original character, one part remained to me: I could write my own hand; and once I had conceived that kindling spark, the way that I must follow became lighted up from end to end.

Thereupon I arranged my clothes as best I could, and summoning a passing hansom, drove to a hotel in Portland Street, the name of which I chanced to remember. At my appearance (which was indeed comical enough, however tragic a fate these garments covered) the driver could not conceal his mirth. I gnashed my teeth upon him with a gust of devilish fury; and the smile withered from his face—happily for him—yet more happily for myself, for in another instant I had certainly dragged him from his perch. At the inn, as I entered, I looked about me with so black a countenance as made the attendants tremble; not a look did they exchange in my presence; but obsequiously took my orders, led me to a private room, and brought me wherewithal to write. Hyde in danger of his life was a creature new to me: shaken with inordinate anger, strung to the pitch of murder, lusting to inflict pain. Yet the creature was astute; mastered his fury with a great effort of the will; composed his two important letters, one to Lanyon and one to Poole; and that he might receive actual evidence of their being posted, sent them out with directions that they should be registered.

Thenceforward, he sat all day over the fire in the private room, gnawing his nails; there he dined, sitting alone with his fears, the waiter visibly quailing before his eye; and then, when the night was fully come, he set forth in the corner of a closed cab, and was driven to and fro about the streets of the city. He, I say—I cannot say, I. That child of Hell had nothing human; nothing lived in him but fear and hatred. And when at last, thinking the driver had begun to grow suspicious, he discharged the cab and ventured on foot, attired in his misfitting clothes, an object marked out for observation, into the midst of the nocturnal passengers, these two base passions raged within him like a tempest. He walked fast, hunted by his fears, chattering to himself, skulking through the less frequented thoroughfares, counting the minutes that still divided him from midnight. Once a woman spoke to him, offering, I think, a box of lights. He smote her in the face, and she fled.

When I came to myself at Lanyon's, the horror of my old friend perhaps affected me somewhat: I do not know; it was at least but a drop in the sea to the abhorrence with which I looked back upon these hours. A change had come over me. It was no longer the fear of the gallows, it was the horror of being Hyde that racked me. I received Lanyon's condemnation partly in a dream; it was partly in a dream that I came home to my own house and got into bed. I slept after the prostration of the day, with a stringent and profound slumber which not even the nightmares that wrung me could avail to break. I awoke in the morning shaken, weakened, but refreshed. I still hated and feared the thought of the brute that slept within me, and I had not, of course, forgotten the appalling dangers of the day before; but I was once more at home, in my own house and close to my drugs; and gratitude for my escape shone so strong in my soul that it almost rivalled the brightness of hope.

I was stepping leisurely across the court after breakfast, drinking the chill of the air with pleasure, when I was seized again with those indescribable sensations that heralded the change; and I had but the time to gain the shelter of my cabinet, before I was once again raging and freezing with the passions of Hyde. It took on this occasion a double dose to recall me to myself; and alas! six hours after, as I sat looking sadly in the fire, the pangs returned, and the drug had to be re-administered. In short, from that day forth it seemed only by a great effort as of gymnastics, and only under the immediate stimulation of the drug, that I was able to wear the countenance of Jekyll. At all hours of the day and night I would be taken with the premonitory shudder; above all, if I slept, or even dozed for a moment in my chair, it was always as Hyde that I awakened. Under the strain of this continually impending doom and by the sleeplessness to which I now condemned myself, ay, even beyond what I had thought possible to man, I became, in my own person, a creature eaten up and emptied by fever, languidly weak both in body and mind, and solely occupied by one thought: the horror of my other self. But when I slept, or when the virtue of the medicine wore off, I would leap almost without transition (for the pangs of transformation grew daily less marked) into the possession of a fancy brimming with images of terror, a soul boiling with causeless hatreds, and a body that seemed not strong enough to contain the raging energies of life. The powers of Hyde seemed to have grown with the sickliness of Jekyll. And certainly the hate that now divided them was equal on each side. With Jekyll, it was a thing of vital instinct. He had now seen the full deformity of that creature that shared with him some of the phenomena of consciousness, and was co-heir with him to death: and beyond these links of community, which in themselves made the most poignant part of his distress, he thought of Hyde, for all his energy of life, as of something not only hellish but inorganic. This was the shocking thing; that the slime of the pit seemed to utter cries and voices; that the amorphous dust gesticulated and sinned; that what was dead, and had no shape, should usurp the offices of life. And this again, that that insurgent horror was knit to him closer than a wife, closer than an eye; lay caged in his flesh, where he heard it mutter and felt it struggle to be born; and at every hour of weakness, and in the confidence of slumber, prevailed against him, and deposed him out of life. The hatred of

Hyde for Jekyll was of a different order. His terror of the gallows drove him continually to commit temporary suicide, and return to his subordinate station of a part instead of a person; but he loathed the necessity, he loathed the despondency into which Jekyll was now fallen, and he resented the dislike with which he was himself regarded. Hence the ape-like tricks that he would play me, scrawling in my own hand blasphemies on the pages of my books, burning the letters and destroying the portrait of my father; and indeed, had it not been for his fear of death, he would long ago have ruined himself in order to involve me in the ruin. But his love of life is wonderful; I go further: I, who sicken and freeze at the mere thought of him, when I recall the abjection and passion of this attachment, and when I know how he fears my power to cut him off by suicide, I find it in my heart to pity him.

It is useless, and the time awfully fails me, to prolong this description; no one has ever suffered such torments, let that suffice; and yet even to these, habit brought—no, not alleviation—but a certain callousness of soul, a certain acquiescence of despair; and my punishment might have gone on for years, but for the last calamity which has now fallen, and which has finally severed me from my own face and nature. My provision of the salt, which had never been renewed since the date of the first experiment, began to run low. I sent out for a fresh supply, and mixed the draught; the ebullition followed, and the first change of colour, not the second; I drank it and it was without efficiency. You will learn from Poole how I have had London ransacked; it was in vain; and I am now persuaded that my first supply was impure, and that it was that unknown impurity which lent efficacy to the draught.

About a week has passed, and I am now finishing this statement under the influence of the last of the old powders. This, then, is the last time, short of a miracle, that Henry Jekyll can think his own thoughts or see his own face (now how sadly altered!) in the glass. Nor must I delay too long to bring my writing to an end; for if my narrative has hitherto escaped destruction, it has been by a combination of great prudence and great good luck. Should the throes of change take me in the act of writing it, Hyde will tear it in pieces; but if some time shall have elapsed after I have laid it by, his wonderful selfishness and circumscription to the moment will probably save it once again from the action of his ape-like spite. And indeed the doom that is closing on us both has already changed and crushed him. Half an hour from now, when I shall again and for ever re-indue that hated personality, I know how I shall sit shuddering and weeping in my chair, or continue, with the most strained and fearstruck ecstasy of listening, to pace up and down this room (my last earthly refuge) and give ear to every sound of menace. Will Hyde die upon the scaffold? or will he find the courage to release himself at the last moment? God knows; I am careless; this is my true hour of death, and what is to follow concerns another than myself. Here then, as I lay down the pen and proceed to seal up my confession, I bring the life of that unhappy Henry Jekyll to an end.